LAST PICK

RISE UP

JASON WALZ

COLOR BY **JON PROCTOR** AND **JOE FLOOD**

:01
First Second
NEW YORK

Copyright © 2020 by Jason Walz

Published by First Second
First Second is an imprint of Roaring Brook Press,
a division of Holtzbrinck Publishing Holdings Limited Partnership
120 Broadway, New York, NY 10271

Don't miss your next favorite book from First Second!
For the latest updates go to firstsecondnewsletter.com and sign up for our enewsletter.

Library of Congress Control Number: 2019947767
Paperback ISBN: 978-1-62672-895-0
Hardcover ISBN: 978-1-62672-894-3

Our books may be purchased in bulk for promotional, educational, or business use.
Please contact your local bookseller or the Macmillan Corporate and Premium Sales Department
at (800) 221-7945 ext. 5442 or by email at MacmillanSpecialMarkets@macmillan.com.

First edition, 2020

Edited by Connie Hsu and Robyn Chapman
Cover and interior book design by Molly Johanson
Series design by Andrew Arnold
Cover color by Shelli Paroline and Braden Lamb
Interior color by Jon Proctor and Joe Flood
Printed in China

Paperback: 10 9 8 7 6 5 4 3 2 1
Hardcover: 10 9 8 7 6 5 4 3 2 1

Thumbnailed and roughed with pencil and paper,
then tightened up in ProCreate on an iPad Pro, and inked and lettered in ClipStudio
using a custom G-pen nib on a Wacom MobileStudio.

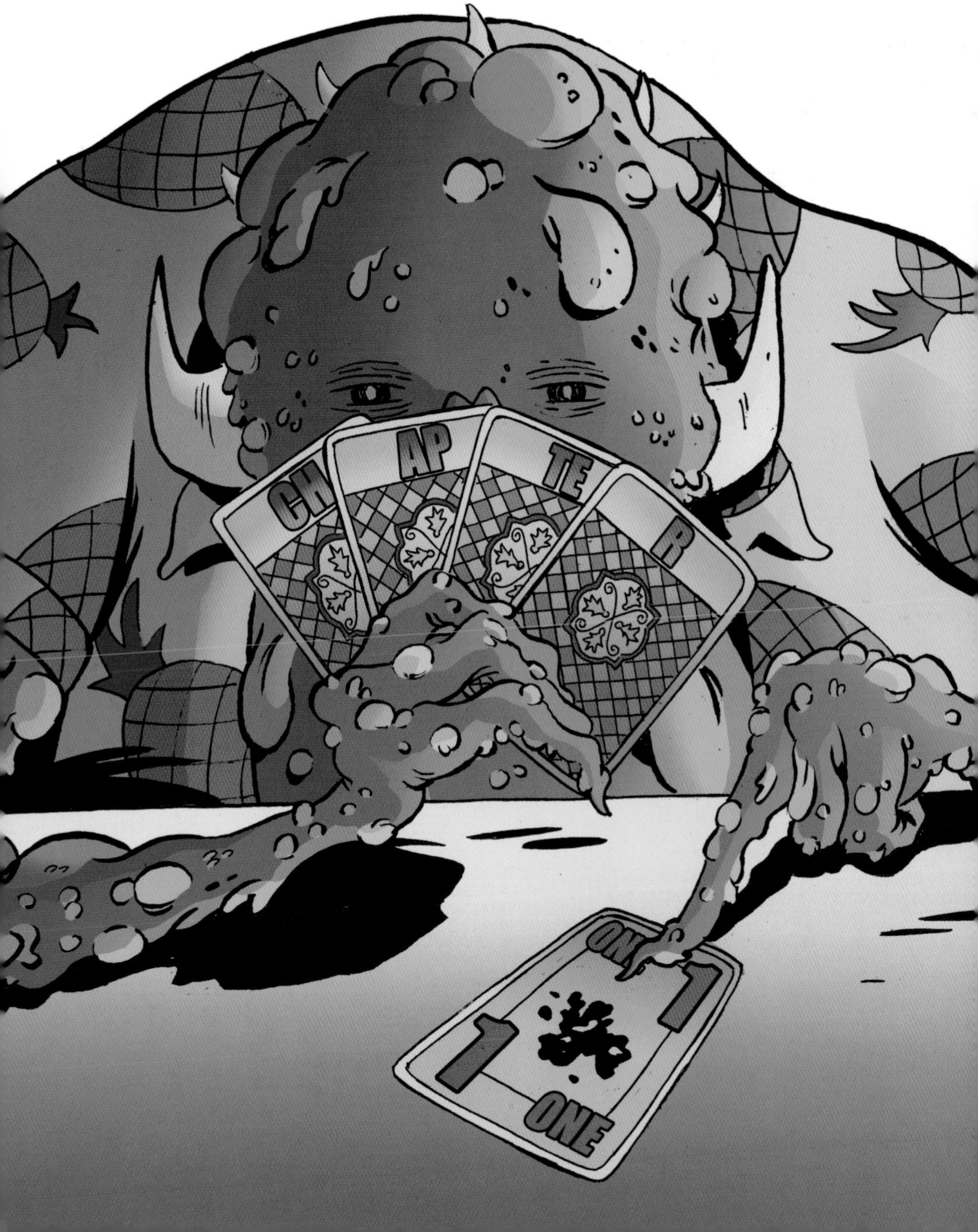

CH
AP
TE
R
ONE
1
1
ONE

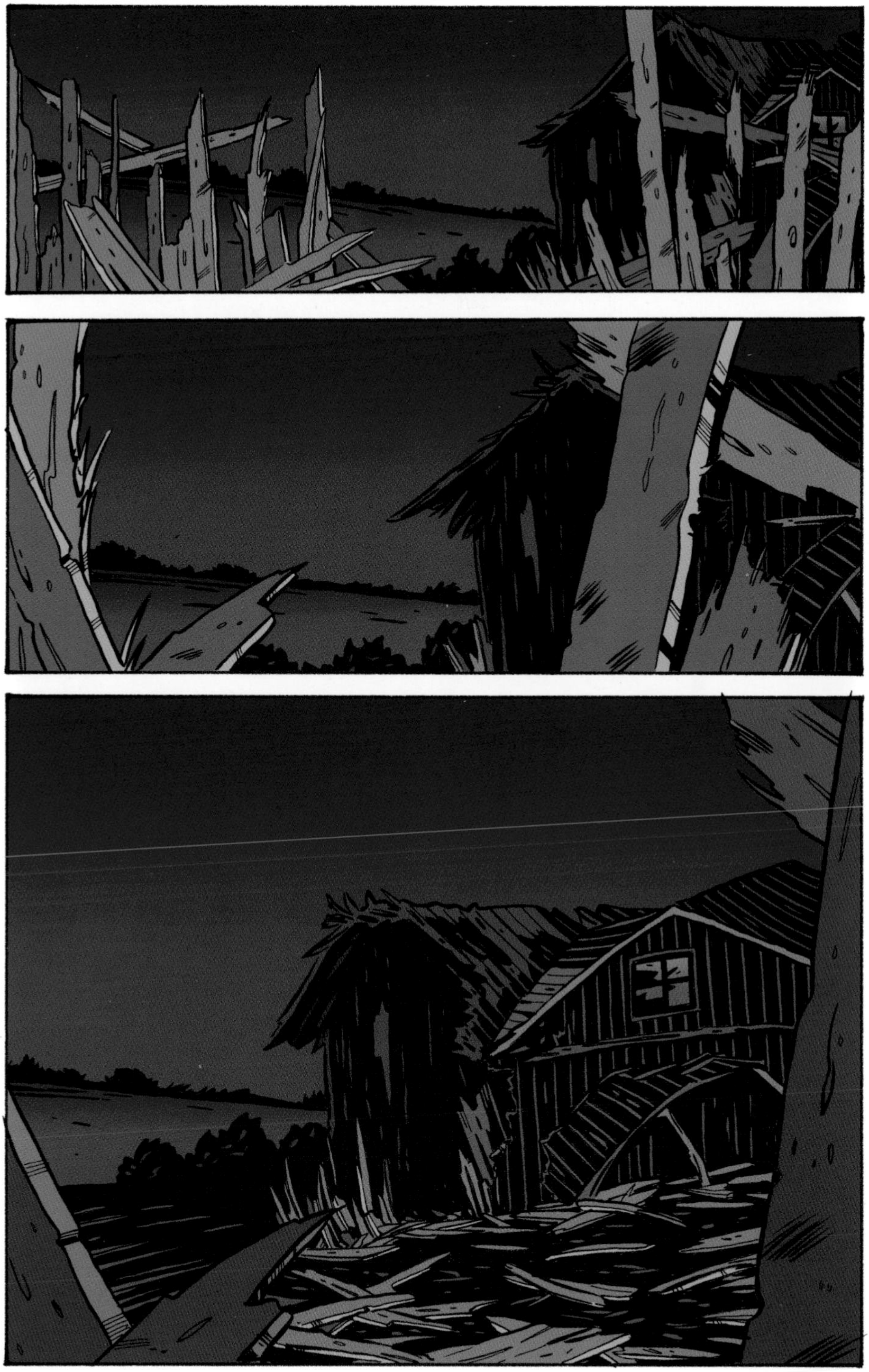

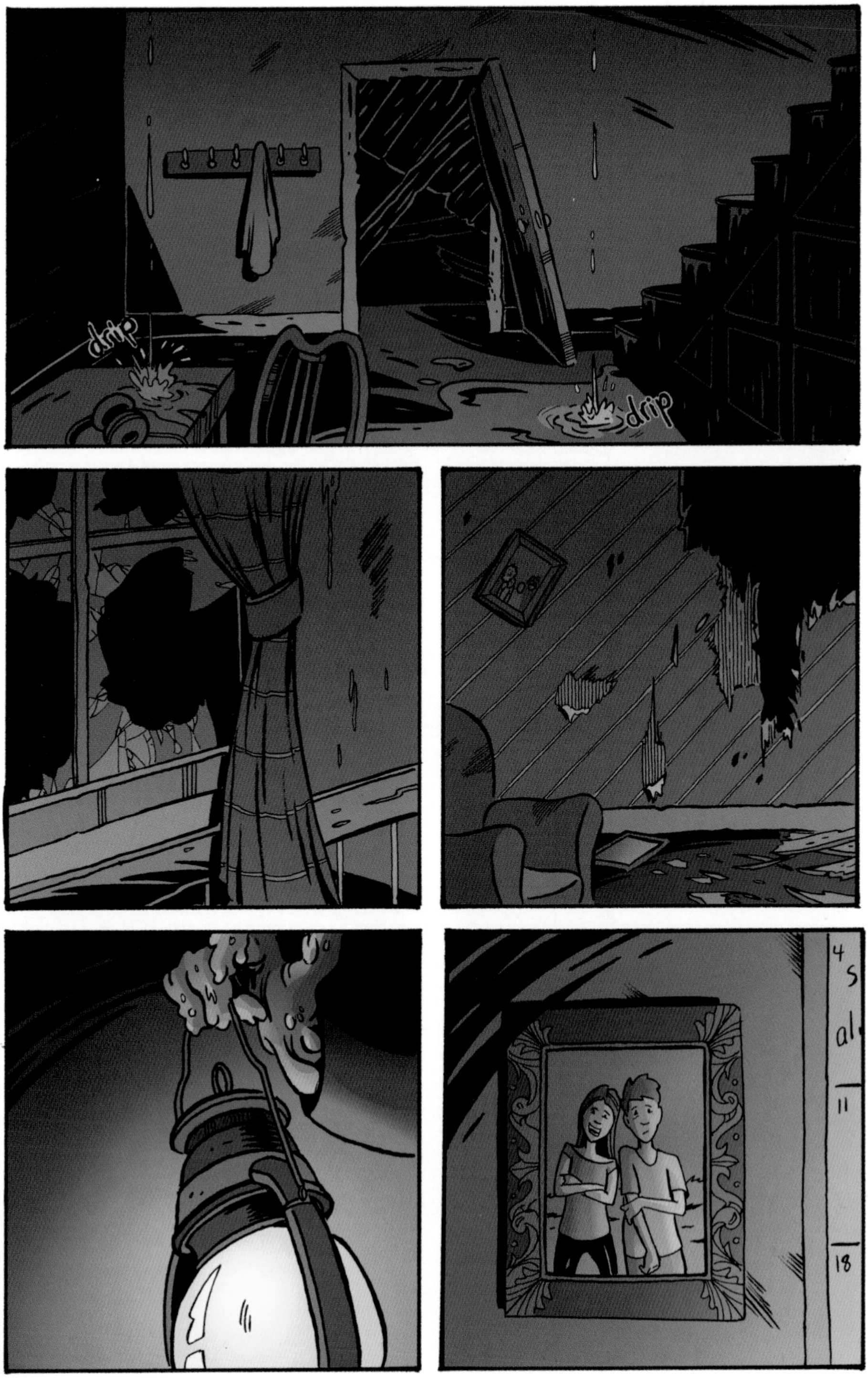
drip
drip

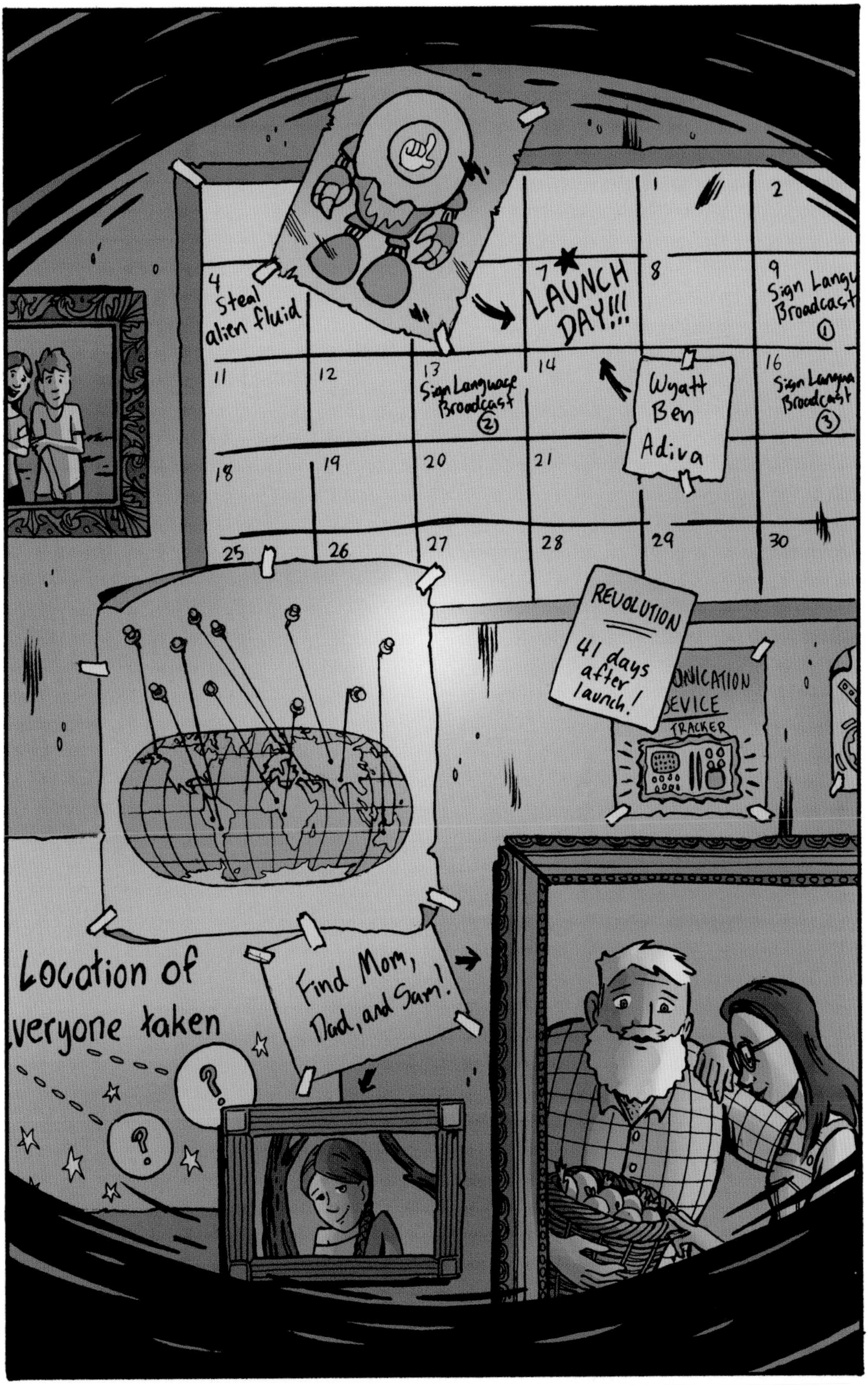

1
2
4 Steal alien fluid
7 LAUNCH DAY!!!
8
9 Sign Langu Broadcast ①
11
12
13 Sign Language Broadcast ②
14
Wyatt Ben Adiva
16 Sign Langua Broadcast ③
18
19
20
21
25
26
27
28
29
30
REVOLUTION 41 days after launch!
DEVICE
TRACKER
Location of everyone taken
Find Mom, Dad, and Sam!

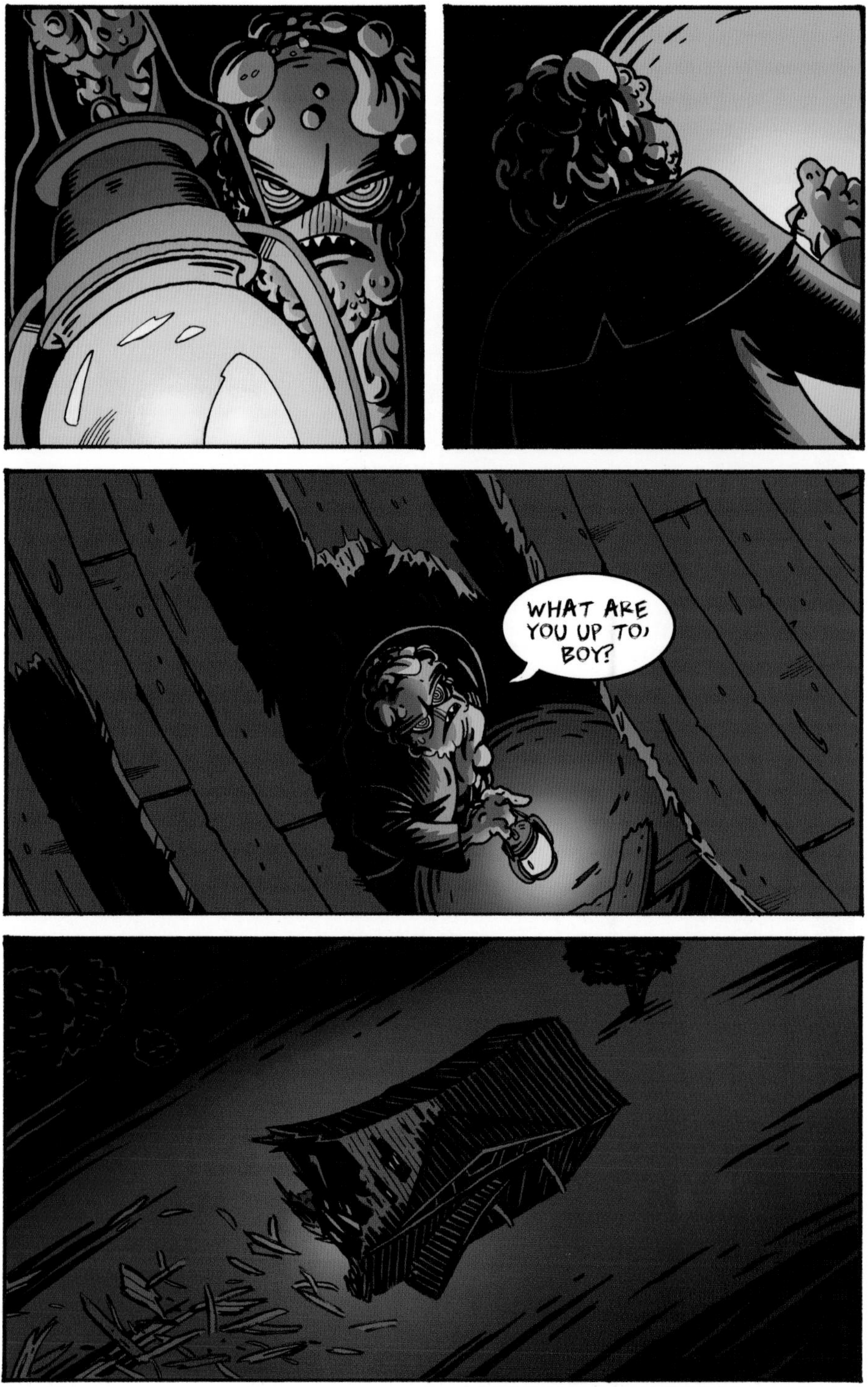
WHAT ARE YOU UP TO, BOY?

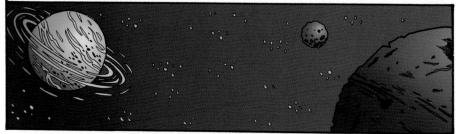

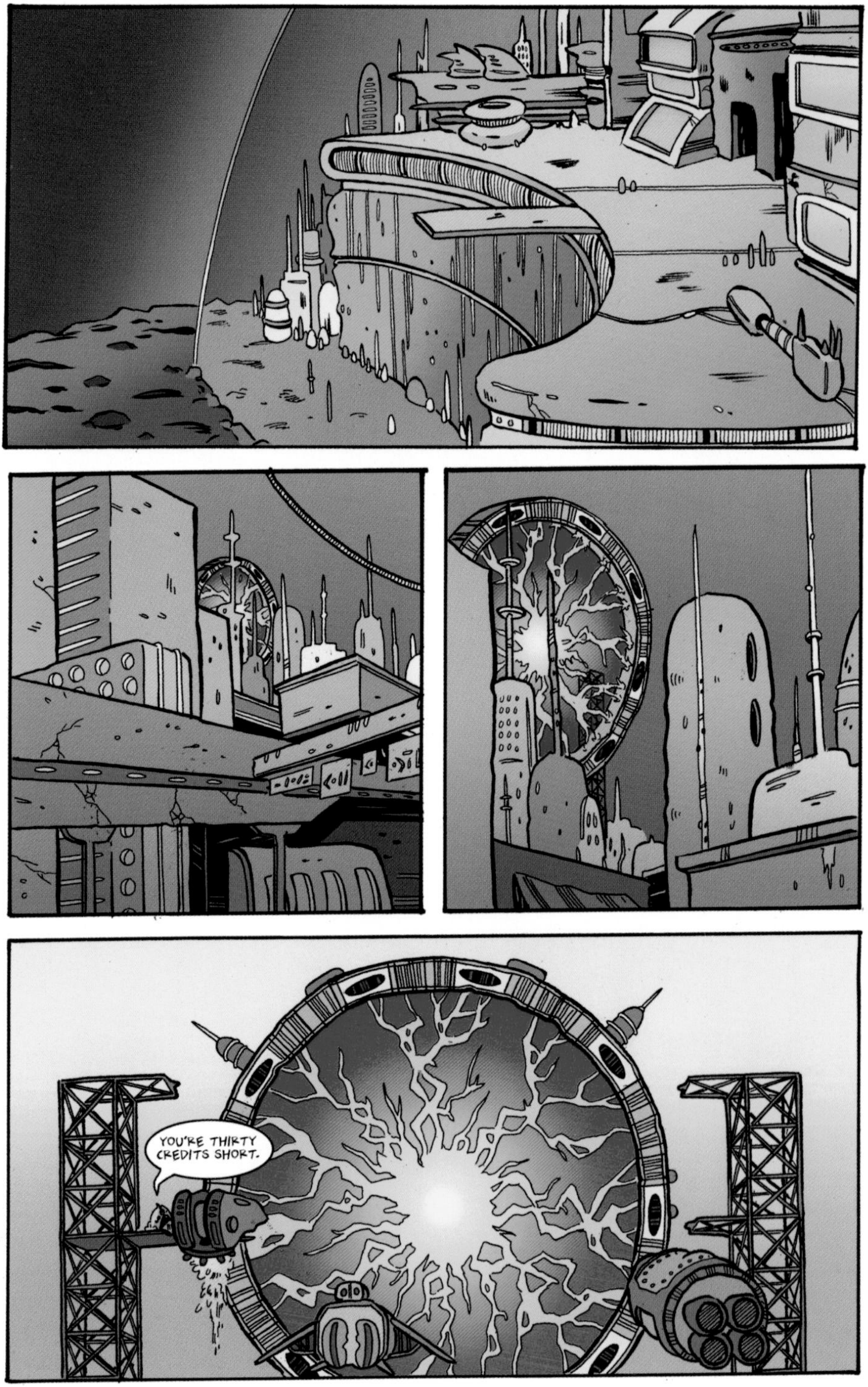
YOU'RE THIRTY CREDITS SHORT.

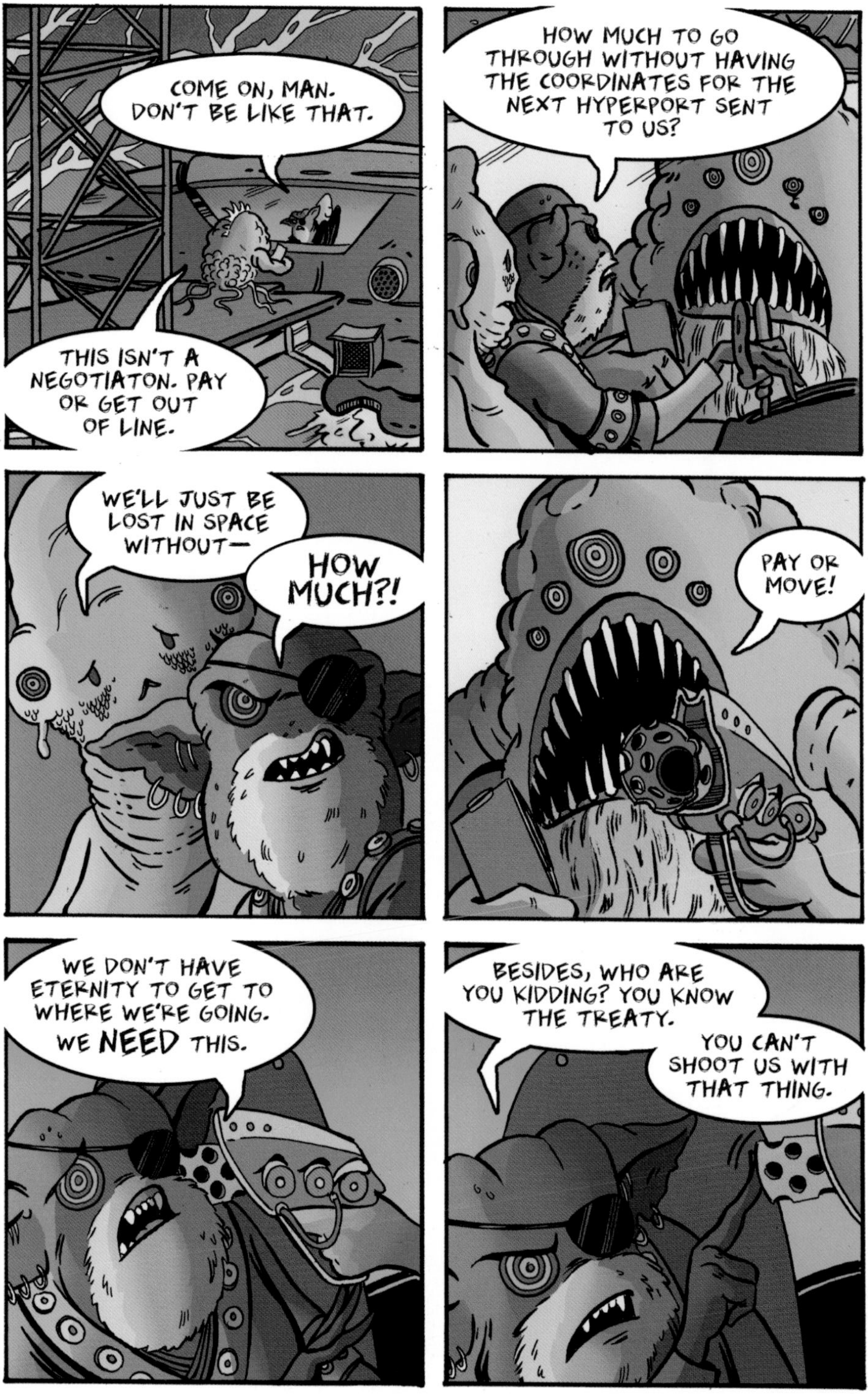
COME ON, MAN. DON'T BE LIKE THAT.
THIS ISN'T A NEGOTIATON. PAY OR GET OUT OF LINE.
HOW MUCH TO GO THROUGH WITHOUT HAVING THE COORDINATES FOR THE NEXT HYPERPORT SENT TO US?
WE'LL JUST BE LOST IN SPACE WITHOUT—
HOW MUCH?!
PAY OR MOVE!
WE DON'T HAVE ETERNITY TO GET TO WHERE WE'RE GOING. WE NEED THIS.
BESIDES, WHO ARE YOU KIDDING? YOU KNOW THE TREATY.
YOU CAN'T SHOOT US WITH THAT THING.

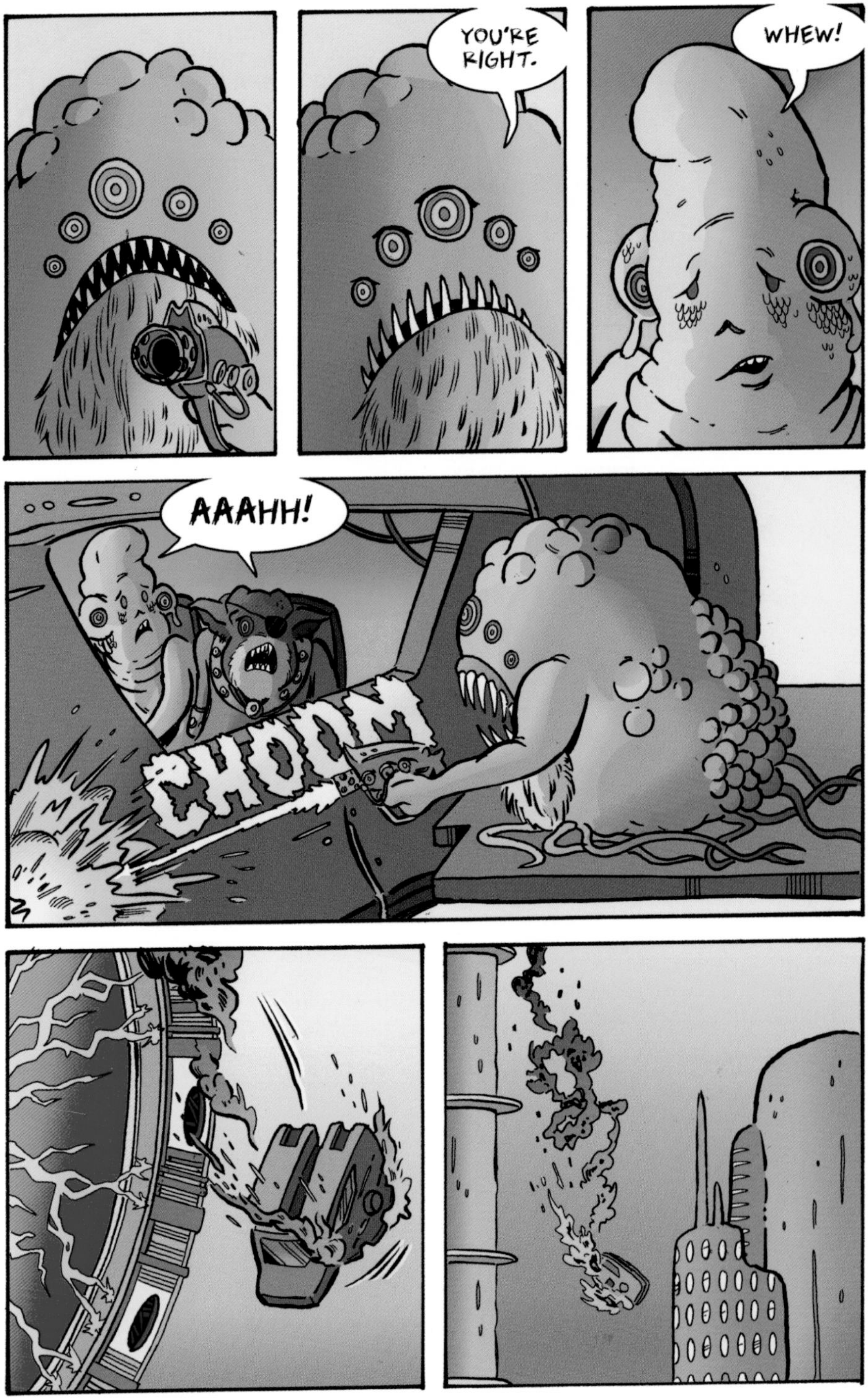

YOU'RE RIGHT.
WHEW!
AAAHH!
CHOOM

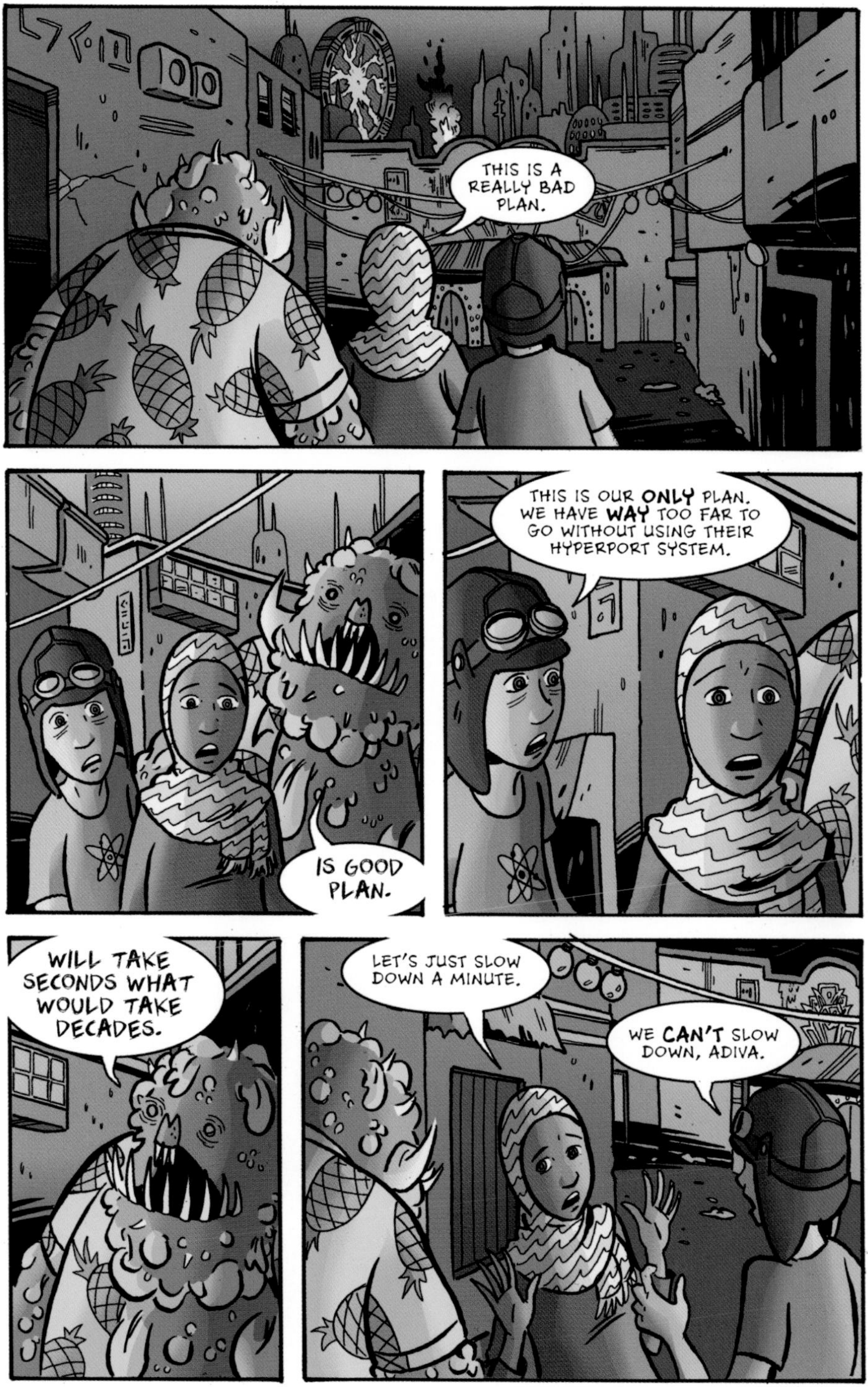
THIS IS A REALLY BAD PLAN.
THIS IS OUR ONLY PLAN. WE HAVE WAY TOO FAR TO GO WITHOUT USING THEIR HYPERPORT SYSTEM.
IS GOOD PLAN.
WILL TAKE SECONDS WHAT WOULD TAKE DECADES.
LET'S JUST SLOW DOWN A MINUTE.
WE CAN'T SLOW DOWN, ADIVA.

WE'VE BEEN TRAVELING FOR WEEKS AND WE'VE ONLY GOTTEN THIS FAR!

HOW CAN WE BE EXPECTED TO HELP ANYONE WHEN WE CAN'T EVEN GET TO WHERE WE'RE GOING?

THIS IS OUR LAST CHANCE TO GET TO—

TALK TO ME LIKE THAT AGAIN, HUMAN, I RIP OFF LIMBS AND DRINK BODILY FLUIDS.

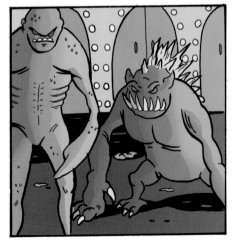

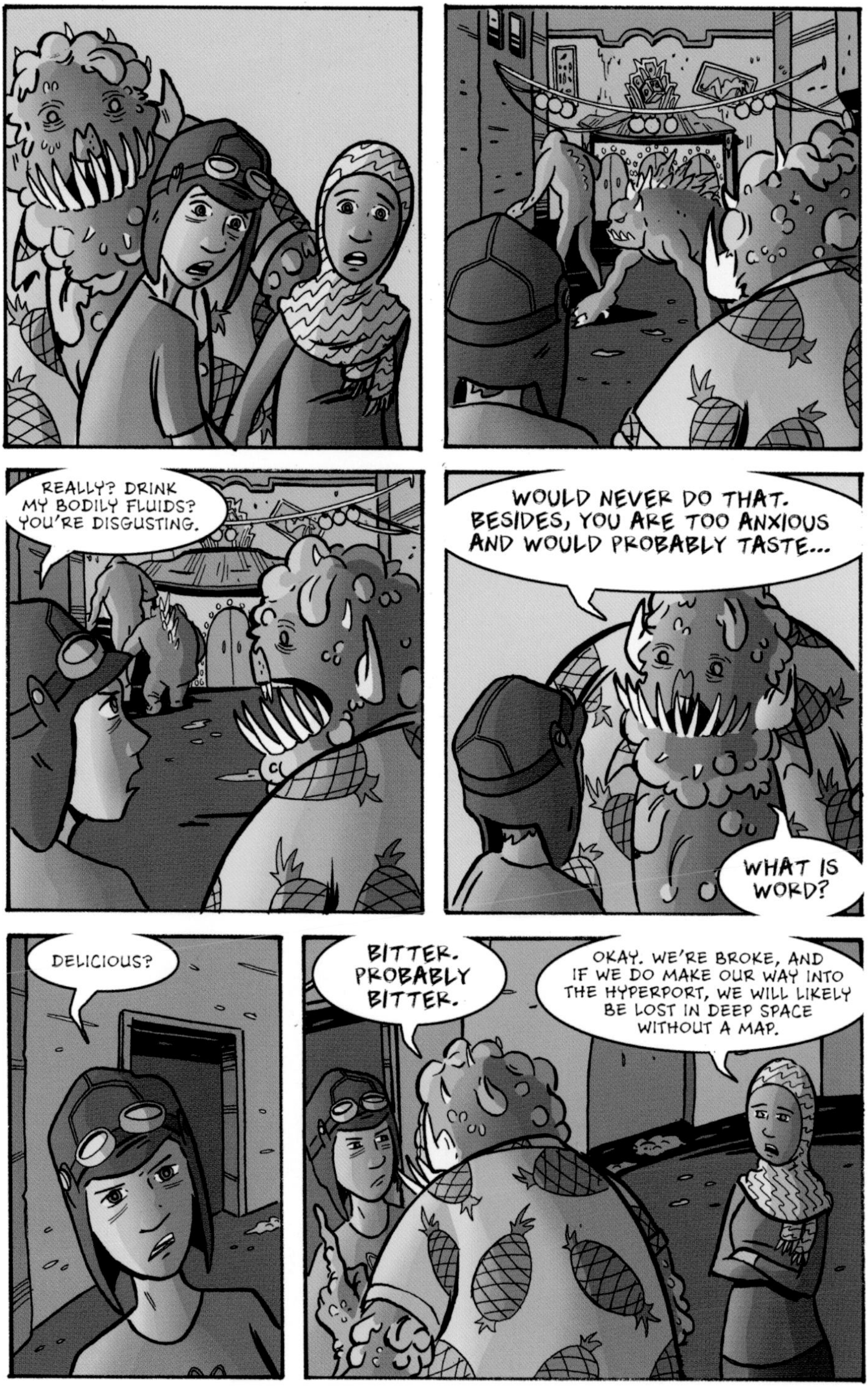
REALLY? DRINK MY BODILY FLUIDS? YOU'RE DISGUSTING.
WOULD NEVER DO THAT. BESIDES, YOU ARE TOO ANXIOUS AND WOULD PROBABLY TASTE...
WHAT IS WORD?
DELICIOUS?
BITTER. PROBABLY BITTER.
OKAY. WE'RE BROKE, AND IF WE DO MAKE OUR WAY INTO THE HYPERPORT, WE WILL LIKELY BE LOST IN DEEP SPACE WITHOUT A MAP.

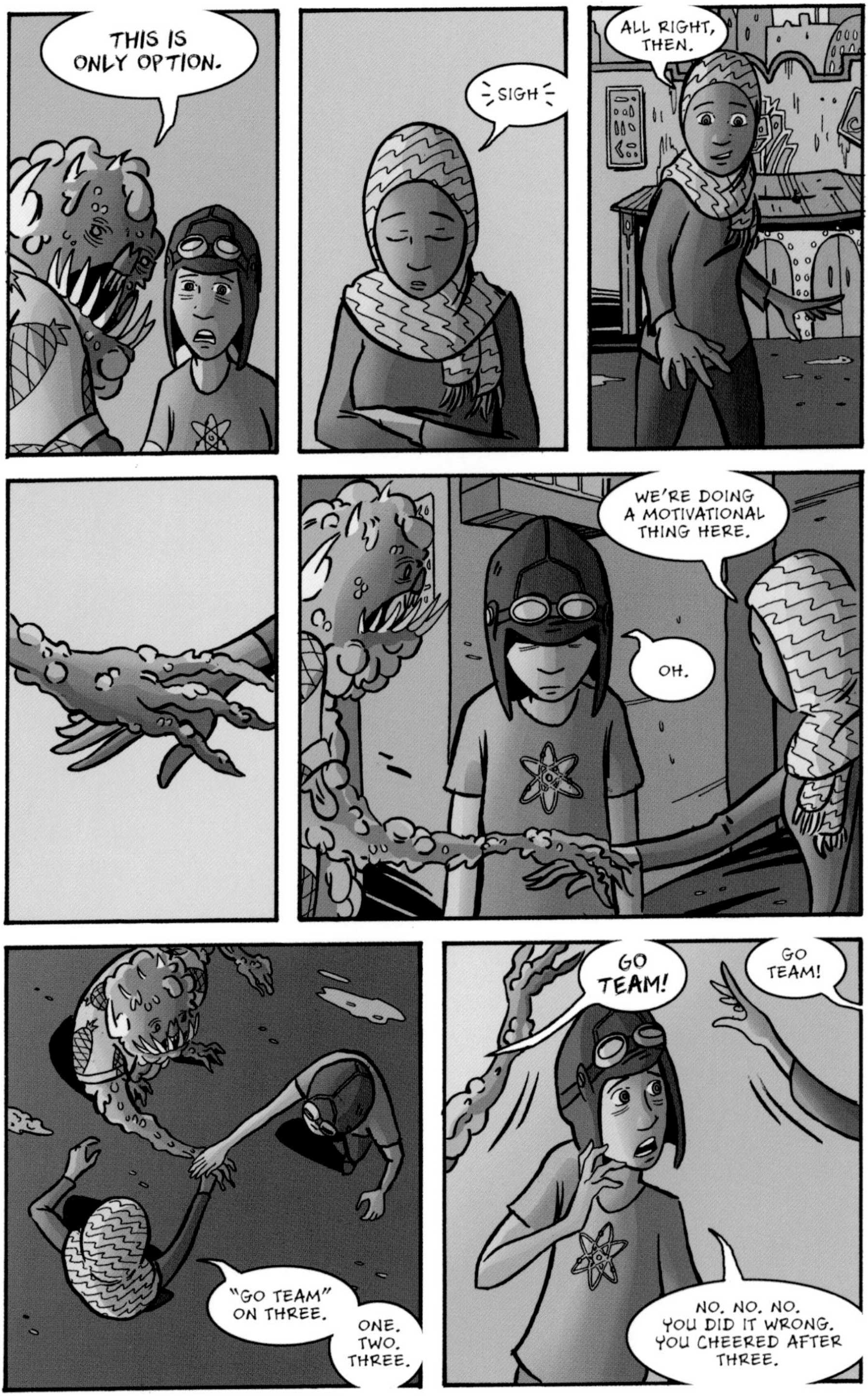
THIS IS ONLY OPTION.
SIGH
ALL RIGHT, THEN.
WE'RE DOING A MOTIVATIONAL THING HERE.
OH.
"GO TEAM" ON THREE.
ONE. TWO. THREE.
GO TEAM!
GO TEAM!
NO. NO. NO. YOU DID IT WRONG. YOU CHEERED AFTER THREE.

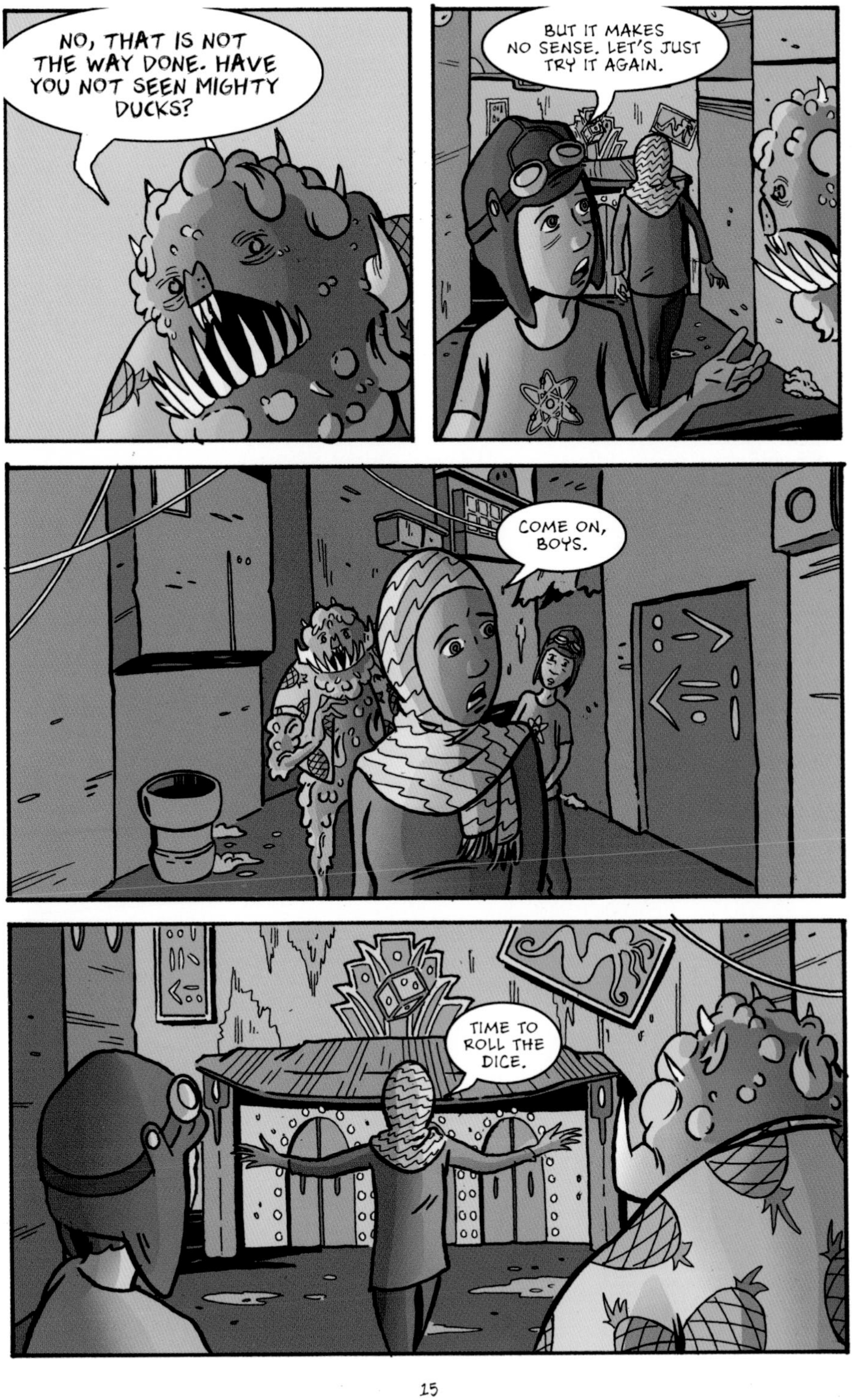
NO, THAT IS NOT THE WAY DONE. HAVE YOU NOT SEEN MIGHTY DUCKS?
BUT IT MAKES NO SENSE. LET'S JUST TRY IT AGAIN.
COME ON, BOYS.
TIME TO ROLL THE DICE.

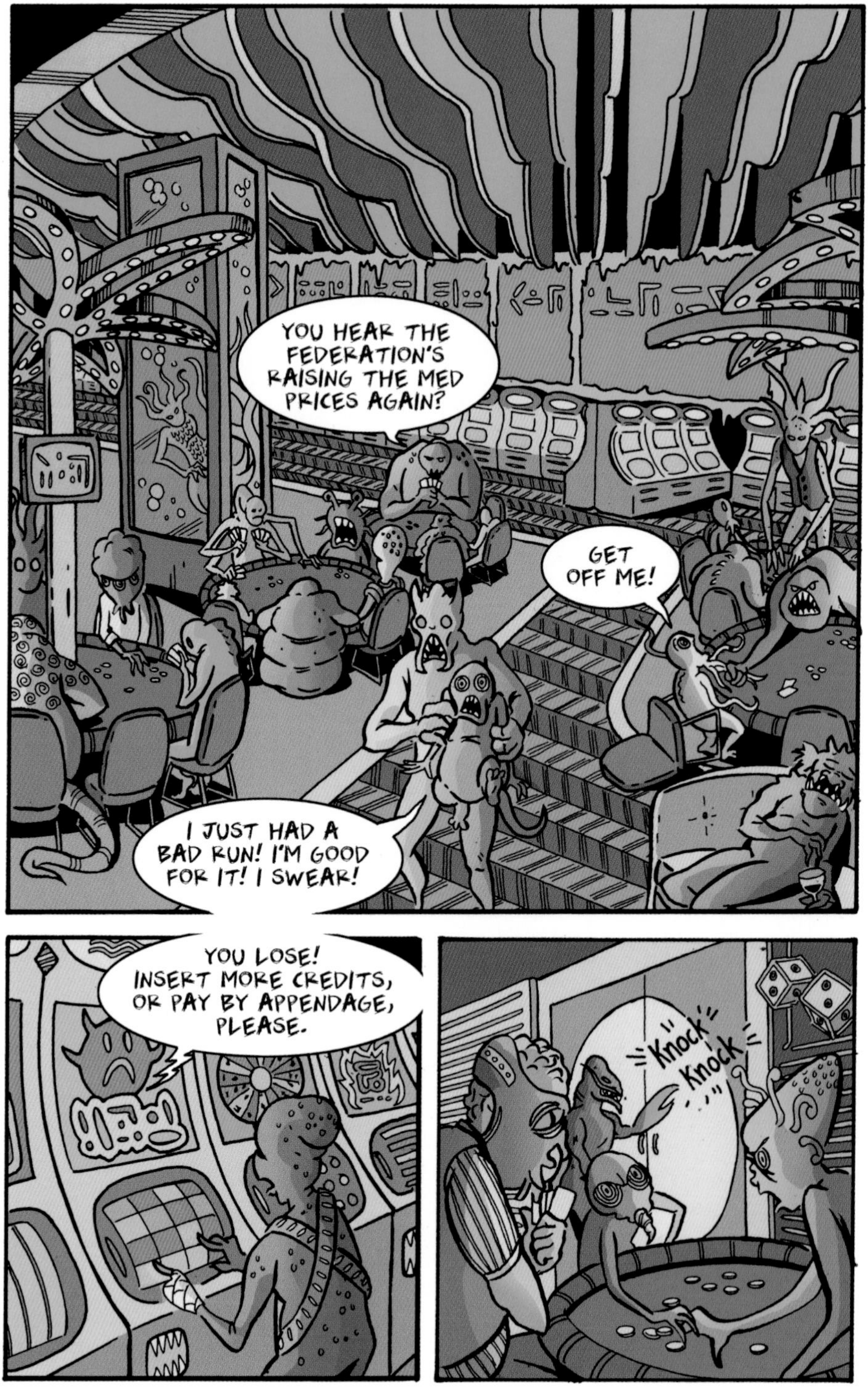
YOU HEAR THE FEDERATION'S RAISING THE MED PRICES AGAIN?
GET OFF ME!
I JUST HAD A BAD RUN! I'M GOOD FOR IT! I SWEAR!
YOU LOSE! INSERT MORE CREDITS, OR PAY BY APPENDAGE, PLEASE.
Knock Knock

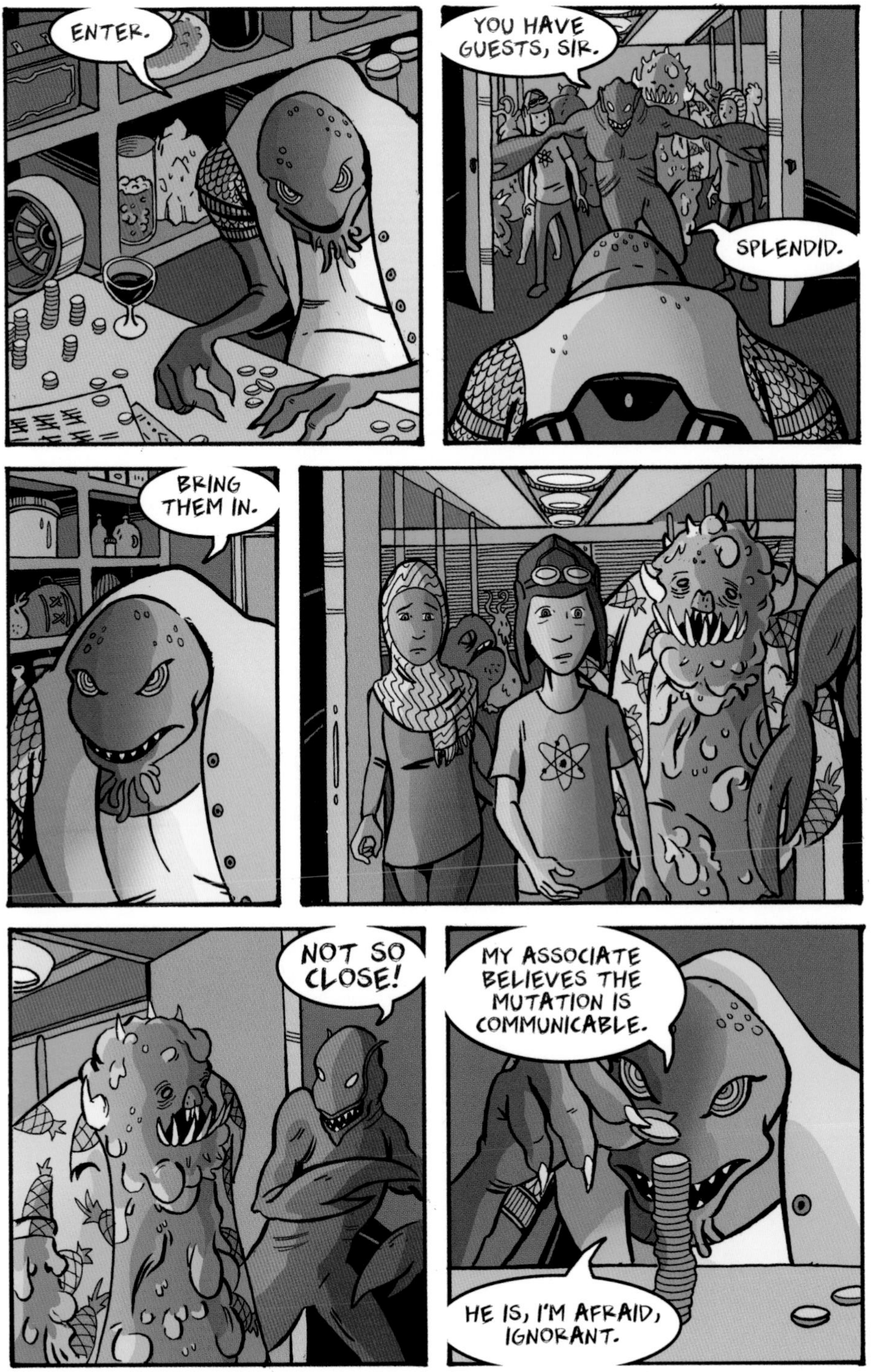
ENTER.
YOU HAVE GUESTS, SIR.
SPLENDID.
BRING THEM IN.
NOT SO CLOSE!
MY ASSOCIATE BELIEVES THE MUTATION IS COMMUNICABLE.
HE IS, I'M AFRAID, IGNORANT.

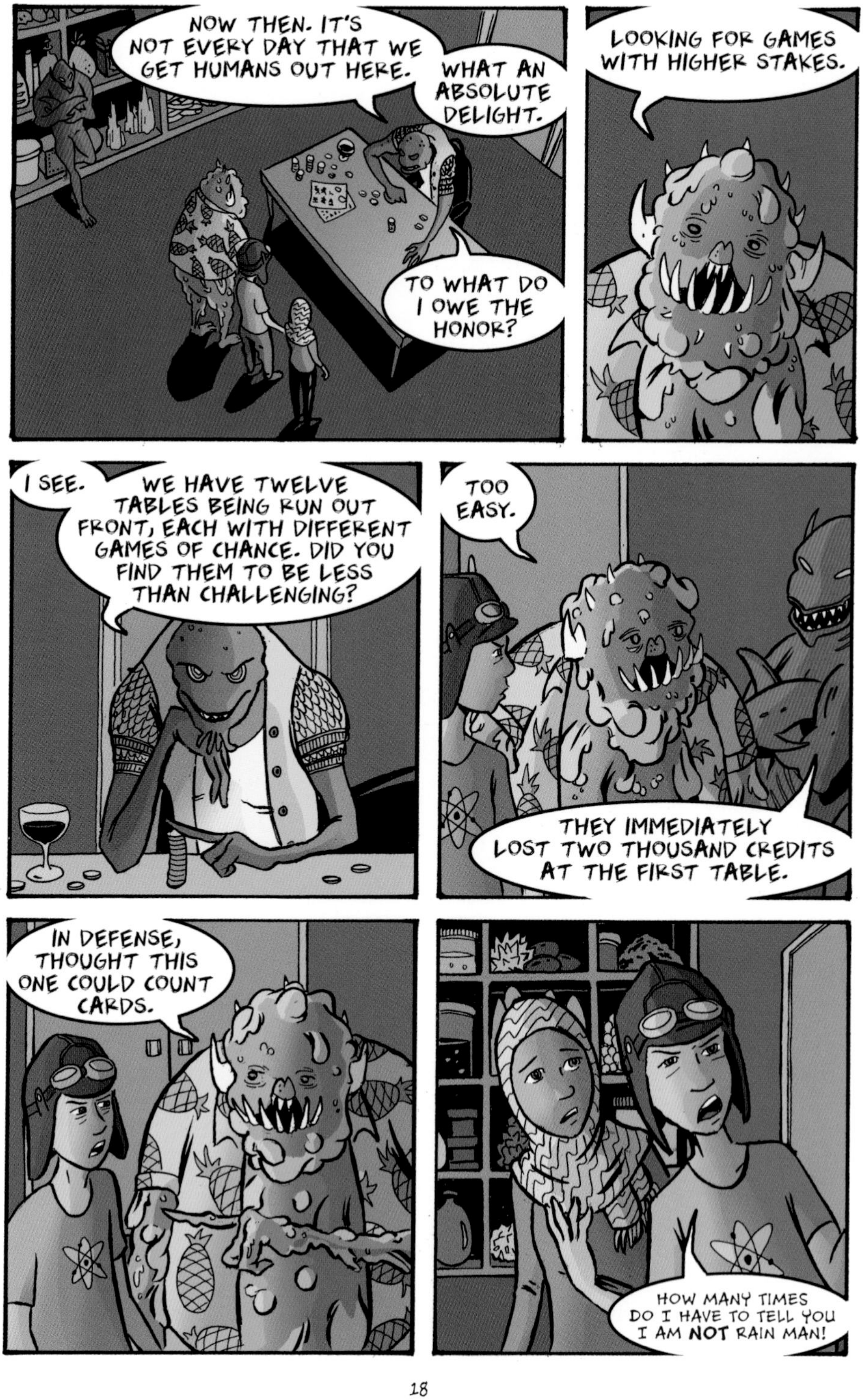
NOW THEN. IT'S NOT EVERY DAY THAT WE GET HUMANS OUT HERE.
WHAT AN ABSOLUTE DELIGHT.
TO WHAT DO I OWE THE HONOR?
LOOKING FOR GAMES WITH HIGHER STAKES.
I SEE.
WE HAVE TWELVE TABLES BEING RUN OUT FRONT, EACH WITH DIFFERENT GAMES OF CHANCE. DID YOU FIND THEM TO BE LESS THAN CHALLENGING?
TOO EASY.
THEY IMMEDIATELY LOST TWO THOUSAND CREDITS AT THE FIRST TABLE.
IN DEFENSE, THOUGHT THIS ONE COULD COUNT CARDS.
HOW MANY TIMES DO I HAVE TO TELL YOU I AM **NOT** RAIN MAN!

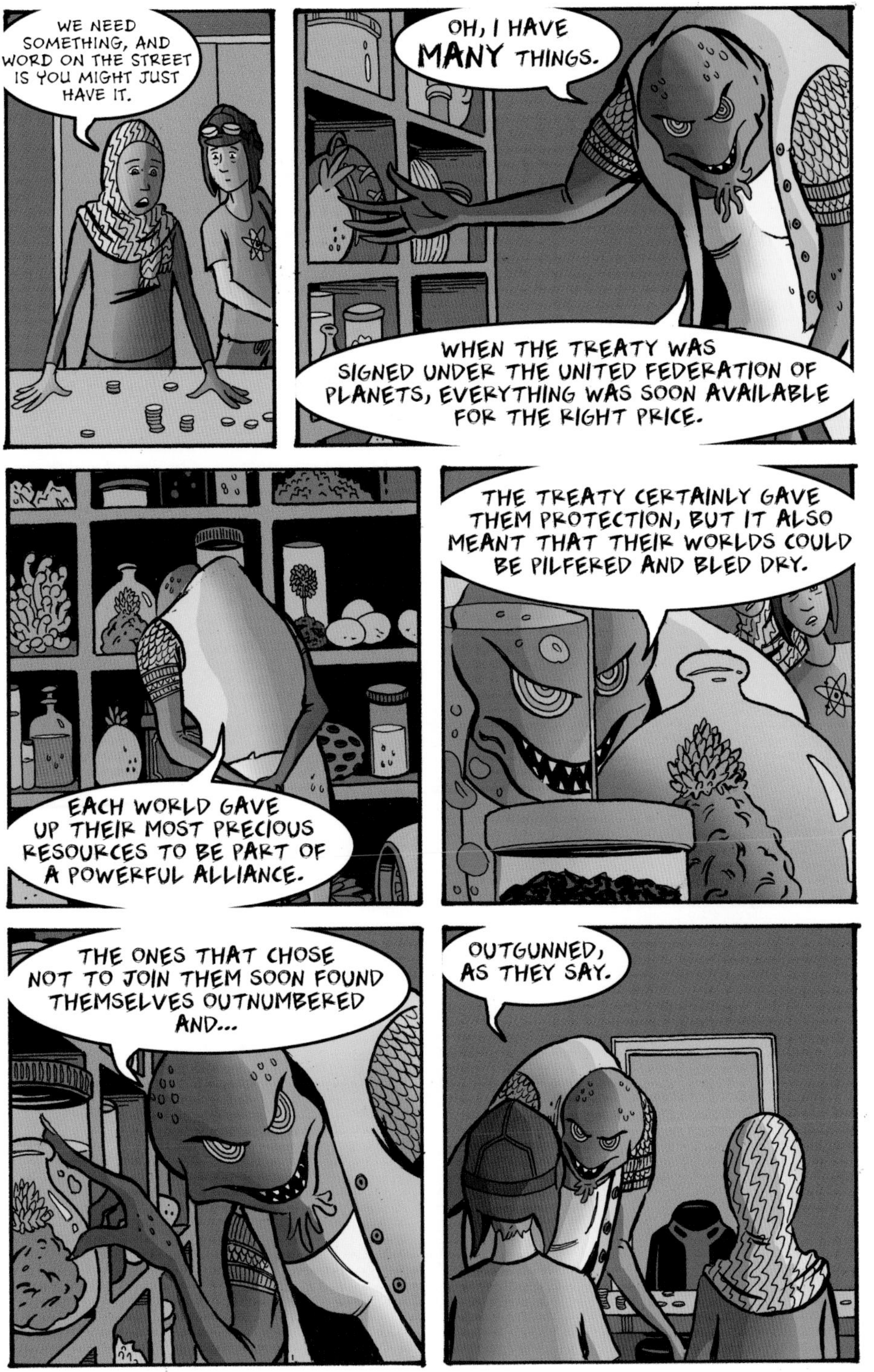
WE NEED SOMETHING, AND WORD ON THE STREET IS YOU MIGHT JUST HAVE IT.
OH, I HAVE MANY THINGS.
WHEN THE TREATY WAS SIGNED UNDER THE UNITED FEDERATION OF PLANETS, EVERYTHING WAS SOON AVAILABLE FOR THE RIGHT PRICE.
EACH WORLD GAVE UP THEIR MOST PRECIOUS RESOURCES TO BE PART OF A POWERFUL ALLIANCE.
THE TREATY CERTAINLY GAVE THEM PROTECTION, BUT IT ALSO MEANT THAT THEIR WORLDS COULD BE PILFERED AND BLED DRY.
THE ONES THAT CHOSE NOT TO JOIN THEM SOON FOUND THEMSELVES OUTNUMBERED AND...
OUTGUNNED, AS THEY SAY.

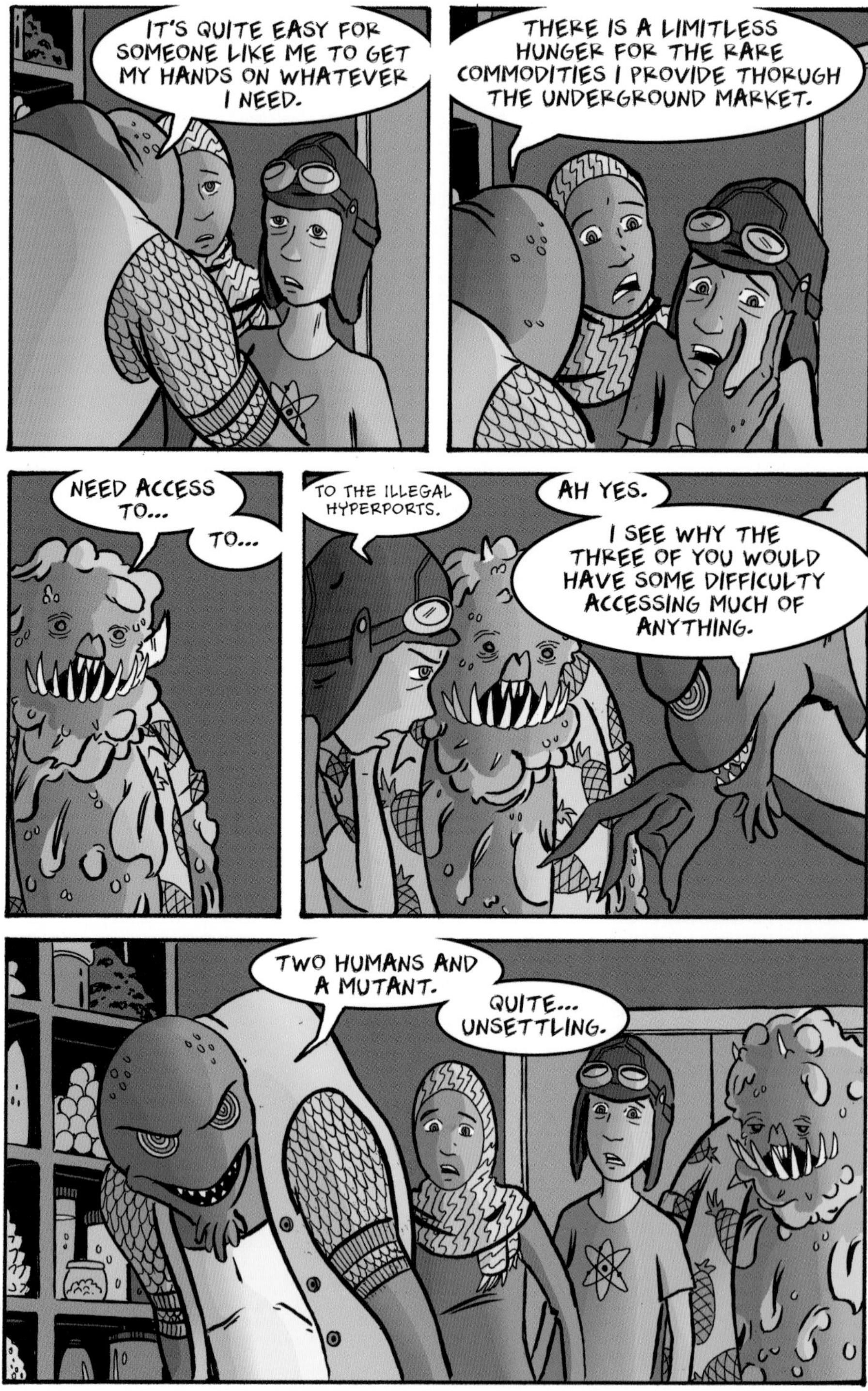
IT'S QUITE EASY FOR SOMEONE LIKE ME TO GET MY HANDS ON WHATEVER I NEED.
THERE IS A LIMITLESS HUNGER FOR THE RARE COMMODITIES I PROVIDE THORUGH THE UNDERGROUND MARKET.
NEED ACCESS TO...
TO...
TO THE ILLEGAL HYPERPORTS.
AH YES.
I SEE WHY THE THREE OF YOU WOULD HAVE SOME DIFFICULTY ACCESSING MUCH OF ANYTHING.
TWO HUMANS AND A MUTANT.
QUITE... UNSETTLING.

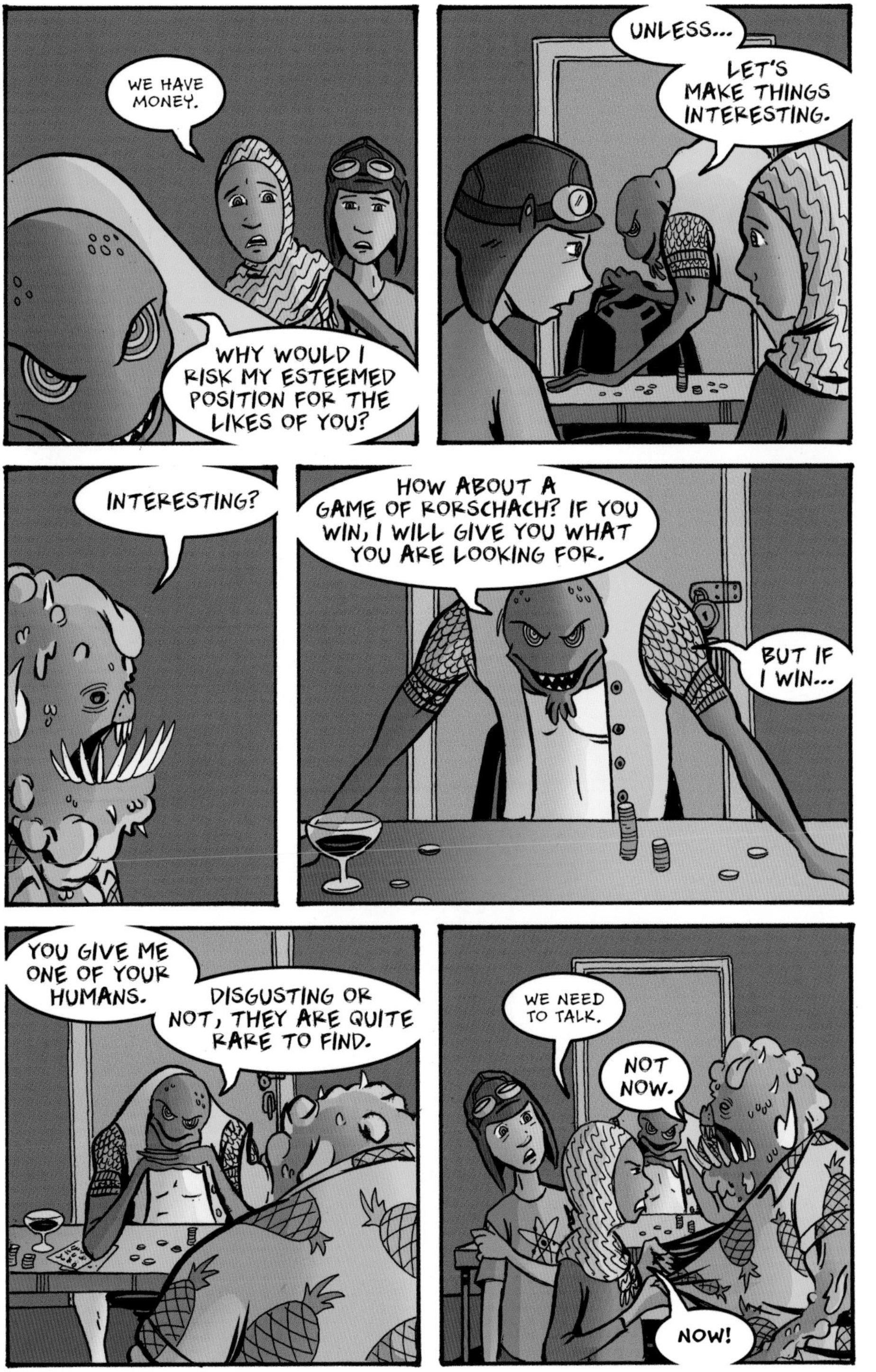
WE HAVE MONEY.
WHY WOULD I RISK MY ESTEEMED POSITION FOR THE LIKES OF YOU?
UNLESS...
LET'S MAKE THINGS INTERESTING.
INTERESTING?
HOW ABOUT A GAME OF RORSCHACH? IF YOU WIN, I WILL GIVE YOU WHAT YOU ARE LOOKING FOR.
BUT IF I WIN...
YOU GIVE ME ONE OF YOUR HUMANS.
DISGUSTING OR NOT, THEY ARE QUITE RARE TO FIND.
WE NEED TO TALK.
NOT NOW.
NOW!

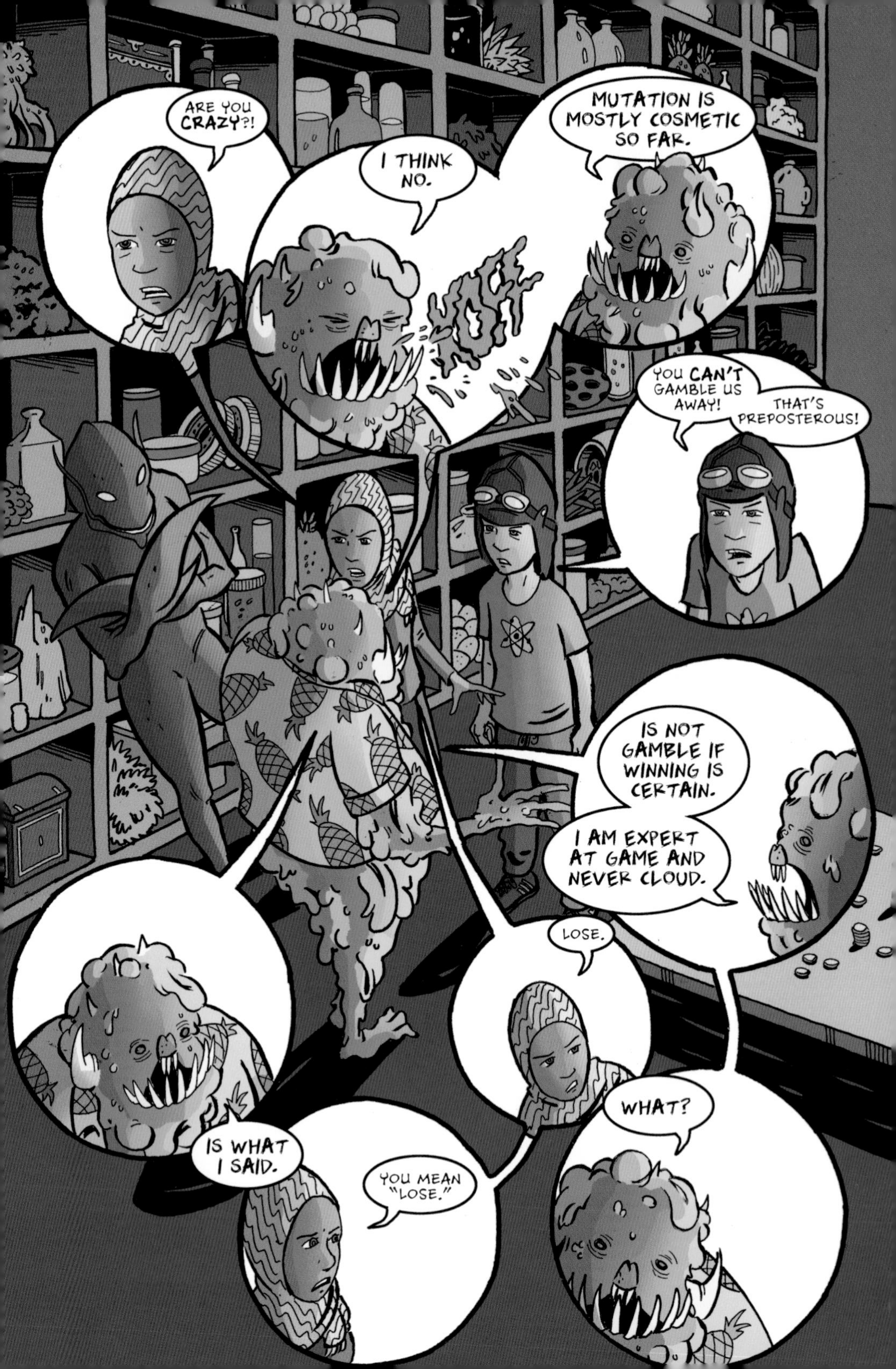
ARE YOU CRAZY?!
I THINK NO.
MUTATION IS MOSTLY COSMETIC SO FAR.
YOU CAN'T GAMBLE US AWAY!
THAT'S PREPOSTEROUS!
IS NOT GAMBLE IF WINNING IS CERTAIN.
I AM EXPERT AT GAME AND NEVER CLOUD.
LOSE.
WHAT?
IS WHAT I SAID.
YOU MEAN "LOSE."

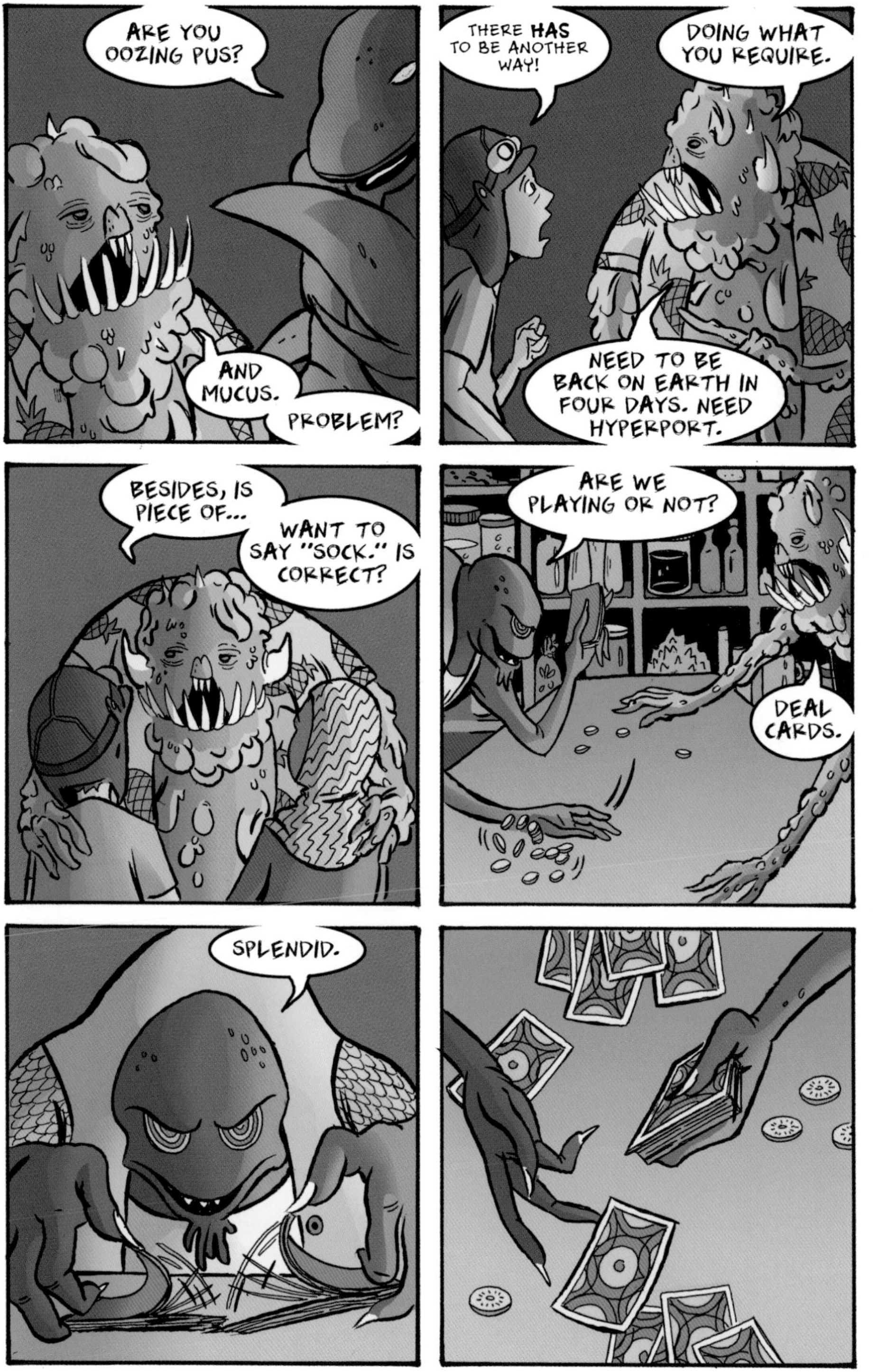
ARE YOU OOZING PUS?
AND MUCUS.
PROBLEM?
THERE HAS TO BE ANOTHER WAY!
DOING WHAT YOU REQUIRE.
NEED TO BE BACK ON EARTH IN FOUR DAYS. NEED HYPERPORT.
BESIDES, IS PIECE OF...
WANT TO SAY "SOCK." IS CORRECT?
ARE WE PLAYING OR NOT?
DEAL CARDS.
SPLENDID.

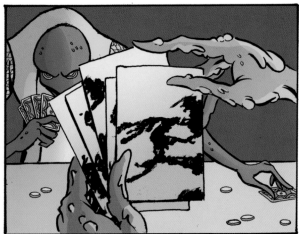

SUN RISING OVER THE DUNES ON OPHESIAN'S MOON.

FOUR CARDS.

NOT BAD.

NOT AS GOOD AS **THIS.**

ALL CARDS.

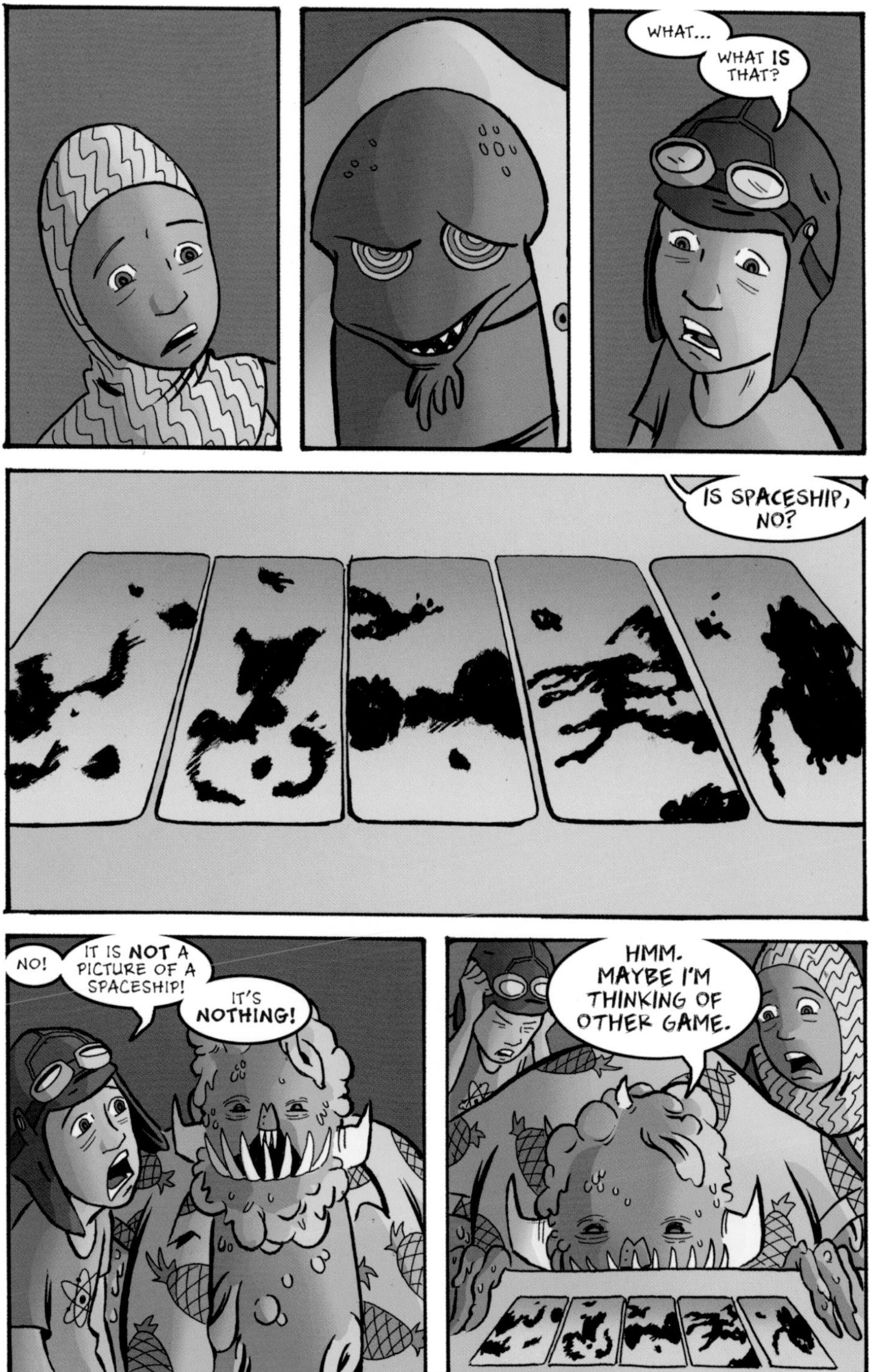
WHAT...
WHAT IS THAT?
IS SPACESHIP, NO?
NO!
IT IS NOT A PICTURE OF A SPACESHIP!
IT'S NOTHING!
HMM. MAYBE I'M THINKING OF OTHER GAME.

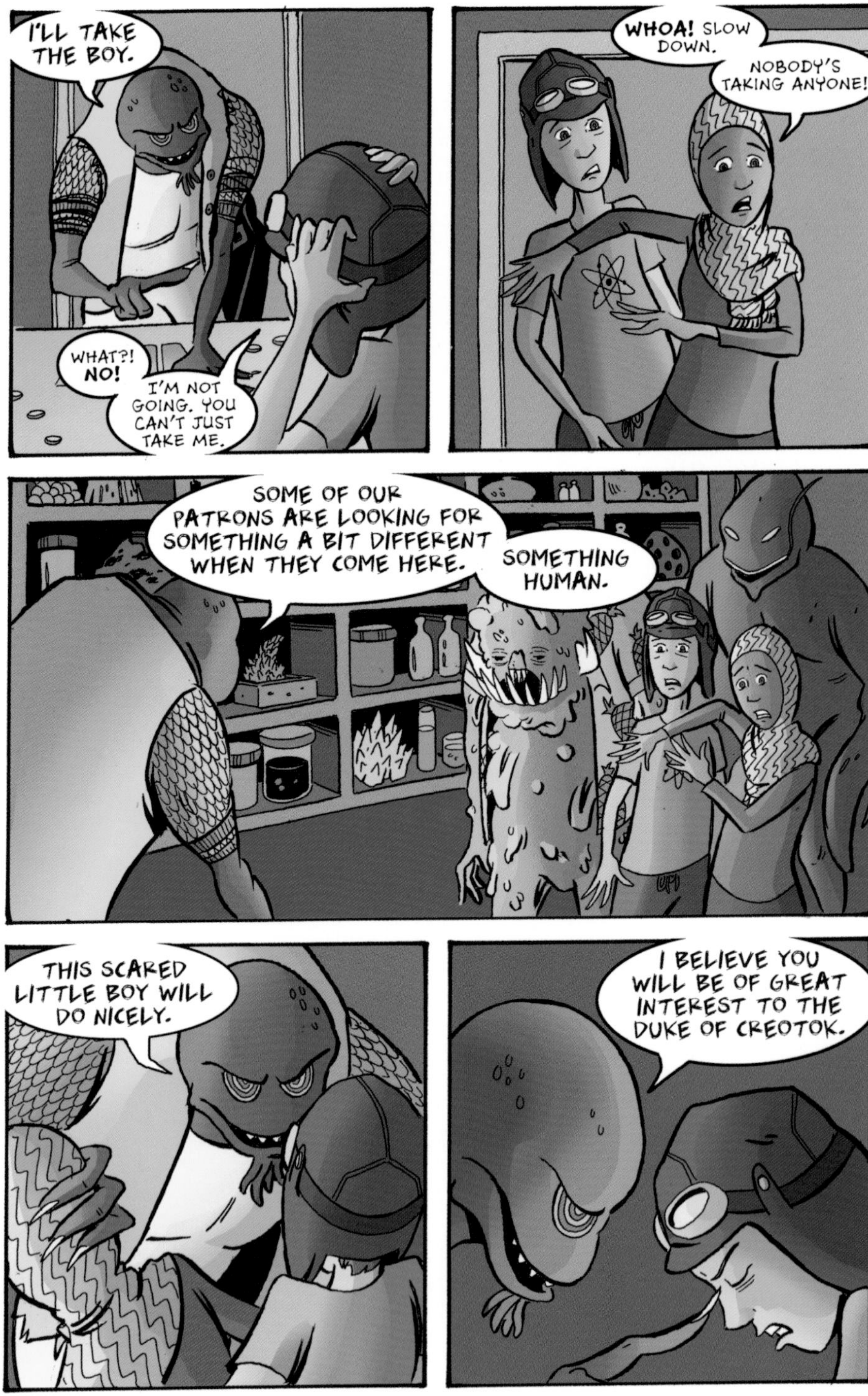
I'LL TAKE THE BOY.
WHAT?! NO!
I'M NOT GOING. YOU CAN'T JUST TAKE ME.
WHOA! SLOW DOWN.
NOBODY'S TAKING ANYONE!
SOME OF OUR PATRONS ARE LOOKING FOR SOMETHING A BIT DIFFERENT WHEN THEY COME HERE.
SOMETHING HUMAN.
THIS SCARED LITTLE BOY WILL DO NICELY.
I BELIEVE YOU WILL BE OF GREAT INTEREST TO THE DUKE OF CREOTOK.

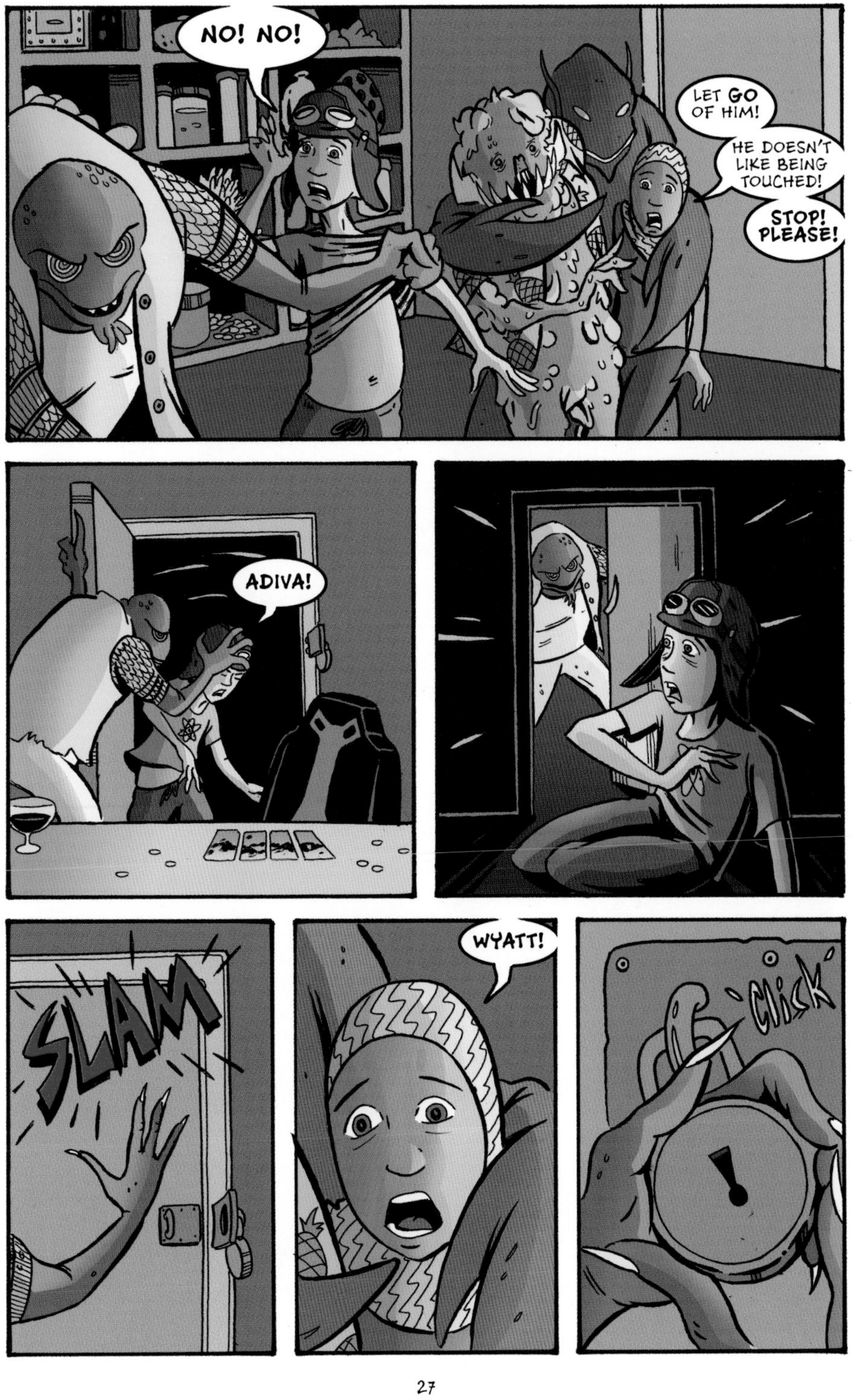
NO! NO!
LET GO OF HIM!
HE DOESN'T LIKE BEING TOUCHED!
STOP! PLEASE!
ADIVA!
SLAM
WYATT!
CLICK

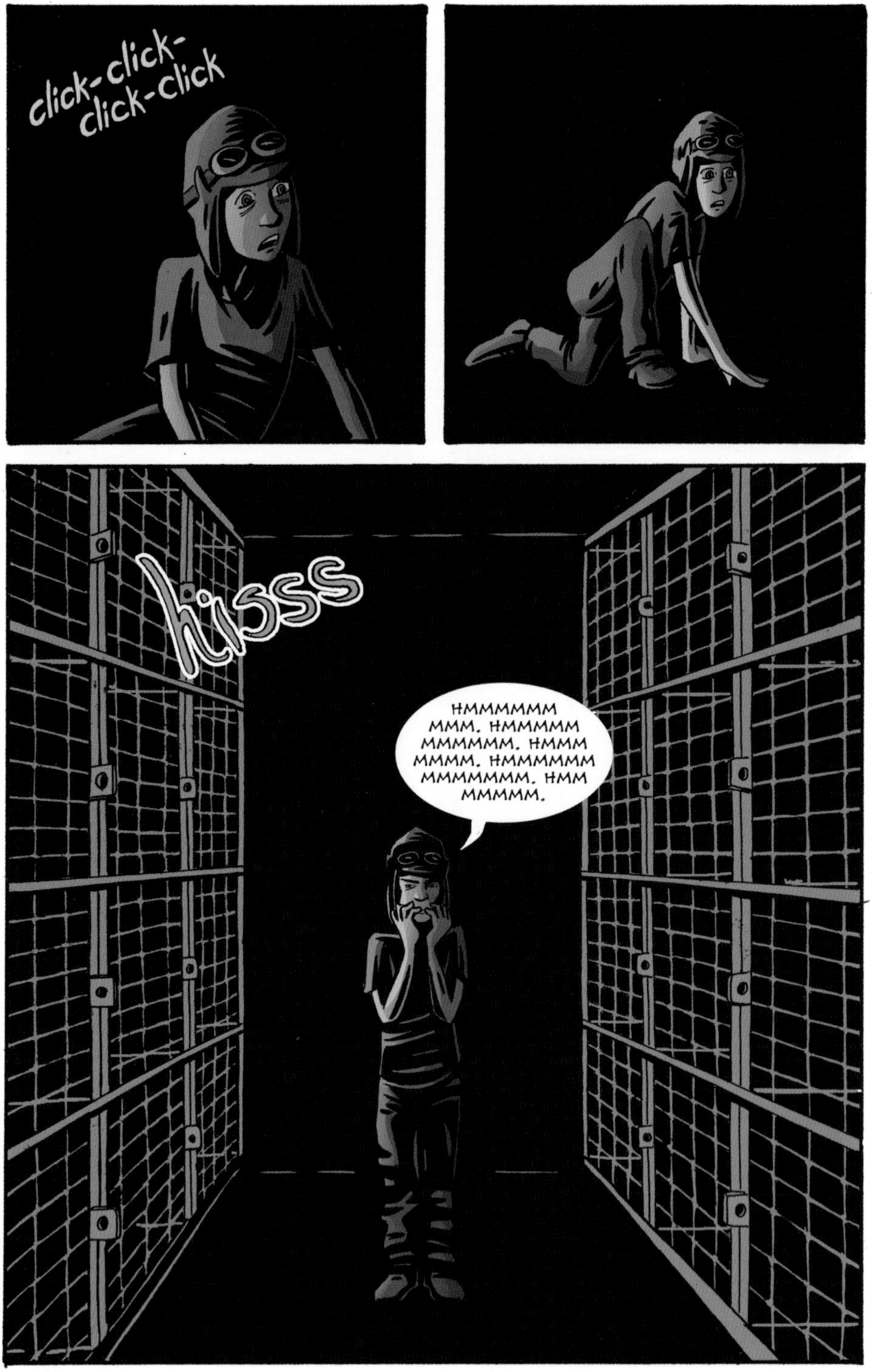
click-click-
click-click
hisss
HMMMMMM MMM. HMMMMM MMMMMM. HMMM MMMM. HMMMMMM MMMMMMM. HMM MMMMM.

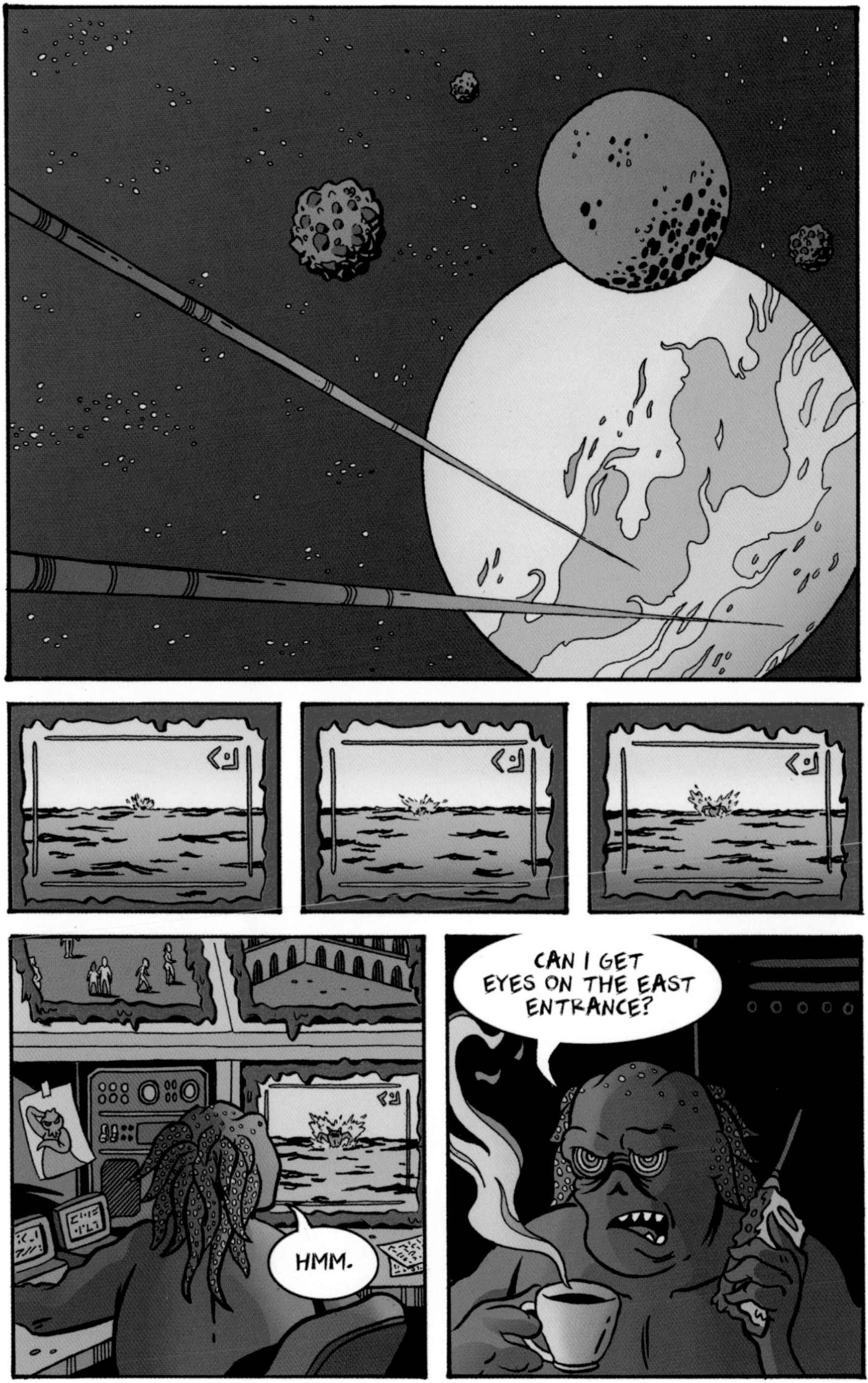
HMM.
CAN I GET EYES ON THE EAST ENTRANCE?

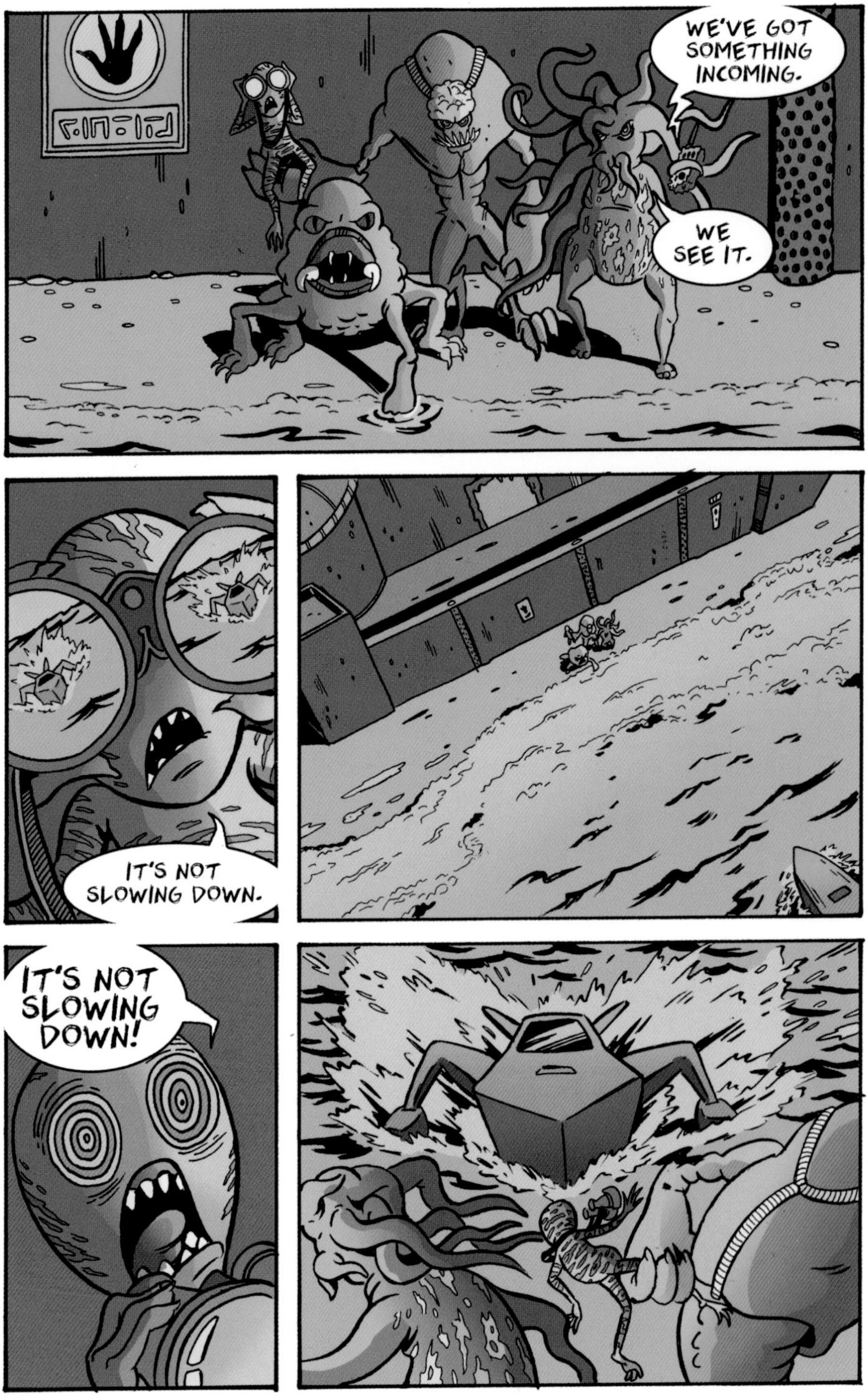
WE'VE GOT SOMETHING INCOMING.
WE SEE IT.
IT'S NOT SLOWING DOWN.
IT'S NOT SLOWING DOWN!

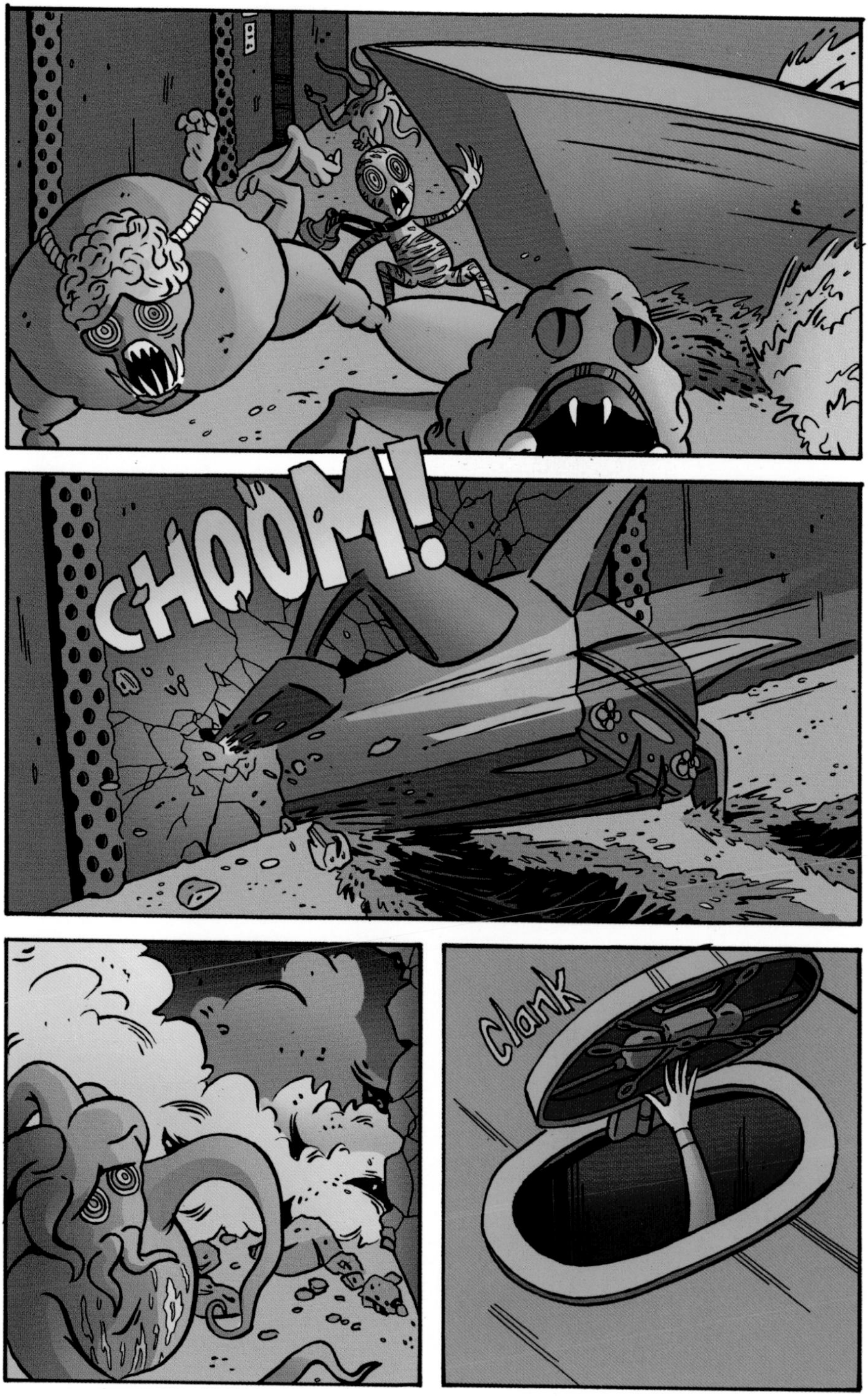
CHOOM!
Clank

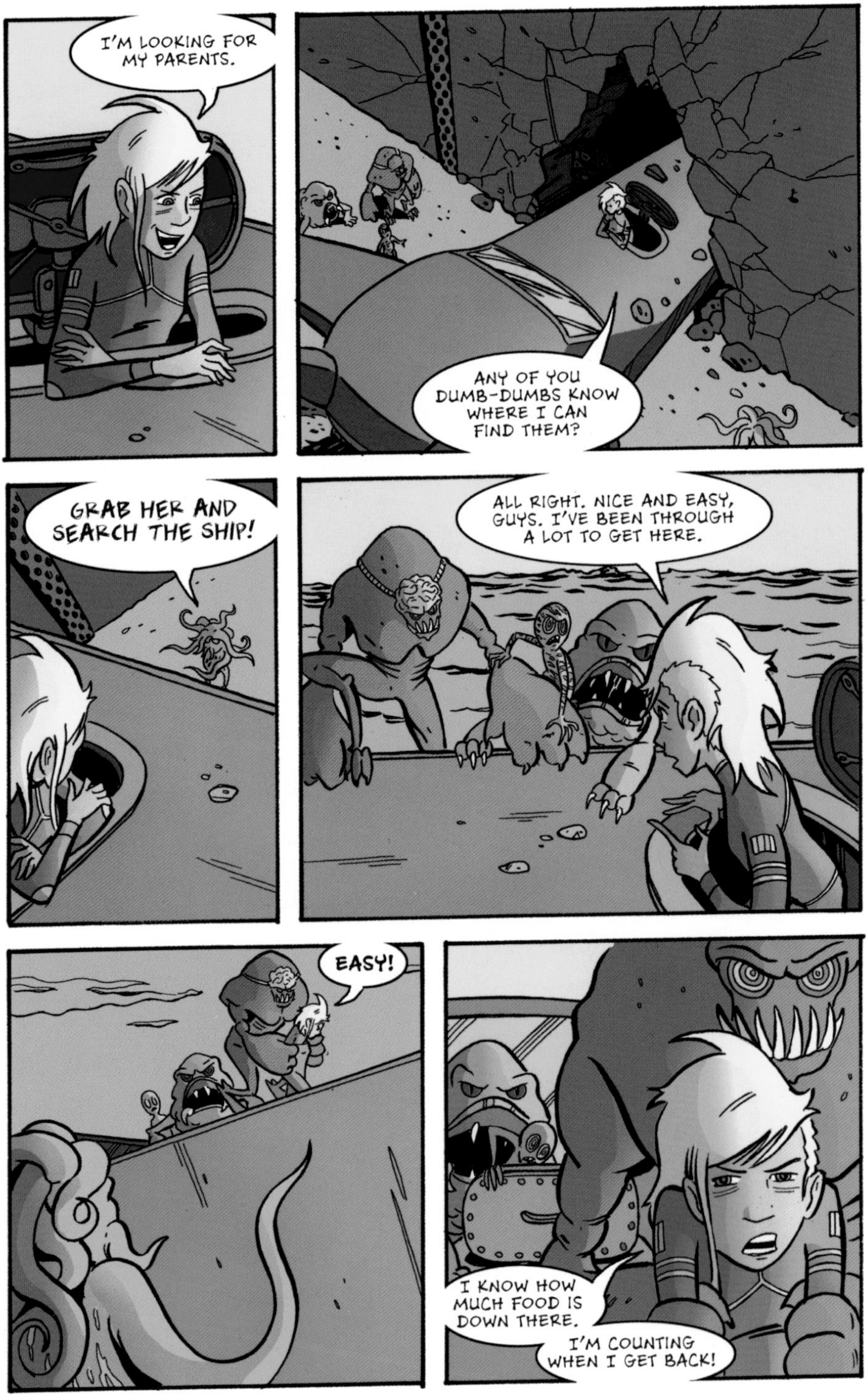

I'M LOOKING FOR MY PARENTS.
ANY OF YOU DUMB-DUMBS KNOW WHERE I CAN FIND THEM?
GRAB HER AND SEARCH THE SHIP!
ALL RIGHT. NICE AND EASY, GUYS. I'VE BEEN THROUGH A LOT TO GET HERE.
EASY!
I KNOW HOW MUCH FOOD IS DOWN THERE.
I'M COUNTING WHEN I GET BACK!

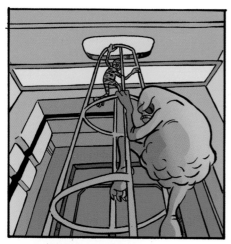

NO ONE HERE.

YEAH. I THINK SHE WAS THE ONLY ONE.

WHAT WAS SHE THINKING?

DO HUMANS REALLY THINK ABOUT MUCH OF ANYTHING?

click

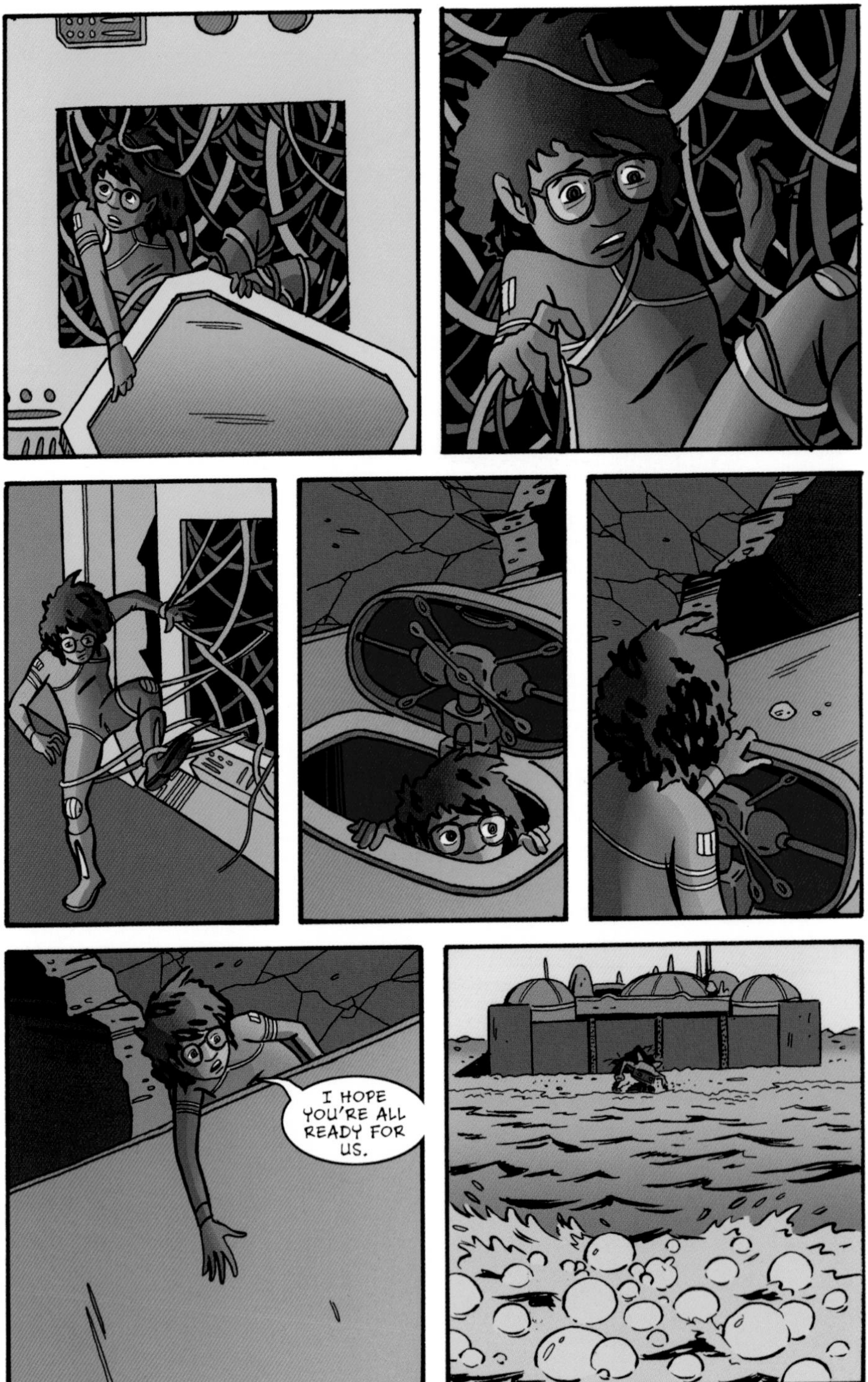
I HOPE YOU'RE ALL READY FOR US.

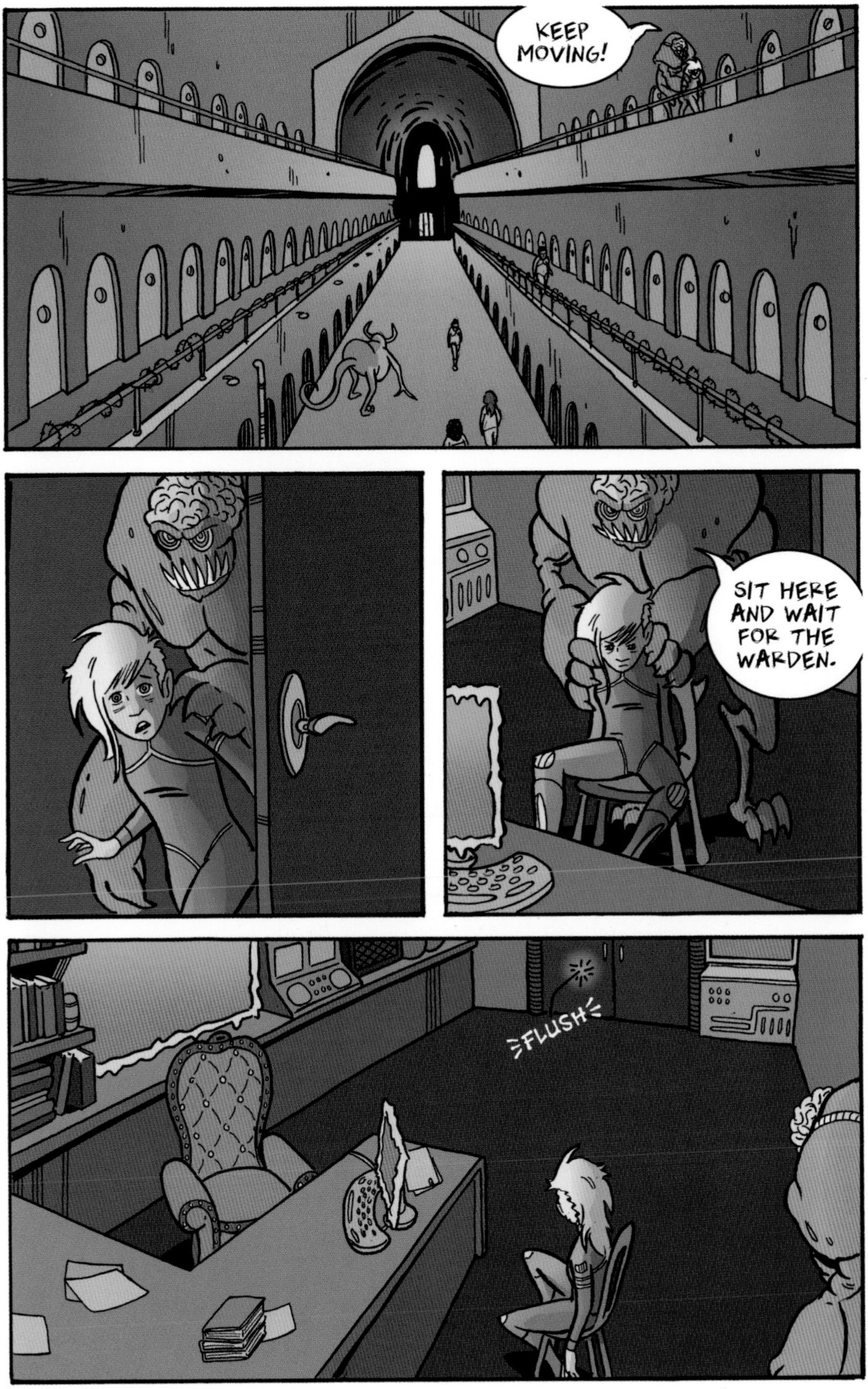
KEEP MOVING!
SIT HERE AND WAIT FOR THE WARDEN.
FLUSH

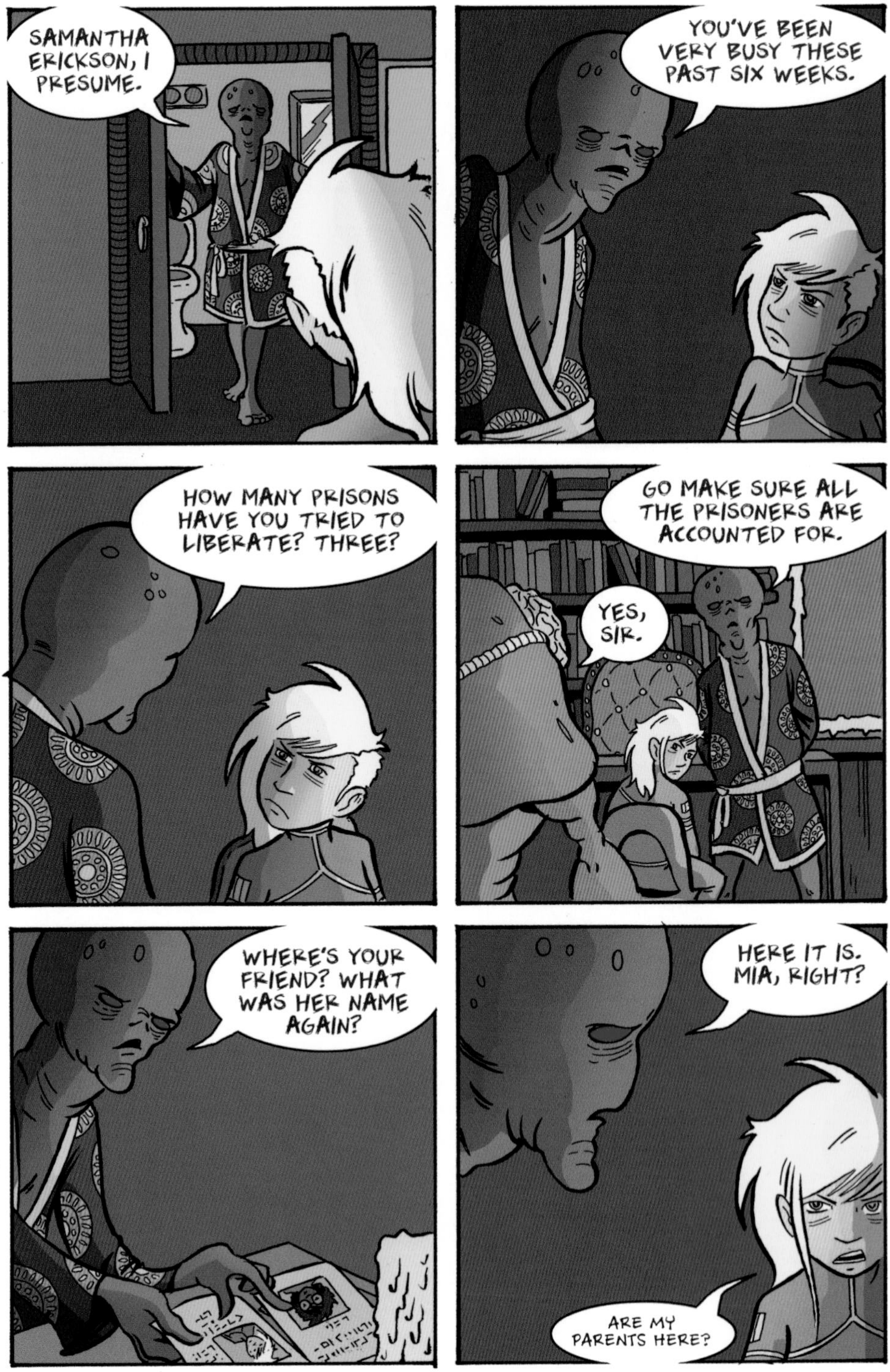
SAMANTHA ERICKSON, I PRESUME.
YOU'VE BEEN VERY BUSY THESE PAST SIX WEEKS.
HOW MANY PRISONS HAVE YOU TRIED TO LIBERATE? THREE?
GO MAKE SURE ALL THE PRISONERS ARE ACCOUNTED FOR.
YES, SIR.
WHERE'S YOUR FRIEND? WHAT WAS HER NAME AGAIN?
HERE IT IS. MIA, RIGHT?
ARE MY PARENTS HERE?

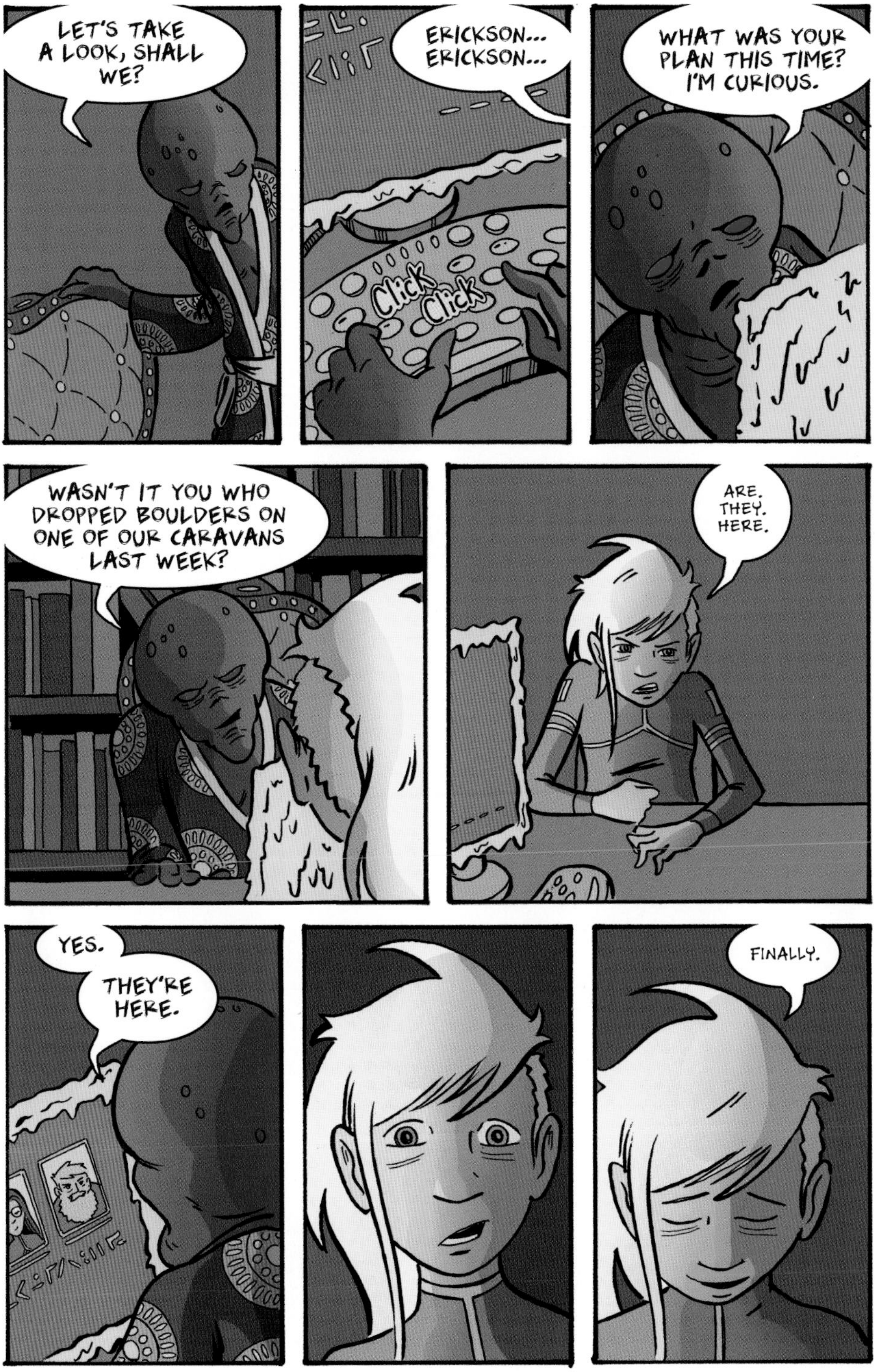
LET'S TAKE A LOOK, SHALL WE?
ERICKSON... ERICKSON...
CLICK CLICK
WHAT WAS YOUR PLAN THIS TIME? I'M CURIOUS.
WASN'T IT YOU WHO DROPPED BOULDERS ON ONE OF OUR CARAVANS LAST WEEK?
ARE. THEY. HERE.
YES.
THEY'RE HERE.
FINALLY.

FOUR.

EXCUSE ME?

WE'VE ATTACKED FOUR DIFFERENT PRISONS.

AH YES. AND IT LOOKS LIKE THEY WERE ALL UNMITIGATED FAILURES ON YOUR PART.

YOU KNOW WHAT THEY SAY...

thump

PRACTICE MAKES PERFECT.

thump

HMM. I'VE BEEN GIVEN PERMISSION TO KILL YOU.

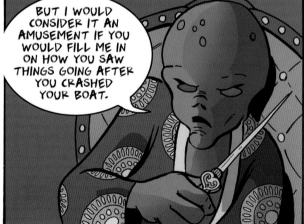

BUT I WOULD CONSIDER IT AN AMUSEMENT IF YOU WOULD FILL ME IN ON HOW YOU SAW THINGS GOING AFTER YOU CRASHED YOUR BOAT.

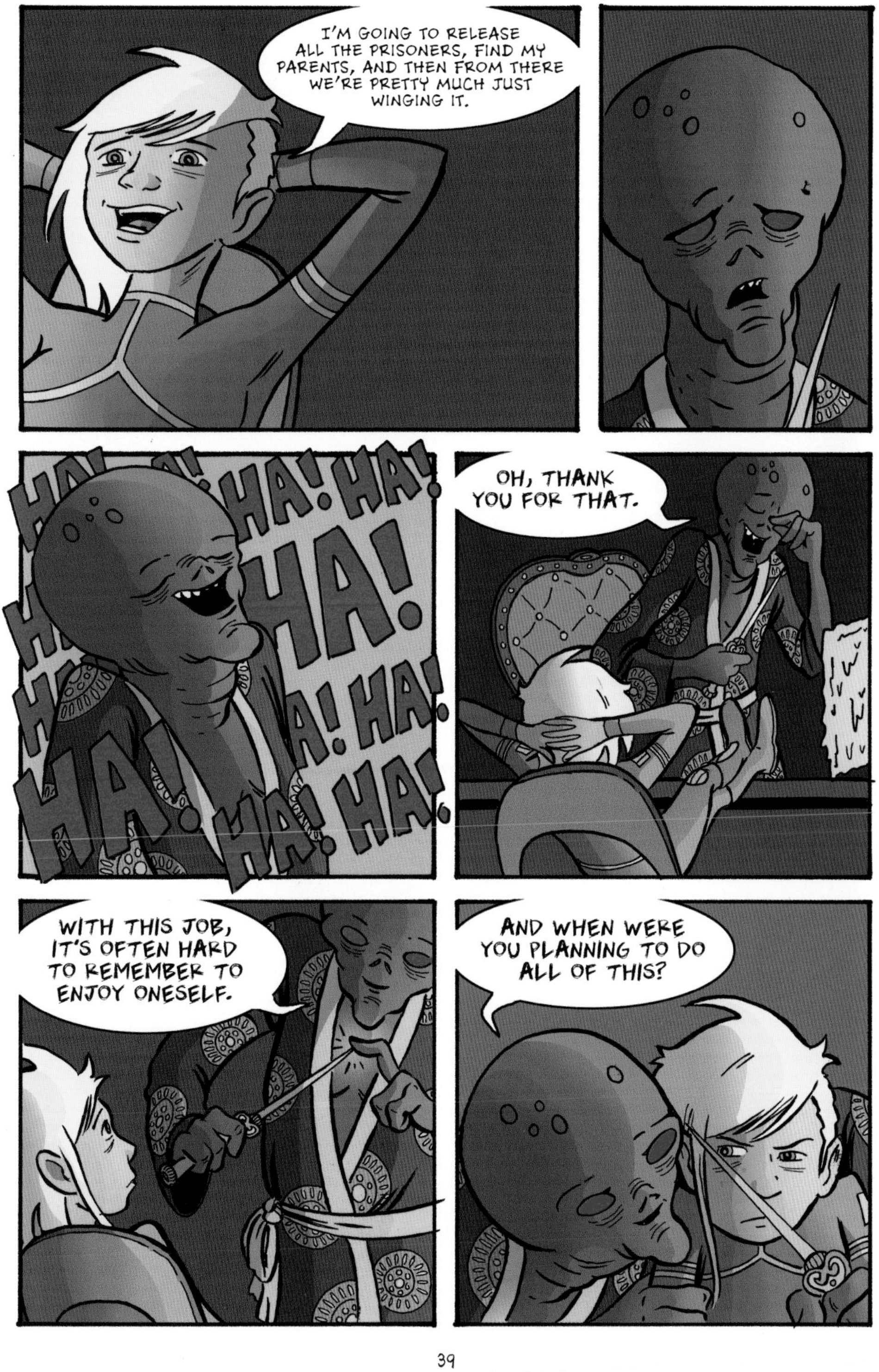
I'M GOING TO RELEASE ALL THE PRISONERS, FIND MY PARENTS, AND THEN FROM THERE WE'RE PRETTY MUCH JUST WINGING IT.
HA! HA! HA! HA! HA! HA! HA! HA! HA! HA!
OH, THANK YOU FOR THAT.
WITH THIS JOB, IT'S OFTEN HARD TO REMEMBER TO ENJOY ONESELF.
AND WHEN WERE YOU PLANNING TO DO ALL OF THIS?

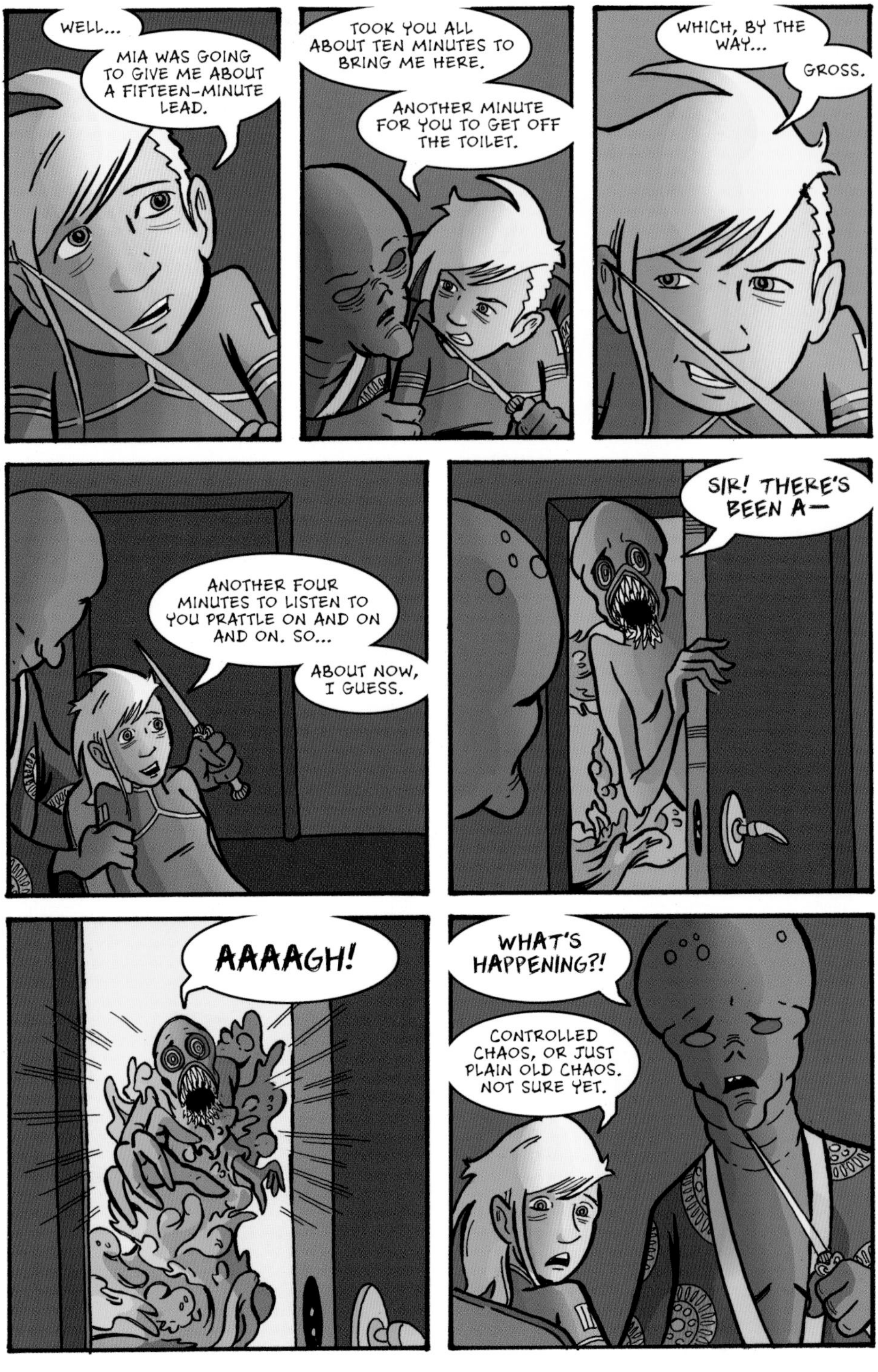
WELL...
MIA WAS GOING TO GIVE ME ABOUT A FIFTEEN-MINUTE LEAD.
TOOK YOU ALL ABOUT TEN MINUTES TO BRING ME HERE.
ANOTHER MINUTE FOR YOU TO GET OFF THE TOILET.
WHICH, BY THE WAY...
GROSS.
ANOTHER FOUR MINUTES TO LISTEN TO YOU PRATTLE ON AND ON AND ON. SO...
ABOUT NOW, I GUESS.
SIR! THERE'S BEEN A—
AAAAGH!
WHAT'S HAPPENING?!
CONTROLLED CHAOS, OR JUST PLAIN OLD CHAOS. NOT SURE YET.

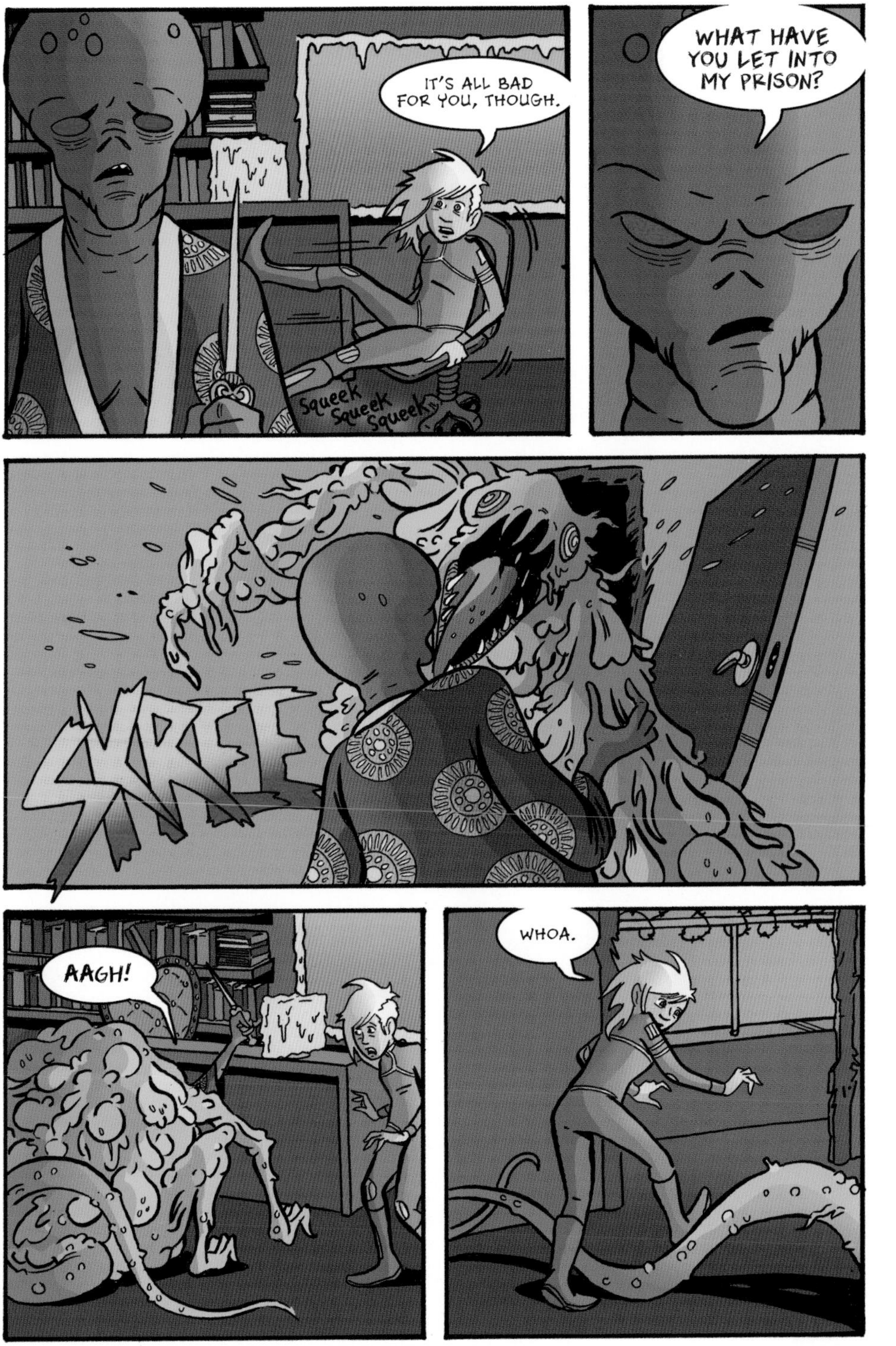
IT'S ALL BAD FOR YOU, THOUGH.
Squeek Squeek Squeek
WHAT HAVE YOU LET INTO MY PRISON?
SKREE
AAGH!
WHOA.

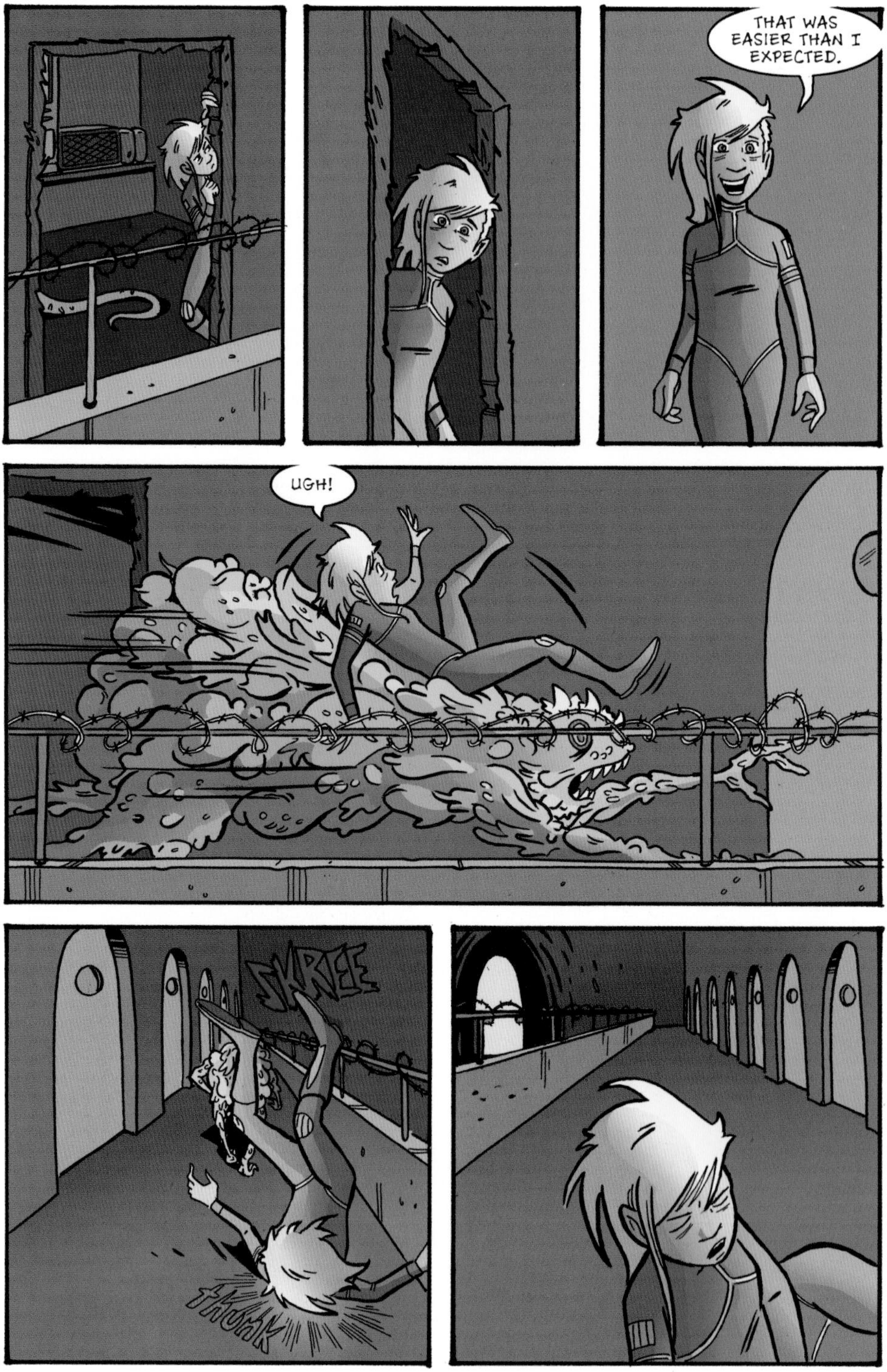
THAT WAS EASIER THAN I EXPECTED.
UGH!
SKREE
THUNK

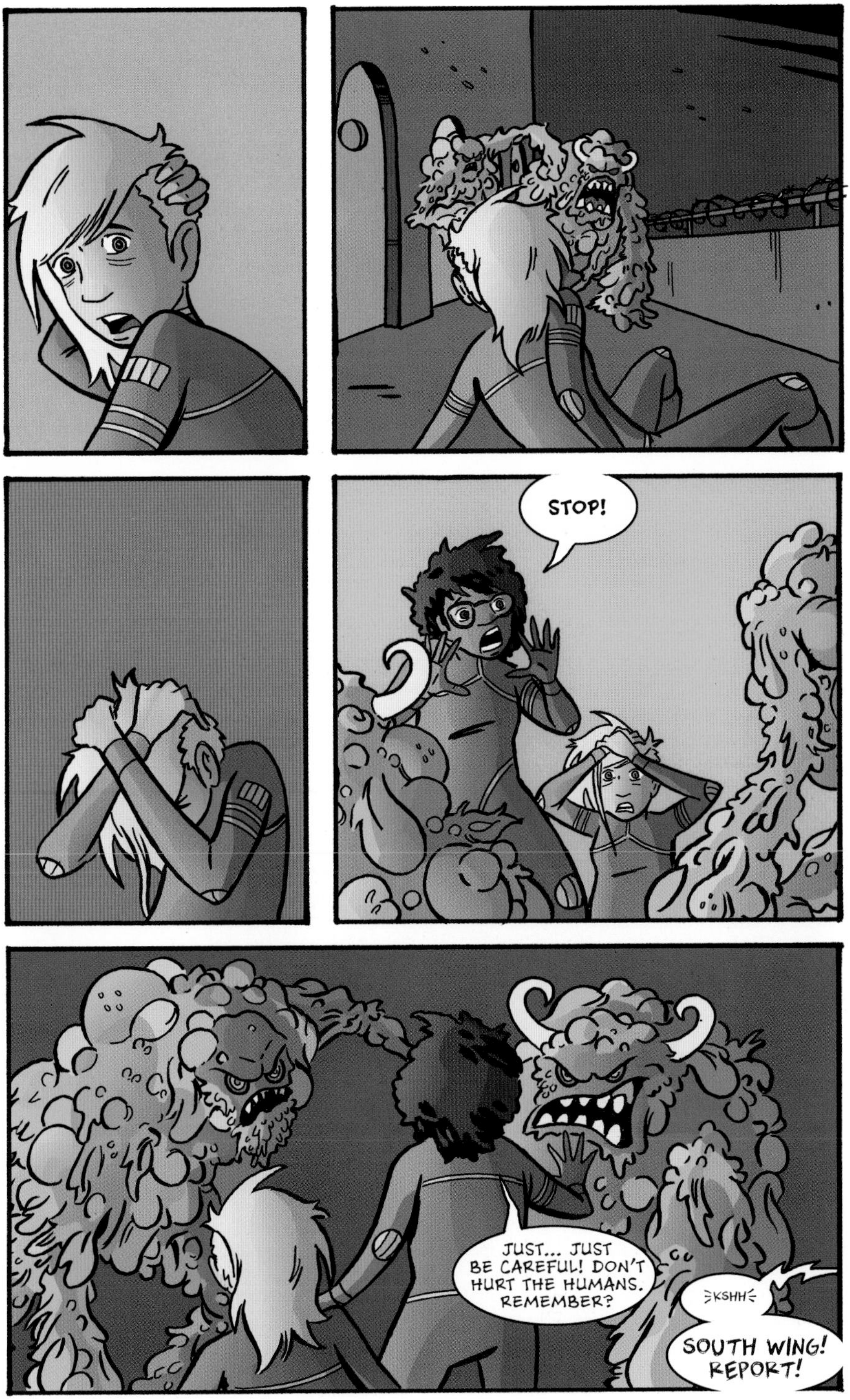
STOP!
JUST... JUST BE CAREFUL! DON'T HURT THE HUMANS. REMEMBER?
KSHH
SOUTH WING! REPORT!

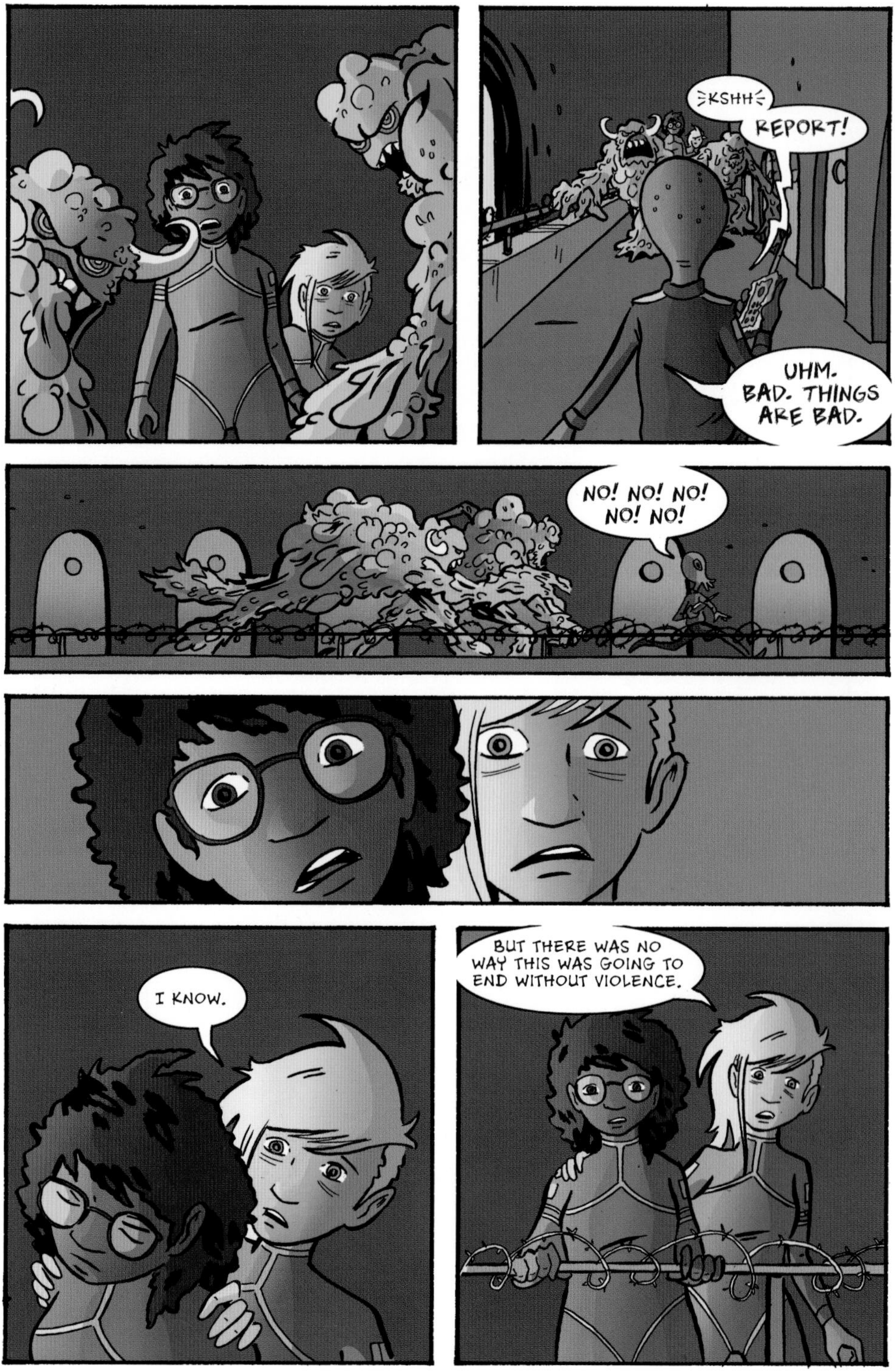
KSHH
REPORT!
UHM. BAD. THINGS ARE BAD.
NO! NO! NO! NO! NO!
I KNOW.
BUT THERE WAS NO WAY THIS WAS GOING TO END WITHOUT VIOLENCE.

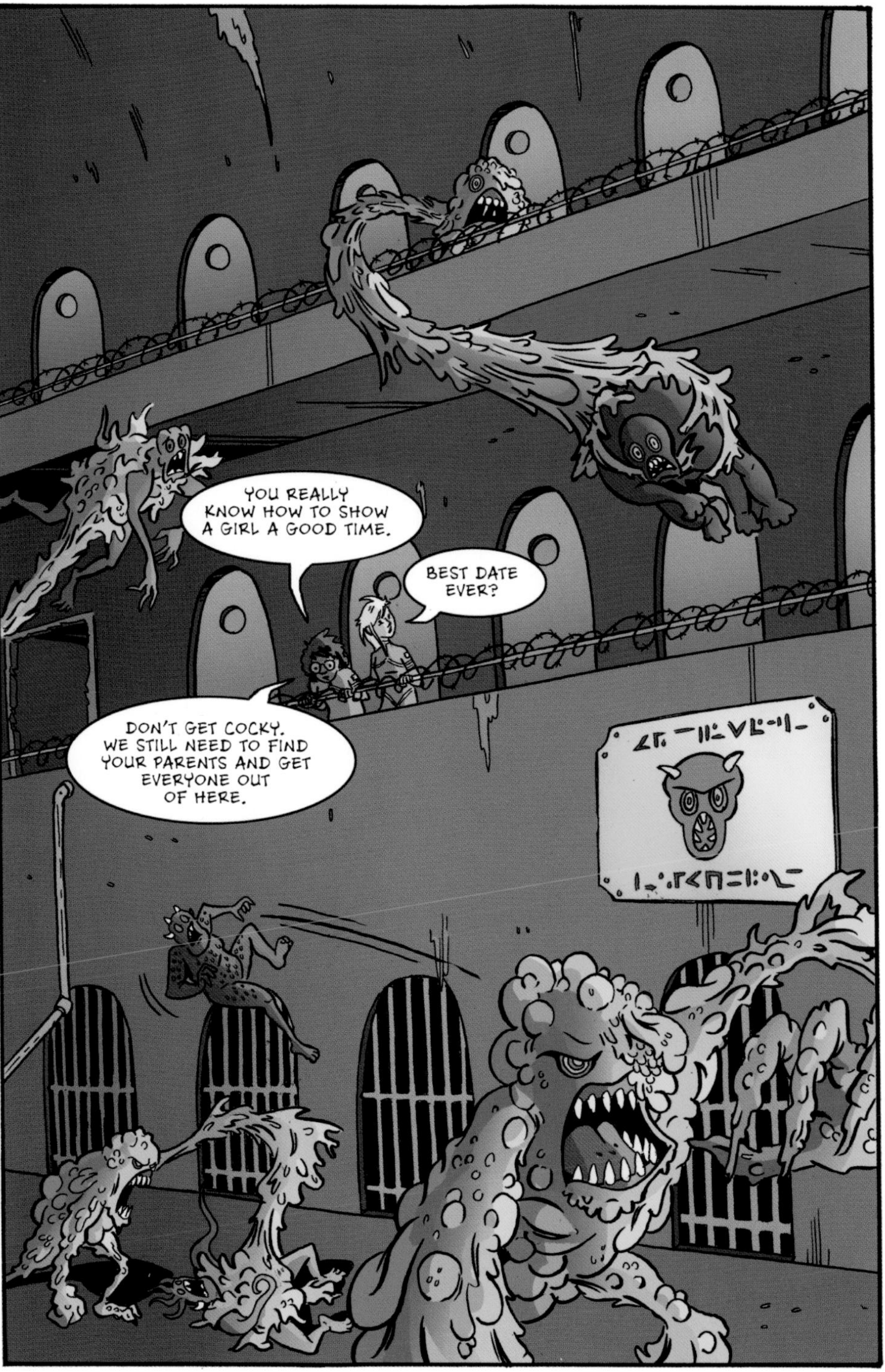

YOU REALLY KNOW HOW TO SHOW A GIRL A GOOD TIME.
BEST DATE EVER?
DON'T GET COCKY. WE STILL NEED TO FIND YOUR PARENTS AND GET EVERYONE OUT OF HERE.

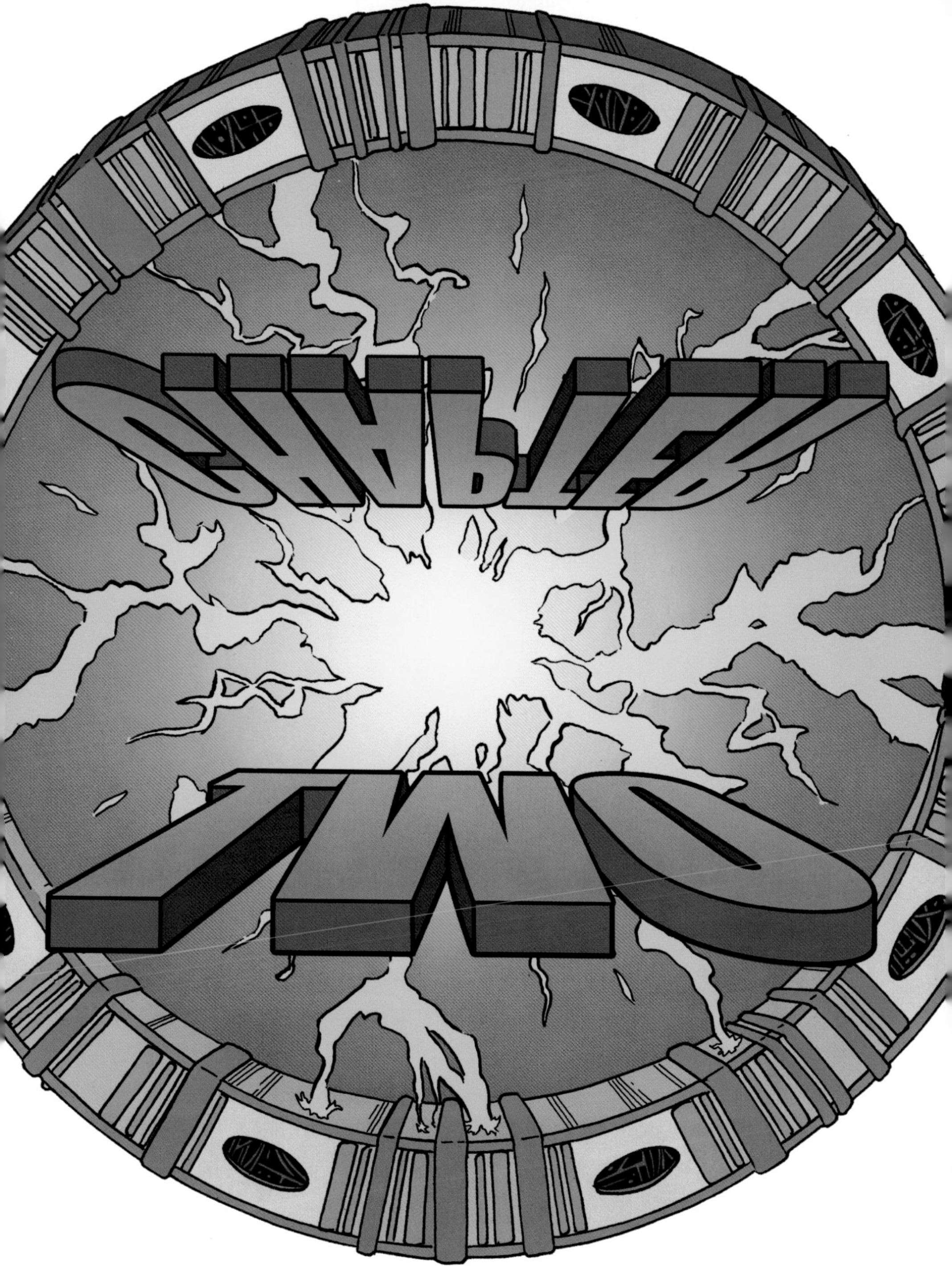
CHAPTER
TWO

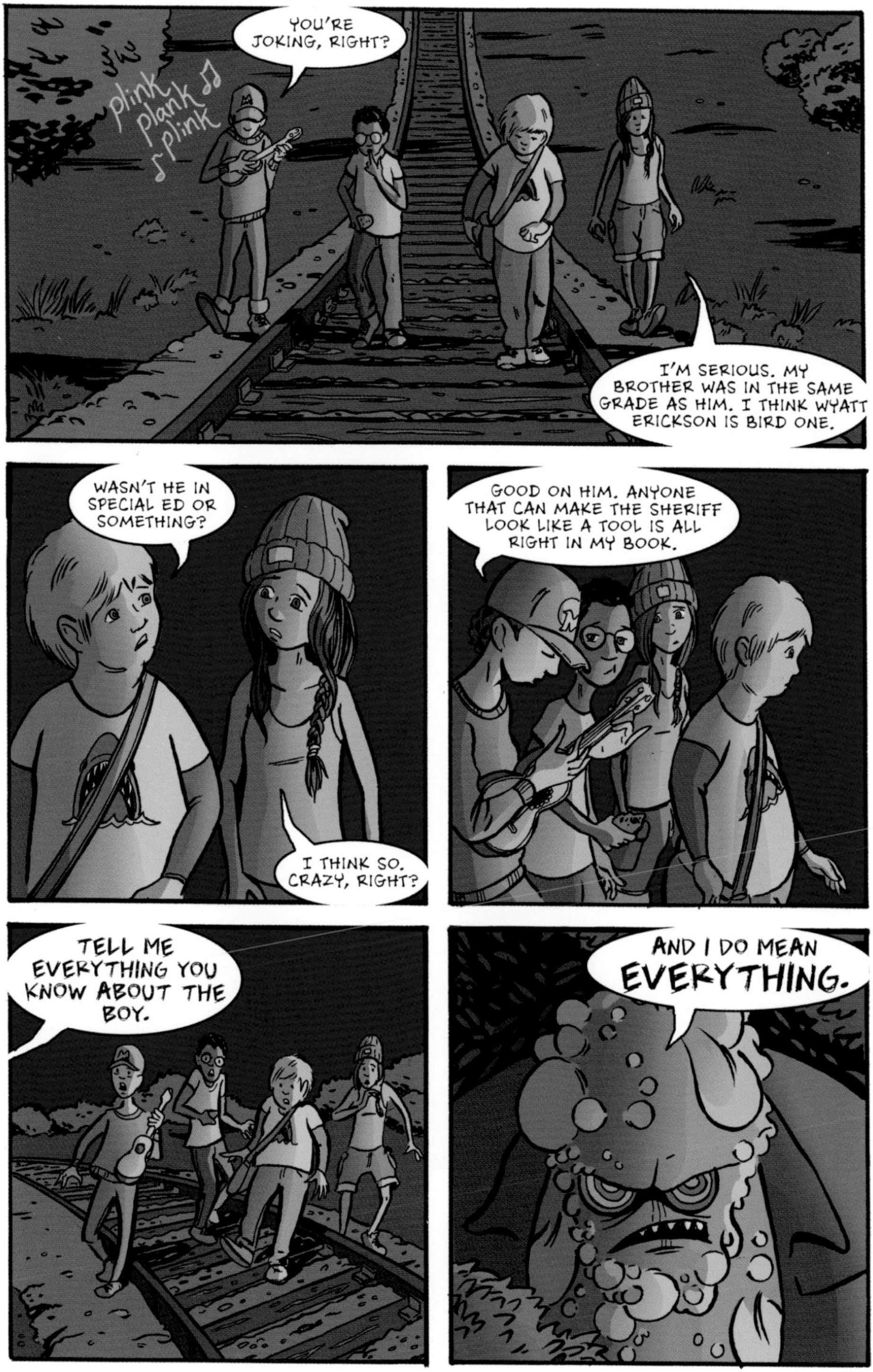
plink plank plink
YOU'RE JOKING, RIGHT?
I'M SERIOUS. MY BROTHER WAS IN THE SAME GRADE AS HIM. I THINK WYATT ERICKSON IS BIRD ONE.
WASN'T HE IN SPECIAL ED OR SOMETHING?
I THINK SO. CRAZY, RIGHT?
GOOD ON HIM. ANYONE THAT CAN MAKE THE SHERIFF LOOK LIKE A TOOL IS ALL RIGHT IN MY BOOK.
TELL ME EVERYTHING YOU KNOW ABOUT THE BOY.
AND I DO MEAN **EVERYTHING.**

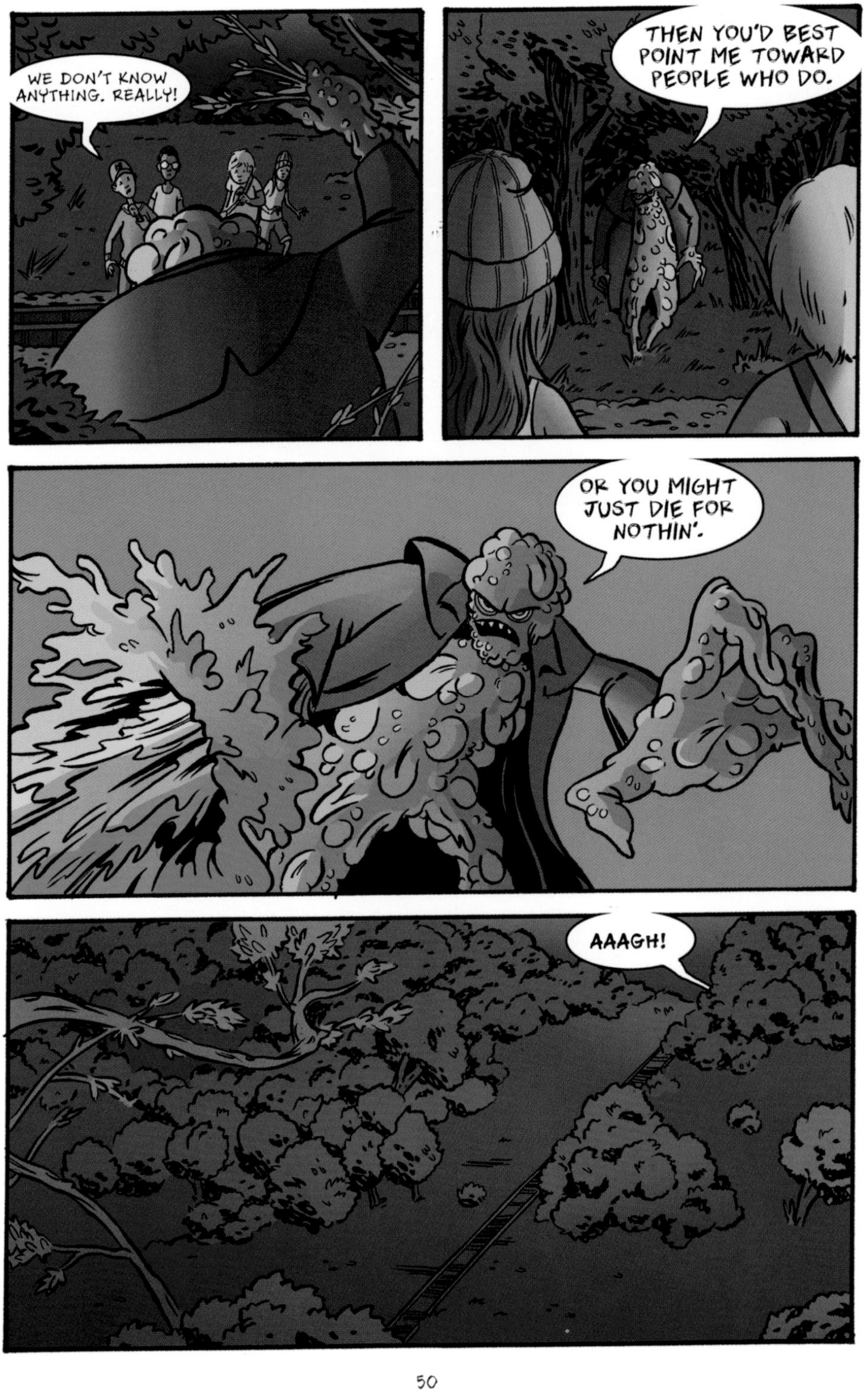
WE DON'T KNOW ANYTHING. REALLY!
THEN YOU'D BEST POINT ME TOWARD PEOPLE WHO DO.
OR YOU MIGHT JUST DIE FOR NOTHIN'.
AAAGH!

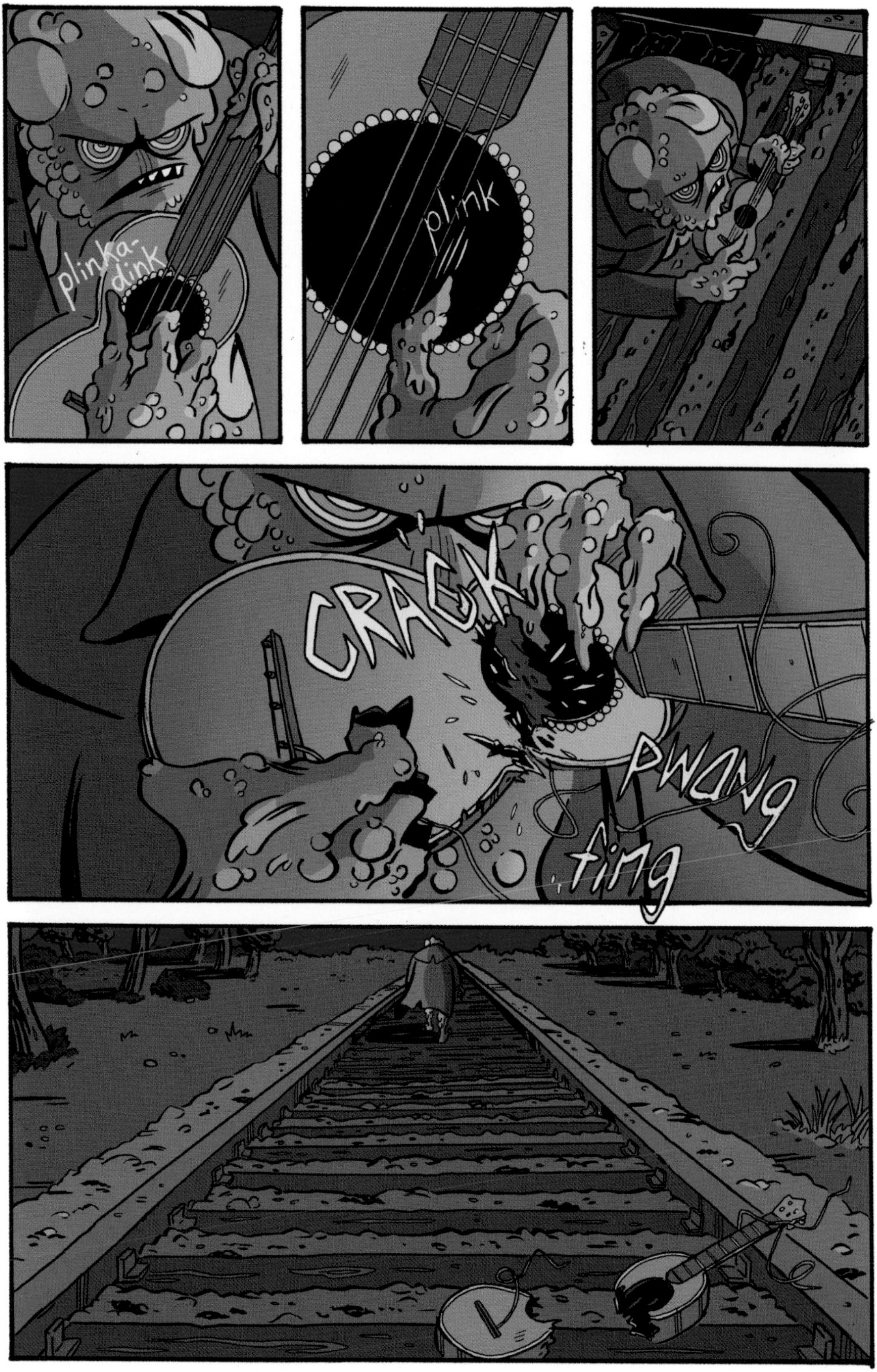
plinka-
dink
plink
CRACK
PWANG
fing

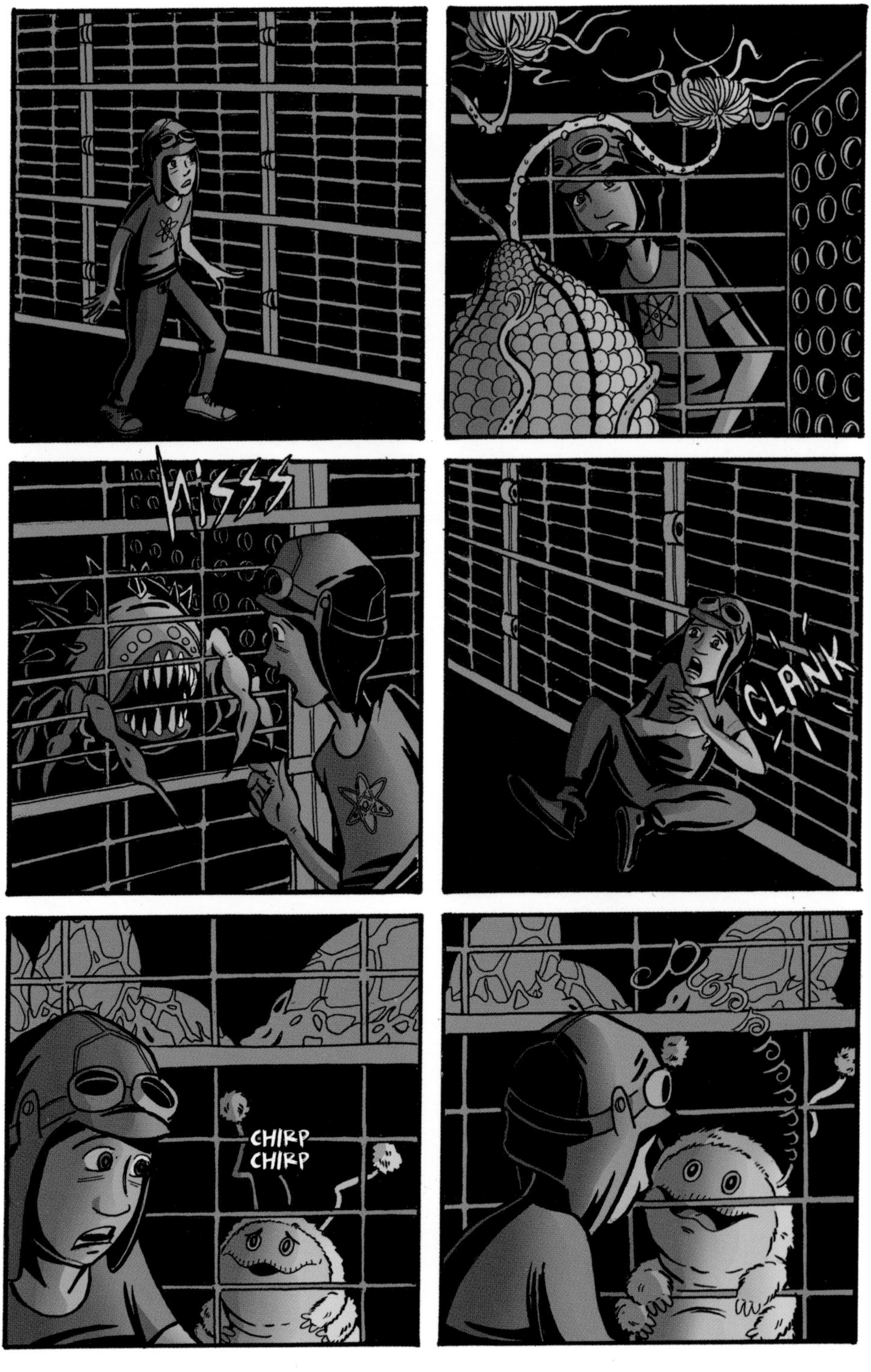
HISSS
CLANK
CHIRP
CHIRP
Purrrrrrrr

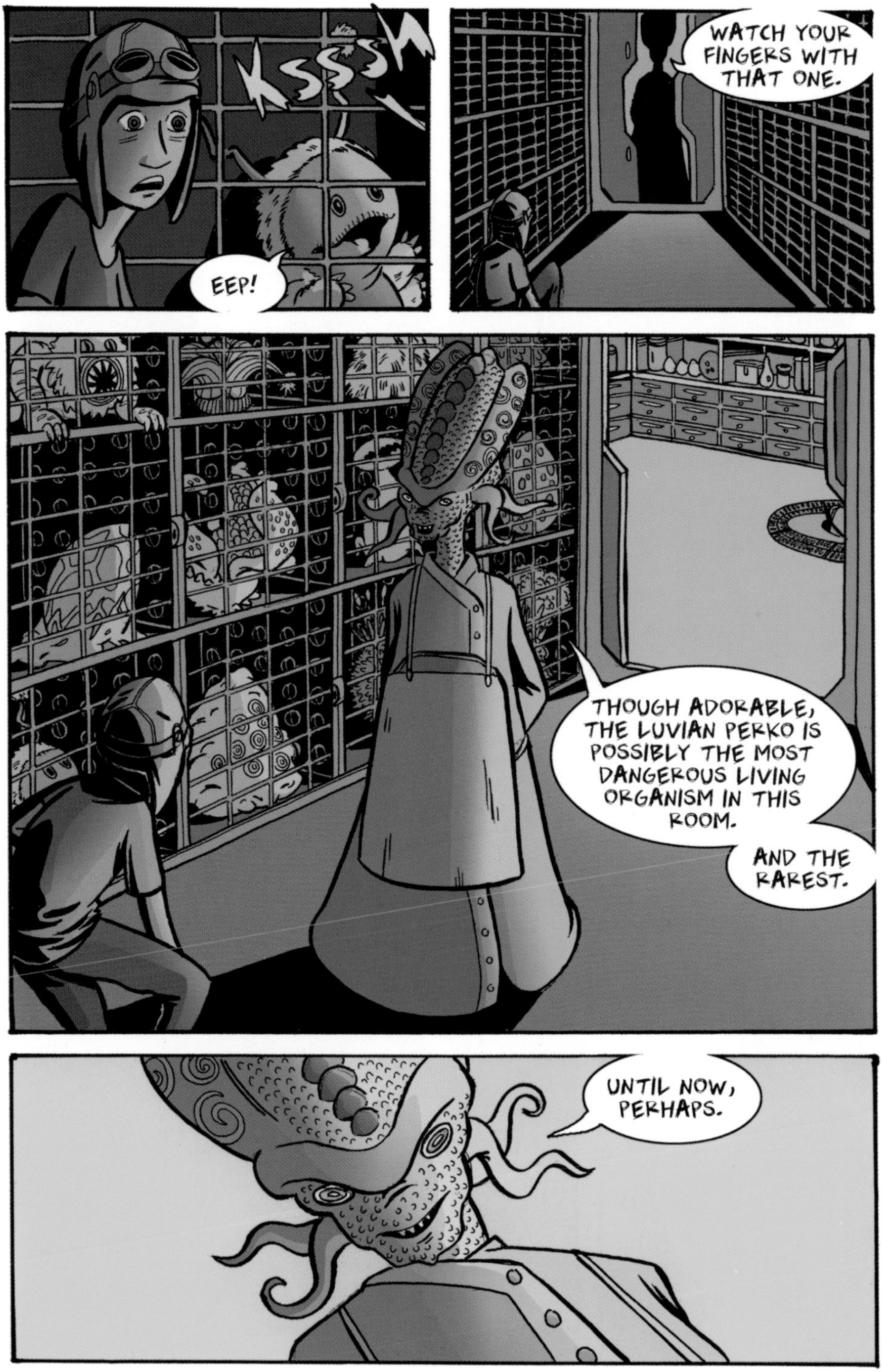
KSSS
EEP!
WATCH YOUR FINGERS WITH THAT ONE.
THOUGH ADORABLE, THE LUVIAN PERKO IS POSSIBLY THE MOST DANGEROUS LIVING ORGANISM IN THIS ROOM.
AND THE RAREST.
UNTIL NOW, PERHAPS.

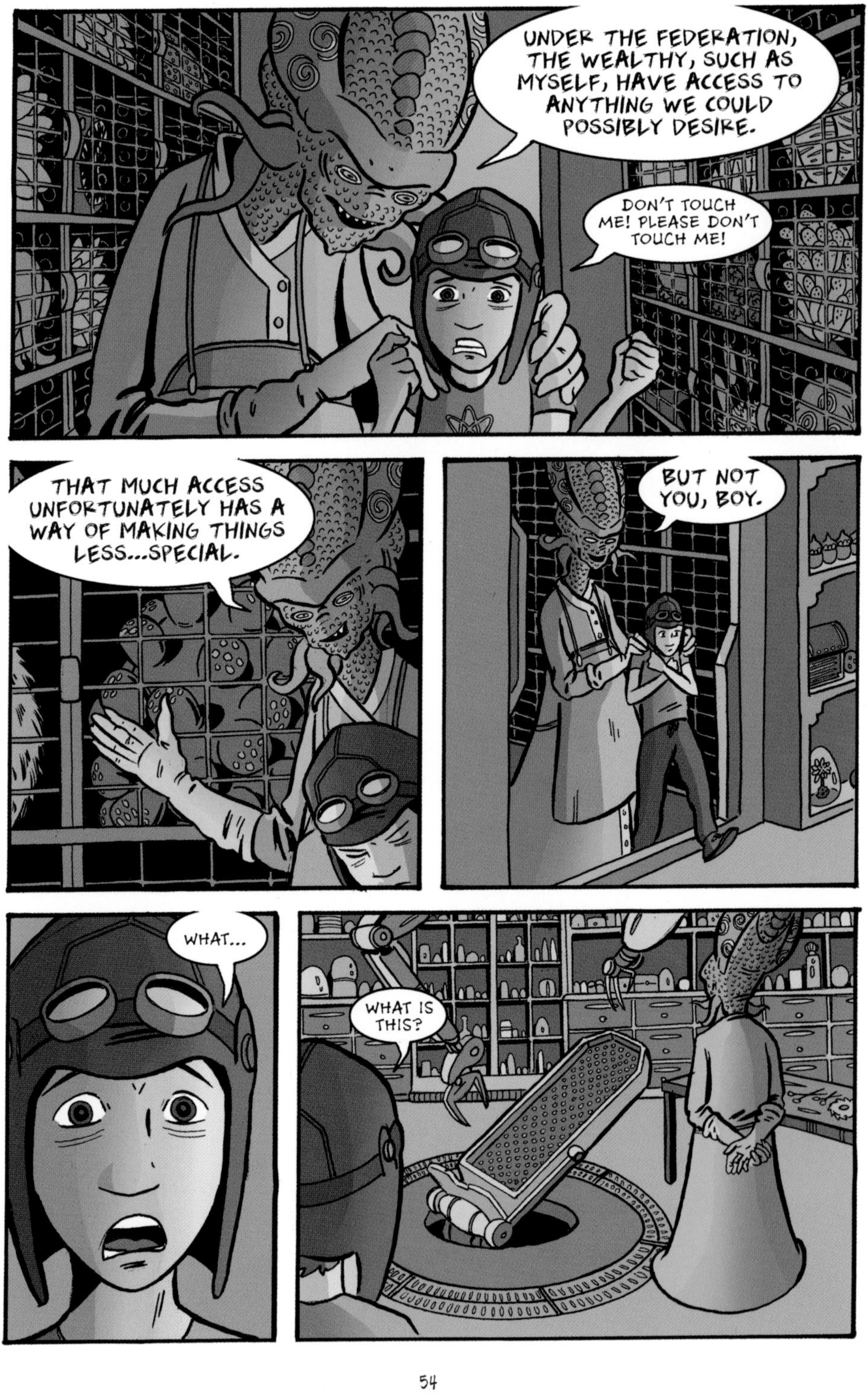
UNDER THE FEDERATION, THE WEALTHY, SUCH AS MYSELF, HAVE ACCESS TO ANYTHING WE COULD POSSIBLY DESIRE.
DON'T TOUCH ME! PLEASE DON'T TOUCH ME!
THAT MUCH ACCESS UNFORTUNATELY HAS A WAY OF MAKING THINGS LESS...SPECIAL.
BUT NOT YOU, BOY.
WHAT...
WHAT IS THIS?

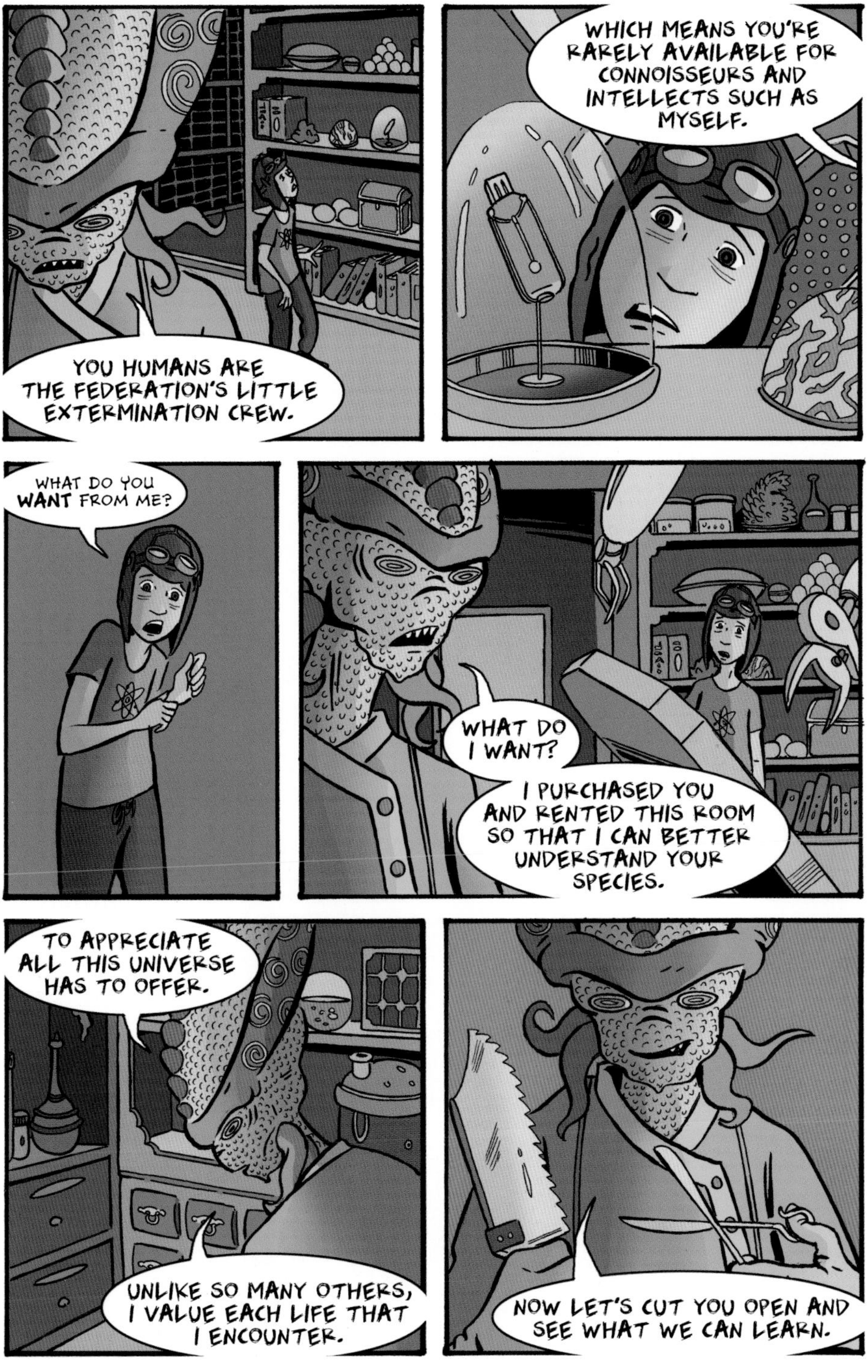

YOU HUMANS ARE THE FEDERATION'S LITTLE EXTERMINATION CREW.
WHICH MEANS YOU'RE RARELY AVAILABLE FOR CONNOISSEURS AND INTELLECTS SUCH AS MYSELF.
WHAT DO YOU WANT FROM ME?
WHAT DO I WANT?
I PURCHASED YOU AND RENTED THIS ROOM SO THAT I CAN BETTER UNDERSTAND YOUR SPECIES.
TO APPRECIATE ALL THIS UNIVERSE HAS TO OFFER.
UNLIKE SO MANY OTHERS, I VALUE EACH LIFE THAT I ENCOUNTER.
NOW LET'S CUT YOU OPEN AND SEE WHAT WE CAN LEARN.

GET AWAY FROM ME!

CAN I OFFER YOU A PARALYZING AGENT? IT WOULD MAKE MY WORK SO MUCH EASIER.

WAIT WAIT **WAIT!** JUST **WAIT!**

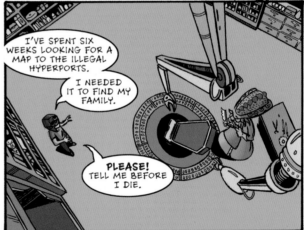

I'VE SPENT SIX WEEKS LOOKING FOR A MAP TO THE ILLEGAL HYPERPORTS.

I NEEDED IT TO FIND MY FAMILY.

PLEASE! TELL ME BEFORE I DIE.

WAS I CLOSE?

I HAVE TO KNOW.

HOW CAN I DENY A LAST REQUEST FROM SUCH A RARE SCIENTIFIC FIND?

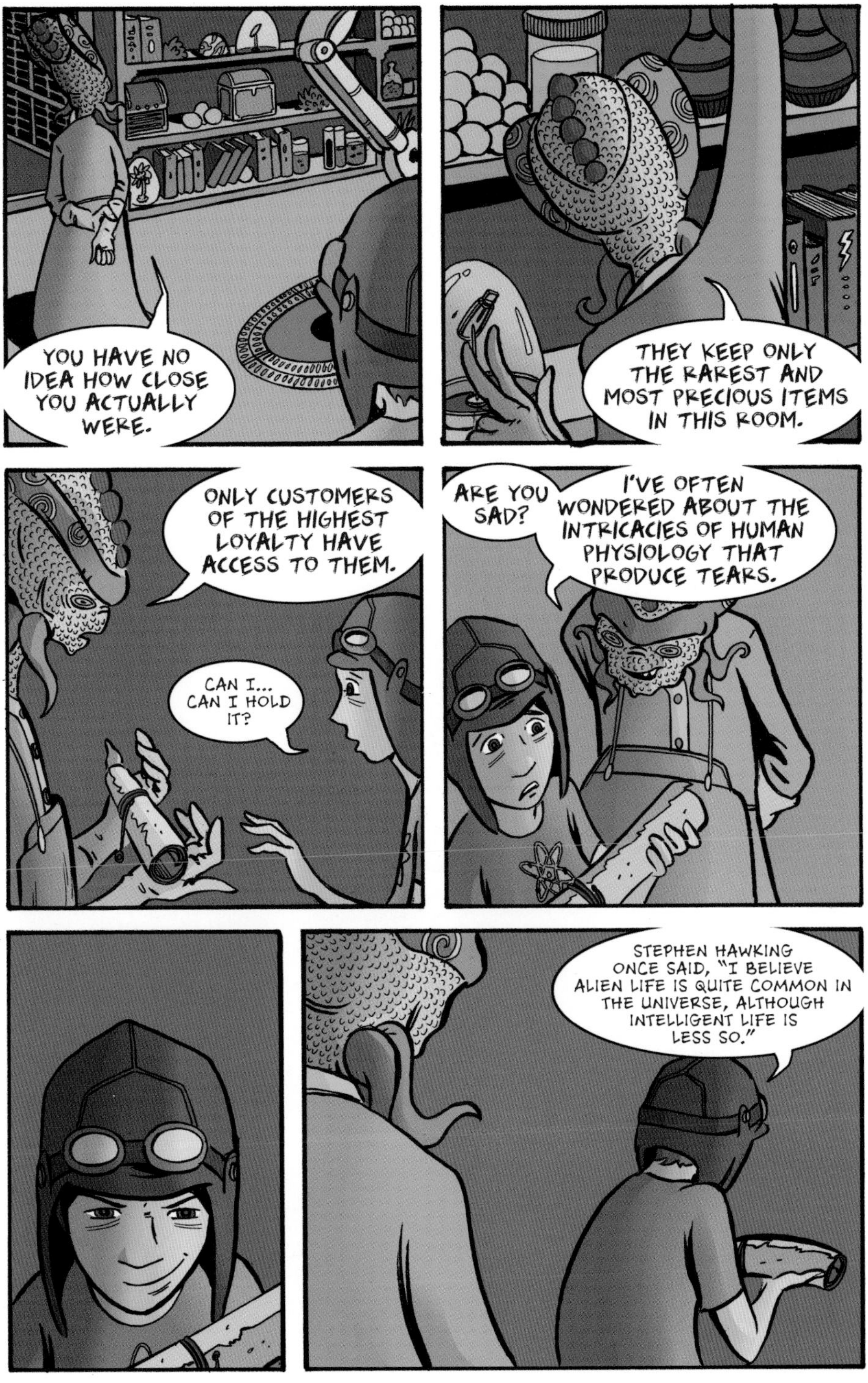
YOU HAVE NO IDEA HOW CLOSE YOU ACTUALLY WERE.
THEY KEEP ONLY THE RAREST AND MOST PRECIOUS ITEMS IN THIS ROOM.
ONLY CUSTOMERS OF THE HIGHEST LOYALTY HAVE ACCESS TO THEM.
CAN I... CAN I HOLD IT?
ARE YOU SAD?
I'VE OFTEN WONDERED ABOUT THE INTRICACIES OF HUMAN PHYSIOLOGY THAT PRODUCE TEARS.
STEPHEN HAWKING ONCE SAID, "I BELIEVE ALIEN LIFE IS QUITE COMMON IN THE UNIVERSE, ALTHOUGH INTELLIGENT LIFE IS LESS SO."

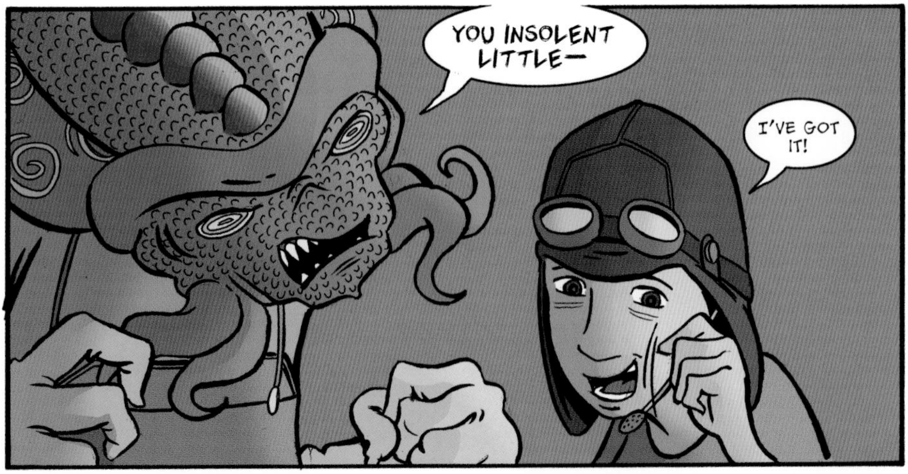
YOU INSOLENT LITTLE—
I'VE GOT IT!

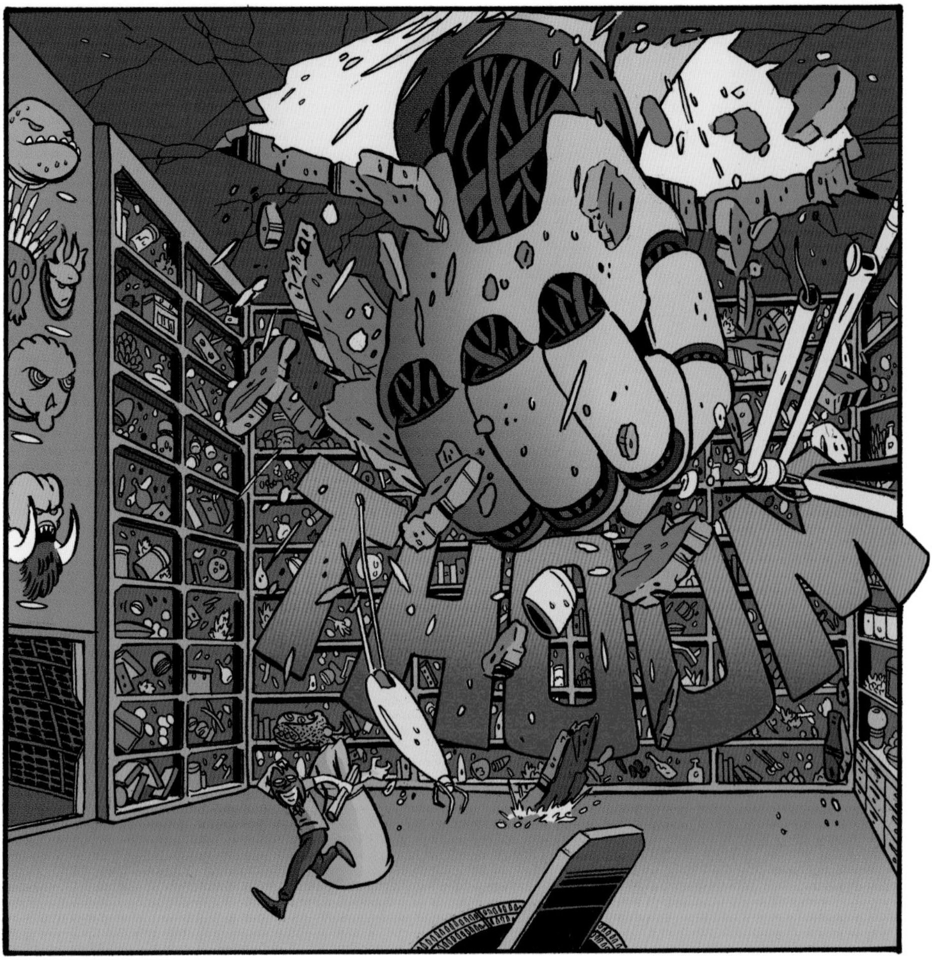
THOOM

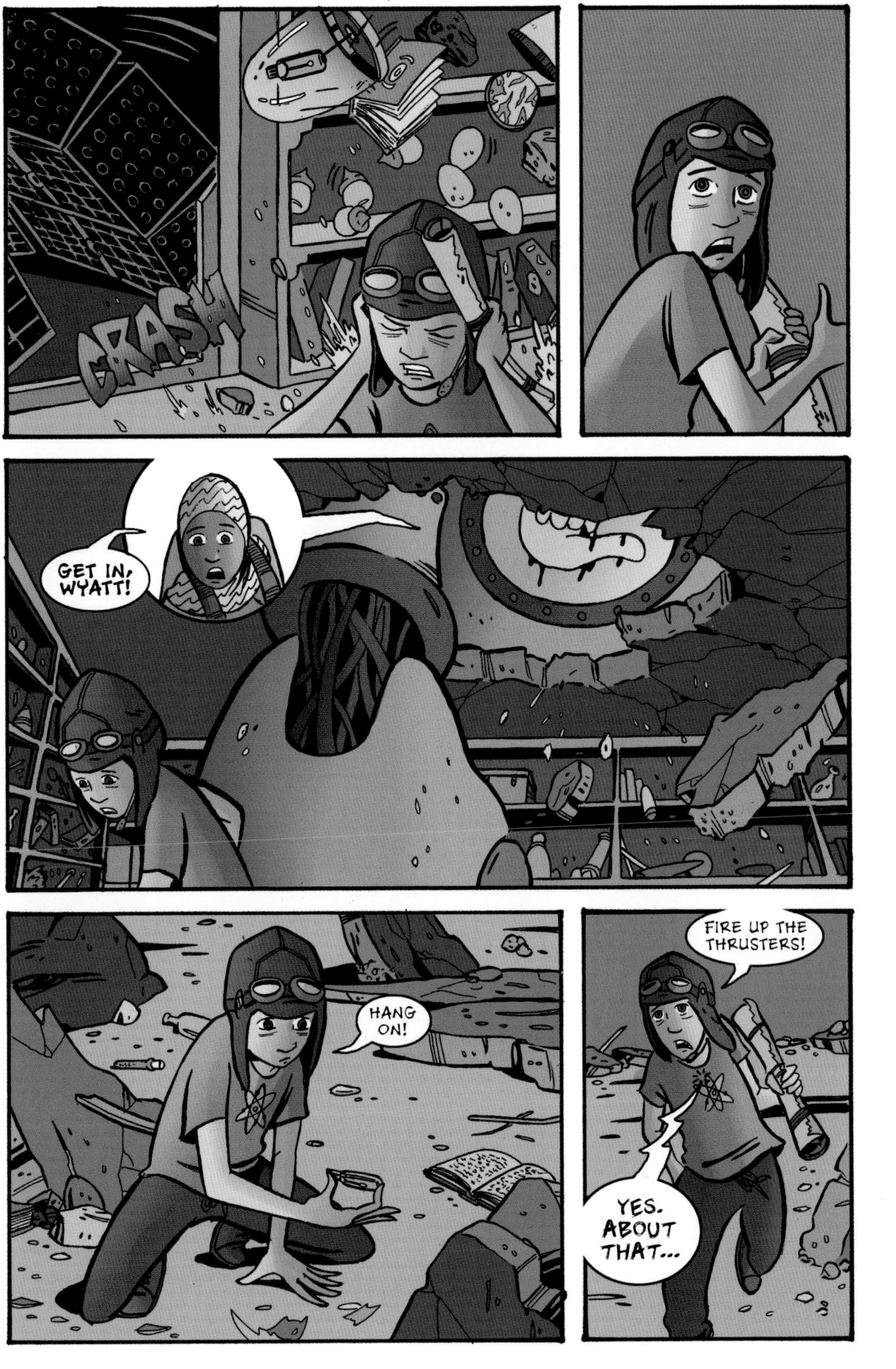
CRASH
GET IN, WYATT!
HANG ON!
FIRE UP THE THRUSTERS!
YES. ABOUT THAT...

DON'T GO! PLEASE!

WHAT IF I JUST EXAMINE YOUR BRAIN?

JUST THE BRAIN!

pupppp

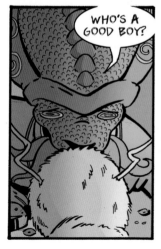

WHO'S A GOOD BOY?

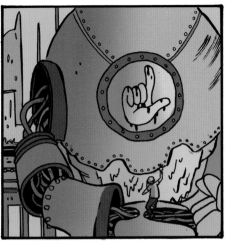

ARE YOU OKAY?

YES, NO, I DON'T KNOW! HE WAS GOING TO DISSECT ME!

WHY DID I HAVE TO BE THE ONE CHOSEN?

IS IT WEIRD THAT I'M A LITTLE OFFENDED?

I MEAN, IT'S NOT LIKE YOU WERE THE ONLY HUMAN THERE.

YOU HAVE MAP?

I'VE GOT IT.

THEN GOOD PLAN. I AM BRILLIANT MASTERMIND.

LET'S GET TO THE HYPERPORT.

LIKE DR. DOOM, BUT GOOD GUY, NO?

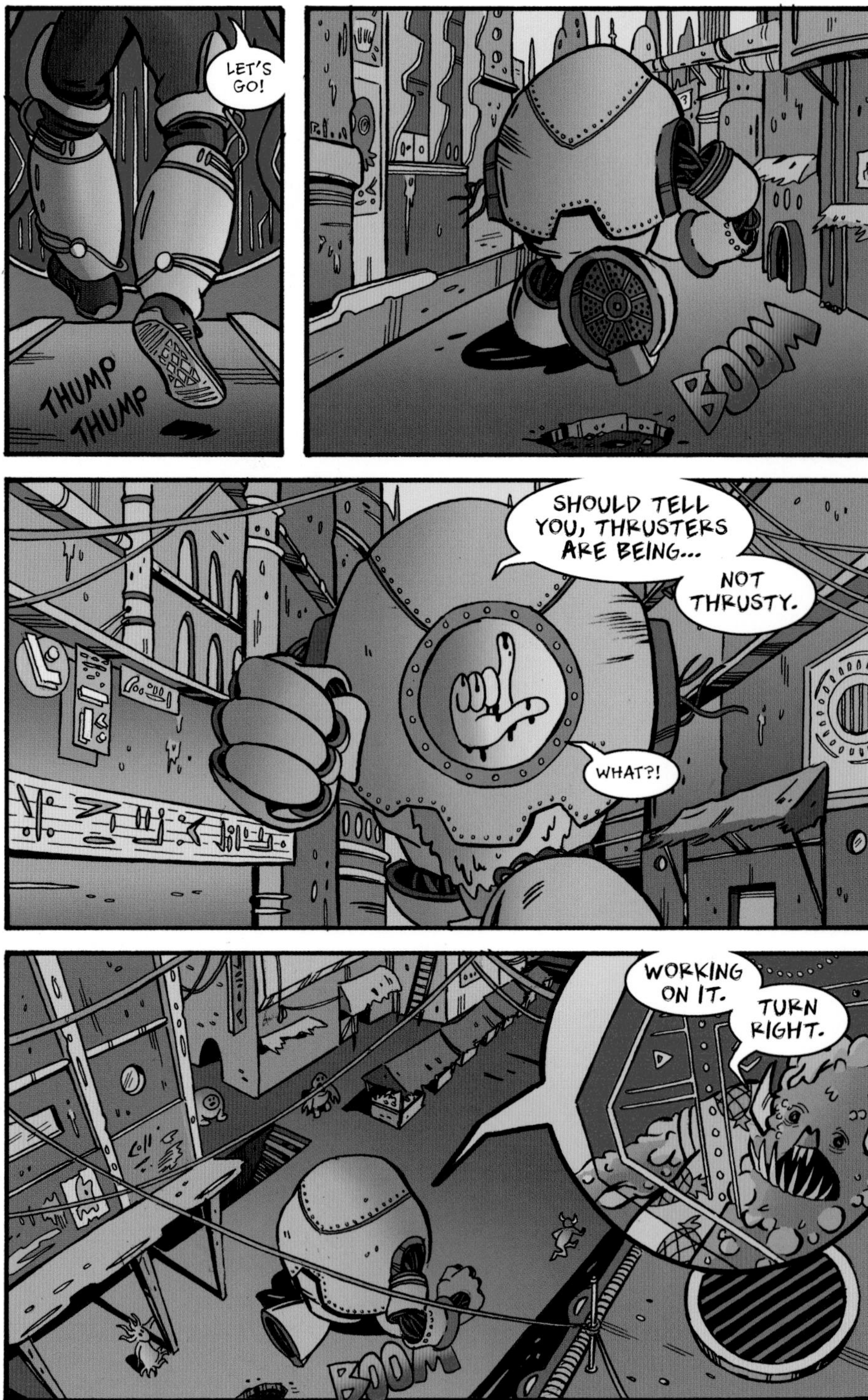
LET'S GO!
THUMP THUMP
BOOM
SHOULD TELL YOU, THRUSTERS ARE BEING...
NOT THRUSTY.
WHAT?!
WORKING ON IT.
TURN RIGHT.
BOOM

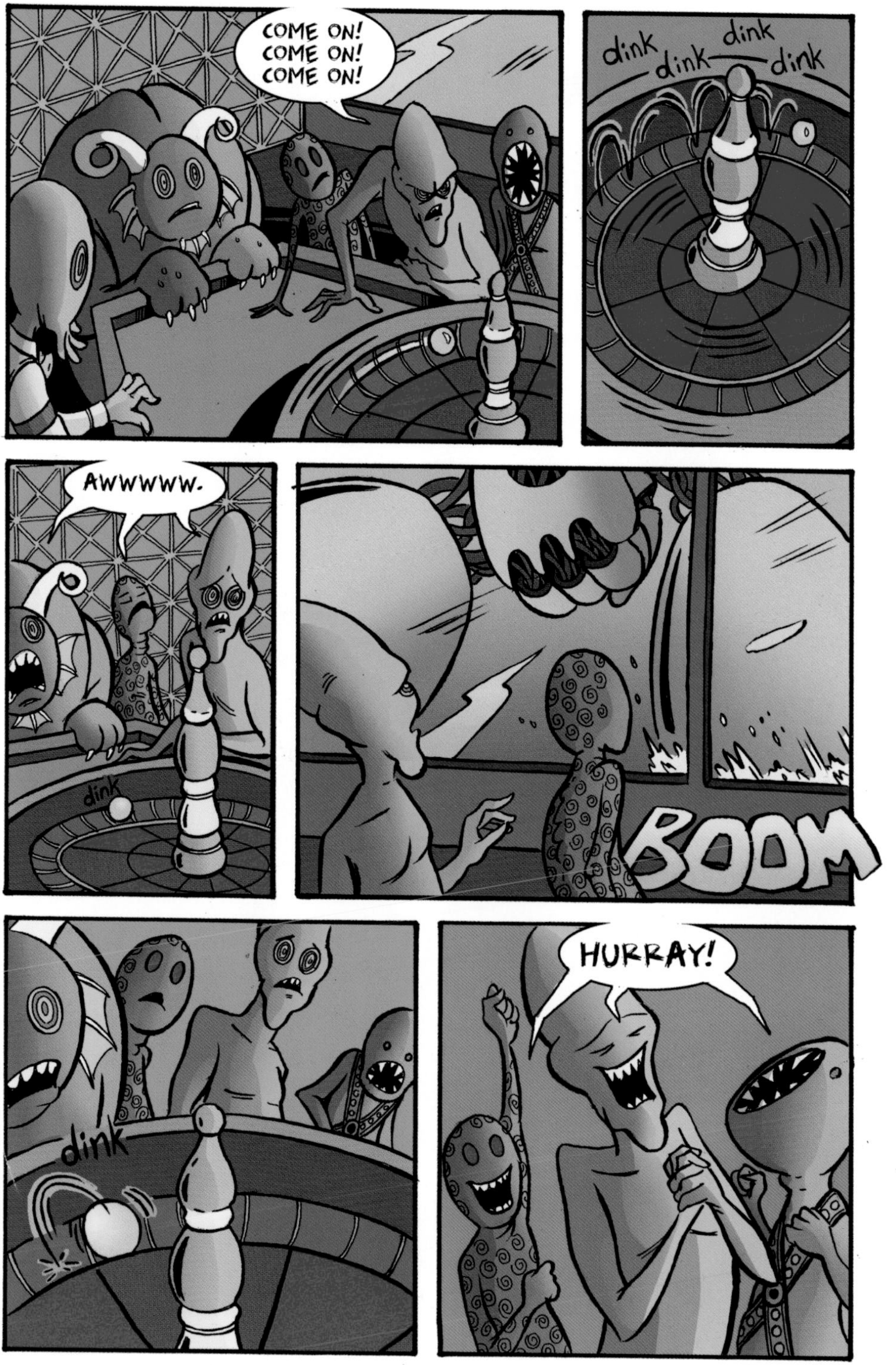
COME ON!
COME ON!
COME ON!
dink dink dink dink
AWWWWW.
dink
BOOM
dink
HURRAY!

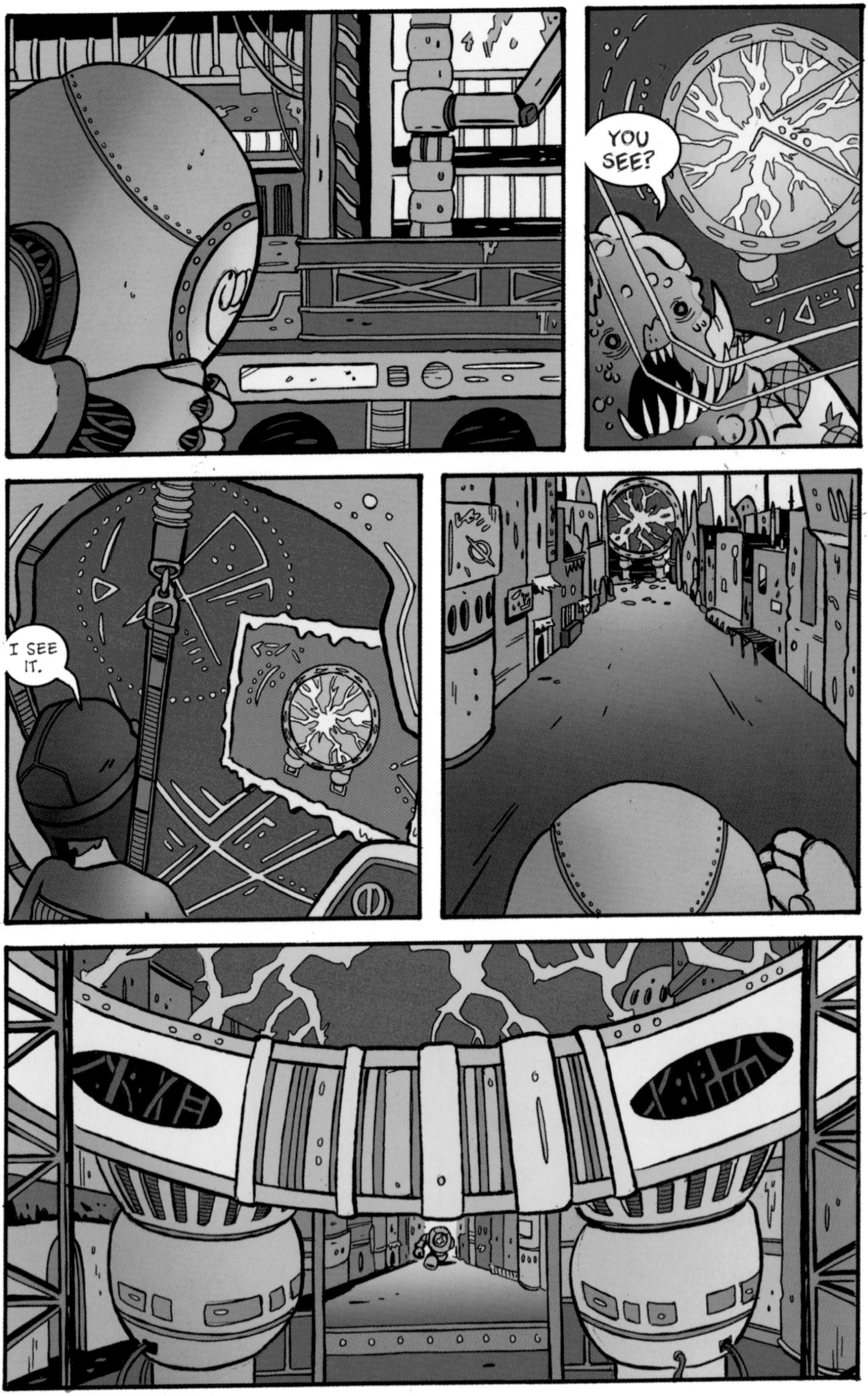
YOU SEE?
I SEE IT.

BWEEP BWEEP BWEEP

UH-OH.

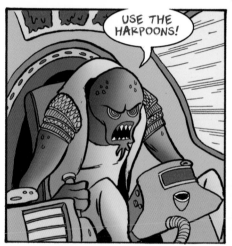

USE THE HARPOONS!

DON'T LET THEM REACH THE HYPERPORT!

HITCH ROUTE FORTY-NINE!

GOT IT!

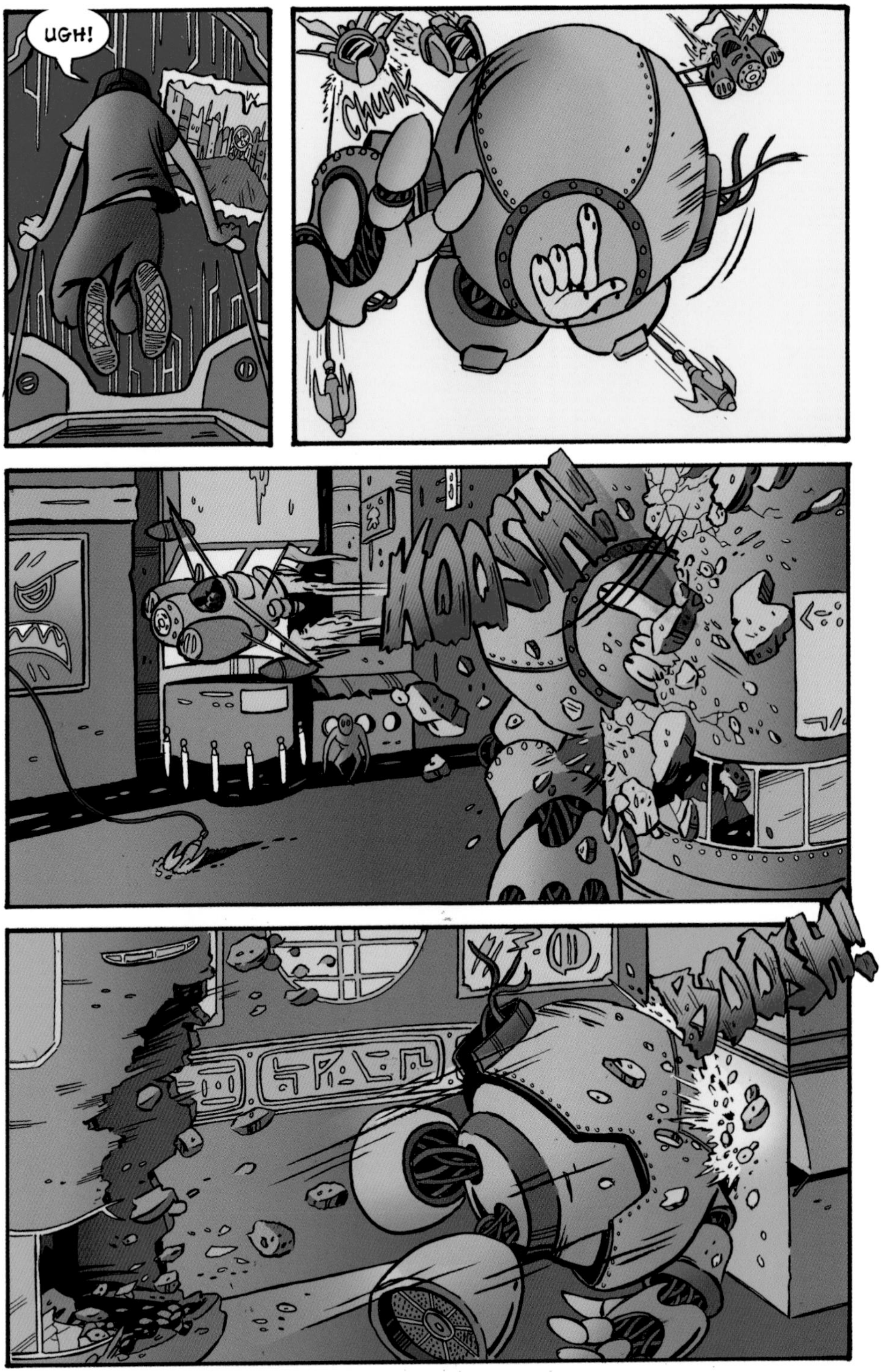
UGH!
CHUNK
KOOSH!
BOOSH!

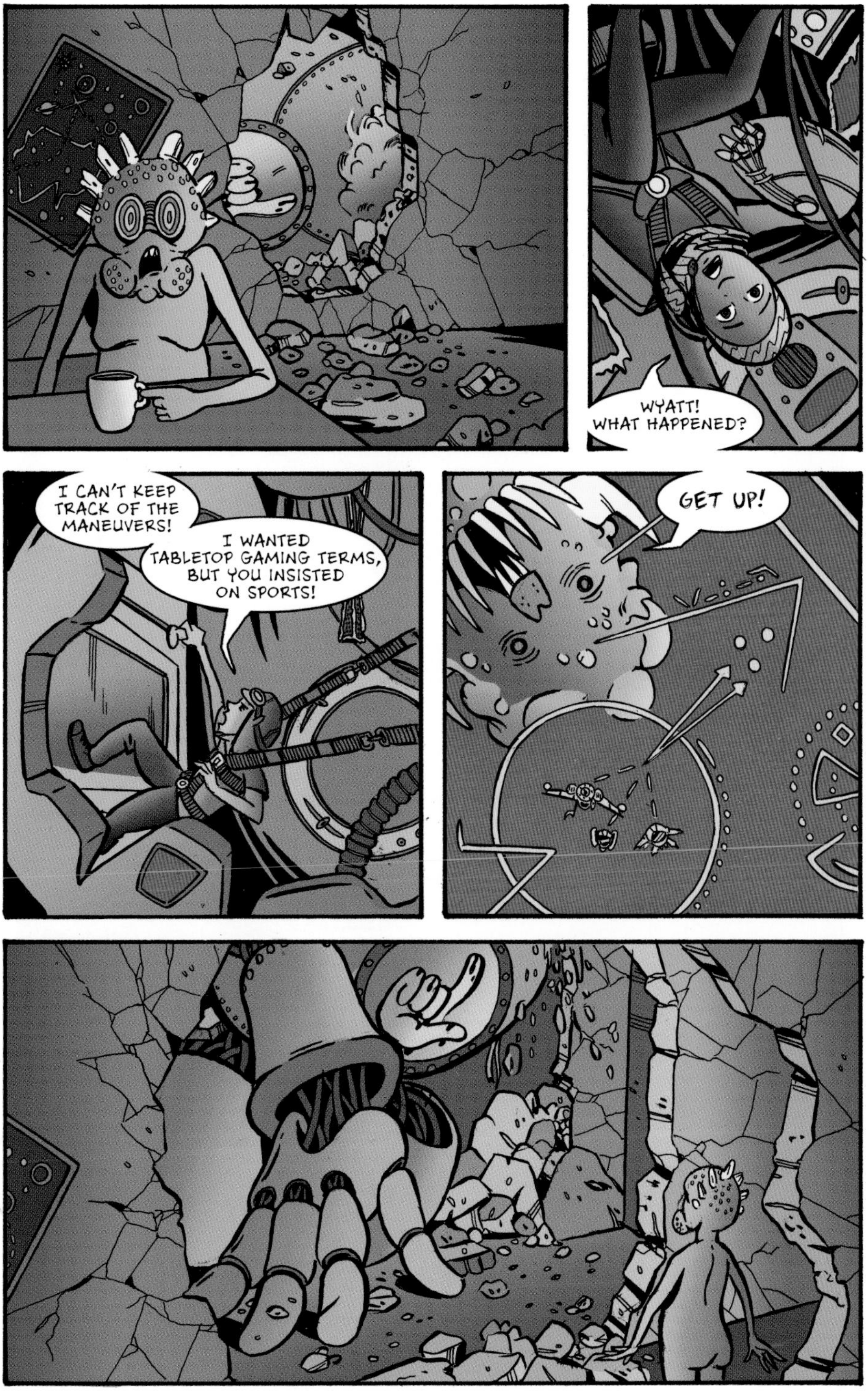
WYATT!
WHAT HAPPENED?
I CAN'T KEEP TRACK OF THE MANEUVERS!
I WANTED TABLETOP GAMING TERMS, BUT YOU INSISTED ON SPORTS!
GET UP!

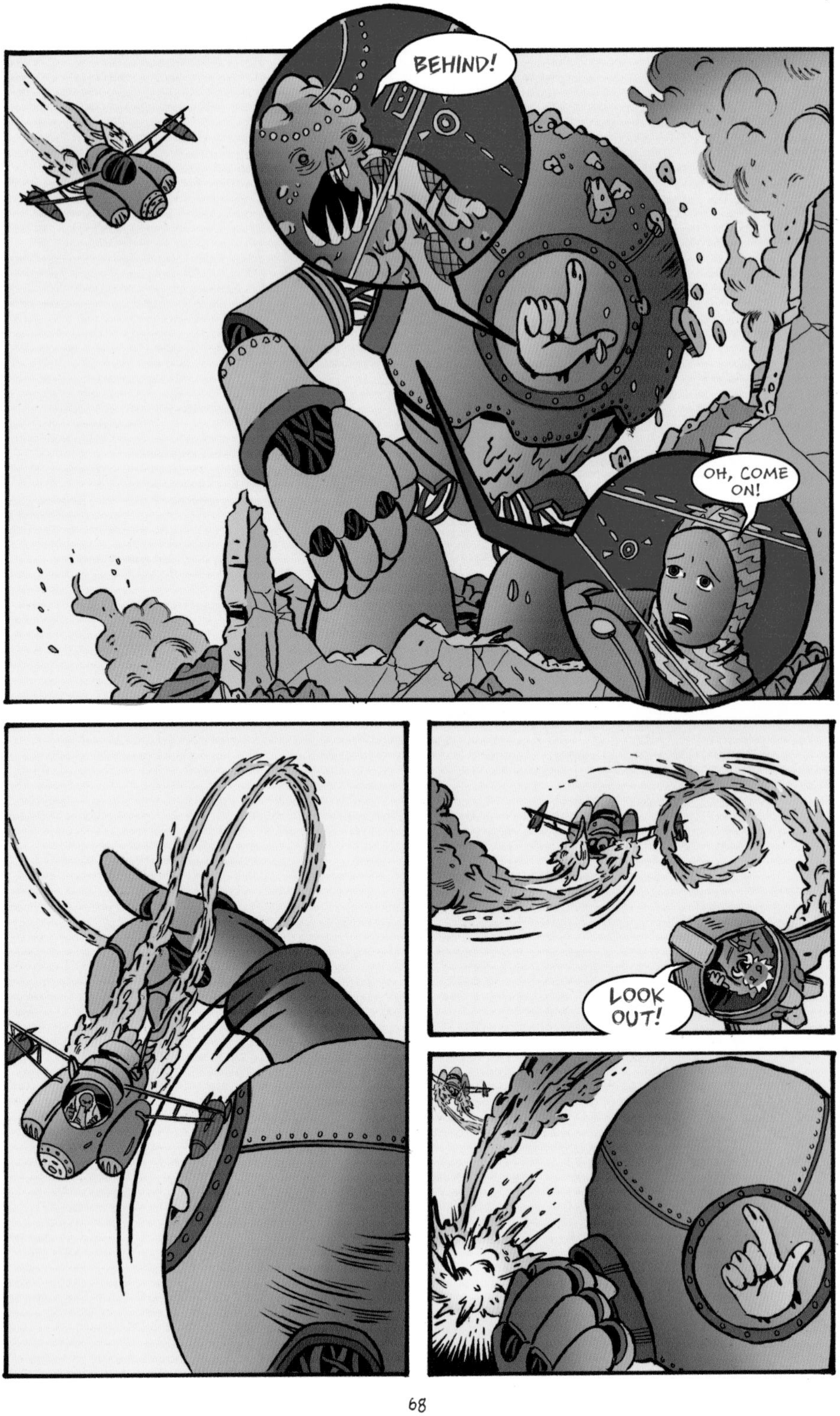
BEHIND!
OH, COME ON!
LOOK OUT!

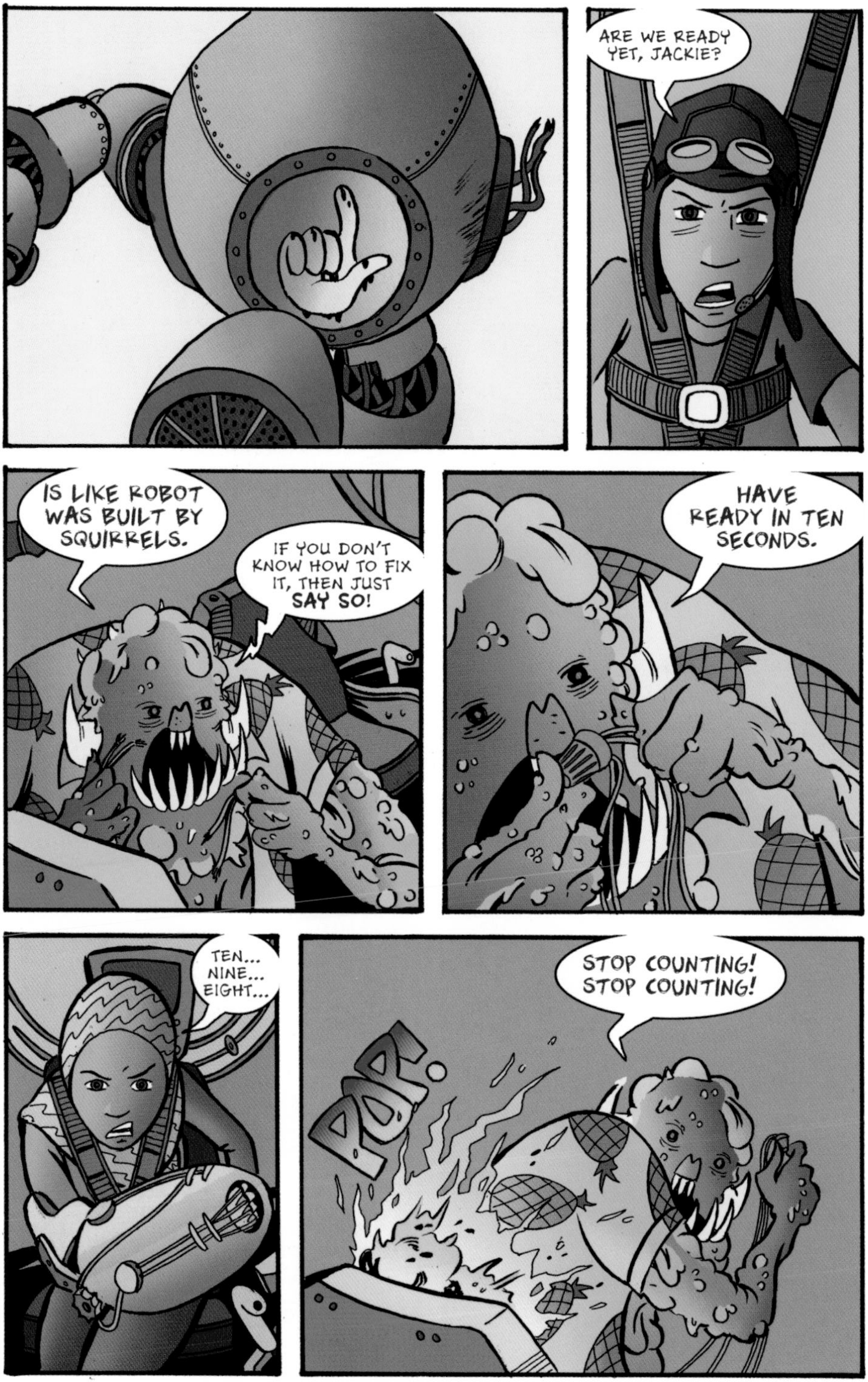
ARE WE READY YET, JACKIE?
IS LIKE ROBOT WAS BUILT BY SQUIRRELS.
IF YOU DON'T KNOW HOW TO FIX IT, THEN JUST SAY SO!
HAVE READY IN TEN SECONDS.
TEN... NINE... EIGHT...
STOP COUNTING! STOP COUNTING!
POP!

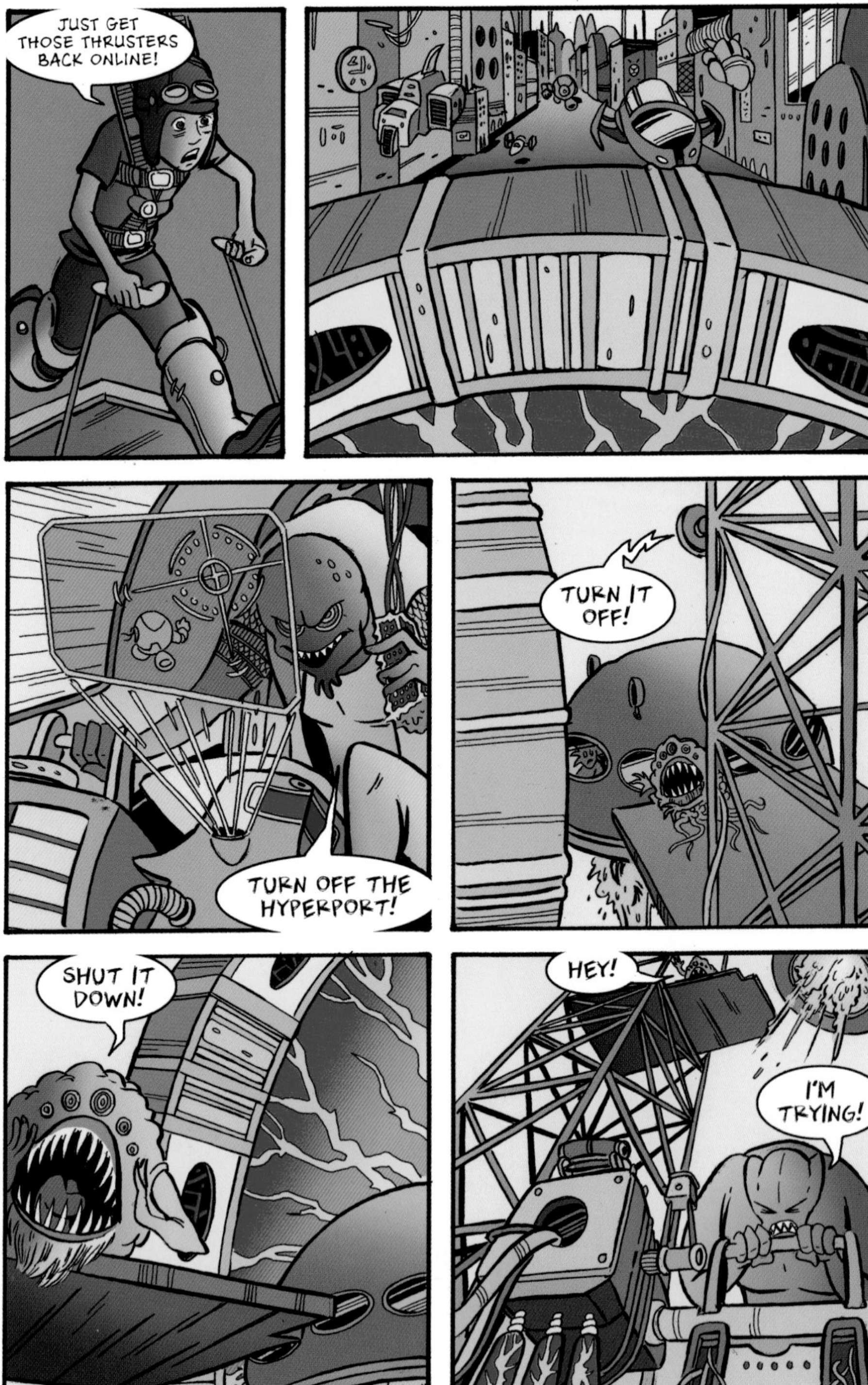
JUST GET THOSE THRUSTERS BACK ONLINE!
TURN OFF THE HYPERPORT!
TURN IT OFF!
SHUT IT DOWN!
HEY!
I'M TRYING!

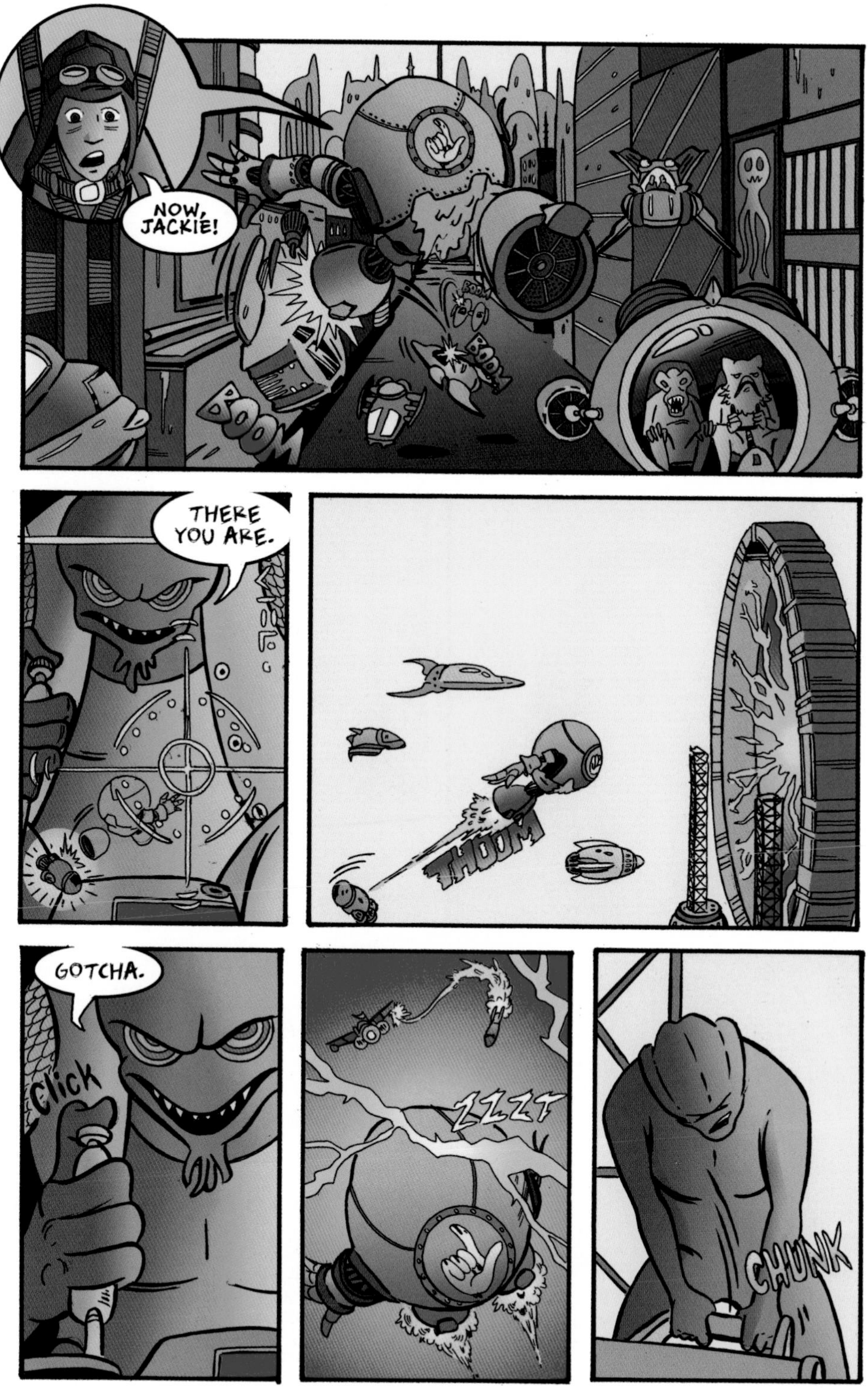
NOW, JACKIE!
BOOM
BOOM
BOOM
THERE YOU ARE.
THOOM
GOTCHA.
CLICK
ZZZT
CHUNK

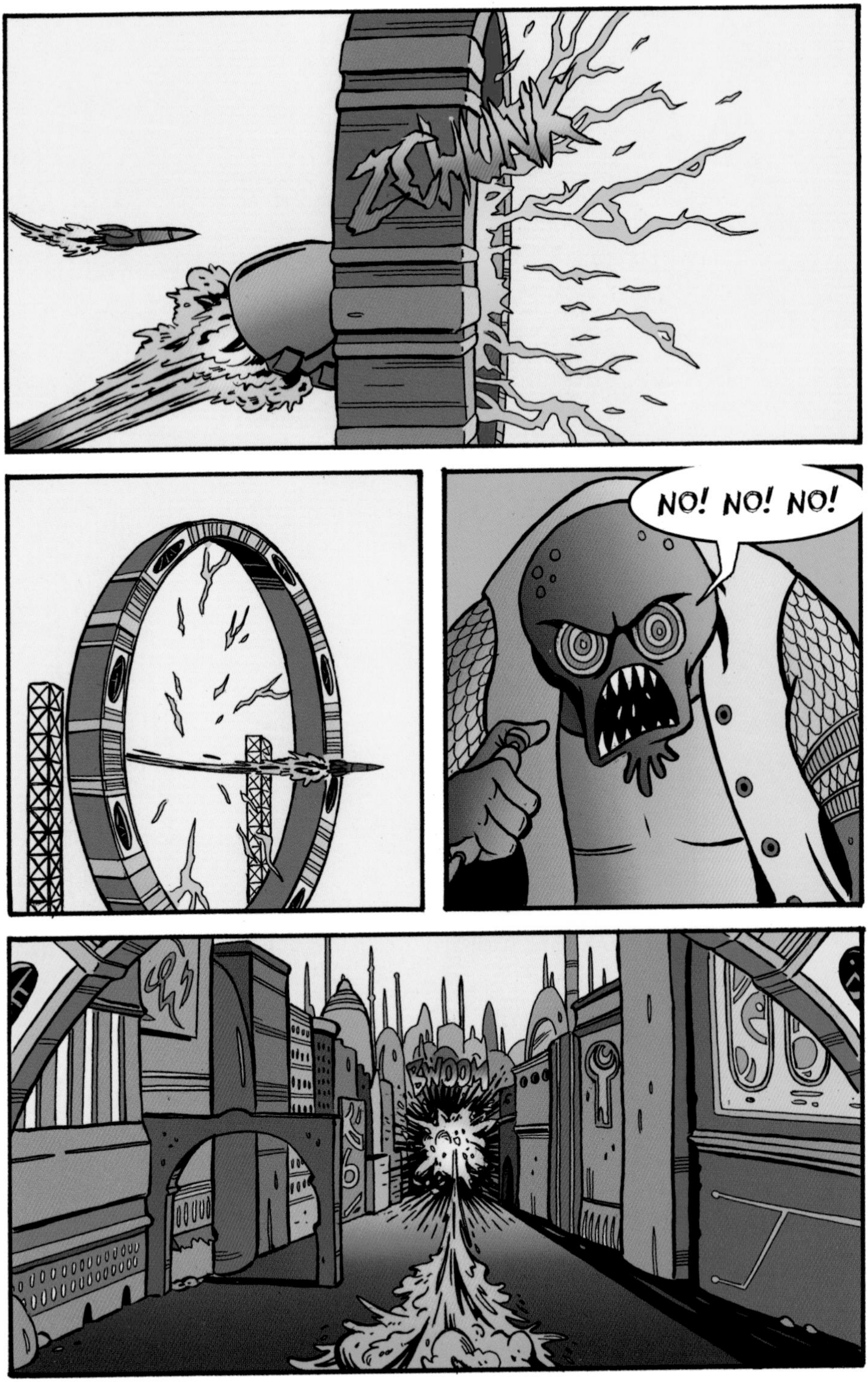
ZCHUNK
NO! NO! NO!
BWOOM

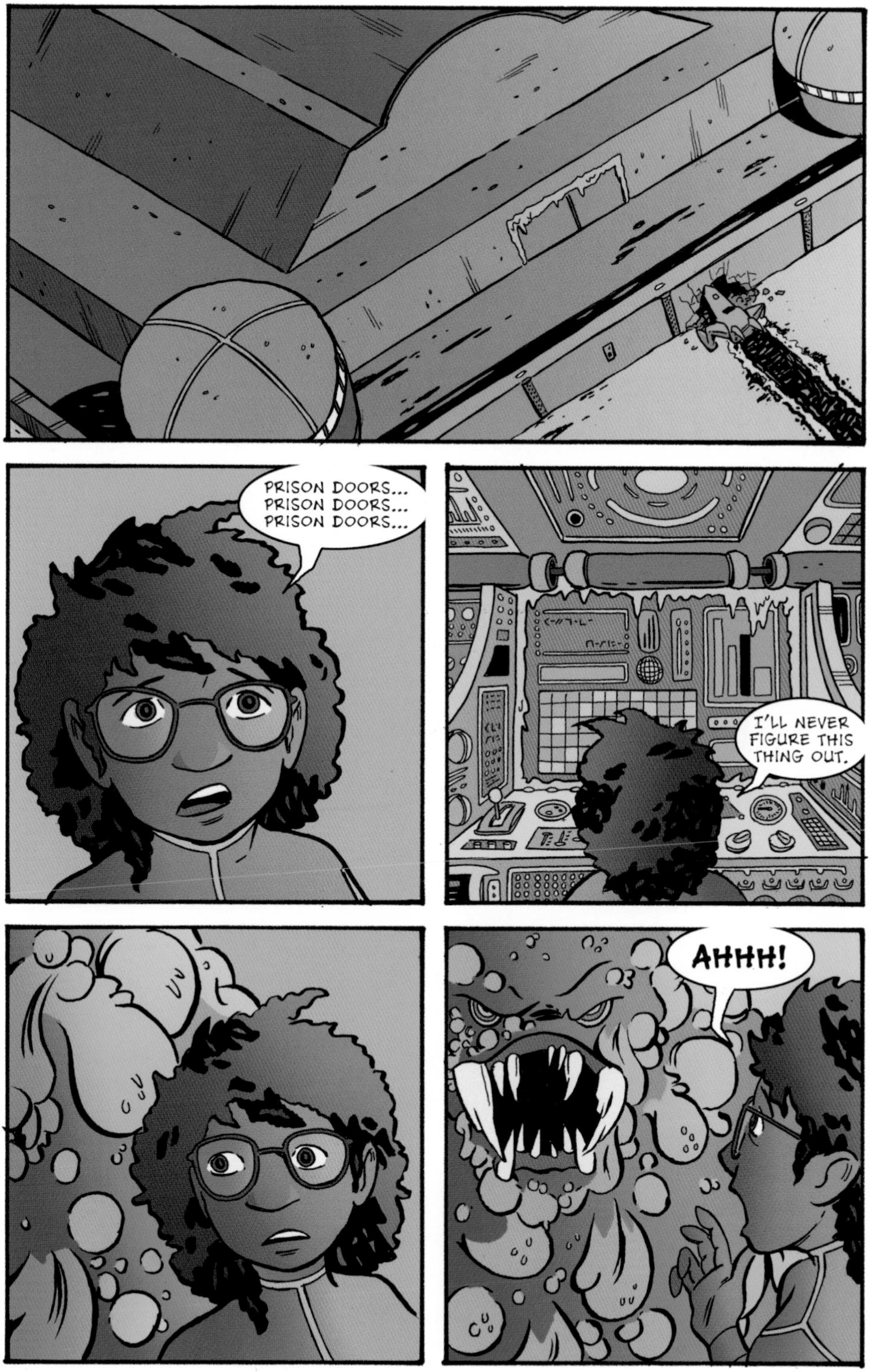
PRISON DOORS...
PRISON DOORS...
PRISON DOORS...
I'LL NEVER FIGURE THIS THING OUT.
AHHH!

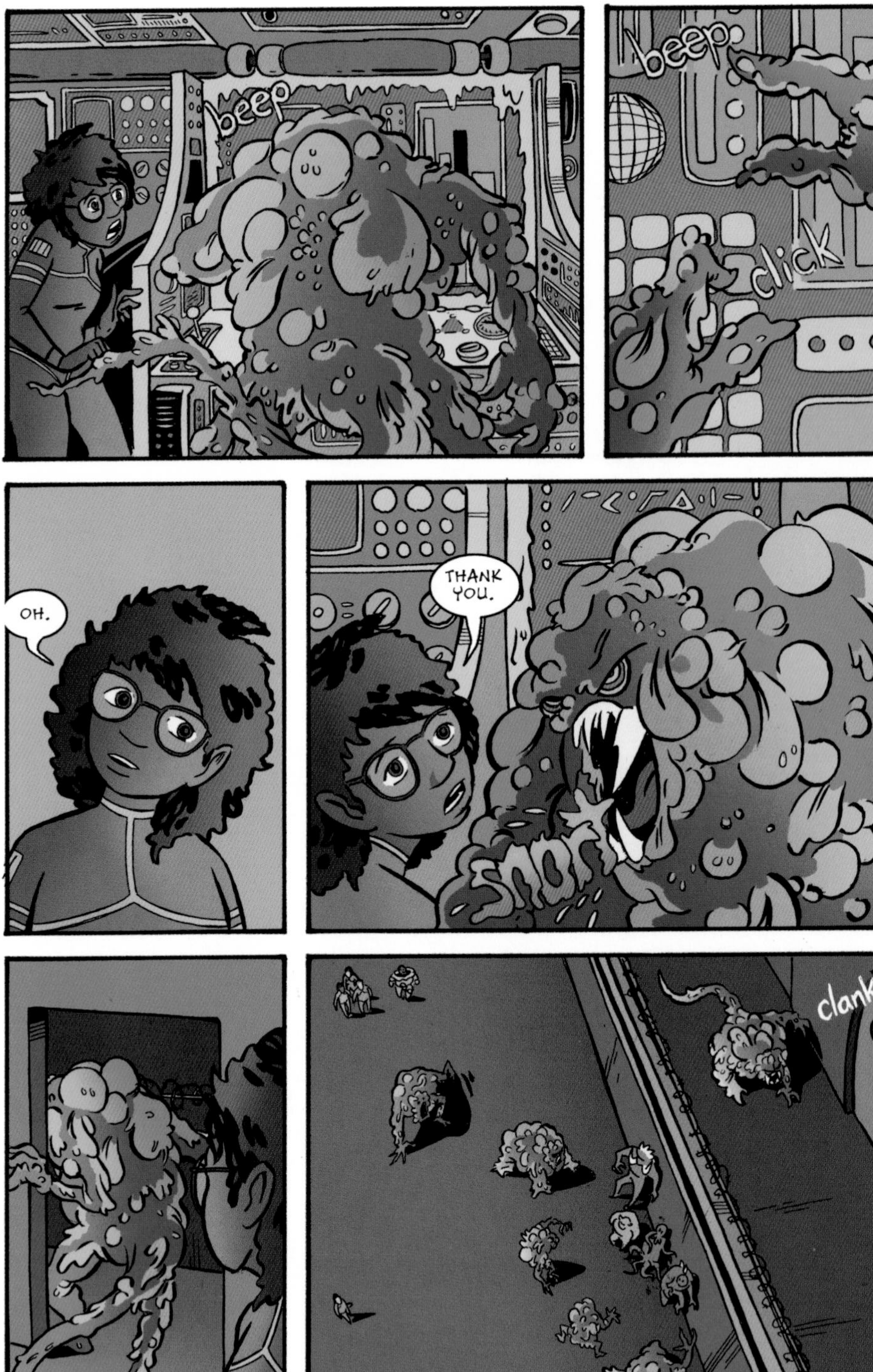
beep
beep
click
OH.
THANK YOU.
snort
clank

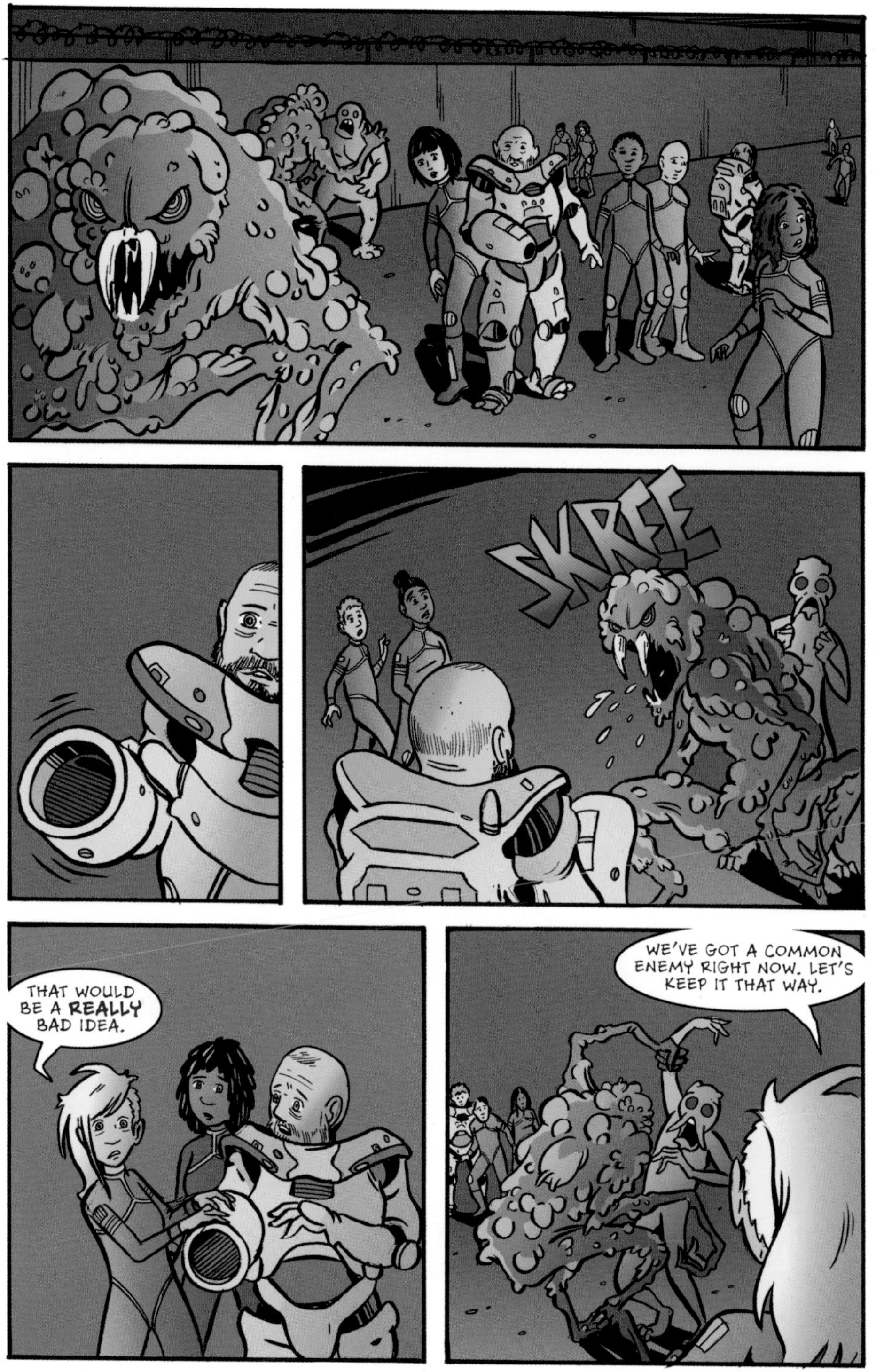
SKREE
THAT WOULD BE A **REALLY** BAD IDEA.
WE'VE GOT A COMMON ENEMY RIGHT NOW. LET'S KEEP IT THAT WAY.

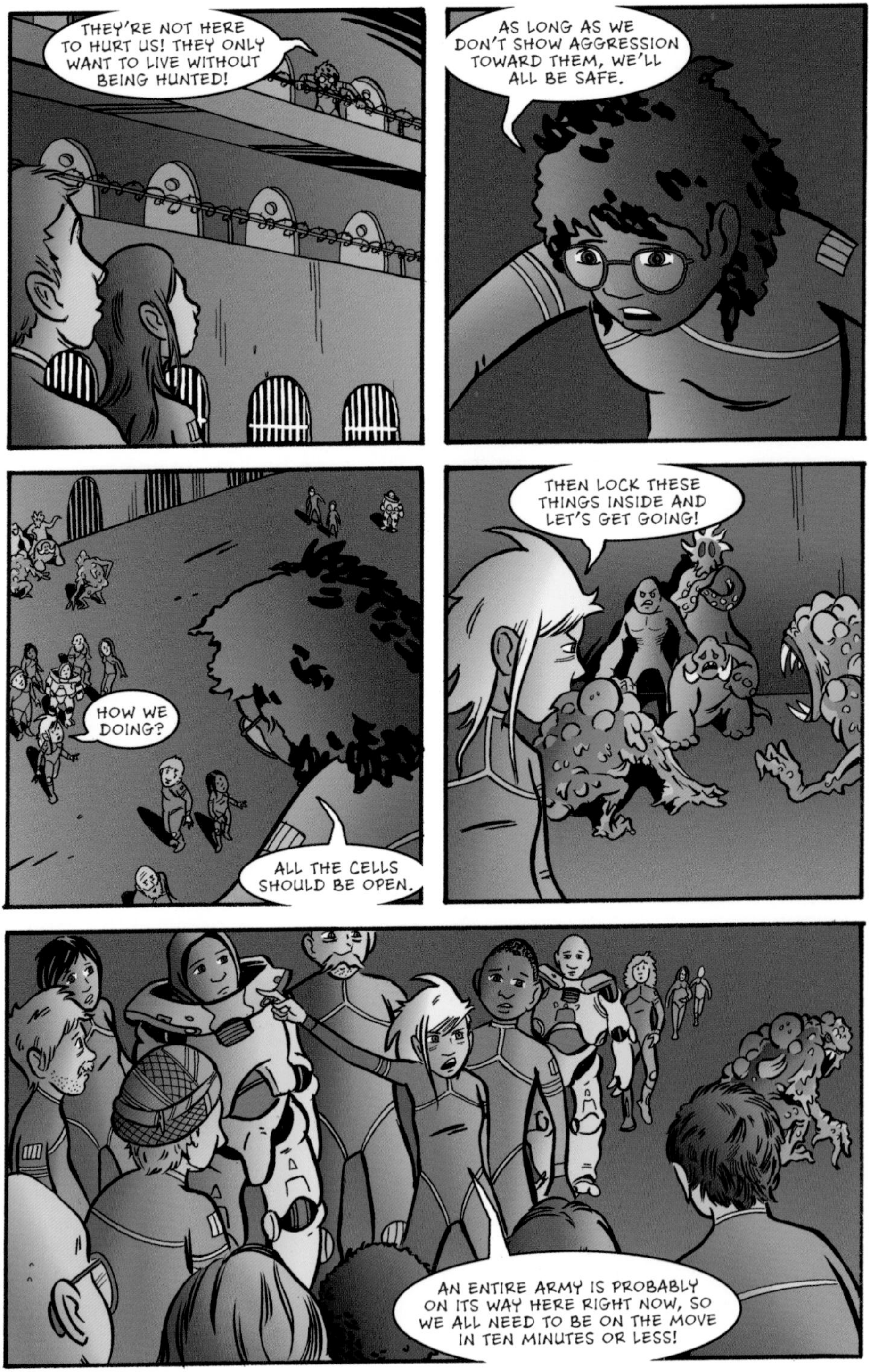
THEY'RE NOT HERE TO HURT US! THEY ONLY WANT TO LIVE WITHOUT BEING HUNTED!
AS LONG AS WE DON'T SHOW AGGRESSION TOWARD THEM, WE'LL ALL BE SAFE.
HOW WE DOING?
ALL THE CELLS SHOULD BE OPEN.
THEN LOCK THESE THINGS INSIDE AND LET'S GET GOING!
AN ENTIRE ARMY IS PROBABLY ON ITS WAY HERE RIGHT NOW, SO WE ALL NEED TO BE ON THE MOVE IN TEN MINUTES OR LESS!

GATHER TWO TEAMS. ONE TO COLLECT WATER AND FOOD, AND THE OTHER TO HELP GET THE INJURED READY TO GO.

DON'T BOTHER WITH THE BLASTERS SINCE THEY WON'T WORK AGAINST—

HEY!

I WOULD RATHER DIE THAN TO BE IMPRISONED BY YOUR KIND!

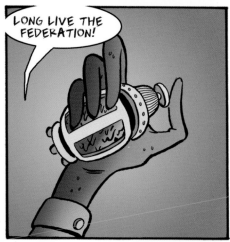

LONG LIVE THE FEDERATION!

THUNK

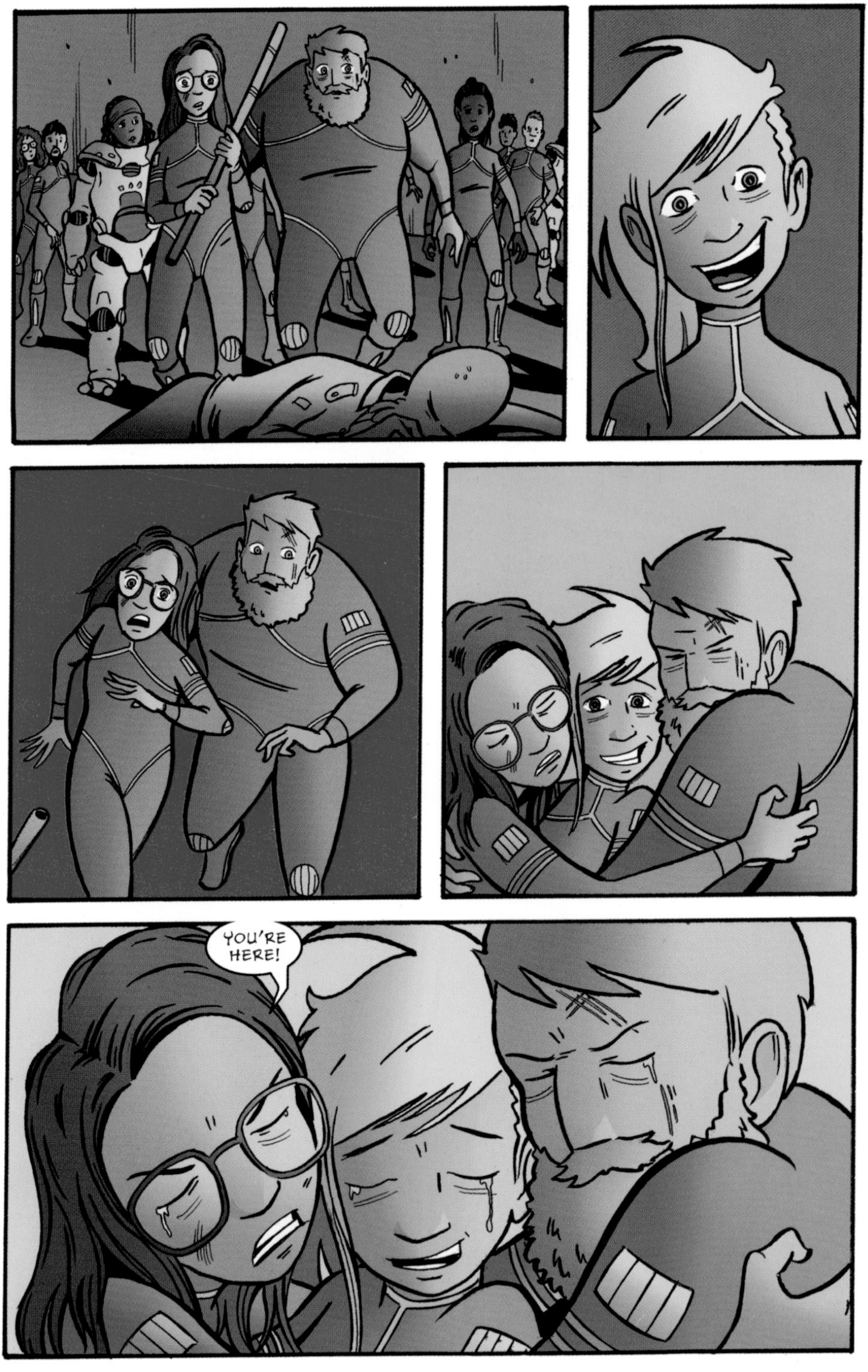
YOU'RE HERE!

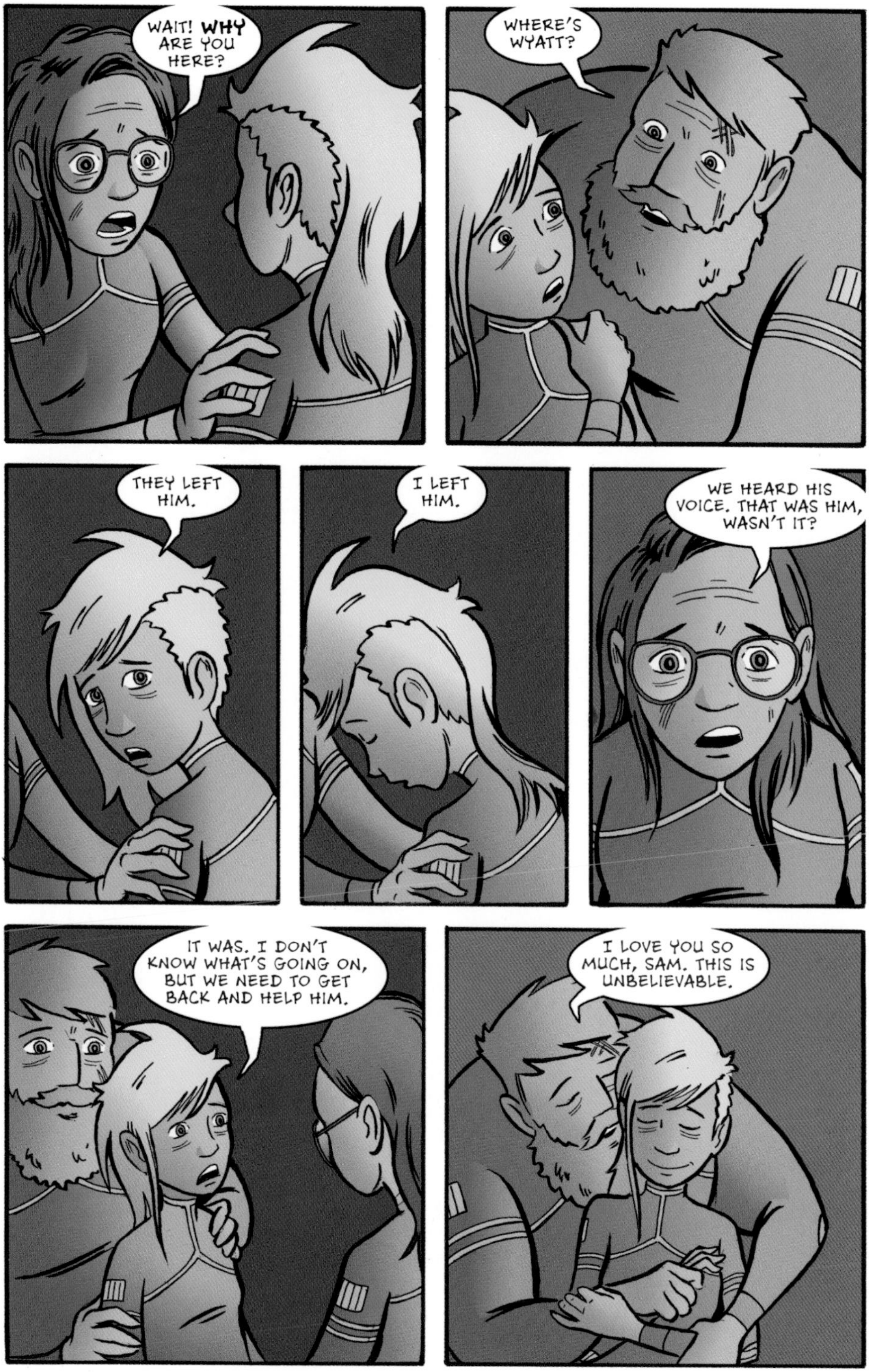
WAIT! **WHY** ARE YOU HERE?
WHERE'S WYATT?
THEY LEFT HIM.
I LEFT HIM.
WE HEARD HIS VOICE. THAT WAS HIM, WASN'T IT?
IT WAS. I DON'T KNOW WHAT'S GOING ON, BUT WE NEED TO GET BACK AND HELP HIM.
I LOVE YOU SO MUCH, SAM. THIS IS UNBELIEVABLE.

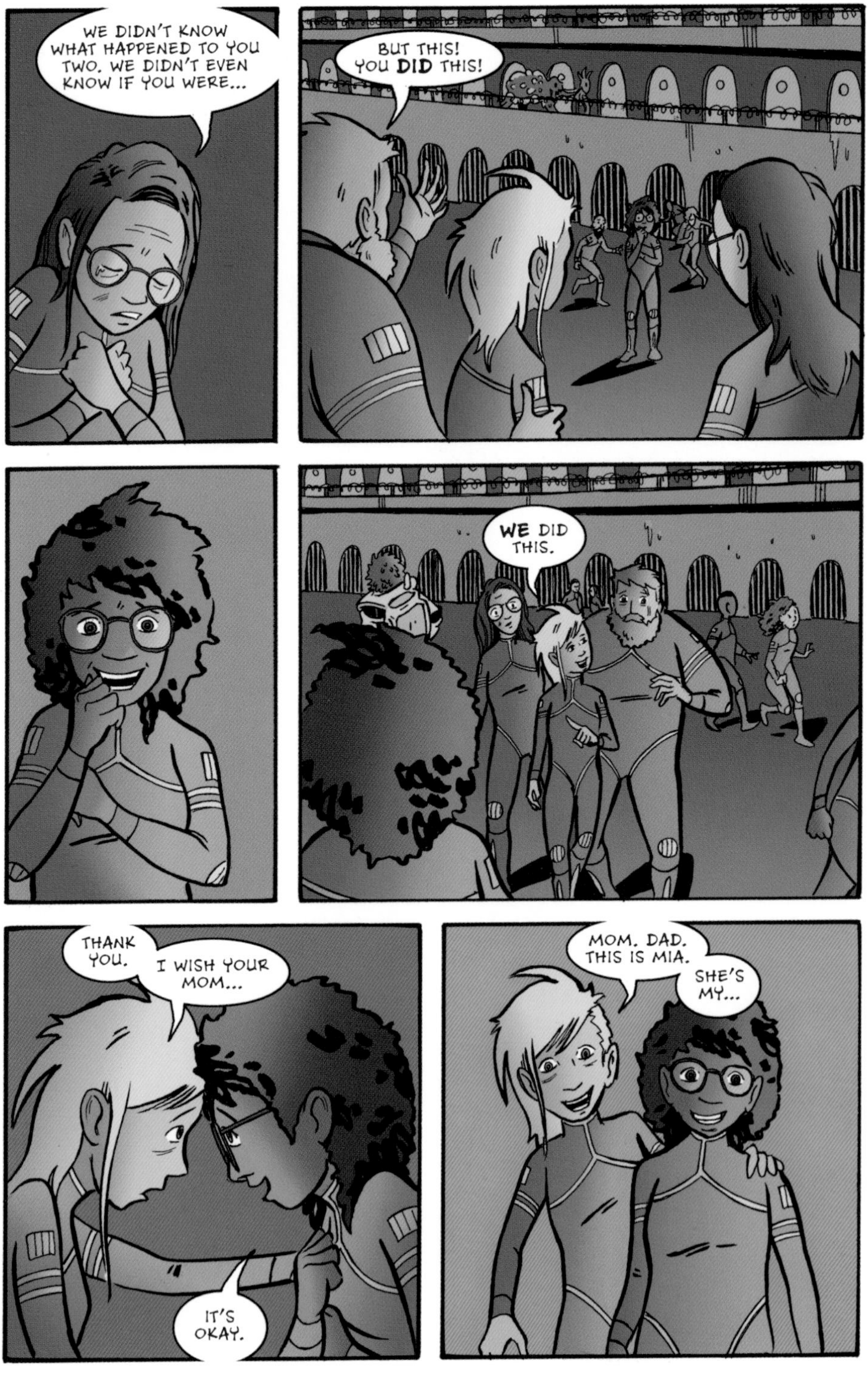
WE DIDN'T KNOW WHAT HAPPENED TO YOU TWO. WE DIDN'T EVEN KNOW IF YOU WERE...
BUT THIS! YOU **DID** THIS!
WE DID THIS.
THANK YOU.
I WISH YOUR MOM...
IT'S OKAY.
MOM. DAD. THIS IS MIA.
SHE'S MY...

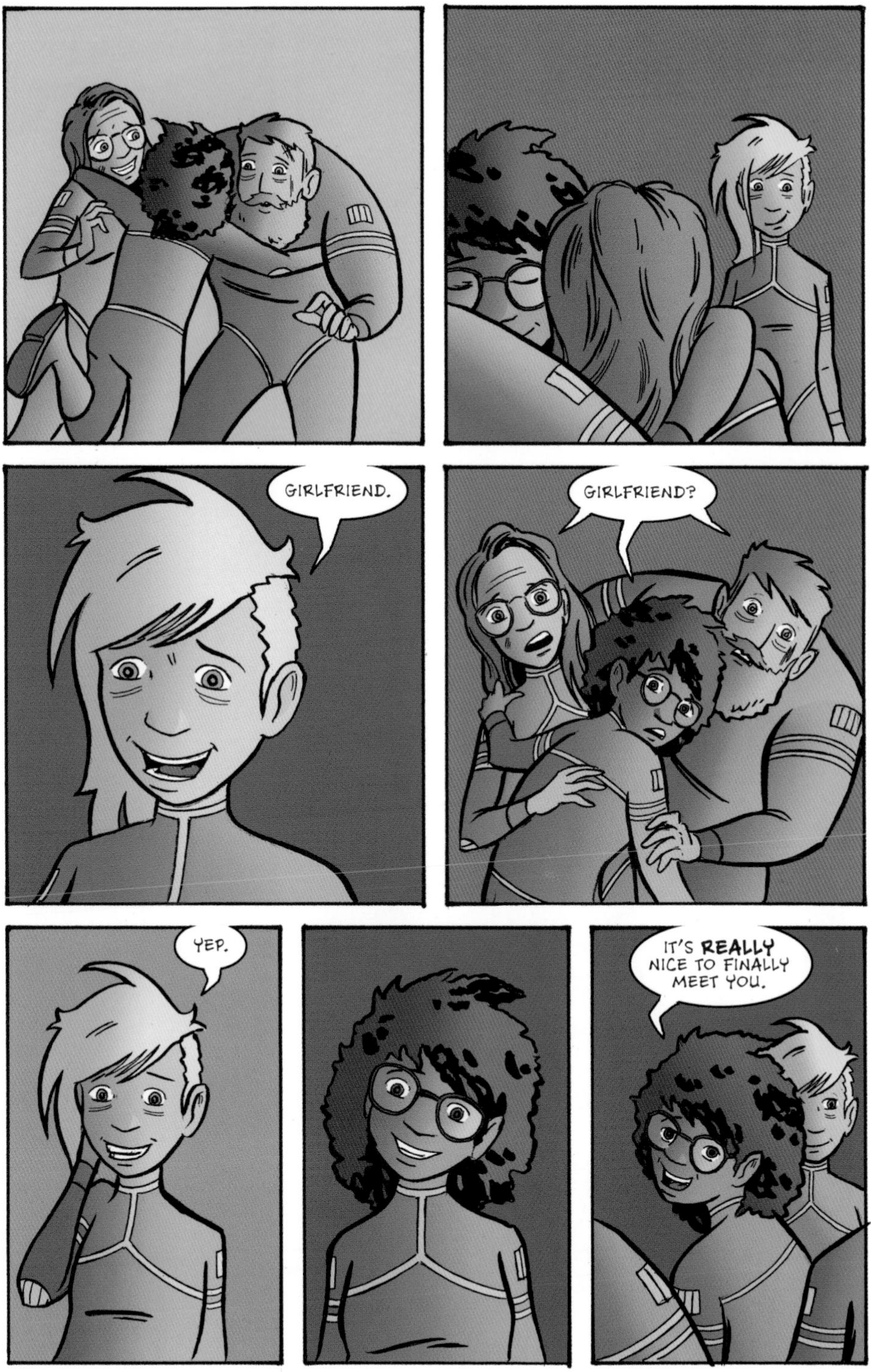
GIRLFRIEND.
GIRLFRIEND?
YEP.
IT'S **REALLY** NICE TO FINALLY MEET YOU.

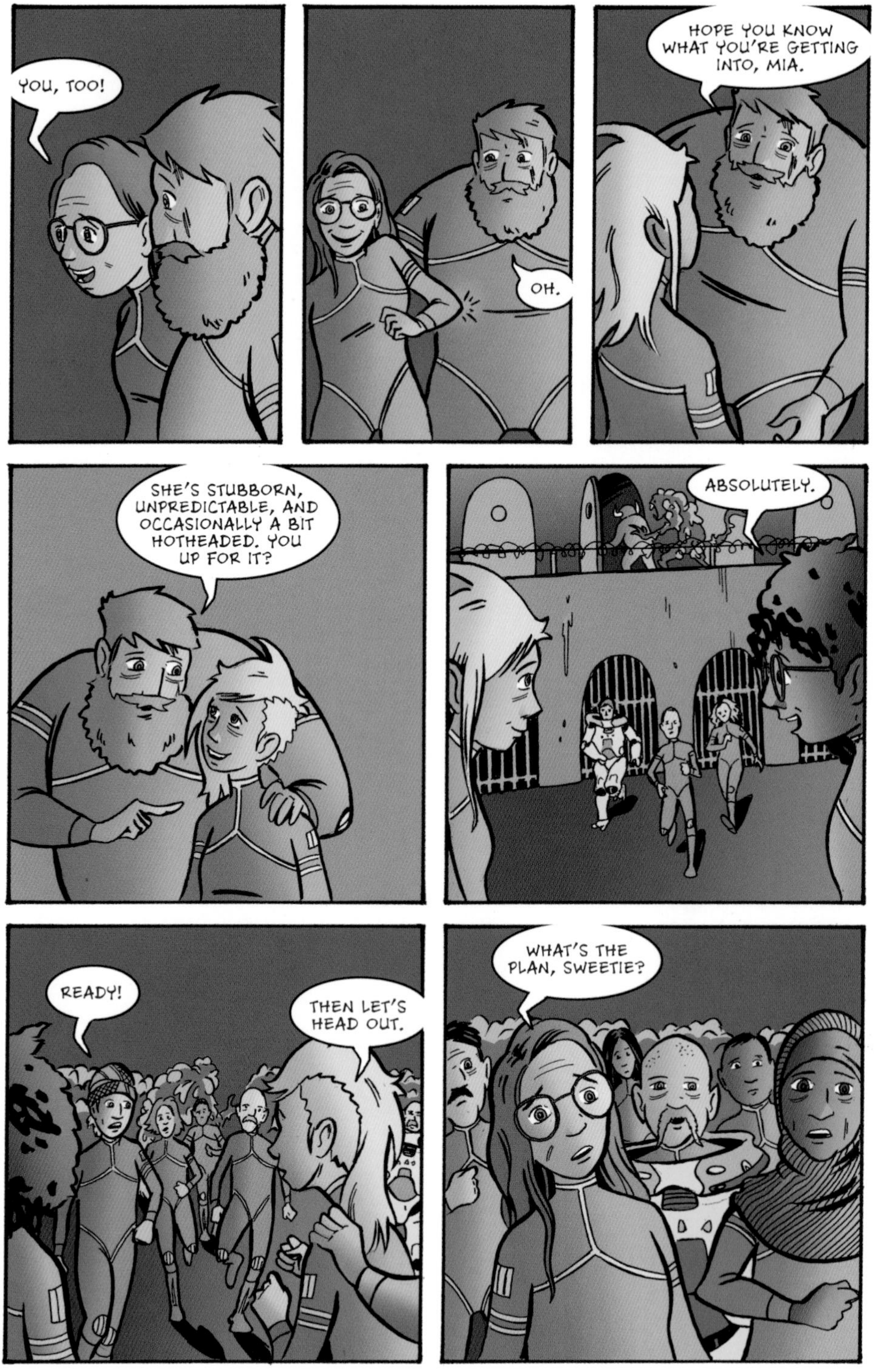
YOU, TOO!
OH.
HOPE YOU KNOW WHAT YOU'RE GETTING INTO, MIA.
SHE'S STUBBORN, UNPREDICTABLE, AND OCCASIONALLY A BIT HOTHEADED. YOU UP FOR IT?
ABSOLUTELY.
READY!
THEN LET'S HEAD OUT.
WHAT'S THE PLAN, SWEETIE?

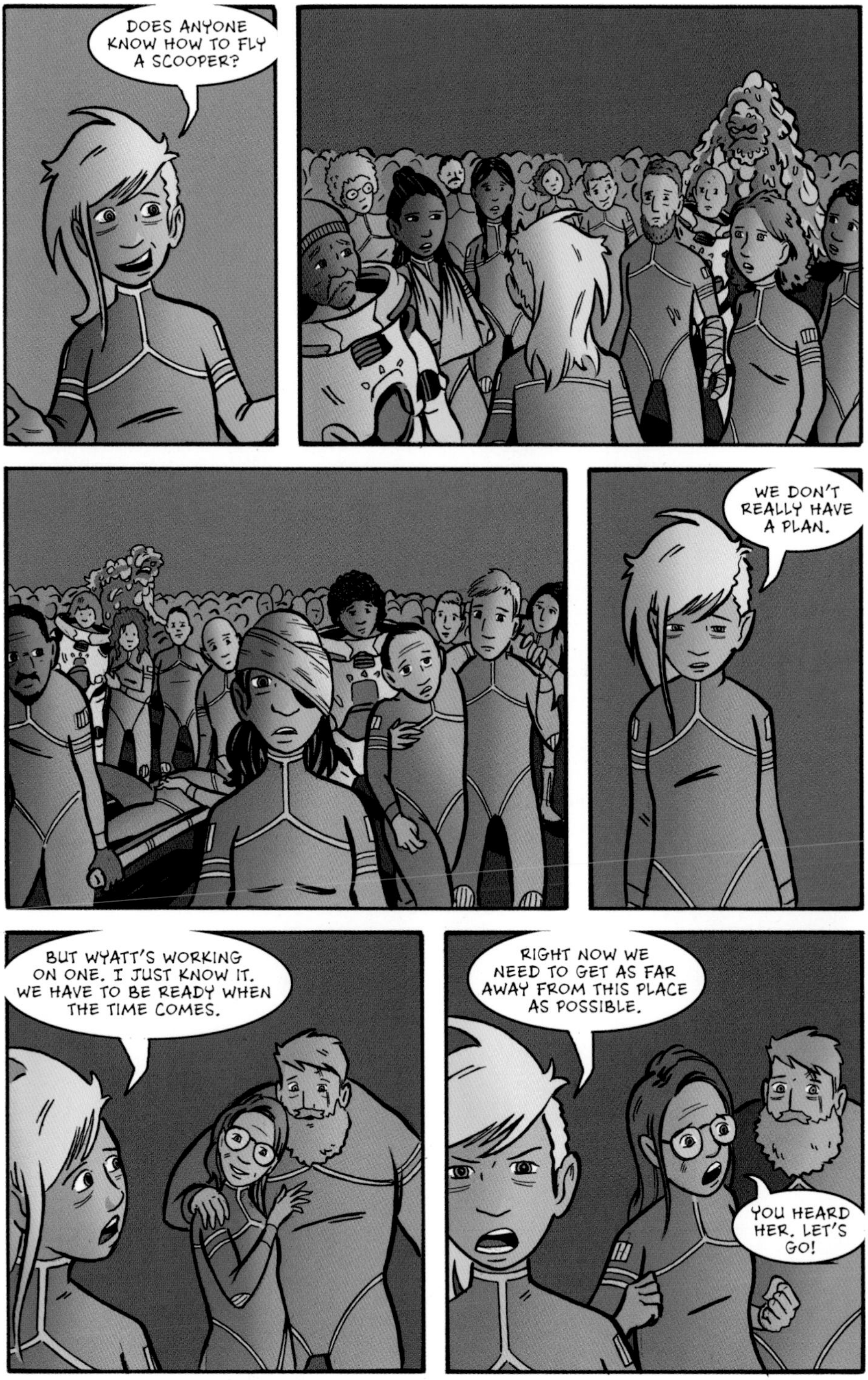
DOES ANYONE KNOW HOW TO FLY A SCOOPER?
WE DON'T REALLY HAVE A PLAN.
BUT WYATT'S WORKING ON ONE. I JUST KNOW IT. WE HAVE TO BE READY WHEN THE TIME COMES.
RIGHT NOW WE NEED TO GET AS FAR AWAY FROM THIS PLACE AS POSSIBLE.
YOU HEARD HER. LET'S GO!

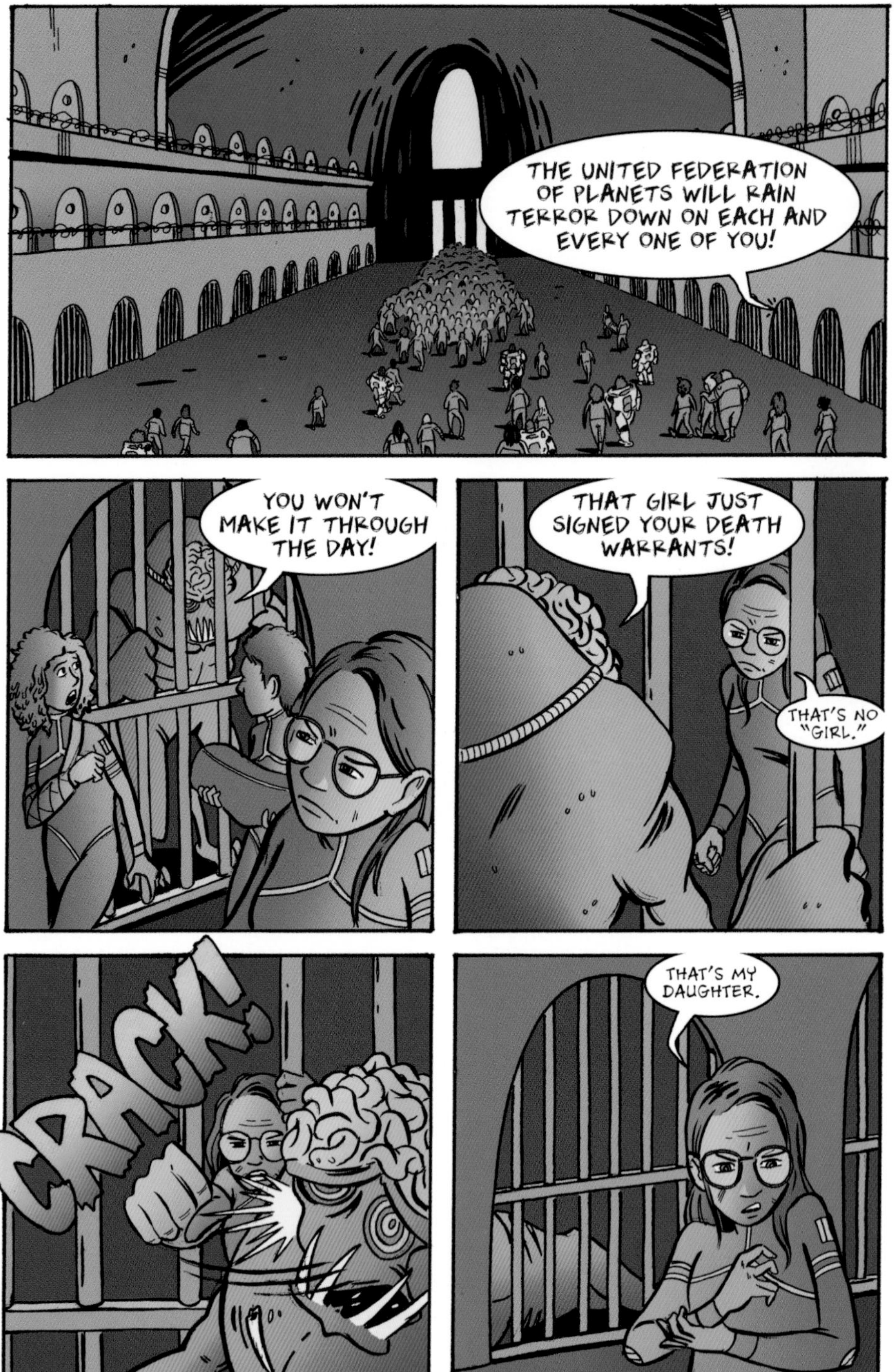
THE UNITED FEDERATION OF PLANETS WILL RAIN TERROR DOWN ON EACH AND EVERY ONE OF YOU!
YOU WON'T MAKE IT THROUGH THE DAY!
THAT GIRL JUST SIGNED YOUR DEATH WARRANTS!
THAT'S NO "GIRL."
CRACK!
THAT'S MY DAUGHTER.

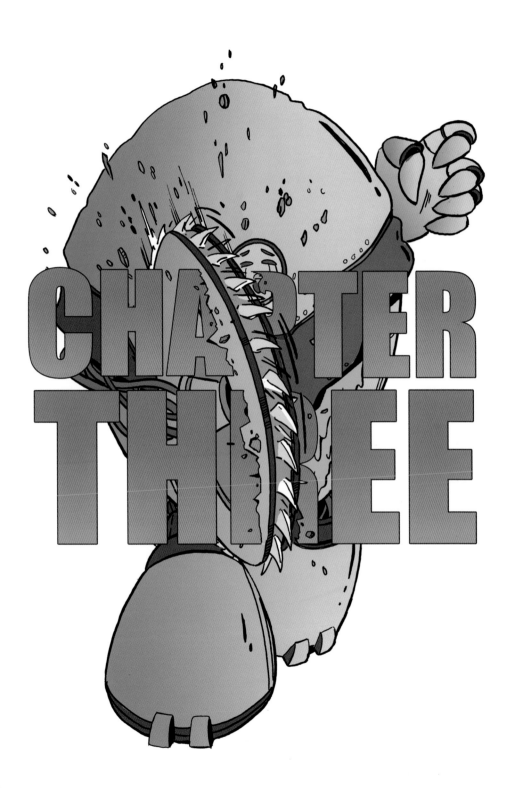

CHAPTER THREE

ANYTIN
EXIT
KNOCK
KNOCK
KNOC

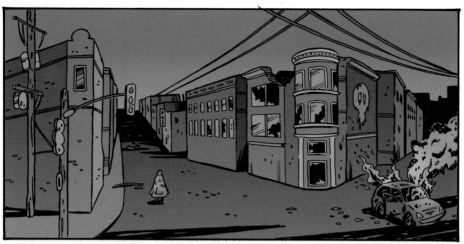

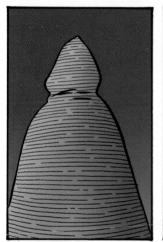

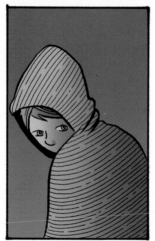

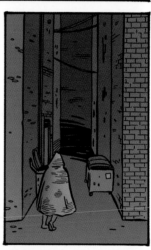

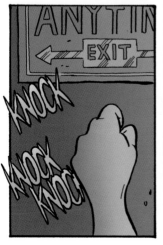

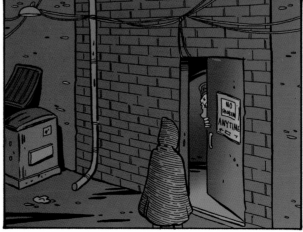

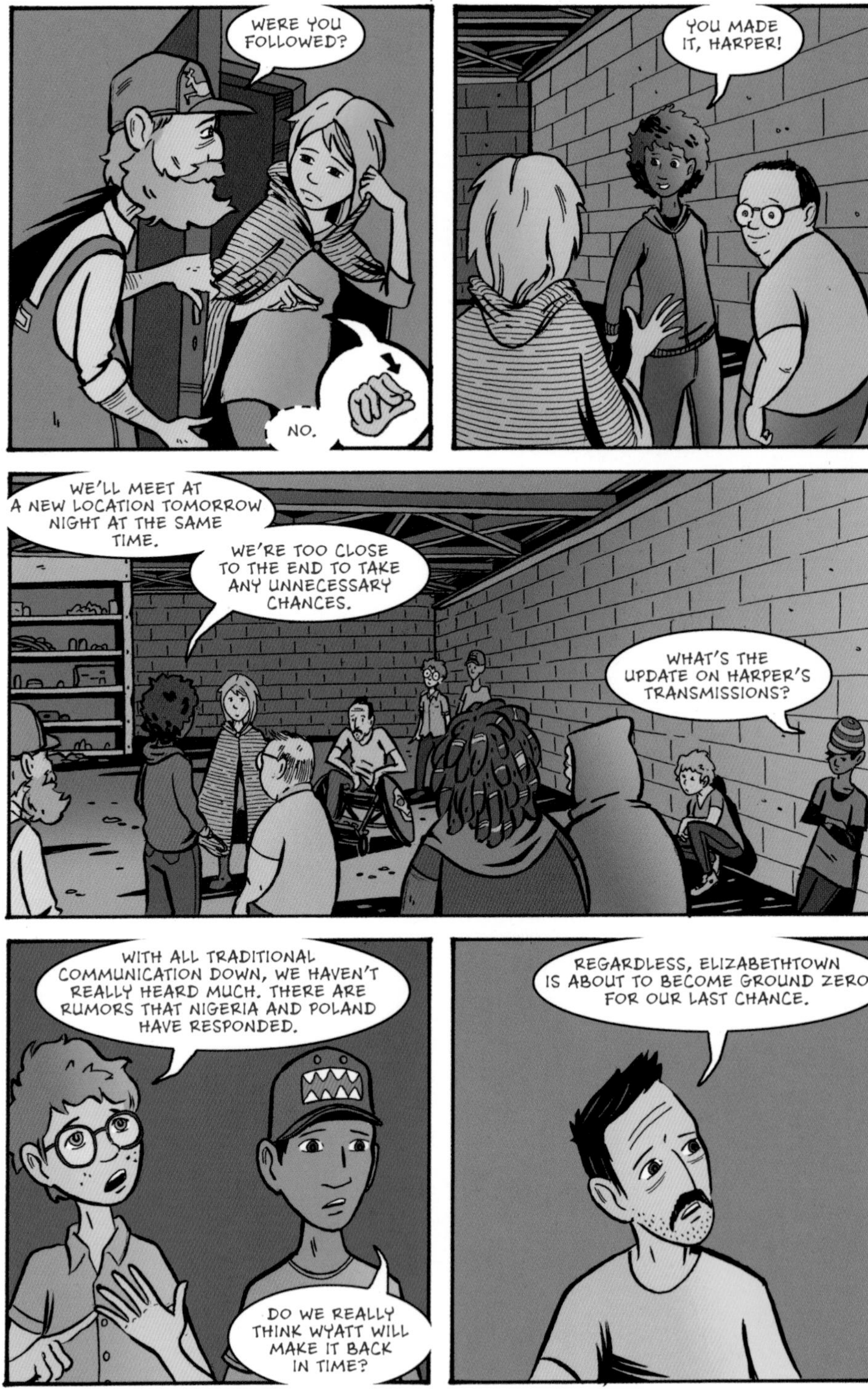
WERE YOU FOLLOWED?
NO.
YOU MADE IT, HARPER!
WE'LL MEET AT A NEW LOCATION TOMORROW NIGHT AT THE SAME TIME.
WE'RE TOO CLOSE TO THE END TO TAKE ANY UNNECESSARY CHANCES.
WHAT'S THE UPDATE ON HARPER'S TRANSMISSIONS?
WITH ALL TRADITIONAL COMMUNICATION DOWN, WE HAVEN'T REALLY HEARD MUCH. THERE ARE RUMORS THAT NIGERIA AND POLAND HAVE RESPONDED.
DO WE REALLY THINK WYATT WILL MAKE IT BACK IN TIME?
REGARDLESS, ELIZABETHTOWN IS ABOUT TO BECOME GROUND ZERO FOR OUR LAST CHANCE.

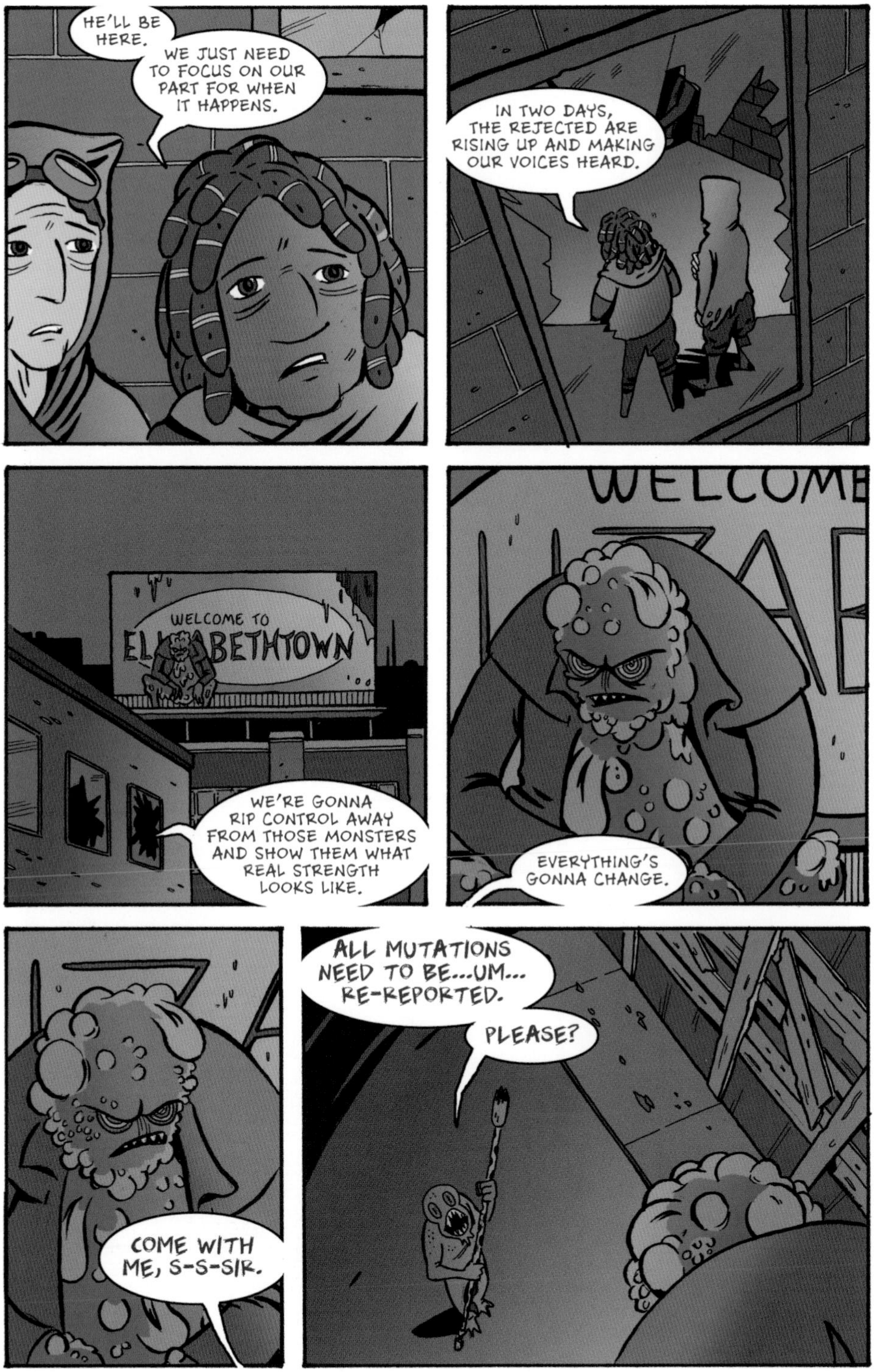
HE'LL BE HERE.
WE JUST NEED TO FOCUS ON OUR PART FOR WHEN IT HAPPENS.
IN TWO DAYS, THE REJECTED ARE RISING UP AND MAKING OUR VOICES HEARD.
WELCOME TO
BETHTOWN
WE'RE GONNA RIP CONTROL AWAY FROM THOSE MONSTERS AND SHOW THEM WHAT REAL STRENGTH LOOKS LIKE.
WELCOM
EVERYTHING'S GONNA CHANGE.
COME WITH ME, S-S-SIR.
ALL MUTATIONS NEED TO BE...UM... RE-REPORTED.
PLEASE?

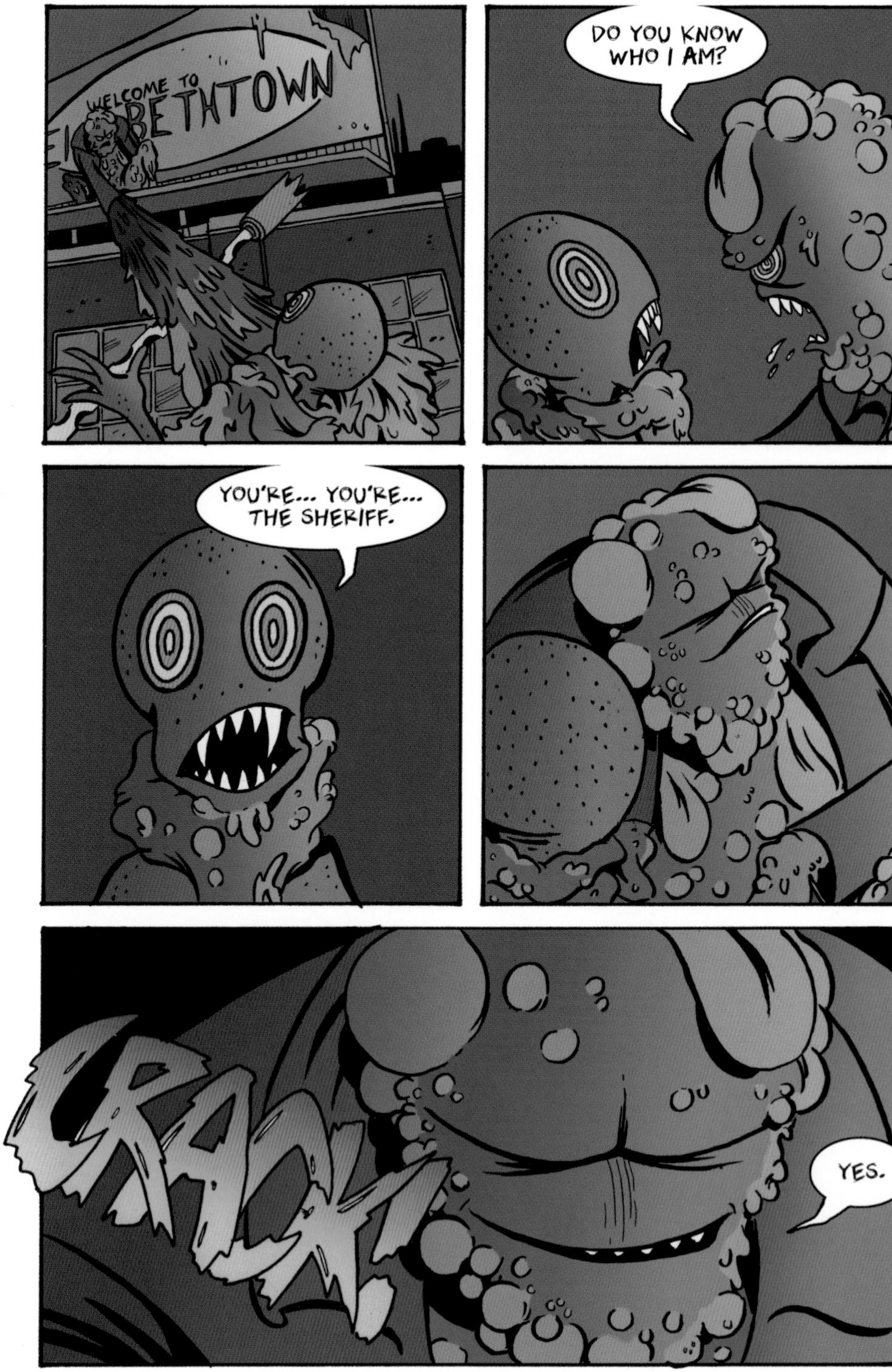
WELCOME TO
BETHTOWN
DO YOU KNOW WHO I AM?
YOU'RE... YOU'RE... THE SHERIFF.
YES.

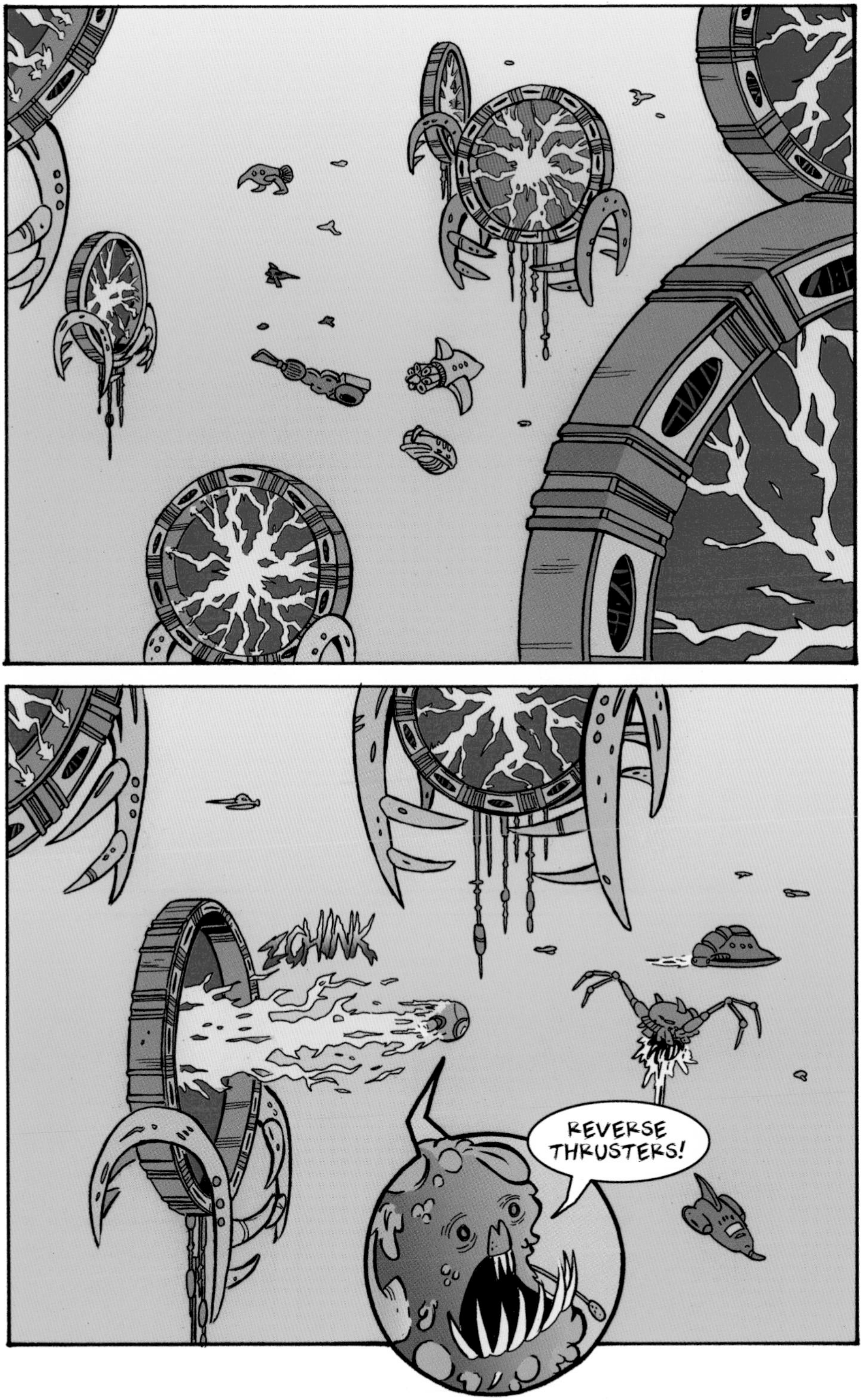
ZCHINK
REVERSE THRUSTERS!

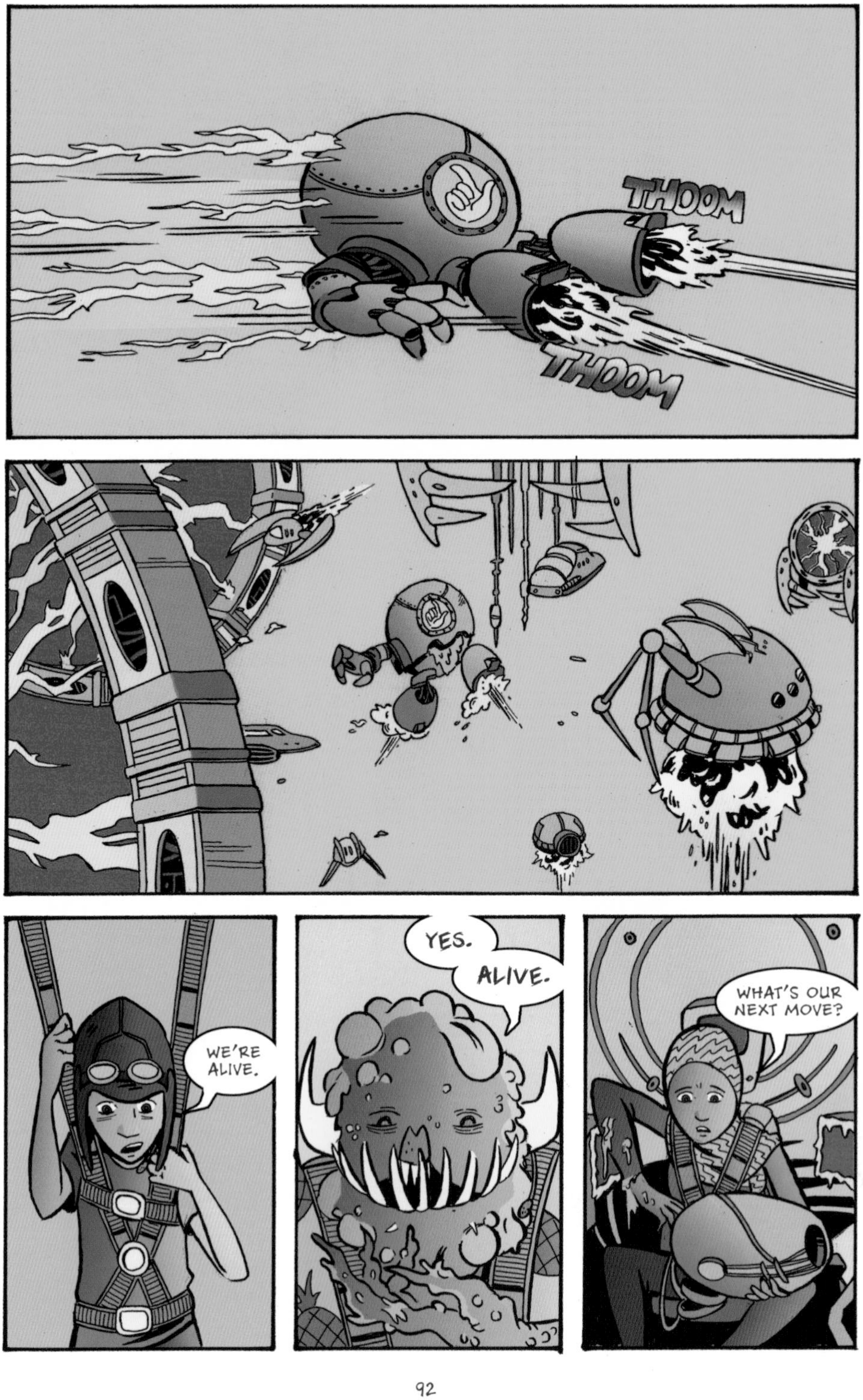
THOOM
THOOM
WE'RE ALIVE.
YES.
ALIVE.
WHAT'S OUR NEXT MOVE?

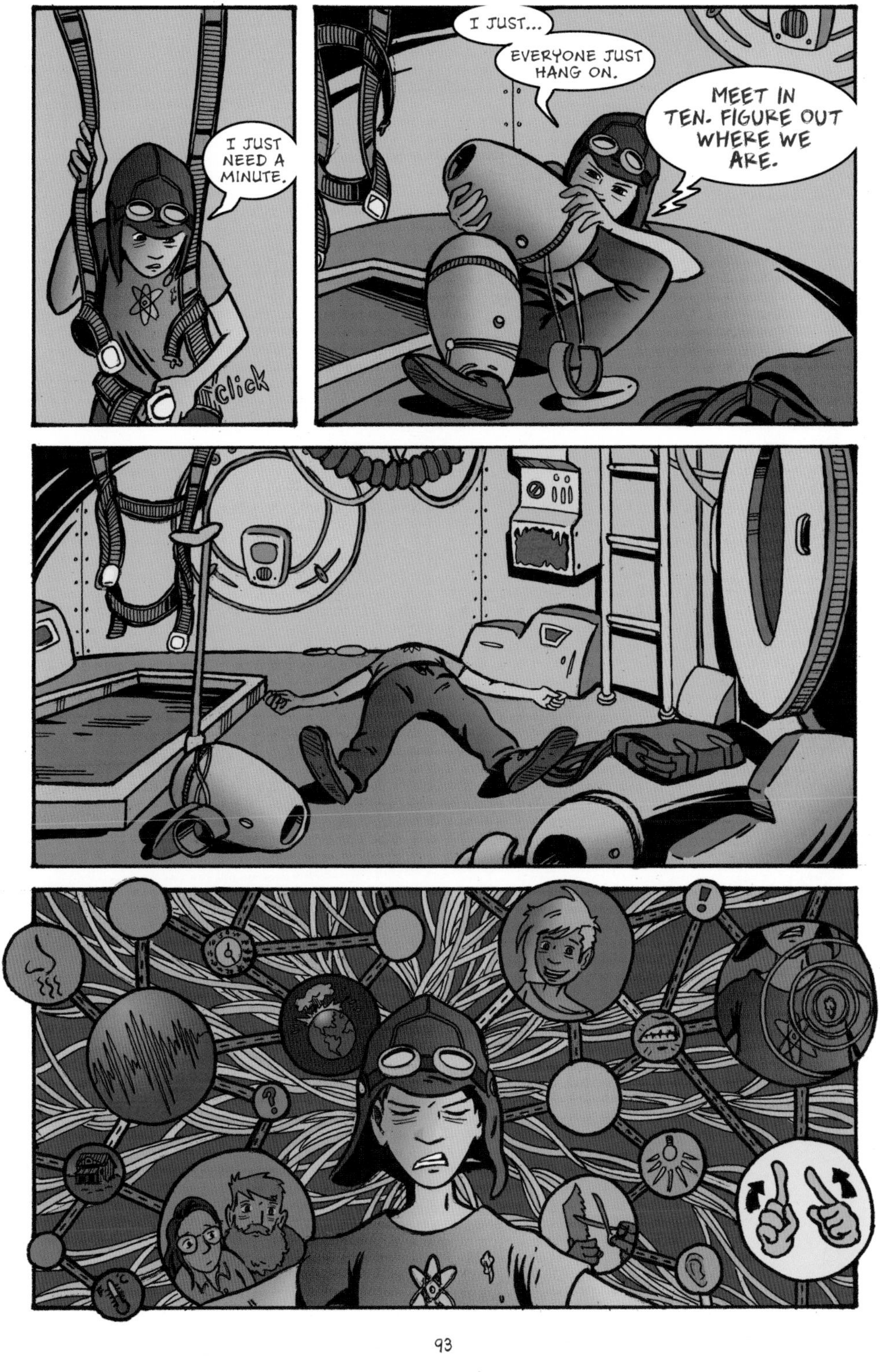
I JUST NEED A MINUTE.
click
I JUST...
EVERYONE JUST HANG ON.
MEET IN TEN. FIGURE OUT WHERE WE ARE.

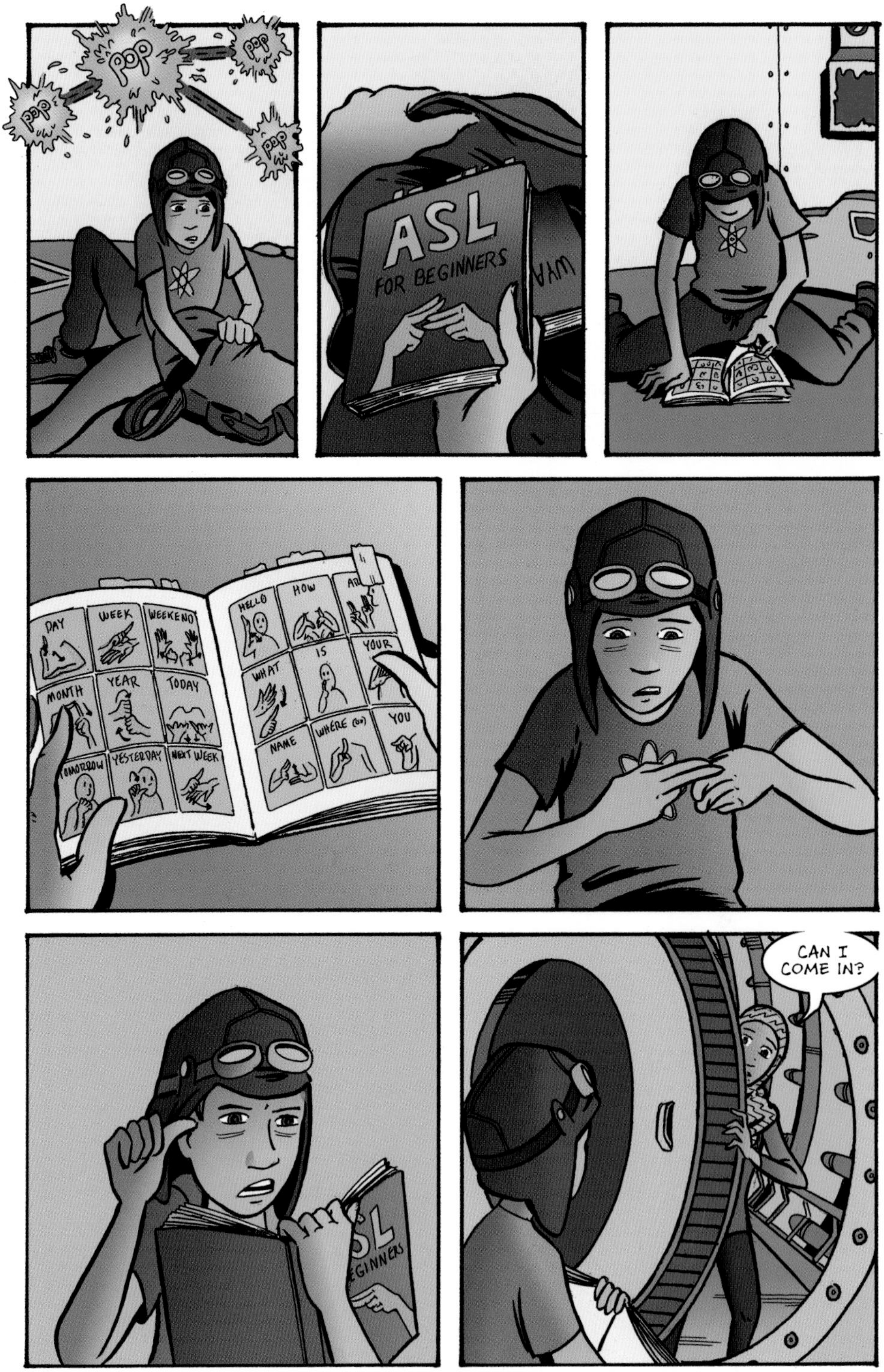
POP
POP
POP
POP
ASL
FOR BEGINNERS
DAY
WEEK
WEEKEND
MONTH
YEAR
TODAY
TOMORROW
YESTERDAY
NEXT WEEK
HELLO
HOW
WHAT
IS
YOUR
NAME
WHERE
YOU
CAN I COME IN?

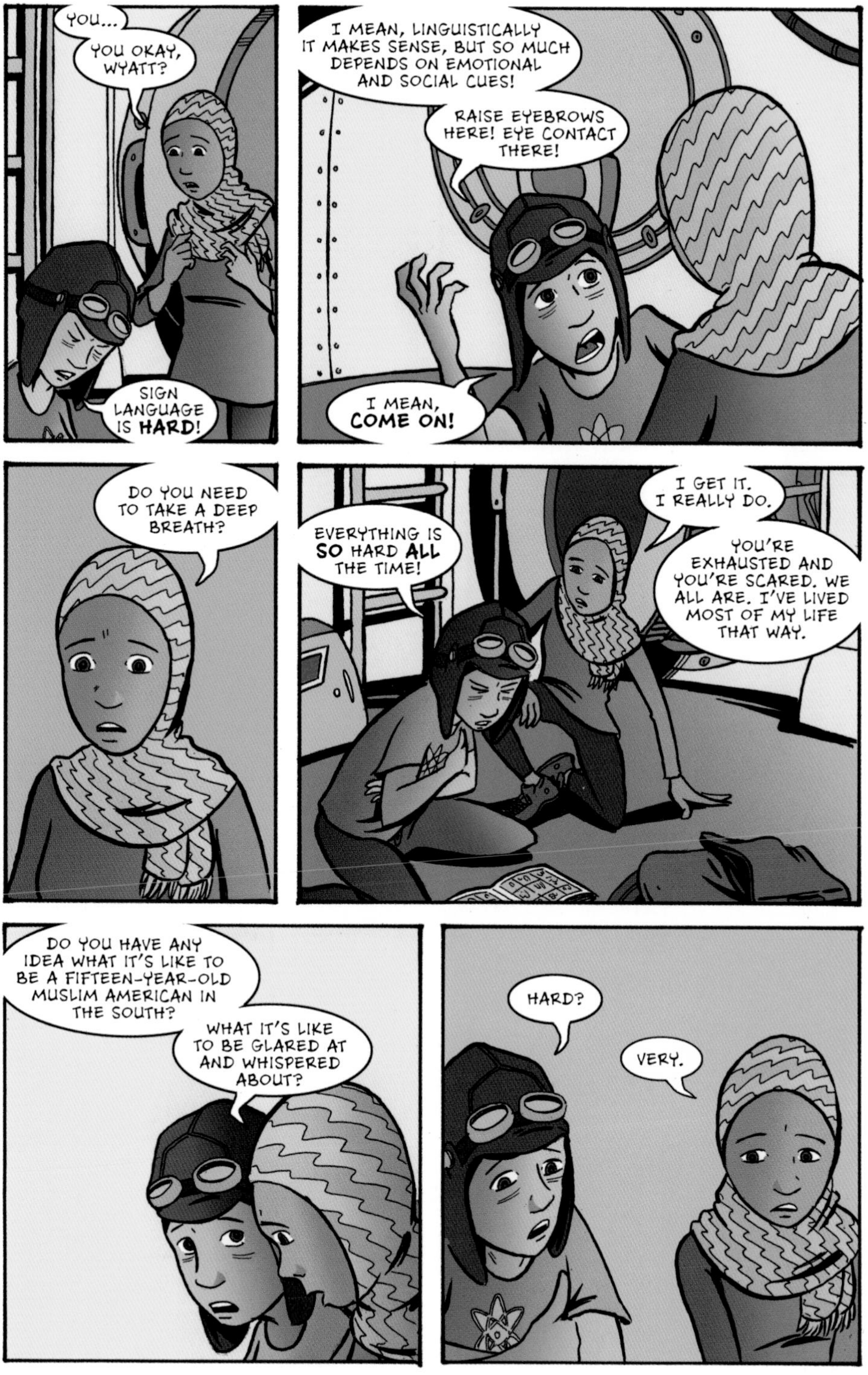
YOU...
YOU OKAY, WYATT?
SIGN LANGUAGE IS **HARD!**
I MEAN, LINGUISTICALLY IT MAKES SENSE, BUT SO MUCH DEPENDS ON EMOTIONAL AND SOCIAL CUES!
RAISE EYEBROWS HERE! EYE CONTACT THERE!
I MEAN, **COME ON!**
DO YOU NEED TO TAKE A DEEP BREATH?
EVERYTHING IS **SO** HARD **ALL** THE TIME!
I GET IT. I REALLY DO.
YOU'RE EXHAUSTED AND YOU'RE SCARED. WE ALL ARE. I'VE LIVED MOST OF MY LIFE THAT WAY.
DO YOU HAVE ANY IDEA WHAT IT'S LIKE TO BE A FIFTEEN-YEAR-OLD MUSLIM AMERICAN IN THE SOUTH?
WHAT IT'S LIKE TO BE GLARED AT AND WHISPERED ABOUT?
HARD?
VERY.

BUT WE'VE GOT FAMILY AND FRIENDS THAT NEED OUR HELP, AND IF WE CAN PULL THIS OFF, LIFE MIGHT BE JUST A LITTLE LESS DIFFICULT.

MY PARENTS ARE OUT THERE, TOO, WYATT.

I NEED THIS TO WORK. WE **ALL** NEED THIS TO WORK.

YOUR PEP TALKS ARE EVEN WORSE THAN MINE.

NOT A PEP TALK. A REALITY CHECK.

SO WHAT DO WE DO NOW?

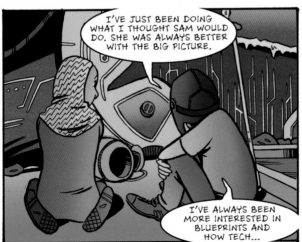

I'VE JUST BEEN DOING WHAT I THOUGHT SAM WOULD DO. SHE WAS ALWAYS BETTER WITH THE BIG PICTURE.

I'VE ALWAYS BEEN MORE INTERESTED IN BLUEPRINTS AND HOW TECH...

I ALMOST FORGOT!

96

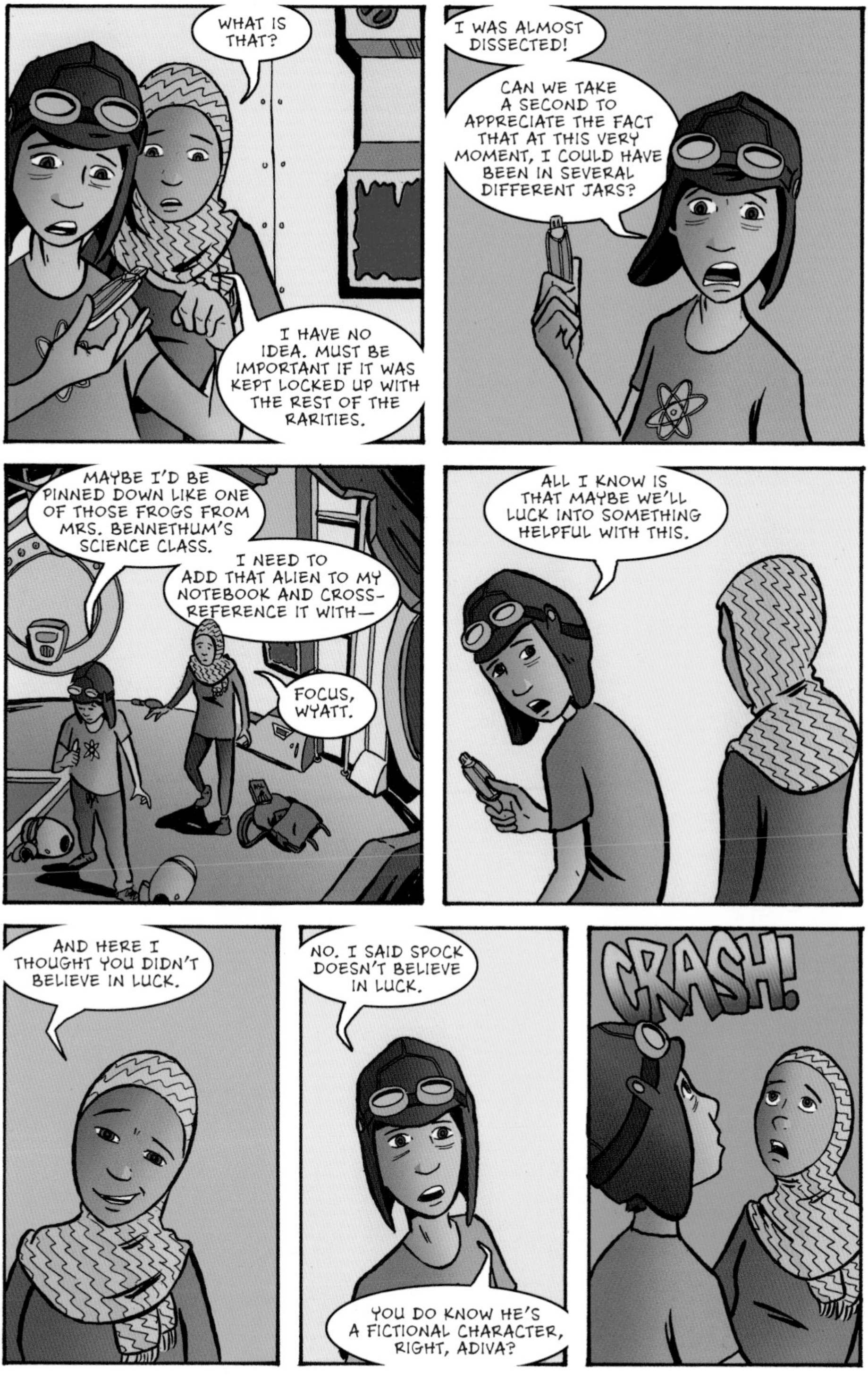
WHAT IS THAT?
I HAVE NO IDEA. MUST BE IMPORTANT IF IT WAS KEPT LOCKED UP WITH THE REST OF THE RARITIES.
I WAS ALMOST DISSECTED!
CAN WE TAKE A SECOND TO APPRECIATE THE FACT THAT AT THIS VERY MOMENT, I COULD HAVE BEEN IN SEVERAL DIFFERENT JARS?
MAYBE I'D BE PINNED DOWN LIKE ONE OF THOSE FROGS FROM MRS. BENNETHUM'S SCIENCE CLASS.
I NEED TO ADD THAT ALIEN TO MY NOTEBOOK AND CROSS-REFERENCE IT WITH—
FOCUS, WYATT.
ALL I KNOW IS THAT MAYBE WE'LL LUCK INTO SOMETHING HELPFUL WITH THIS.
AND HERE I THOUGHT YOU DIDN'T BELIEVE IN LUCK.
NO. I SAID SPOCK DOESN'T BELIEVE IN LUCK.
YOU DO KNOW HE'S A FICTIONAL CHARACTER, RIGHT, ADIVA?
CRASH!

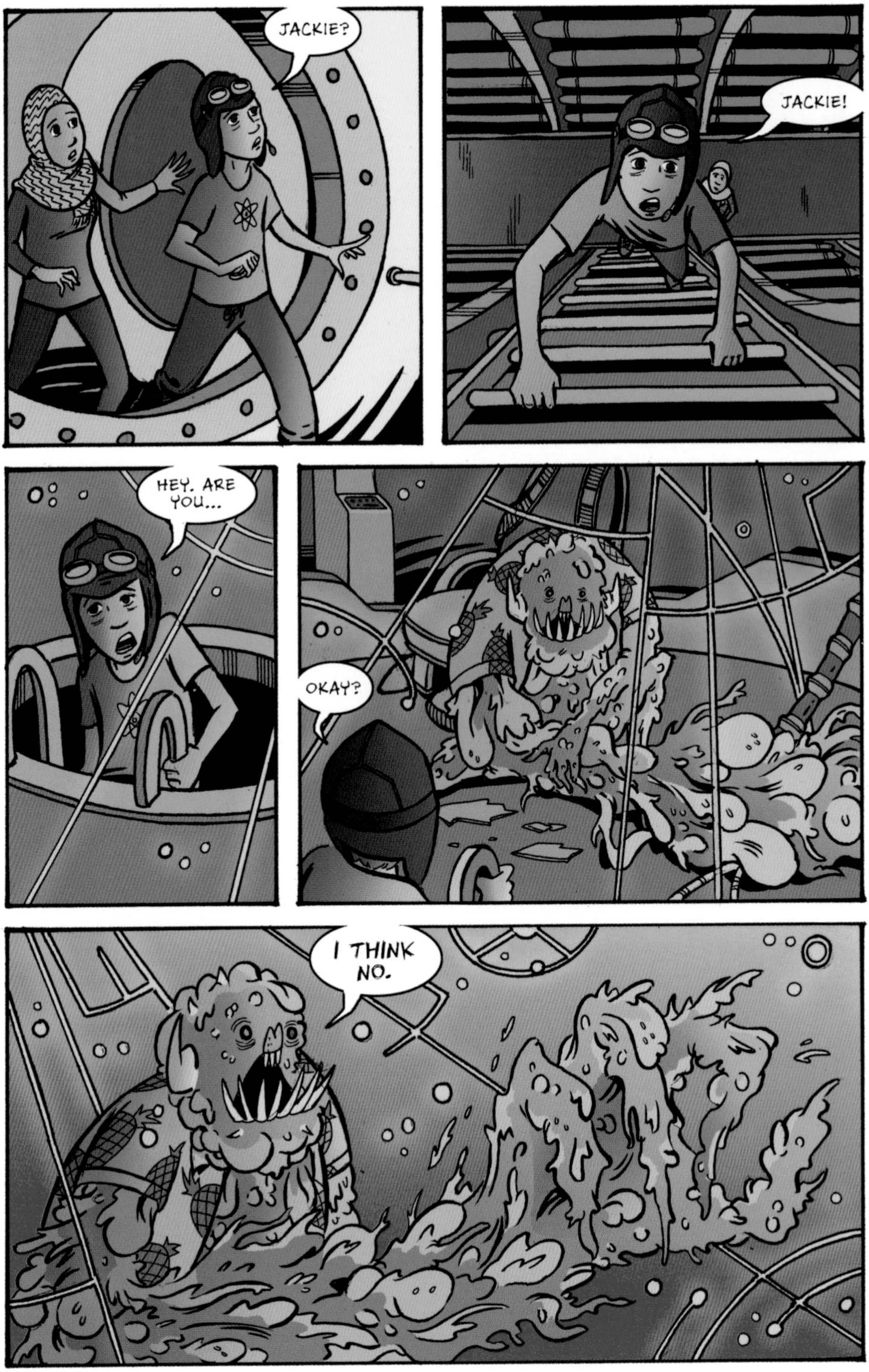
JACKIE?
JACKIE!
HEY. ARE YOU...
OKAY?
I THINK NO.

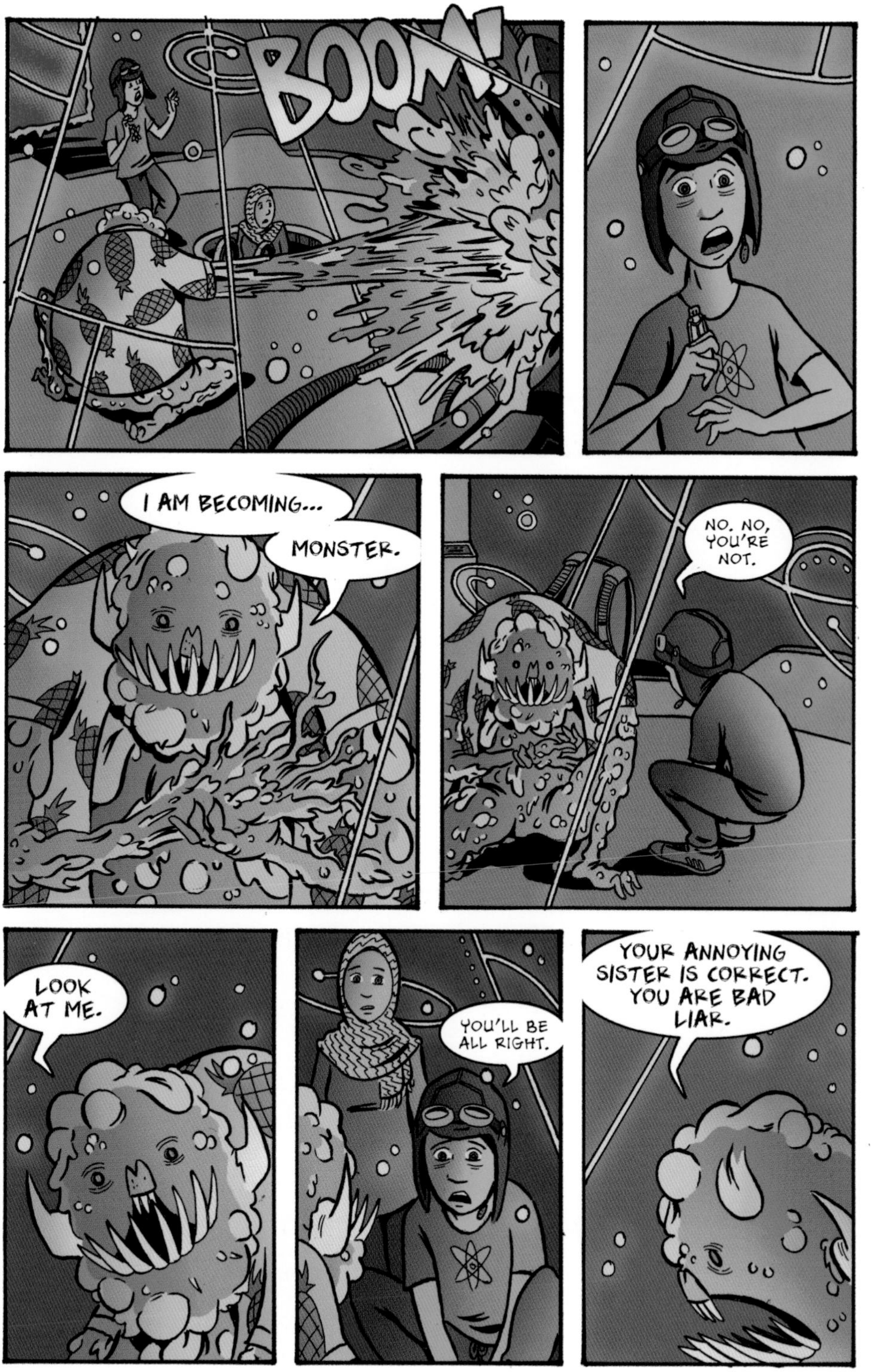
BOOM!
I AM BECOMING...
MONSTER.
NO. NO, YOU'RE NOT.
LOOK AT ME.
YOU'LL BE ALL RIGHT.
YOUR ANNOYING SISTER IS CORRECT. YOU ARE BAD LIAR.

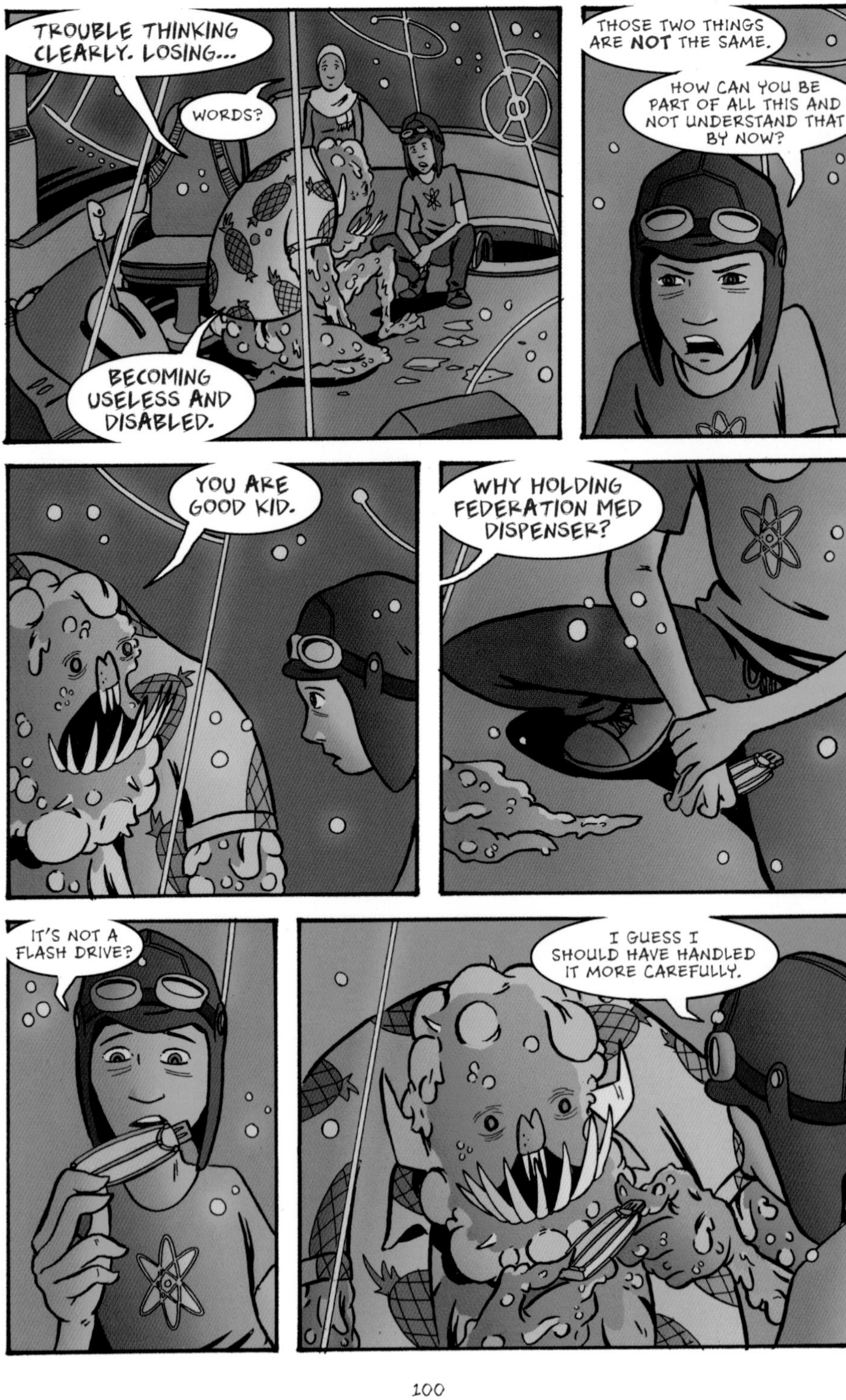
TROUBLE THINKING CLEARLY. LOSING...
WORDS?
BECOMING USELESS AND DISABLED.
THOSE TWO THINGS ARE **NOT** THE SAME.
HOW CAN YOU BE PART OF ALL THIS AND NOT UNDERSTAND THAT BY NOW?
YOU ARE GOOD KID.
WHY HOLDING FEDERATION MED DISPENSER?
IT'S NOT A FLASH DRIVE?
I GUESS I SHOULD HAVE HANDLED IT MORE CAREFULLY.

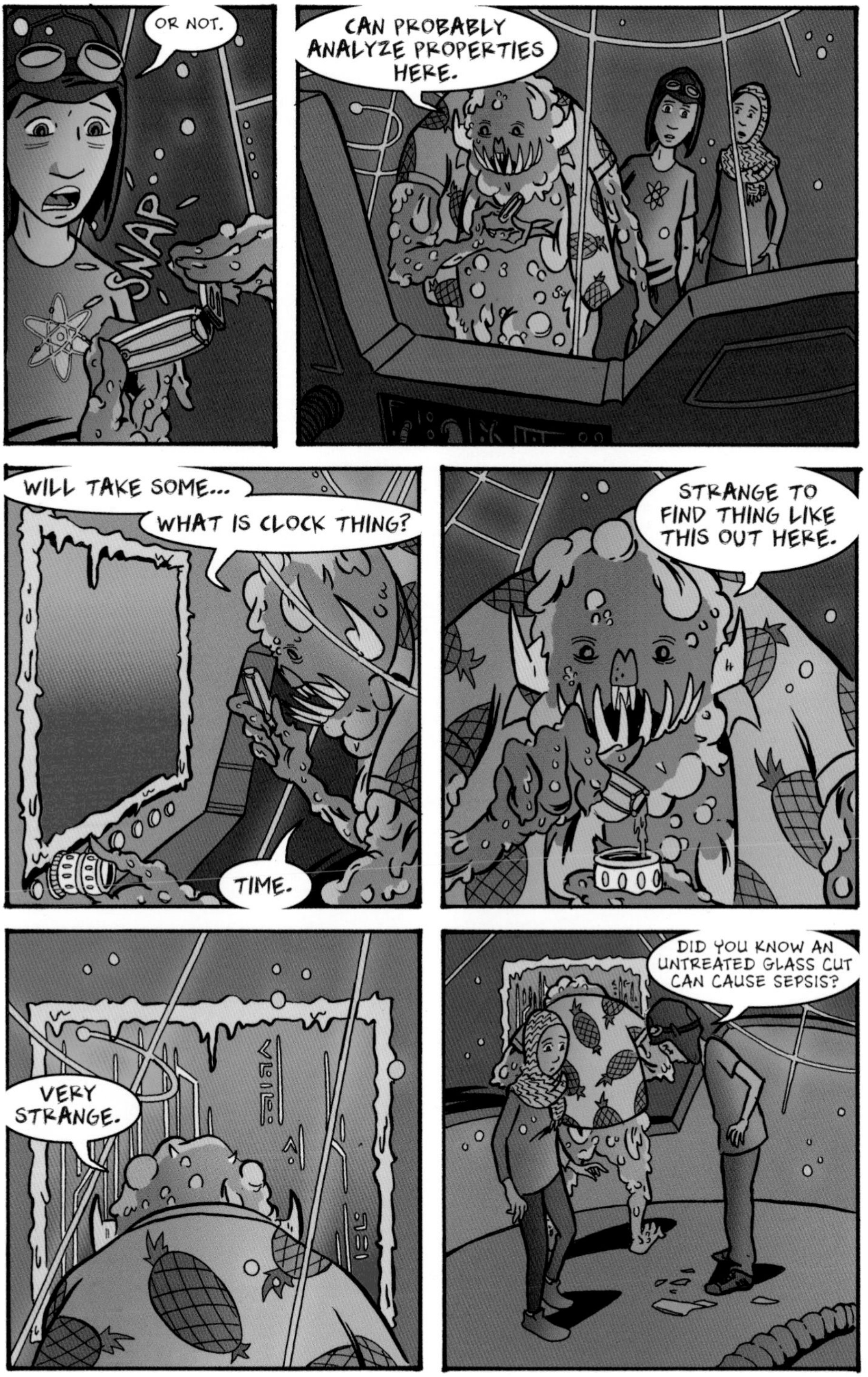
OR NOT.
SNAP
CAN PROBABLY ANALYZE PROPERTIES HERE.
WILL TAKE SOME...
WHAT IS CLOCK THING?
TIME.
STRANGE TO FIND THING LIKE THIS OUT HERE.
VERY STRANGE.
DID YOU KNOW AN UNTREATED GLASS CUT CAN CAUSE SEPSIS?

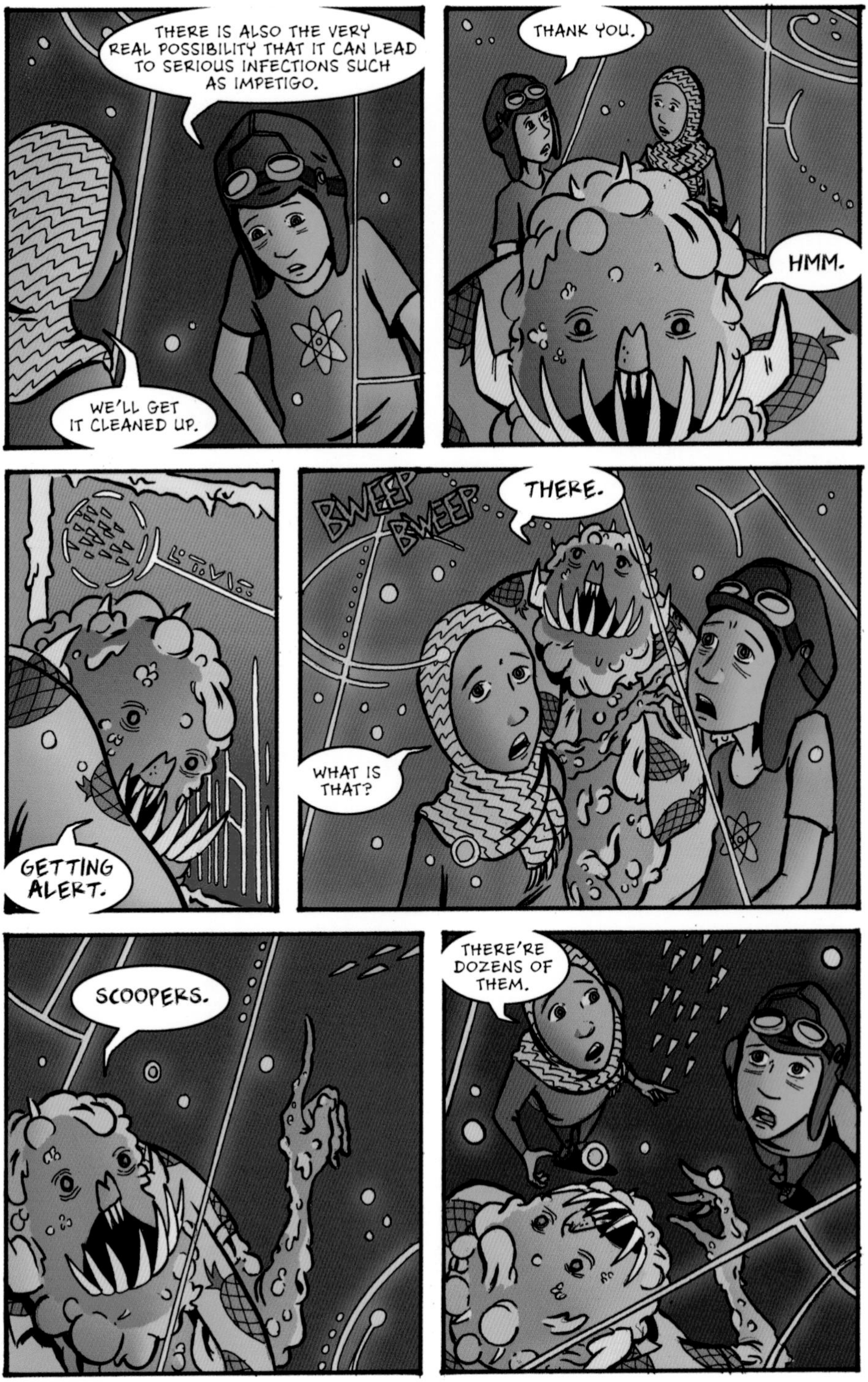
THERE IS ALSO THE VERY REAL POSSIBILITY THAT IT CAN LEAD TO SERIOUS INFECTIONS SUCH AS IMPETIGO.
WE'LL GET IT CLEANED UP.
THANK YOU.
HMM.
GETTING ALERT.
BWEEP BWEEP
THERE.
WHAT IS THAT?
SCOOPERS.
THERE'RE DOZENS OF THEM.

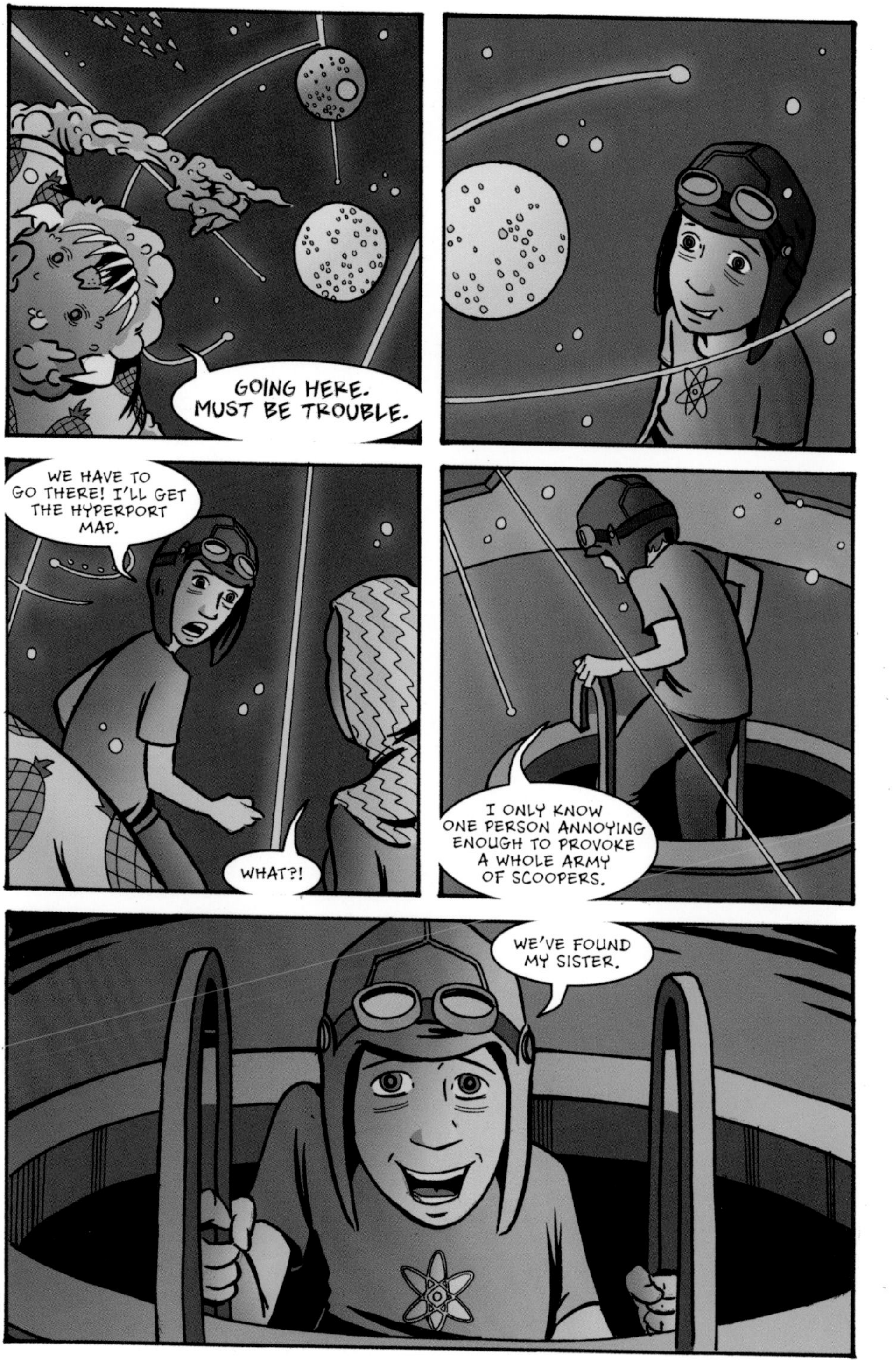
GOING HERE.
MUST BE TROUBLE.
WE HAVE TO GO THERE! I'LL GET THE HYPERPORT MAP.
WHAT?!
I ONLY KNOW ONE PERSON ANNOYING ENOUGH TO PROVOKE A WHOLE ARMY OF SCOOPERS.
WE'VE FOUND MY SISTER.

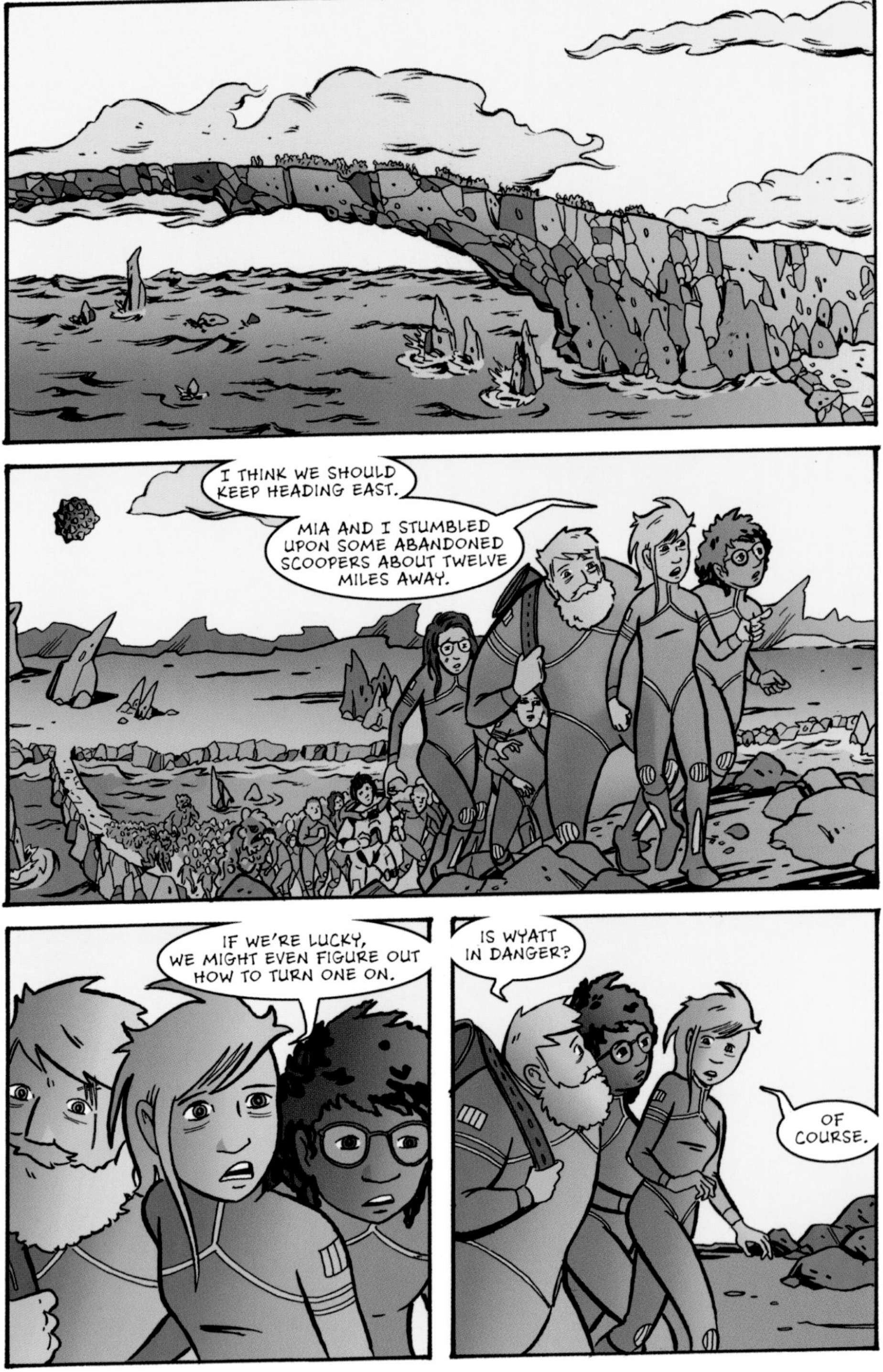
I THINK WE SHOULD KEEP HEADING EAST.
MIA AND I STUMBLED UPON SOME ABANDONED SCOOPERS ABOUT TWELVE MILES AWAY.
IF WE'RE LUCKY, WE MIGHT EVEN FIGURE OUT HOW TO TURN ONE ON.
IS WYATT IN DANGER?
OF COURSE.

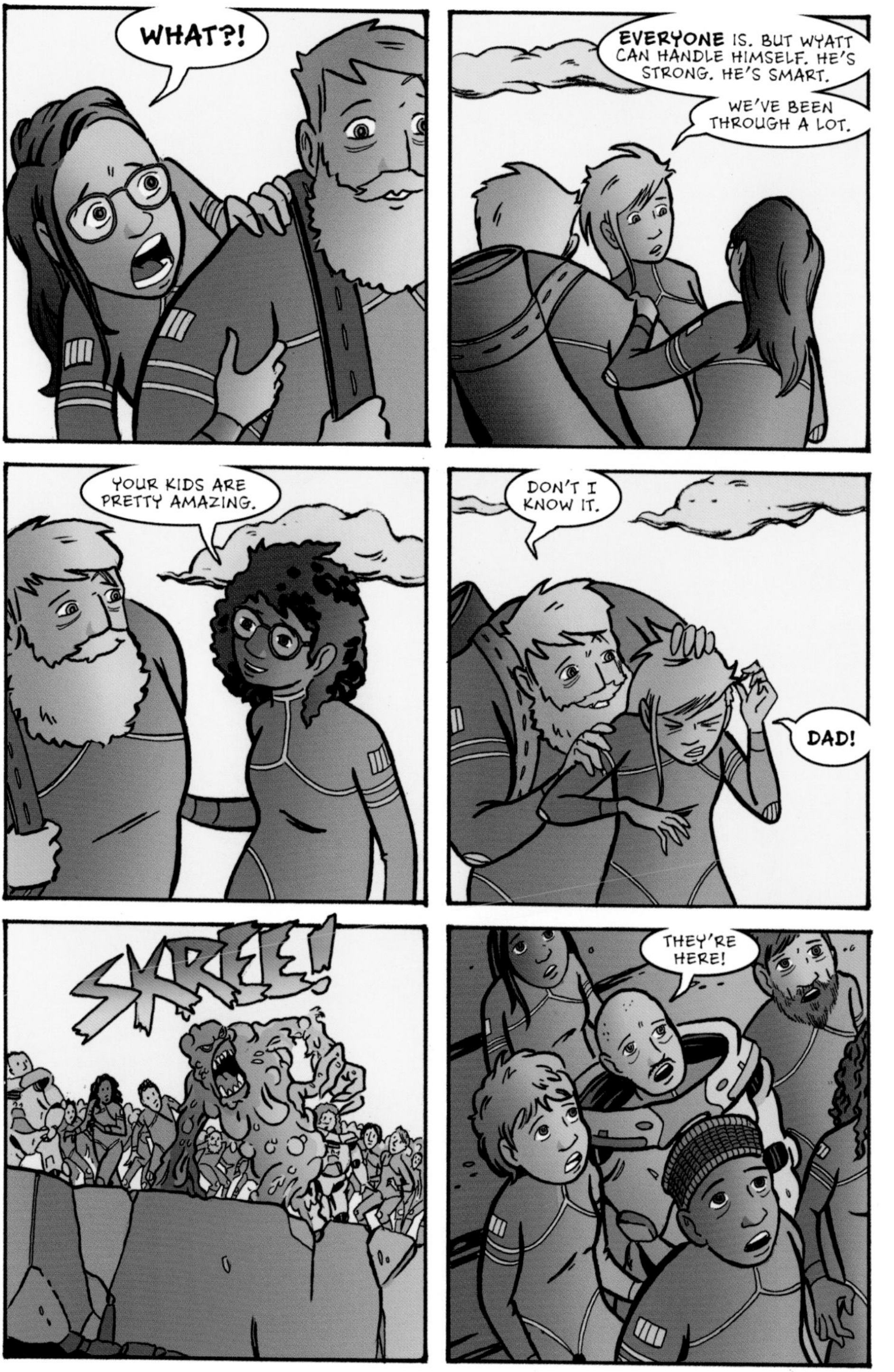
WHAT?!
EVERYONE IS. BUT WYATT CAN HANDLE HIMSELF. HE'S STRONG. HE'S SMART.
WE'VE BEEN THROUGH A LOT.
YOUR KIDS ARE PRETTY AMAZING.
DON'T I KNOW IT.
DAD!
SKREE!
THEY'RE HERE!

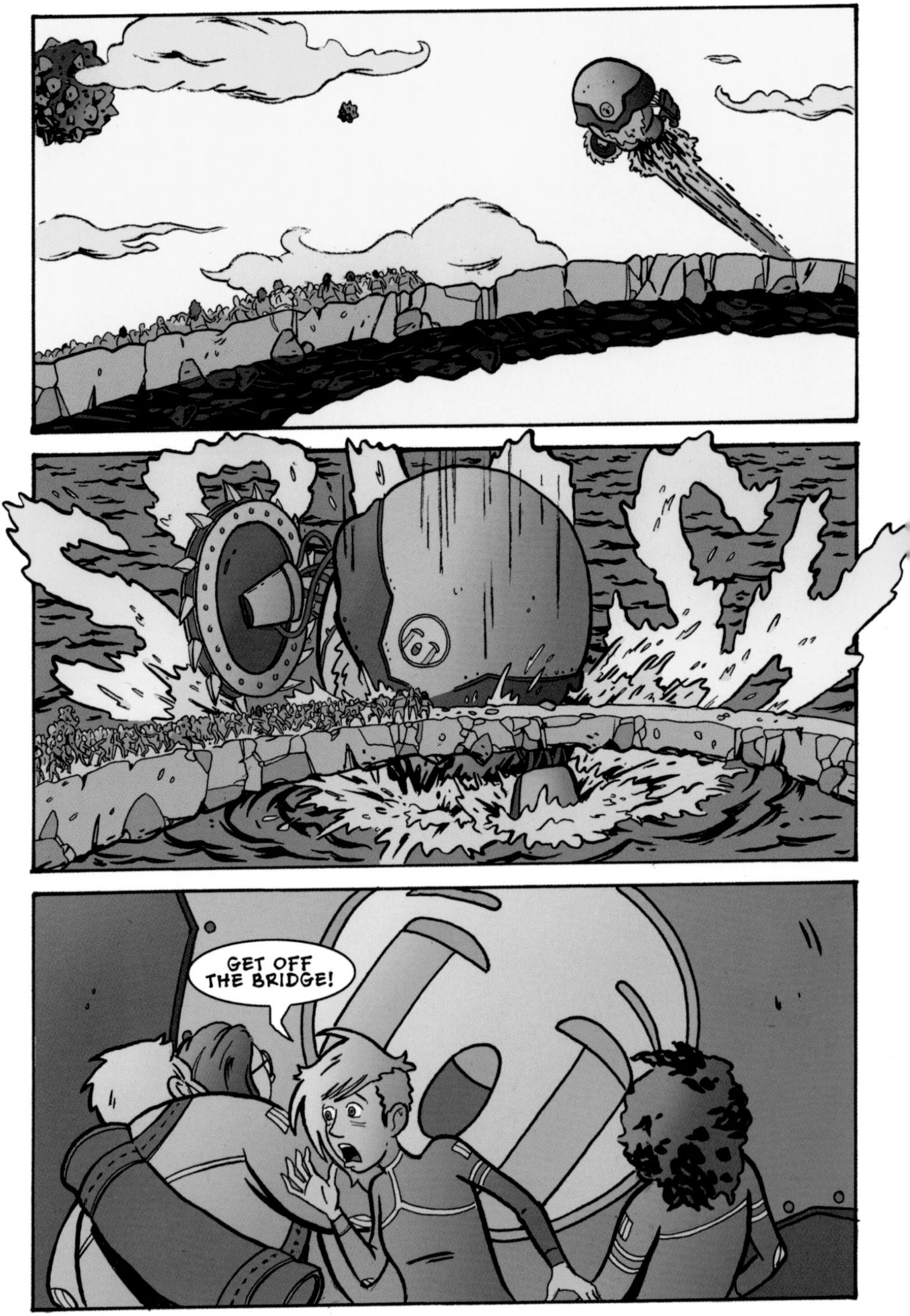
GET OFF THE BRIDGE!

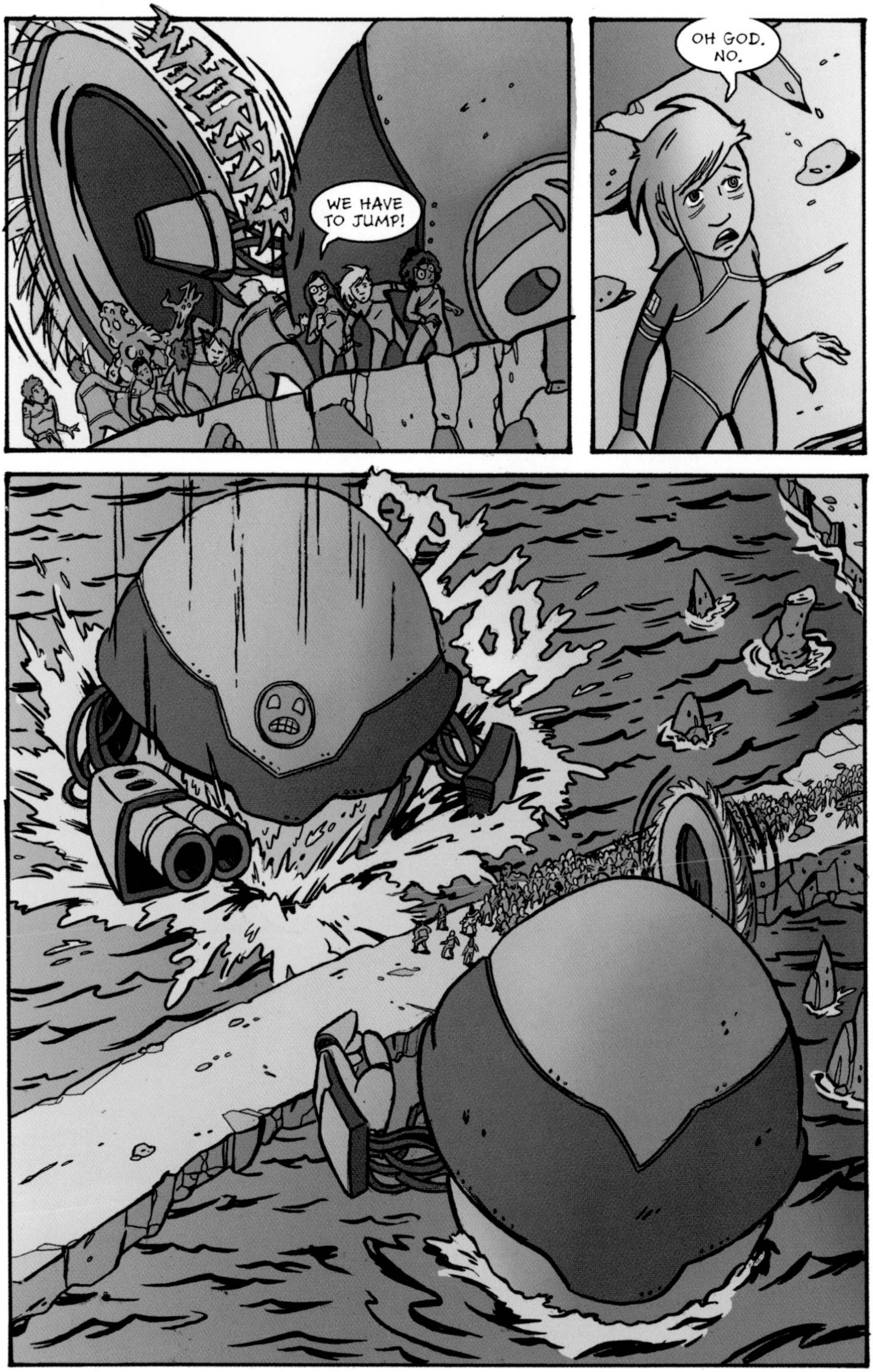
WE HAVE TO JUMP!
OH GOD. NO.

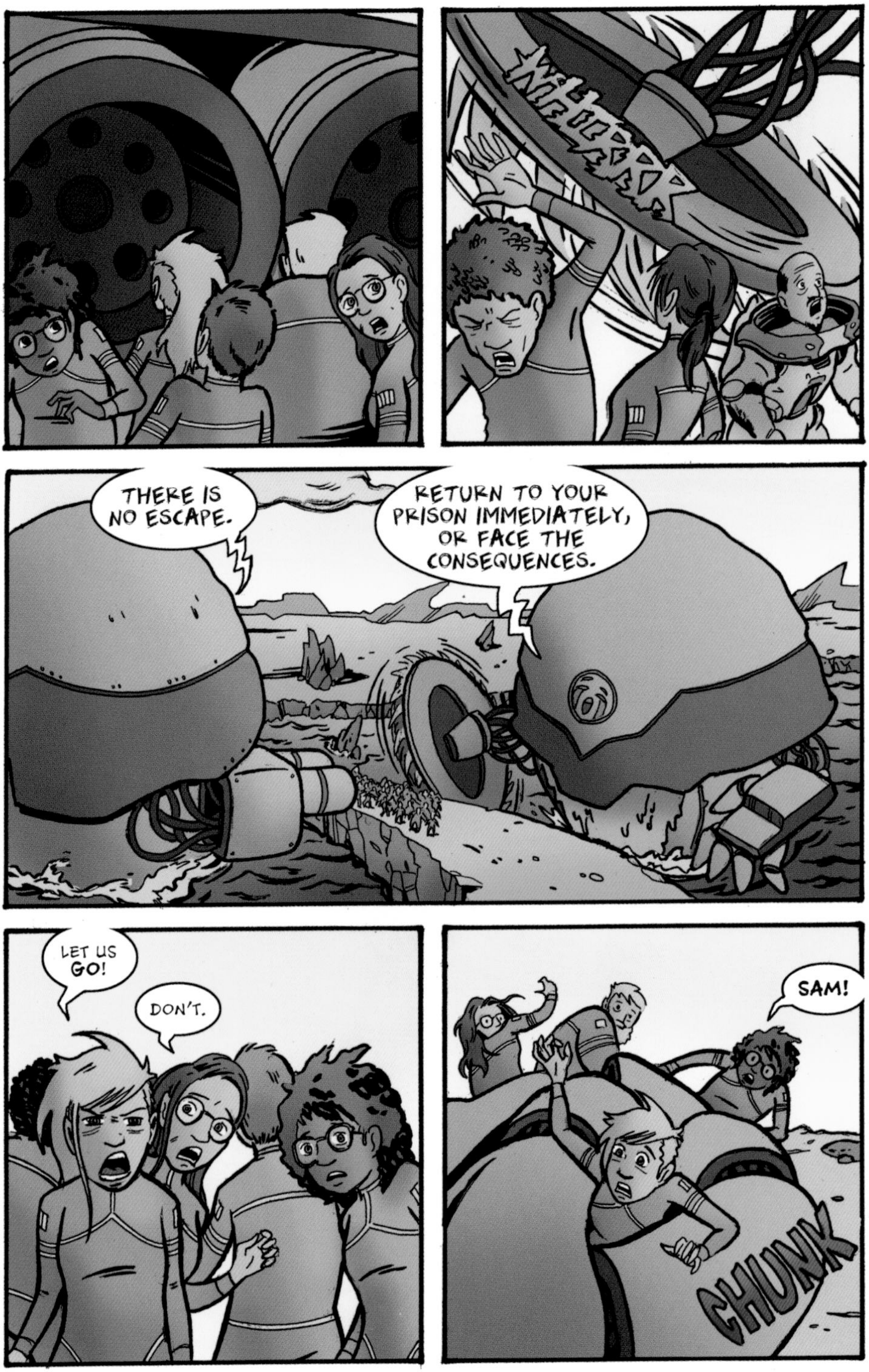
THERE IS NO ESCAPE.
RETURN TO YOUR PRISON IMMEDIATELY, OR FACE THE CONSEQUENCES.
LET US GO!
DON'T.
SAM!
CHUNK

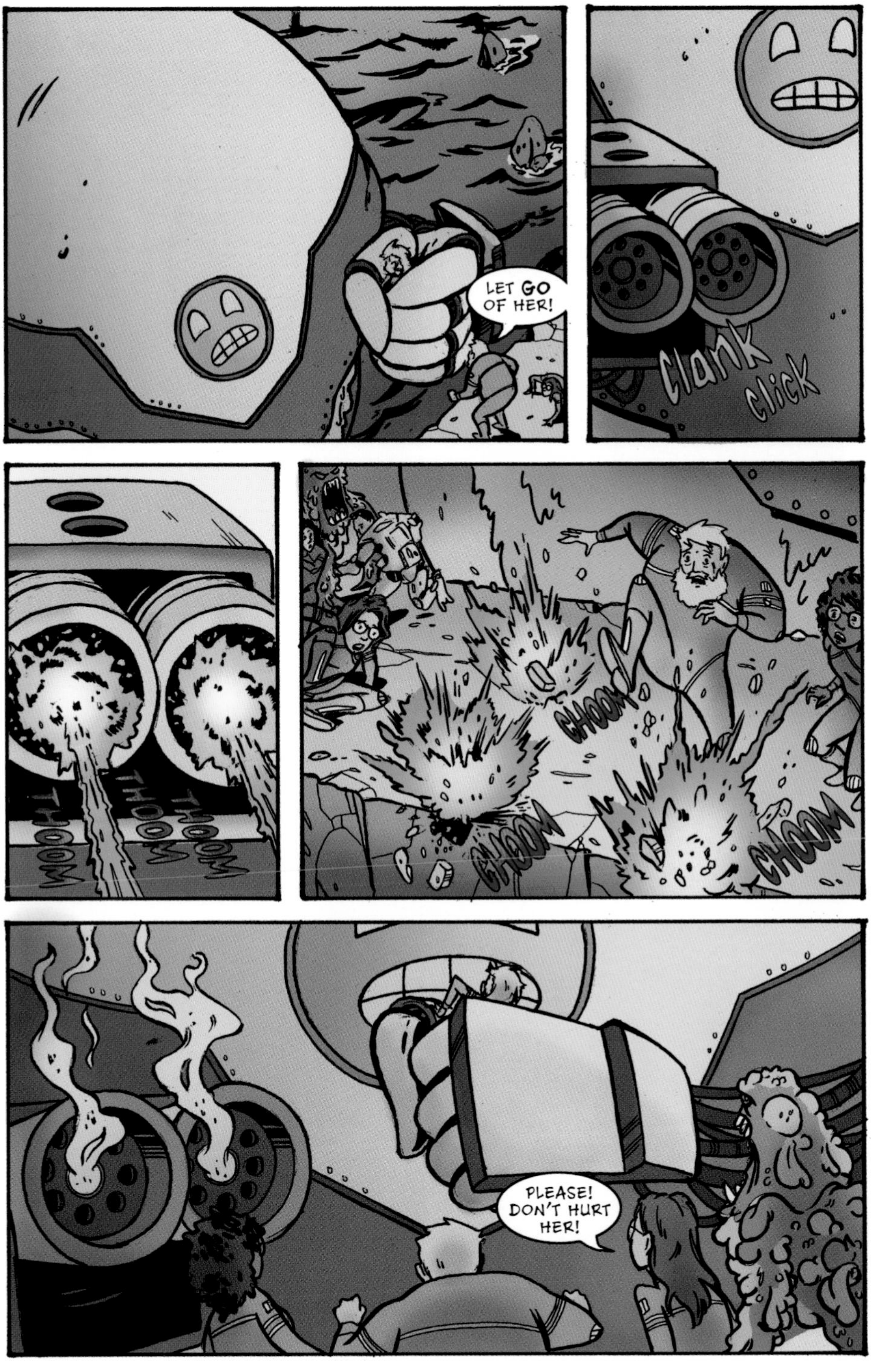
LET GO OF HER!
CLANK
CLICK
THOOM
THOOM
THOOM
CHOOM
CHOOM
CHOOM
PLEASE! DON'T HURT HER!

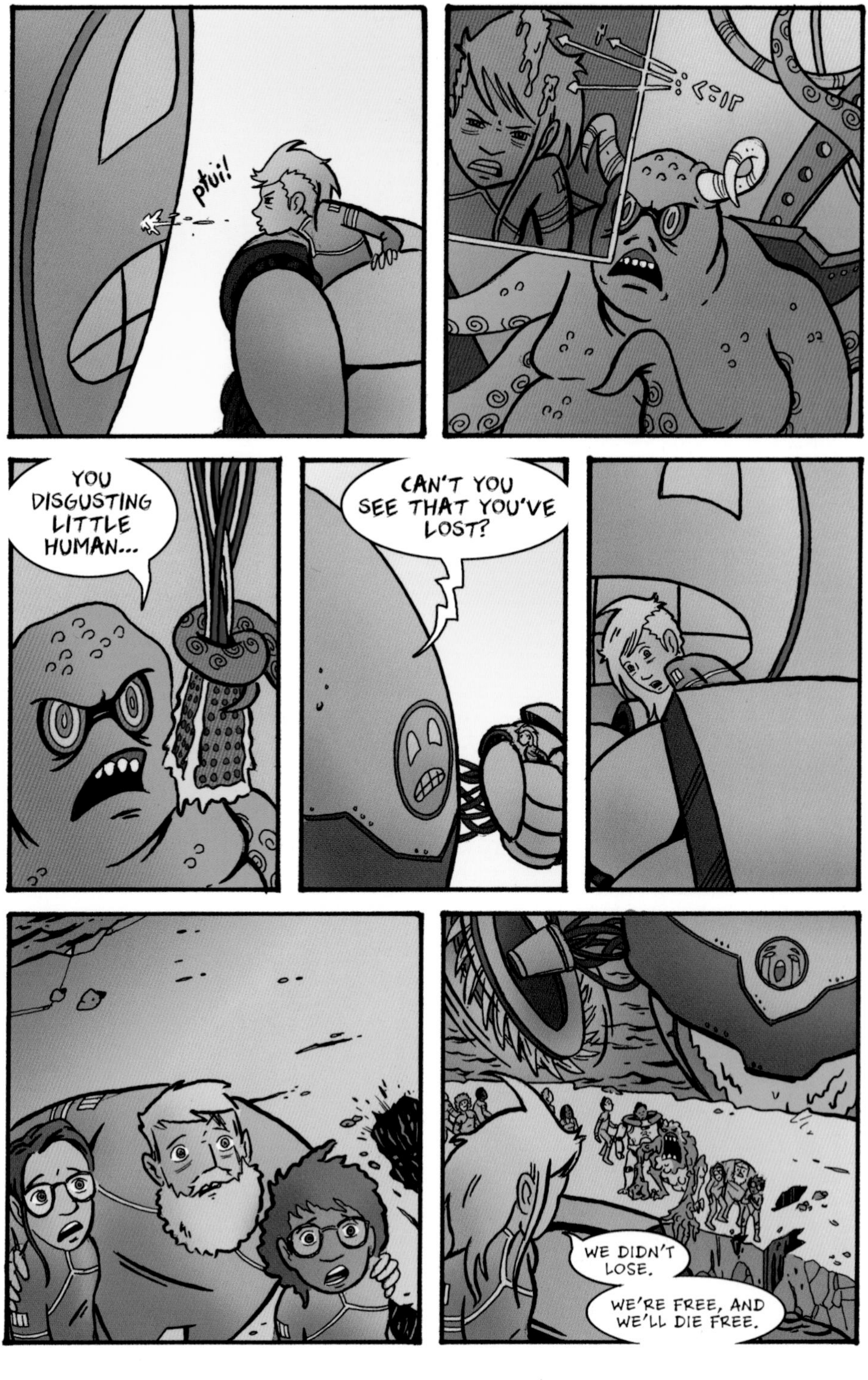
ptui!
YOU DISGUSTING LITTLE HUMAN...
CAN'T YOU SEE THAT YOU'VE LOST?
WE DIDN'T LOSE.
WE'RE FREE, AND WE'LL DIE FREE.

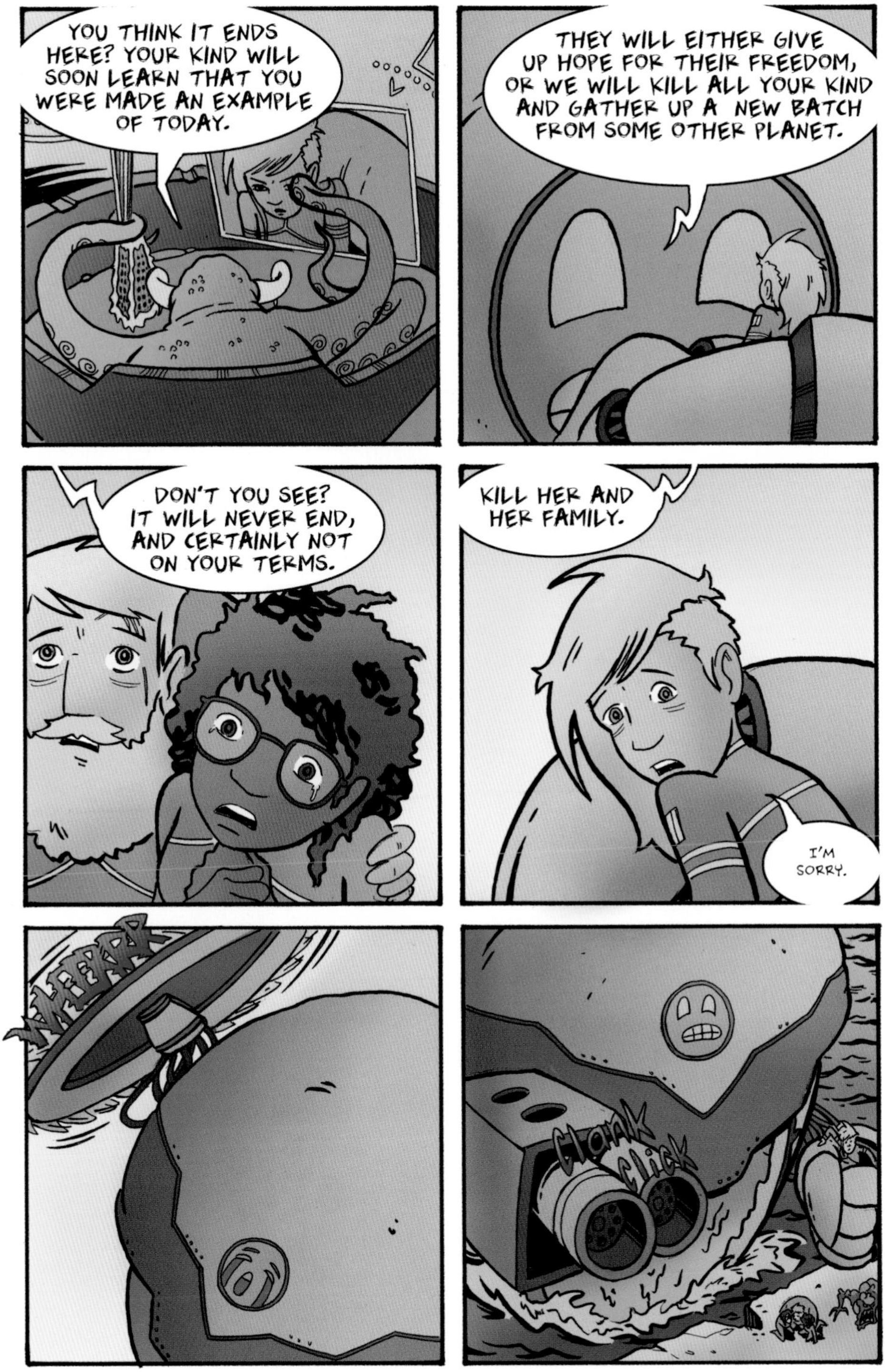
YOU THINK IT ENDS HERE? YOUR KIND WILL SOON LEARN THAT YOU WERE MADE AN EXAMPLE OF TODAY.
THEY WILL EITHER GIVE UP HOPE FOR THEIR FREEDOM, OR WE WILL KILL ALL YOUR KIND AND GATHER UP A NEW BATCH FROM SOME OTHER PLANET.
DON'T YOU SEE? IT WILL NEVER END, AND CERTAINLY NOT ON YOUR TERMS.
KILL HER AND HER FAMILY.
I'M SORRY.
CLANK
CLICK

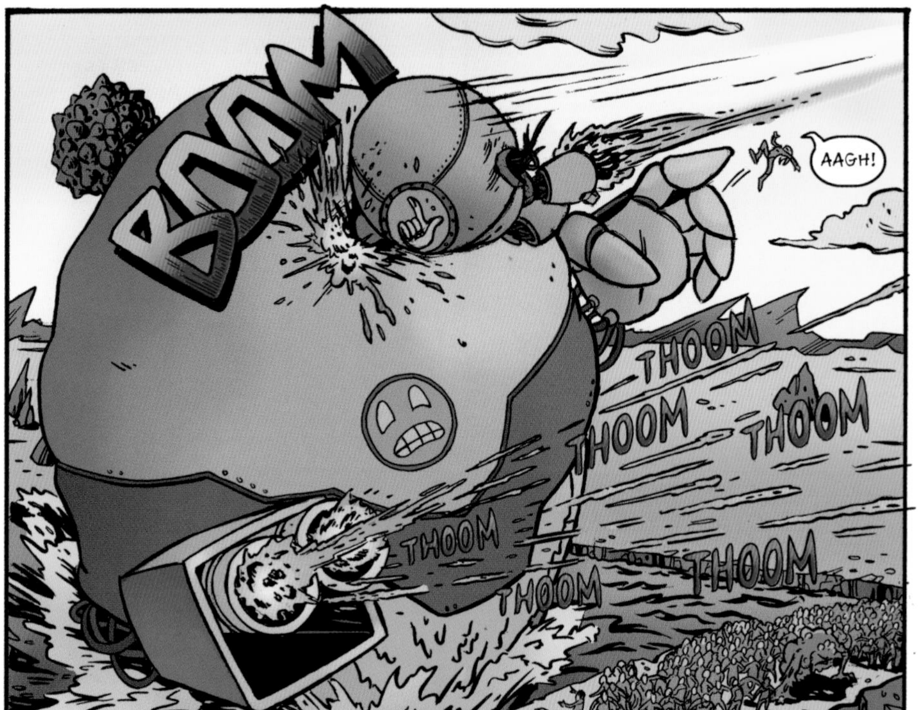
BOOM
AAGH!
THOOM
THOOM
THOOM
THOOM
THOOM
THOOM

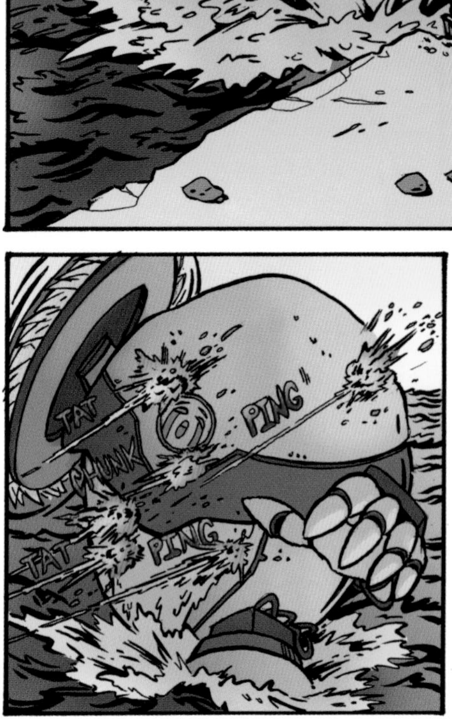
TAT
CHUNK
PING
TAT
PING

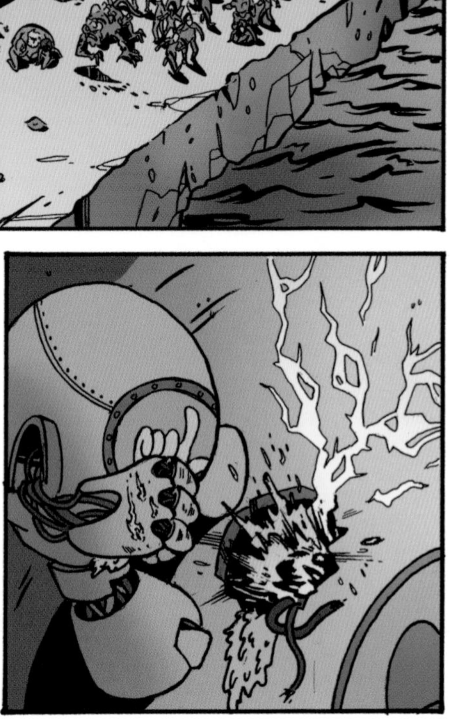

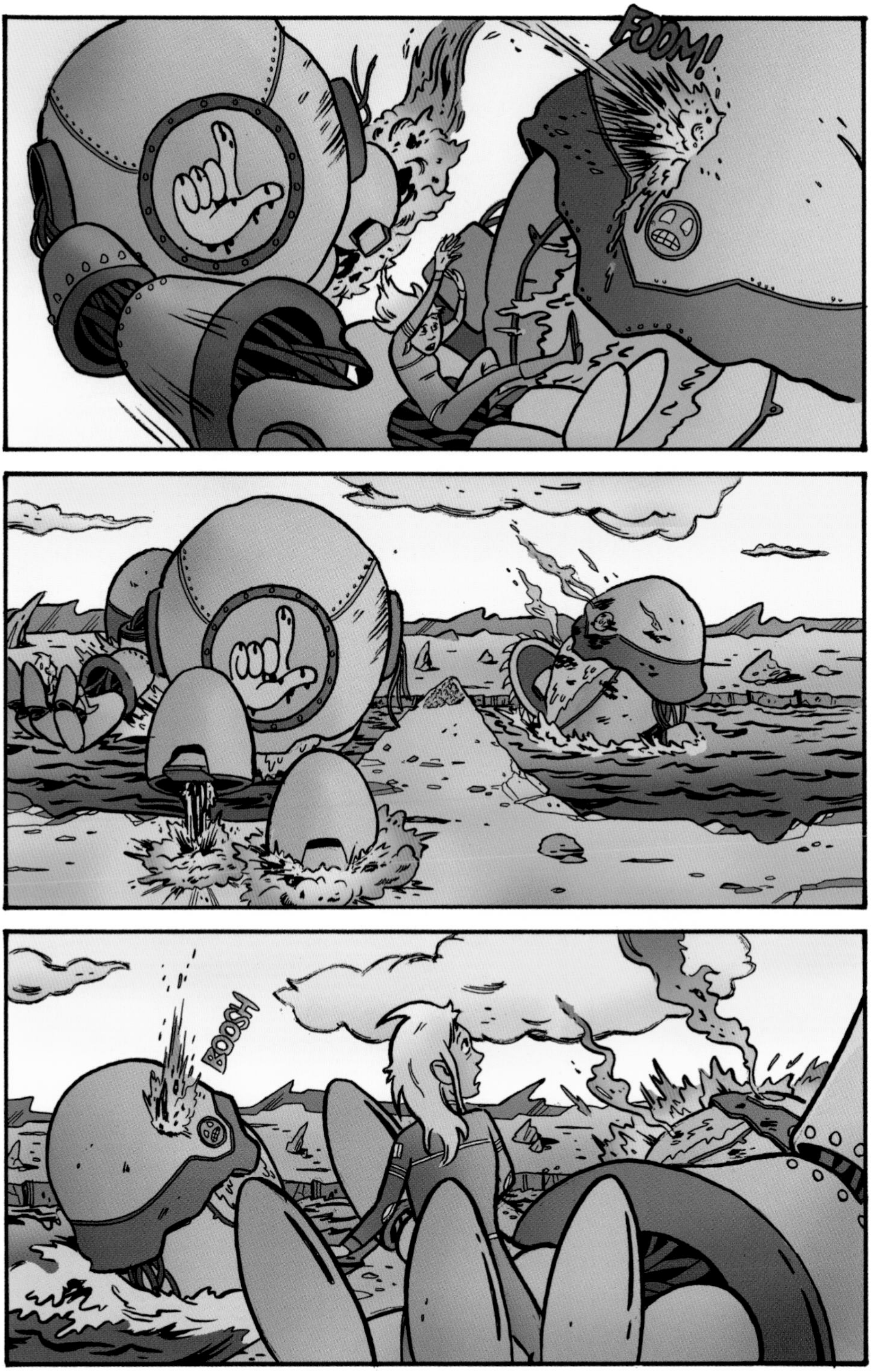
FOOM!
BOOSH

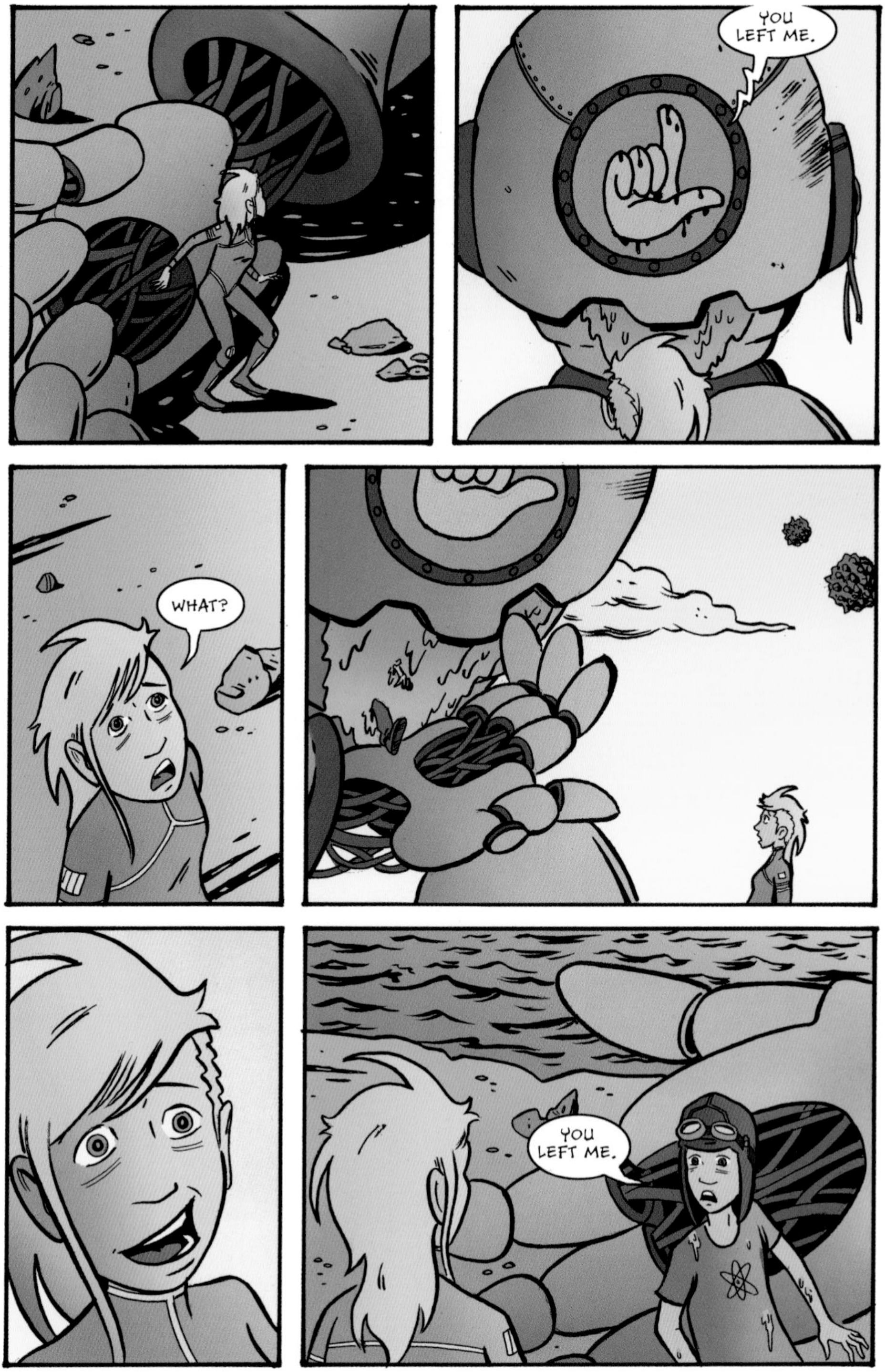
YOU LEFT ME.
WHAT?
YOU LEFT ME.

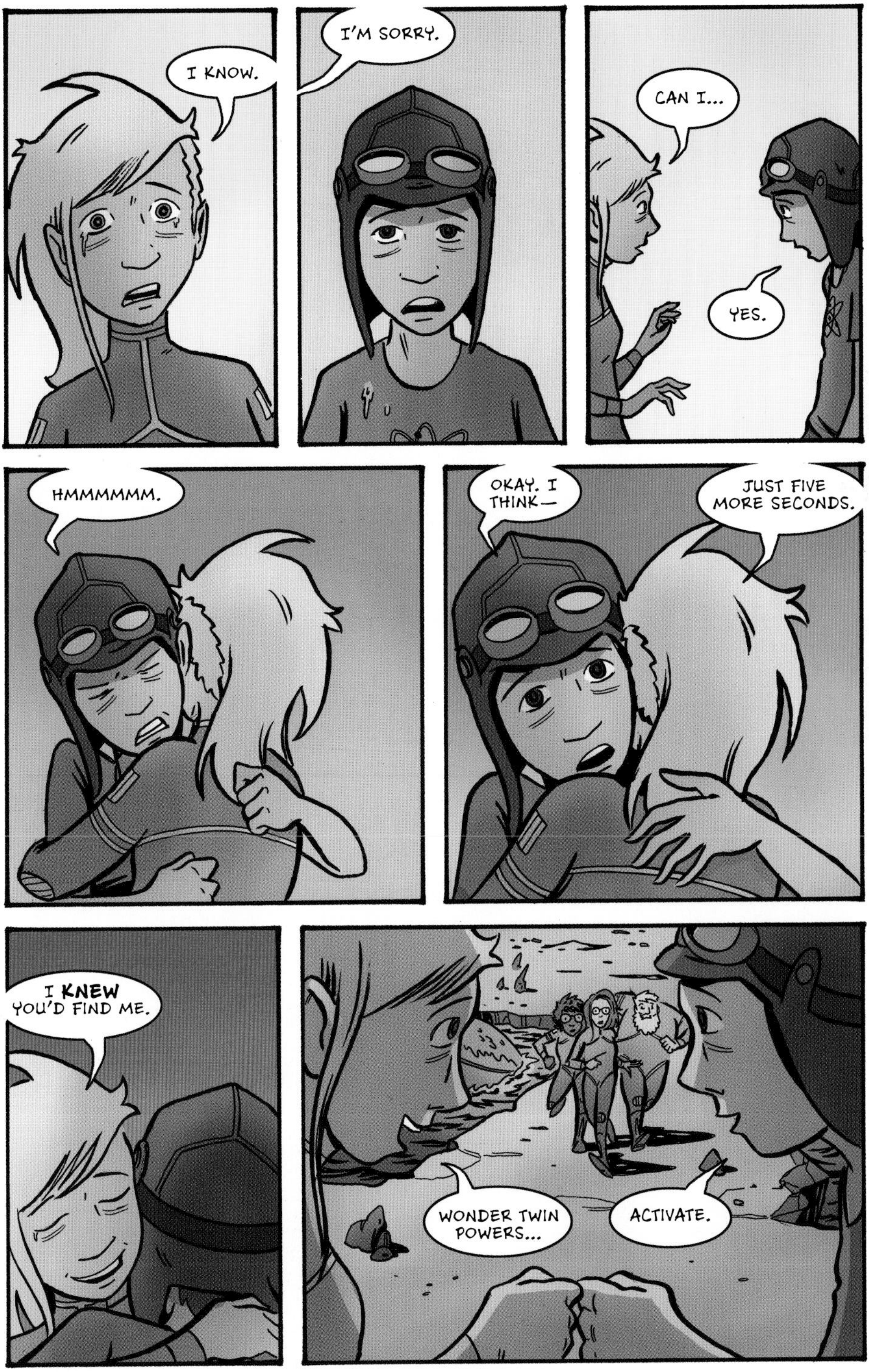

I KNOW.
I'M SORRY.
CAN I...
YES.
HMMMMMM.
OKAY. I THINK—
JUST FIVE MORE SECONDS.
I **KNEW** YOU'D FIND ME.
WONDER TWIN POWERS...
ACTIVATE.

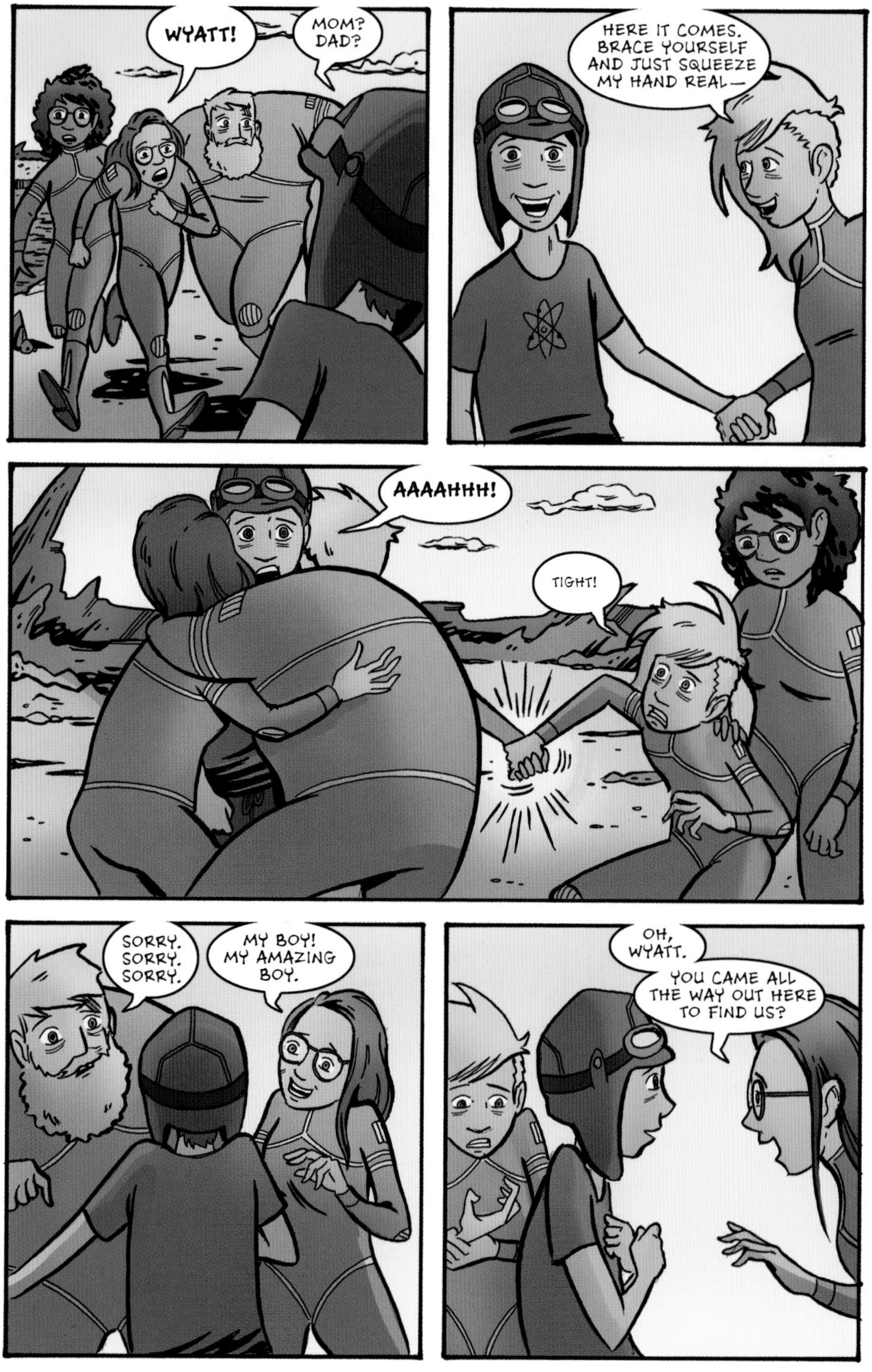
WYATT!
MOM? DAD?
HERE IT COMES. BRACE YOURSELF AND JUST SQUEEZE MY HAND REAL—
AAAAHHH!
TIGHT!
SORRY. SORRY. SORRY.
MY BOY! MY AMAZING BOY.
OH, WYATT.
YOU CAME ALL THE WAY OUT HERE TO FIND US?

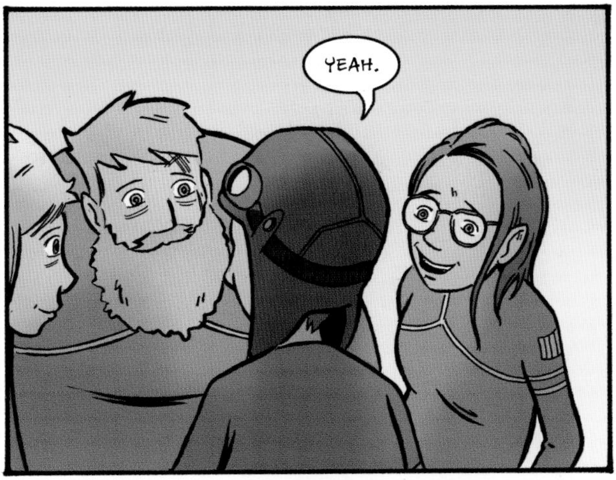
YEAH.

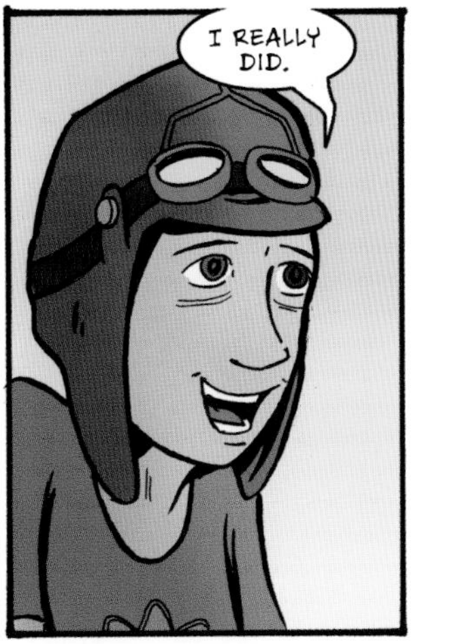
I REALLY DID.

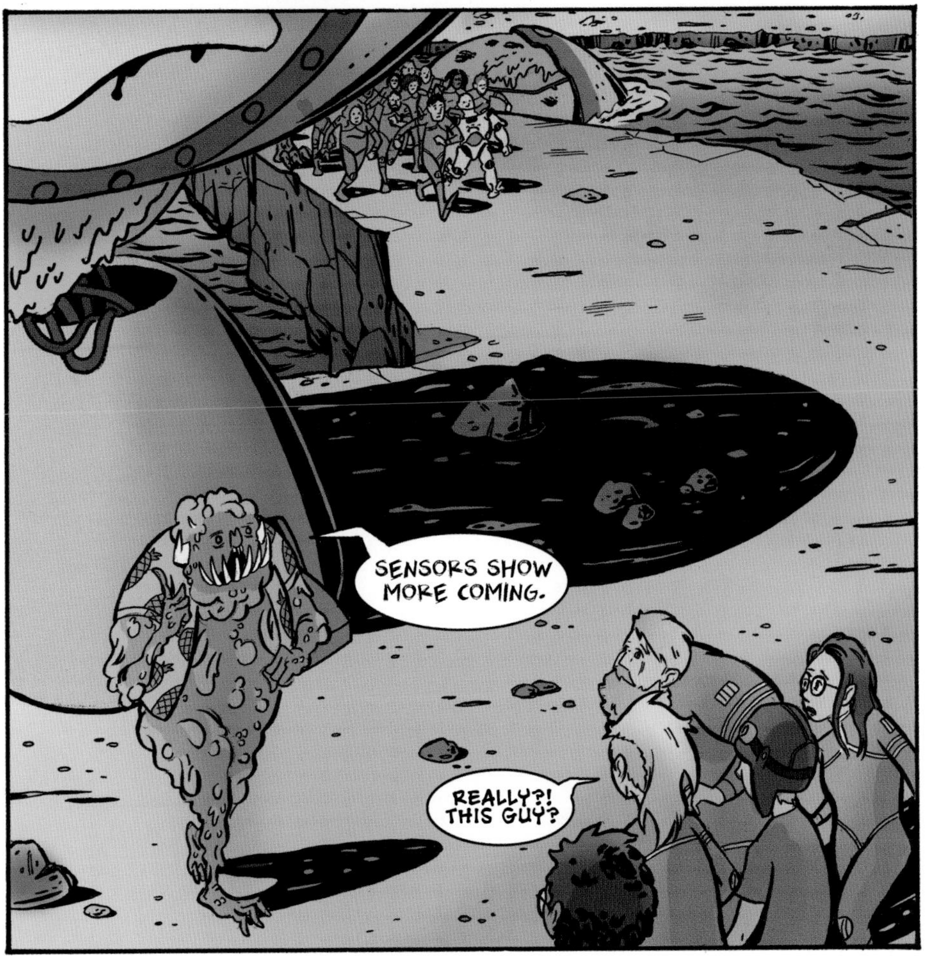
SENSORS SHOW MORE COMING.
REALLY?! THIS GUY?

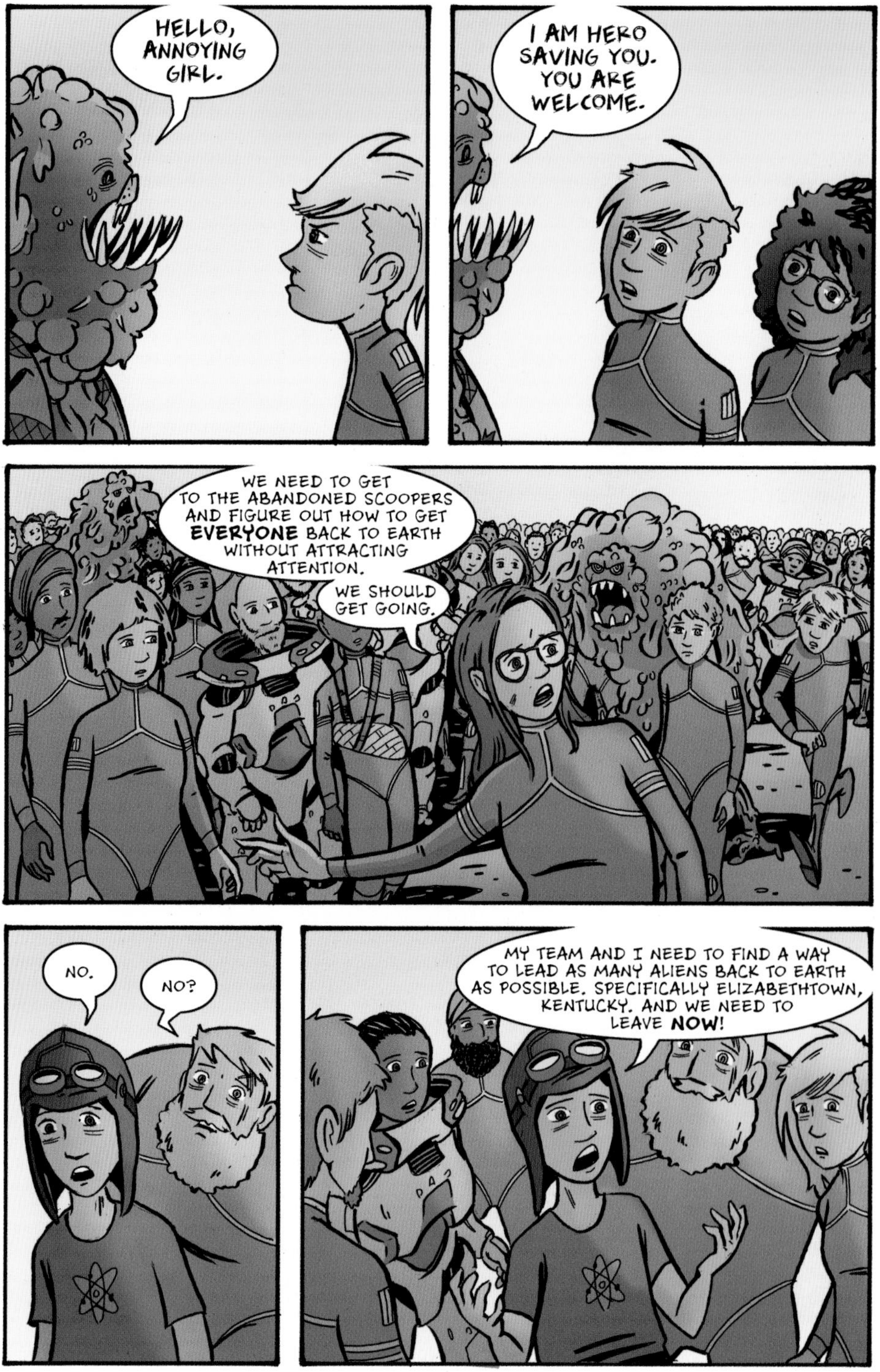
HELLO, ANNOYING GIRL.
I AM HERO SAVING YOU. YOU ARE WELCOME.
WE NEED TO GET TO THE ABANDONED SCOOPERS AND FIGURE OUT HOW TO GET **EVERYONE** BACK TO EARTH WITHOUT ATTRACTING ATTENTION.
WE SHOULD GET GOING.
NO.
NO?
MY TEAM AND I NEED TO FIND A WAY TO LEAD AS MANY ALIENS BACK TO EARTH AS POSSIBLE. SPECIFICALLY ELIZABETHTOWN, KENTUCKY. AND WE NEED TO LEAVE **NOW**!

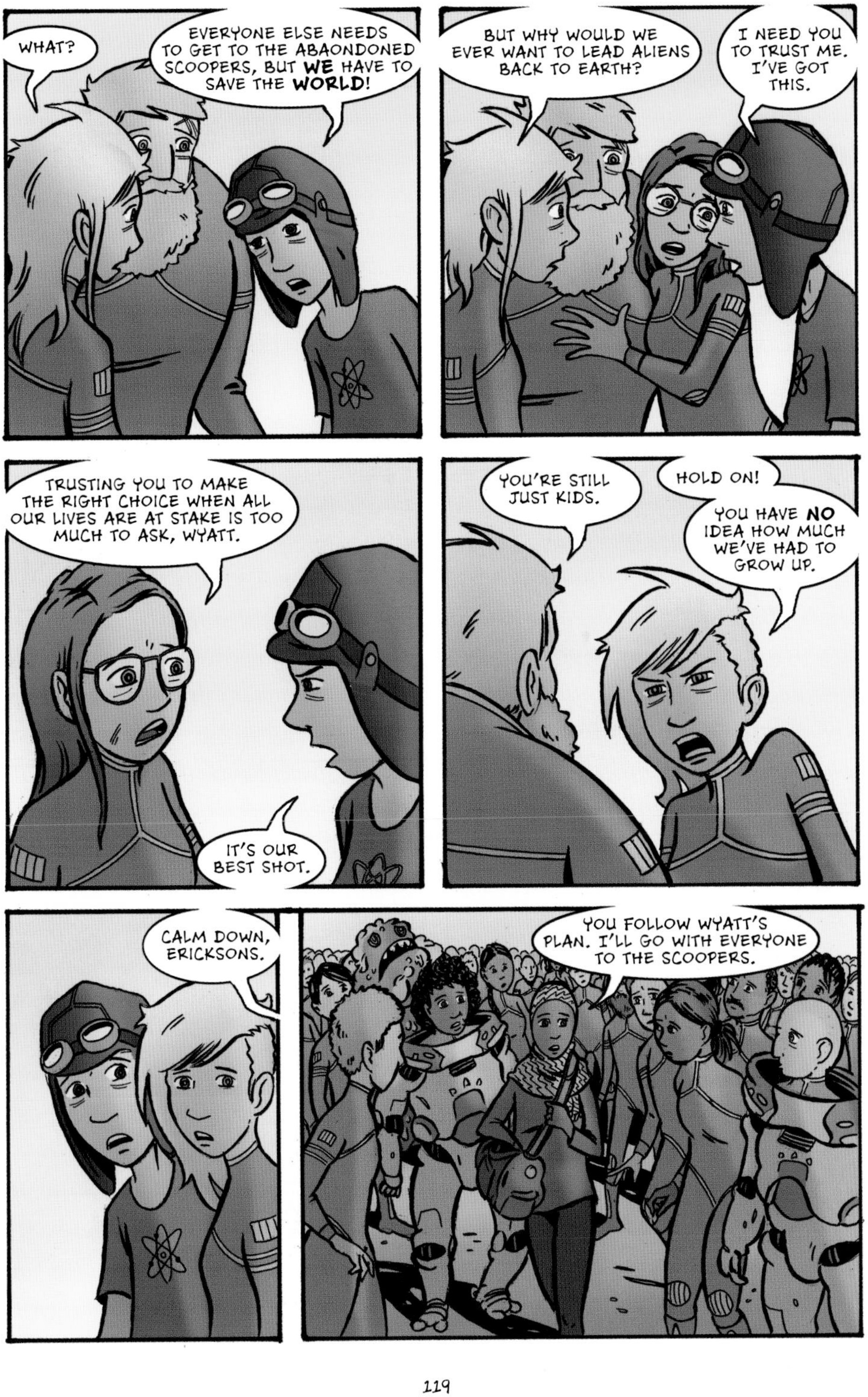
WHAT?
EVERYONE ELSE NEEDS TO GET TO THE ABANDONED SCOOPERS, BUT **WE** HAVE TO SAVE THE **WORLD**!
BUT WHY WOULD WE EVER WANT TO LEAD ALIENS BACK TO EARTH?
I NEED YOU TO TRUST ME. I'VE GOT THIS.
TRUSTING YOU TO MAKE THE RIGHT CHOICE WHEN ALL OUR LIVES ARE AT STAKE IS TOO MUCH TO ASK, WYATT.
IT'S OUR BEST SHOT.
YOU'RE STILL JUST KIDS.
HOLD ON!
YOU HAVE **NO** IDEA HOW MUCH WE'VE HAD TO GROW UP.
CALM DOWN, ERICKSONS.
YOU FOLLOW WYATT'S PLAN. I'LL GO WITH EVERYONE TO THE SCOOPERS.

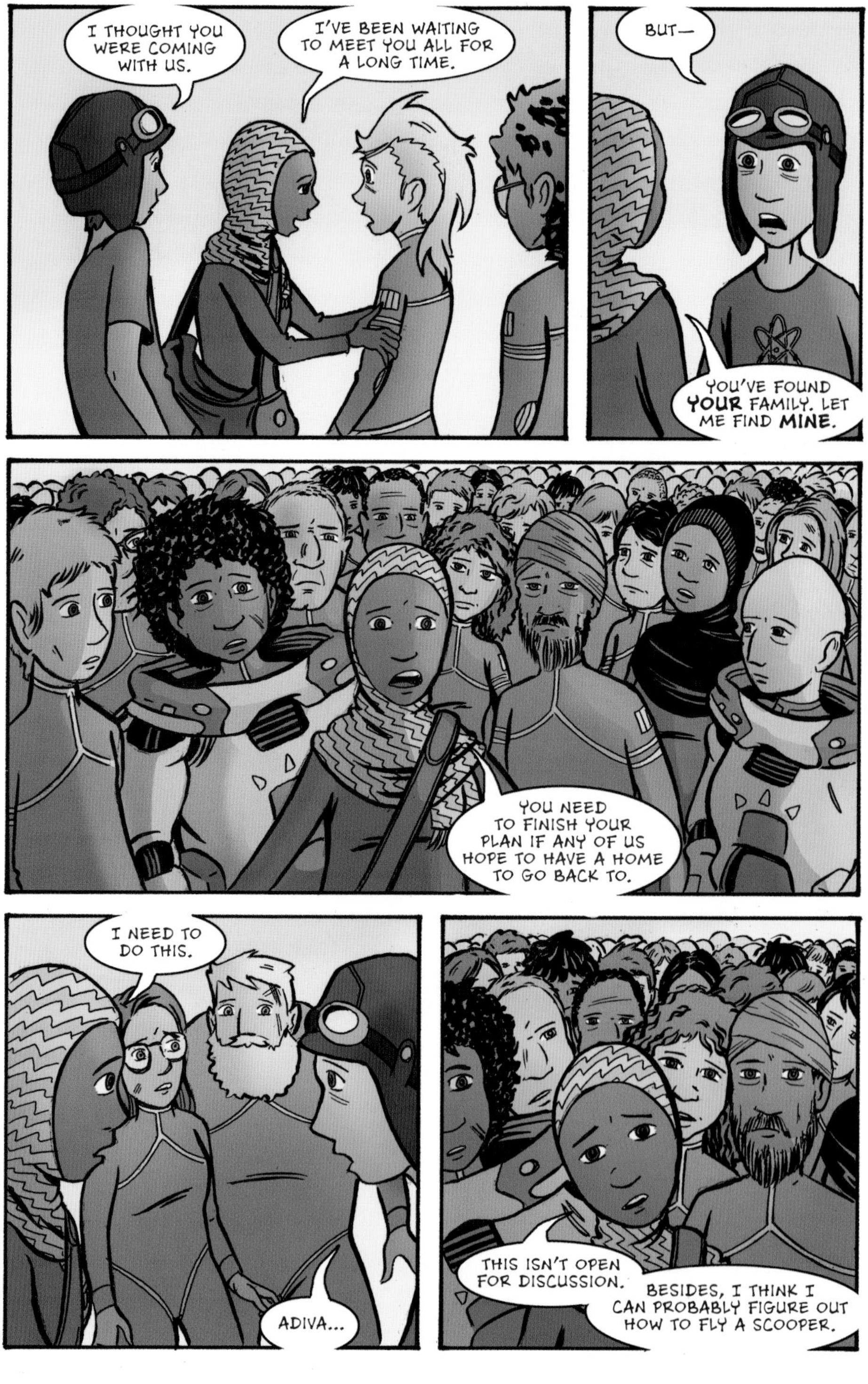
I THOUGHT YOU WERE COMING WITH US.
I'VE BEEN WAITING TO MEET YOU ALL FOR A LONG TIME.
BUT—
YOU'VE FOUND **YOUR** FAMILY. LET ME FIND **MINE**.
YOU NEED TO FINISH YOUR PLAN IF ANY OF US HOPE TO HAVE A HOME TO GO BACK TO.
I NEED TO DO THIS.
ADIVA...
THIS ISN'T OPEN FOR DISCUSSION.
BESIDES, I THINK I CAN PROBABLY FIGURE OUT HOW TO FLY A SCOOPER.

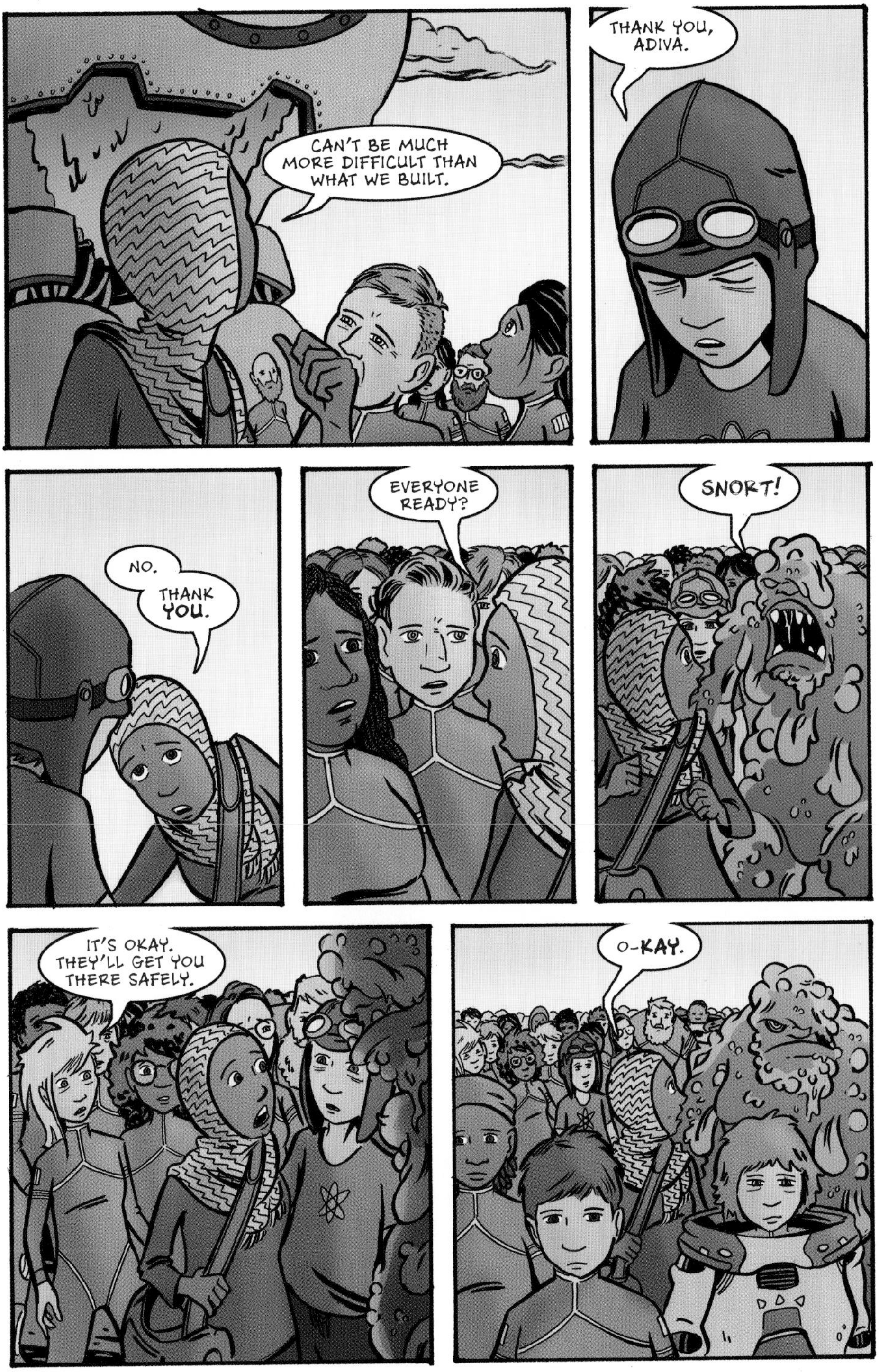
CAN'T BE MUCH MORE DIFFICULT THAN WHAT WE BUILT.
THANK YOU, ADIVA.
NO.
THANK **YOU**.
EVERYONE READY?
SNORT!
IT'S OKAY. THEY'LL GET YOU THERE SAFELY.
O-**KAY**.

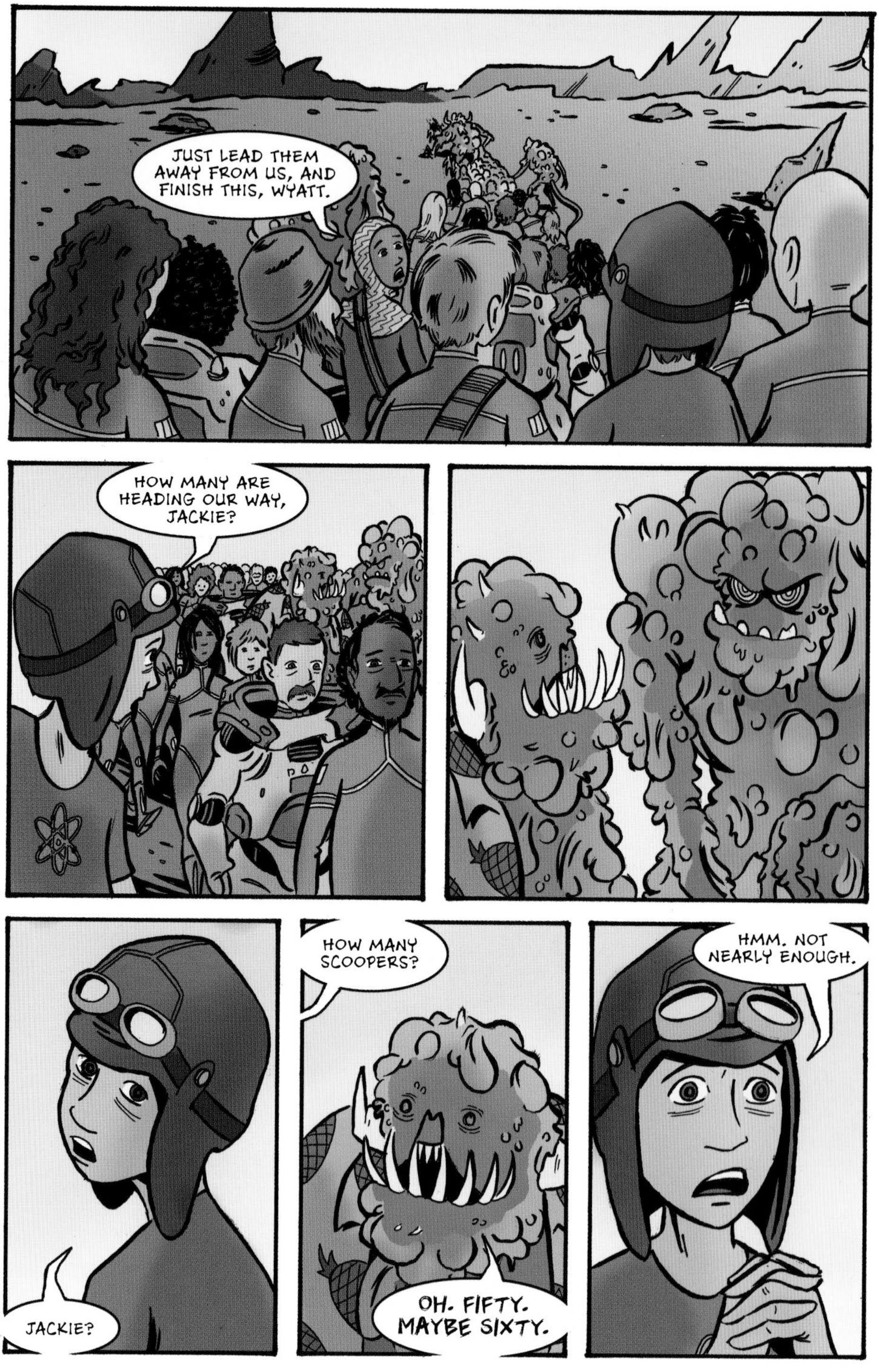
JUST LEAD THEM AWAY FROM US, AND FINISH THIS, WYATT.
HOW MANY ARE HEADING OUR WAY, JACKIE?
JACKIE?
HOW MANY SCOOPERS?
OH. FIFTY. MAYBE SIXTY.
HMM. NOT NEARLY ENOUGH.

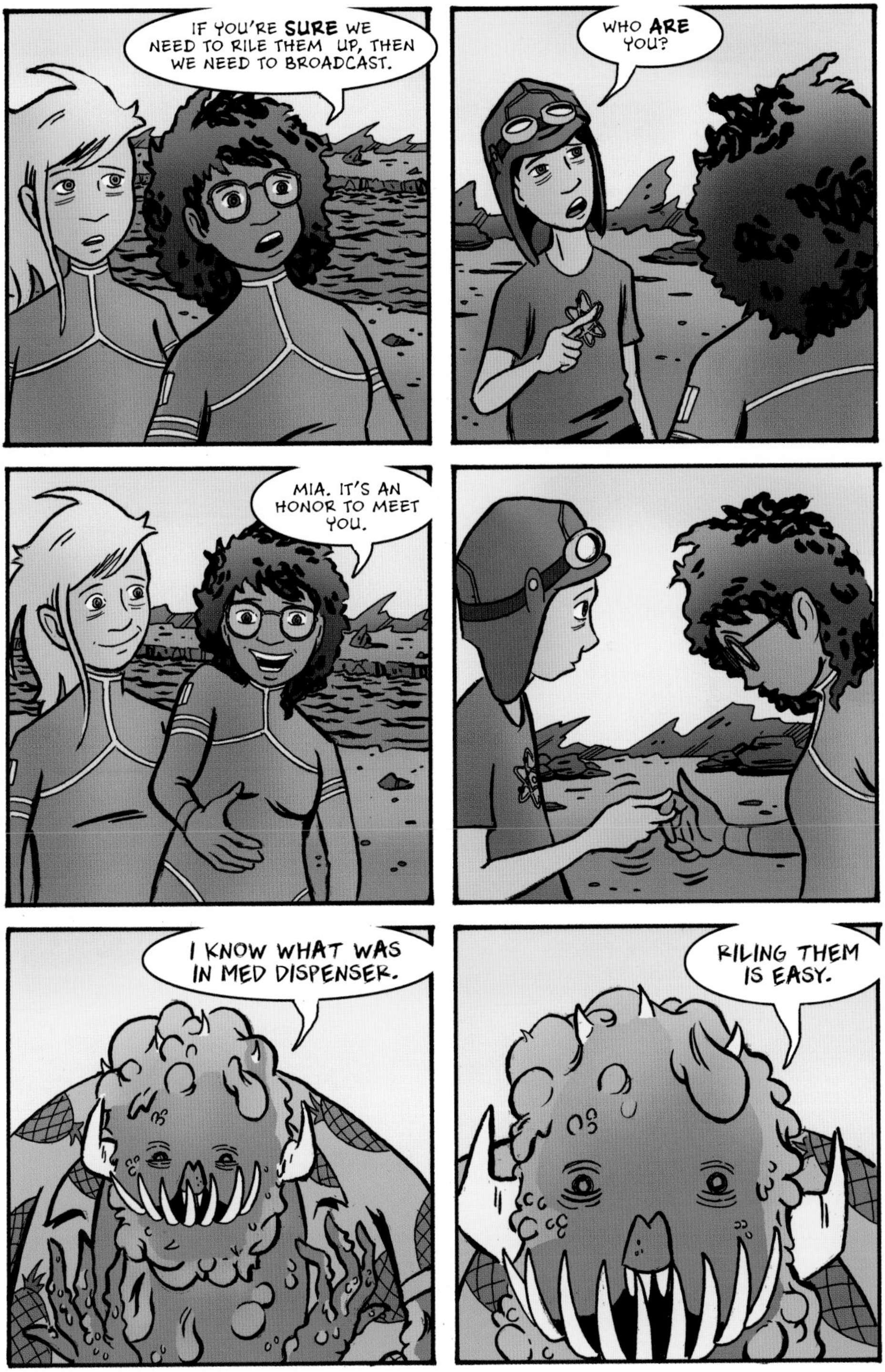
IF YOU'RE SURE WE NEED TO RILE THEM UP, THEN WE NEED TO BROADCAST.
WHO ARE YOU?
MIA. IT'S AN HONOR TO MEET YOU.
I KNOW WHAT WAS IN MED DISPENSER.
RILING THEM IS EASY.

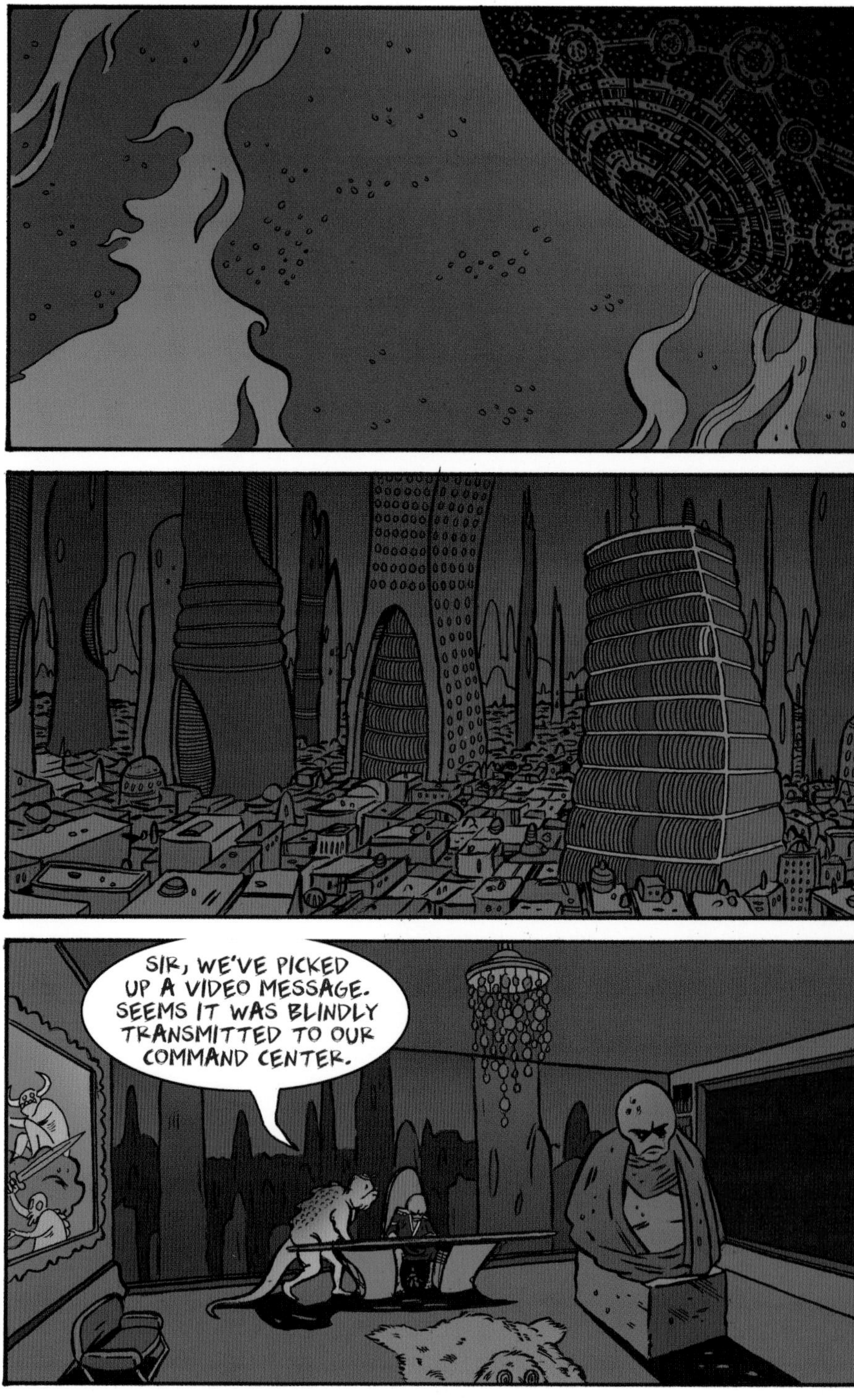
SIR, WE'VE PICKED UP A VIDEO MESSAGE. SEEMS IT WAS BLINDLY TRANSMITTED TO OUR COMMAND CENTER.

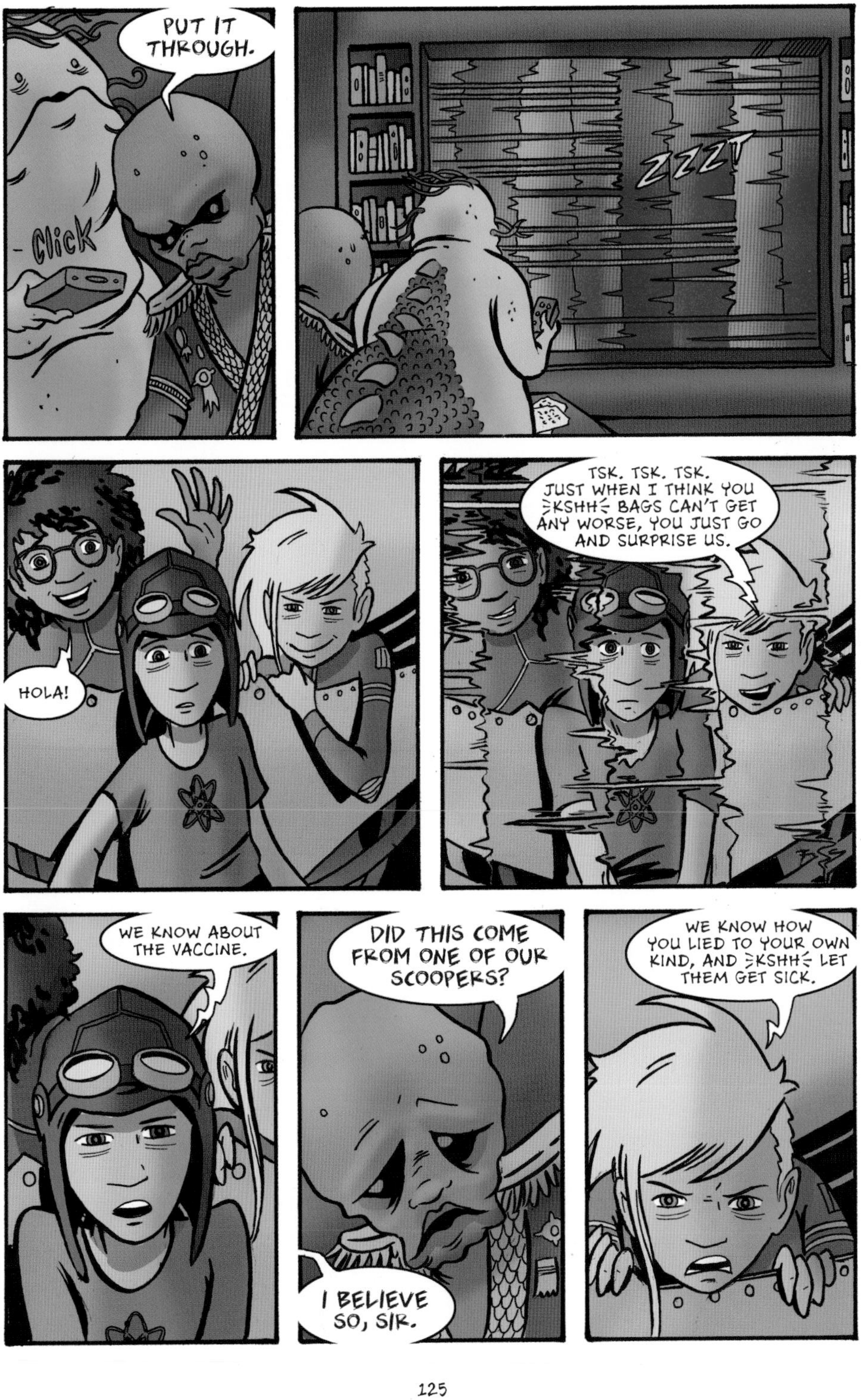
PUT IT THROUGH.
CLICK
ZZZT
HOLA!
TSK. TSK. TSK. JUST WHEN I THINK YOU ⋛KSHH⋚ BAGS CAN'T GET ANY WORSE, YOU JUST GO AND SURPRISE US.
WE KNOW ABOUT THE VACCINE.
DID THIS COME FROM ONE OF OUR SCOOPERS?
I BELIEVE SO, SIR.
WE KNOW HOW YOU LIED TO YOUR OWN KIND, AND ⋛KSHH⋚ LET THEM GET SICK.

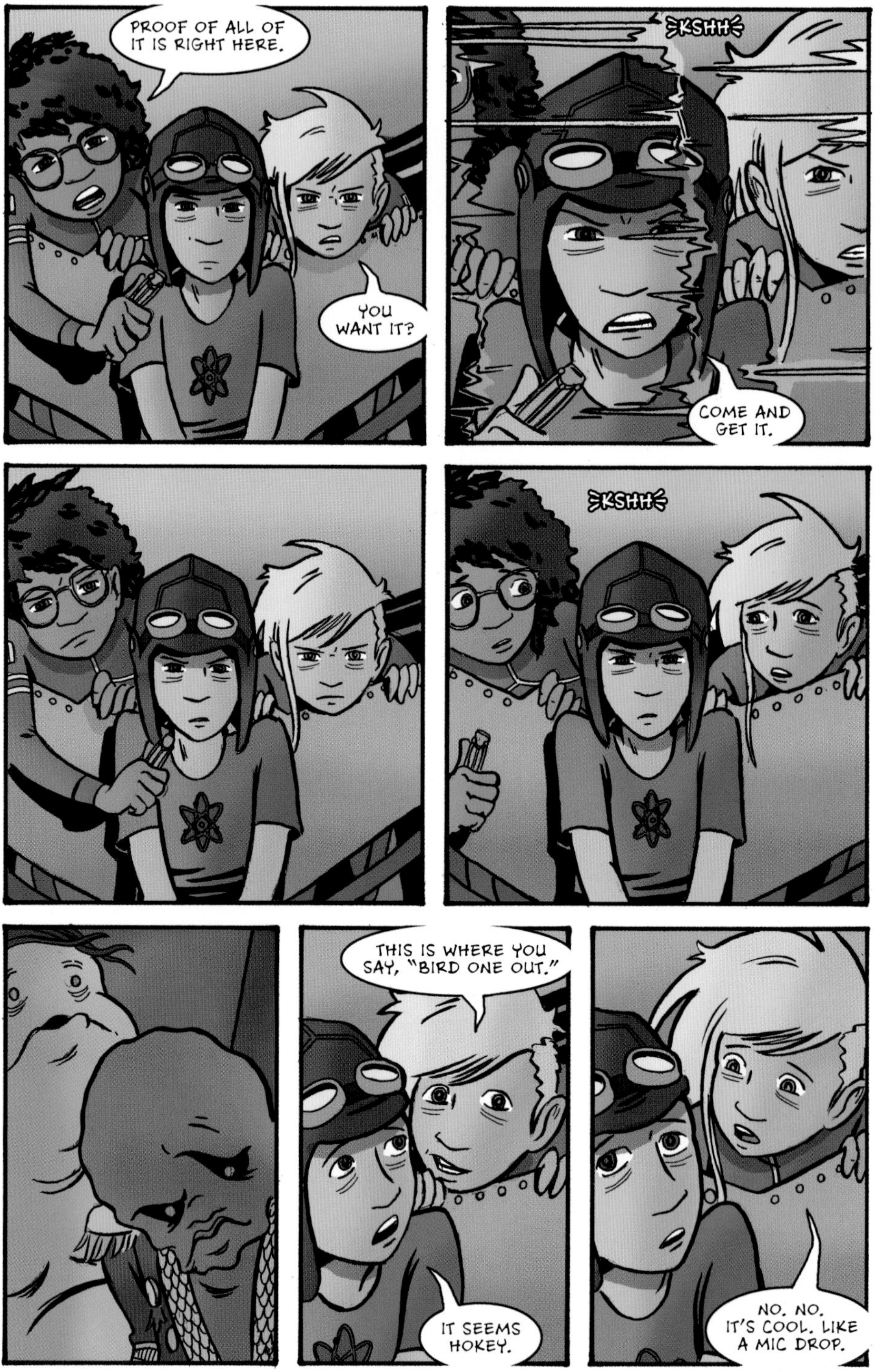
PROOF OF ALL OF IT IS RIGHT HERE.
YOU WANT IT?
KSHH
COME AND GET IT.
KSHH
THIS IS WHERE YOU SAY, "BIRD ONE OUT."
IT SEEMS HOKEY.
NO. NO. IT'S COOL. LIKE A MIC DROP.

FINE.

NEVER MIND. THE MOMENT'S PASSED.

HOW DO YOU TURN THIS THING OFF?

BIRD ONE—

NOT **NOW**. IT DOESN'T WORK **NOW**.

IS IT THE RED BUTTON?

HOW ABOUT "YOU'VE BEEN BIRD ONED"?

THAT'S SO TERRIBLE, I CAN'T EVEN—

ZZZT

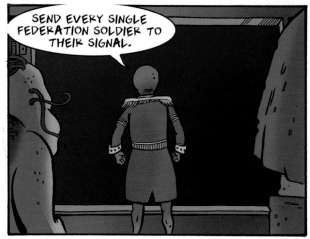

SEND EVERY SINGLE FEDERATION SOLDIER TO THEIR SIGNAL.

I WANT THEM **DEAD!**

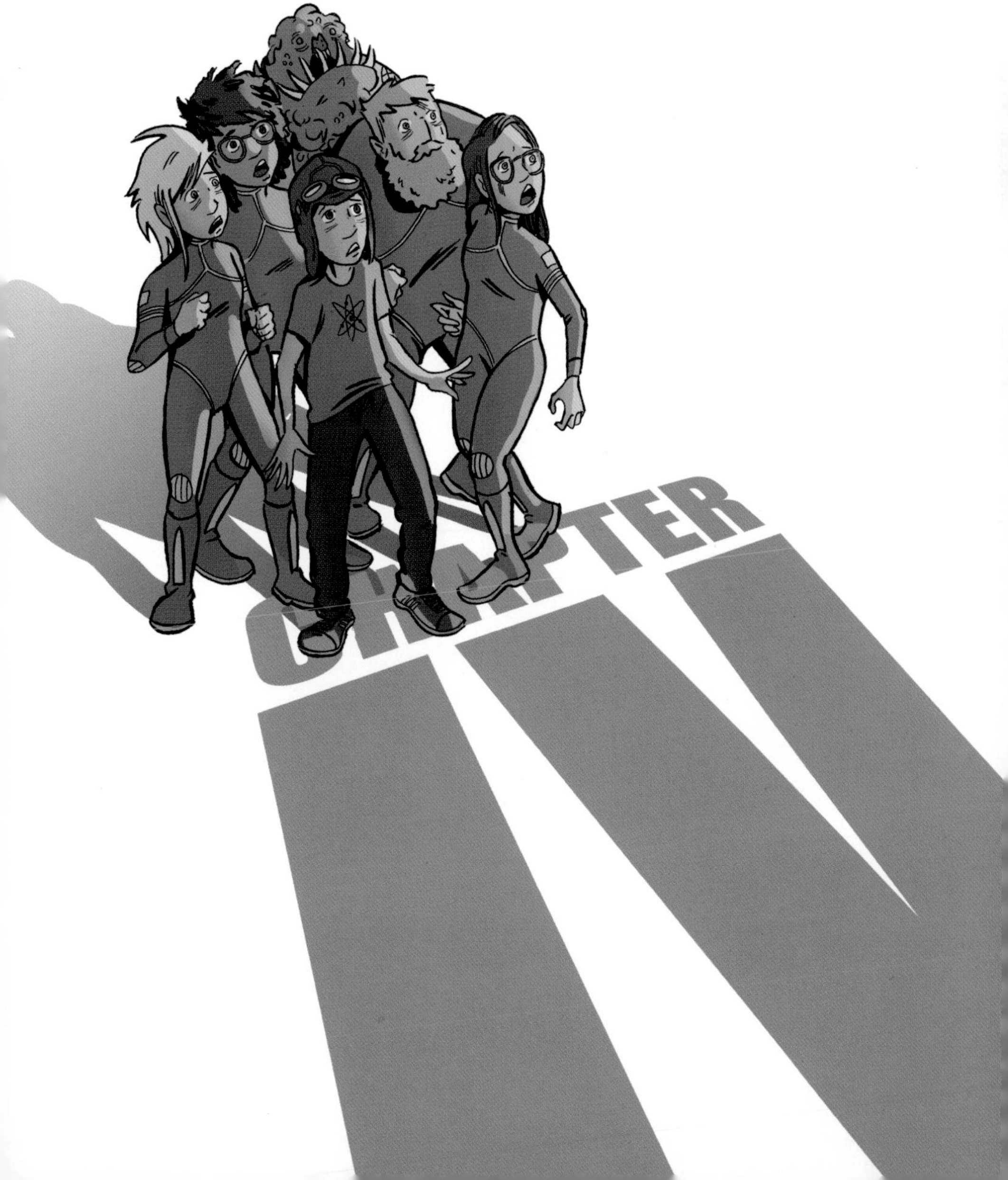
CHAPTER

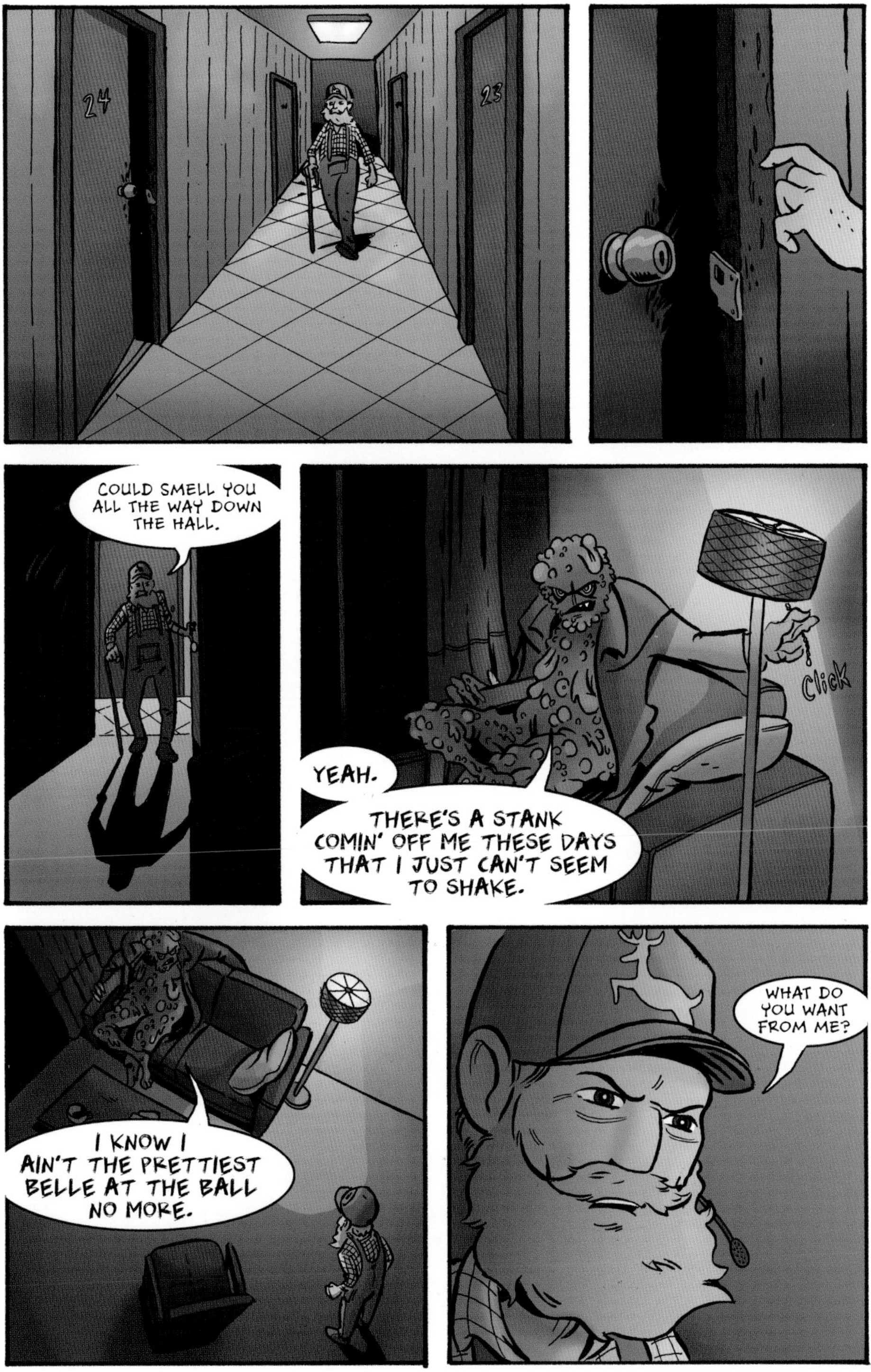
24
23
COULD SMELL YOU ALL THE WAY DOWN THE HALL.
CLICK
YEAH.
THERE'S A STANK COMIN' OFF ME THESE DAYS THAT I JUST CAN'T SEEM TO SHAKE.
I KNOW I AIN'T THE PRETTIEST BELLE AT THE BALL NO MORE.
WHAT DO YOU WANT FROM ME?

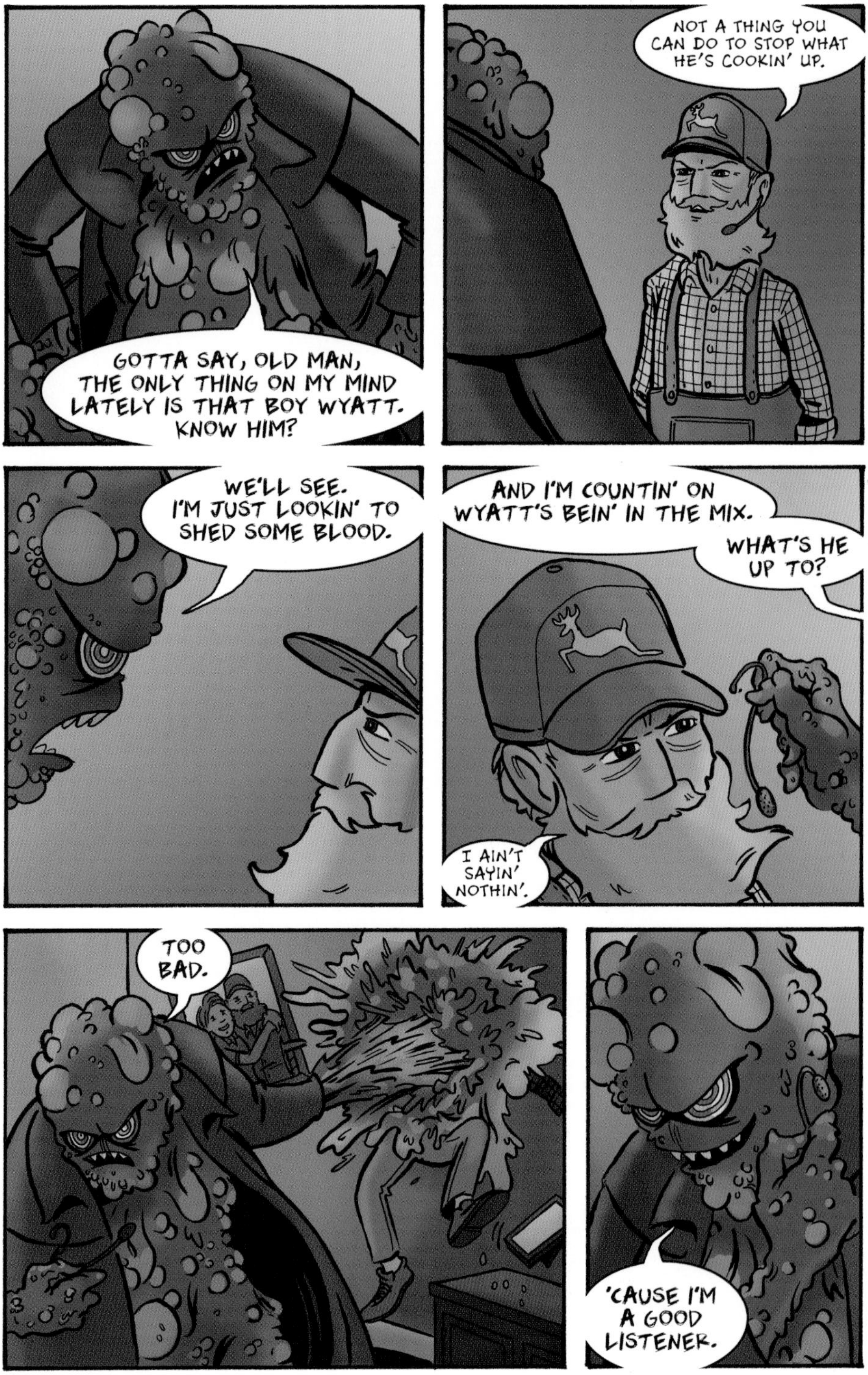
GOTTA SAY, OLD MAN, THE ONLY THING ON MY MIND LATELY IS THAT BOY WYATT. KNOW HIM?
NOT A THING YOU CAN DO TO STOP WHAT HE'S COOKIN' UP.
WE'LL SEE. I'M JUST LOOKIN' TO SHED SOME BLOOD.
AND I'M COUNTIN' ON WYATT'S BEIN' IN THE MIX.
WHAT'S HE UP TO?
I AIN'T SAYIN' NOTHIN'.
TOO BAD.
'CAUSE I'M A GOOD LISTENER.

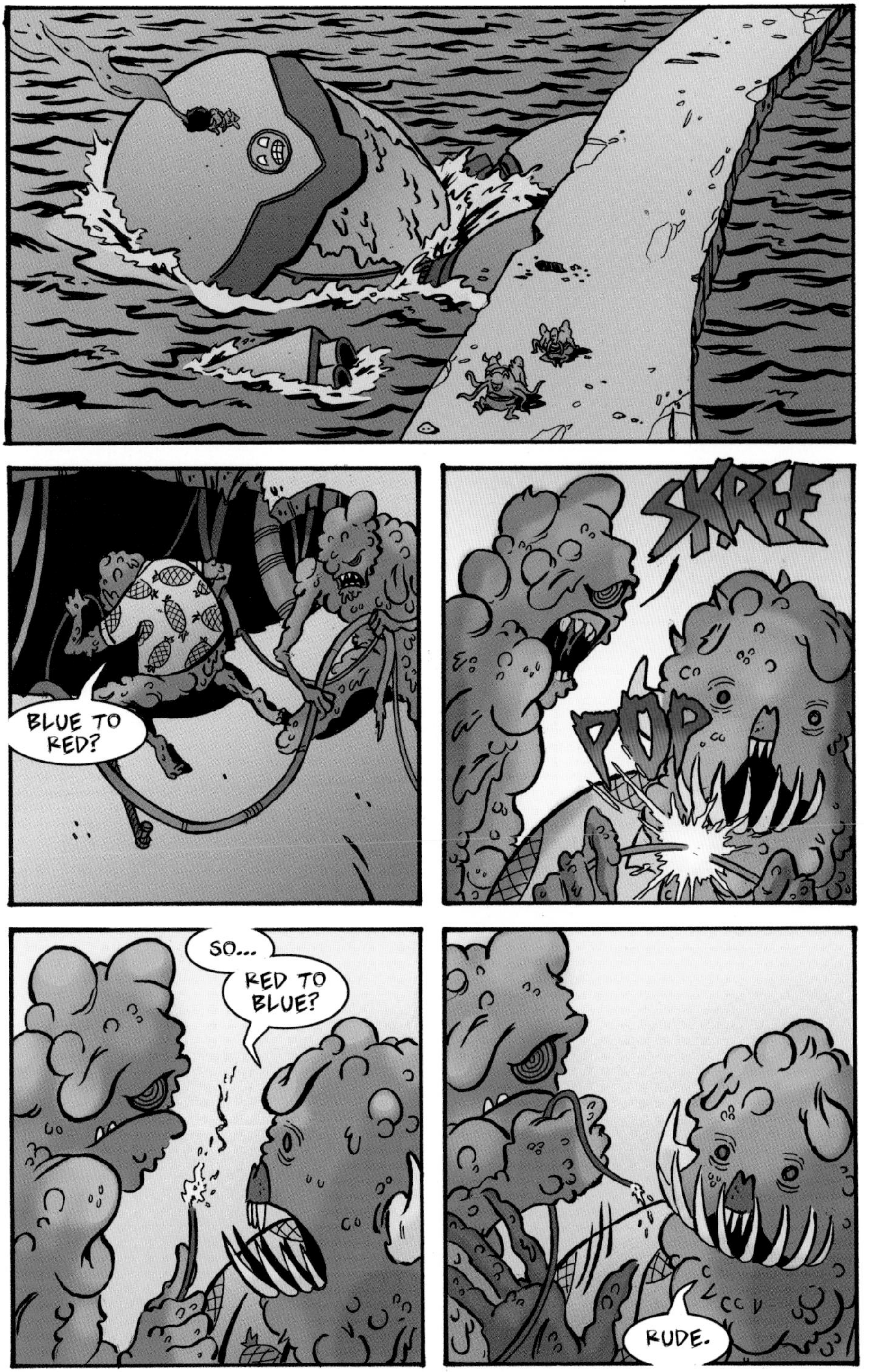
BLUE TO RED?
SKREE
POP
SO...
RED TO BLUE?
RUDE.

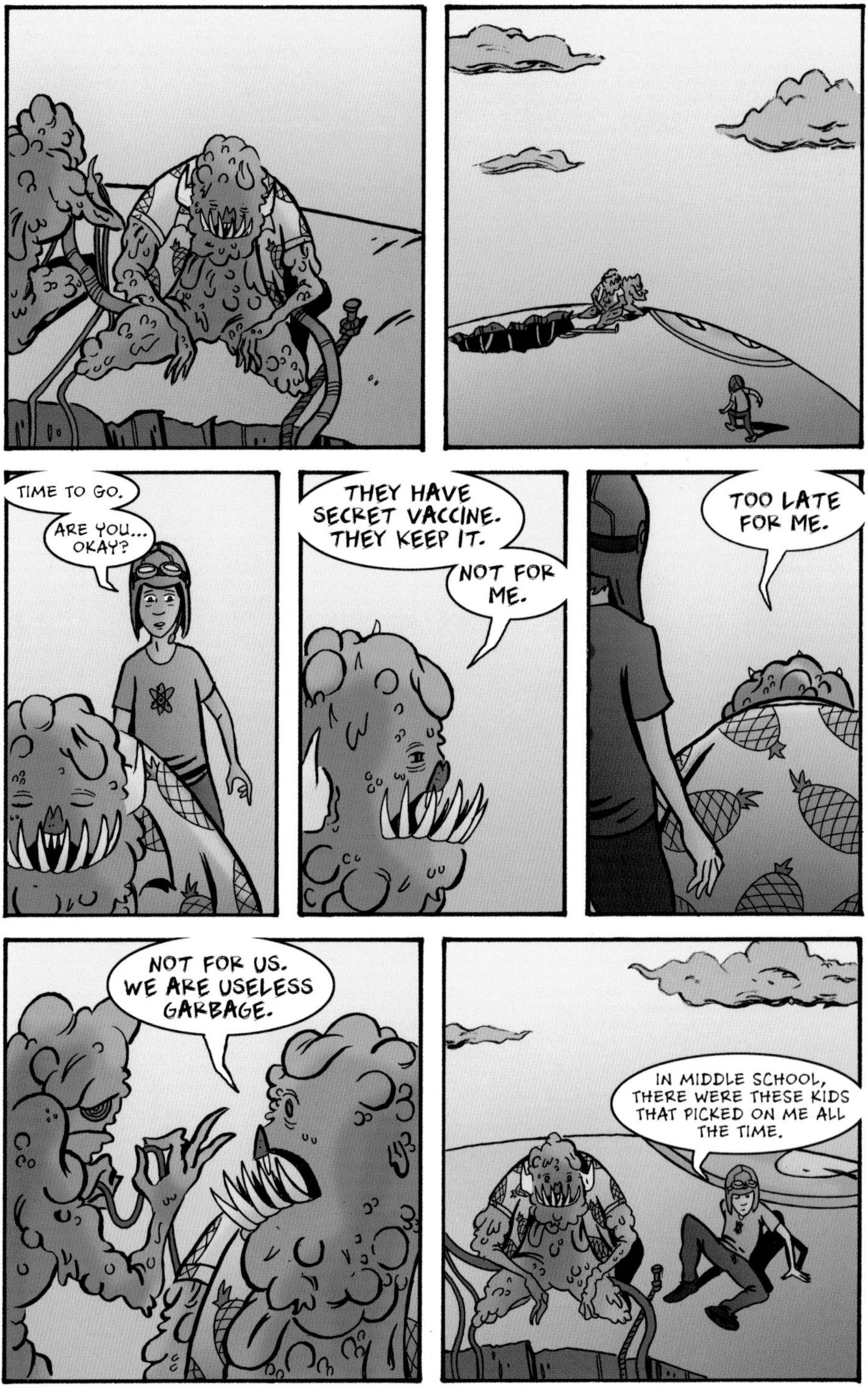
TIME TO GO.
ARE YOU... OKAY?
THEY HAVE SECRET VACCINE. THEY KEEP IT.
NOT FOR ME.
TOO LATE FOR ME.
NOT FOR US. WE ARE USELESS GARBAGE.
IN MIDDLE SCHOOL, THERE WERE THESE KIDS THAT PICKED ON ME ALL THE TIME.

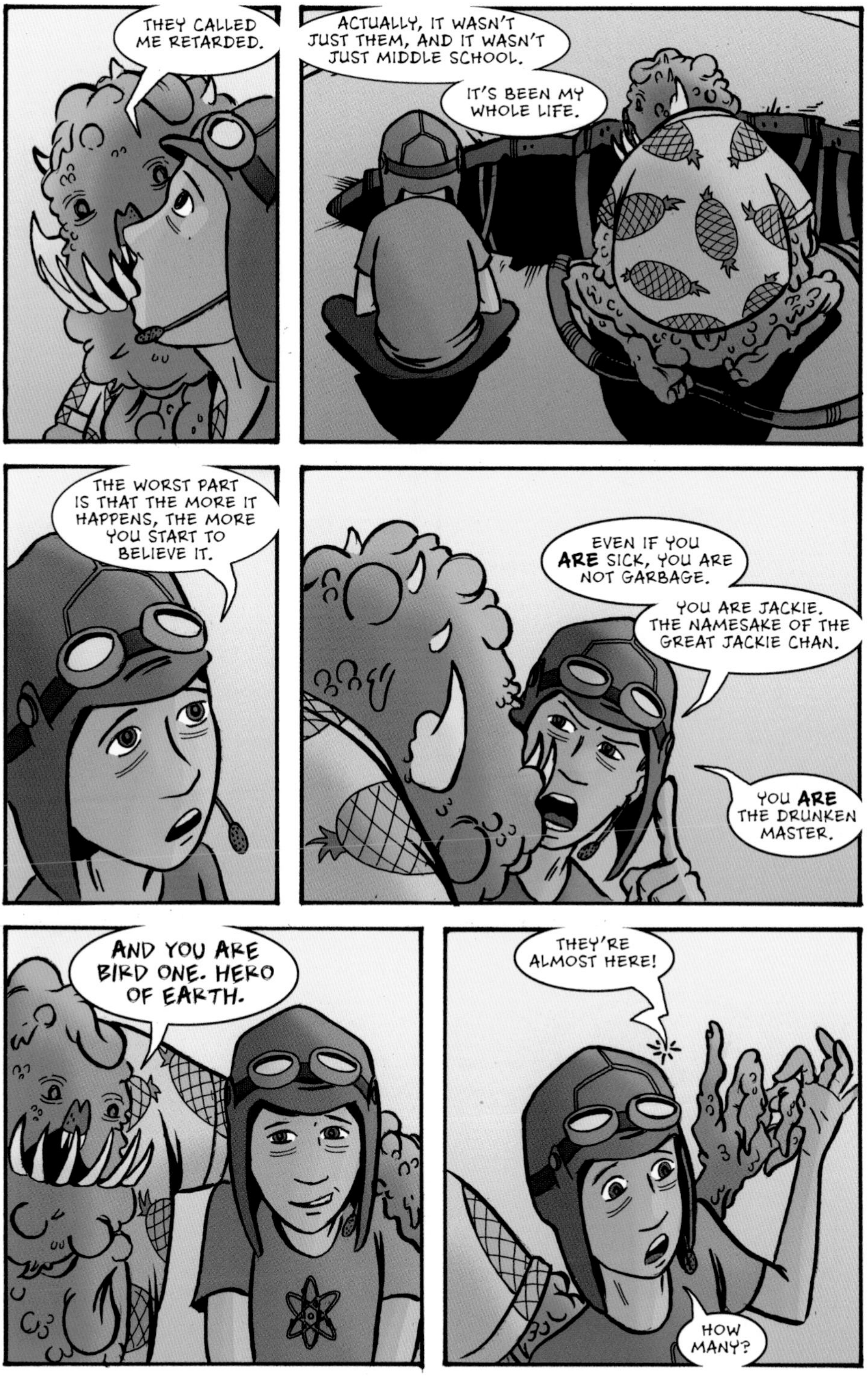
THEY CALLED ME RETARDED.
ACTUALLY, IT WASN'T JUST THEM, AND IT WASN'T JUST MIDDLE SCHOOL.
IT'S BEEN MY WHOLE LIFE.
THE WORST PART IS THAT THE MORE IT HAPPENS, THE MORE YOU START TO BELIEVE IT.
EVEN IF YOU **ARE** SICK, YOU ARE NOT GARBAGE.
YOU ARE JACKIE. THE NAMESAKE OF THE GREAT JACKIE CHAN.
YOU **ARE** THE DRUNKEN MASTER.
AND YOU ARE BIRD ONE. HERO OF EARTH.
THEY'RE ALMOST HERE!
HOW MANY?

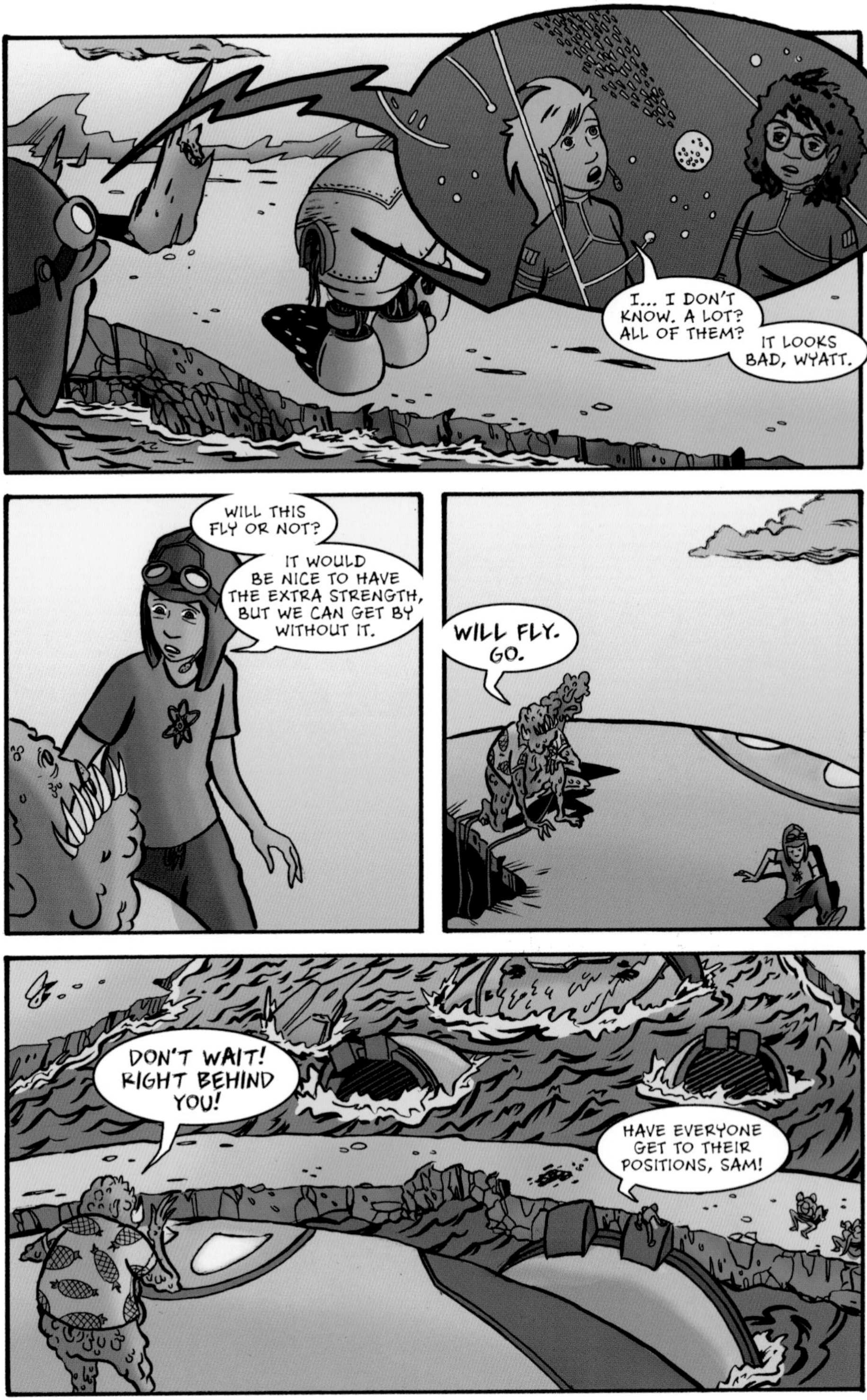
I... I DON'T KNOW. A LOT? ALL OF THEM?
IT LOOKS BAD, WYATT.
WILL THIS FLY OR NOT?
IT WOULD BE NICE TO HAVE THE EXTRA STRENGTH, BUT WE CAN GET BY WITHOUT IT.
WILL FLY. GO.
DON'T WAIT! RIGHT BEHIND YOU!
HAVE EVERYONE GET TO THEIR POSITIONS, SAM!

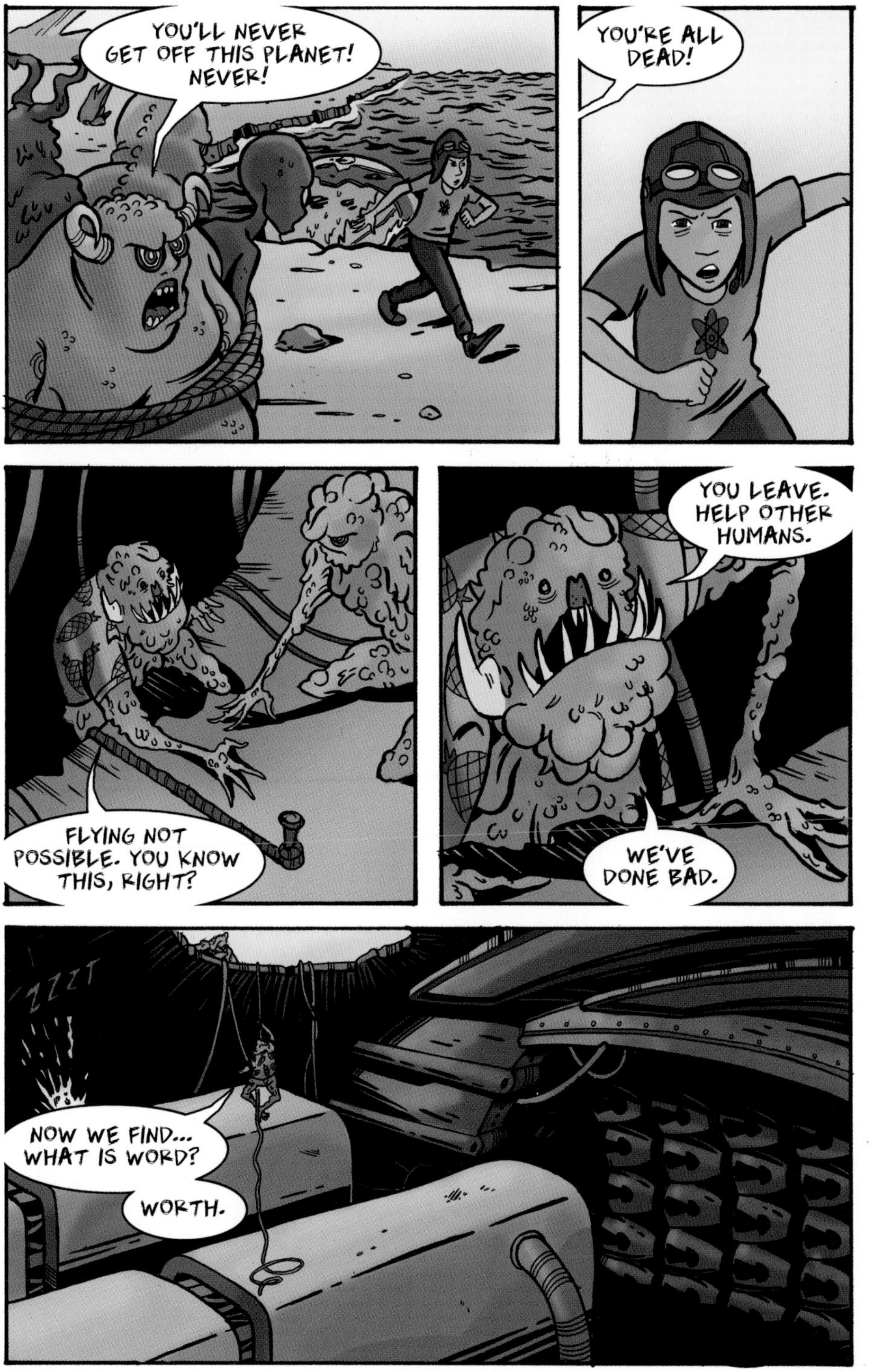
YOU'LL NEVER GET OFF THIS PLANET! NEVER!
YOU'RE ALL DEAD!
FLYING NOT POSSIBLE. YOU KNOW THIS, RIGHT?
YOU LEAVE. HELP OTHER HUMANS.
WE'VE DONE BAD.
ZZZT
NOW WE FIND... WHAT IS WORD?
WORTH.

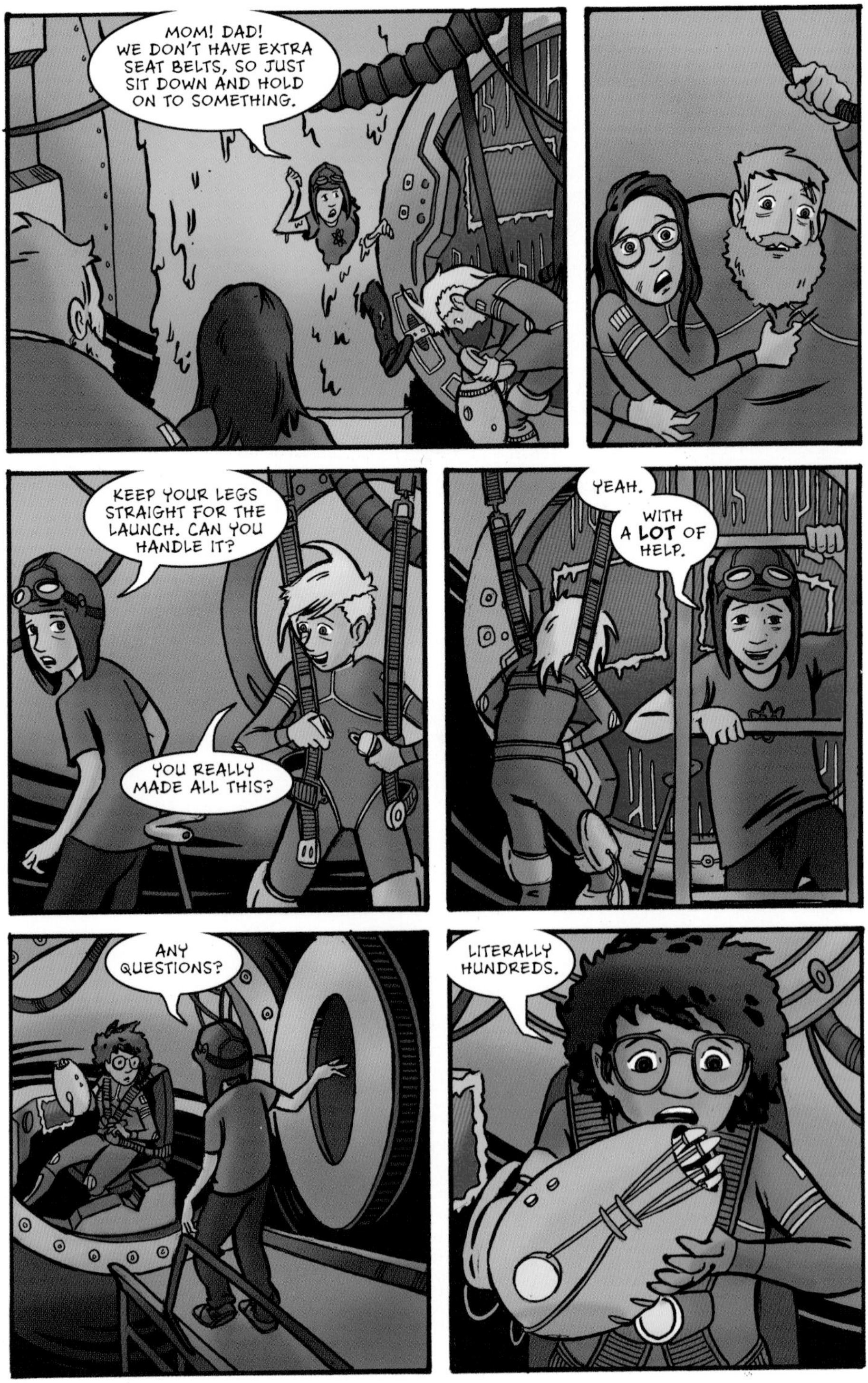
MOM! DAD! WE DON'T HAVE EXTRA SEAT BELTS, SO JUST SIT DOWN AND HOLD ON TO SOMETHING.
KEEP YOUR LEGS STRAIGHT FOR THE LAUNCH. CAN YOU HANDLE IT?
YOU REALLY MADE ALL THIS?
YEAH.
WITH A **LOT** OF HELP.
ANY QUESTIONS?
LITERALLY HUNDREDS.

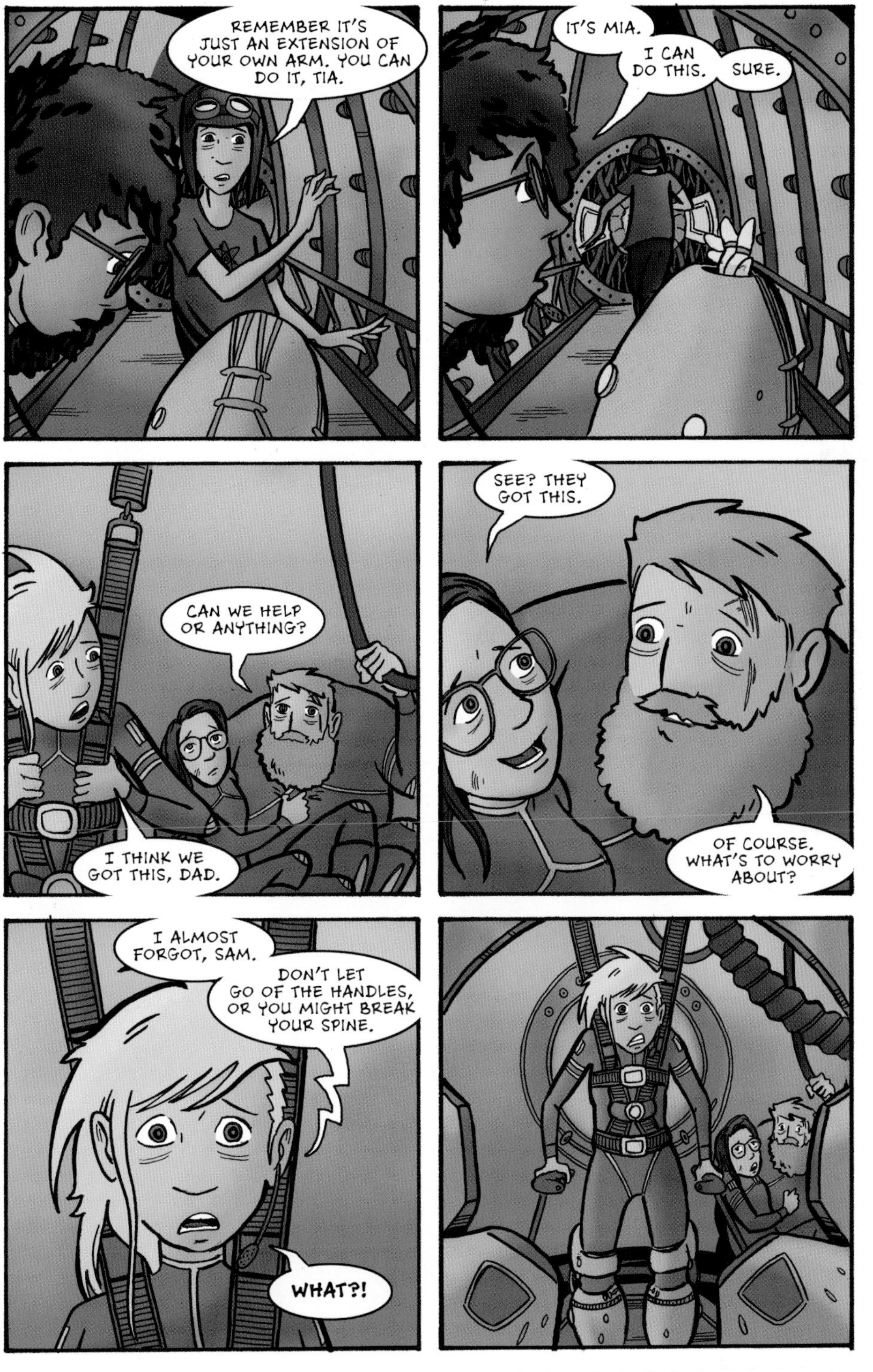
REMEMBER IT'S JUST AN EXTENSION OF YOUR OWN ARM. YOU CAN DO IT, TIA.
IT'S MIA.
I CAN DO THIS.
SURE.
CAN WE HELP OR ANYTHING?
I THINK WE GOT THIS, DAD.
SEE? THEY GOT THIS.
OF COURSE. WHAT'S TO WORRY ABOUT?
I ALMOST FORGOT, SAM.
DON'T LET GO OF THE HANDLES, OR YOU MIGHT BREAK YOUR SPINE.
WHAT?!

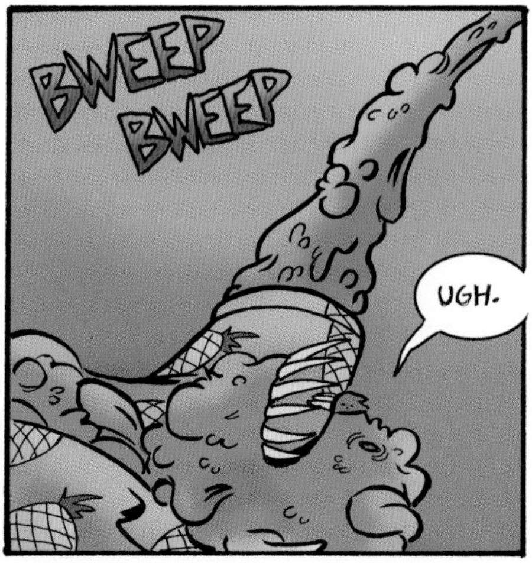
BWEEP
BWEEP
UGH.
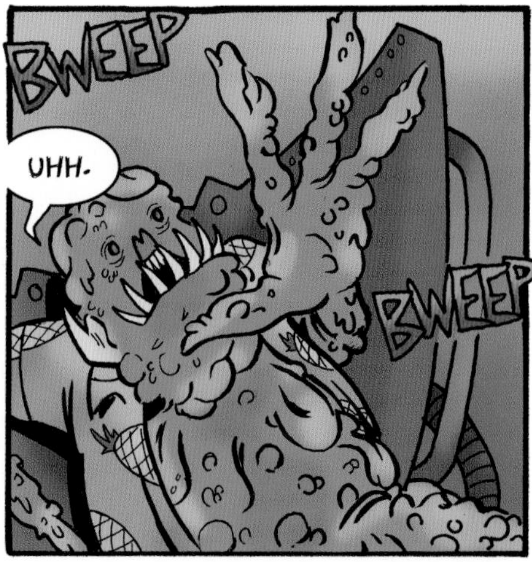
BWEEP
UHH.
BWEEP
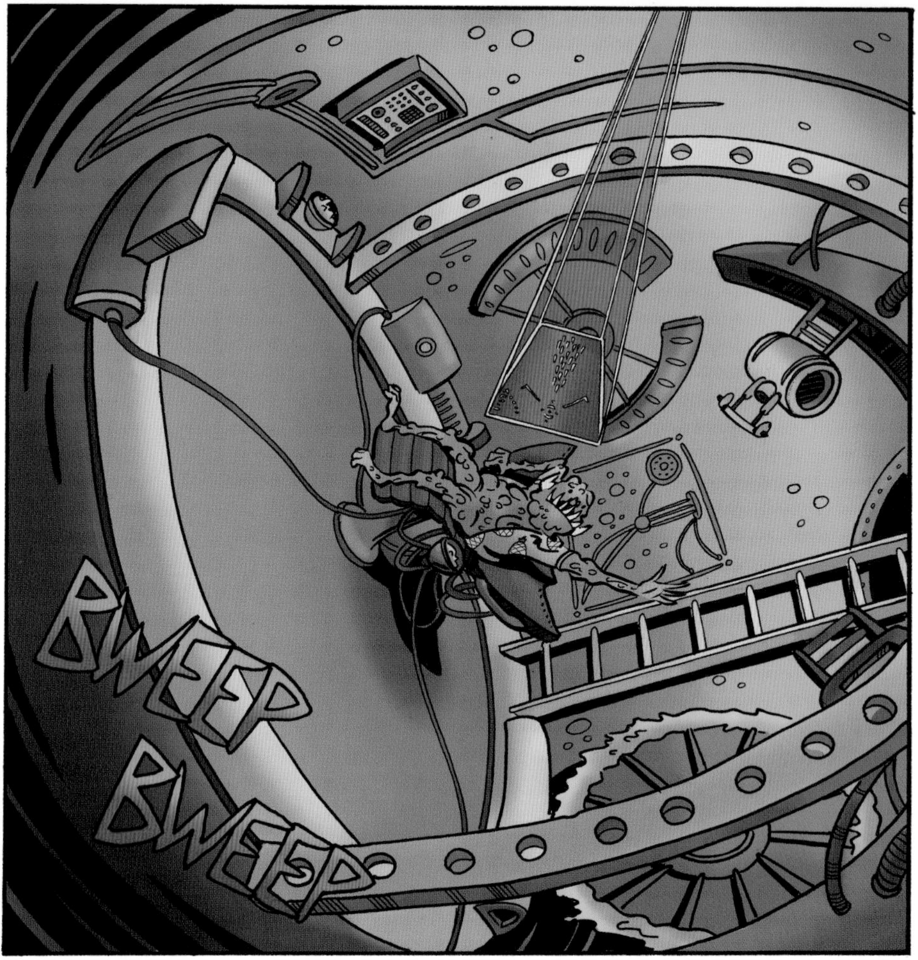
BWEEP
BWEEP

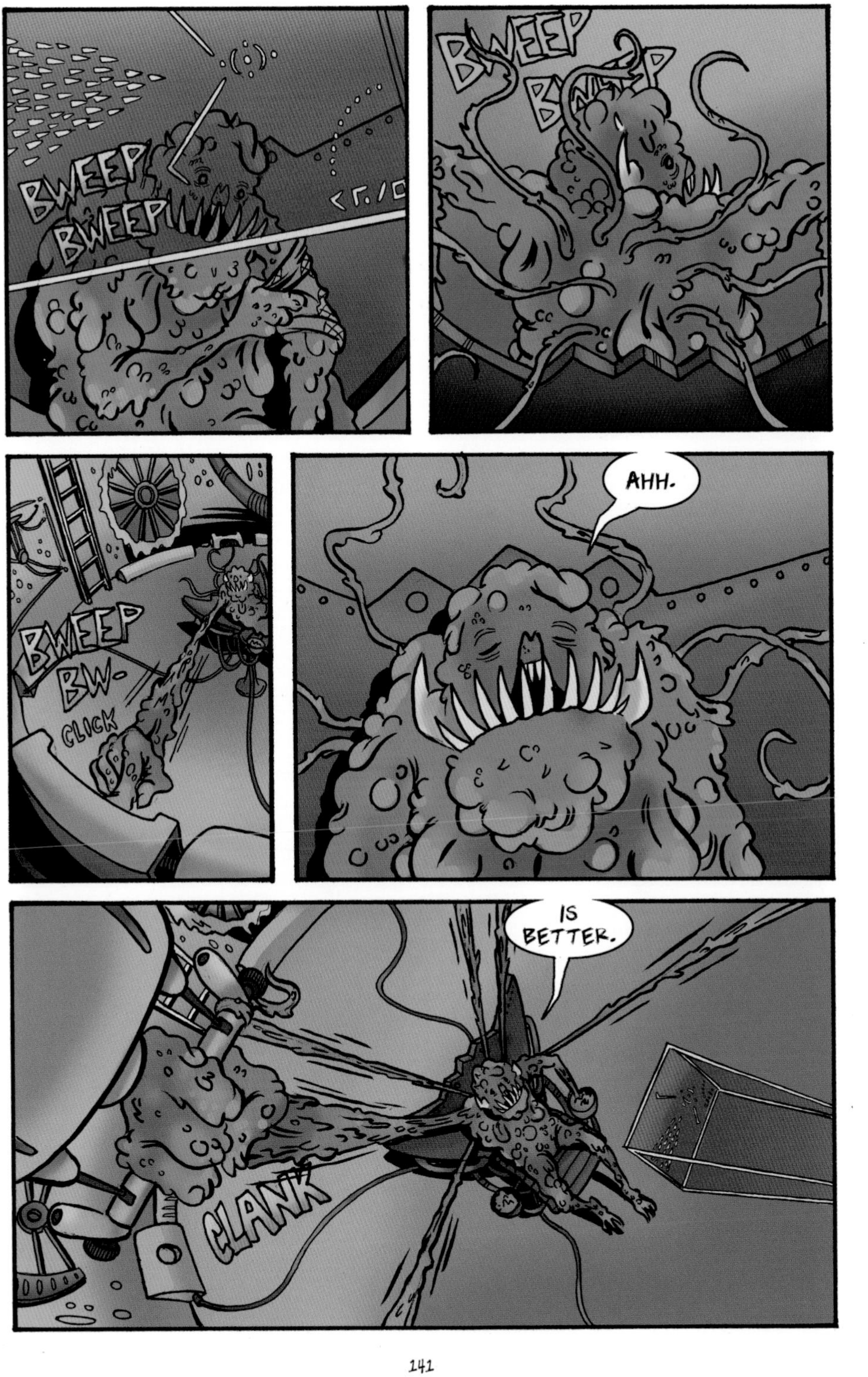
BWEEP
BWEEP
BWEEP
BWEEP
BWEEP
BW-
CLICK
AHH.
IS BETTER.
CLANK

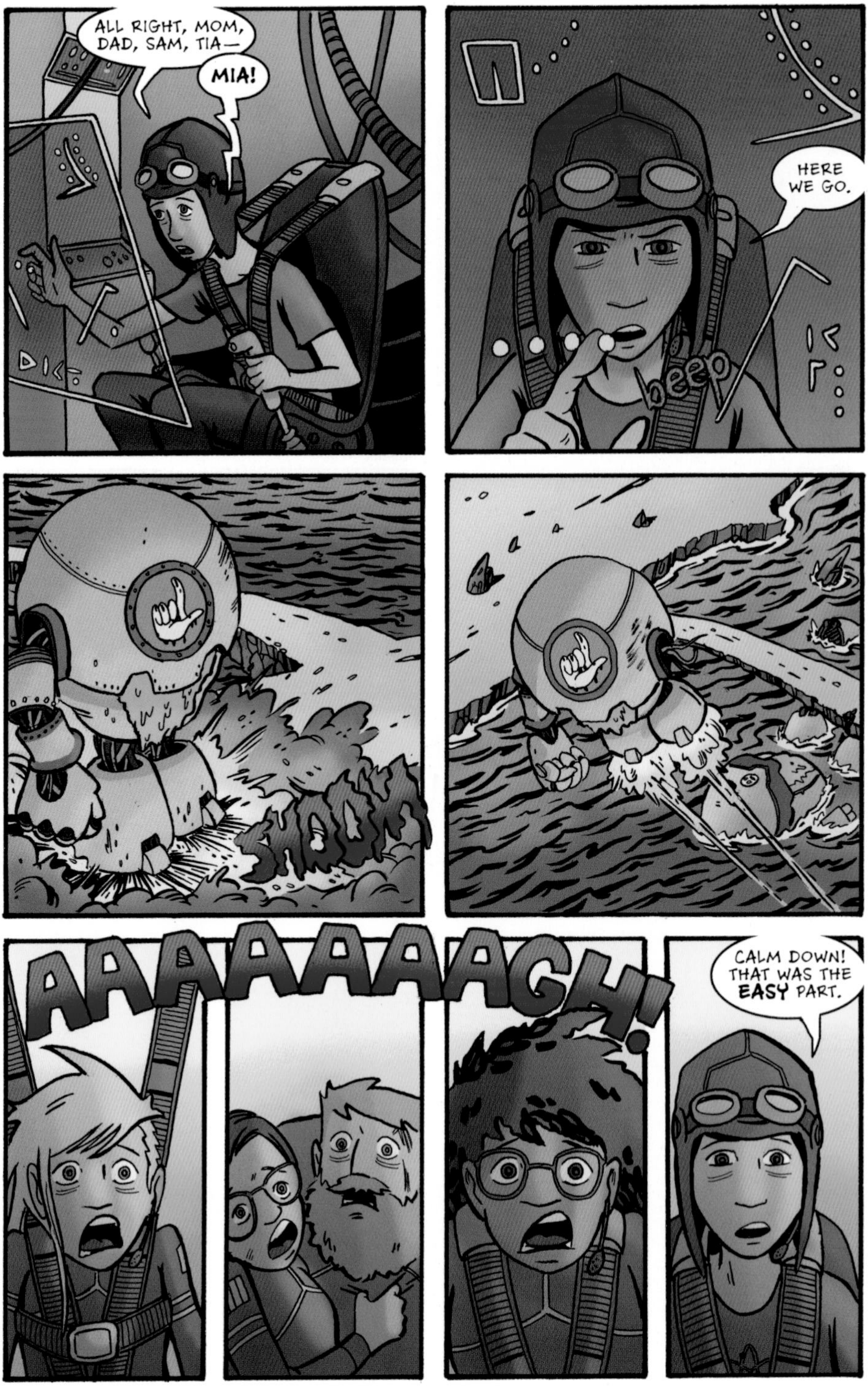
ALL RIGHT, MOM, DAD, SAM, TIA—
MIA!
HERE WE GO.
beep
SHOOM
AAAAAAAAAGH!
CALM DOWN! THAT WAS THE **EASY** PART.

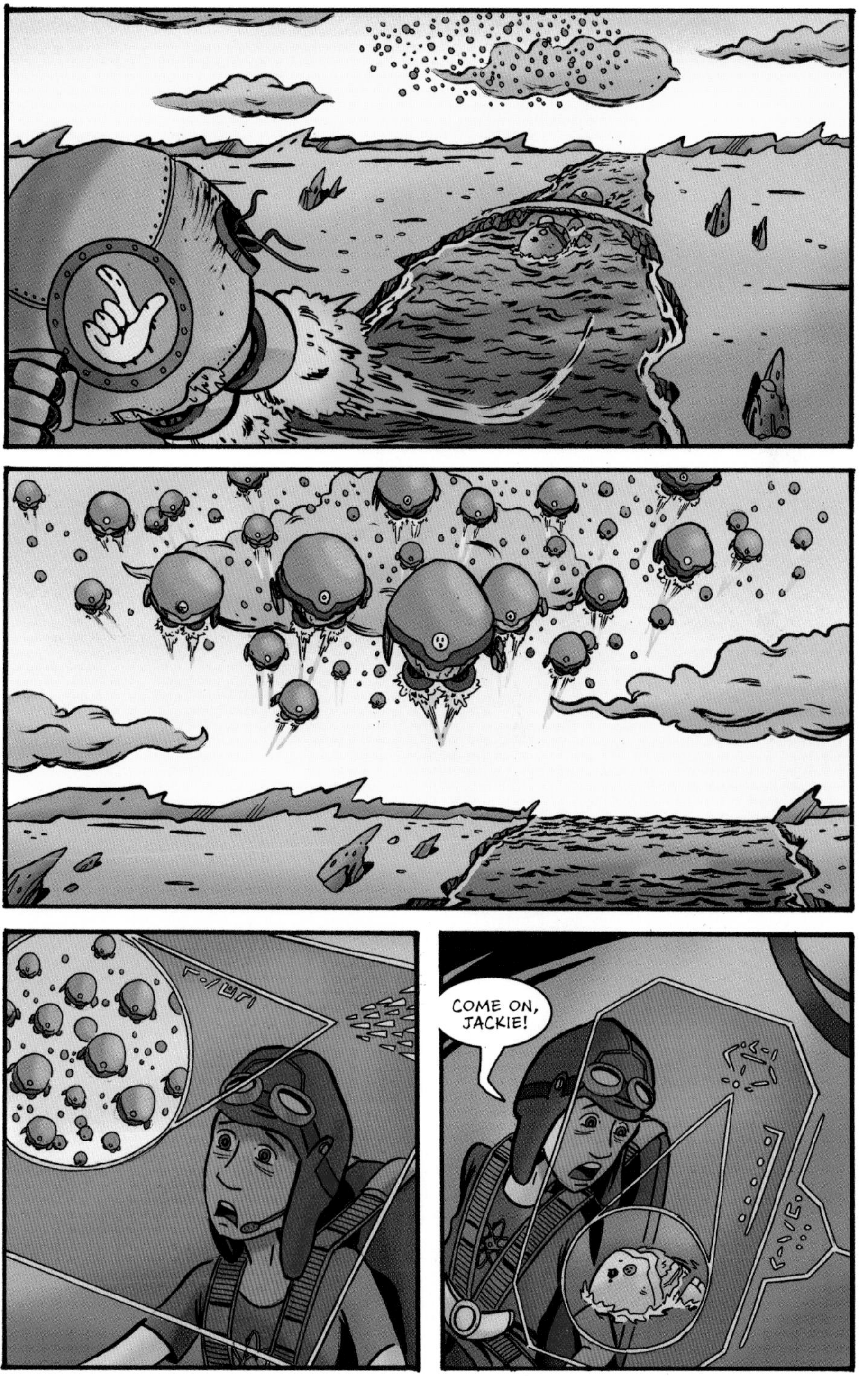
COME ON, JACKIE!

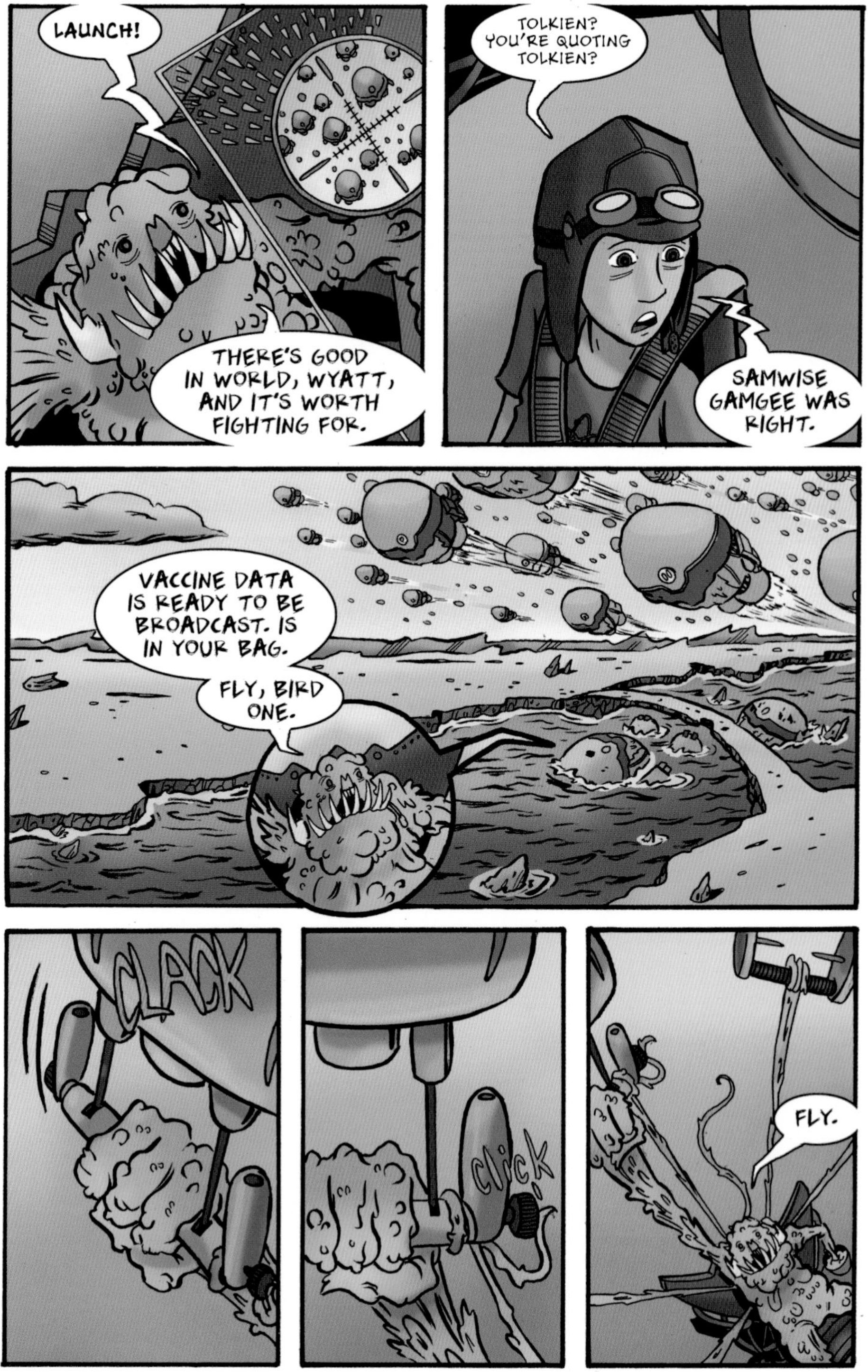
LAUNCH!
THERE'S GOOD IN WORLD, WYATT, AND IT'S WORTH FIGHTING FOR.
TOLKIEN? YOU'RE QUOTING TOLKIEN?
SAMWISE GAMGEE WAS RIGHT.
VACCINE DATA IS READY TO BE BROADCAST. IS IN YOUR BAG.
FLY, BIRD ONE.
CLACK
CLICK
FLY.

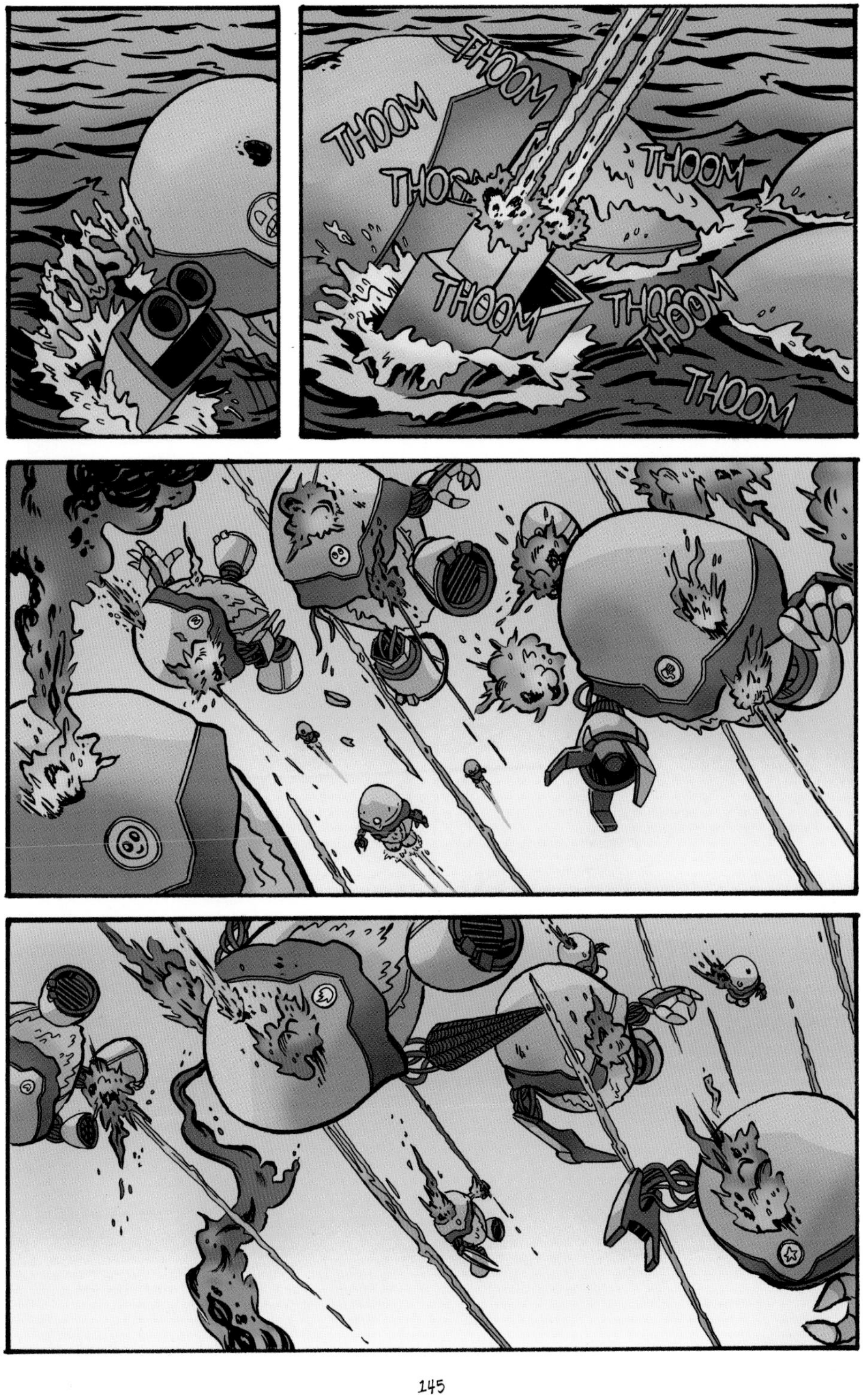
THOOM
THOOM
THOOM
THOOM
THOOM
THOOM
THOOM

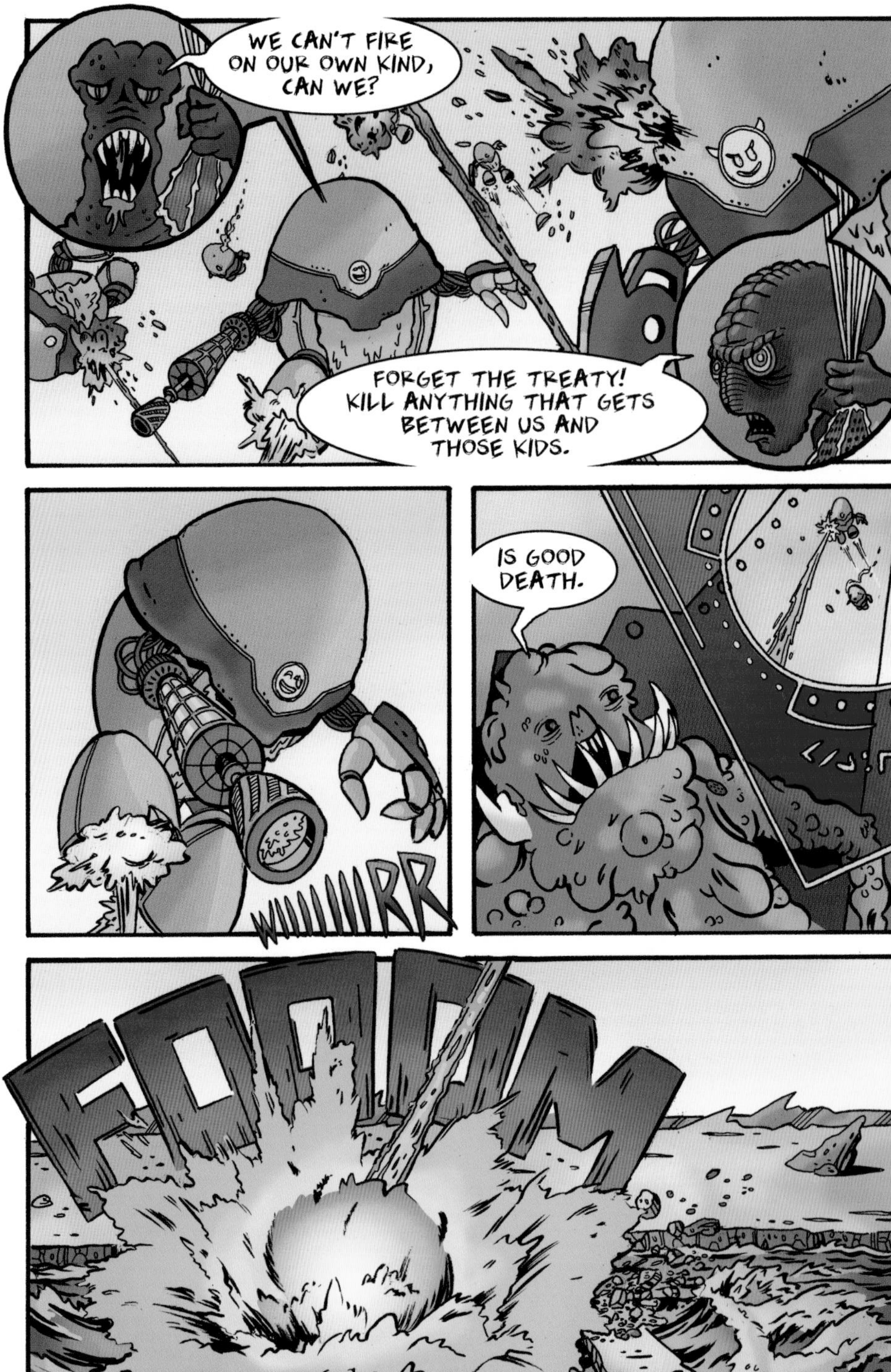
WE CAN'T FIRE ON OUR OWN KIND, CAN WE?
FORGET THE TREATY! KILL ANYTHING THAT GETS BETWEEN US AND THOSE KIDS.
WIIIIIIRR
IS GOOD DEATH.
FOOOM

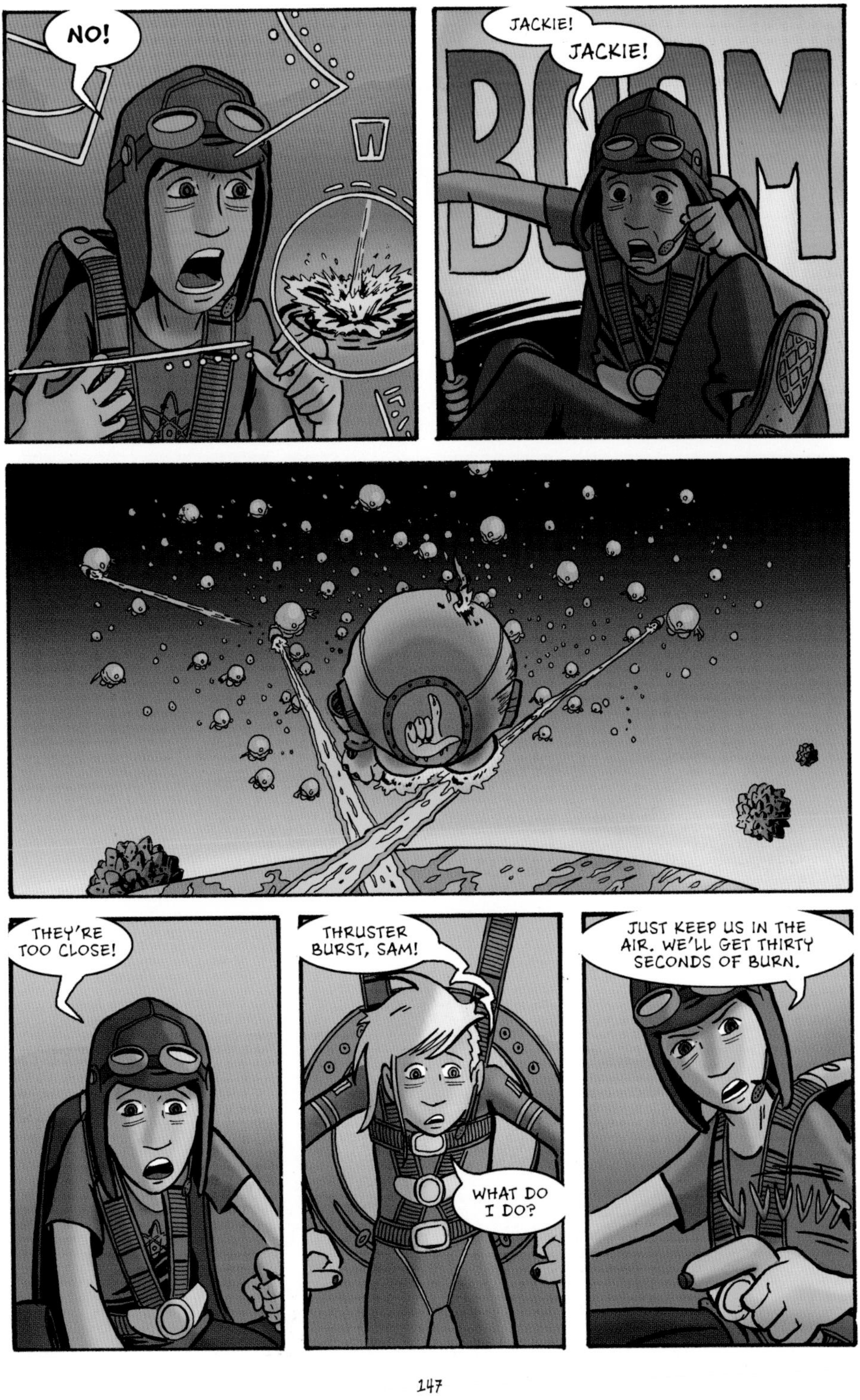
NO!
JACKIE!
JACKIE!
BOOM
THEY'RE TOO CLOSE!
THRUSTER BURST, SAM!
WHAT DO I DO?
JUST KEEP US IN THE AIR. WE'LL GET THIRTY SECONDS OF BURN.

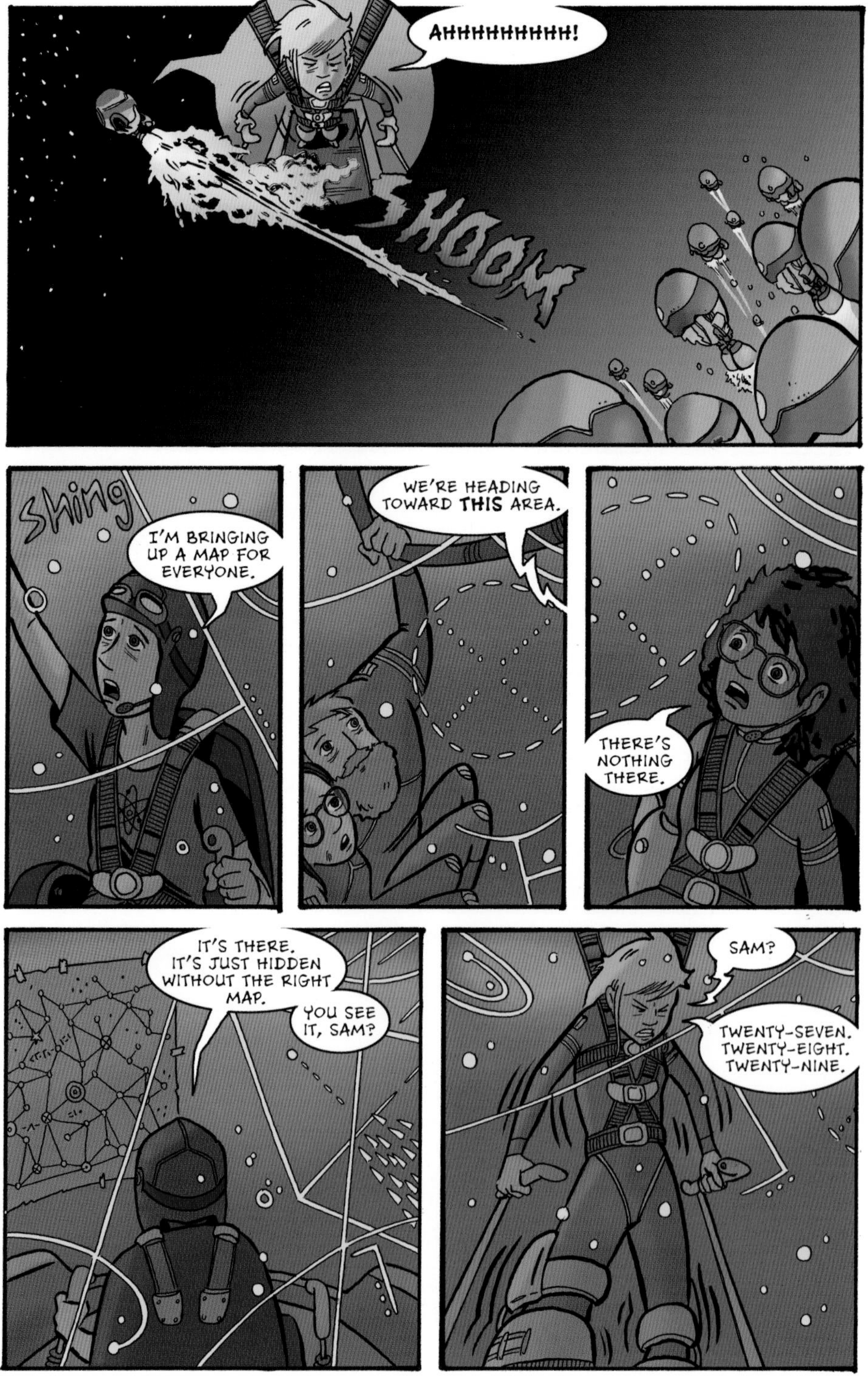
AHHHHHHHHH!
SHOOM
Shing
I'M BRINGING UP A MAP FOR EVERYONE.
WE'RE HEADING TOWARD THIS AREA.
THERE'S NOTHING THERE.
IT'S THERE. IT'S JUST HIDDEN WITHOUT THE RIGHT MAP.
YOU SEE IT, SAM?
SAM?
TWENTY-SEVEN. TWENTY-EIGHT. TWENTY-NINE.

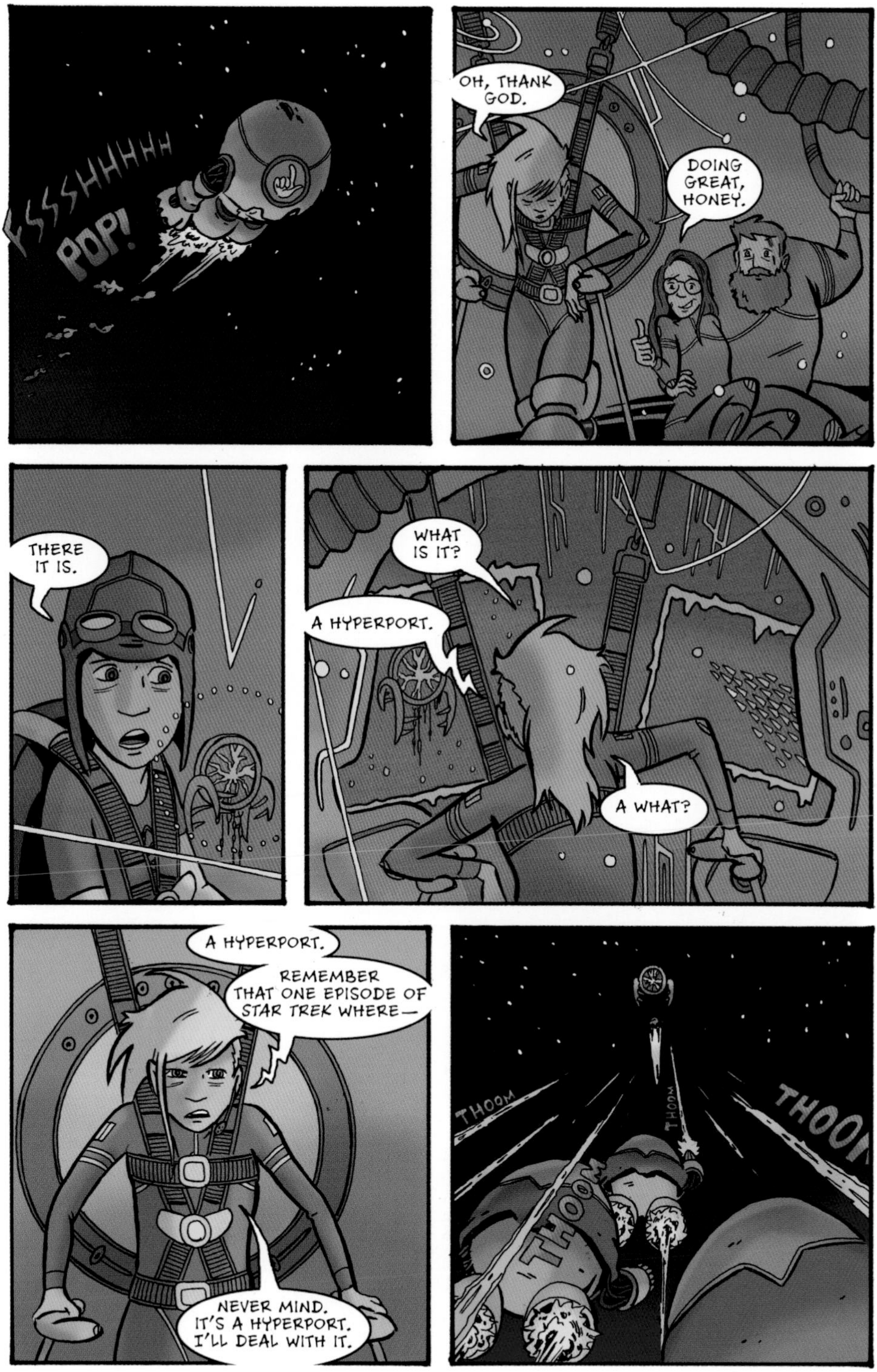
FSSSHHHHHH
POP!
OH, THANK GOD.
DOING GREAT, HONEY.
THERE IT IS.
WHAT IS IT?
A HYPERPORT.
A WHAT?
A HYPERPORT.
REMEMBER THAT ONE EPISODE OF STAR TREK WHERE—
NEVER MIND. IT'S A HYPERPORT. I'LL DEAL WITH IT.
THOOM
THOOM
THOOM
THOOM
THOOM

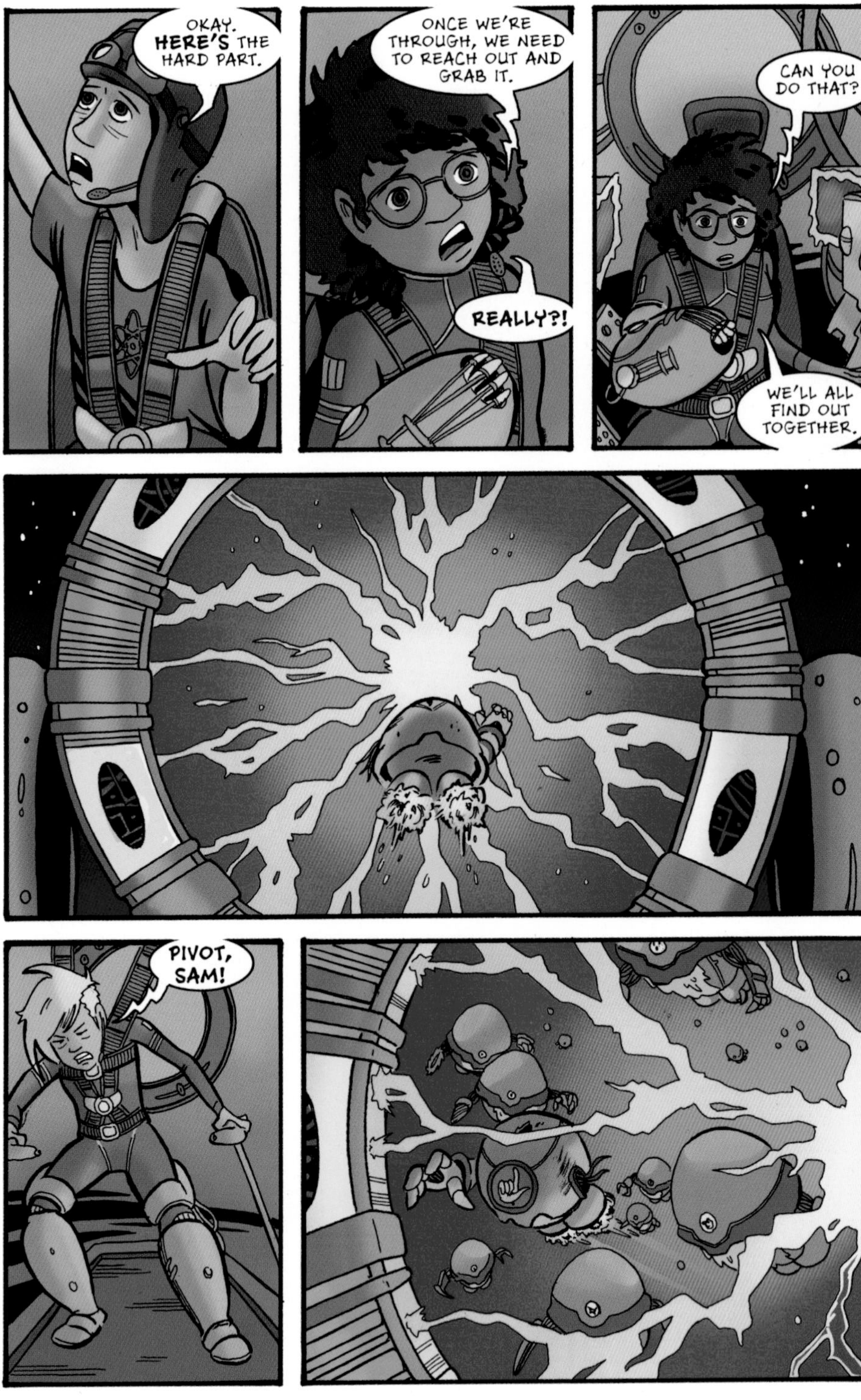
OKAY. **HERE'S** THE HARD PART.
ONCE WE'RE THROUGH, WE NEED TO REACH OUT AND GRAB IT.
REALLY?!
CAN YOU DO THAT?
WE'LL ALL FIND OUT TOGETHER.
PIVOT, SAM!

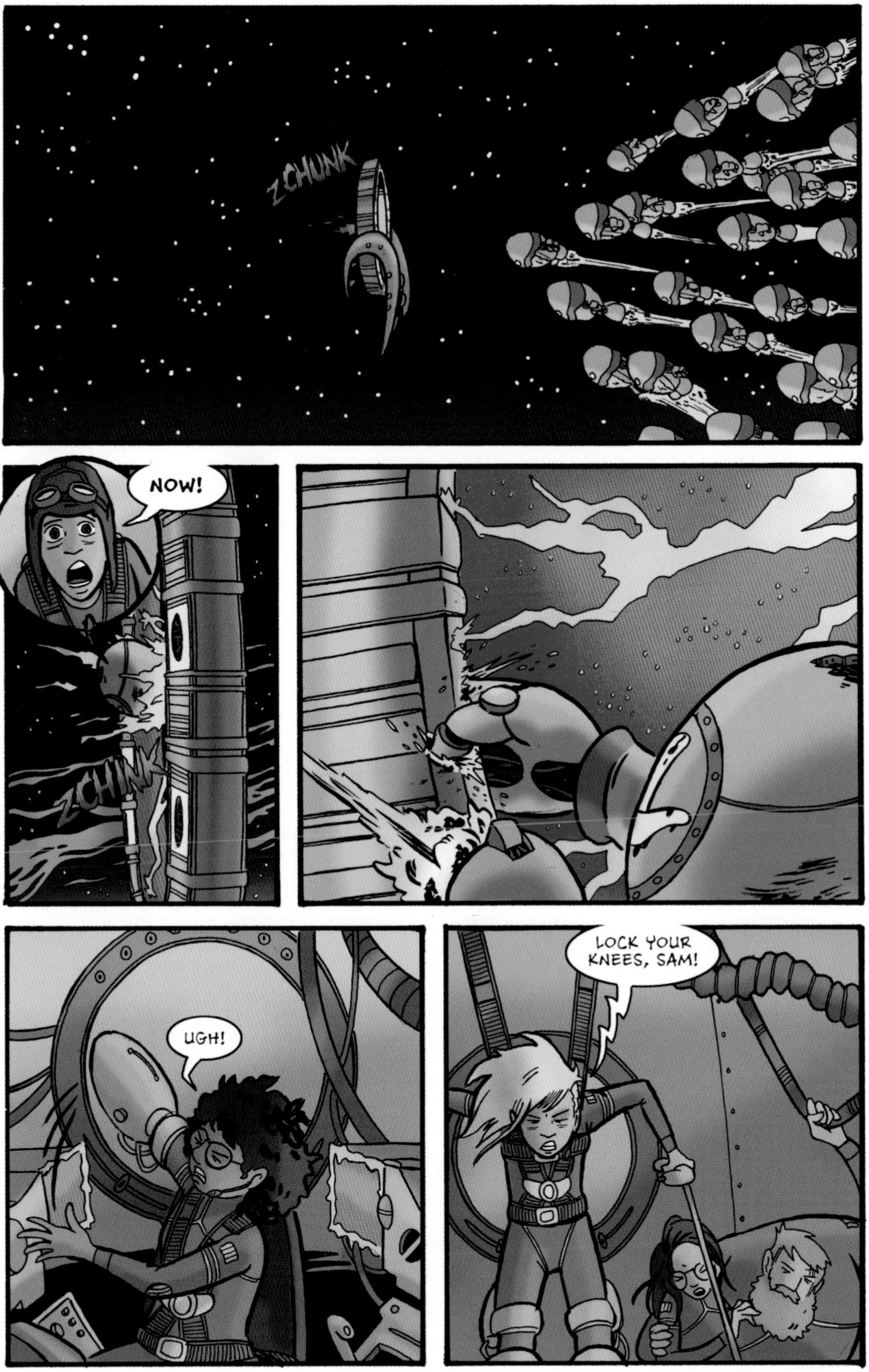
ZCHUNK
NOW!
ZCHUNK
UGH!
LOCK YOUR KNEES, SAM!

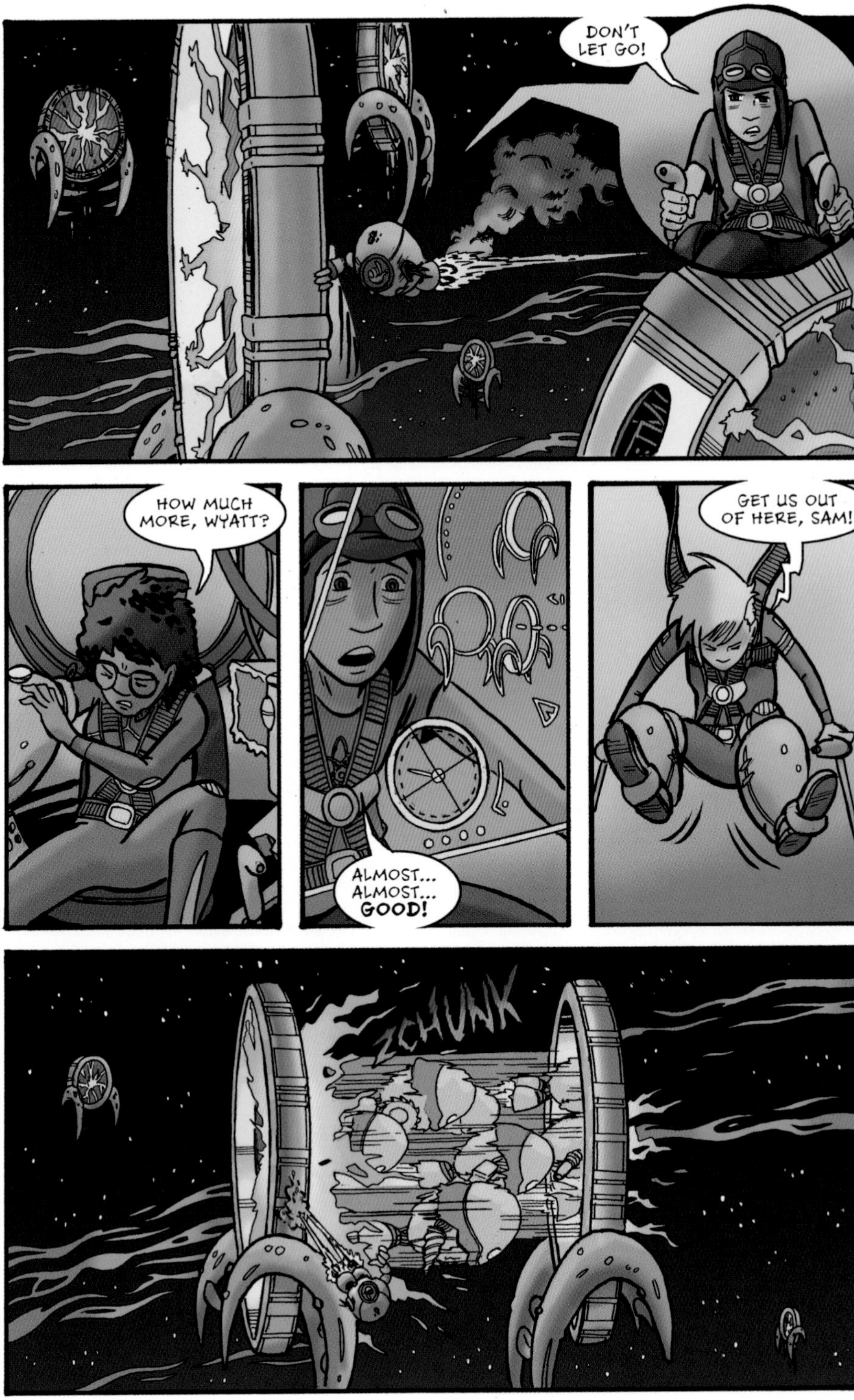
DON'T LET GO!
HOW MUCH MORE, WYATT?
ALMOST... ALMOST... GOOD!
GET US OUT OF HERE, SAM!
ZCHUNK

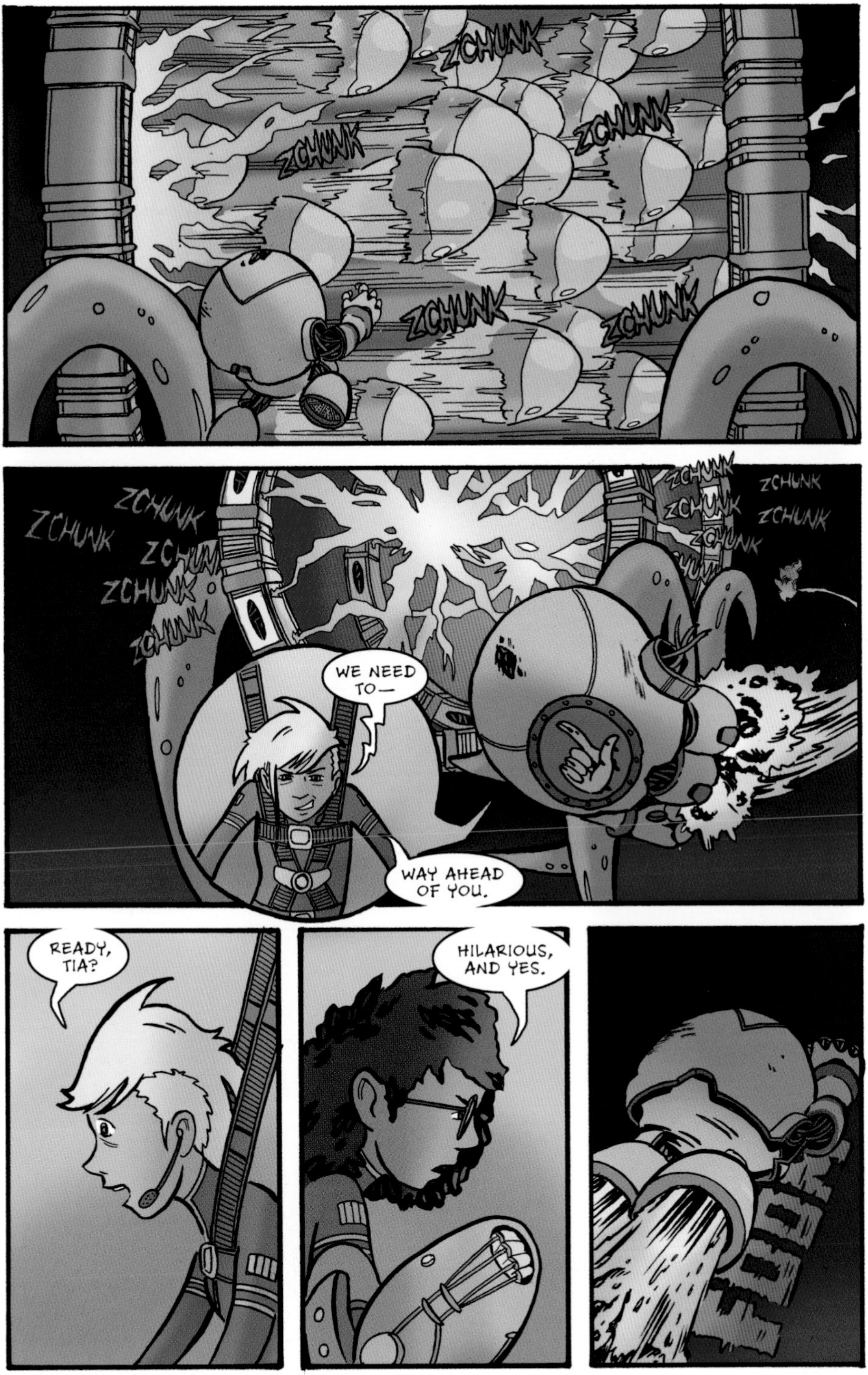
ZCHUNK
ZCHUNK
ZCHUNK
ZCHUNK
ZCHUNK
ZCHUNK
ZCHUNK
ZCHUNK
ZCHUNK
ZCHUNK
ZCHUNK
ZCHUNK
ZCHUNK
ZCHUNK
ZCHUNK
WE NEED TO—
WAY AHEAD OF YOU.
READY, TIA?
HILARIOUS, AND YES.

WAIT, SAM!
WE CAN JUST—

CREEEEAAAAK

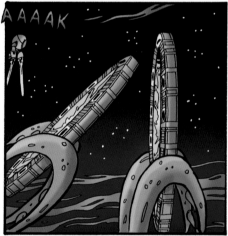

HUH.

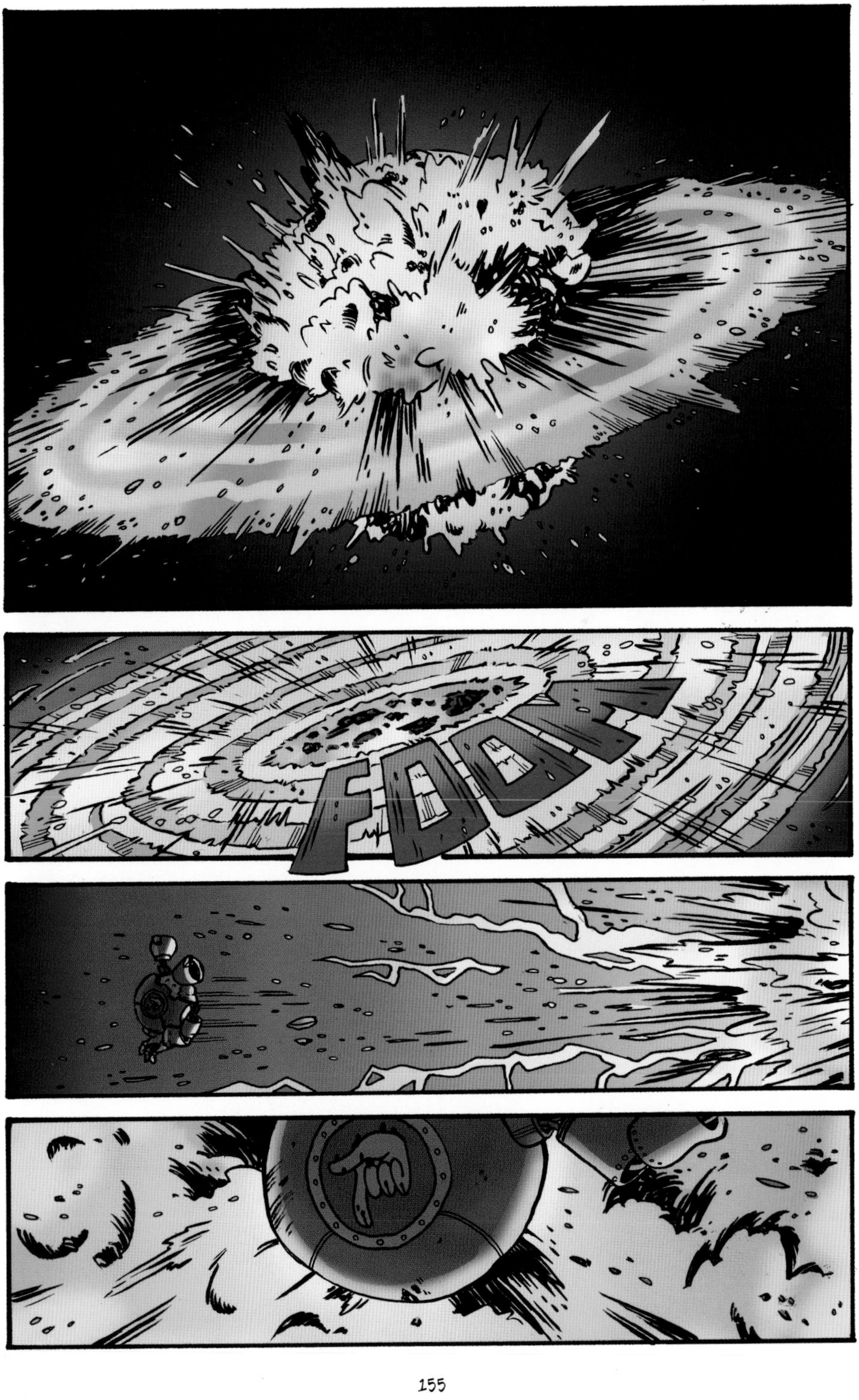
FOOM

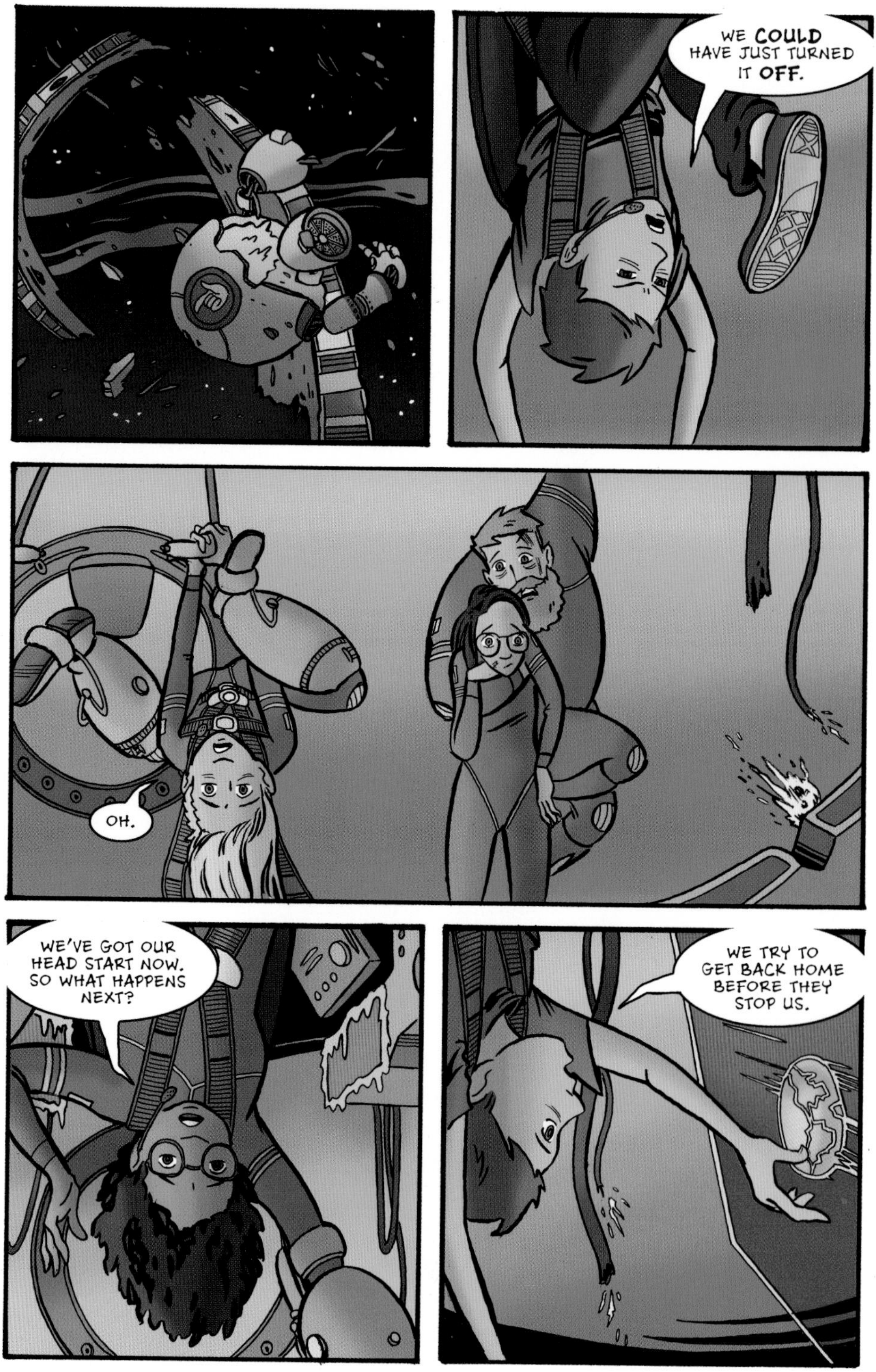
WE COULD HAVE JUST TURNED IT OFF.
OH.
WE'VE GOT OUR HEAD START NOW. SO WHAT HAPPENS NEXT?
WE TRY TO GET BACK HOME BEFORE THEY STOP US.

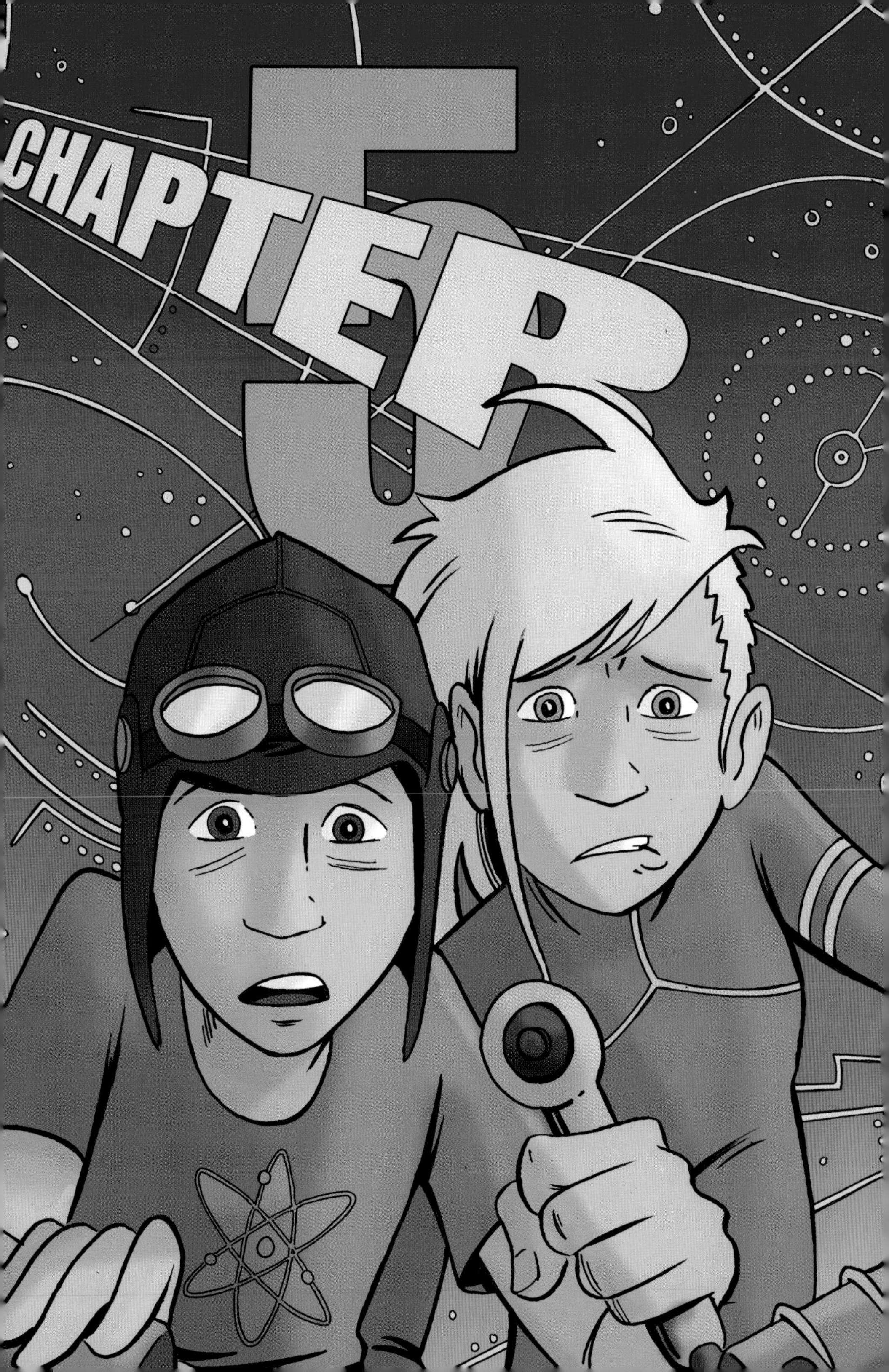
CHAPTER 5

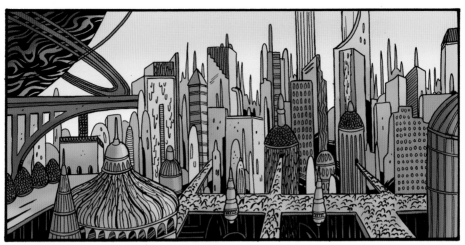

FRESH VELSO ROOT FROM THE OUTER RIM.

GET YOUR HEALING SANDS FROM AXION FOUR.

I HEAR THE FEDERATION HAS TAKEN OVER A NEW PLANET AND THEY HAVE DISCOVERED SOME BEAUTIFUL NEW FABRICS.

PERSONALLY, I PREFER LAST YEAR'S DESIGNS INSPIRED BY THE MOONS OF INTILLION.

IF THEY RAISE THE PRICE OF MEDICATION, I'LL CERTAINLY HAVE TO CUT BACK ON MY RARE EXFOLIANT COLLECTION.

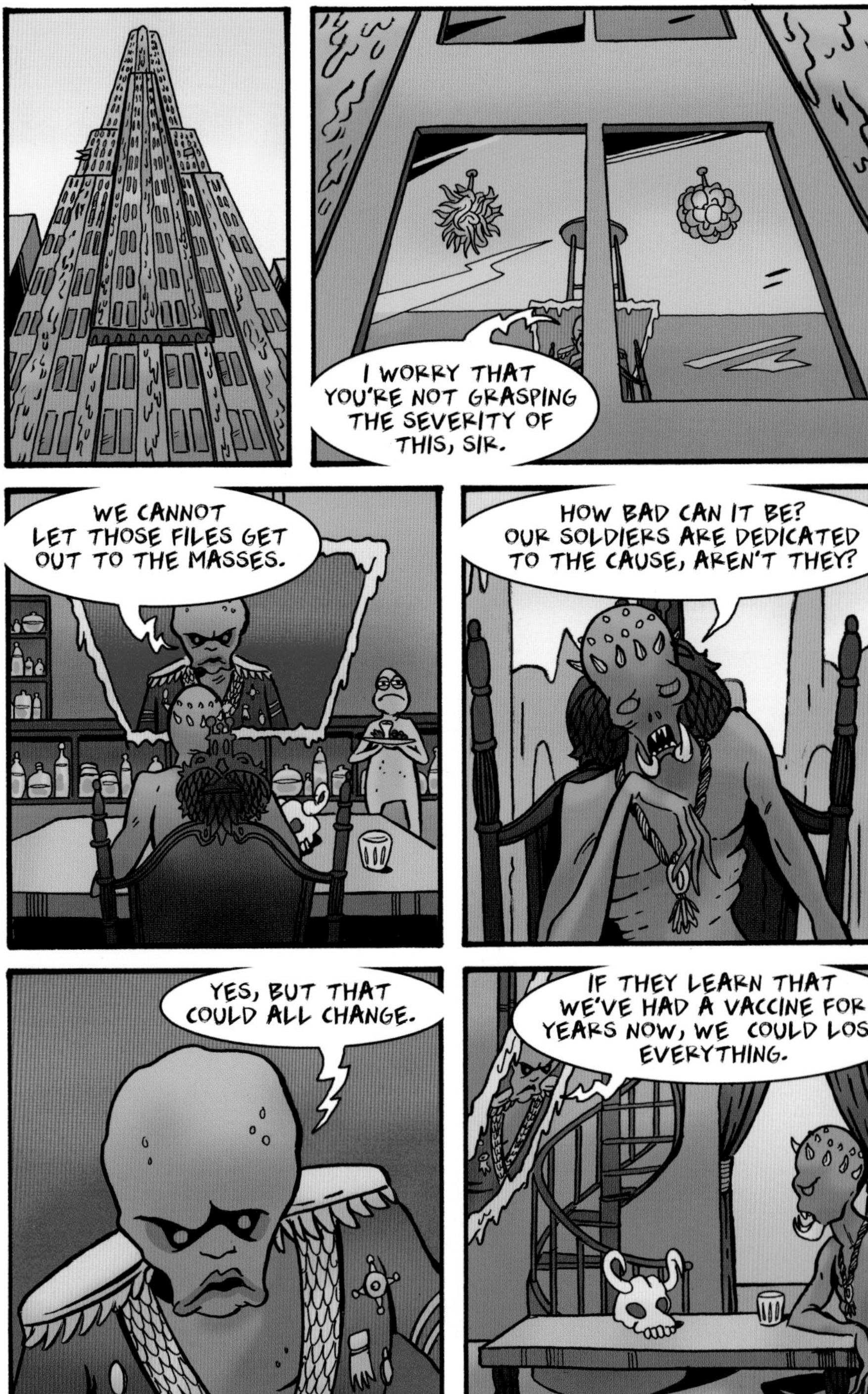
I WORRY THAT YOU'RE NOT GRASPING THE SEVERITY OF THIS, SIR.
WE CANNOT LET THOSE FILES GET OUT TO THE MASSES.
HOW BAD CAN IT BE? OUR SOLDIERS ARE DEDICATED TO THE CAUSE, AREN'T THEY?
YES, BUT THAT COULD ALL CHANGE.
IF THEY LEARN THAT WE'VE HAD A VACCINE FOR YEARS NOW, WE COULD LOSE EVERYTHING.

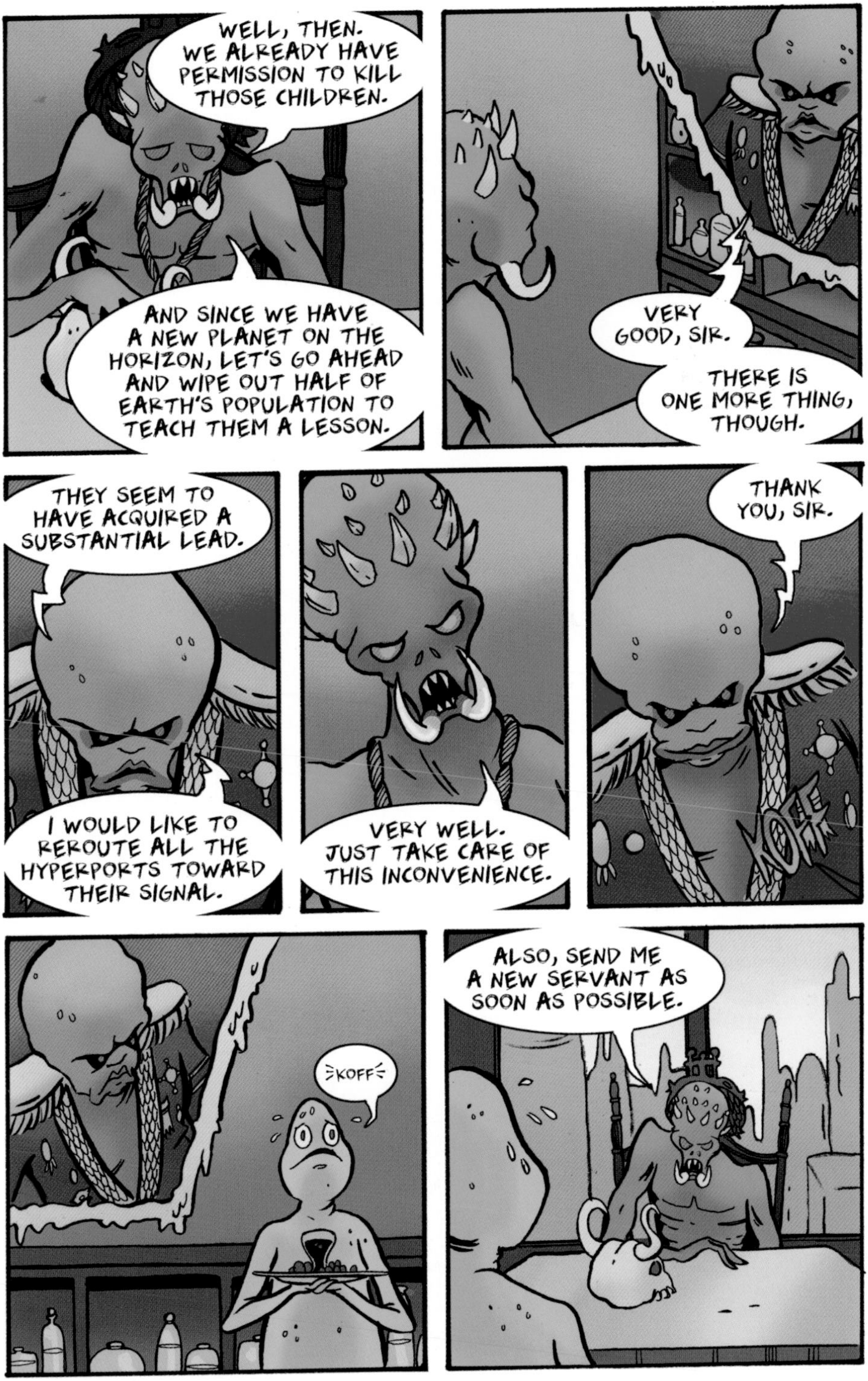
WELL, THEN. WE ALREADY HAVE PERMISSION TO KILL THOSE CHILDREN.
AND SINCE WE HAVE A NEW PLANET ON THE HORIZON, LET'S GO AHEAD AND WIPE OUT HALF OF EARTH'S POPULATION TO TEACH THEM A LESSON.
VERY GOOD, SIR.
THERE IS ONE MORE THING, THOUGH.
THEY SEEM TO HAVE ACQUIRED A SUBSTANTIAL LEAD.
I WOULD LIKE TO REROUTE ALL THE HYPERPORTS TOWARD THEIR SIGNAL.
VERY WELL. JUST TAKE CARE OF THIS INCONVENIENCE.
THANK YOU, SIR.
KOFF
KOFF
ALSO, SEND ME A NEW SERVANT AS SOON AS POSSIBLE.

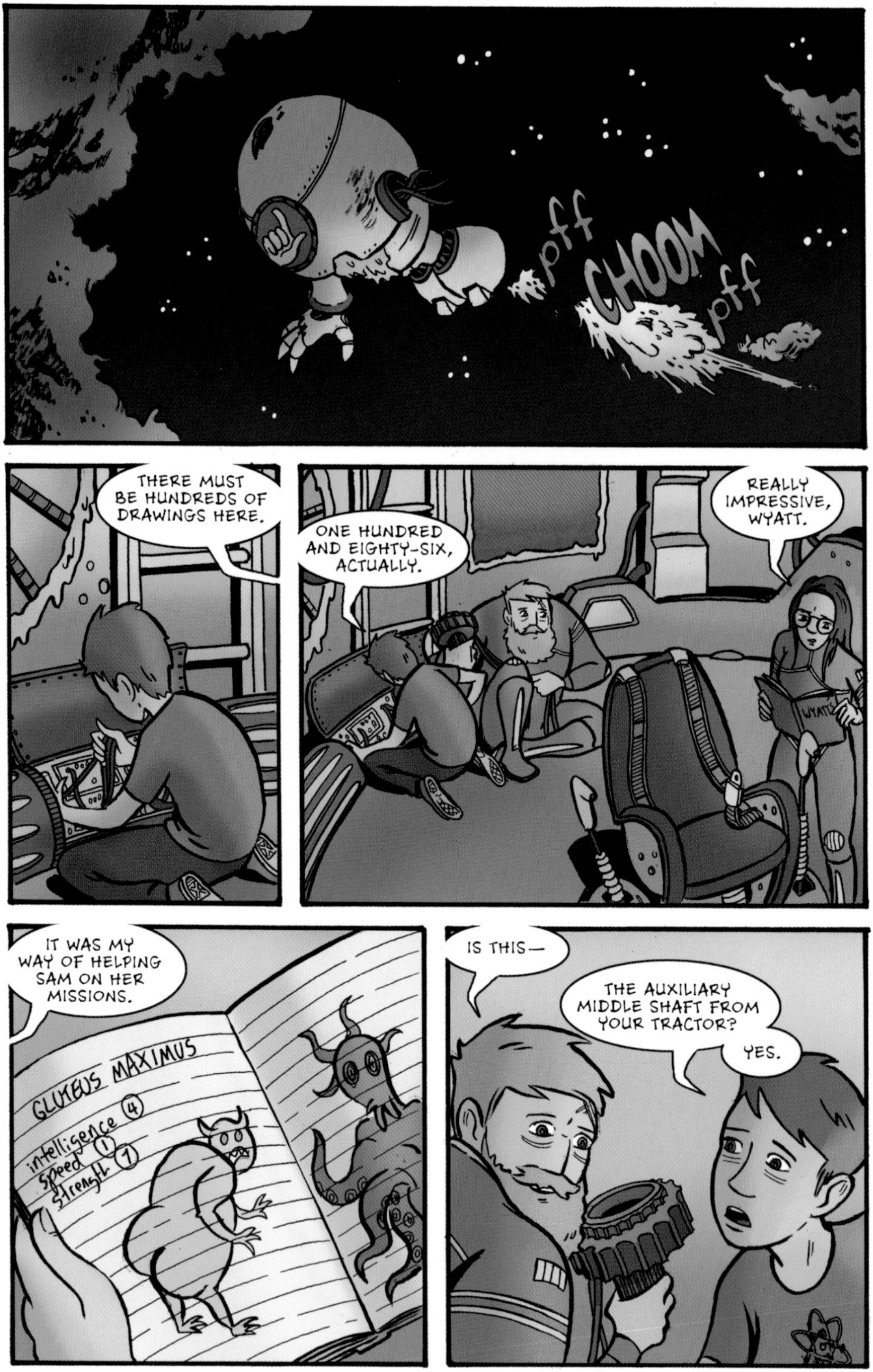
pff
CHOOM
pff
THERE MUST BE HUNDREDS OF DRAWINGS HERE.
ONE HUNDRED AND EIGHTY-SIX, ACTUALLY.
REALLY IMPRESSIVE, WYATT.
WYATT
IT WAS MY WAY OF HELPING SAM ON HER MISSIONS.
GLUTEUS MAXIMUS
intelligence 4
speed 1
strength 1
IS THIS—
THE AUXILIARY MIDDLE SHAFT FROM YOUR TRACTOR?
YES.

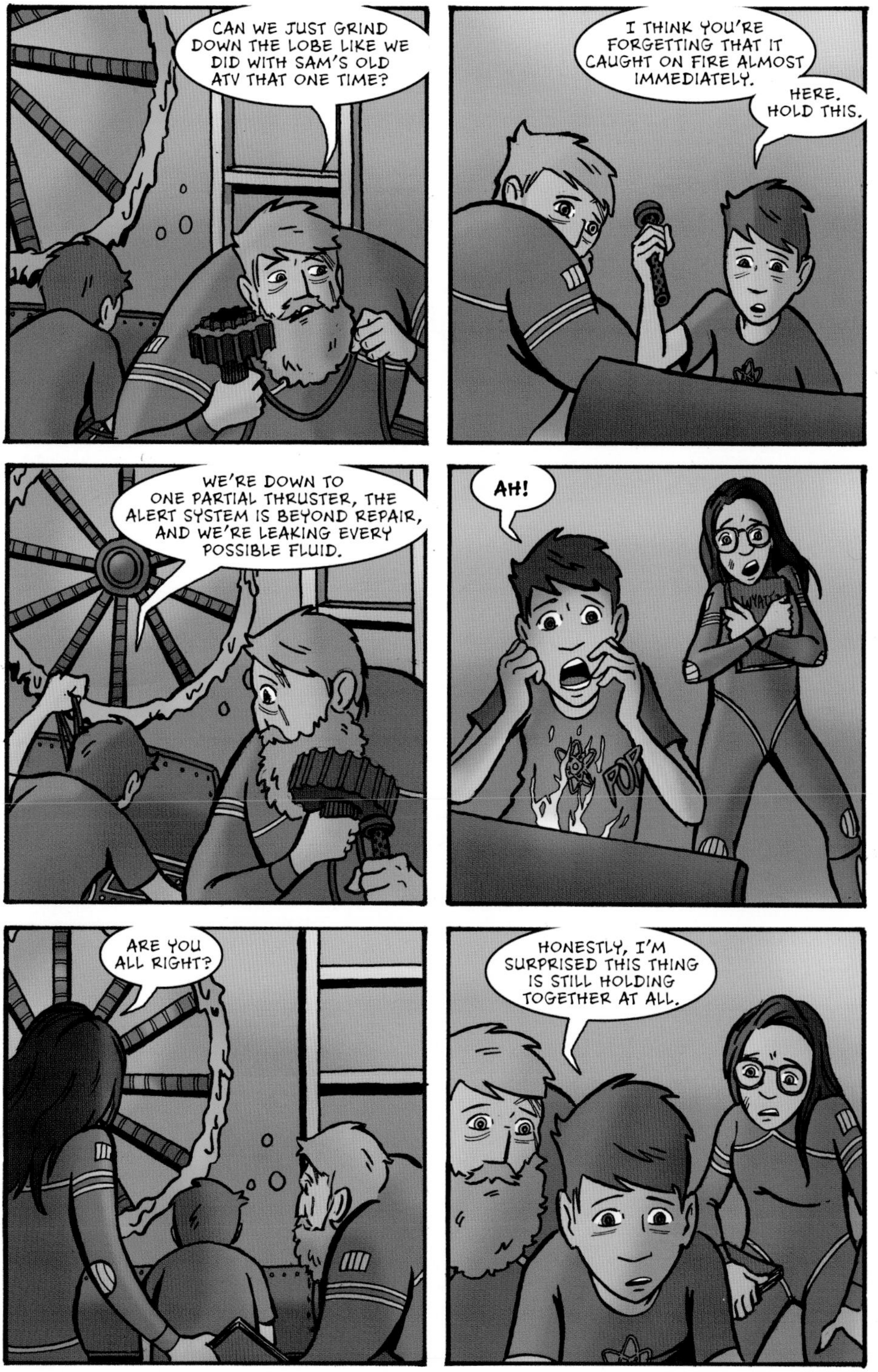
CAN WE JUST GRIND DOWN THE LOBE LIKE WE DID WITH SAM'S OLD ATV THAT ONE TIME?
I THINK YOU'RE FORGETTING THAT IT CAUGHT ON FIRE ALMOST IMMEDIATELY.
HERE. HOLD THIS.
WE'RE DOWN TO ONE PARTIAL THRUSTER, THE ALERT SYSTEM IS BEYOND REPAIR, AND WE'RE LEAKING EVERY POSSIBLE FLUID.
AH!
ARE YOU ALL RIGHT?
HONESTLY, I'M SURPRISED THIS THING IS STILL HOLDING TOGETHER AT ALL.

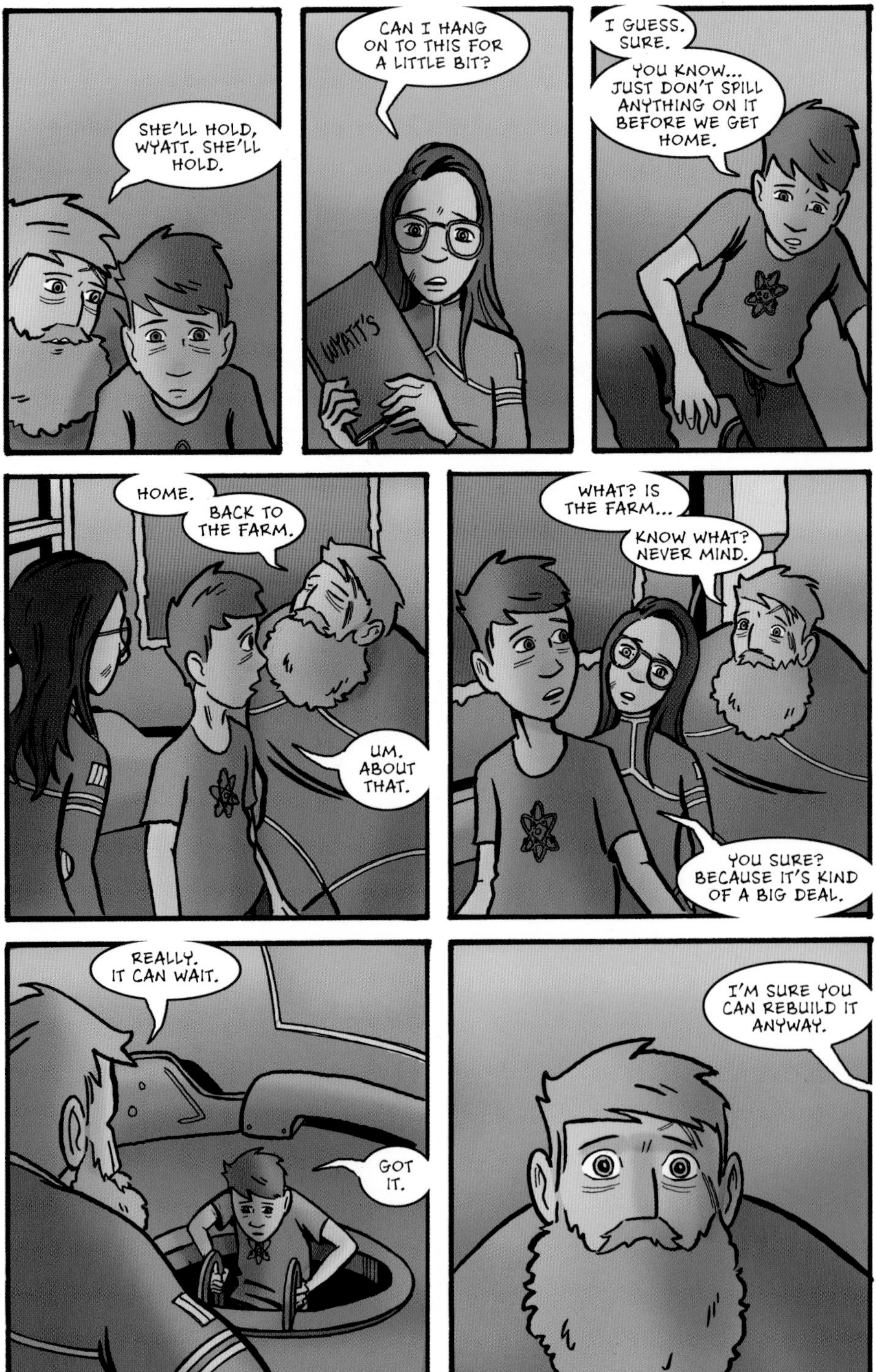
SHE'LL HOLD, WYATT. SHE'LL HOLD.
CAN I HANG ON TO THIS FOR A LITTLE BIT?
WYATT'S
I GUESS. SURE.
YOU KNOW... JUST DON'T SPILL ANYTHING ON IT BEFORE WE GET HOME.
HOME.
BACK TO THE FARM.
UM. ABOUT THAT.
WHAT? IS THE FARM...
KNOW WHAT? NEVER MIND.
YOU SURE? BECAUSE IT'S KIND OF A BIG DEAL.
REALLY. IT CAN WAIT.
GOT IT.
I'M SURE YOU CAN REBUILD IT ANYWAY.

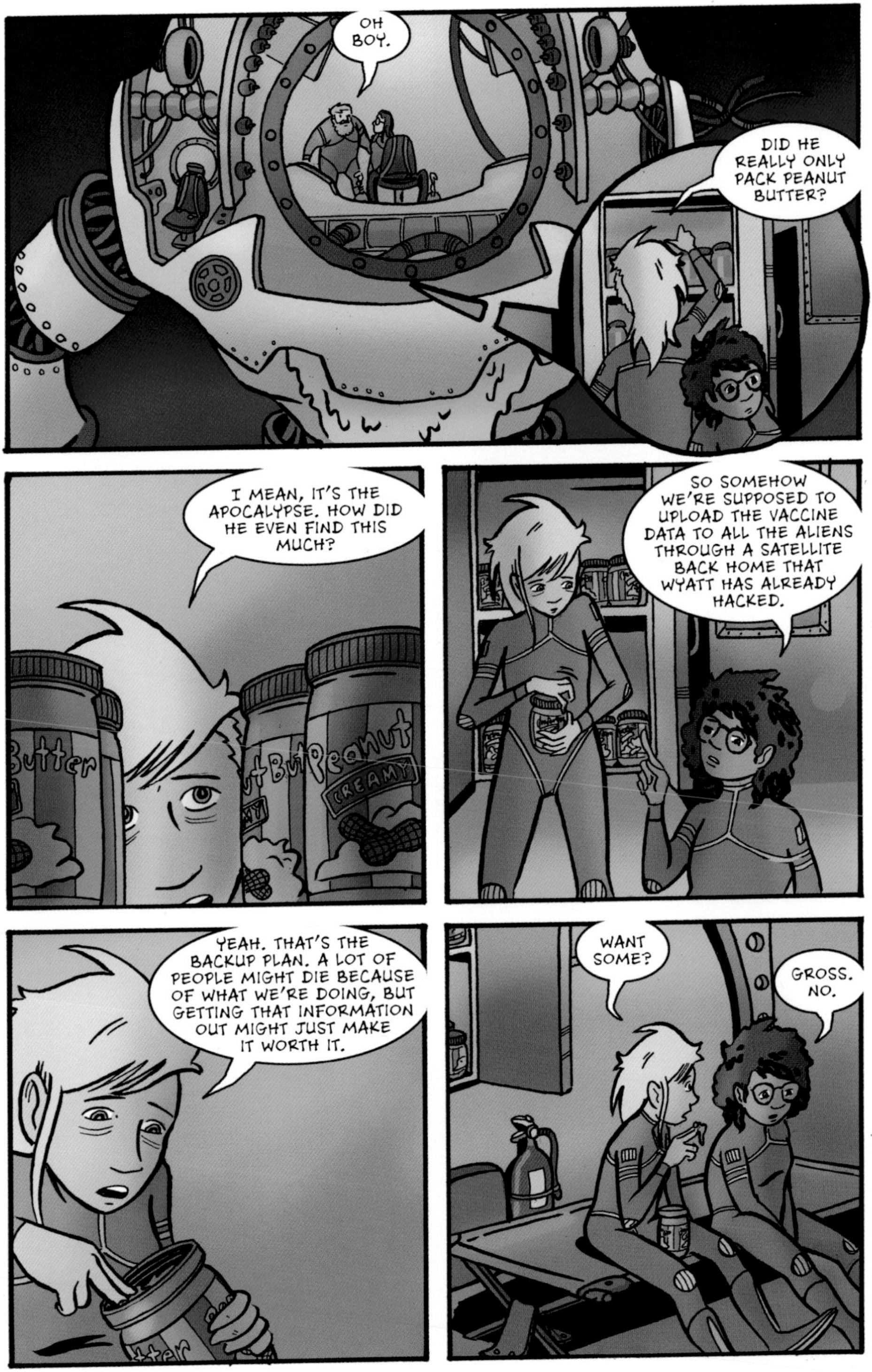
OH BOY.
DID HE REALLY ONLY PACK PEANUT BUTTER?
I MEAN, IT'S THE APOCALYPSE. HOW DID HE EVEN FIND THIS MUCH?
SO SOMEHOW WE'RE SUPPOSED TO UPLOAD THE VACCINE DATA TO ALL THE ALIENS THROUGH A SATELLITE BACK HOME THAT WYATT HAS ALREADY HACKED.
YEAH. THAT'S THE BACKUP PLAN. A LOT OF PEOPLE MIGHT DIE BECAUSE OF WHAT WE'RE DOING, BUT GETTING THAT INFORMATION OUT MIGHT JUST MAKE IT WORTH IT.
WANT SOME?
GROSS. NO.

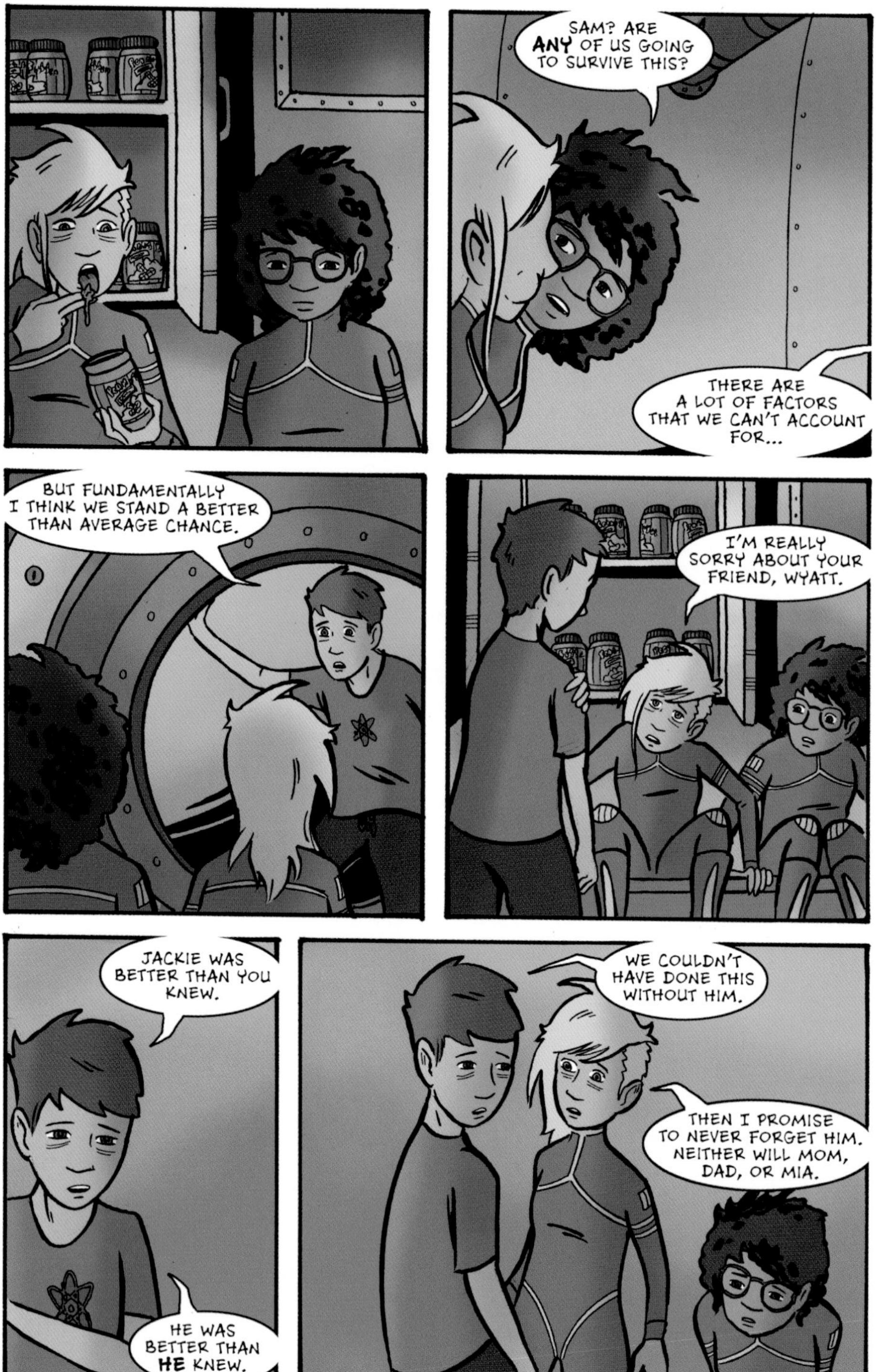
SAM? ARE ANY OF US GOING TO SURVIVE THIS?
THERE ARE A LOT OF FACTORS THAT WE CAN'T ACCOUNT FOR...
BUT FUNDAMENTALLY I THINK WE STAND A BETTER THAN AVERAGE CHANCE.
I'M REALLY SORRY ABOUT YOUR FRIEND, WYATT.
JACKIE WAS BETTER THAN YOU KNEW.
HE WAS BETTER THAN HE KNEW.
WE COULDN'T HAVE DONE THIS WITHOUT HIM.
THEN I PROMISE TO NEVER FORGET HIM. NEITHER WILL MOM, DAD, OR MIA.

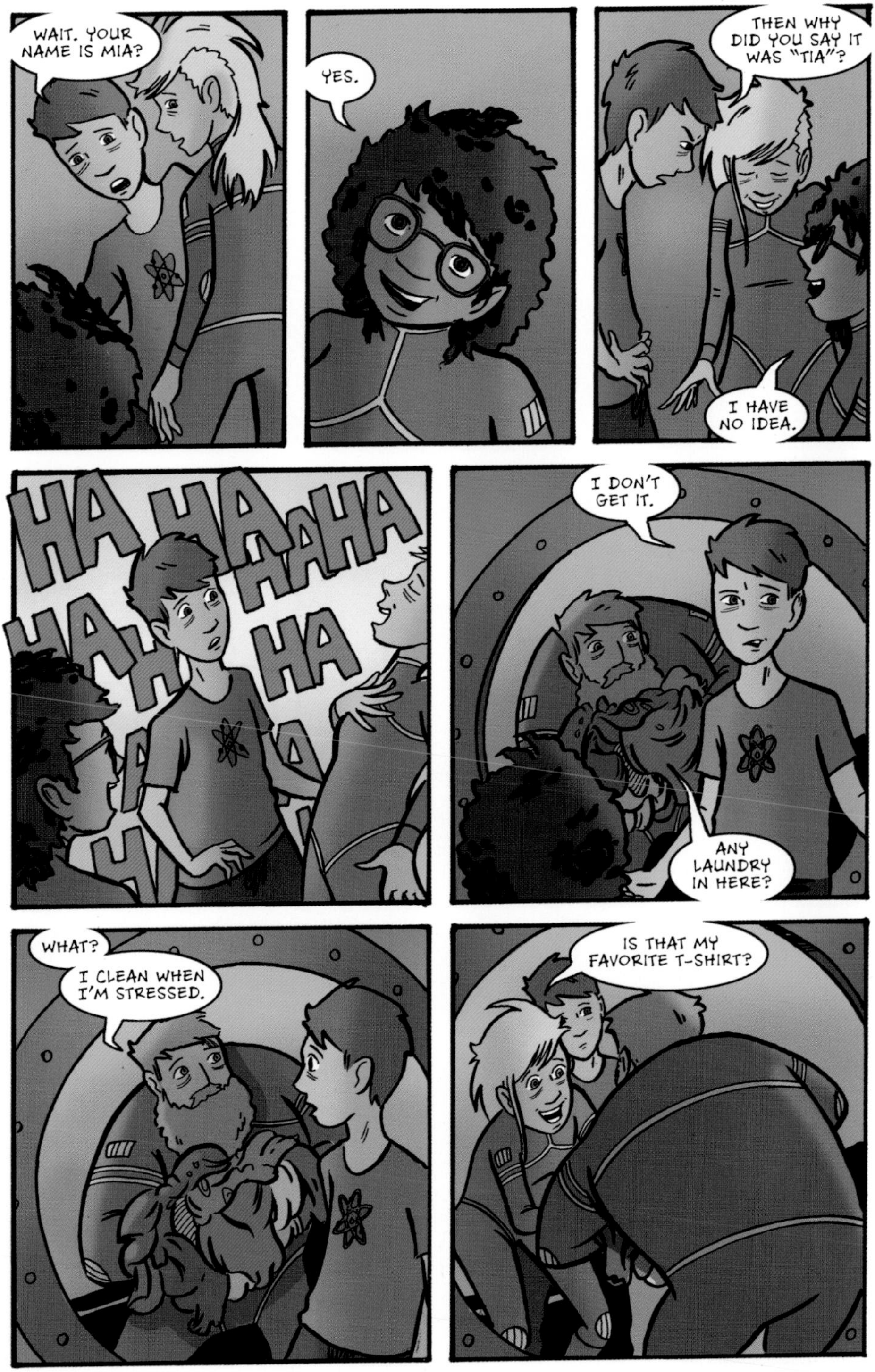
WAIT. YOUR NAME IS MIA?
YES.
THEN WHY DID YOU SAY IT WAS "TIA"?
I HAVE NO IDEA.
HA HA HA HA HA HA HA HA HA HA HA
I DON'T GET IT.
ANY LAUNDRY IN HERE?
WHAT?
I CLEAN WHEN I'M STRESSED.
IS THAT MY FAVORITE T-SHIRT?

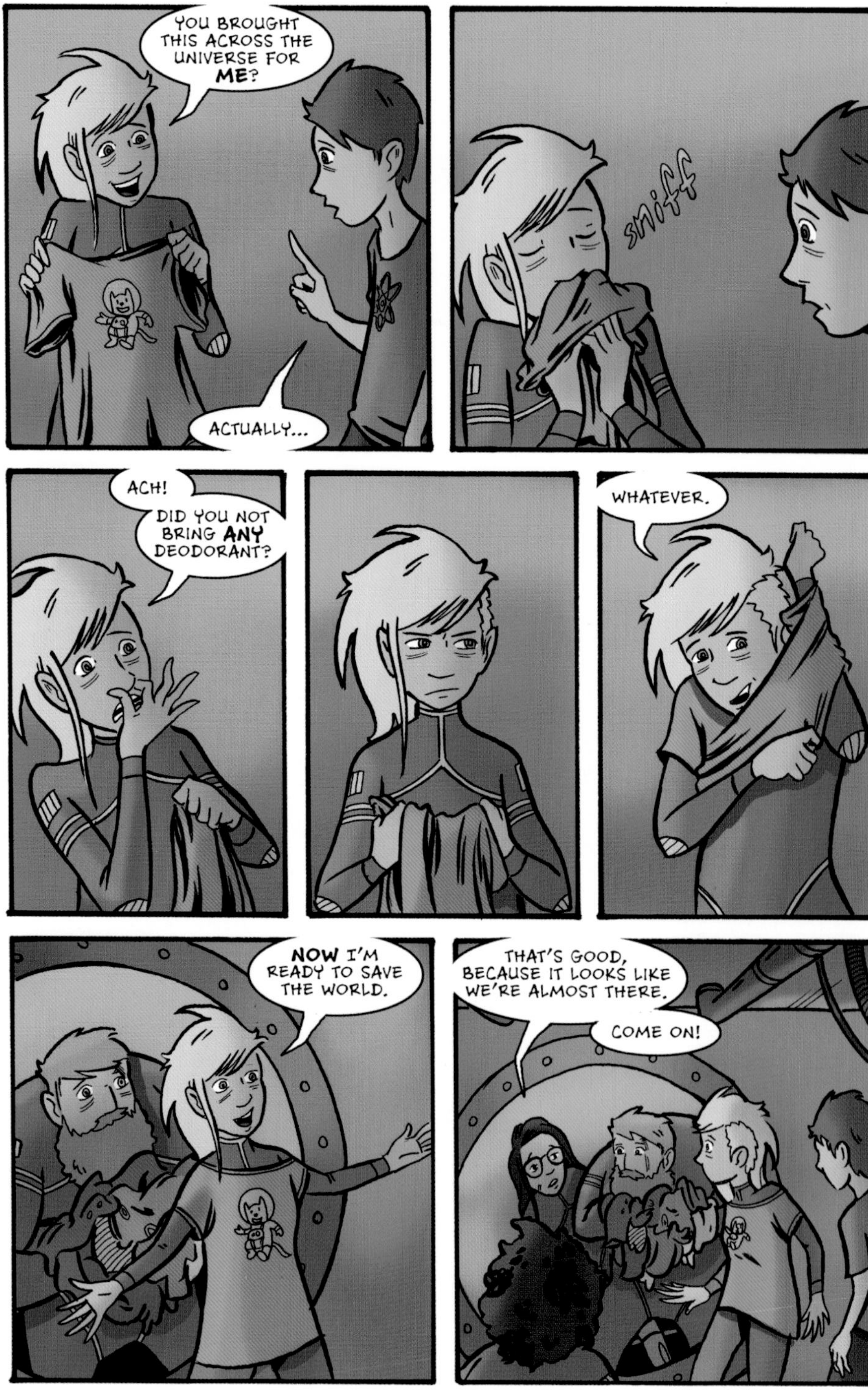
YOU BROUGHT THIS ACROSS THE UNIVERSE FOR **ME**?
ACTUALLY...
sniff
ACH!
DID YOU NOT BRING **ANY** DEODORANT?
WHATEVER.
NOW I'M READY TO SAVE THE WORLD.
THAT'S GOOD, BECAUSE IT LOOKS LIKE WE'RE ALMOST THERE.
COME ON!

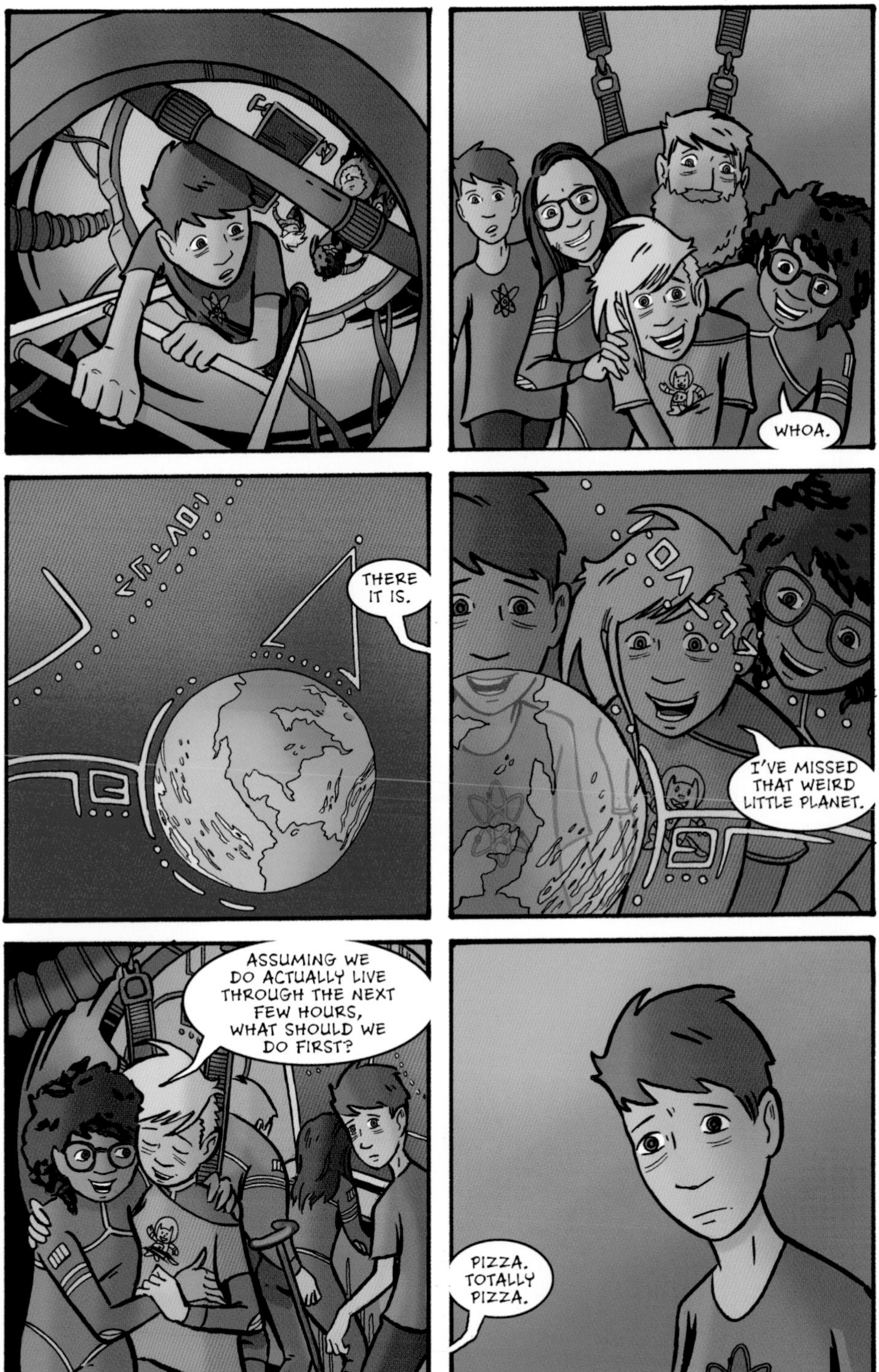
WHOA.
THERE IT IS.
I'VE MISSED THAT WEIRD LITTLE PLANET.
ASSUMING WE DO ACTUALLY LIVE THROUGH THE NEXT FEW HOURS, WHAT SHOULD WE DO FIRST?
PIZZA. TOTALLY PIZZA.

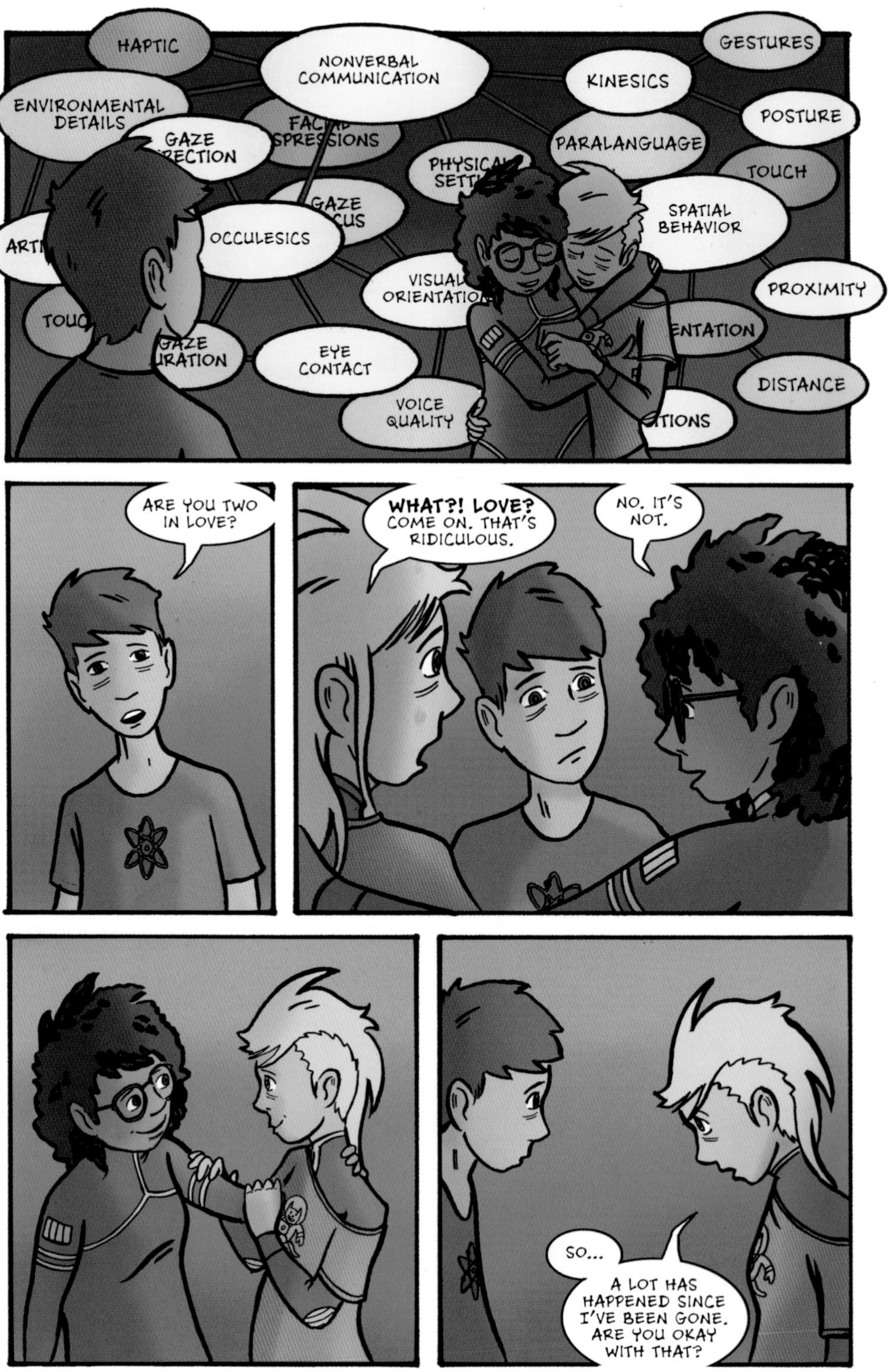

HAPTIC
NONVERBAL COMMUNICATION
GESTURES
KINESICS
ENVIRONMENTAL DETAILS
POSTURE
GAZE
PARALANGUAGE
TOUCH
SPATIAL BEHAVIOR
OCCULESICS
PROXIMITY
EYE CONTACT
DISTANCE
VOICE QUALITY
ARE YOU TWO IN LOVE?
WHAT?! LOVE? COME ON. THAT'S RIDICULOUS.
NO. IT'S NOT.
SO...
A LOT HAS HAPPENED SINCE I'VE BEEN GONE. ARE YOU OKAY WITH THAT?

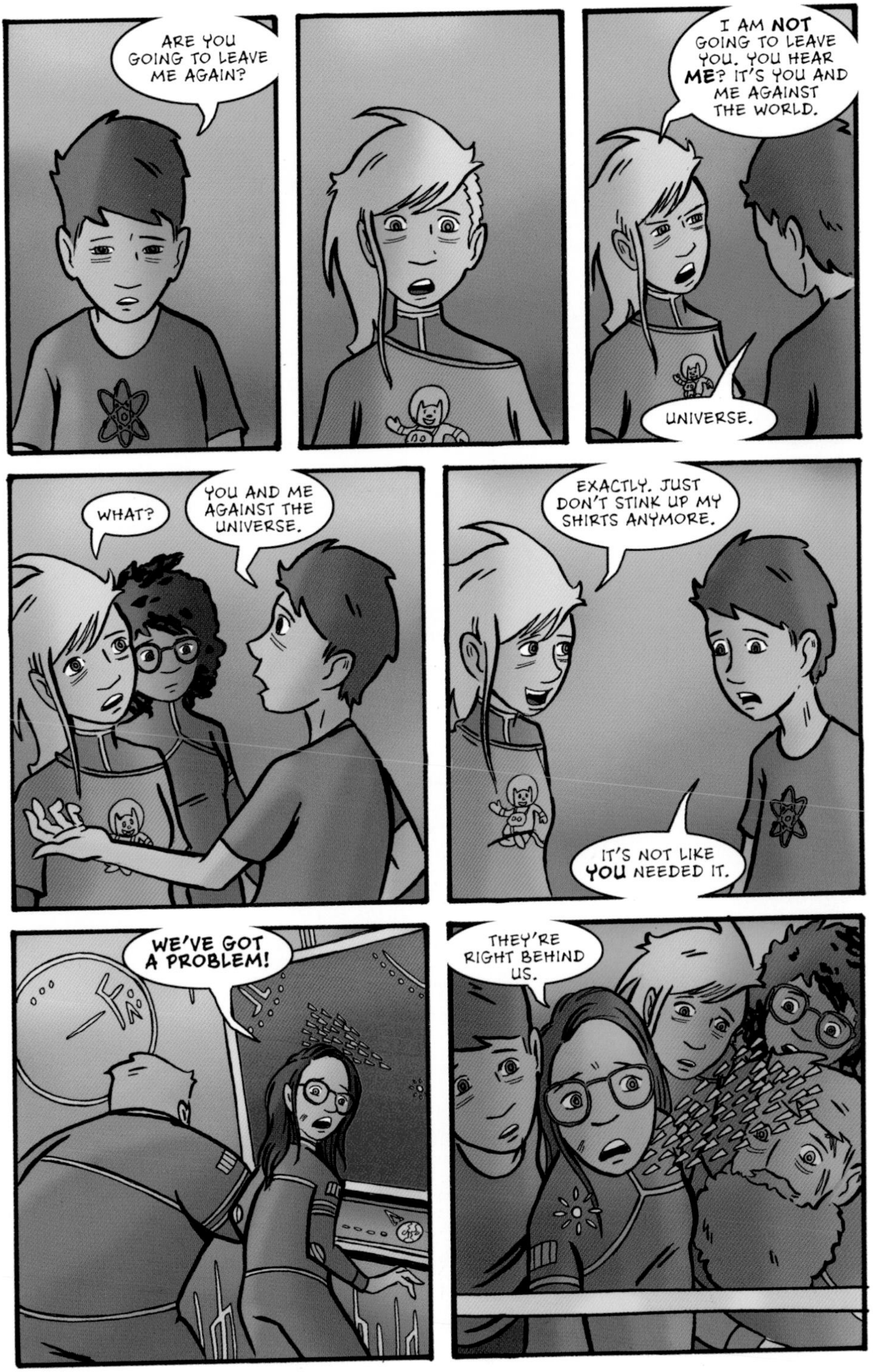
ARE YOU GOING TO LEAVE ME AGAIN?
I AM NOT GOING TO LEAVE YOU. YOU HEAR ME? IT'S YOU AND ME AGAINST THE WORLD.
UNIVERSE.
WHAT?
YOU AND ME AGAINST THE UNIVERSE.
EXACTLY. JUST DON'T STINK UP MY SHIRTS ANYMORE.
IT'S NOT LIKE YOU NEEDED IT.
WE'VE GOT A PROBLEM!
THEY'RE RIGHT BEHIND US.

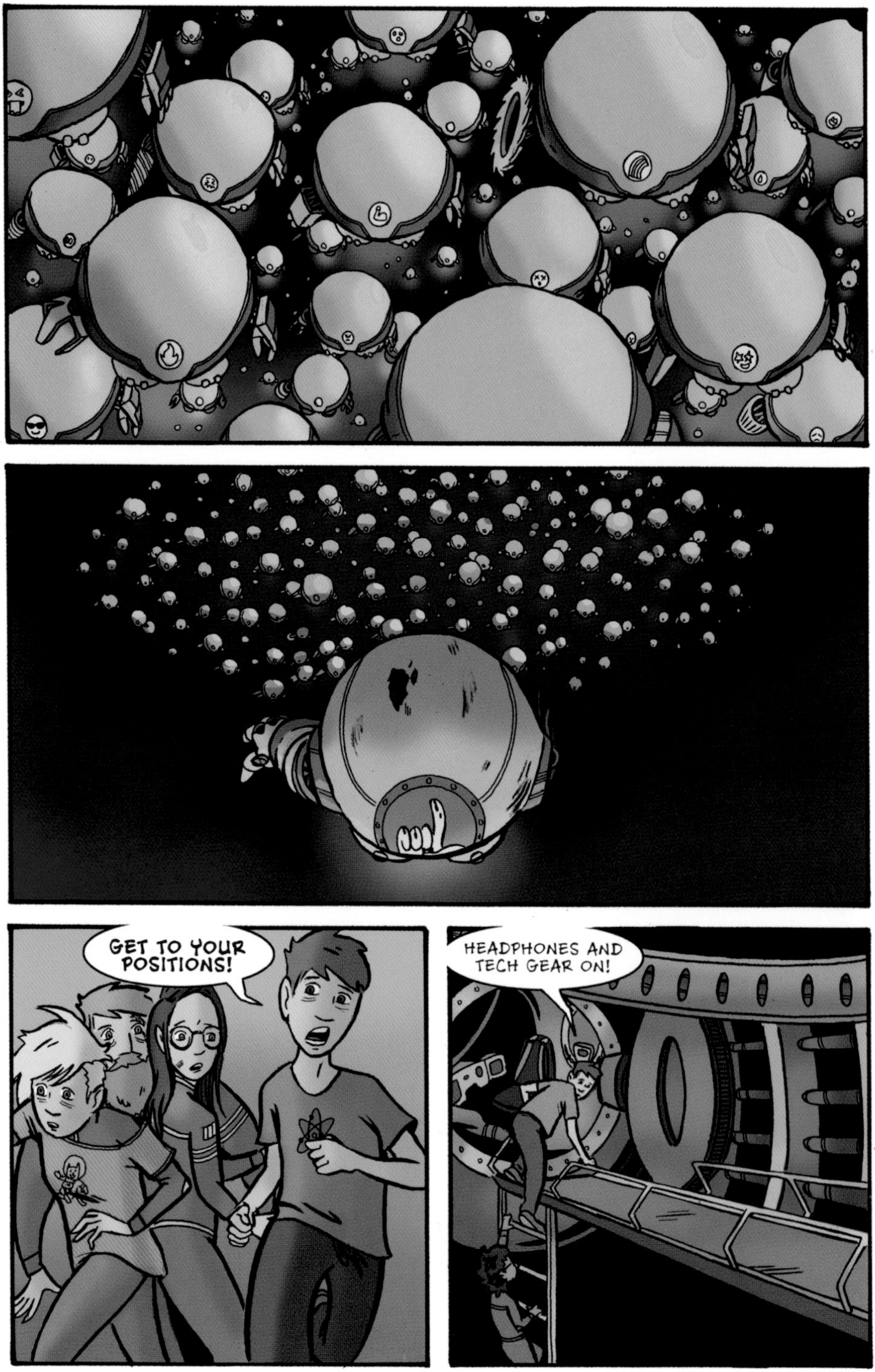
GET TO YOUR POSITIONS!
HEADPHONES AND TECH GEAR ON!

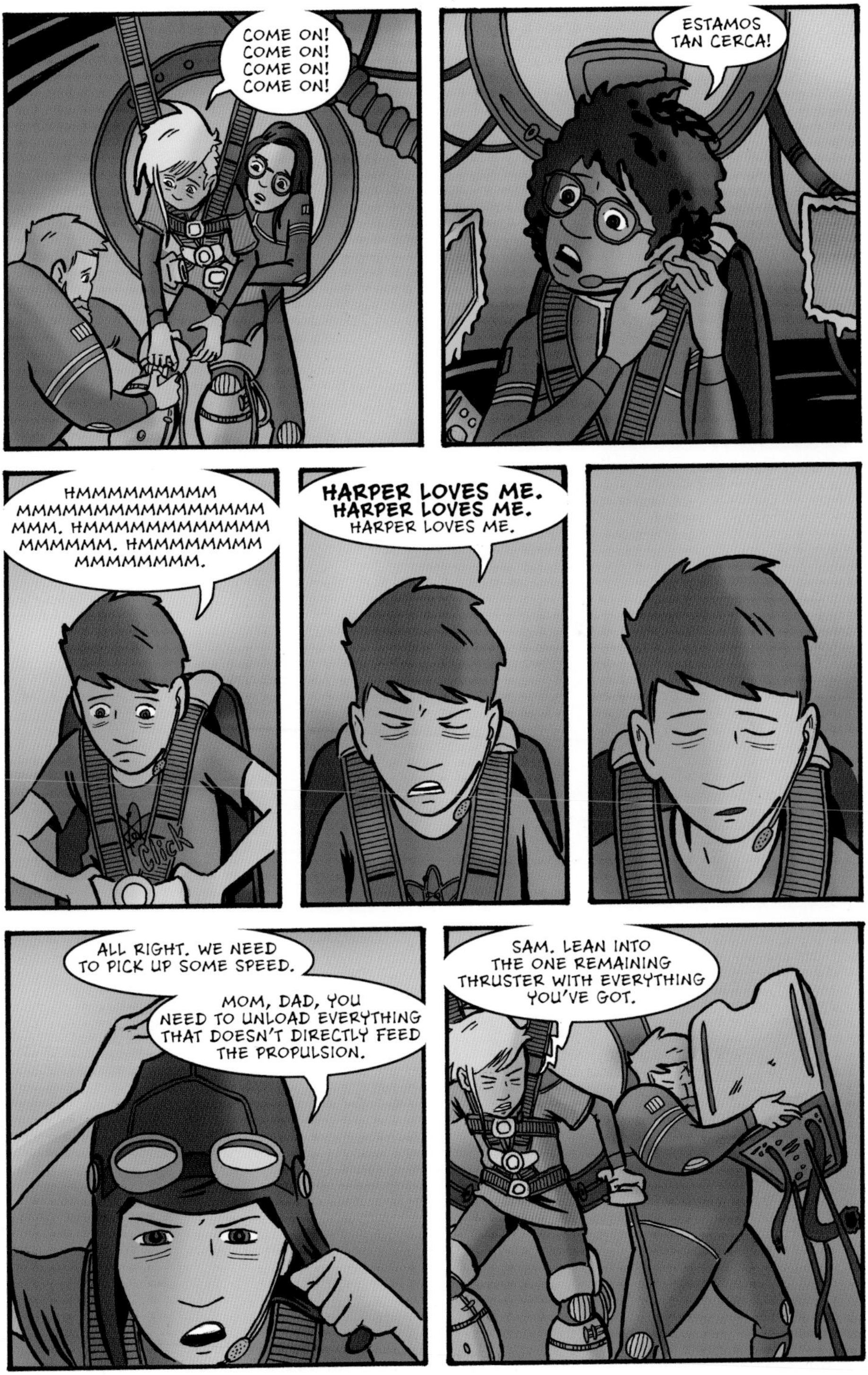
COME ON! COME ON! COME ON! COME ON!
ESTAMOS TAN CERCA!
HMMMMMMMMM MMMMMMMMMMMMMMMMM MMM. HMMMMMMMMMMMMM MMMMMM. HMMMMMMMM MMMMMMMM.
Click
HARPER LOVES ME. HARPER LOVES ME. HARPER LOVES ME.
ALL RIGHT. WE NEED TO PICK UP SOME SPEED.
MOM, DAD, YOU NEED TO UNLOAD EVERYTHING THAT DOESN'T DIRECTLY FEED THE PROPULSION.
SAM. LEAN INTO THE ONE REMAINING THRUSTER WITH EVERYTHING YOU'VE GOT.

MIA, I JUST SENT YOU THE SCHEMATICS FOR THE FAULTY THRUSTER.
FIND ME SOMETHING INSIDE IT THAT STILL SHOWS SIGNS OF LIFE.
NEARLY WITHIN RANGE. READY ALL WEAPONS.
WHAT IS THAT?

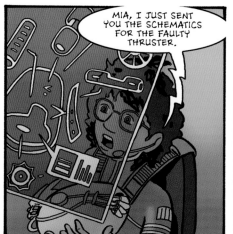

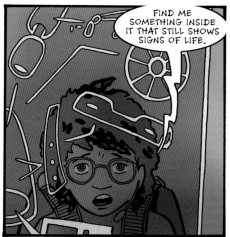

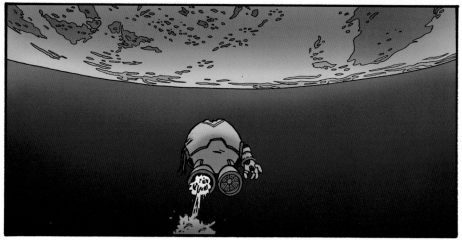

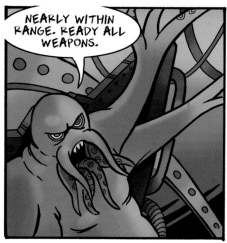

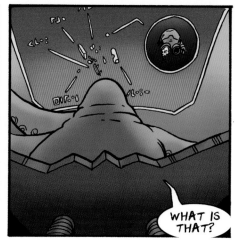

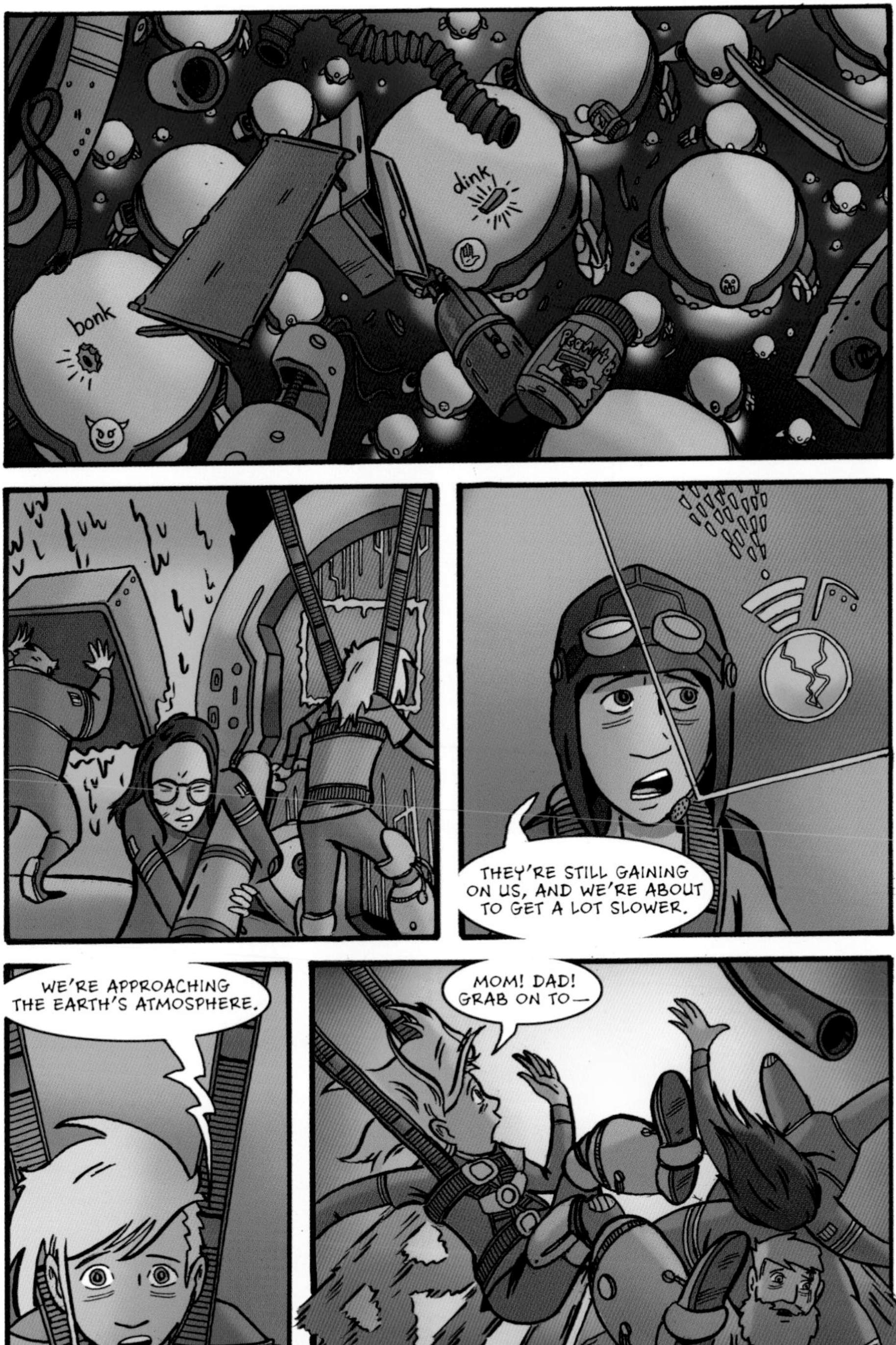
bonk
dink
THEY'RE STILL GAINING ON US, AND WE'RE ABOUT TO GET A LOT SLOWER.
WE'RE APPROACHING THE EARTH'S ATMOSPHERE.
MOM! DAD! GRAB ON TO—

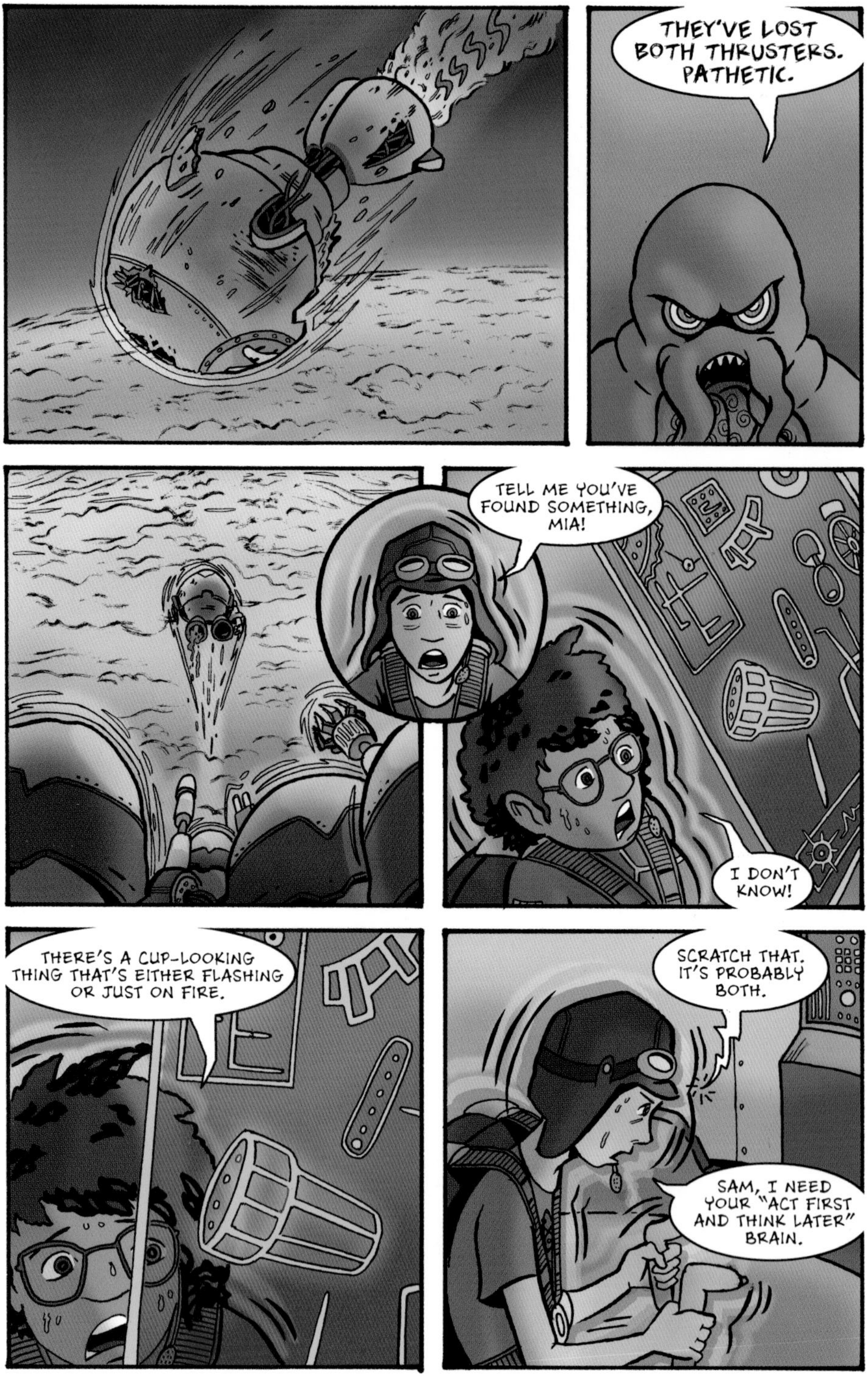
THEY'VE LOST BOTH THRUSTERS. PATHETIC.
TELL ME YOU'VE FOUND SOMETHING, MIA!
I DON'T KNOW!
THERE'S A CUP-LOOKING THING THAT'S EITHER FLASHING OR JUST ON FIRE.
SCRATCH THAT. IT'S PROBABLY BOTH.
SAM, I NEED YOUR "ACT FIRST AND THINK LATER" BRAIN.

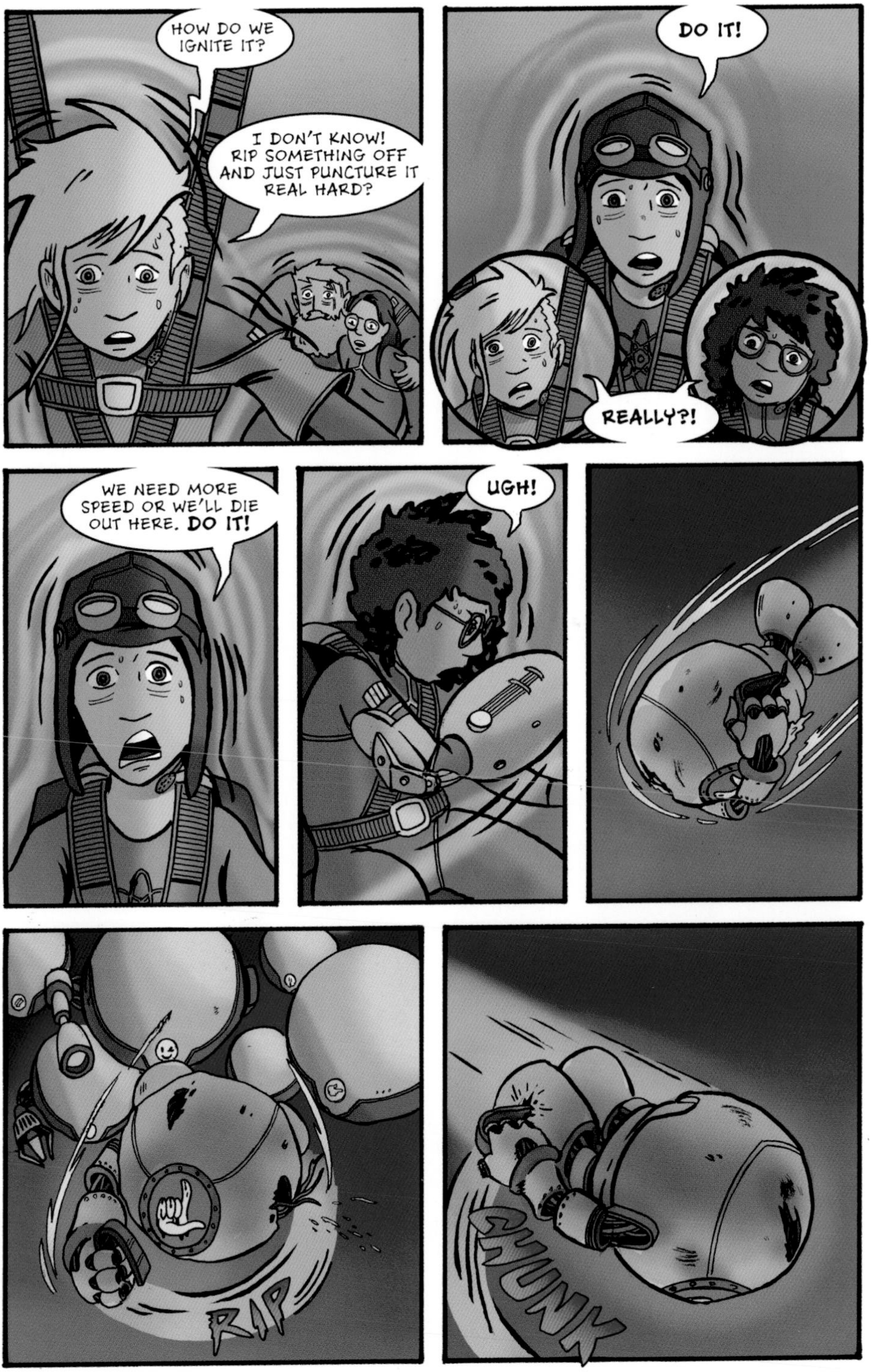
HOW DO WE IGNITE IT?
I DON'T KNOW! RIP SOMETHING OFF AND JUST PUNCTURE IT REAL HARD?
DO IT!
REALLY?!
WE NEED MORE SPEED OR WE'LL DIE OUT HERE. DO IT!
UGH!
RIP
CHUNK

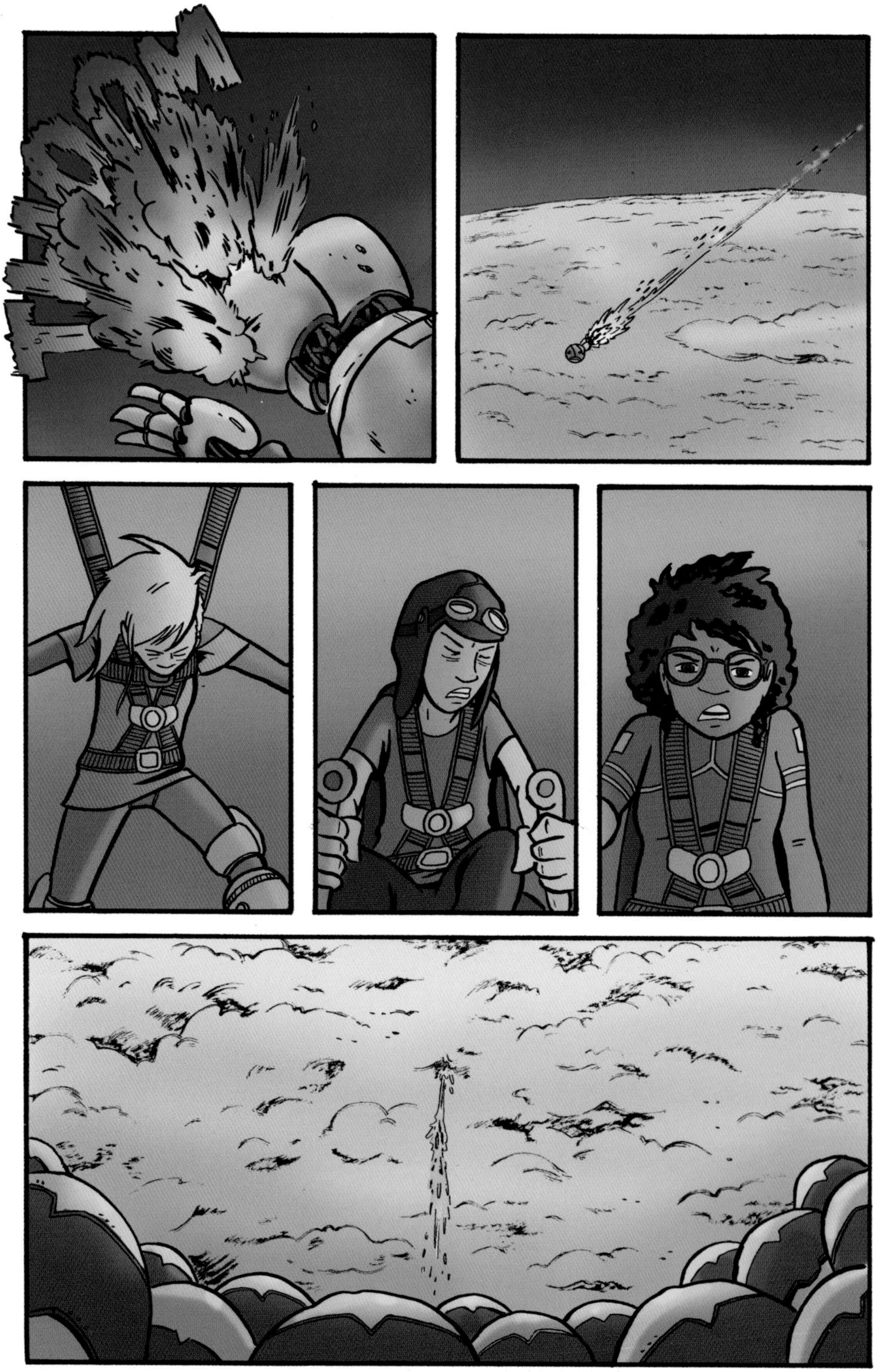
THOOM

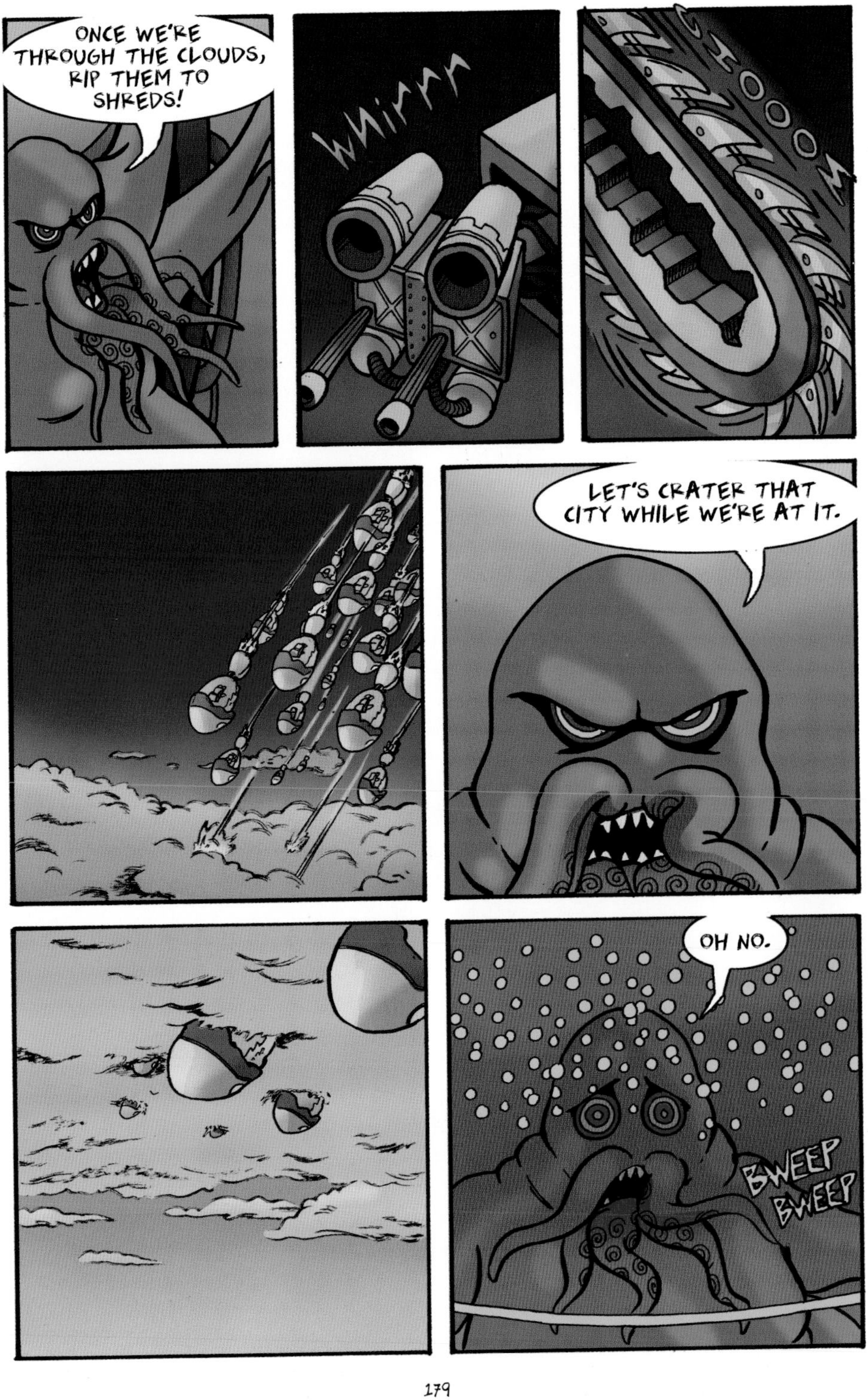
ONCE WE'RE THROUGH THE CLOUDS, RIP THEM TO SHREDS!
WHIRRR
CHOOOM
LET'S CRATER THAT CITY WHILE WE'RE AT IT.
OH NO.
BWEEP BWEEP

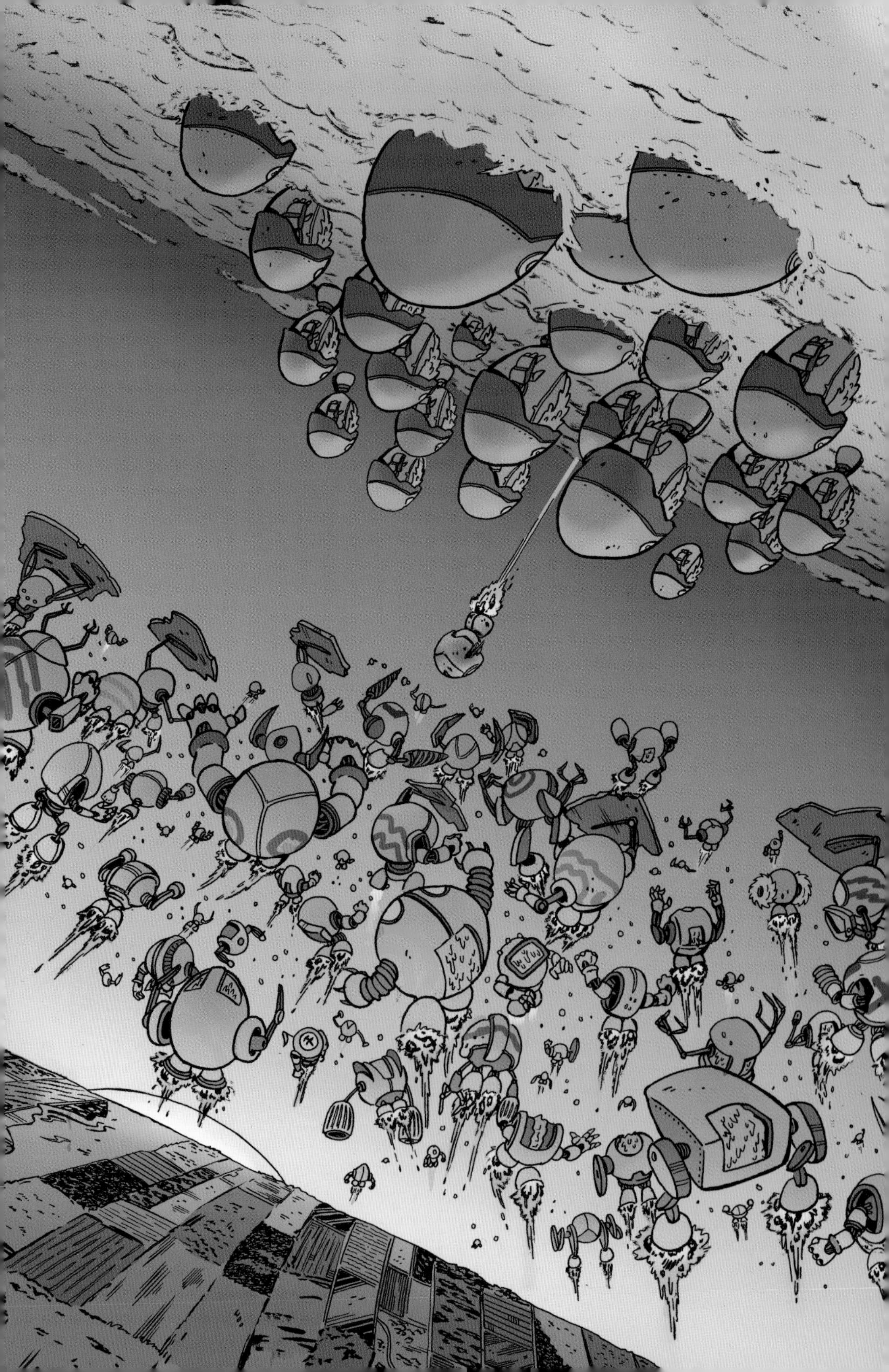

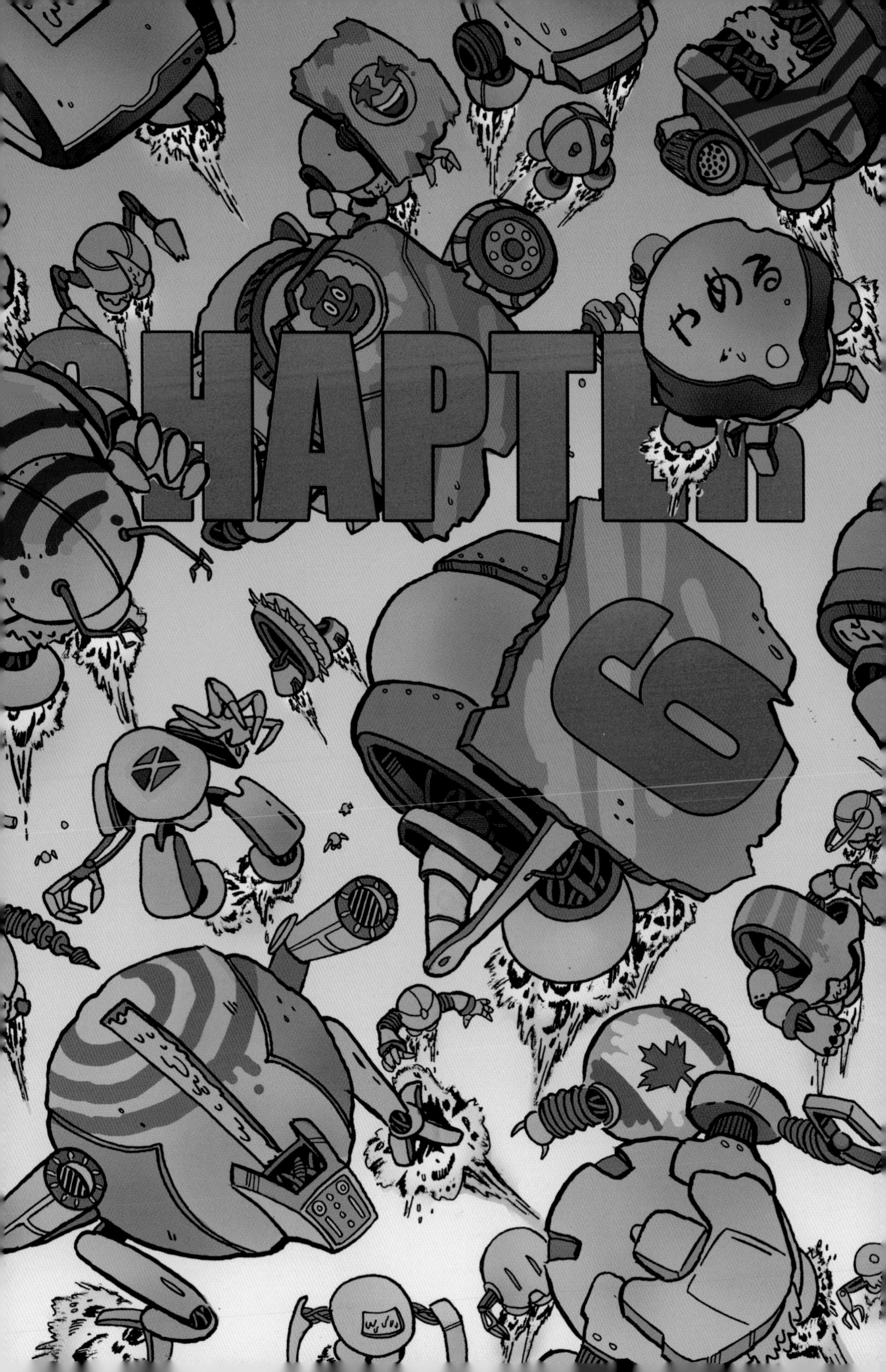
CHAPTER
6

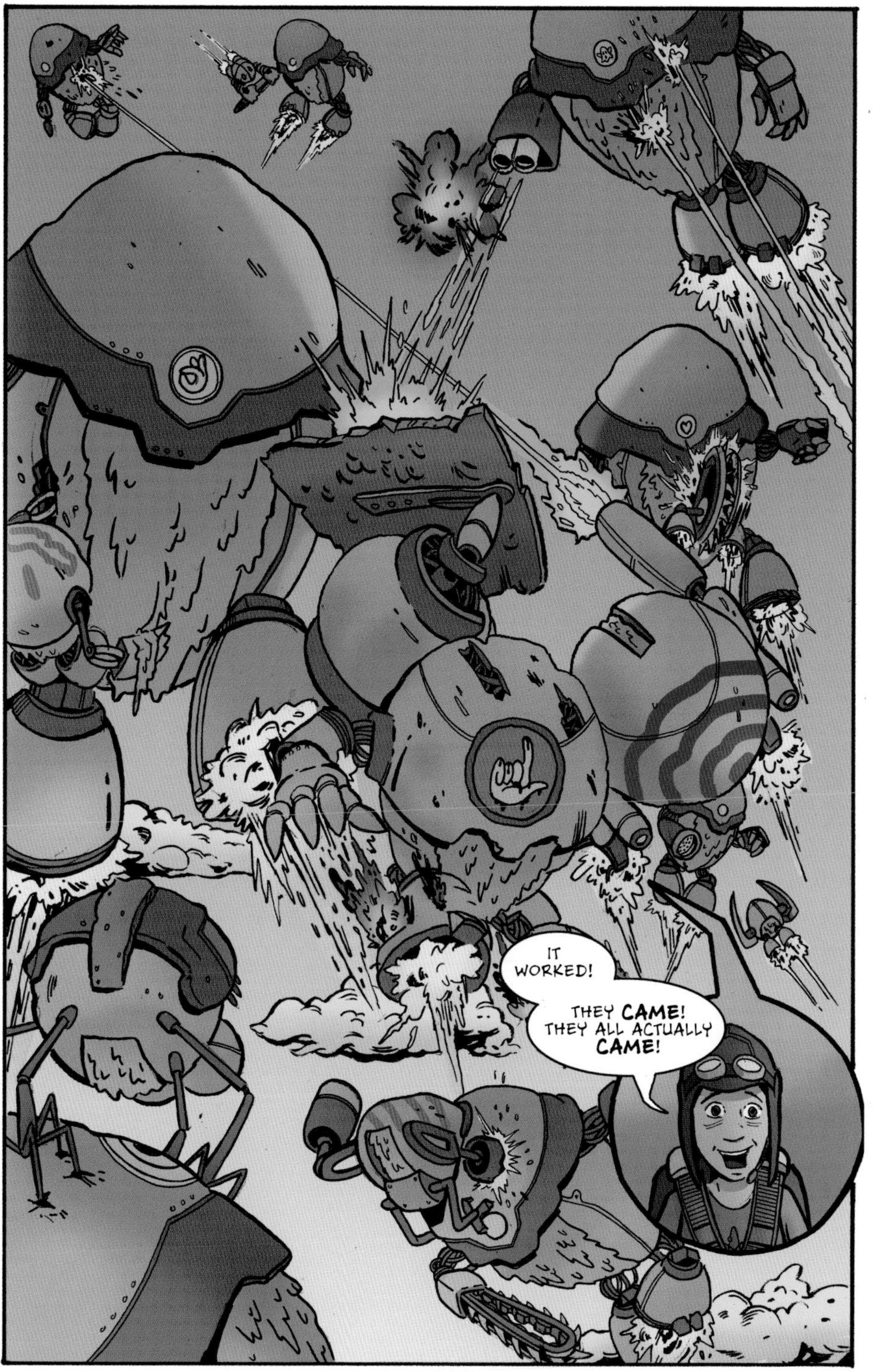
IT WORKED!
THEY CAME! THEY ALL ACTUALLY CAME!

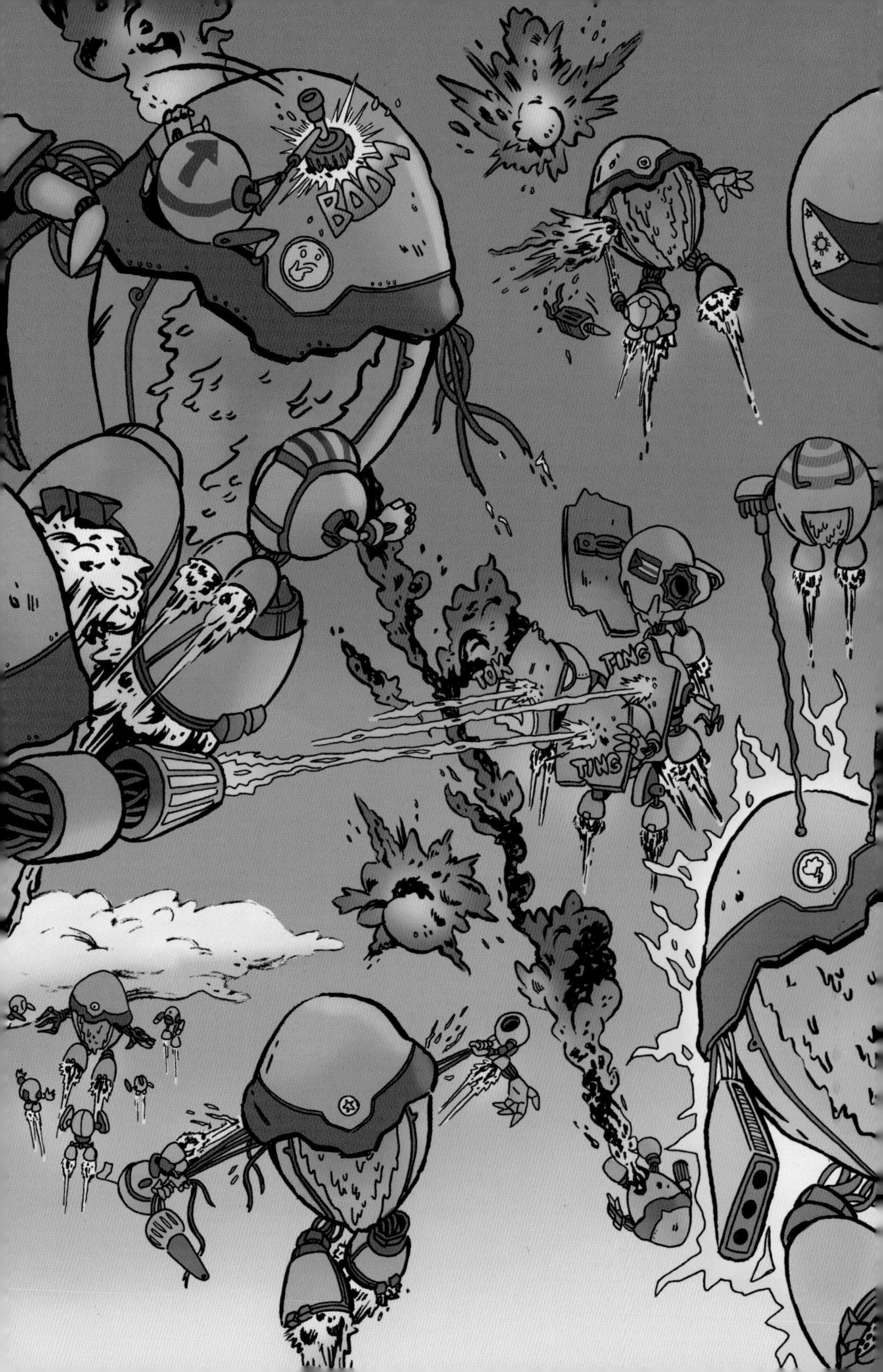
BOOM
TOK
TING
TING

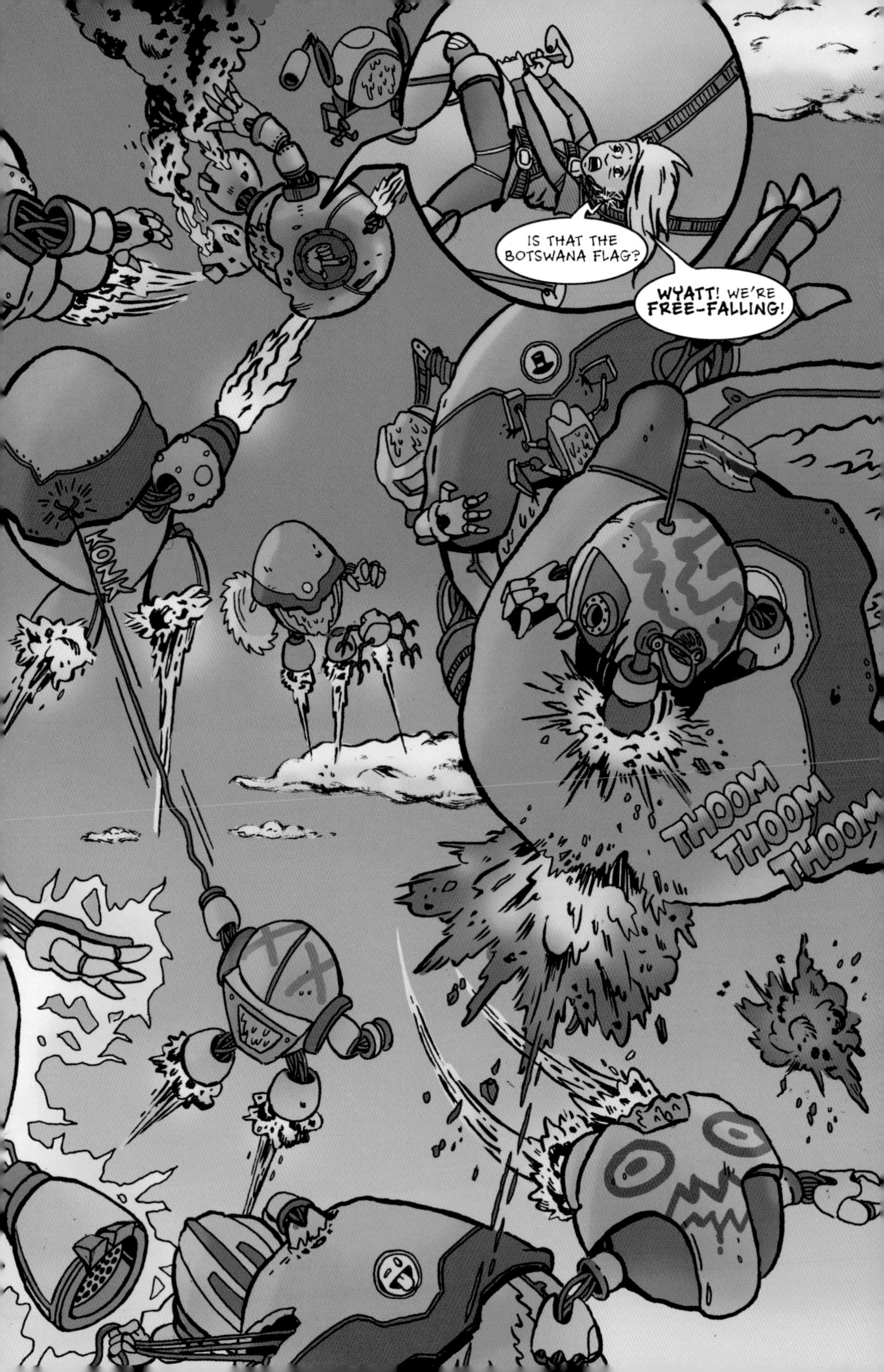

IS THAT THE BOTSWANA FLAG?
WYATT! WE'RE FREE-FALLING!
KONK
THOOM THOOM THOOM

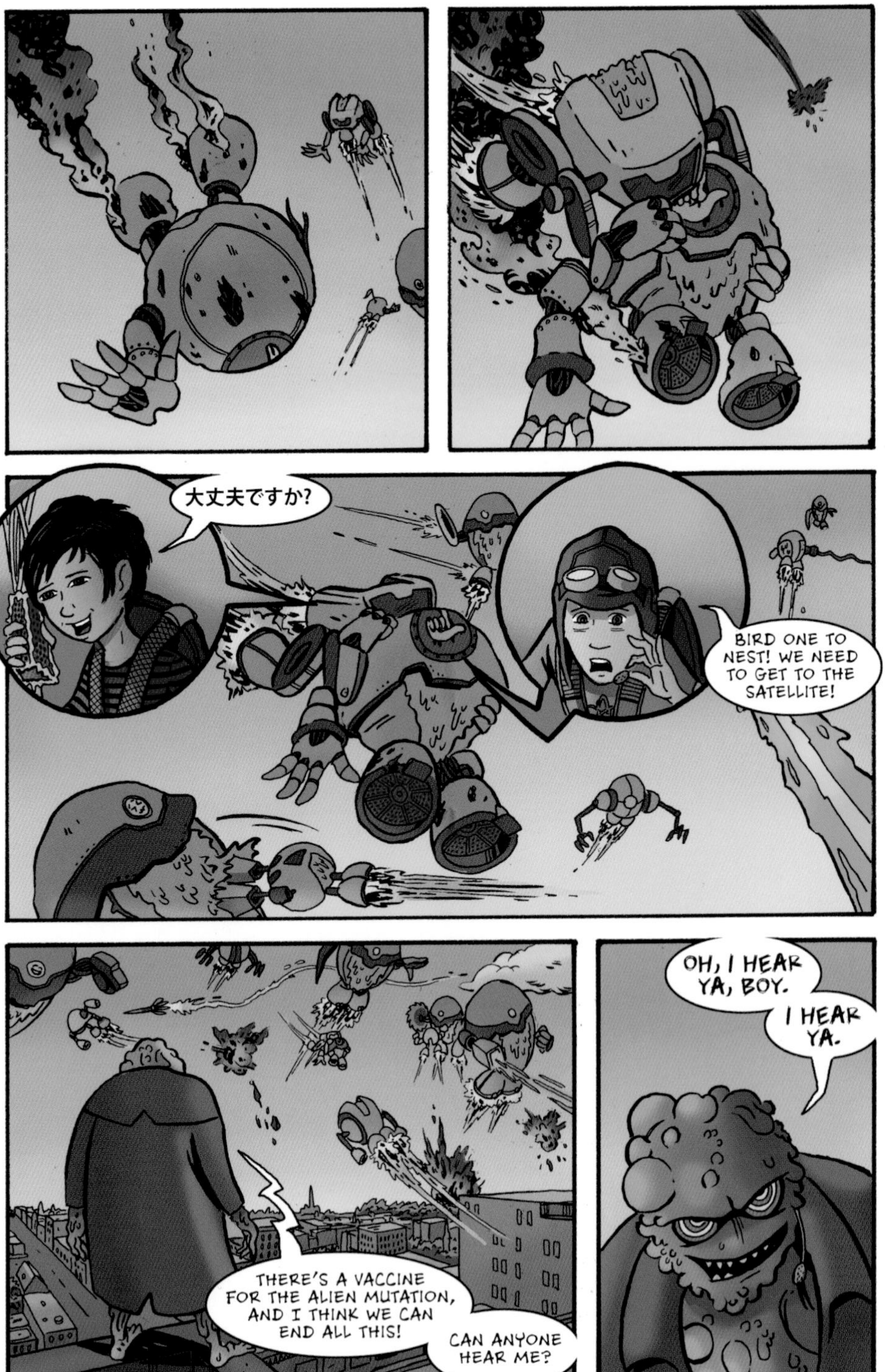
大丈夫ですか?
BIRD ONE TO NEST! WE NEED TO GET TO THE SATELLITE!
THERE'S A VACCINE FOR THE ALIEN MUTATION, AND I THINK WE CAN END ALL THIS!
CAN ANYONE HEAR ME?
OH, I HEAR YA, BOY.
I HEAR YA.

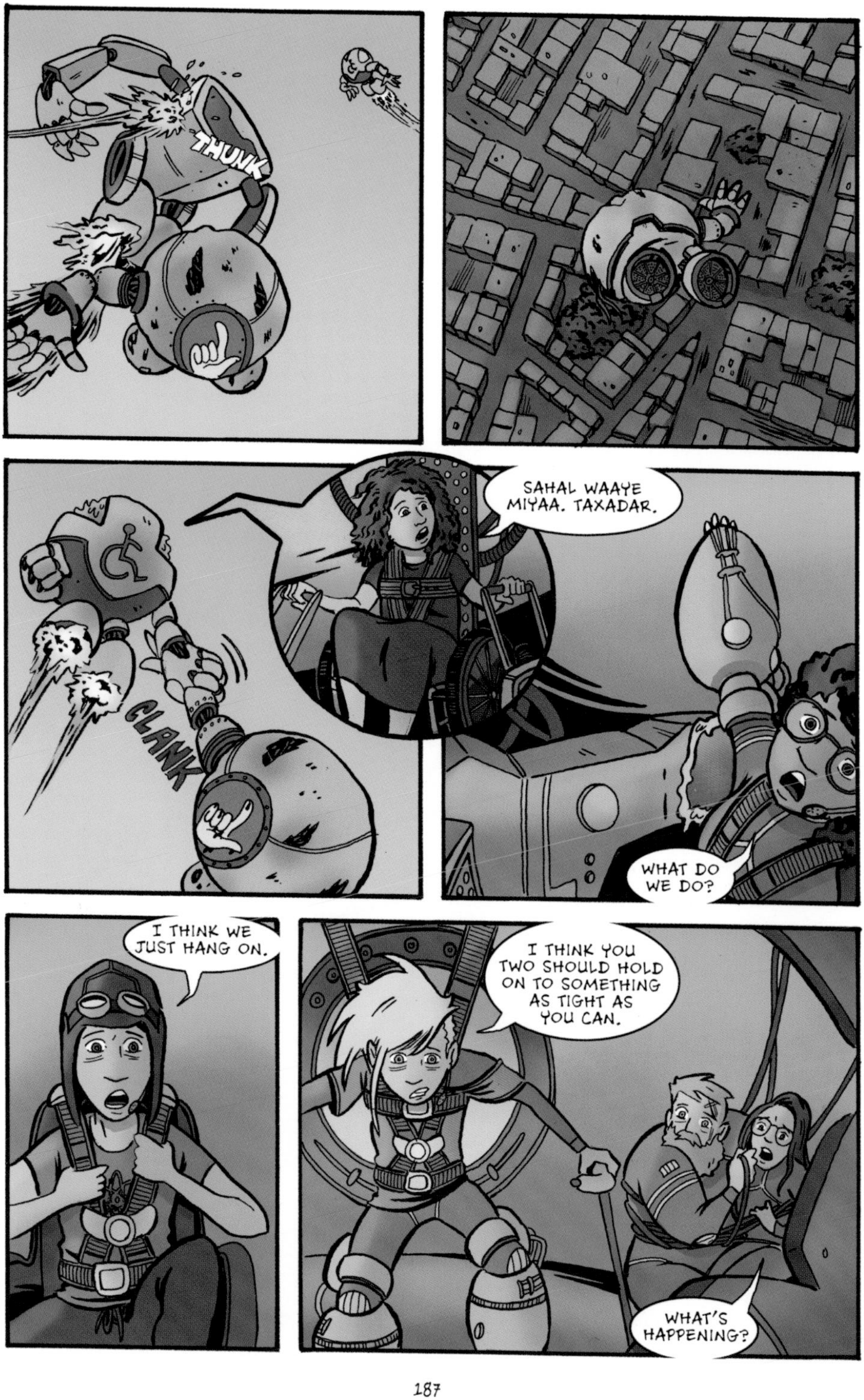
THUNK
SAHAL WAAYE MIYAA. TAXADAR.
CLANK
WHAT DO WE DO?
I THINK WE JUST HANG ON.
I THINK YOU TWO SHOULD HOLD ON TO SOMETHING AS TIGHT AS YOU CAN.
WHAT'S HAPPENING?

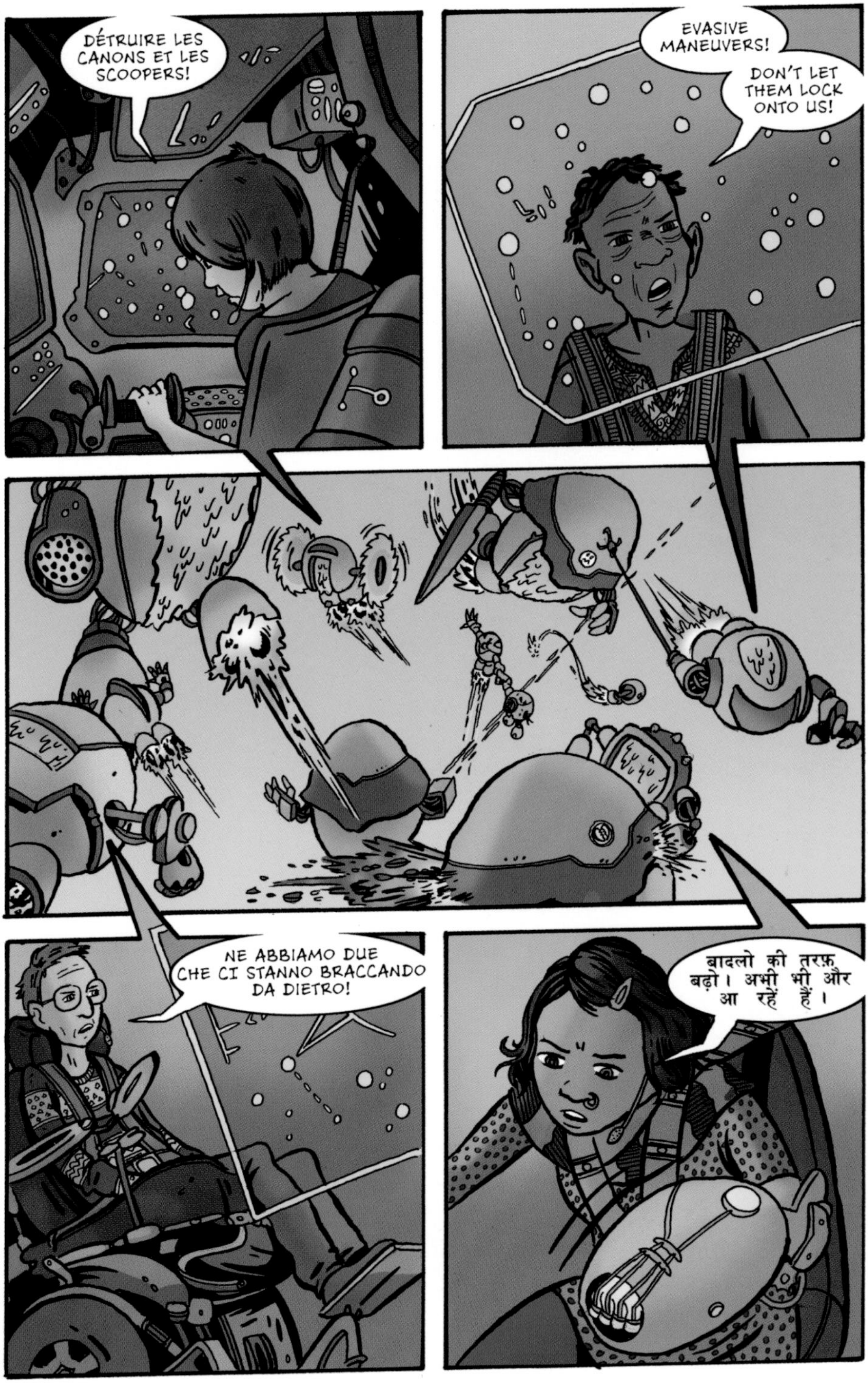
DÉTRUIRE LES CANONS ET LES SCOOPERS!
EVASIVE MANEUVERS!
DON'T LET THEM LOCK ONTO US!
NE ABBIAMO DUE CHE CI STANNO BRACCANDO DA DIETRO!
बादलो की तरफ़ बढ़ो। अभी भी और आ रहें हैं।

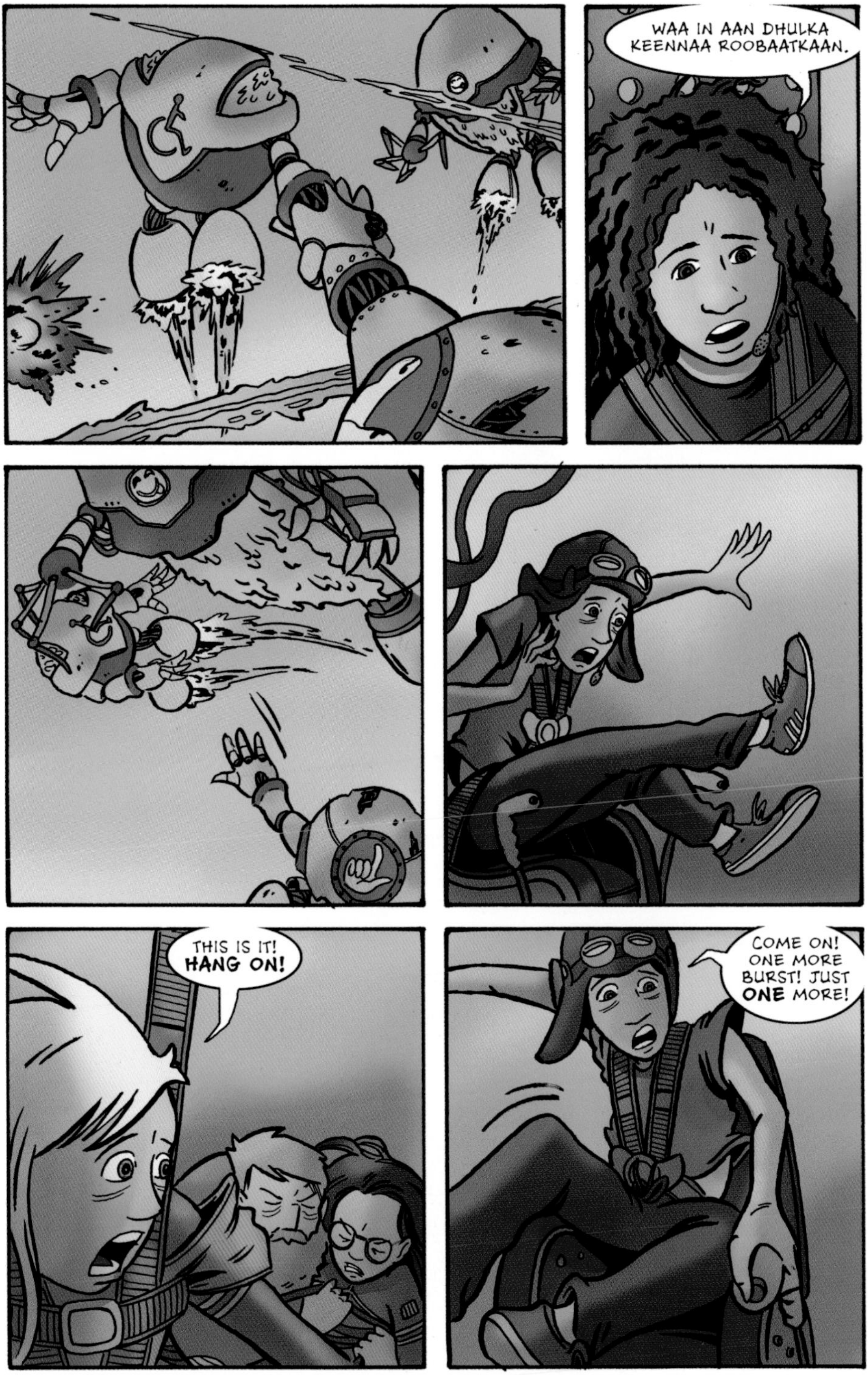

WAA IN AAN DHULKA KEENNAA ROOBAATKAAN.
THIS IS IT! HANG ON!
COME ON! ONE MORE BURST! JUST ONE MORE!

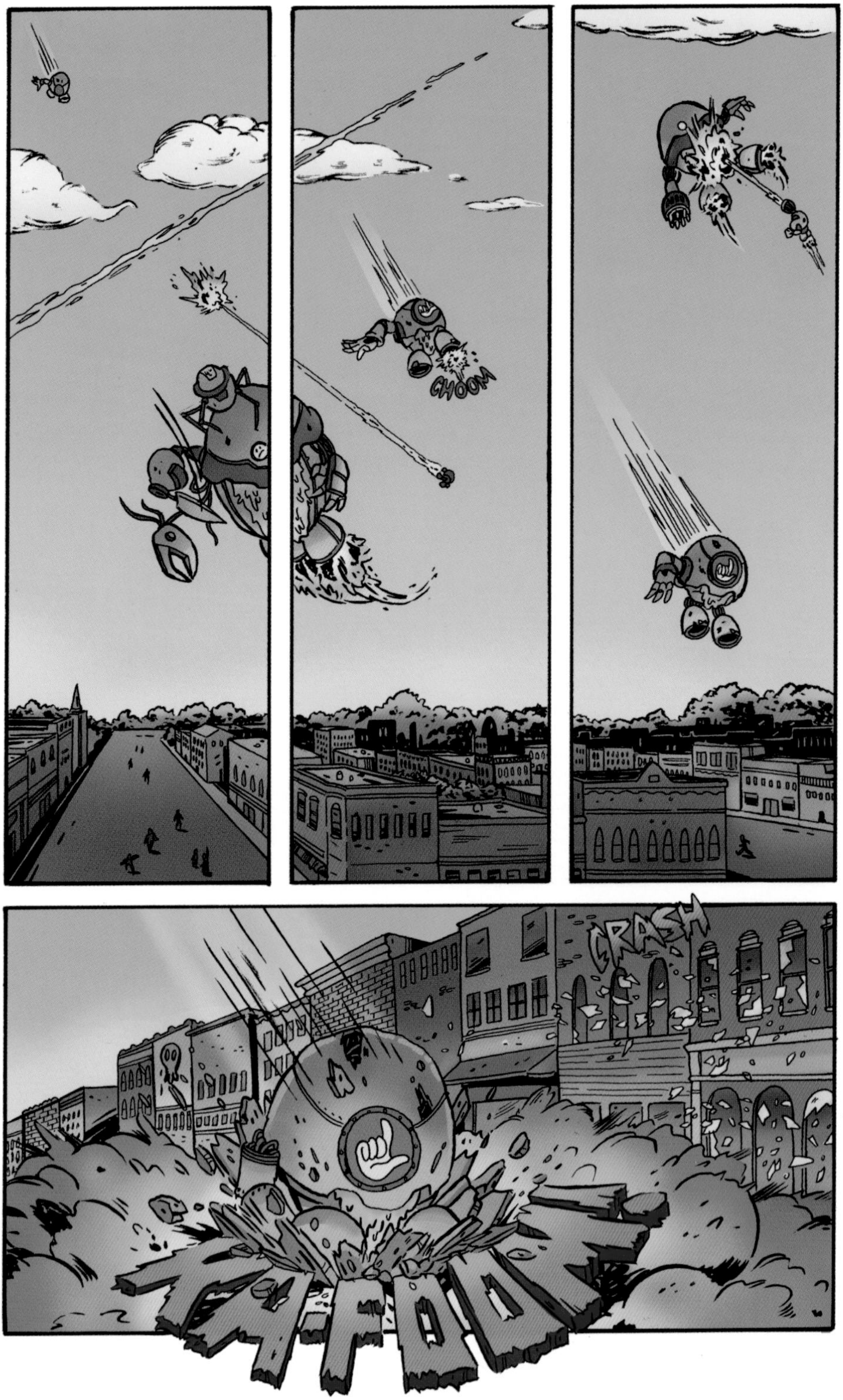
CHOOM
CRASH
KA-FOOM

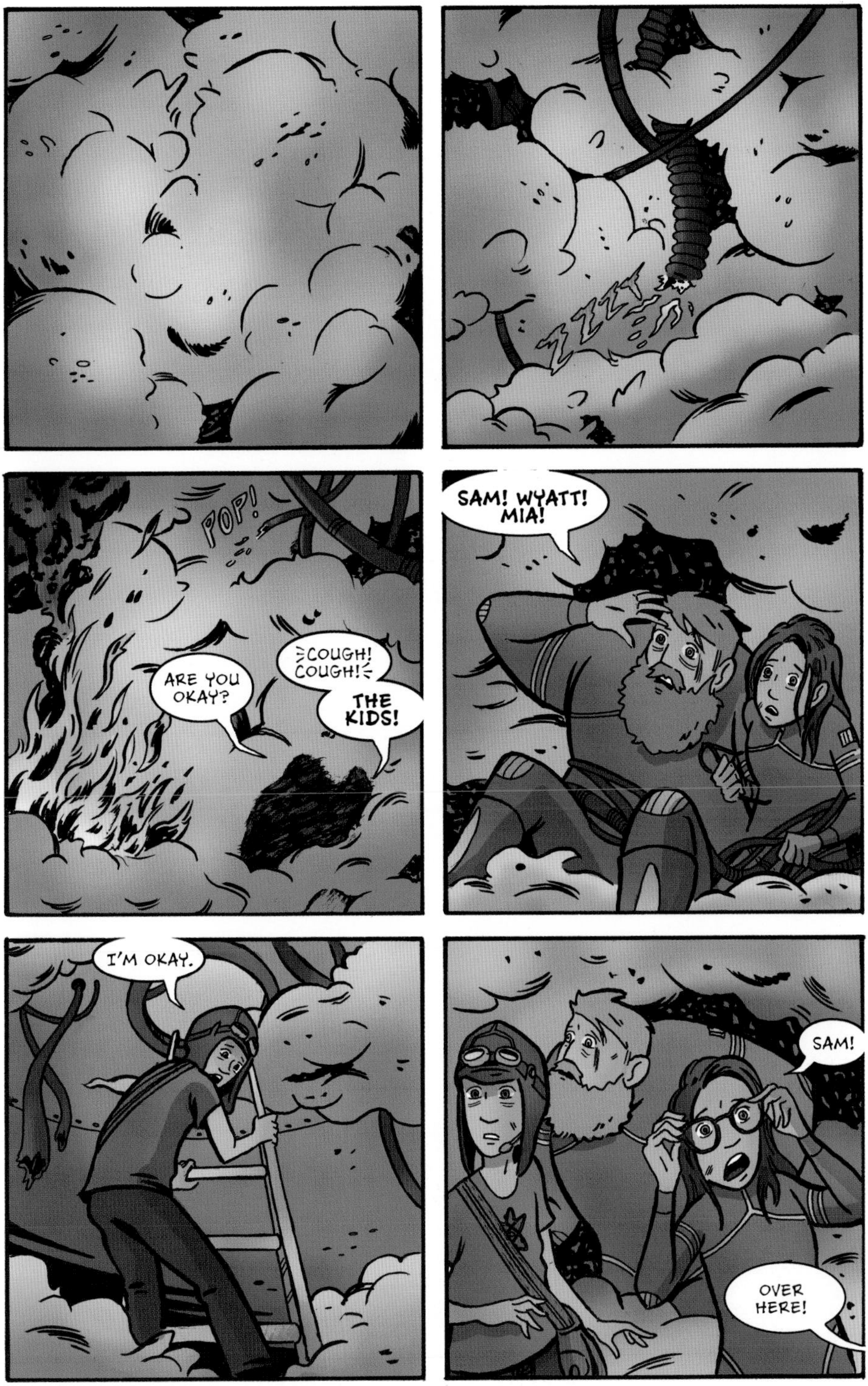
ZZZZT
POP!
ARE YOU OKAY?
COUGH! COUGH!
THE KIDS!
SAM! WYATT! MIA!
I'M OKAY.
SAM!
OVER HERE!

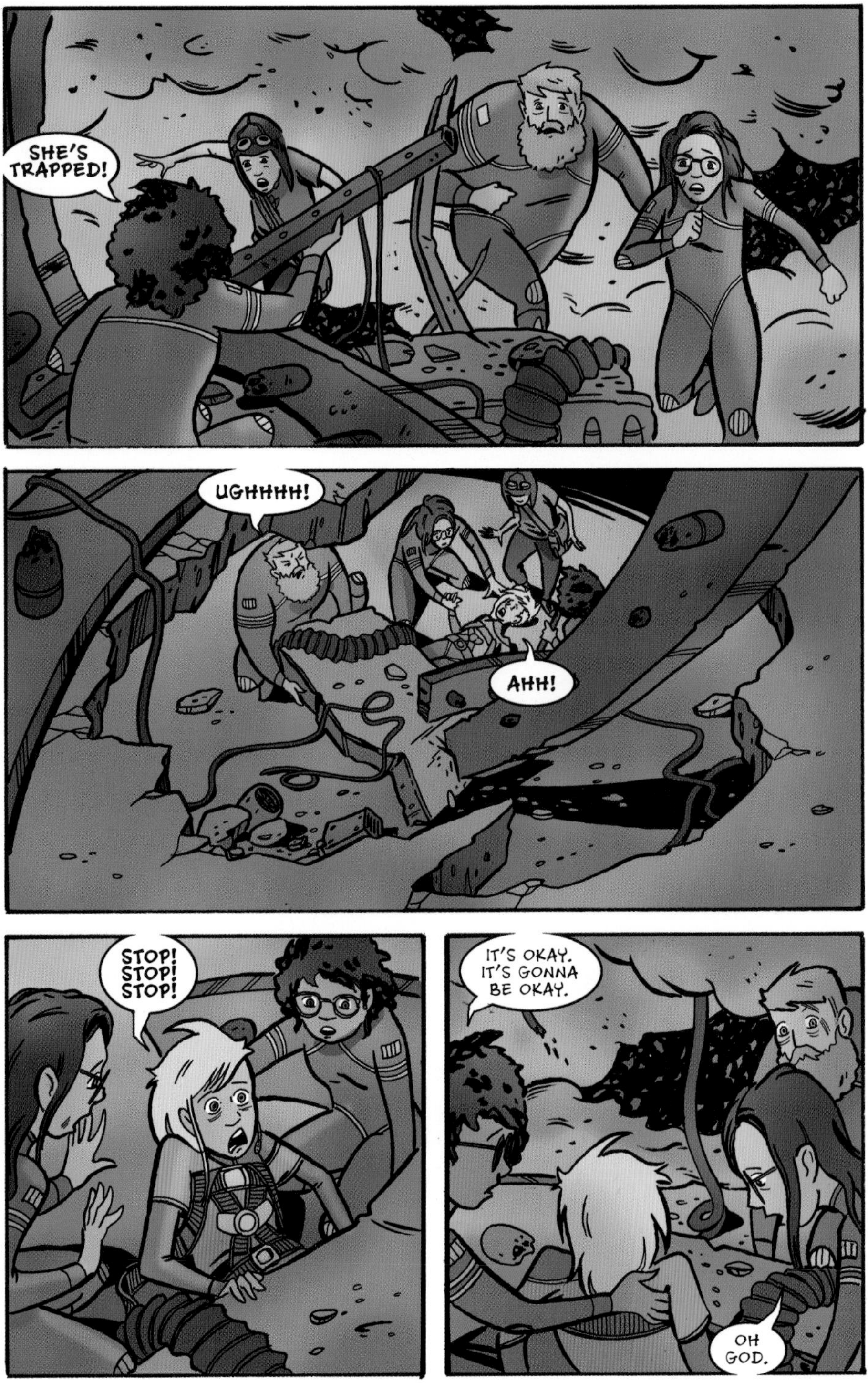
SHE'S TRAPPED!
UGHHHH!
AHH!
STOP! STOP! STOP!
IT'S OKAY. IT'S GONNA BE OKAY.
OH GOD.

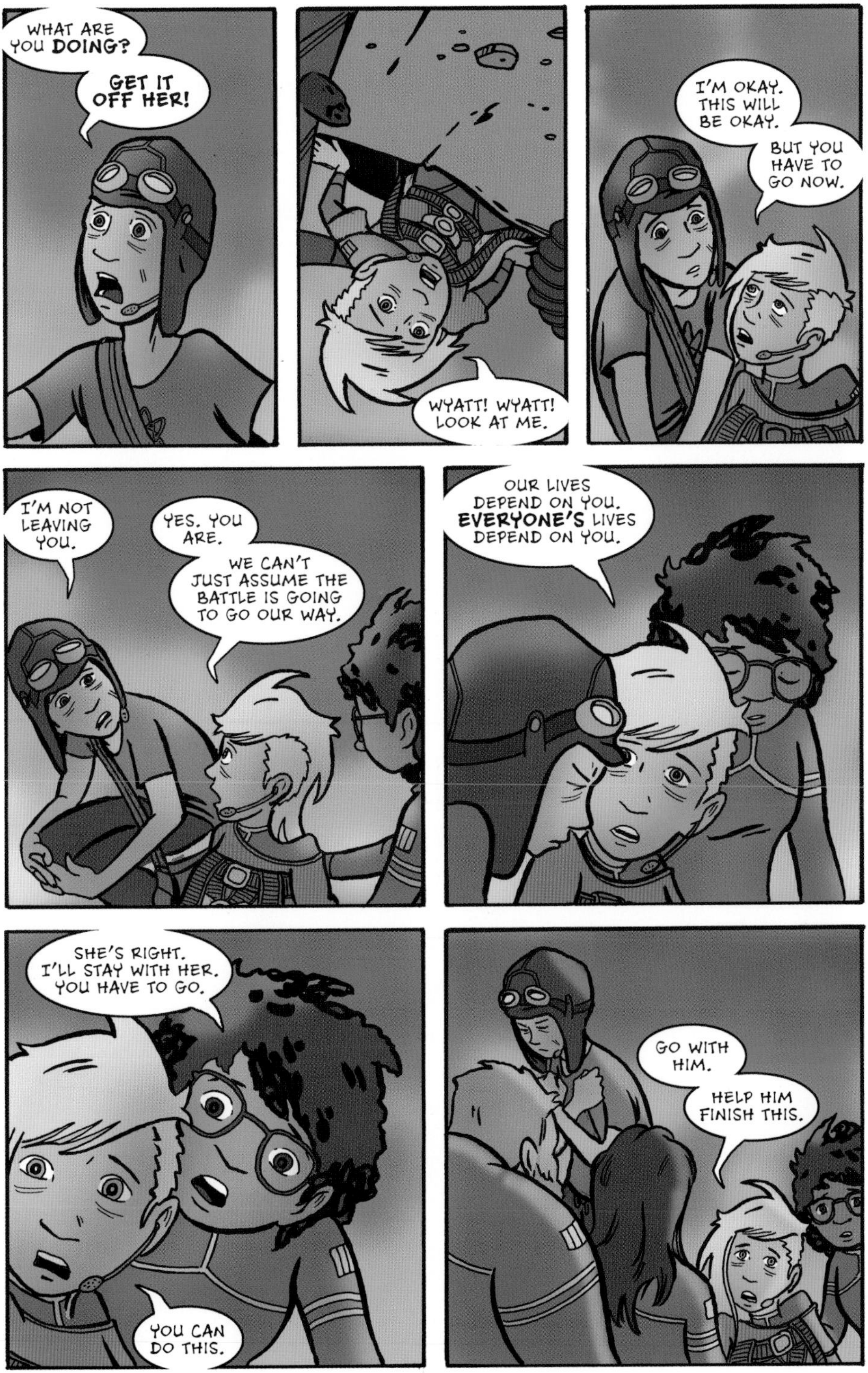
WHAT ARE YOU DOING?
GET IT OFF HER!
WYATT! WYATT! LOOK AT ME.
I'M OKAY. THIS WILL BE OKAY.
BUT YOU HAVE TO GO NOW.
I'M NOT LEAVING YOU.
YES. YOU ARE.
WE CAN'T JUST ASSUME THE BATTLE IS GOING TO GO OUR WAY.
OUR LIVES DEPEND ON YOU. EVERYONE'S LIVES DEPEND ON YOU.
SHE'S RIGHT. I'LL STAY WITH HER. YOU HAVE TO GO.
YOU CAN DO THIS.
GO WITH HIM.
HELP HIM FINISH THIS.

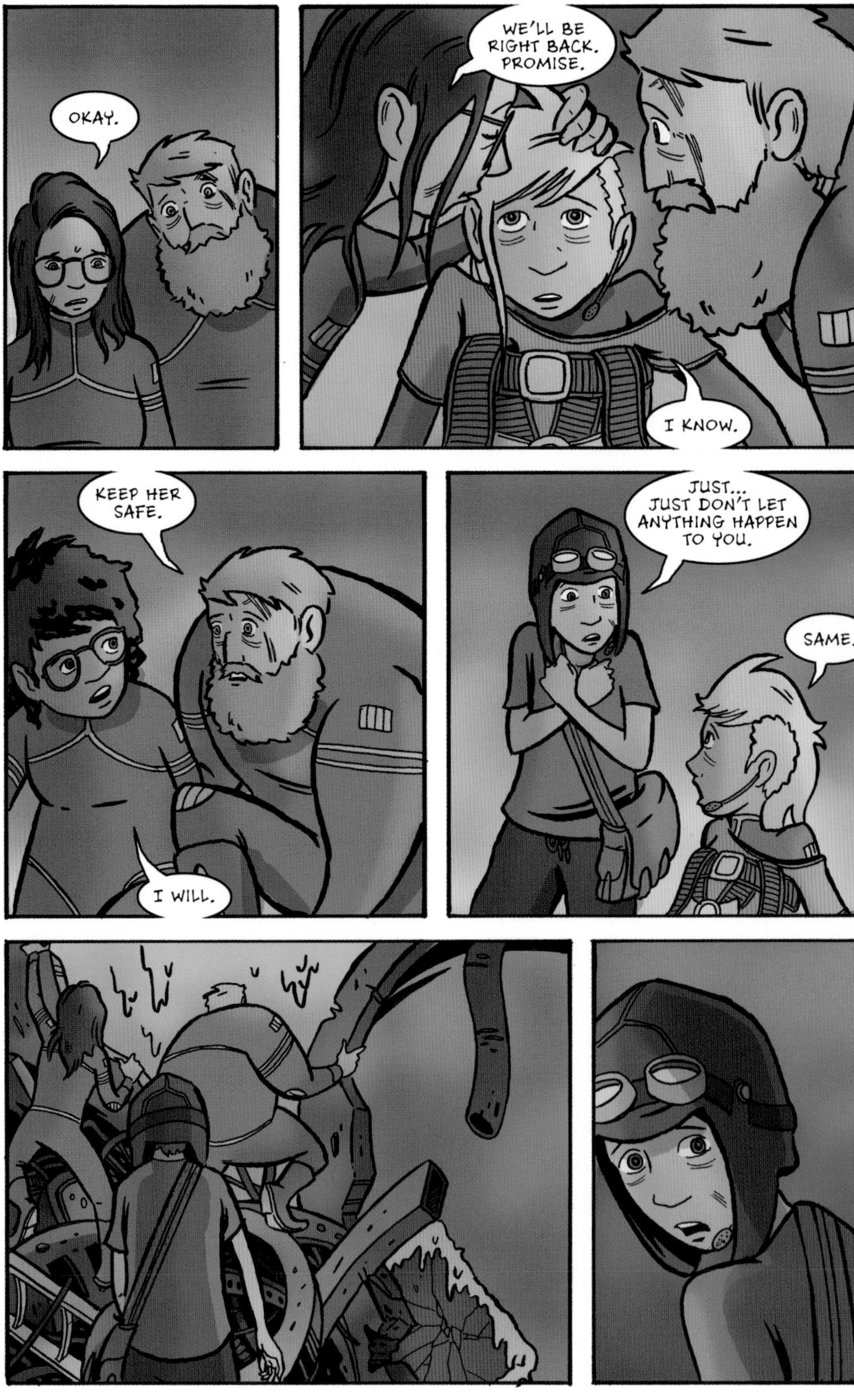
OKAY.
WE'LL BE RIGHT BACK. PROMISE.
I KNOW.
KEEP HER SAFE.
I WILL.
JUST... JUST DON'T LET ANYTHING HAPPEN TO YOU.
SAME.

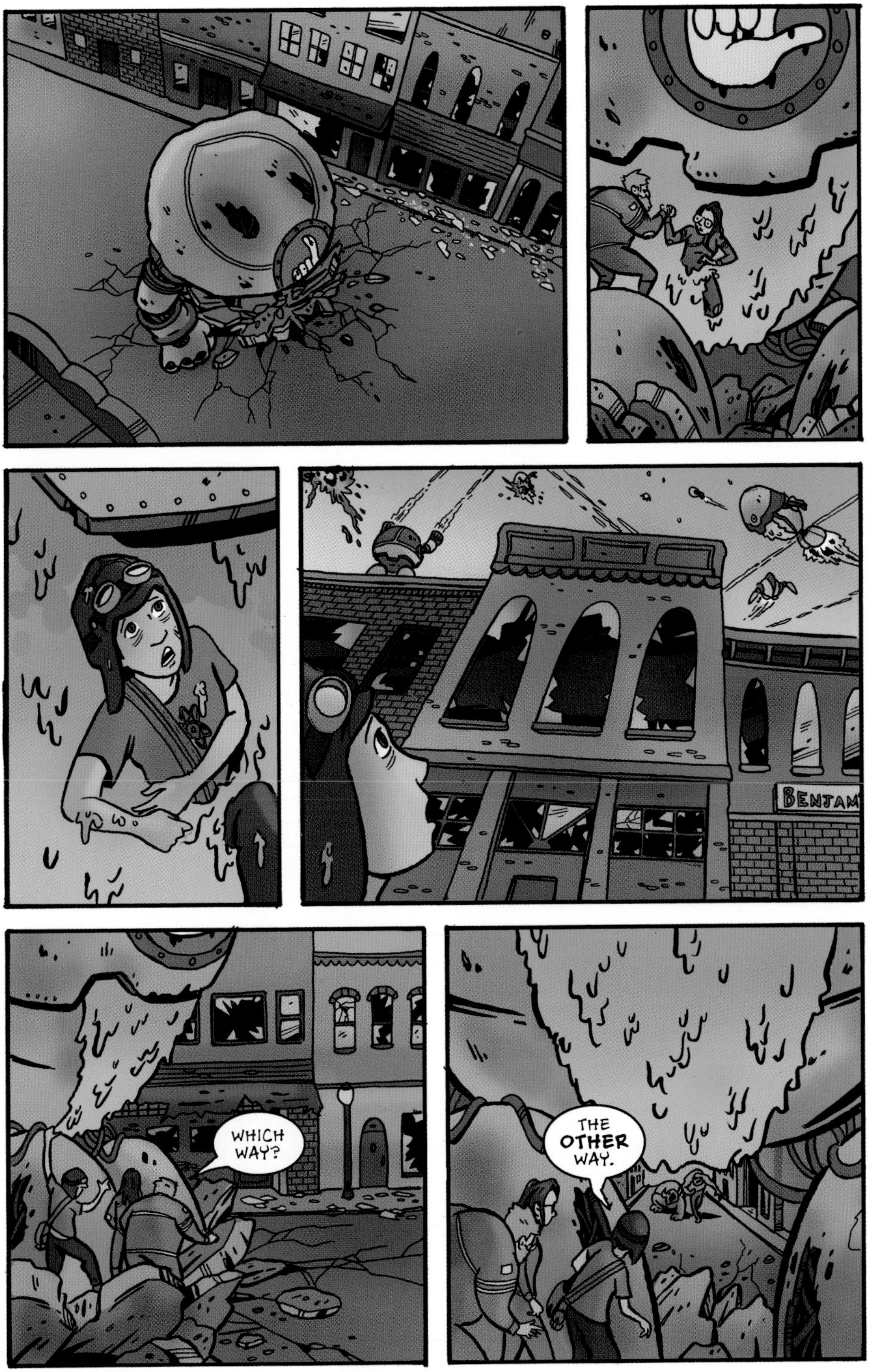
BENJAM
WHICH WAY?
THE OTHER WAY.

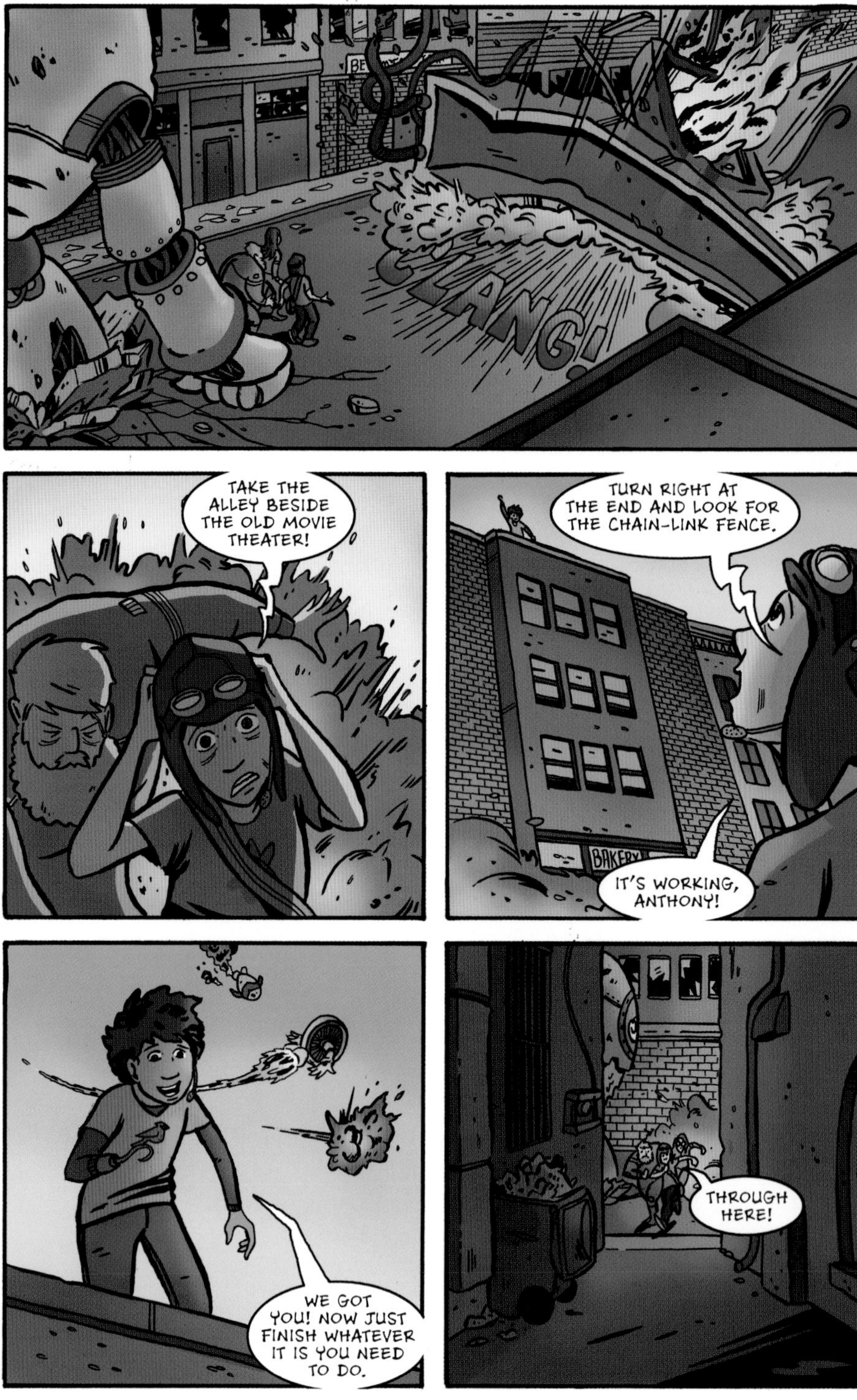
CLANG!
TAKE THE ALLEY BESIDE THE OLD MOVIE THEATER!
TURN RIGHT AT THE END AND LOOK FOR THE CHAIN-LINK FENCE.
BAKERY
IT'S WORKING, ANTHONY!
WE GOT YOU! NOW JUST FINISH WHATEVER IT IS YOU NEED TO DO.
THROUGH HERE!

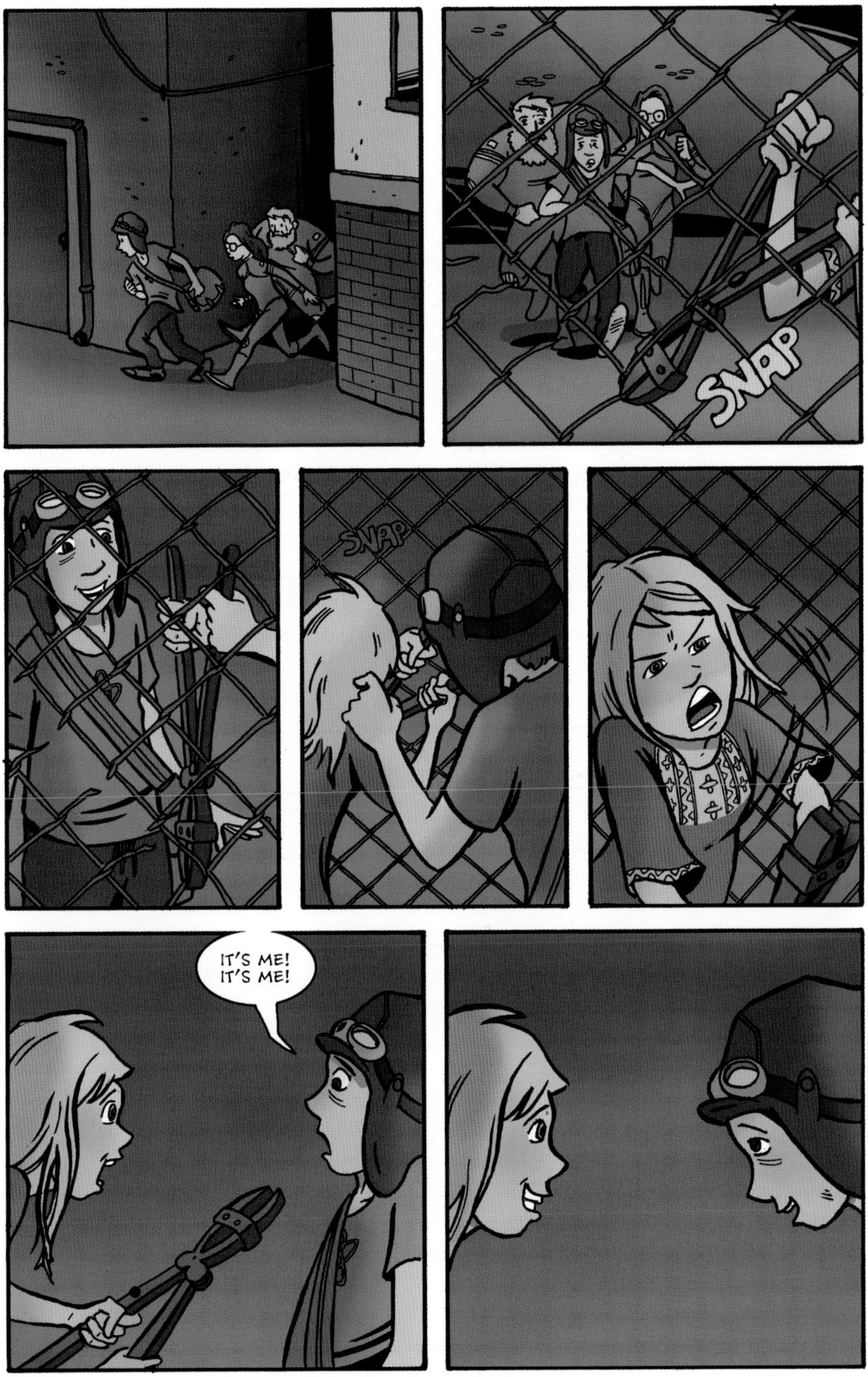
SNAP
SNAP
IT'S ME! IT'S ME!

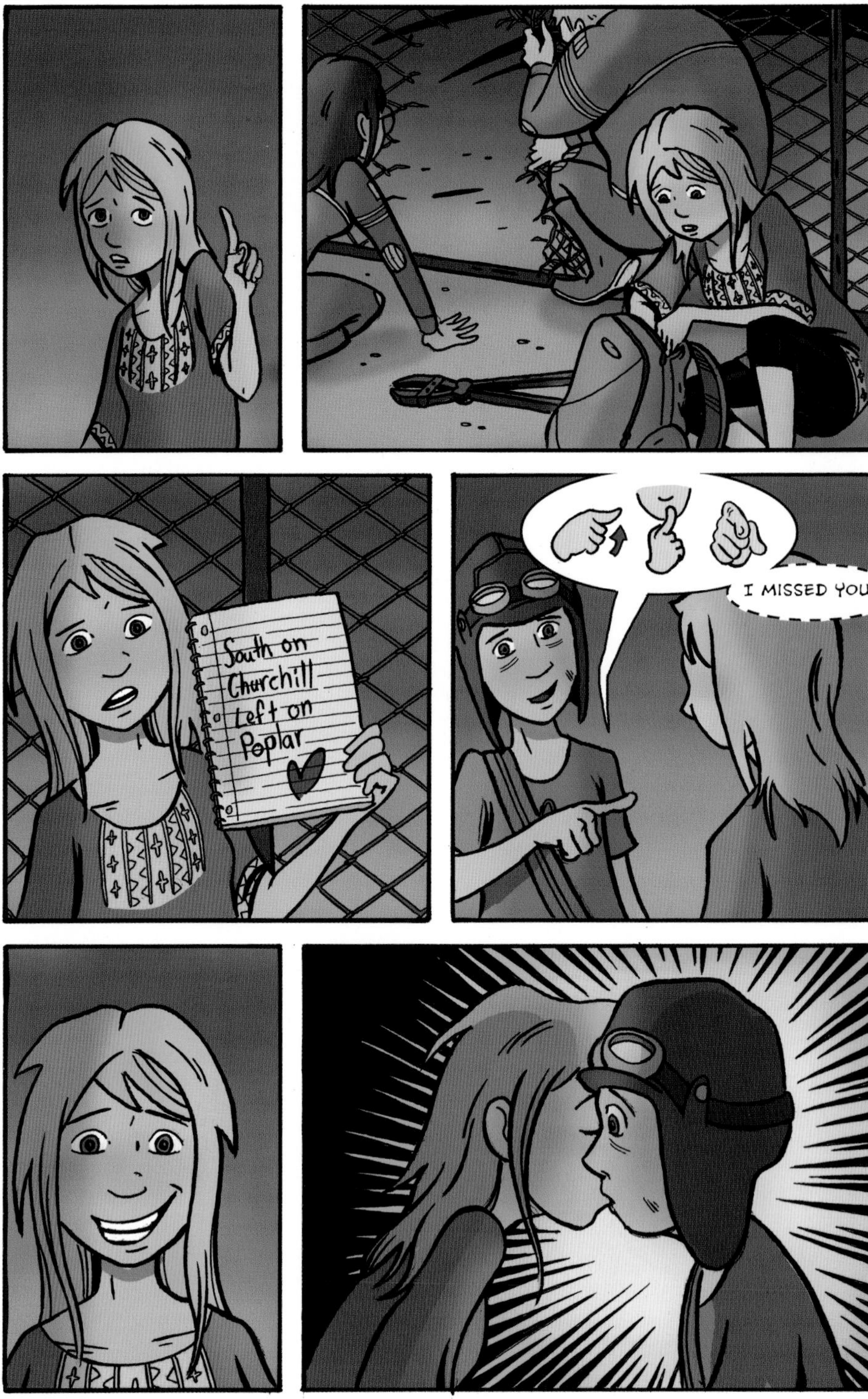
South on Churchill
Left on Poplar
I MISSED YOU.

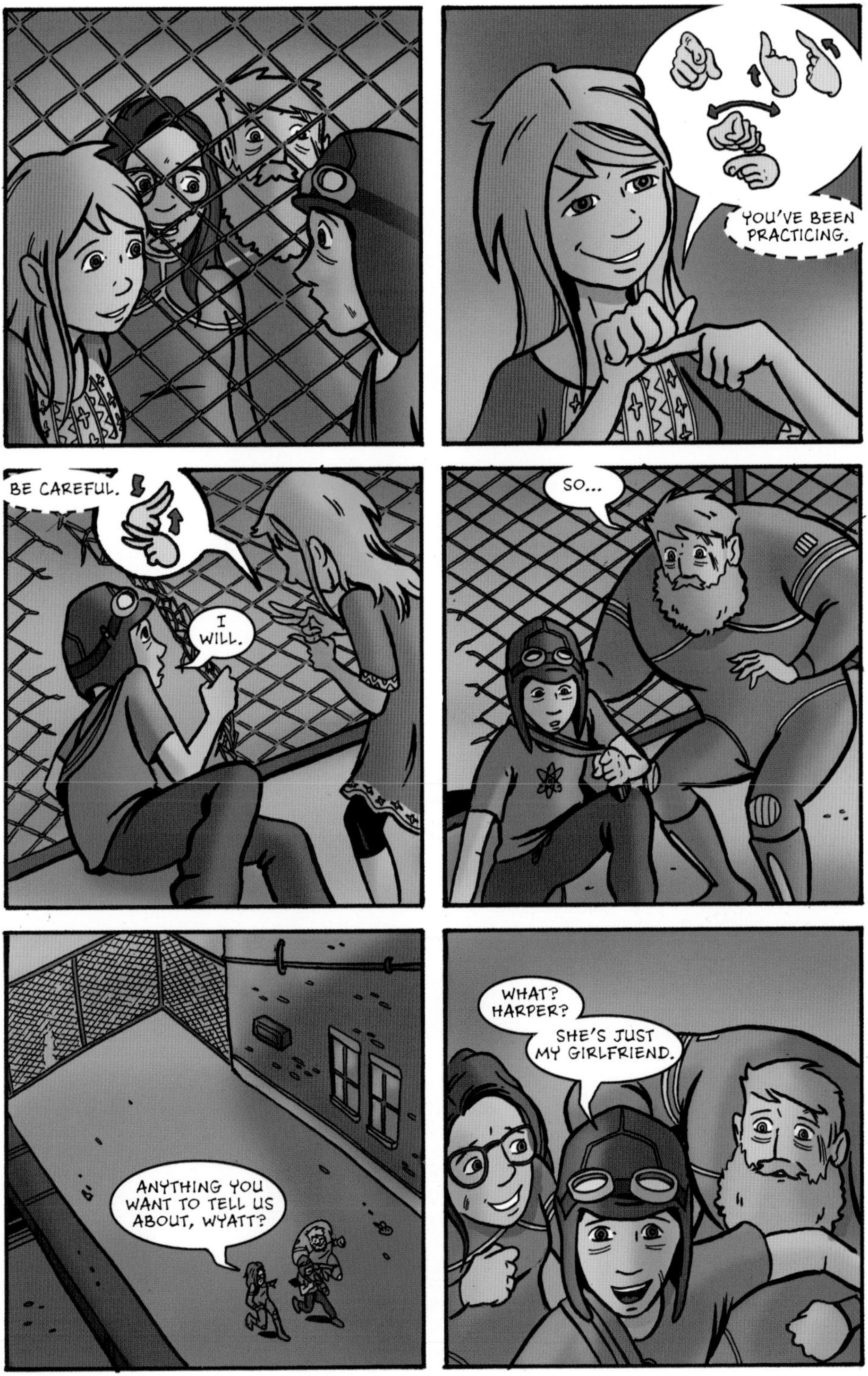
YOU'VE BEEN PRACTICING.
BE CAREFUL.
I WILL.
SO...
ANYTHING YOU WANT TO TELL US ABOUT, WYATT?
WHAT? HARPER?
SHE'S JUST MY GIRLFRIEND.

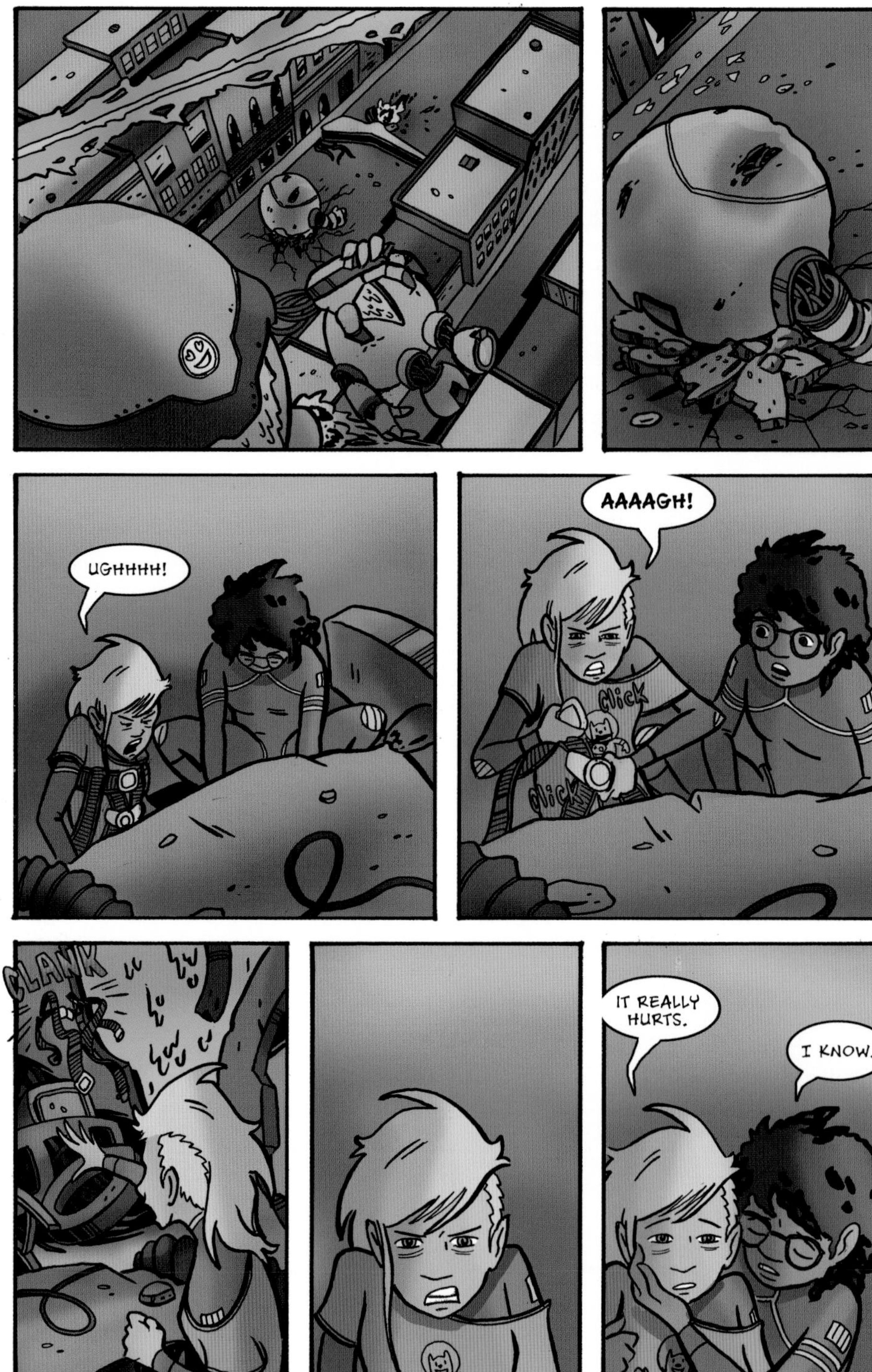
UGHHHH!
AAAAGH!
CLICK
CLICK
CLANK
IT REALLY HURTS.
I KNOW.

AFTER EVERYTHING, WHEN IT COUNTS THE MOST, I'M PINNED DOWN AND STUCK HERE.

HE'LL BE OKAY. JUST TRY TO BREATHE SLOWLY.

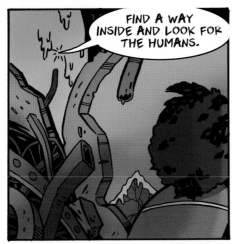

FIND A WAY INSIDE AND LOOK FOR THE HUMANS.

LEAVE NO SURVIVORS!

YOU NEED TO BARRICADE THE ENTRANCE.

FAST.

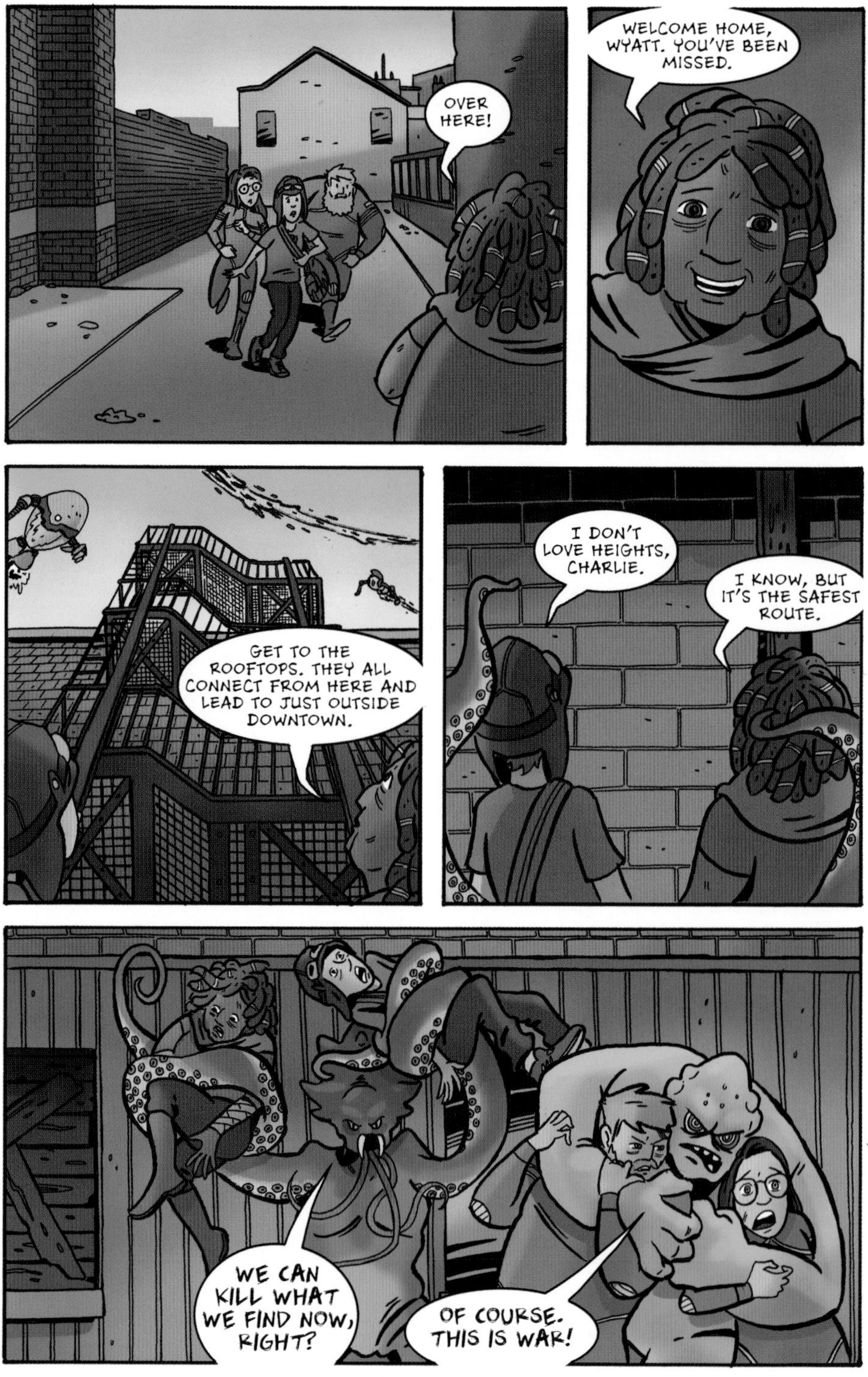
OVER HERE!
WELCOME HOME, WYATT. YOU'VE BEEN MISSED.
GET TO THE ROOFTOPS. THEY ALL CONNECT FROM HERE AND LEAD TO JUST OUTSIDE DOWNTOWN.
I DON'T LOVE HEIGHTS, CHARLIE.
I KNOW, BUT IT'S THE SAFEST ROUTE.
WE CAN KILL WHAT WE FIND NOW, RIGHT?
OF COURSE. THIS IS WAR!

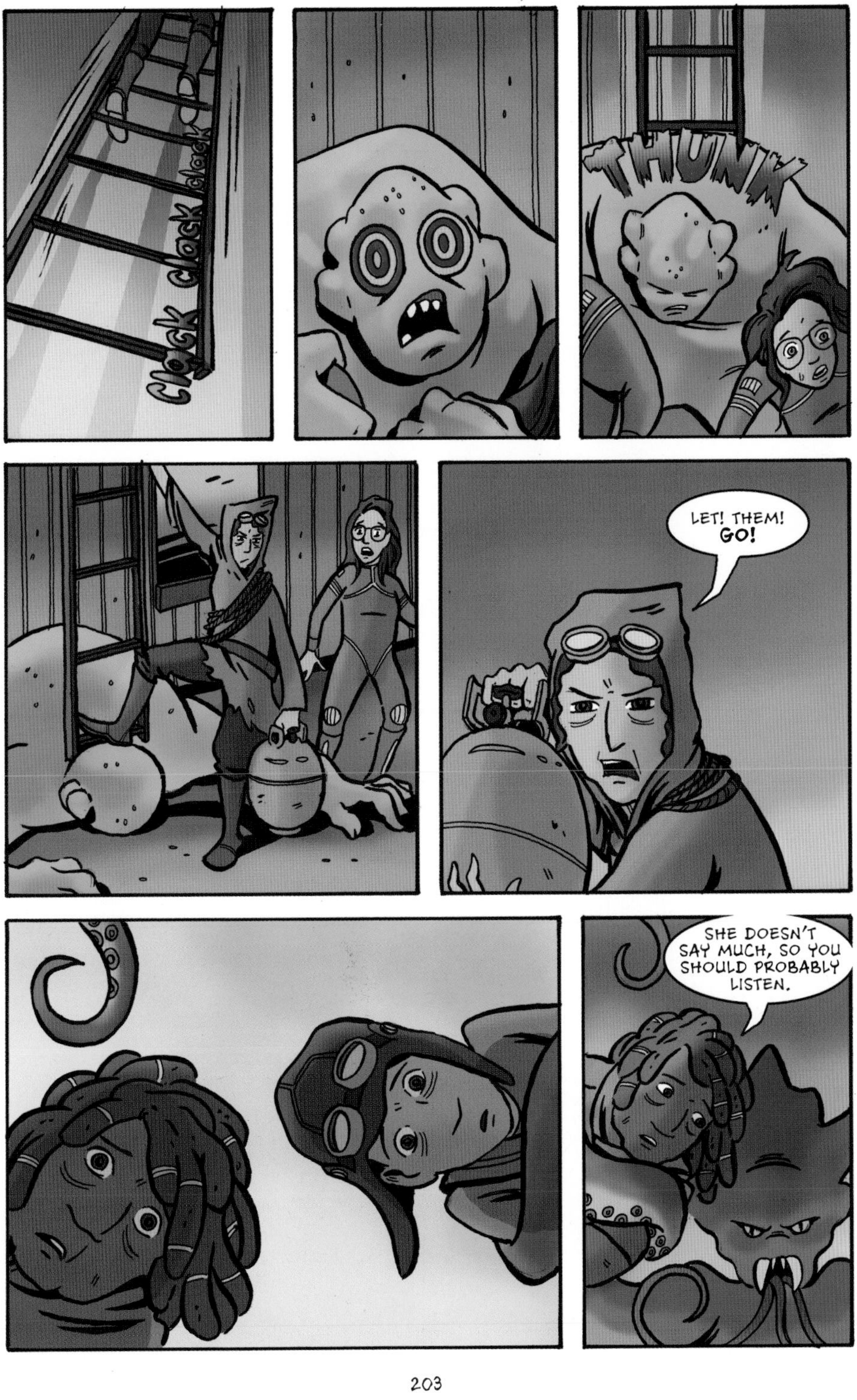
CLACK CLACK clack clack
THUNK
LET! THEM! GO!
SHE DOESN'T SAY MUCH, SO YOU SHOULD PROBABLY LISTEN.

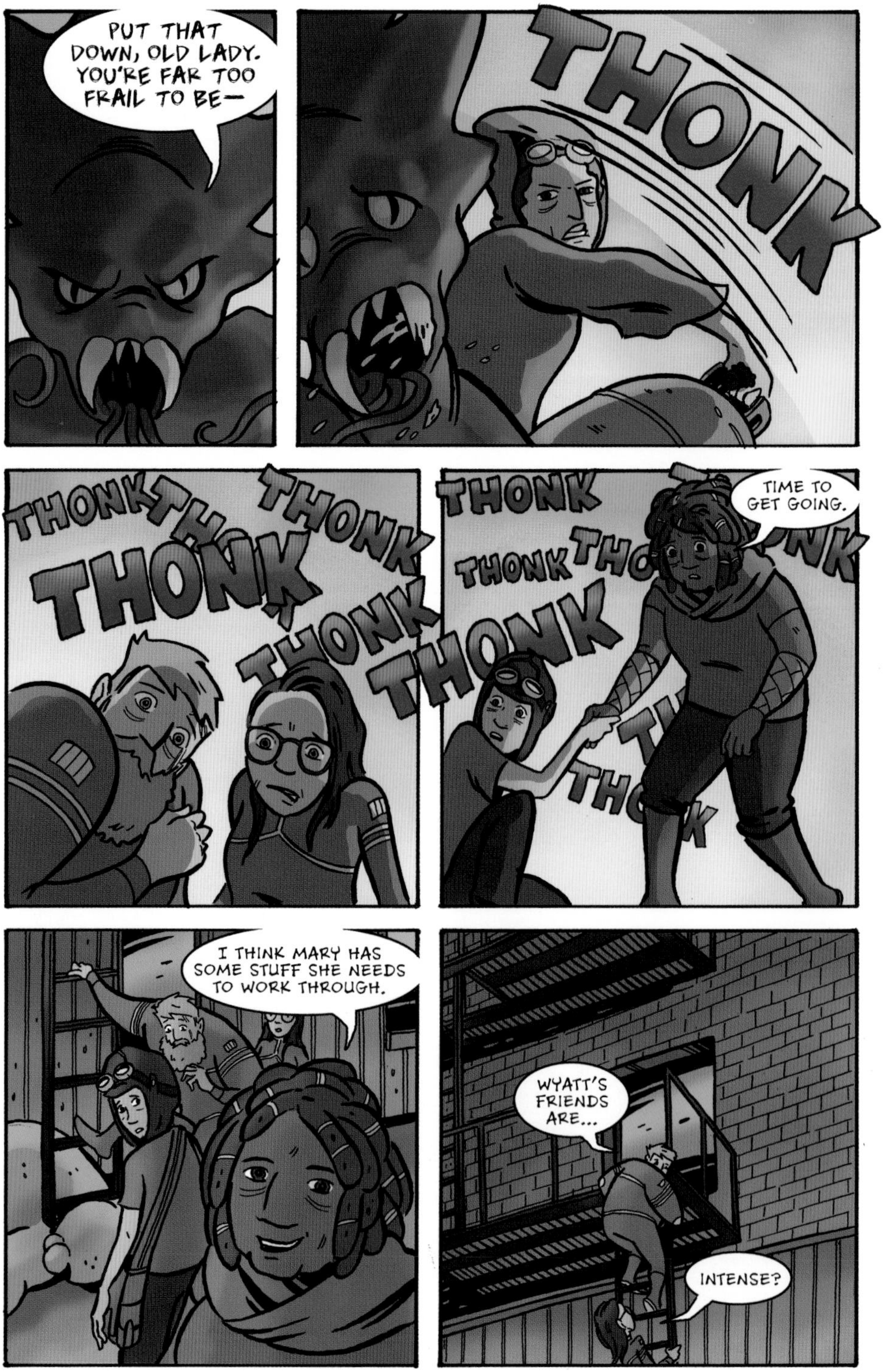
PUT THAT DOWN, OLD LADY. YOU'RE FAR TOO FRAIL TO BE—
THONK
THONK
THONK
THONK
THONK
THONK
TIME TO GET GOING.
THONK
THONK
I THINK MARY HAS SOME STUFF SHE NEEDS TO WORK THROUGH.
WYATT'S FRIENDS ARE...
INTENSE?

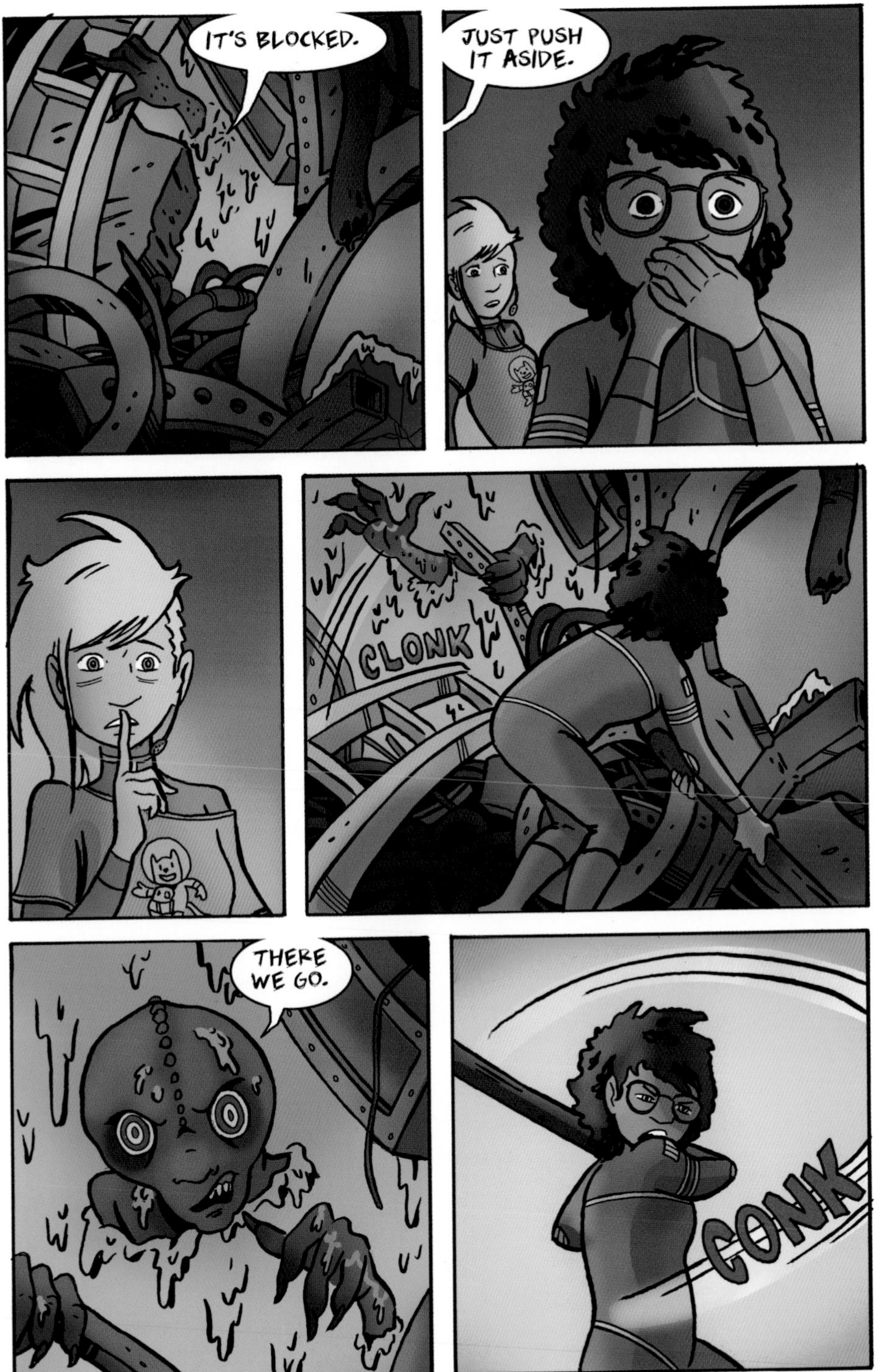
IT'S BLOCKED.
JUST PUSH IT ASIDE.
CLONK
THERE WE GO.
CONK

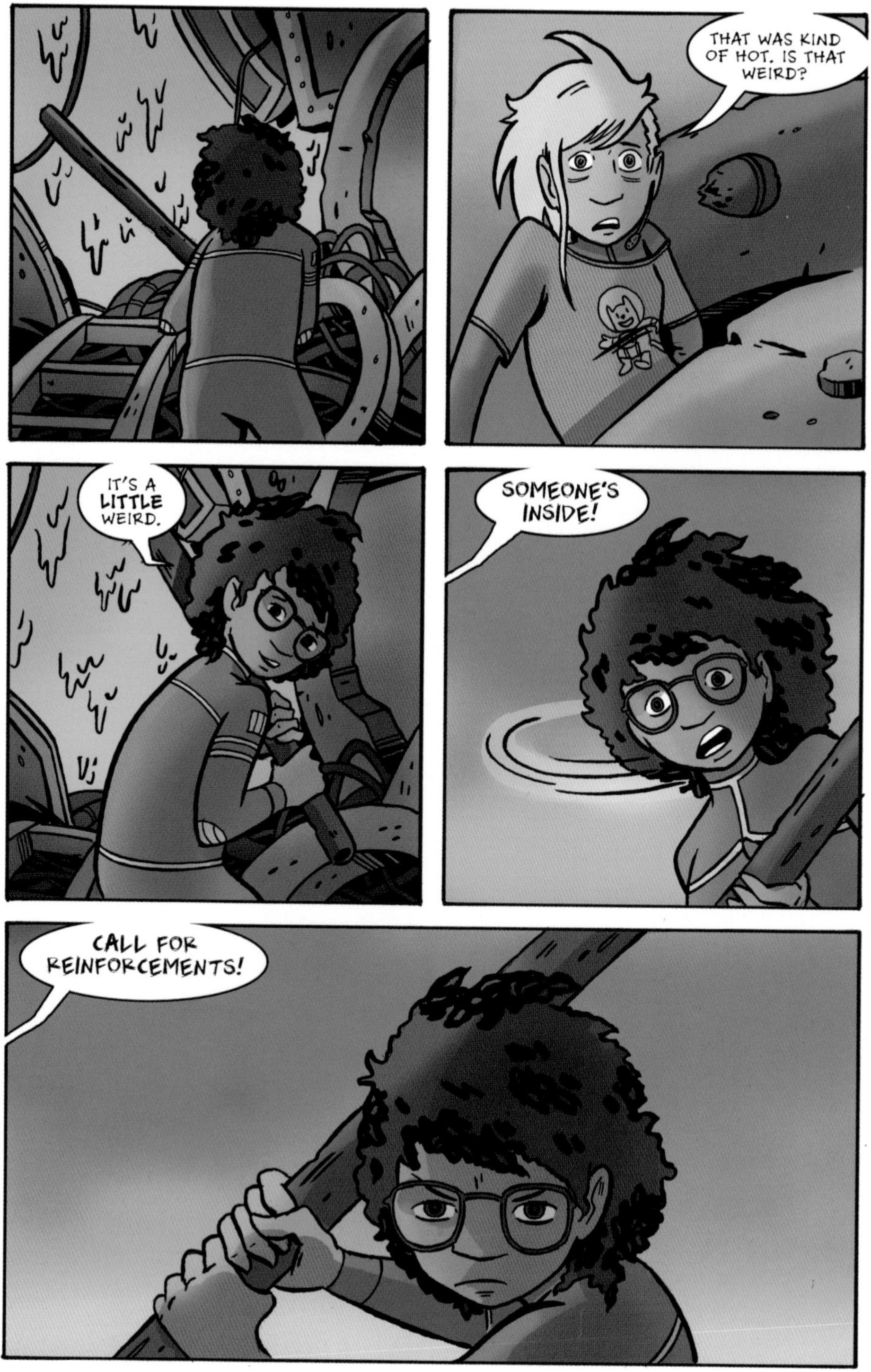
THAT WAS KIND OF HOT. IS THAT WEIRD?
IT'S A LITTLE WEIRD.
SOMEONE'S INSIDE!
CALL FOR REINFORCEMENTS!

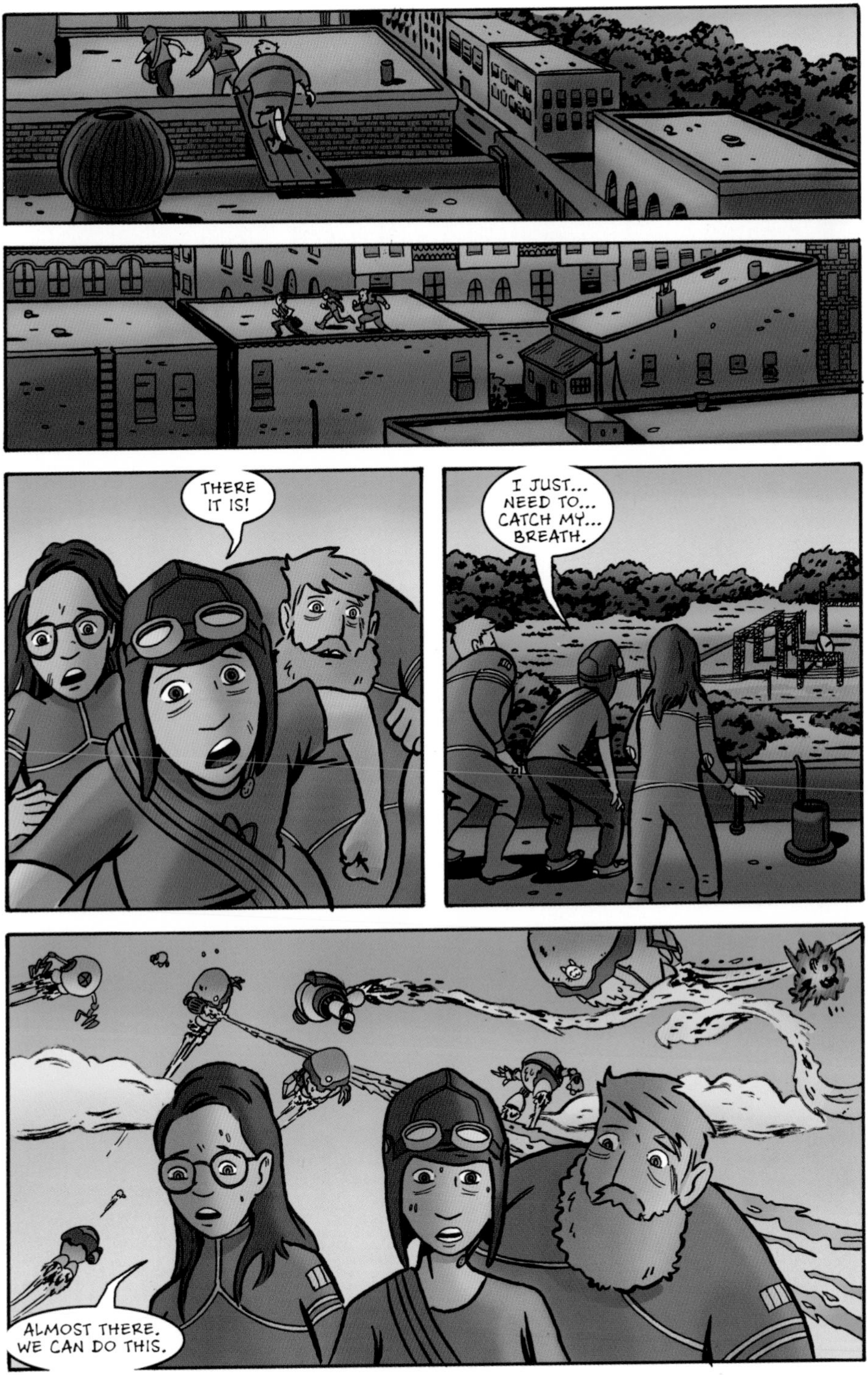
THERE IT IS!
I JUST... NEED TO... CATCH MY... BREATH.
ALMOST THERE. WE CAN DO THIS.

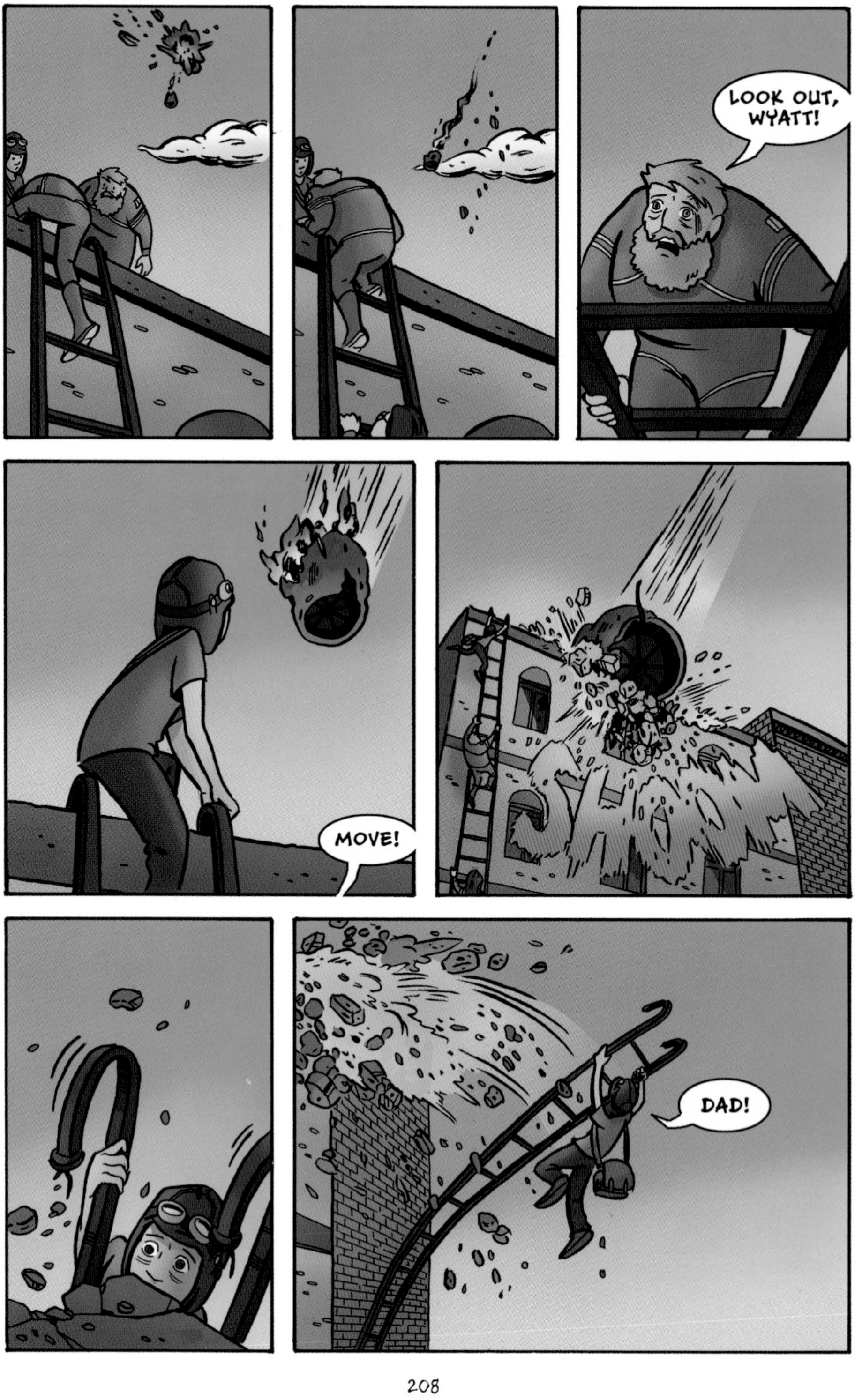
LOOK OUT, WYATT!
MOVE!
DAD!

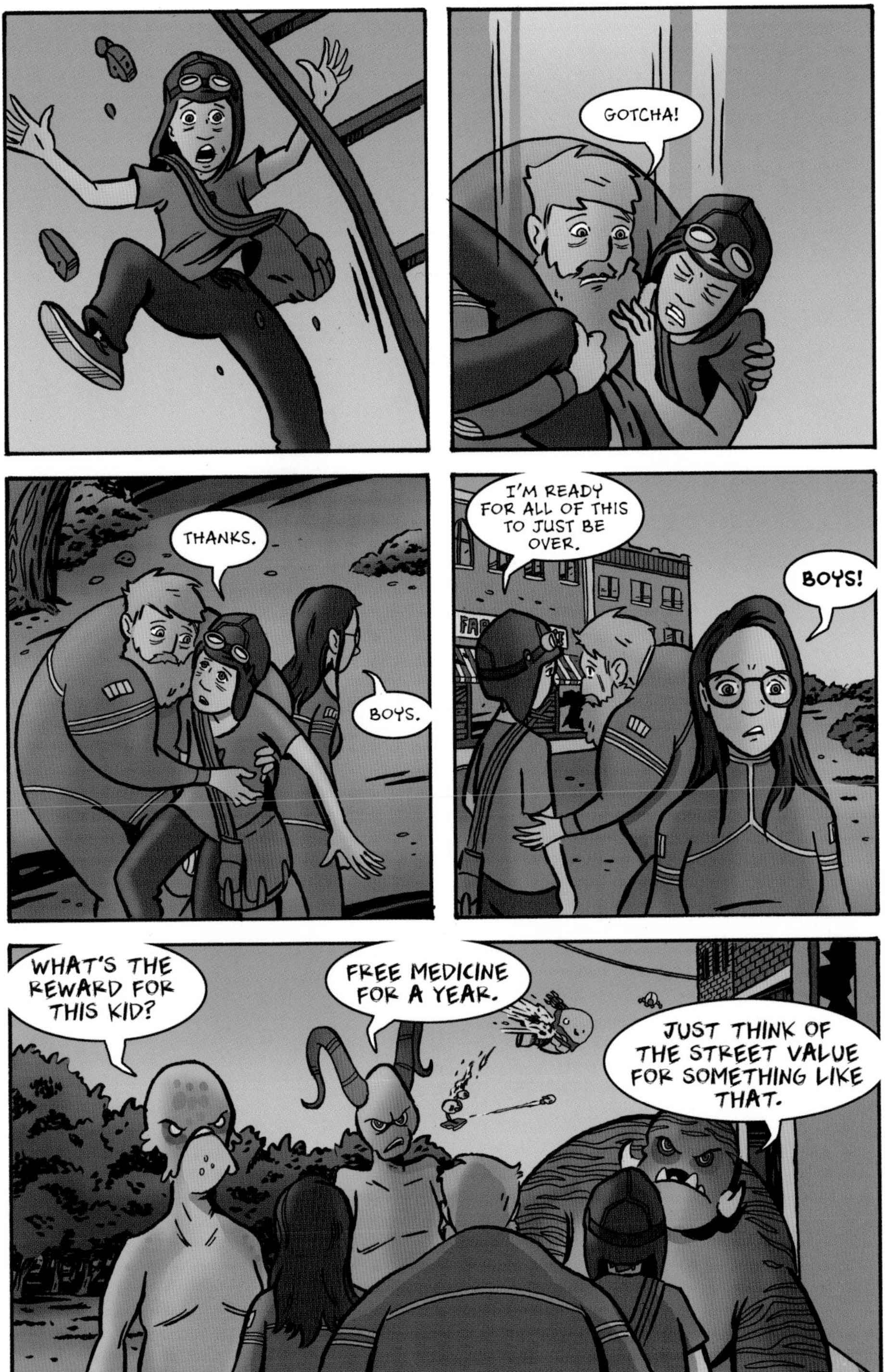
GOTCHA!
THANKS.
BOYS.
I'M READY FOR ALL OF THIS TO JUST BE OVER.
BOYS!
WHAT'S THE REWARD FOR THIS KID?
FREE MEDICINE FOR A YEAR.
JUST THINK OF THE STREET VALUE FOR SOMETHING LIKE THAT.

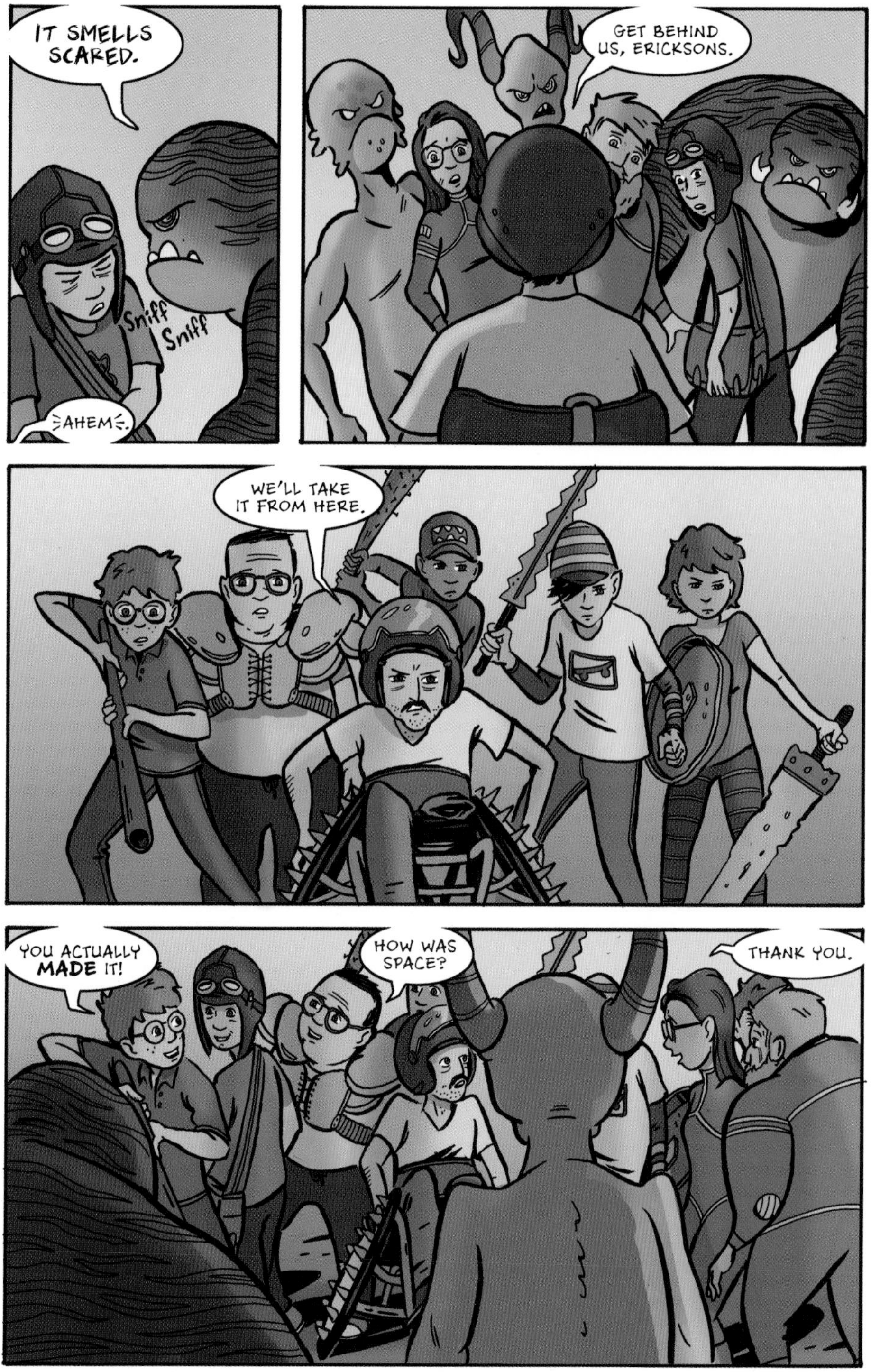
IT SMELLS SCARED.
Sniff Sniff
AHEM
GET BEHIND US, ERICKSONS.
WE'LL TAKE IT FROM HERE.
YOU ACTUALLY **MADE** IT!
HOW WAS SPACE?
THANK YOU.

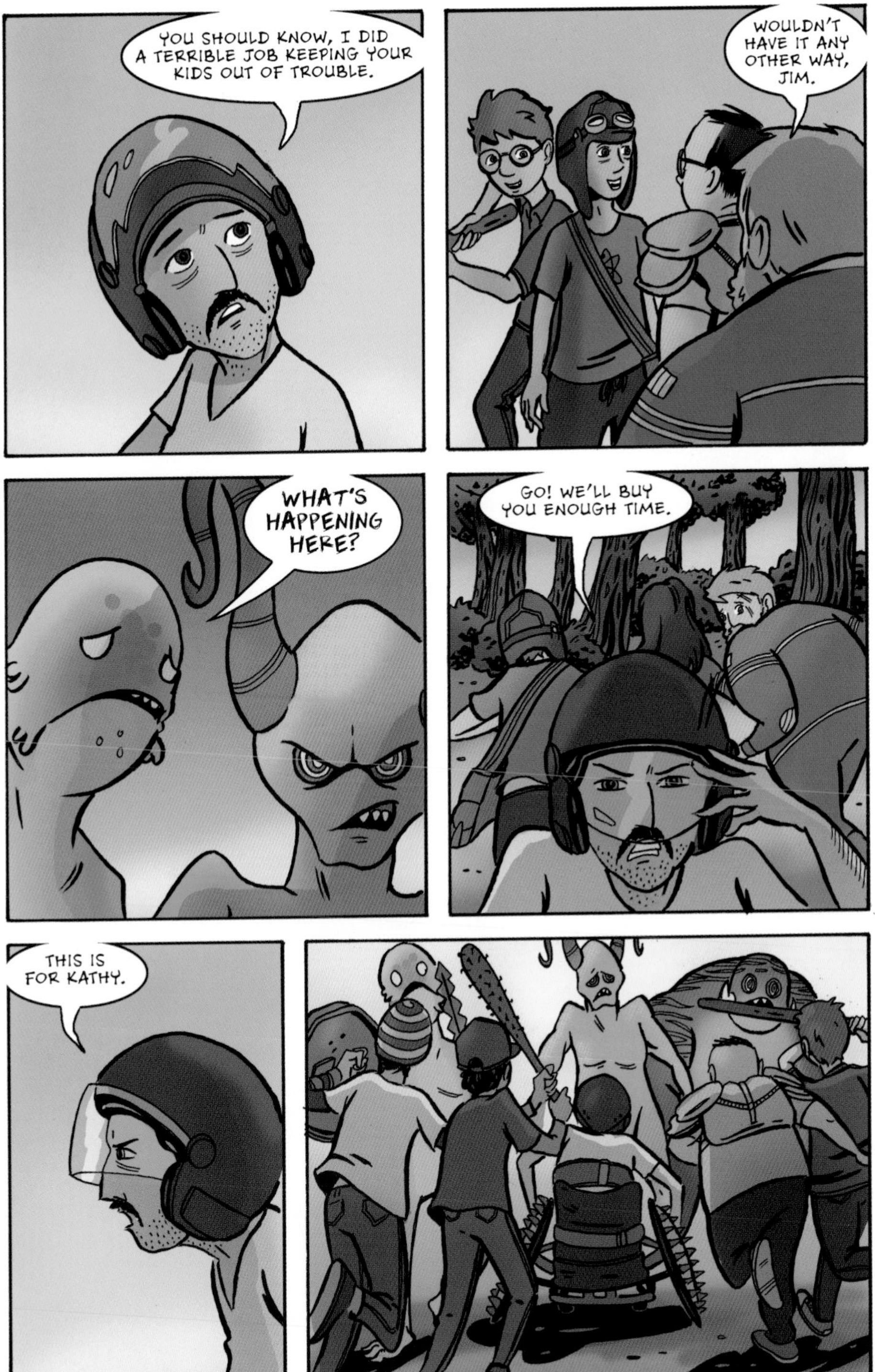
YOU SHOULD KNOW, I DID A TERRIBLE JOB KEEPING YOUR KIDS OUT OF TROUBLE.
WOULDN'T HAVE IT ANY OTHER WAY, JIM.
WHAT'S HAPPENING HERE?
GO! WE'LL BUY YOU ENOUGH TIME.
THIS IS FOR KATHY.

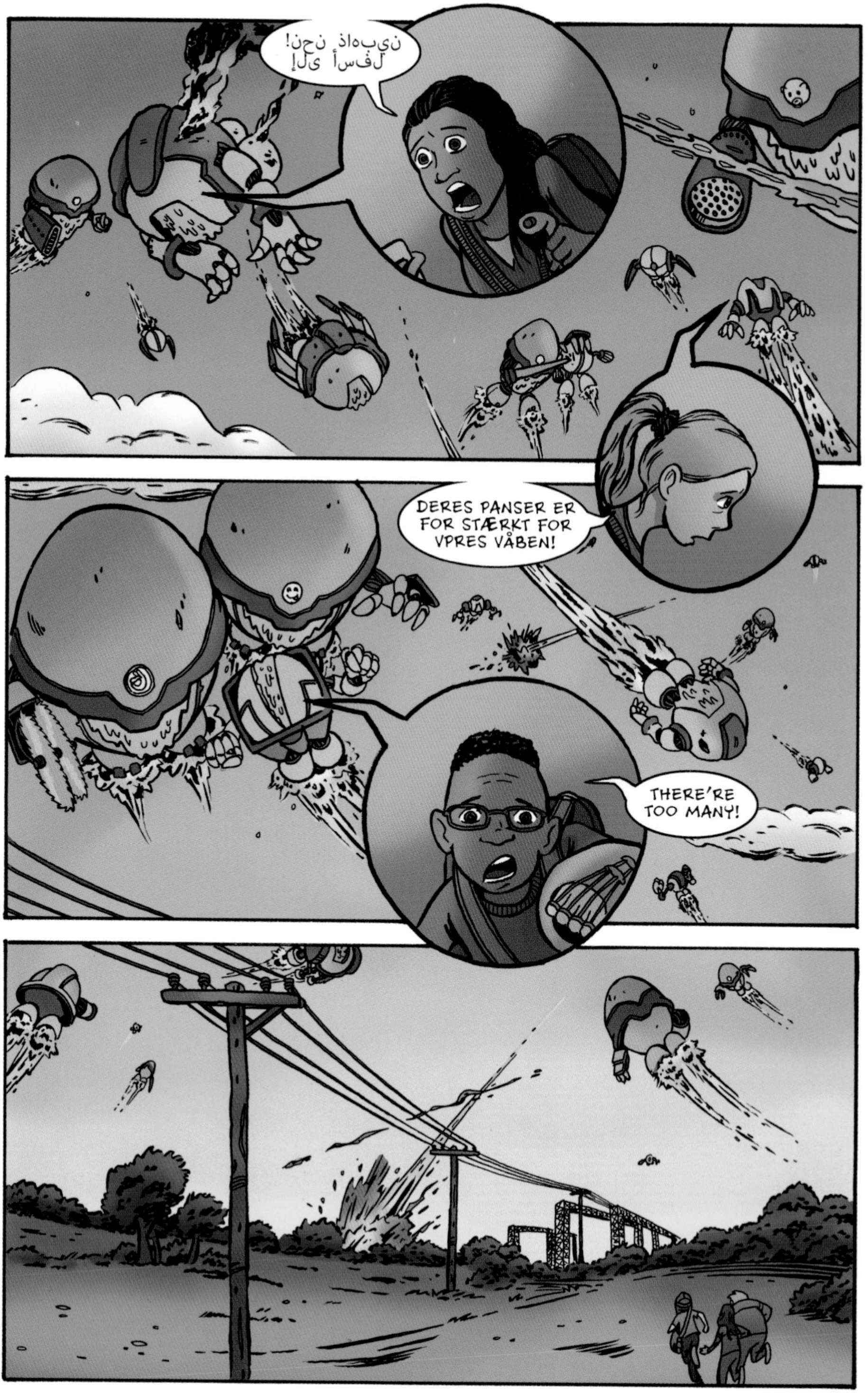

نحن ذاهبين!
إلى أسفل
DERES PANSER ER FOR STÆRKT FOR VPRES VÅBEN!
THERE'RE TOO MANY!

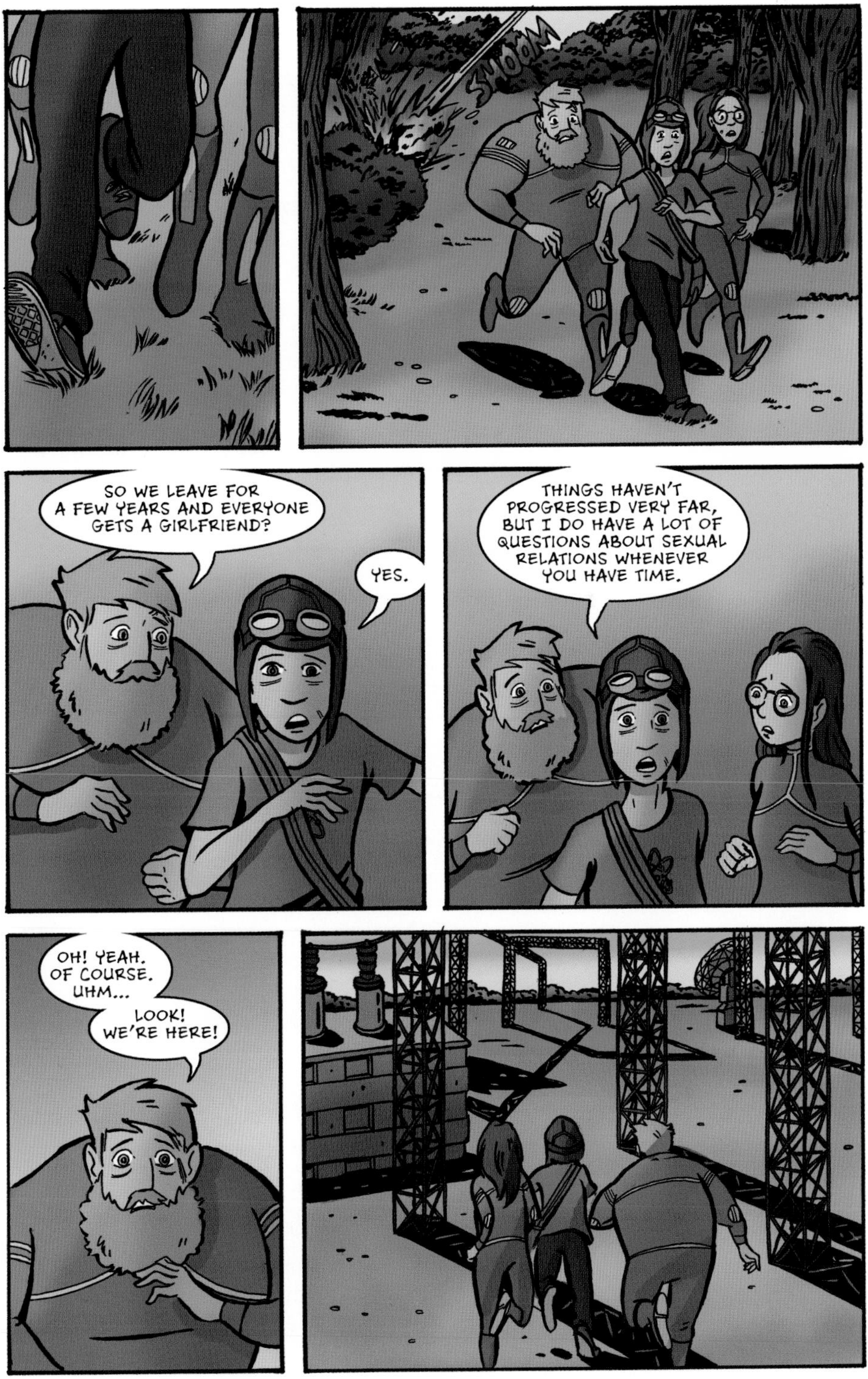
SNOOM
SO WE LEAVE FOR A FEW YEARS AND EVERYONE GETS A GIRLFRIEND?
YES.
THINGS HAVEN'T PROGRESSED VERY FAR, BUT I DO HAVE A LOT OF QUESTIONS ABOUT SEXUAL RELATIONS WHENEVER YOU HAVE TIME.
OH! YEAH. OF COURSE. UHM...
LOOK! WE'RE HERE!

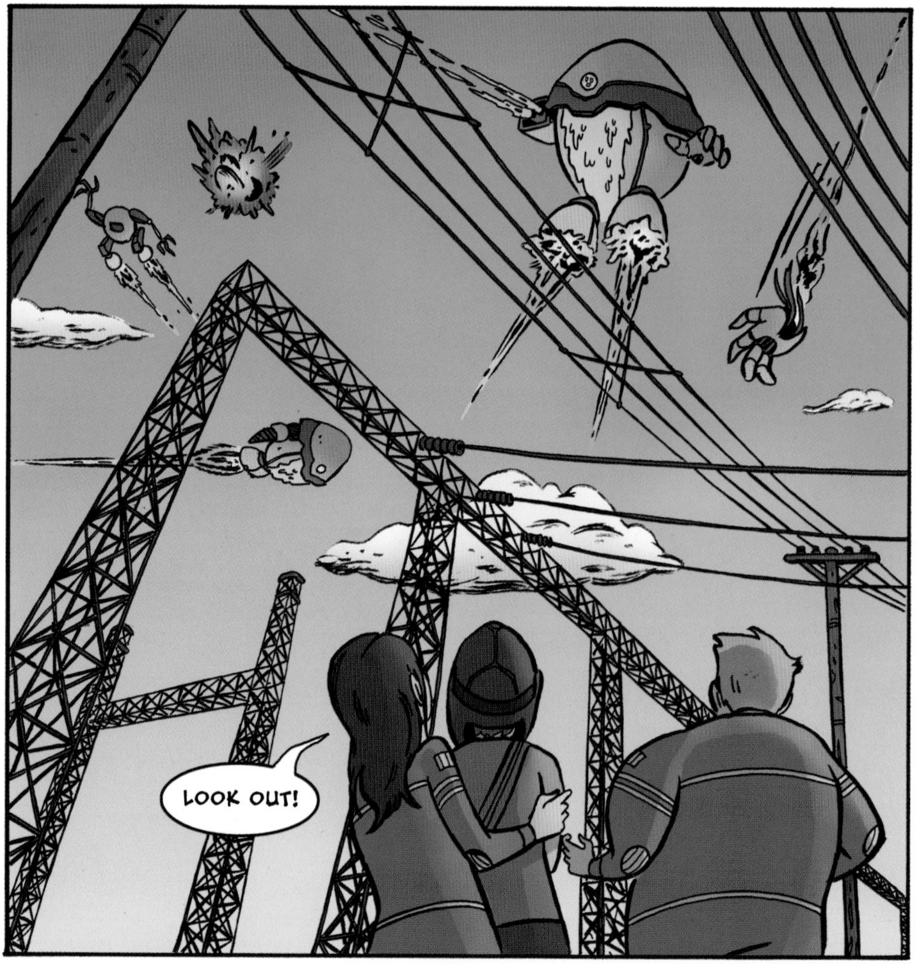
LOOK OUT!

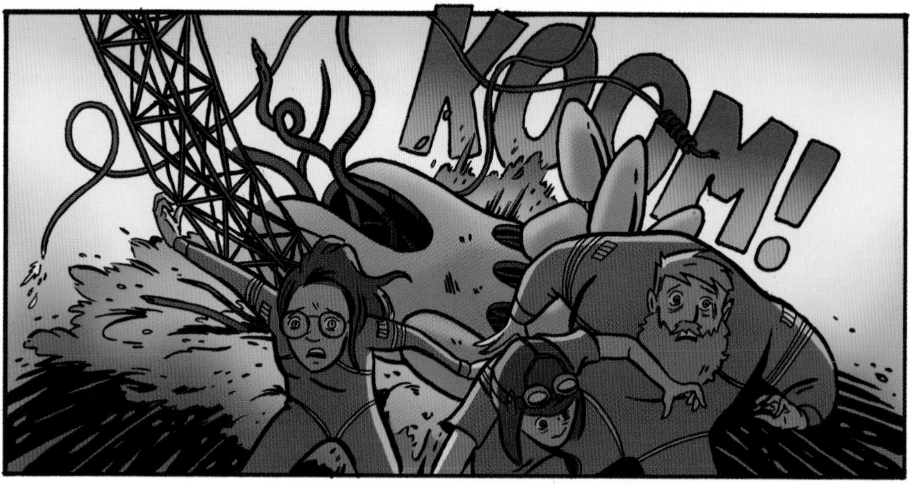
KOOM!

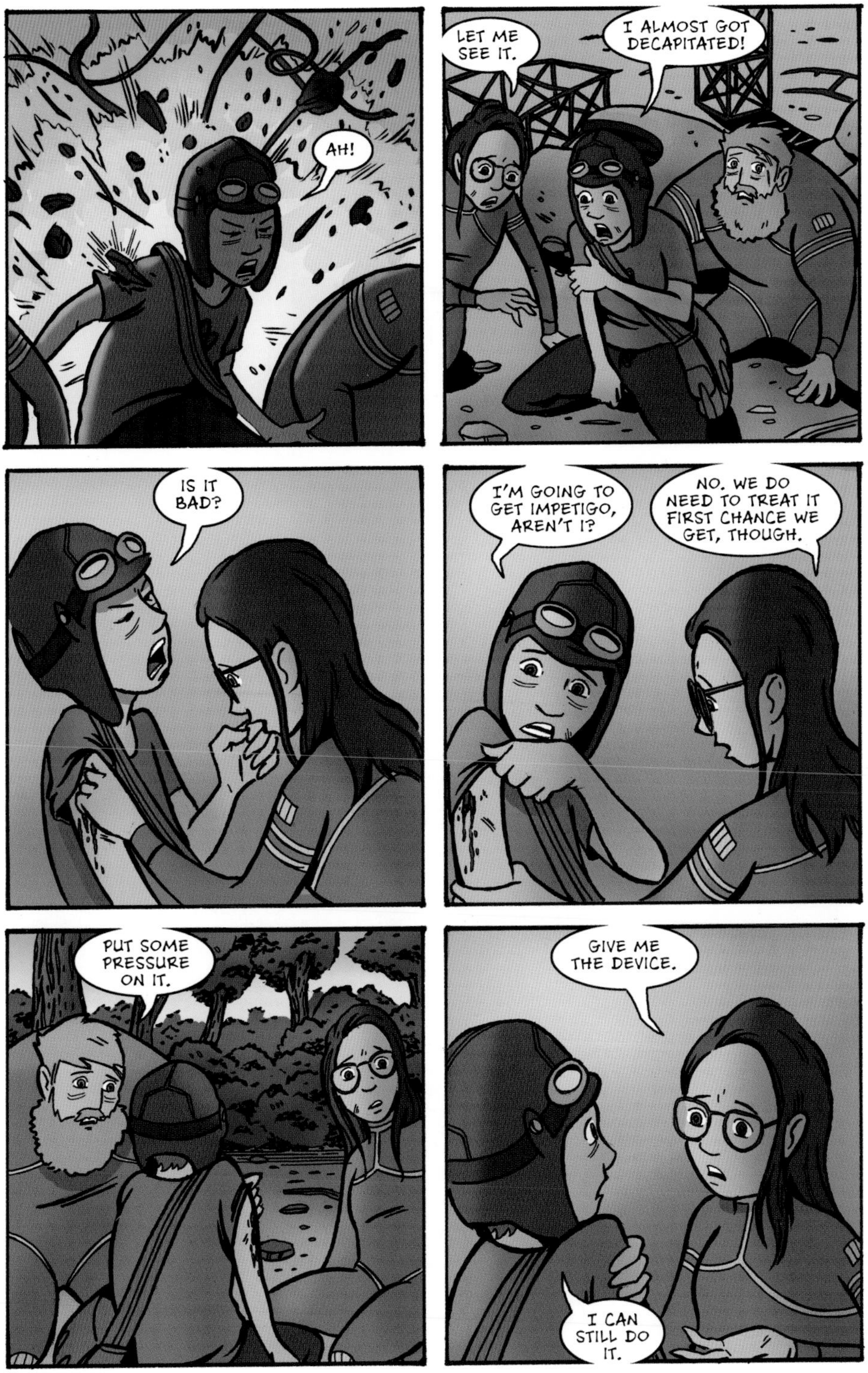
AH!
LET ME SEE IT.
I ALMOST GOT DECAPITATED!
IS IT BAD?
I'M GOING TO GET IMPETIGO, AREN'T I?
NO. WE DO NEED TO TREAT IT FIRST CHANCE WE GET, THOUGH.
PUT SOME PRESSURE ON IT.
GIVE ME THE DEVICE.
I CAN STILL DO IT.

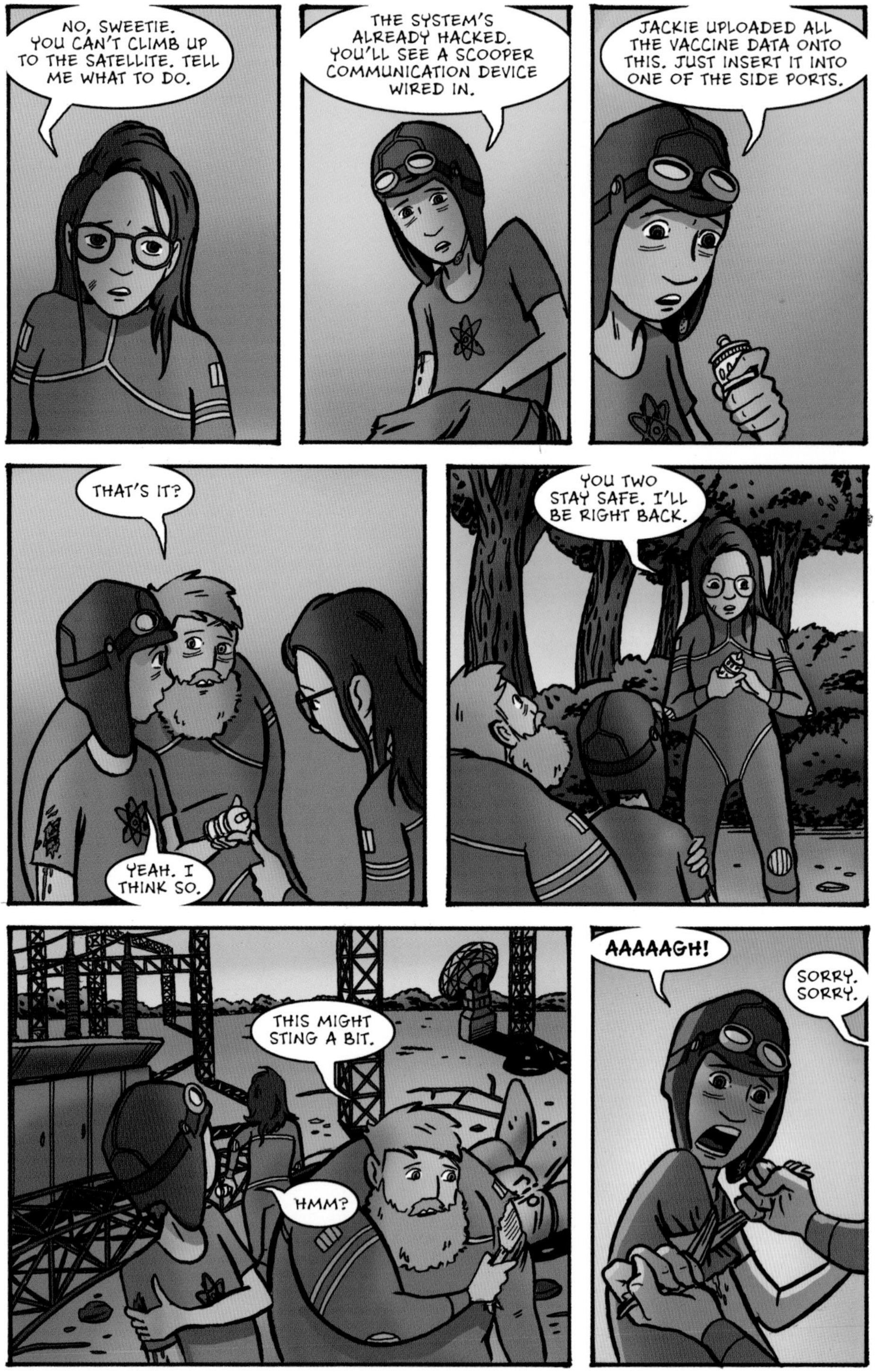

NO, SWEETIE. YOU CAN'T CLIMB UP TO THE SATELLITE. TELL ME WHAT TO DO.
THE SYSTEM'S ALREADY HACKED. YOU'LL SEE A SCOOPER COMMUNICATION DEVICE WIRED IN.
JACKIE UPLOADED ALL THE VACCINE DATA ONTO THIS. JUST INSERT IT INTO ONE OF THE SIDE PORTS.
THAT'S IT?
YEAH. I THINK SO.
YOU TWO STAY SAFE. I'LL BE RIGHT BACK.
THIS MIGHT STING A BIT.
HMM?
AAAAAGH!
SORRY. SORRY.

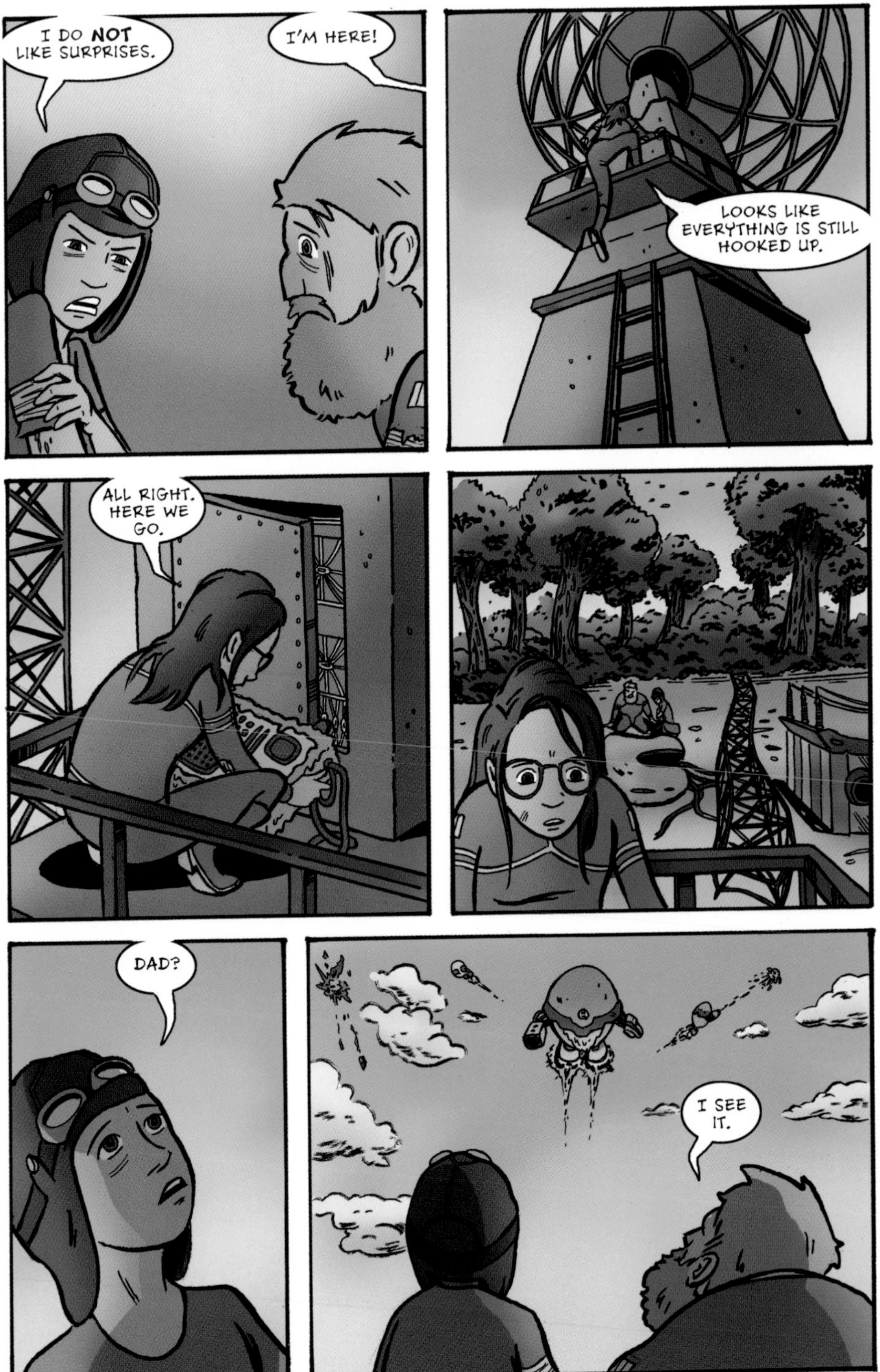
I DO **NOT** LIKE SURPRISES.
I'M HERE!
LOOKS LIKE EVERYTHING IS STILL HOOKED UP.
ALL RIGHT. HERE WE GO.
DAD?
I SEE IT.

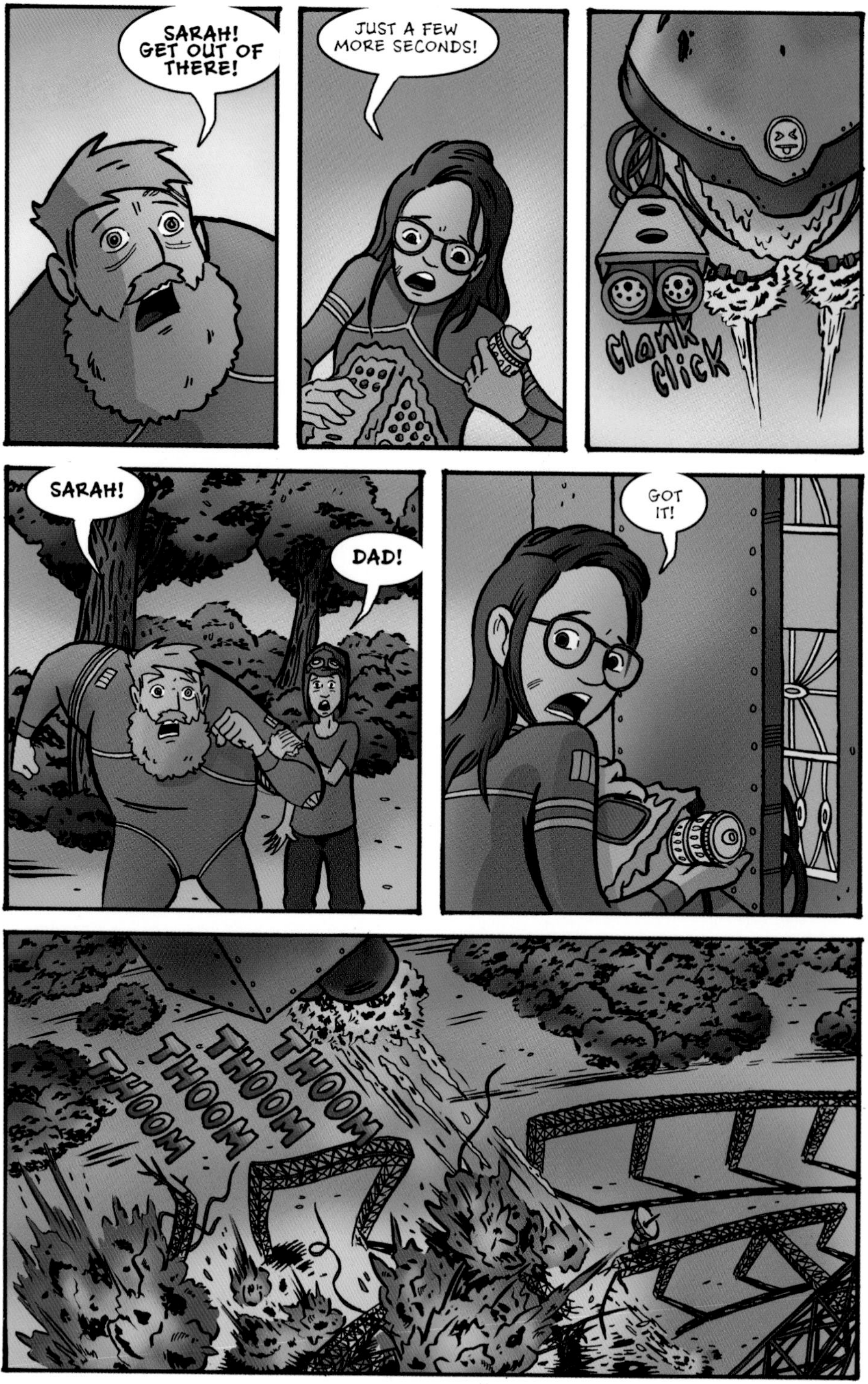
SARAH! GET OUT OF THERE!
JUST A FEW MORE SECONDS!
CLANK CLICK
SARAH!
DAD!
GOT IT!
THOOM
THOOM
THOOM
THOOM

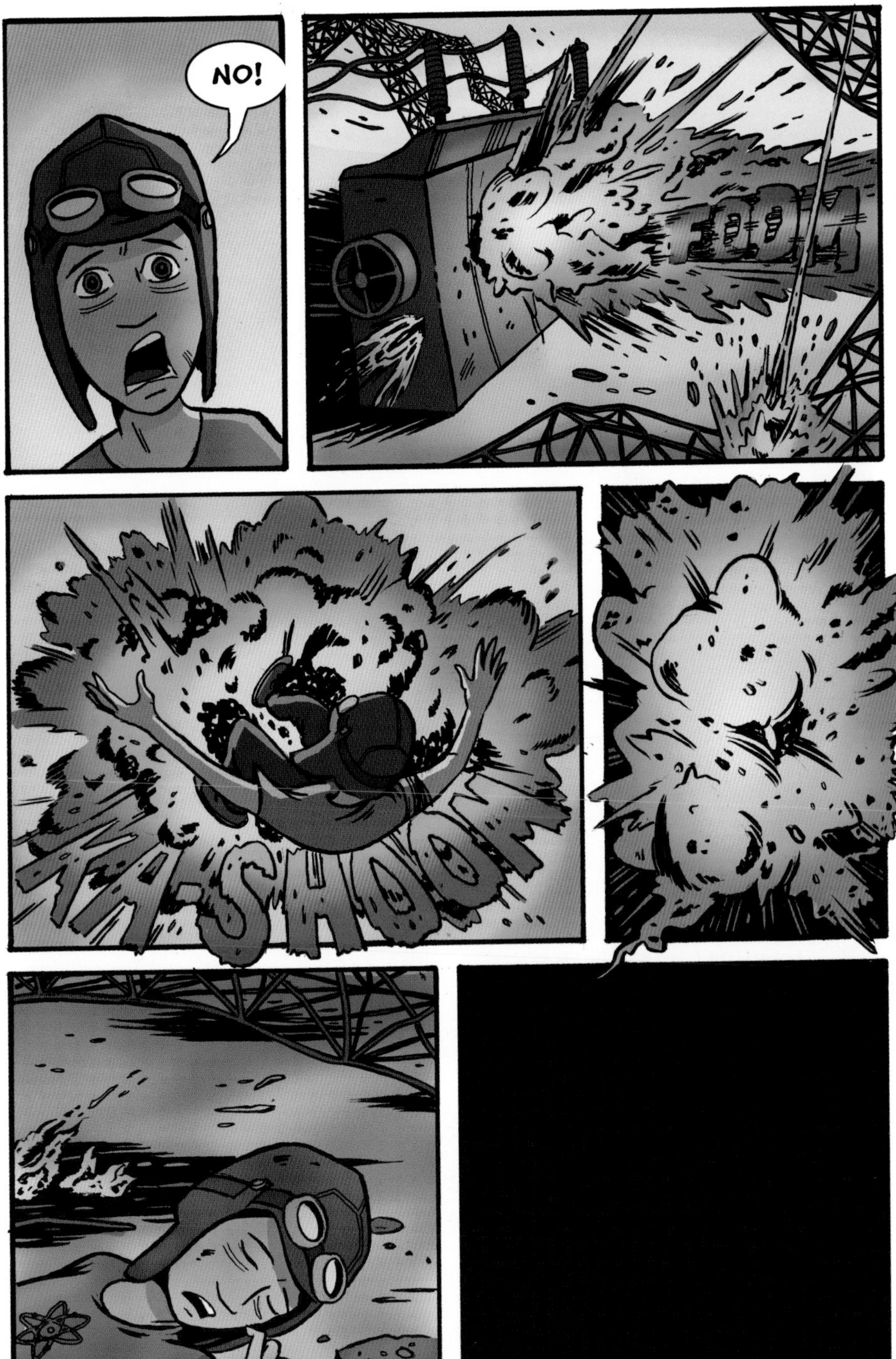
NO!
FOOM
KA-SHOOM

MOM!
DAD!
I CAN'T HANG ON!
IT'S OKAY. YOU DON'T HAVE TO ANYMORE.
IT'S SLIPPING!
JUST LET GO.
NO! YOU CAN'T LEAVE ME AGAIN! I HAVE TO SAVE YOU!

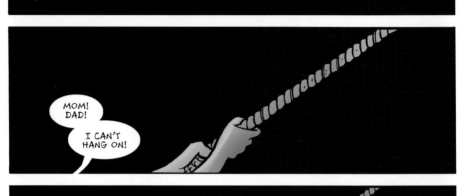

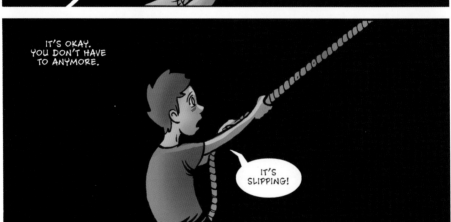

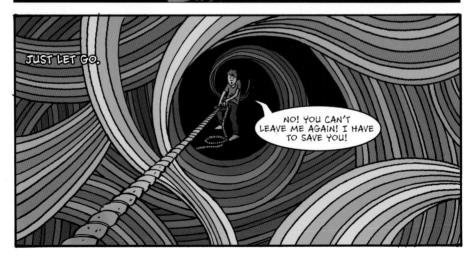

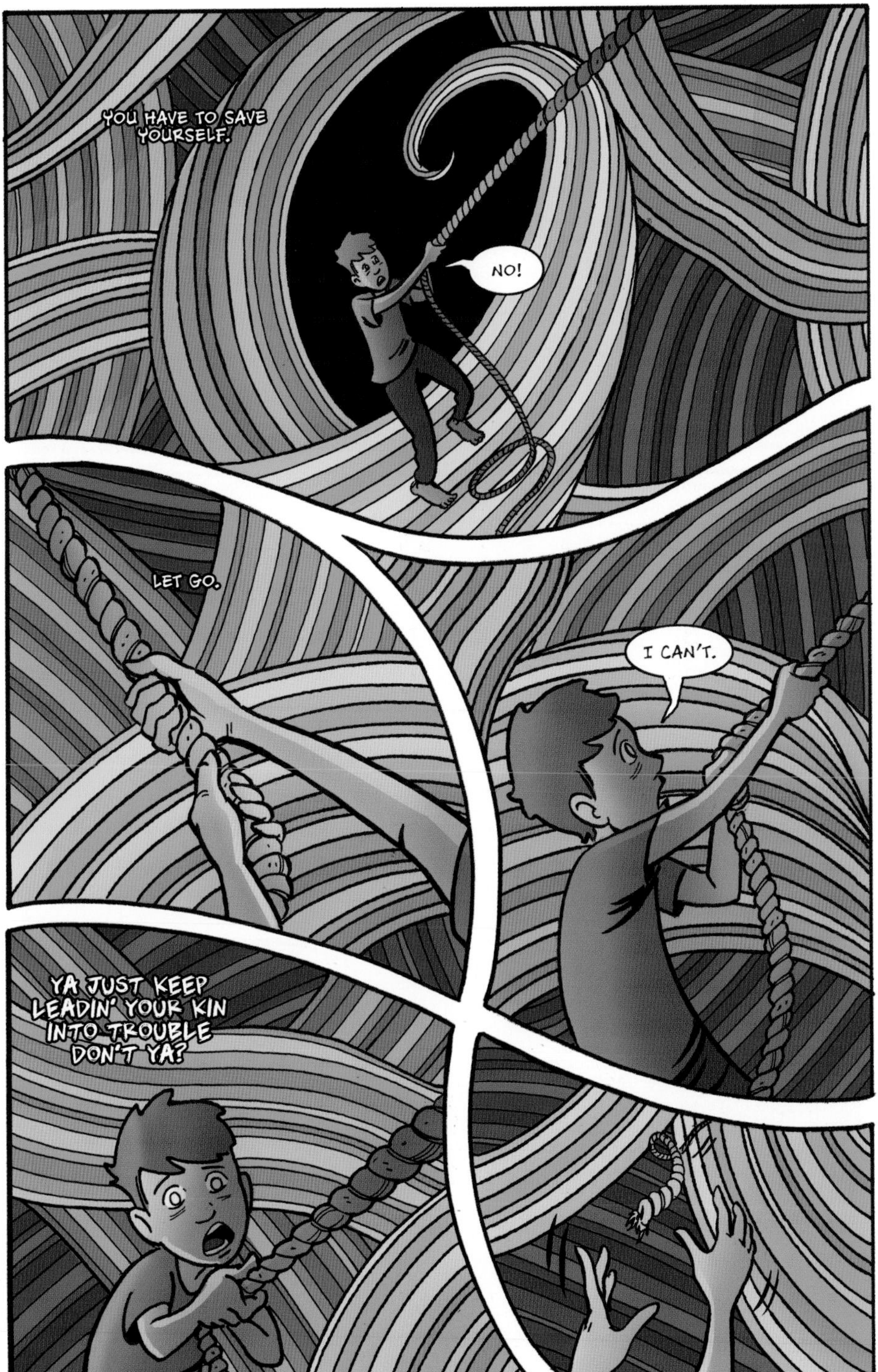
YOU HAVE TO SAVE YOURSELF.
NO!
LET GO.
I CAN'T.
YA JUST KEEP LEADIN' YOUR KIN INTO TROUBLE DON'T YA?

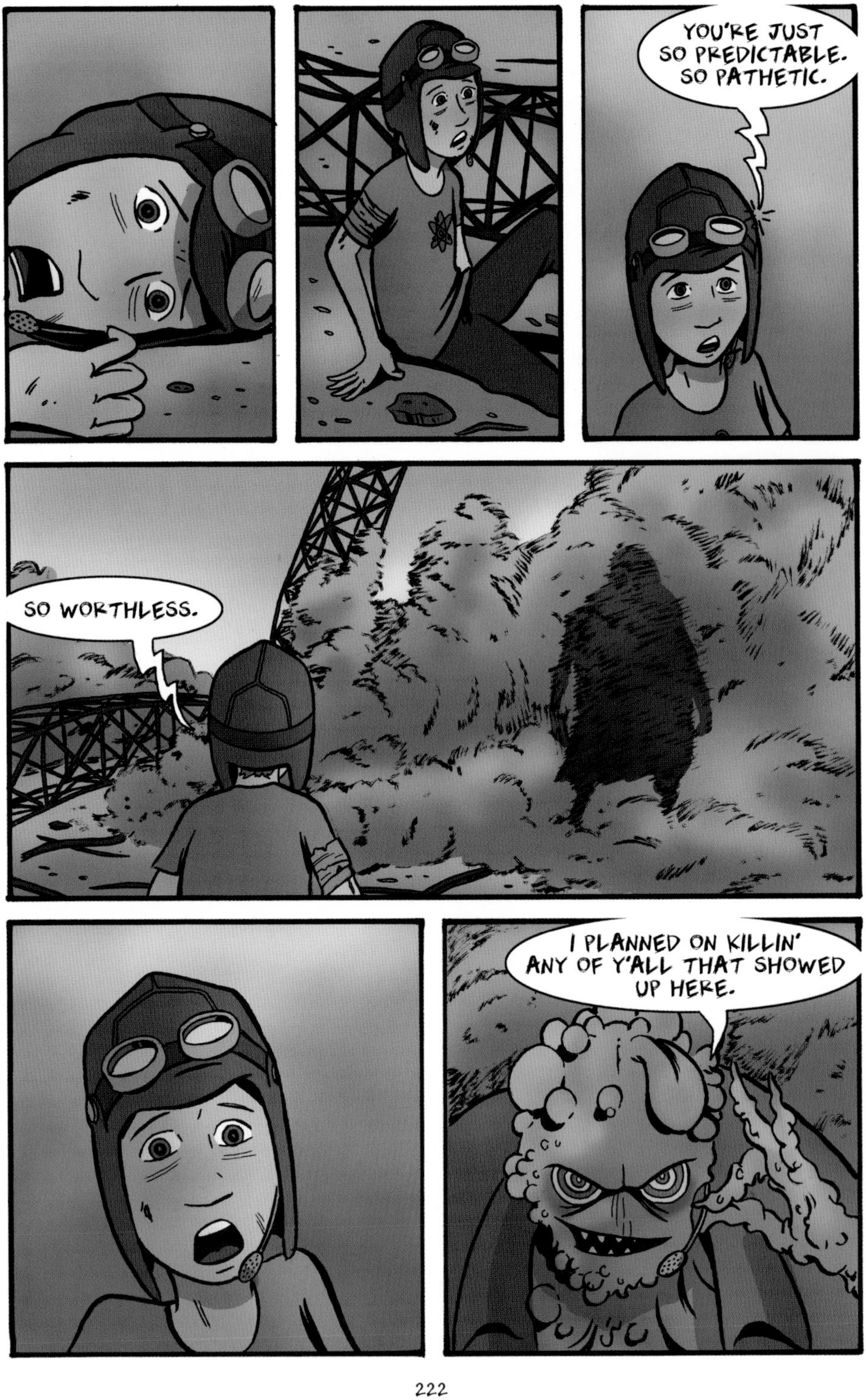
YOU'RE JUST SO PREDICTABLE. SO PATHETIC.
SO WORTHLESS.
I PLANNED ON KILLIN' ANY OF Y'ALL THAT SHOWED UP HERE.

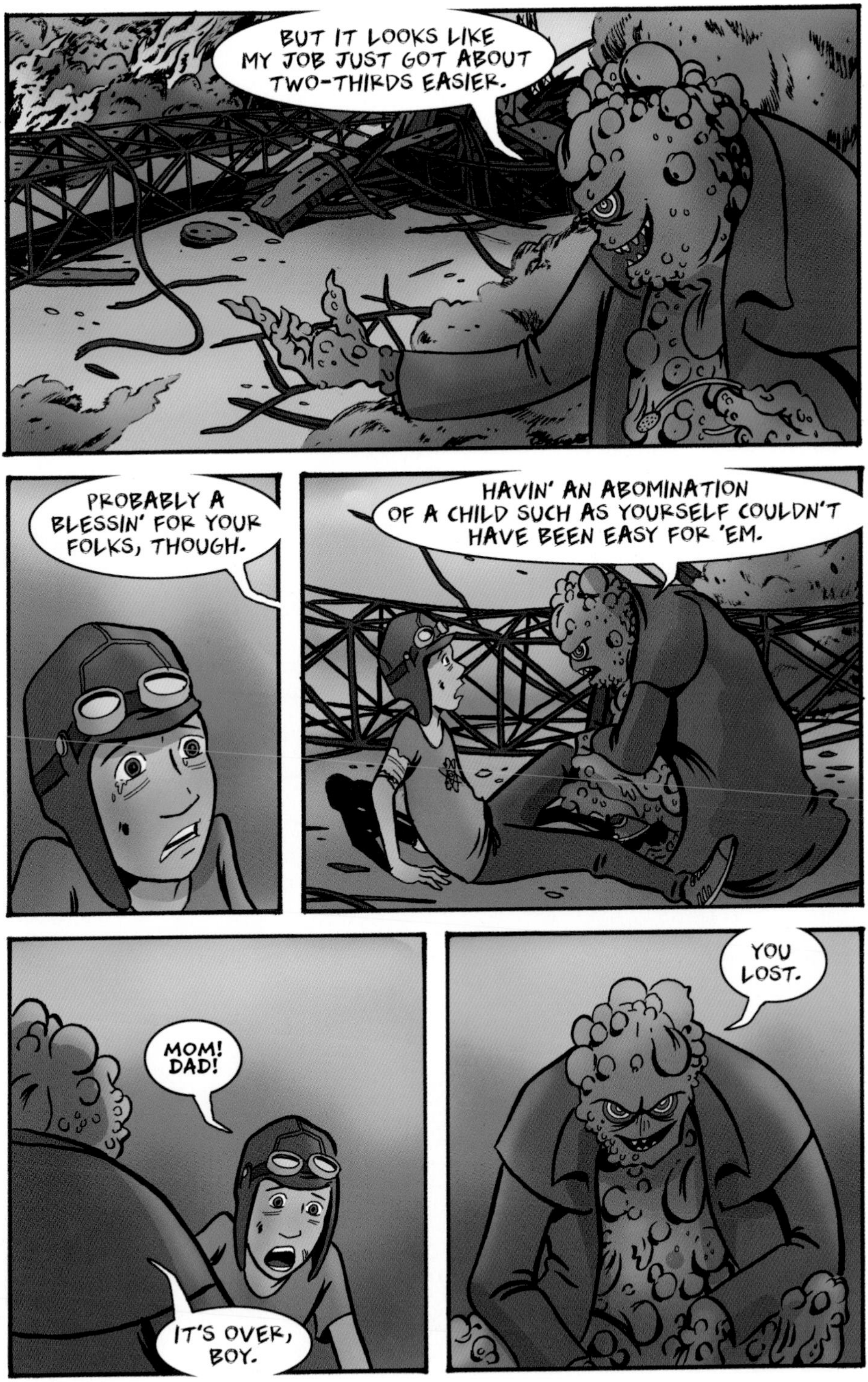
BUT IT LOOKS LIKE MY JOB JUST GOT ABOUT TWO-THIRDS EASIER.
PROBABLY A BLESSIN' FOR YOUR FOLKS, THOUGH.
HAVIN' AN ABOMINATION OF A CHILD SUCH AS YOURSELF COULDN'T HAVE BEEN EASY FOR 'EM.
MOM! DAD!
IT'S OVER, BOY.
YOU LOST.

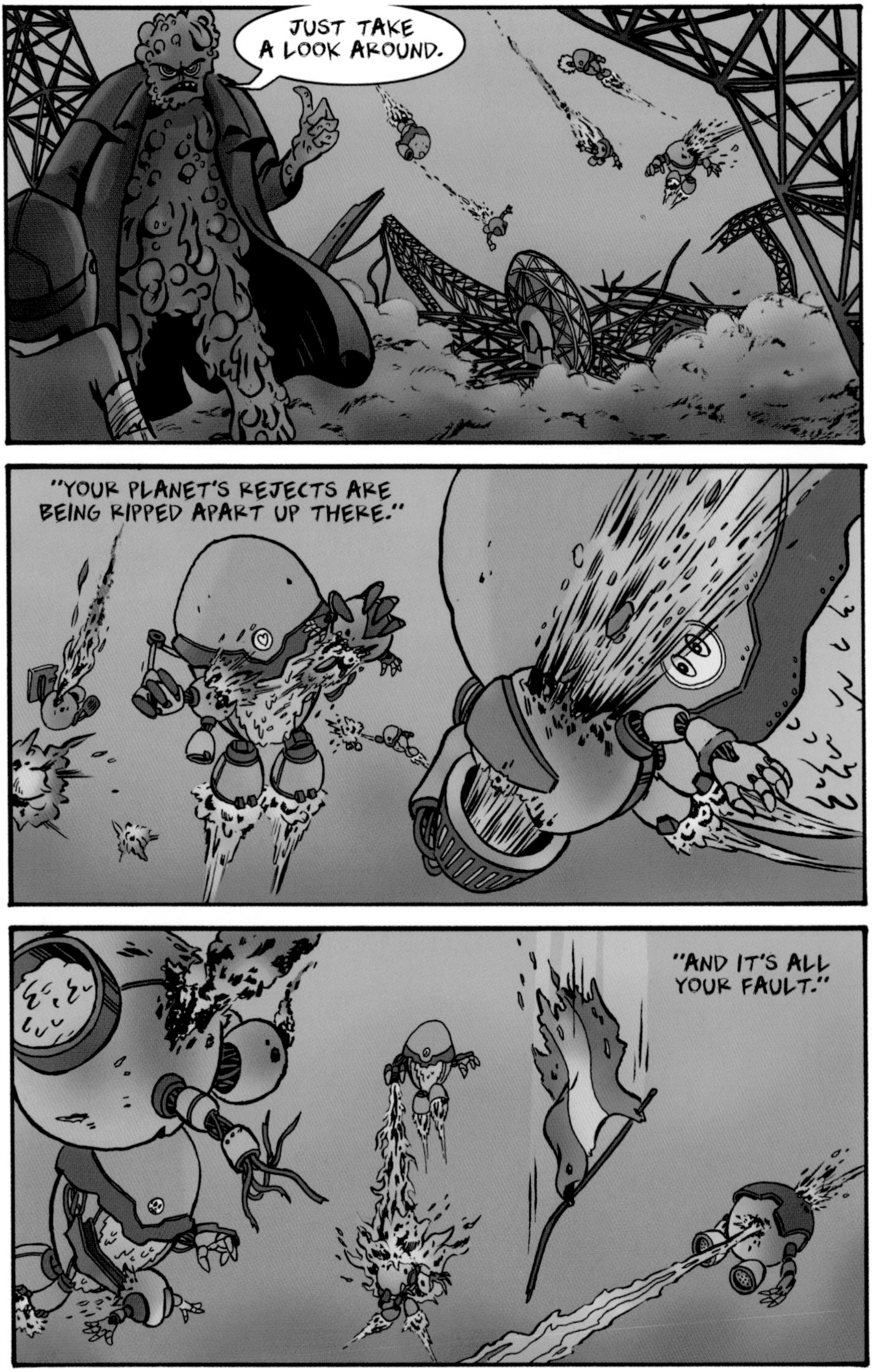
JUST TAKE A LOOK AROUND.
"YOUR PLANET'S REJECTS ARE BEING RIPPED APART UP THERE."
"AND IT'S ALL YOUR FAULT."

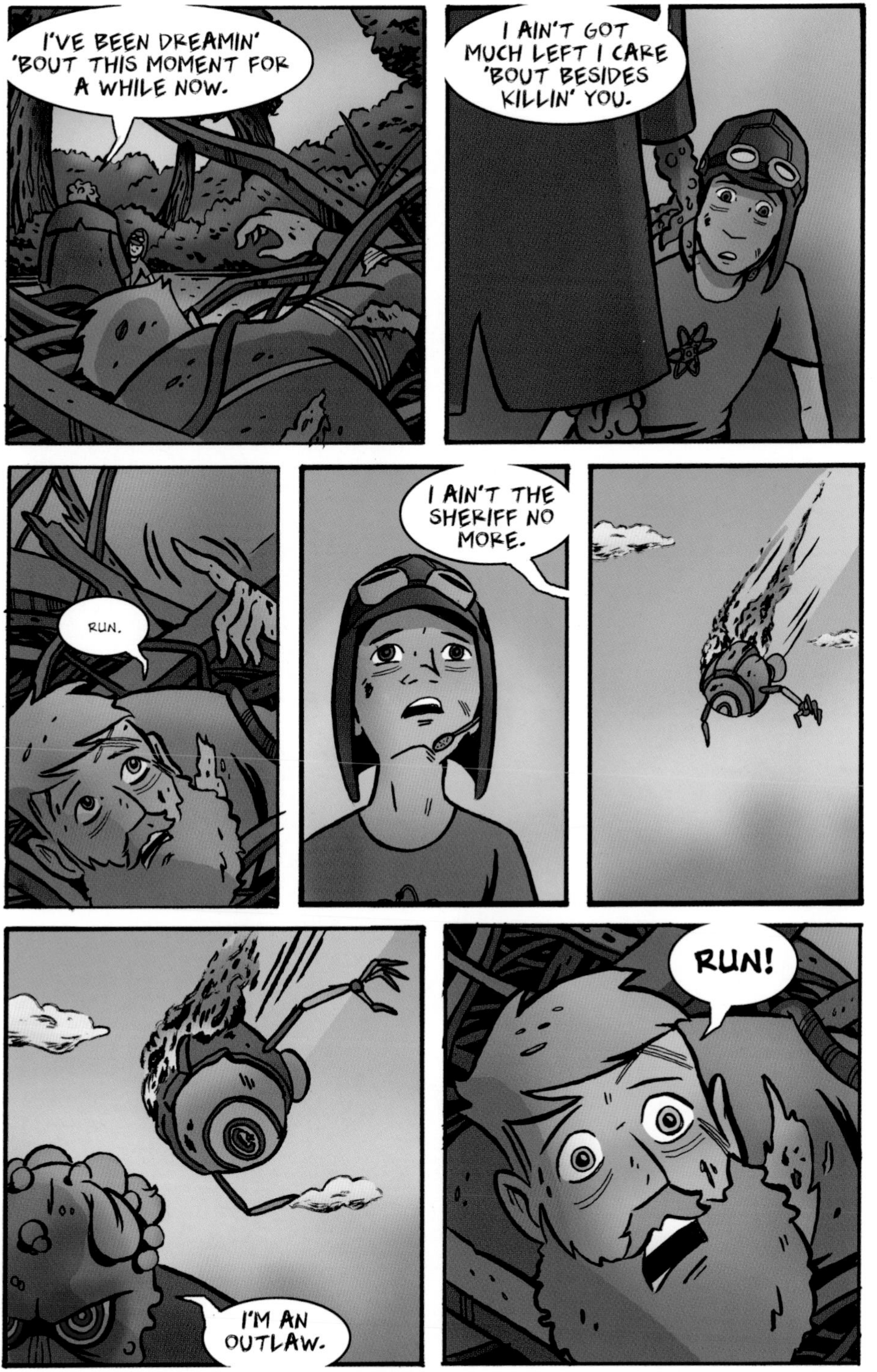
I'VE BEEN DREAMIN' 'BOUT THIS MOMENT FOR A WHILE NOW.
I AIN'T GOT MUCH LEFT I CARE 'BOUT BESIDES KILLIN' YOU.
RUN.
I AIN'T THE SHERIFF NO MORE.
I'M AN OUTLAW.
RUN!

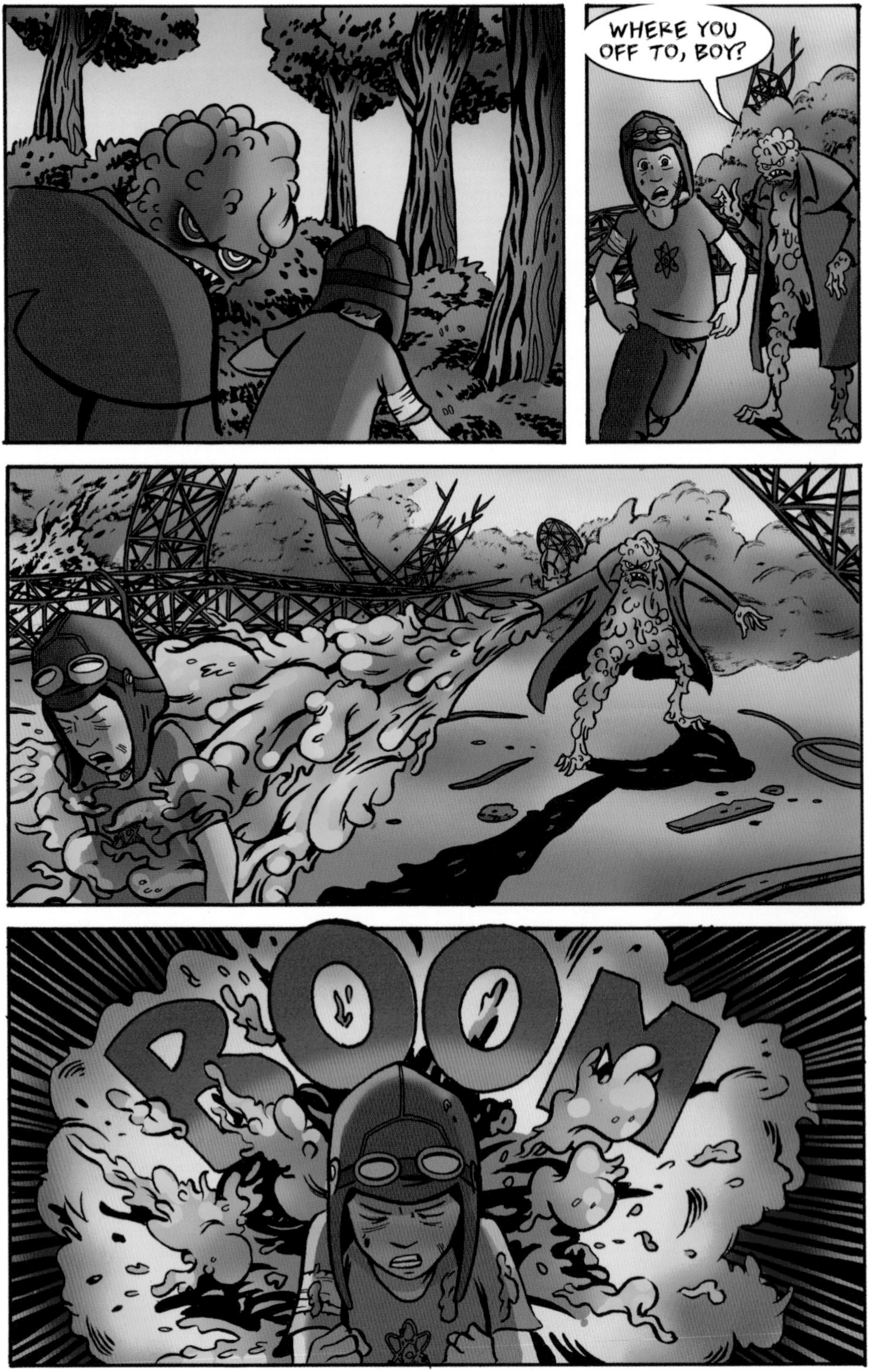
WHERE YOU OFF TO, BOY?
BOOM

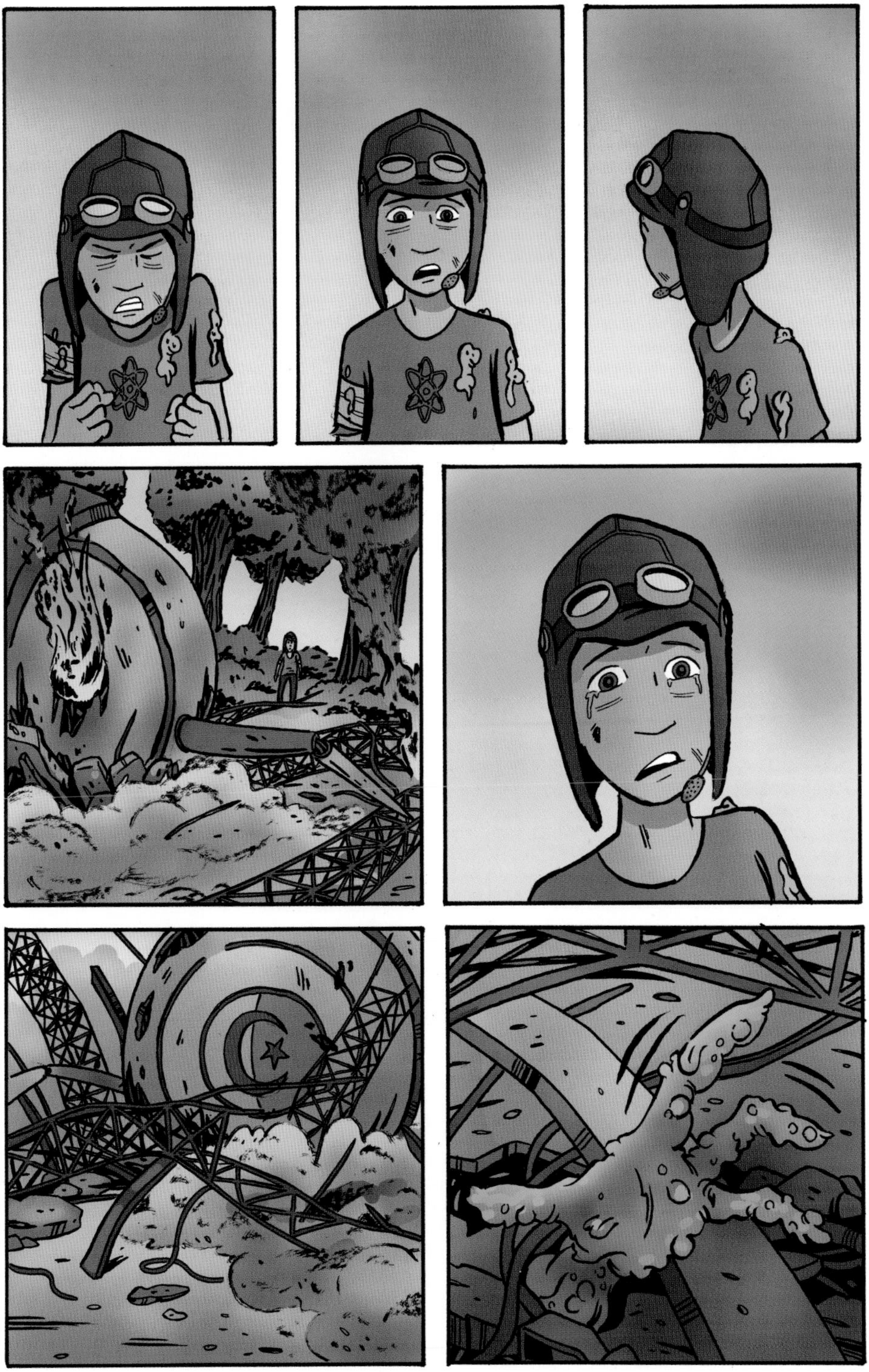

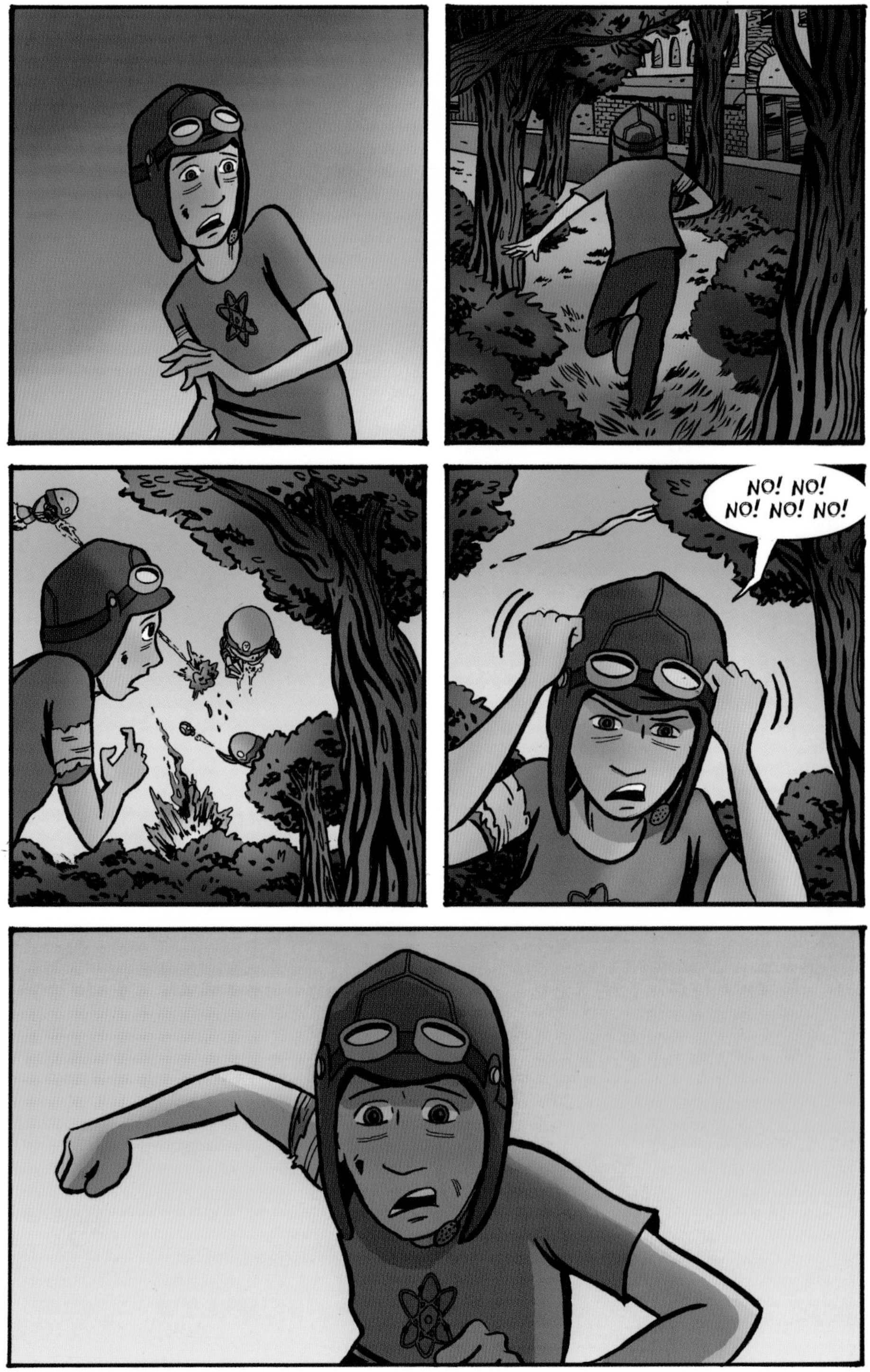
NO! NO!
NO! NO! NO!

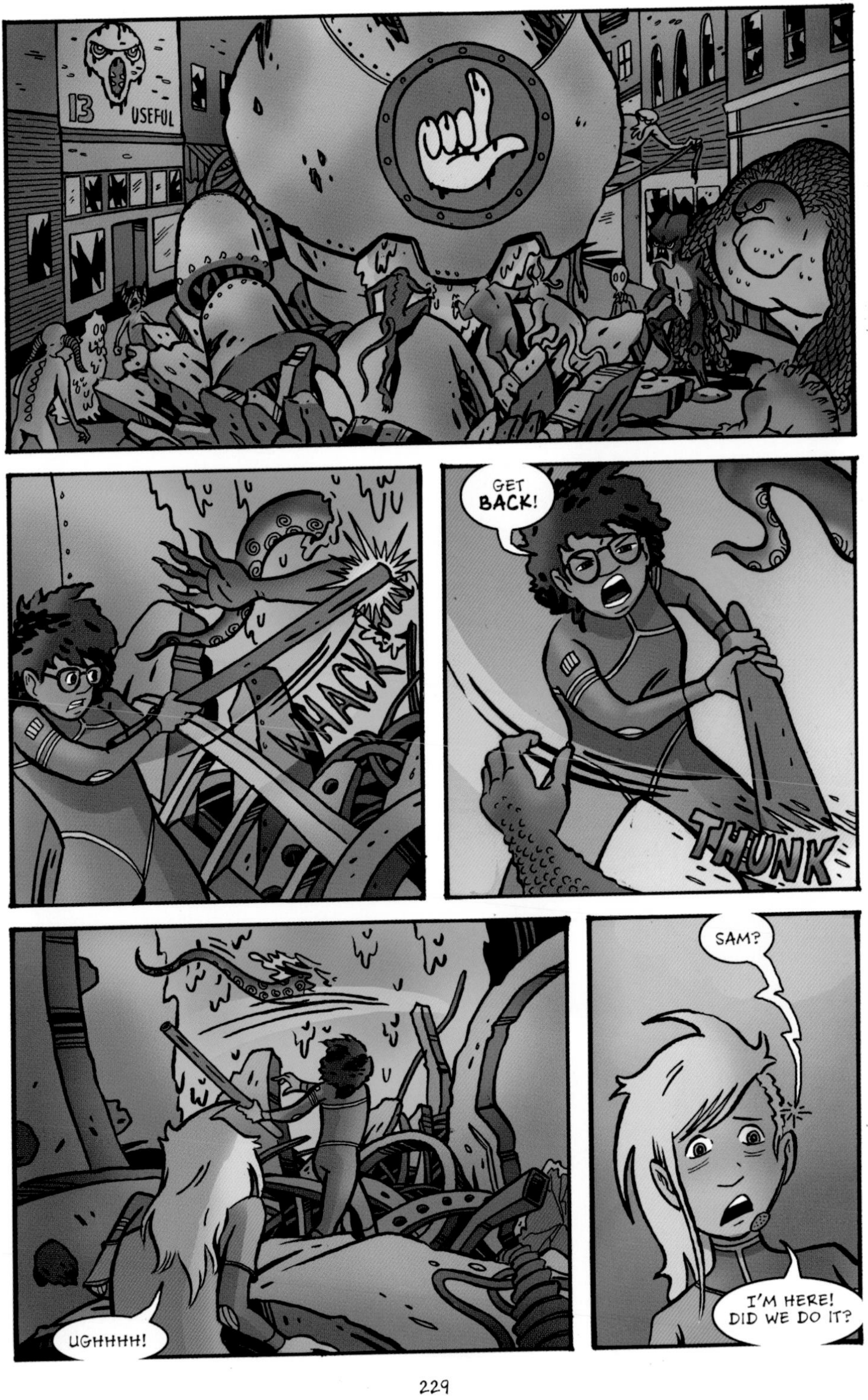
13
USEFUL
WHACK
GET BACK!
THUNK
UGHHHH!
SAM?
I'M HERE! DID WE DO IT?

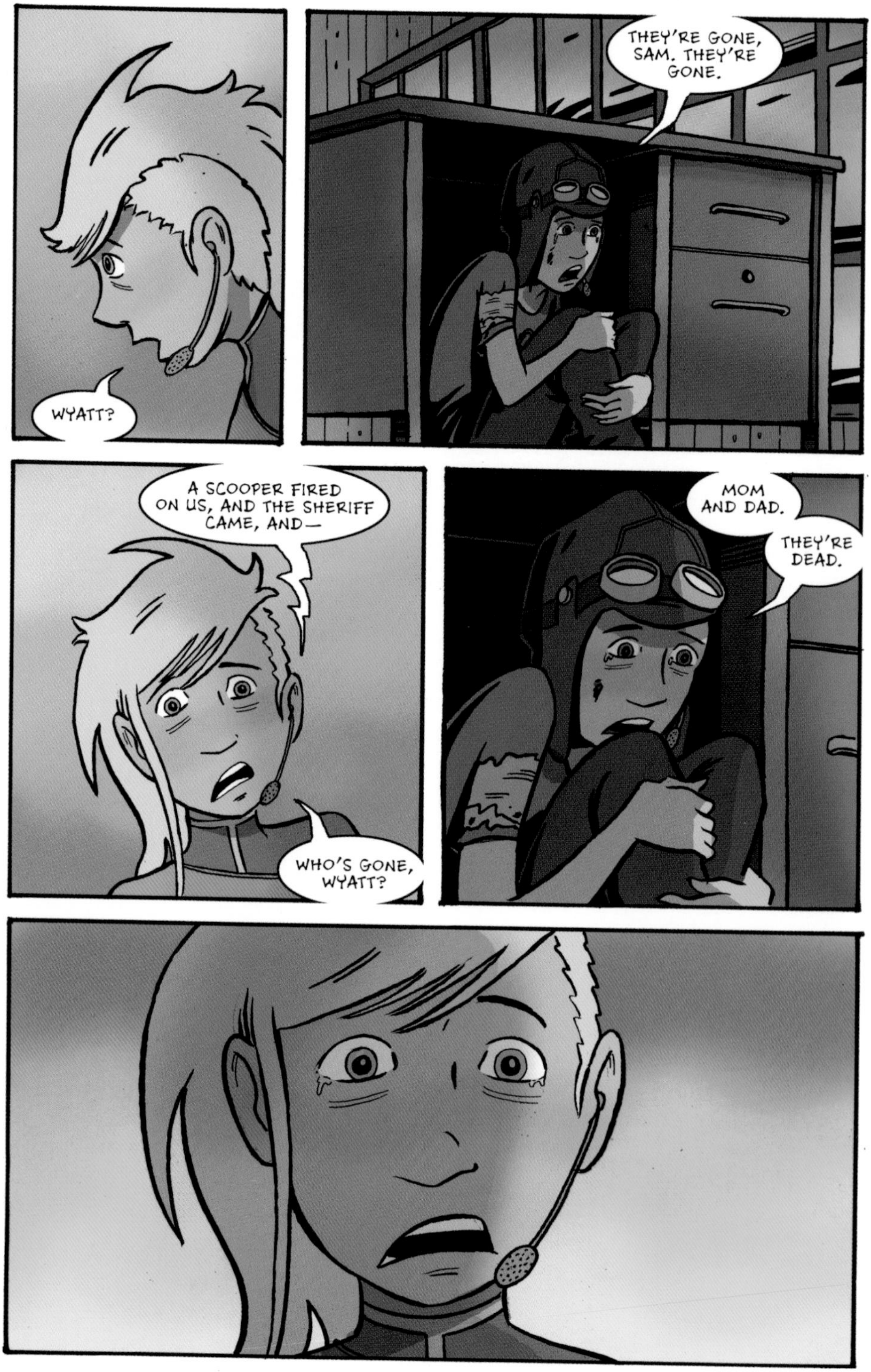
WYATT?
THEY'RE GONE, SAM. THEY'RE GONE.
A SCOOPER FIRED ON US, AND THE SHERIFF CAME, AND—
WHO'S GONE, WYATT?
MOM AND DAD.
THEY'RE DEAD.

ARE YOU SAFE?

IT'S MY FAULT.

DON'T YOU DARE SAY THAT. IT IS **NOT** YOUR FAULT.

ARE YOU SAFE, WYATT?

I KNOW YOU'RE HERE, BOY. I COULD NEARLY FOLLOW YOUR TEARS.

YOU'RE A SPECIAL PIECE OF THE PUZZ

HE'S HERE.

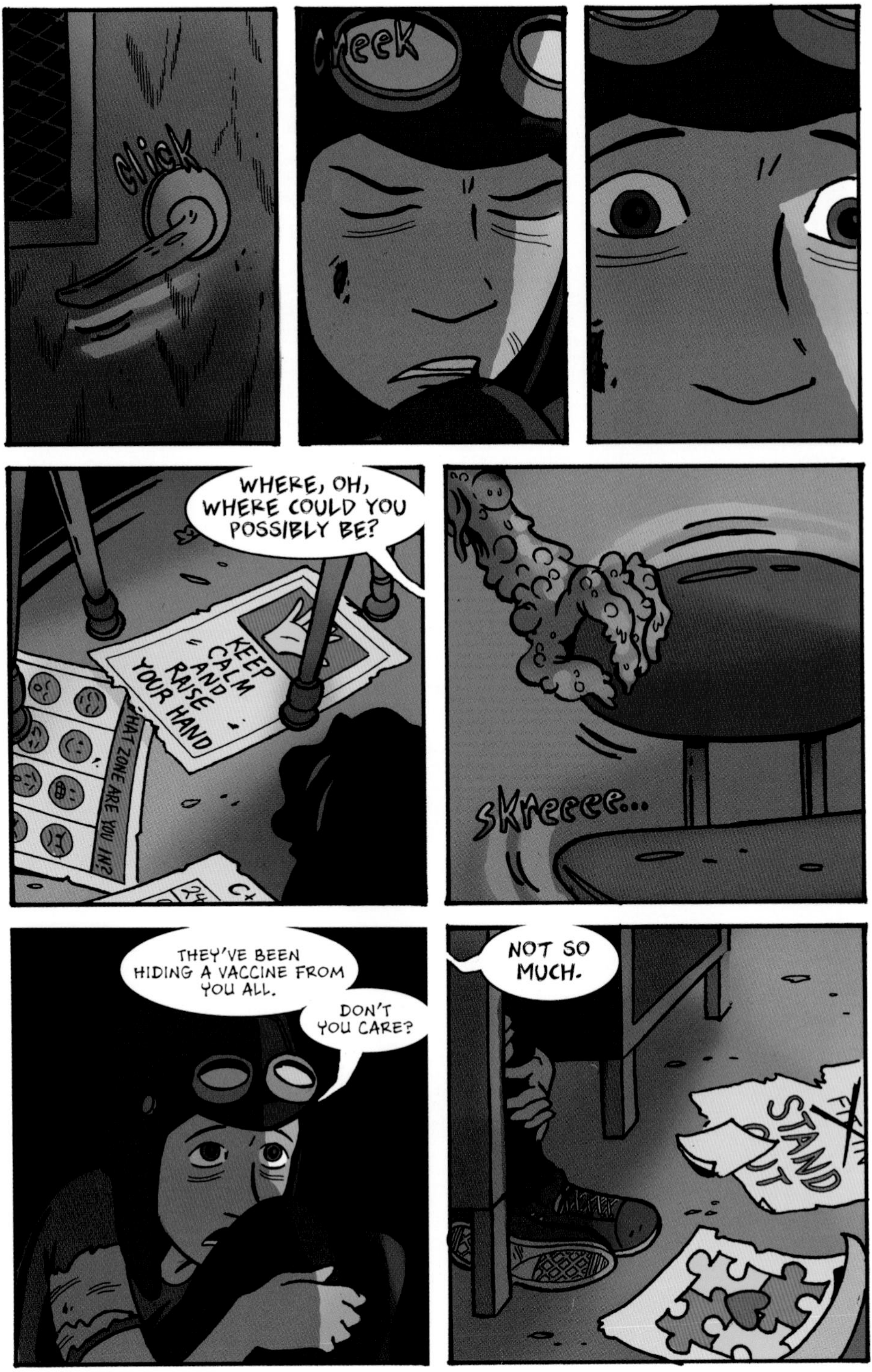
click
cReek
WHERE, OH, WHERE COULD YOU POSSIBLY BE?
KEEP CALM AND RAISE YOUR HAND
HAT ZONE ARE YOU IN?
sKreeee...
THEY'VE BEEN HIDING A VACCINE FROM YOU ALL.
DON'T YOU CARE?
NOT SO MUCH.
STAND OUT

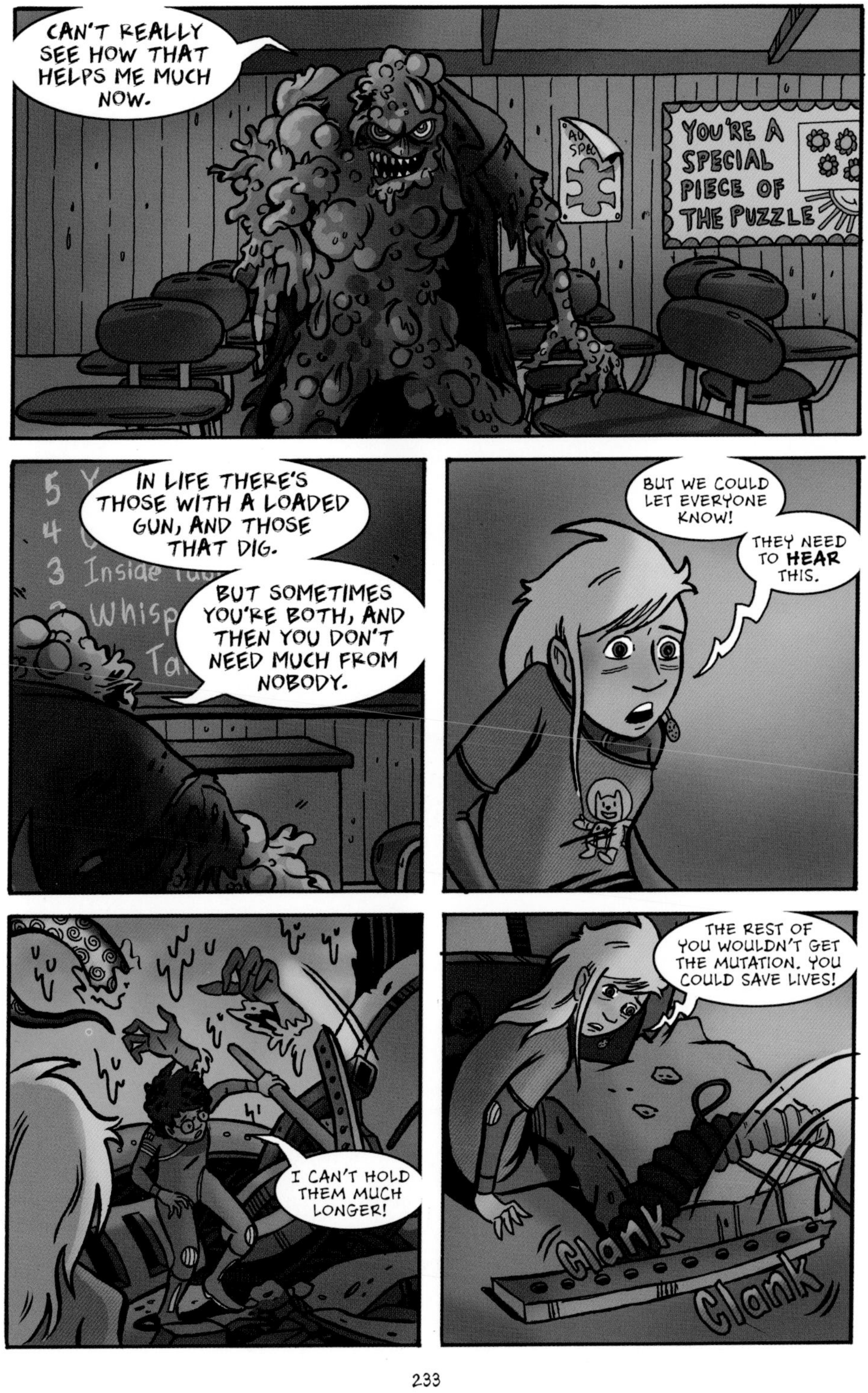
CAN'T REALLY SEE HOW THAT HELPS ME MUCH NOW.
YOU'RE A SPECIAL PIECE OF THE PUZZLE
IN LIFE THERE'S THOSE WITH A LOADED GUN, AND THOSE THAT DIG.
BUT SOMETIMES YOU'RE BOTH, AND THEN YOU DON'T NEED MUCH FROM NOBODY.
BUT WE COULD LET EVERYONE KNOW!
THEY NEED TO HEAR THIS.
I CAN'T HOLD THEM MUCH LONGER!
THE REST OF YOU WOULDN'T GET THE MUTATION. YOU COULD SAVE LIVES!
Clank
Clank

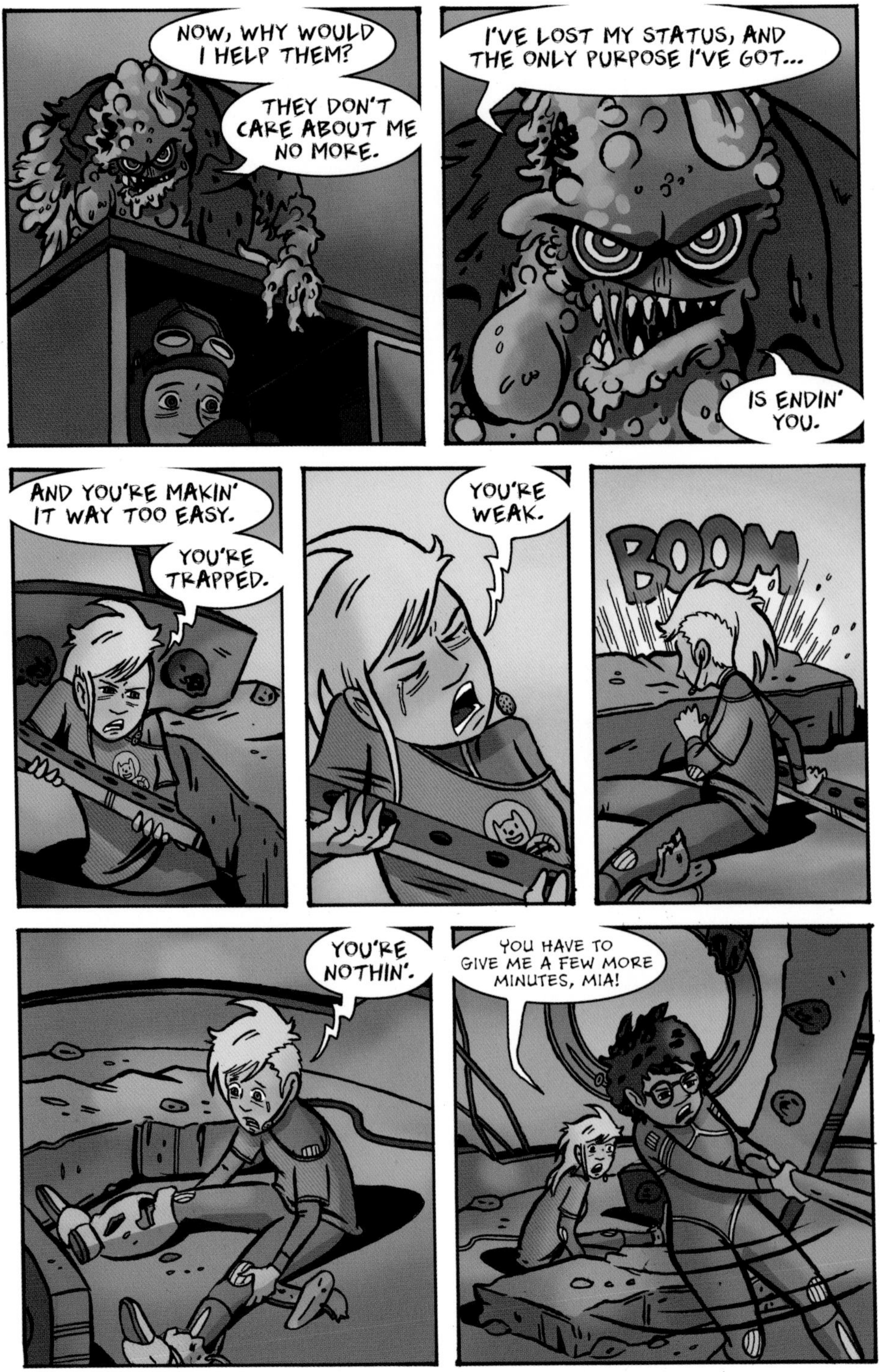
NOW, WHY WOULD I HELP THEM?
THEY DON'T CARE ABOUT ME NO MORE.
I'VE LOST MY STATUS, AND THE ONLY PURPOSE I'VE GOT...
IS ENDIN' YOU.
AND YOU'RE MAKIN' IT WAY TOO EASY.
YOU'RE TRAPPED.
YOU'RE WEAK.
BOOM
YOU'RE NOTHIN'.
YOU HAVE TO GIVE ME A FEW MORE MINUTES, MIA!

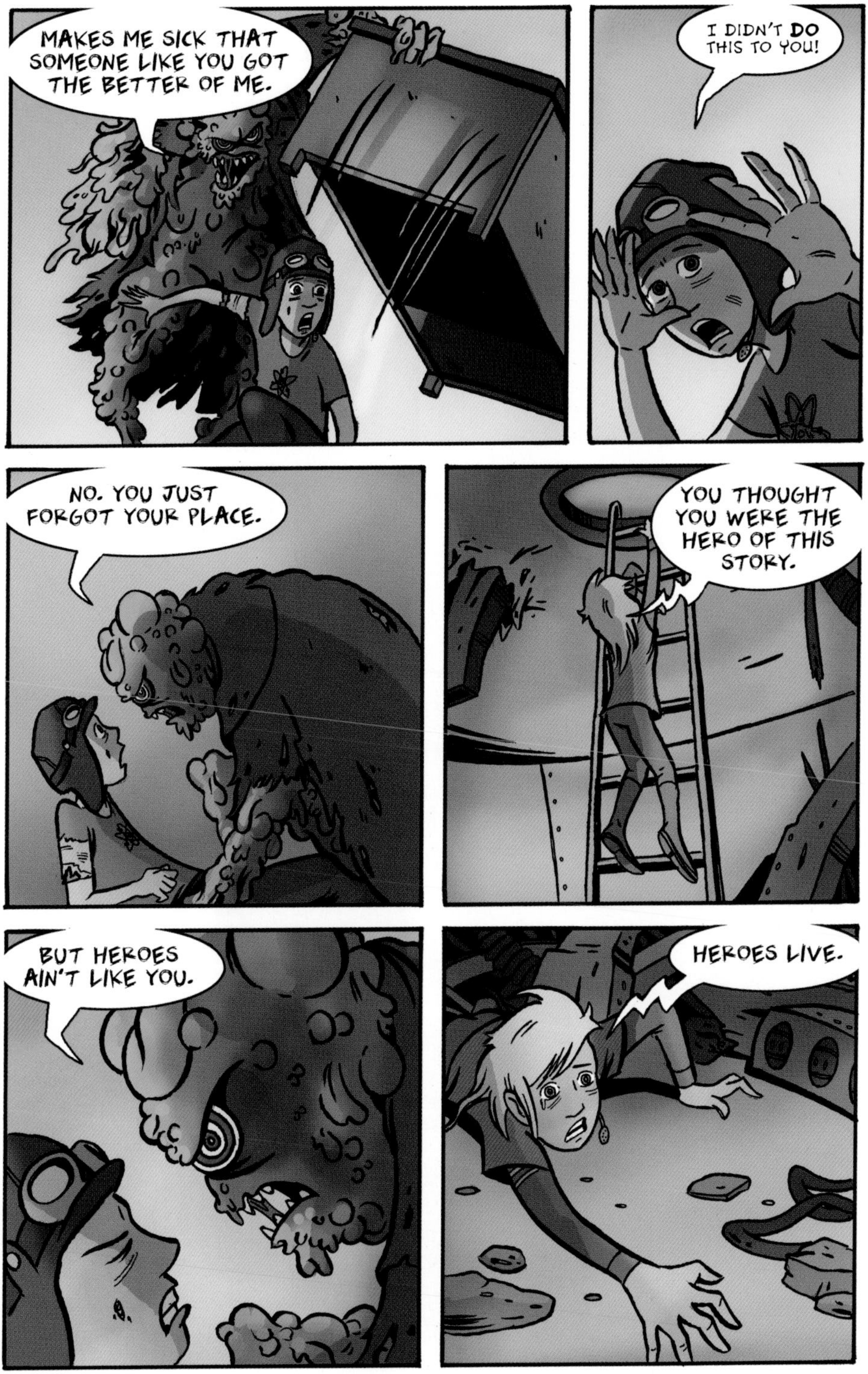
MAKES ME SICK THAT SOMEONE LIKE YOU GOT THE BETTER OF ME.
I DIDN'T DO THIS TO YOU!
NO. YOU JUST FORGOT YOUR PLACE.
YOU THOUGHT YOU WERE THE HERO OF THIS STORY.
BUT HEROES AIN'T LIKE YOU.
HEROES LIVE.

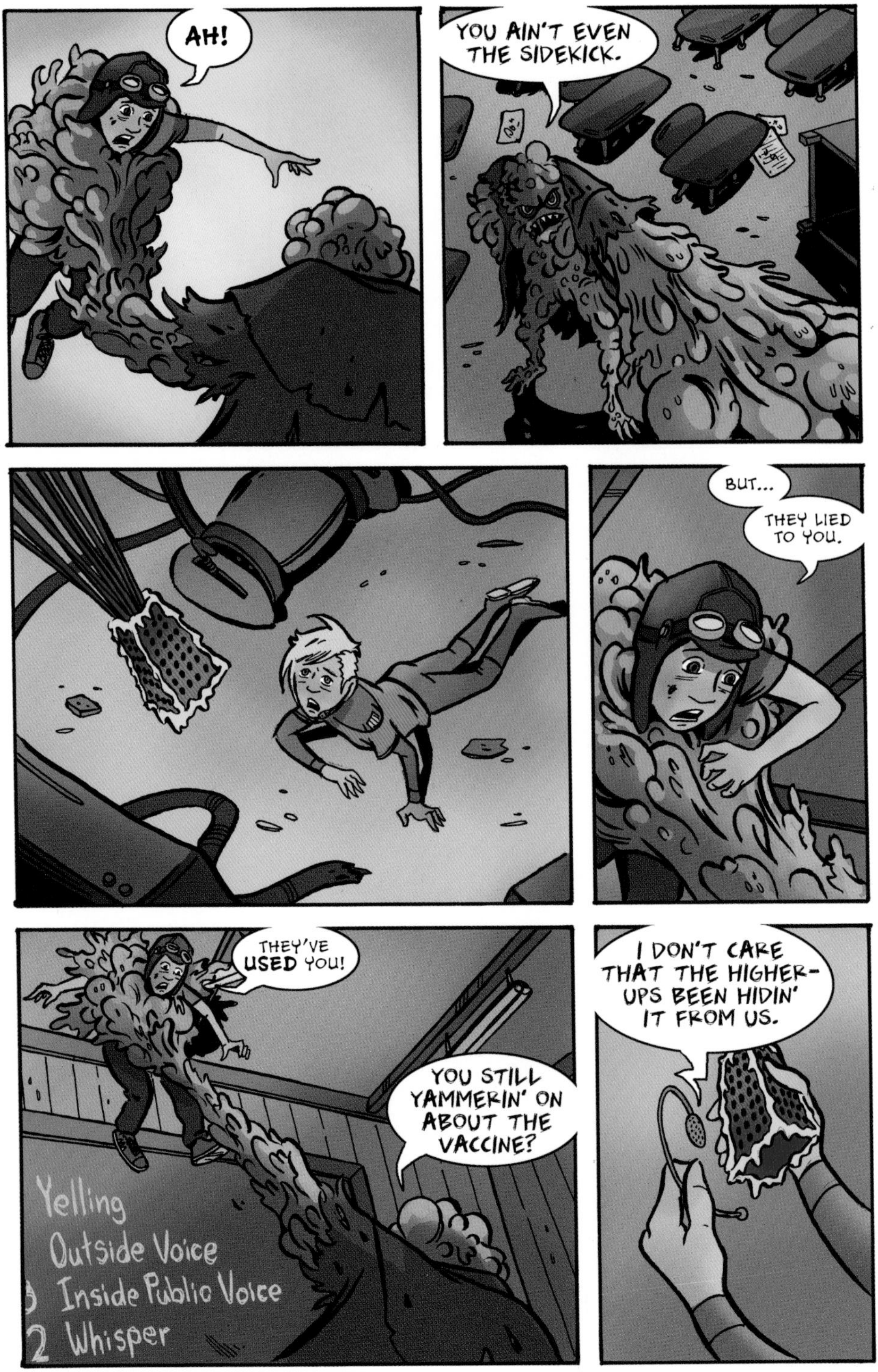
AH!
YOU AIN'T EVEN THE SIDEKICK.
BUT...
THEY LIED TO YOU.
THEY'VE **USED** YOU!
YOU STILL YAMMERIN' ON ABOUT THE VACCINE?
Yelling
Outside Voice
Inside Public Voice
2 Whisper
I DON'T CARE THAT THE HIGHER-UPS BEEN HIDIN' IT FROM US.

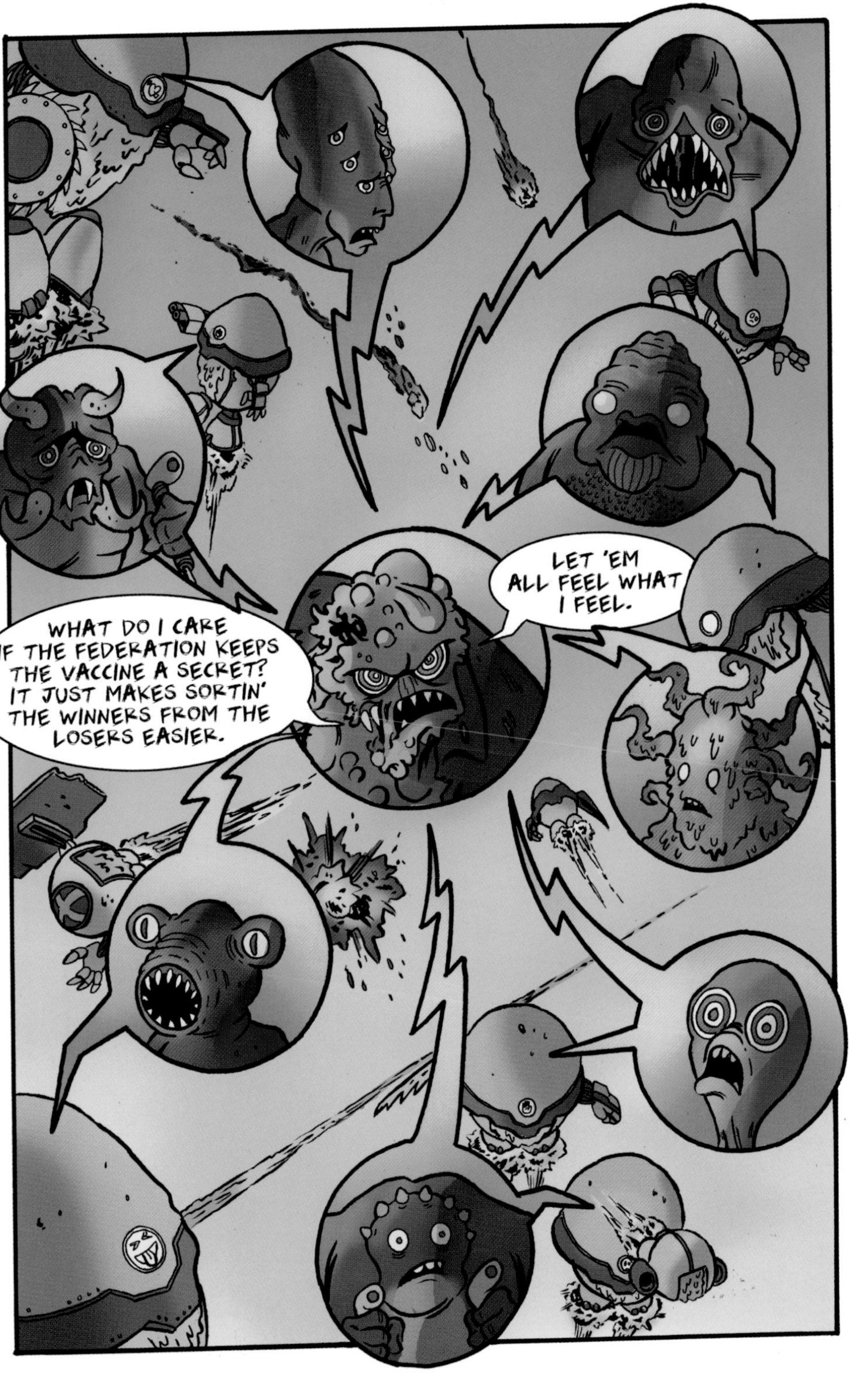
LET 'EM ALL FEEL WHAT I FEEL.
WHAT DO I CARE IF THE FEDERATION KEEPS THE VACCINE A SECRET? IT JUST MAKES SORTIN' THE WINNERS FROM THE LOSERS EASIER.

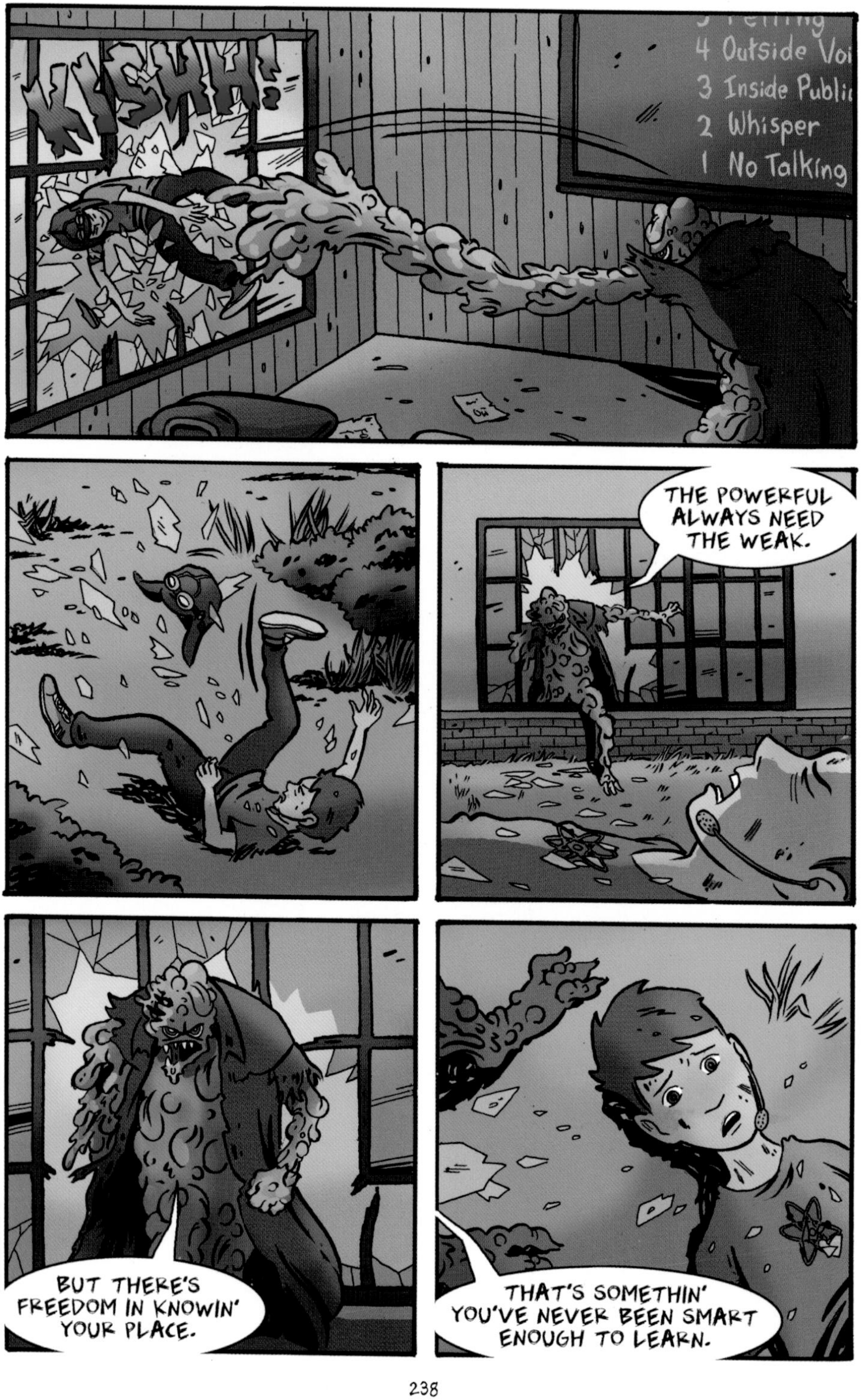
KISHH!
4 Outside Voi
3 Inside Publi
2 Whisper
1 No Talking
THE POWERFUL ALWAYS NEED THE WEAK.
BUT THERE'S FREEDOM IN KNOWIN' YOUR PLACE.
THAT'S SOMETHIN' YOU'VE NEVER BEEN SMART ENOUGH TO LEARN.

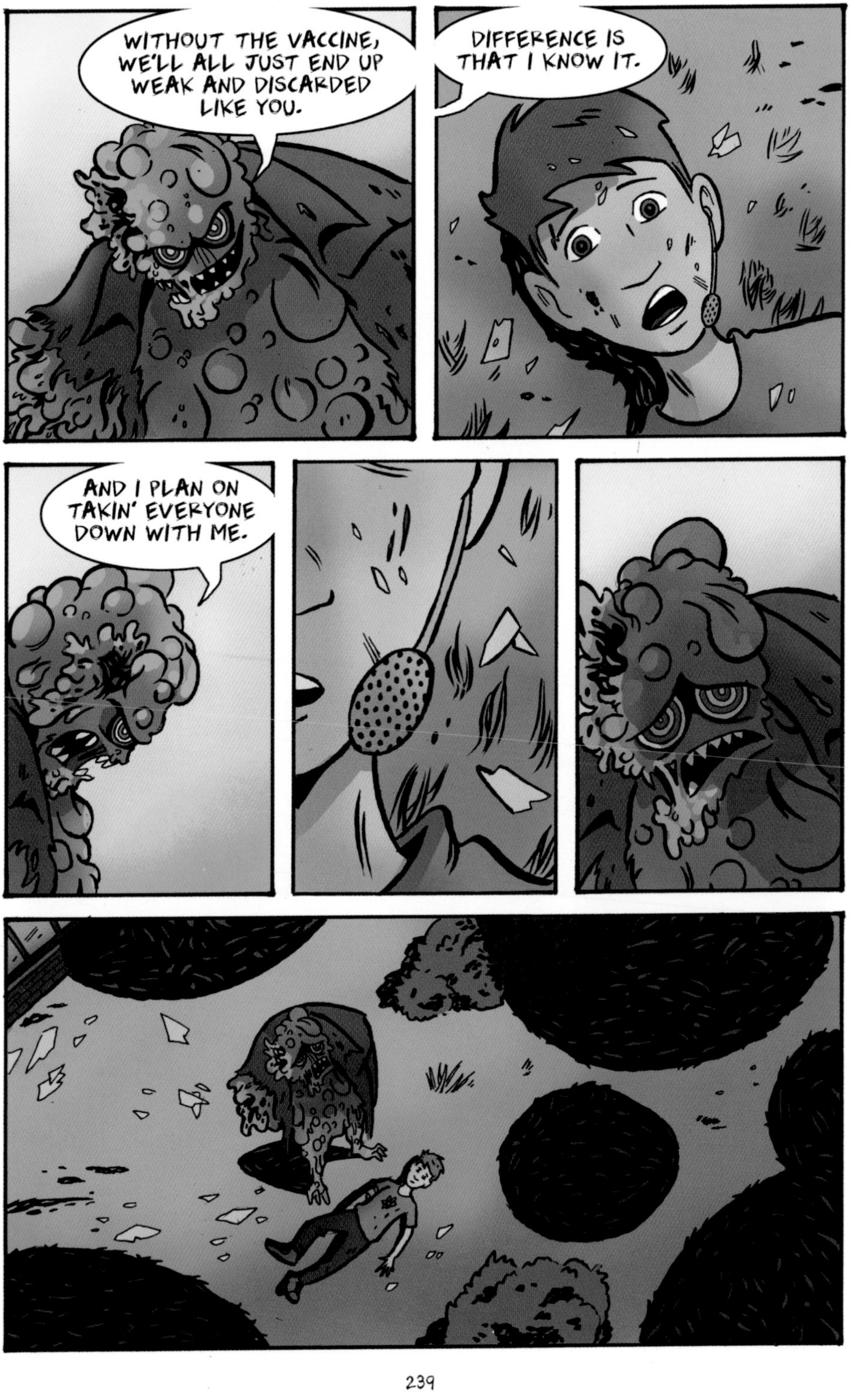
WITHOUT THE VACCINE, WE'LL ALL JUST END UP WEAK AND DISCARDED LIKE YOU.
DIFFERENCE IS THAT I KNOW IT.
AND I PLAN ON TAKIN' EVERYONE DOWN WITH ME.

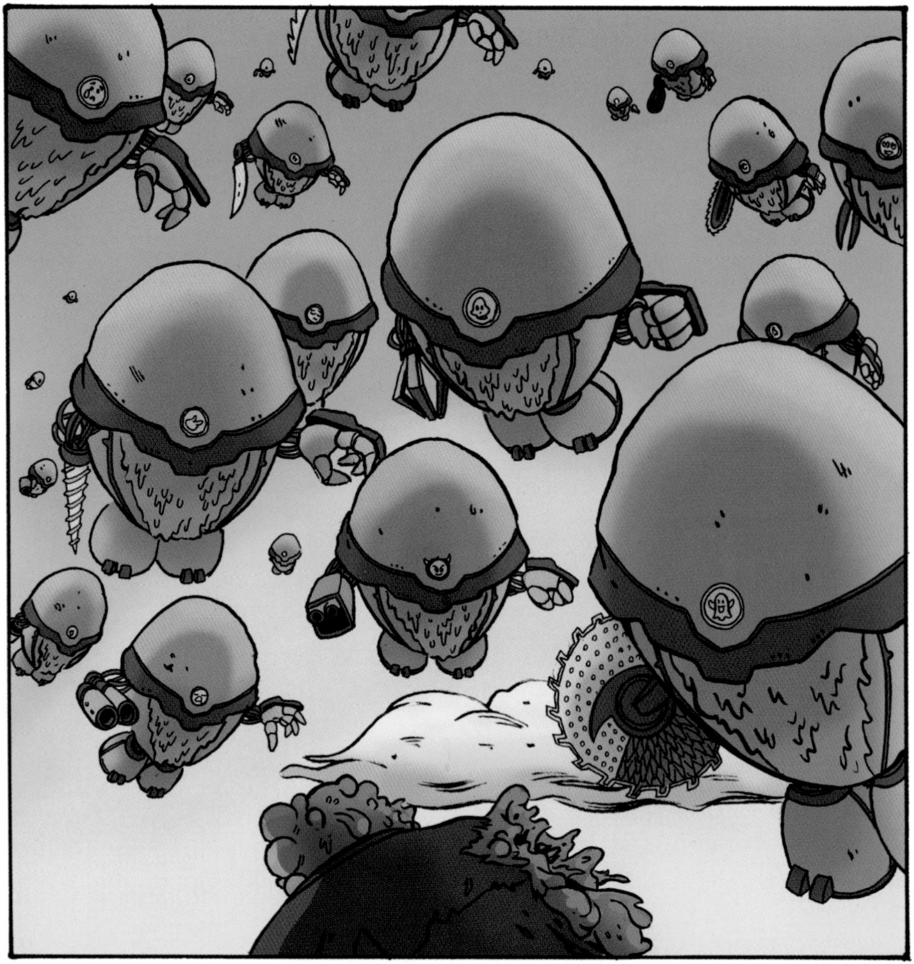

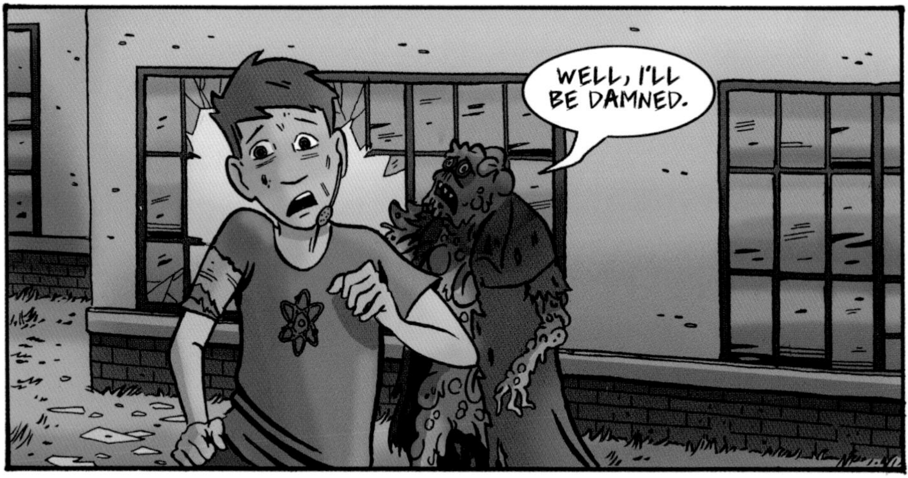
WELL, I'LL BE DAMNED.

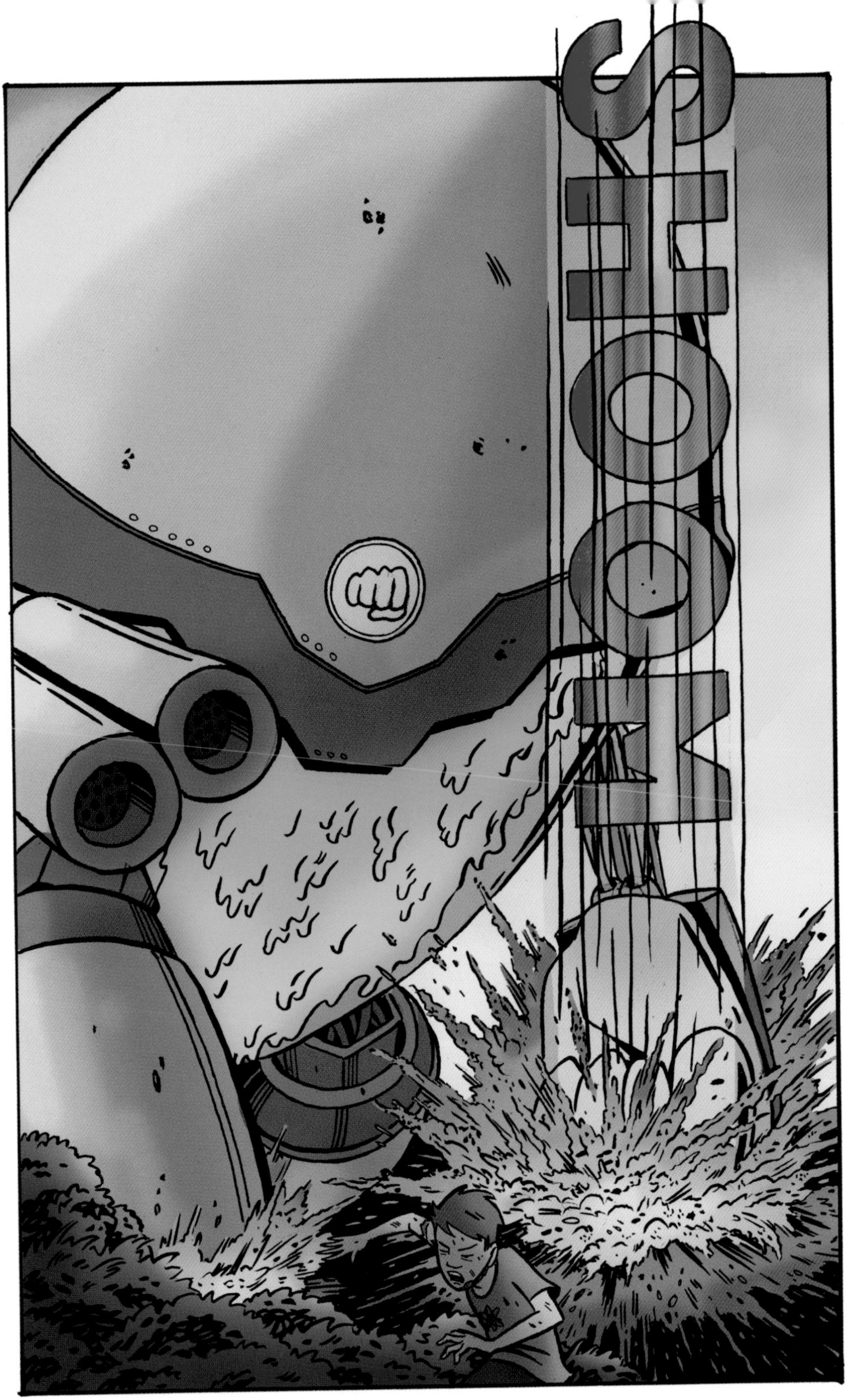
SHOOM

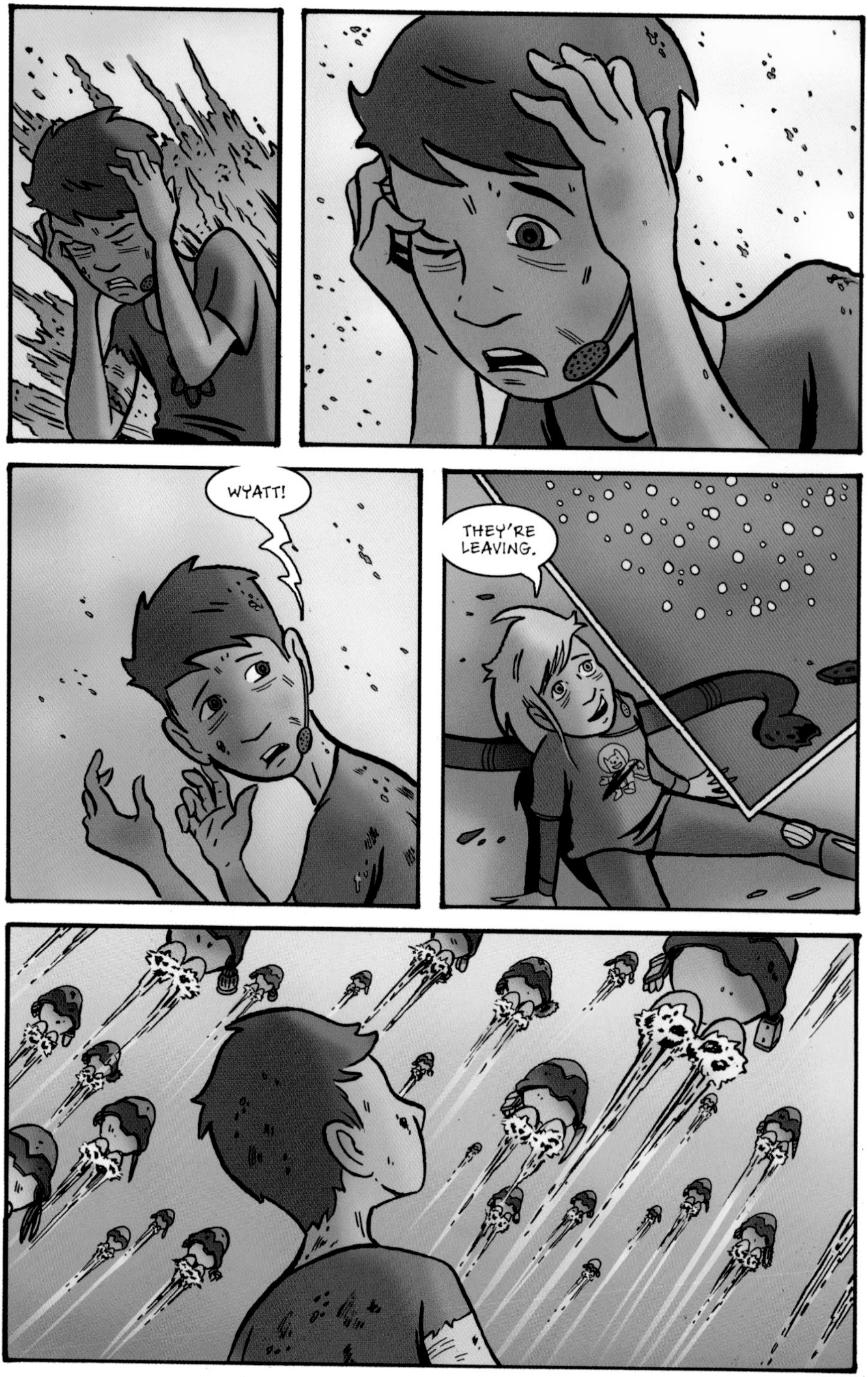
WYATT!
THEY'RE LEAVING.

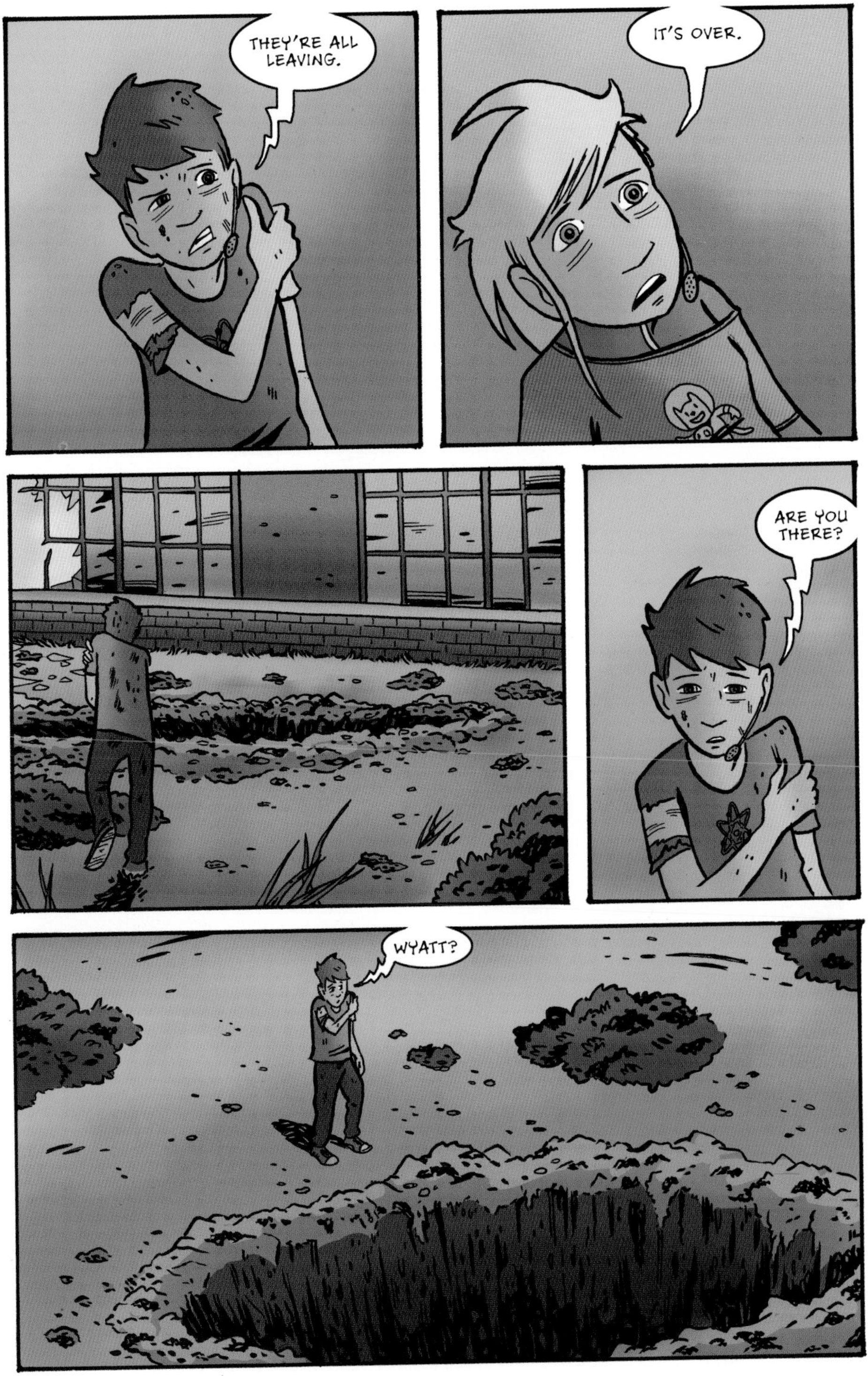
THEY'RE ALL LEAVING.
IT'S OVER.
ARE YOU THERE?
WYATT?

EPILOGUE

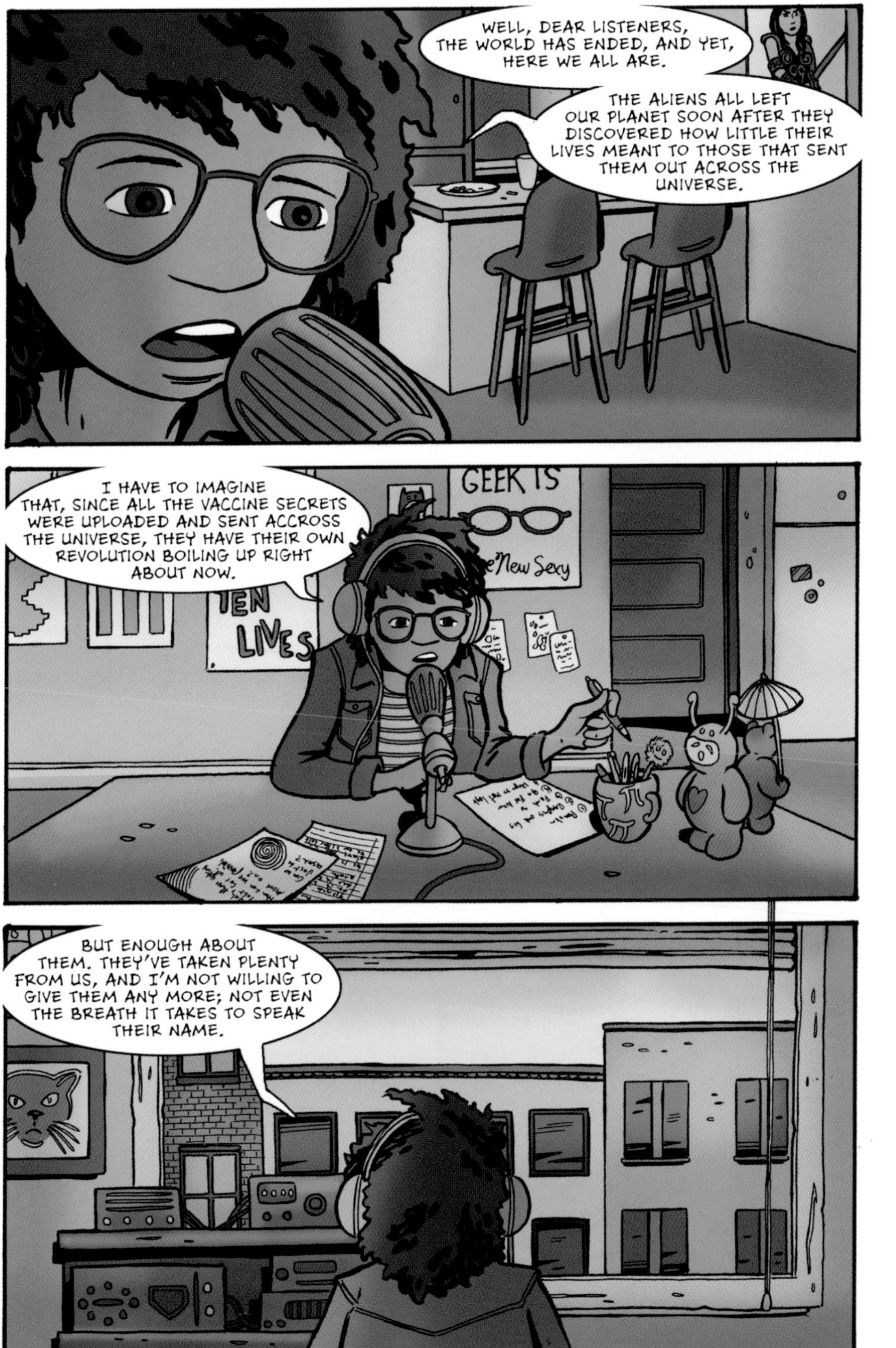
WELL, DEAR LISTENERS, THE WORLD HAS ENDED, AND YET, HERE WE ALL ARE.
THE ALIENS ALL LEFT OUR PLANET SOON AFTER THEY DISCOVERED HOW LITTLE THEIR LIVES MEANT TO THOSE THAT SENT THEM OUT ACROSS THE UNIVERSE.
I HAVE TO IMAGINE THAT, SINCE ALL THE VACCINE SECRETS WERE UPLOADED AND SENT ACCROSS THE UNIVERSE, THEY HAVE THEIR OWN REVOLUTION BOILING UP RIGHT ABOUT NOW.
GEEK IS
BUT ENOUGH ABOUT THEM. THEY'VE TAKEN PLENTY FROM US, AND I'M NOT WILLING TO GIVE THEM ANY MORE; NOT EVEN THE BREATH IT TAKES TO SPEAK THEIR NAME.

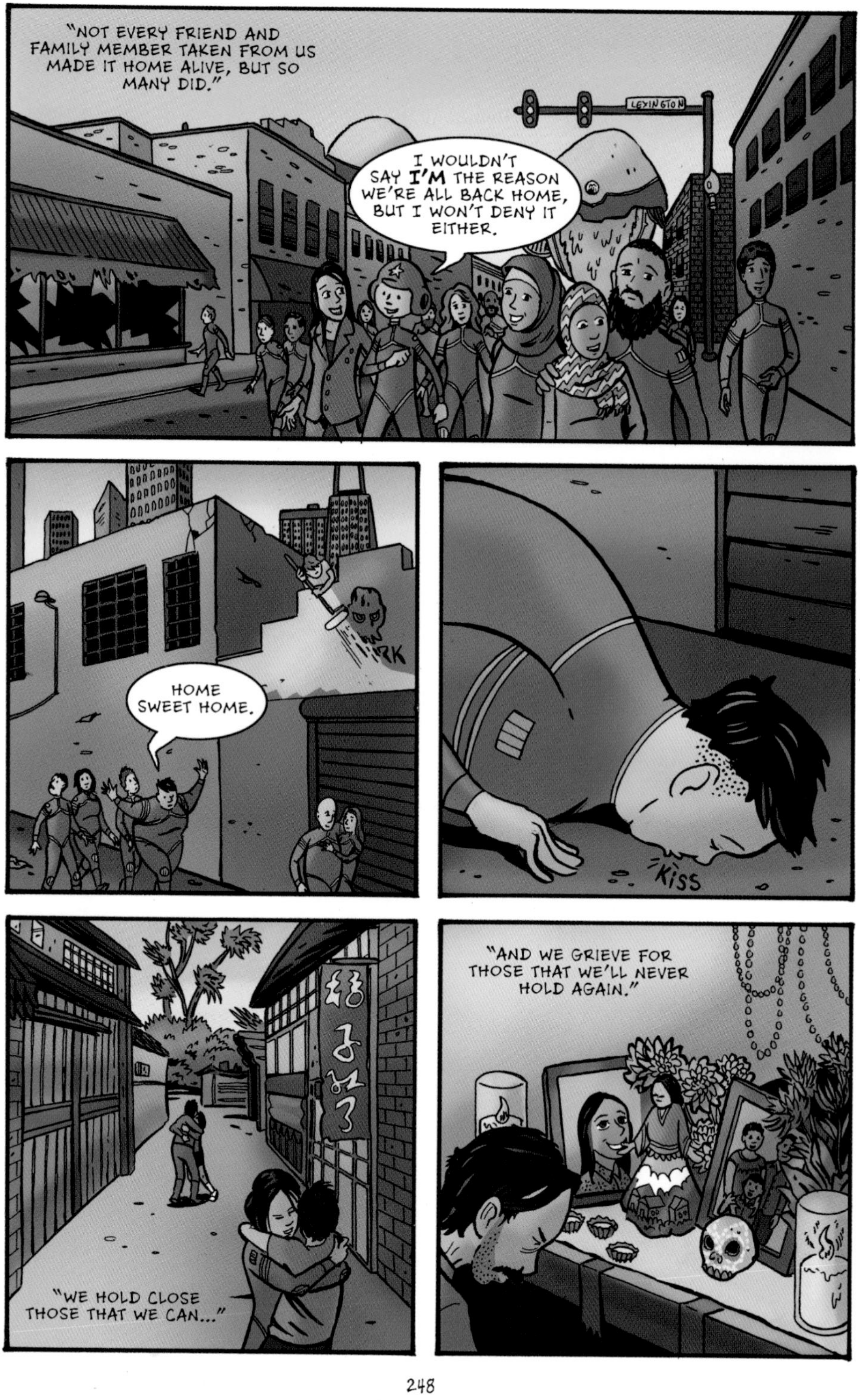
"NOT EVERY FRIEND AND FAMILY MEMBER TAKEN FROM US MADE IT HOME ALIVE, BUT SO MANY DID."
LEXINGTON
I WOULDN'T SAY **I'M** THE REASON WE'RE ALL BACK HOME, BUT I WON'T DENY IT EITHER.
HOME SWEET HOME.
KISS
"WE HOLD CLOSE THOSE THAT WE CAN..."
"AND WE GRIEVE FOR THOSE THAT WE'LL NEVER HOLD AGAIN."

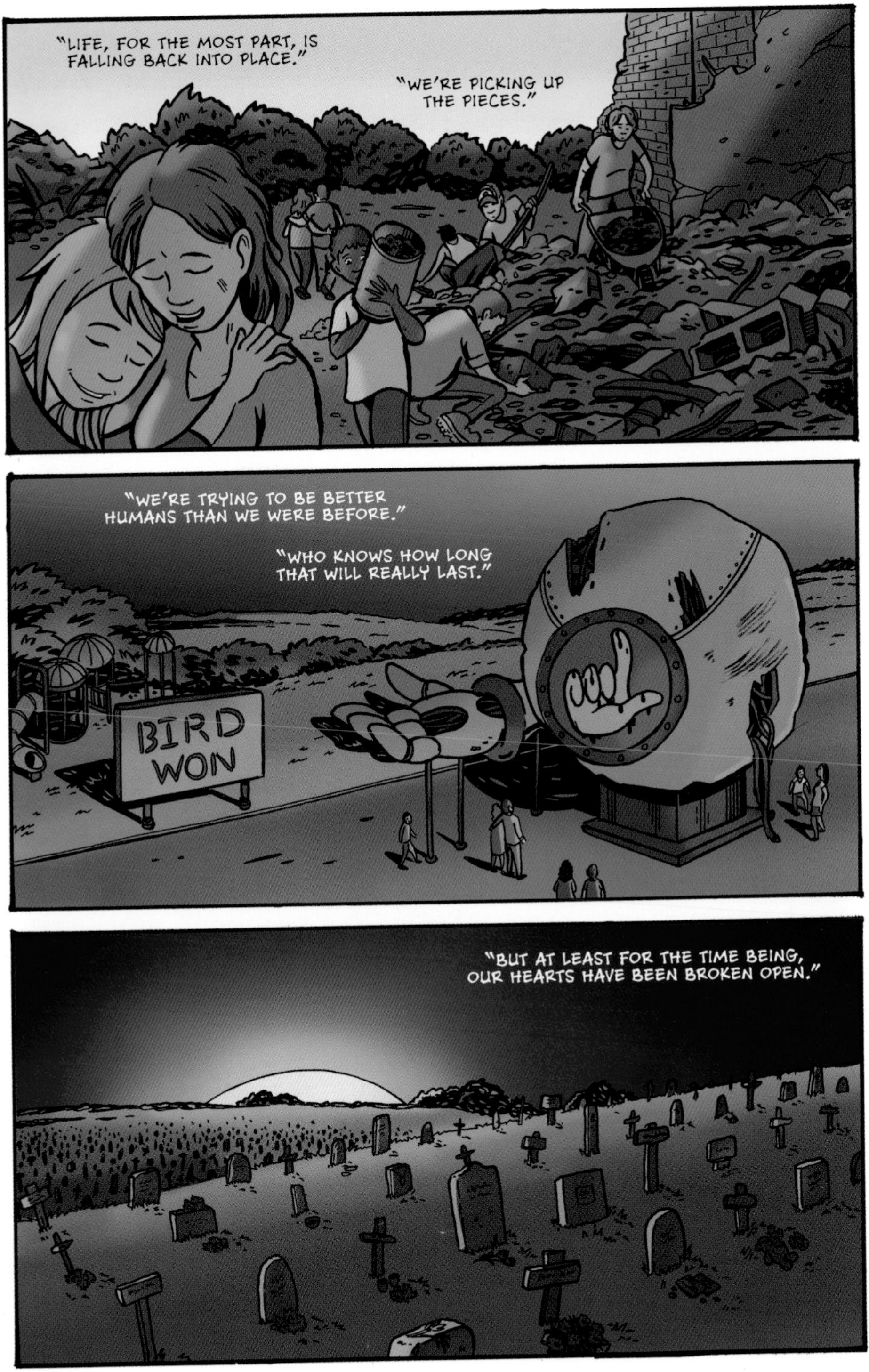
"LIFE, FOR THE MOST PART, IS FALLING BACK INTO PLACE."
"WE'RE PICKING UP THE PIECES."
"WE'RE TRYING TO BE BETTER HUMANS THAN WE WERE BEFORE."
"WHO KNOWS HOW LONG THAT WILL REALLY LAST."
BIRD WON
"BUT AT LEAST FOR THE TIME BEING, OUR HEARTS HAVE BEEN BROKEN OPEN."

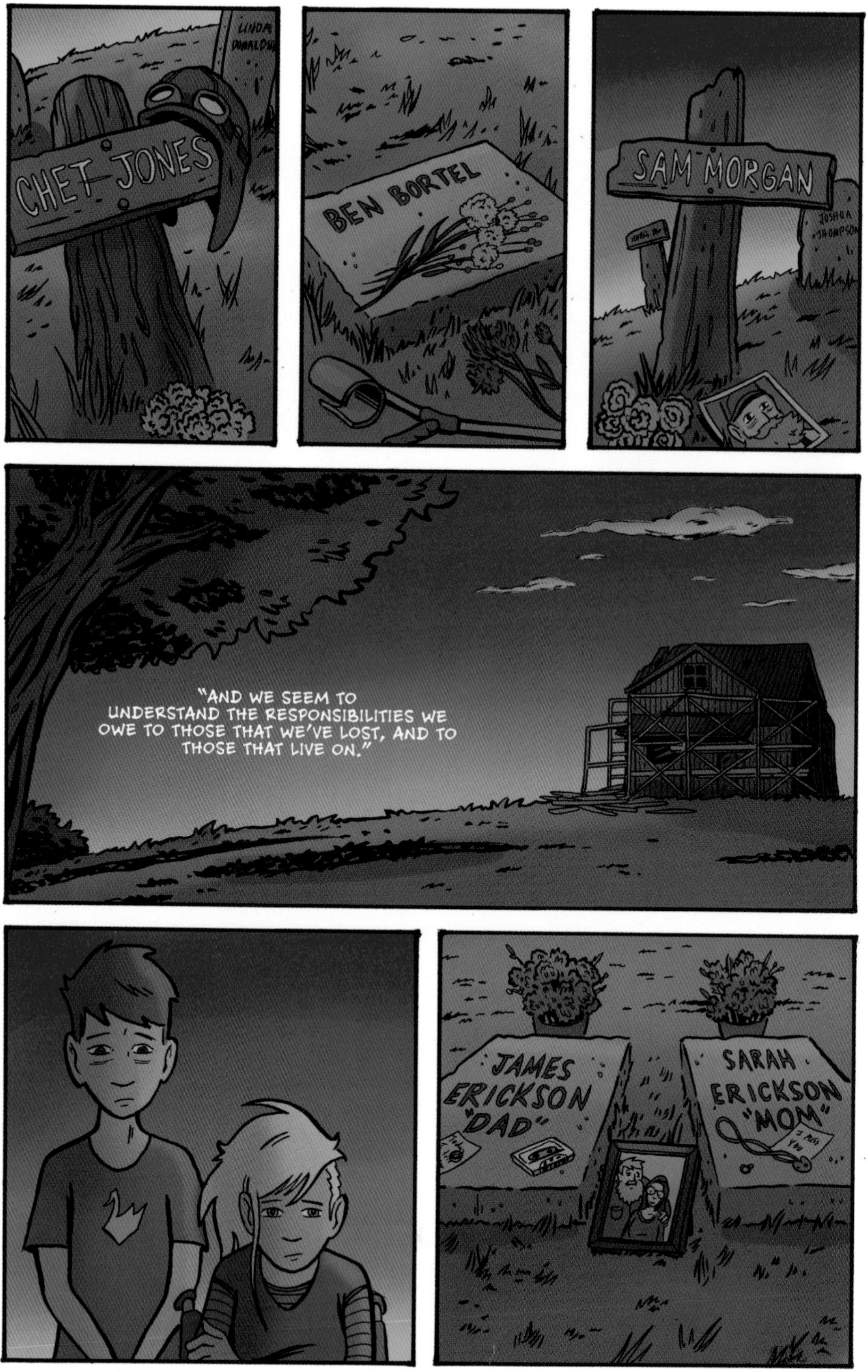
CHET JONES
BEN BORTEL
SAM MORGAN
"AND WE SEEM TO UNDERSTAND THE RESPONSIBILITIES WE OWE TO THOSE THAT WE'VE LOST, AND TO THOSE THAT LIVE ON."
JAMES ERICKSON "DAD"
SARAH ERICKSON "MOM"

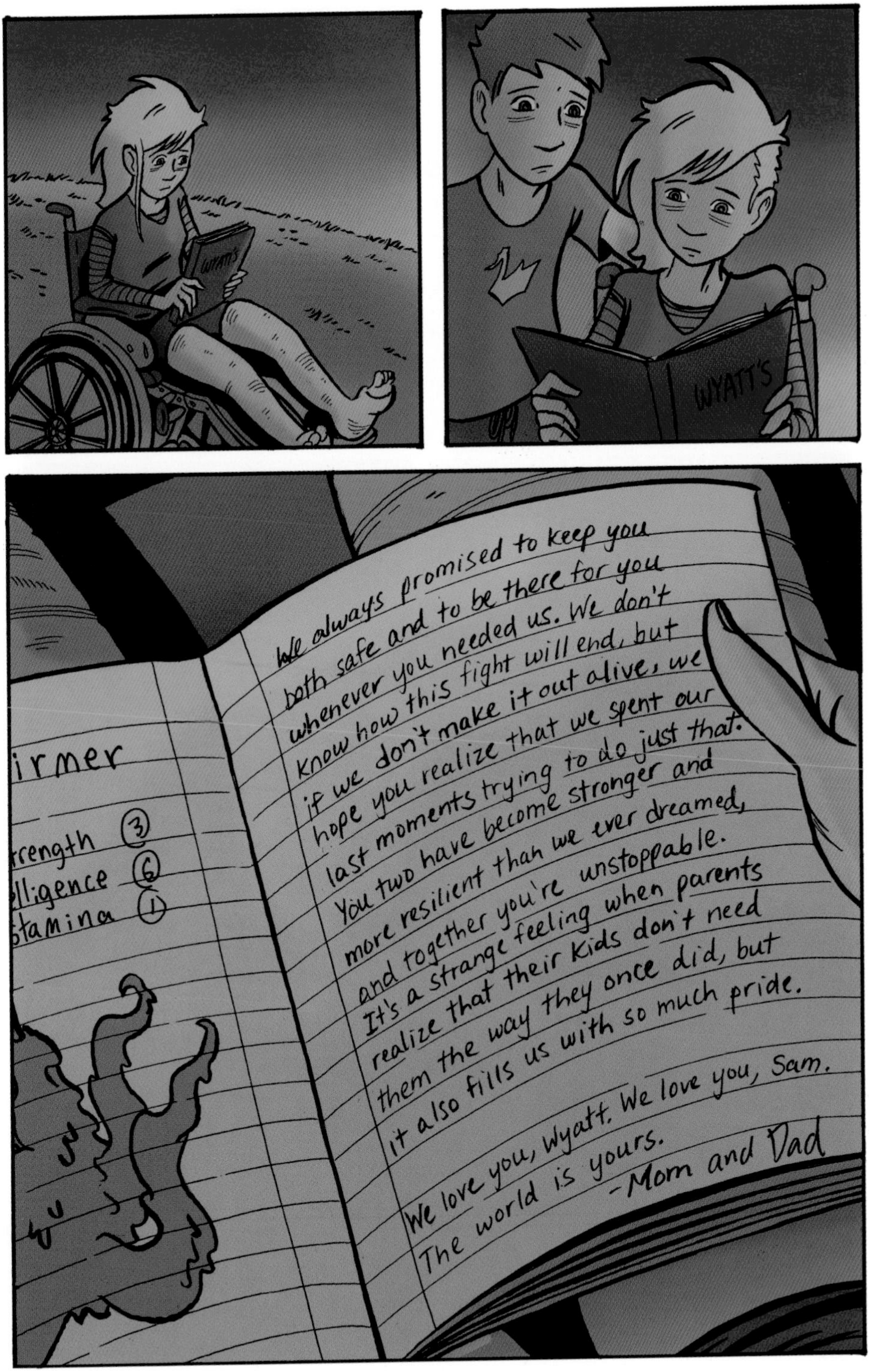
WYATT'S
WYATT'S
irmer
rength 3
lligence 6
stamina 1
We always promised to keep you both safe and to be there for you whenever you needed us. We don't know how this fight will end, but if we don't make it out alive, we hope you realize that we spent our last moments trying to do just that.
You two have become stronger and more resilient than we ever dreamed, and together you're unstoppable.
It's a strange feeling when parents realize that their kids don't need them the way they once did, but it also fills us with so much pride.
We love you, Wyatt. We love you, Sam.
The world is yours.
-Mom and Dad

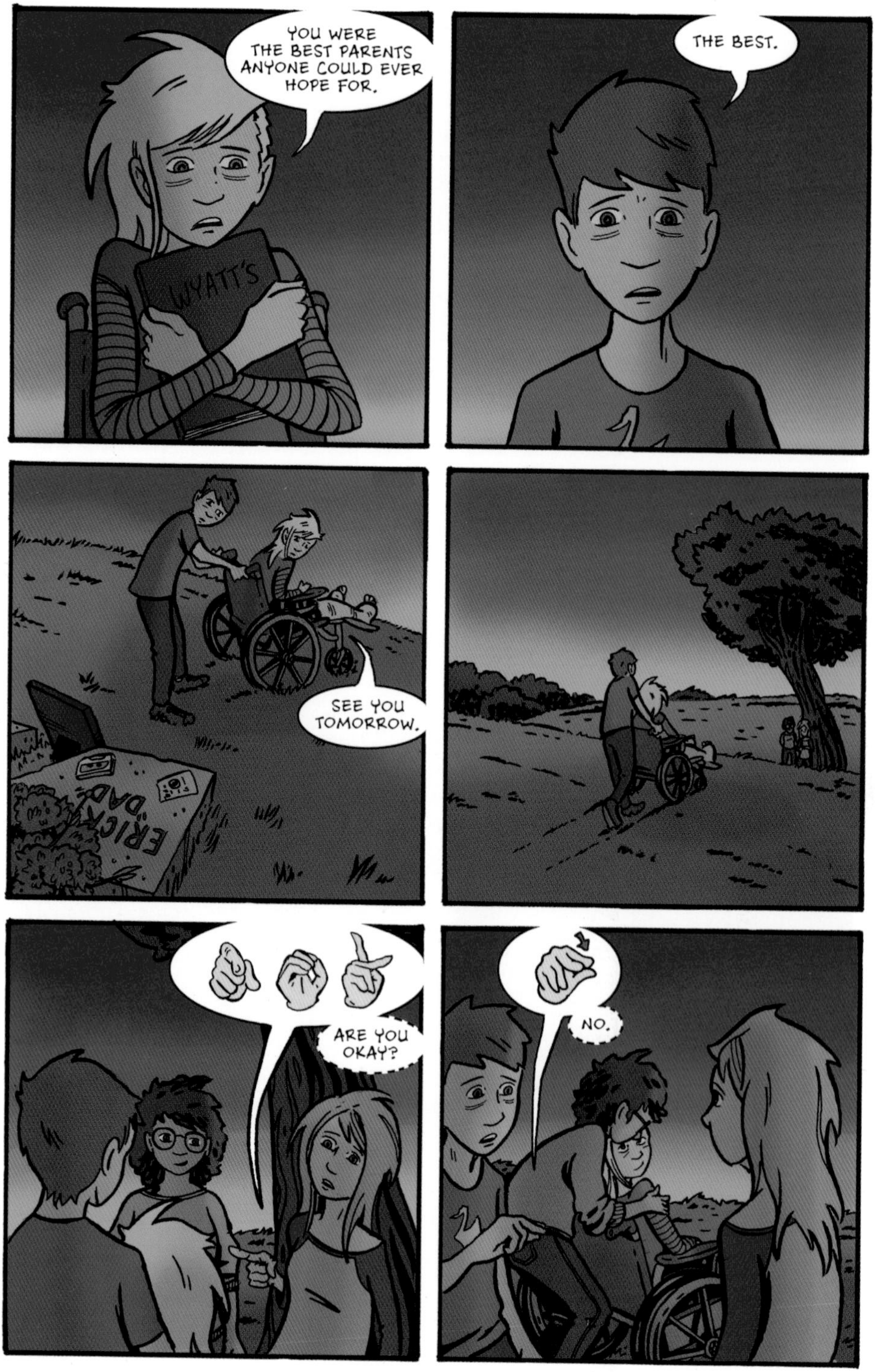
YOU WERE THE BEST PARENTS ANYONE COULD EVER HOPE FOR.
WYATT'S
THE BEST.
ERIC DAD
SEE YOU TOMORROW.
ARE YOU OKAY?
NO.

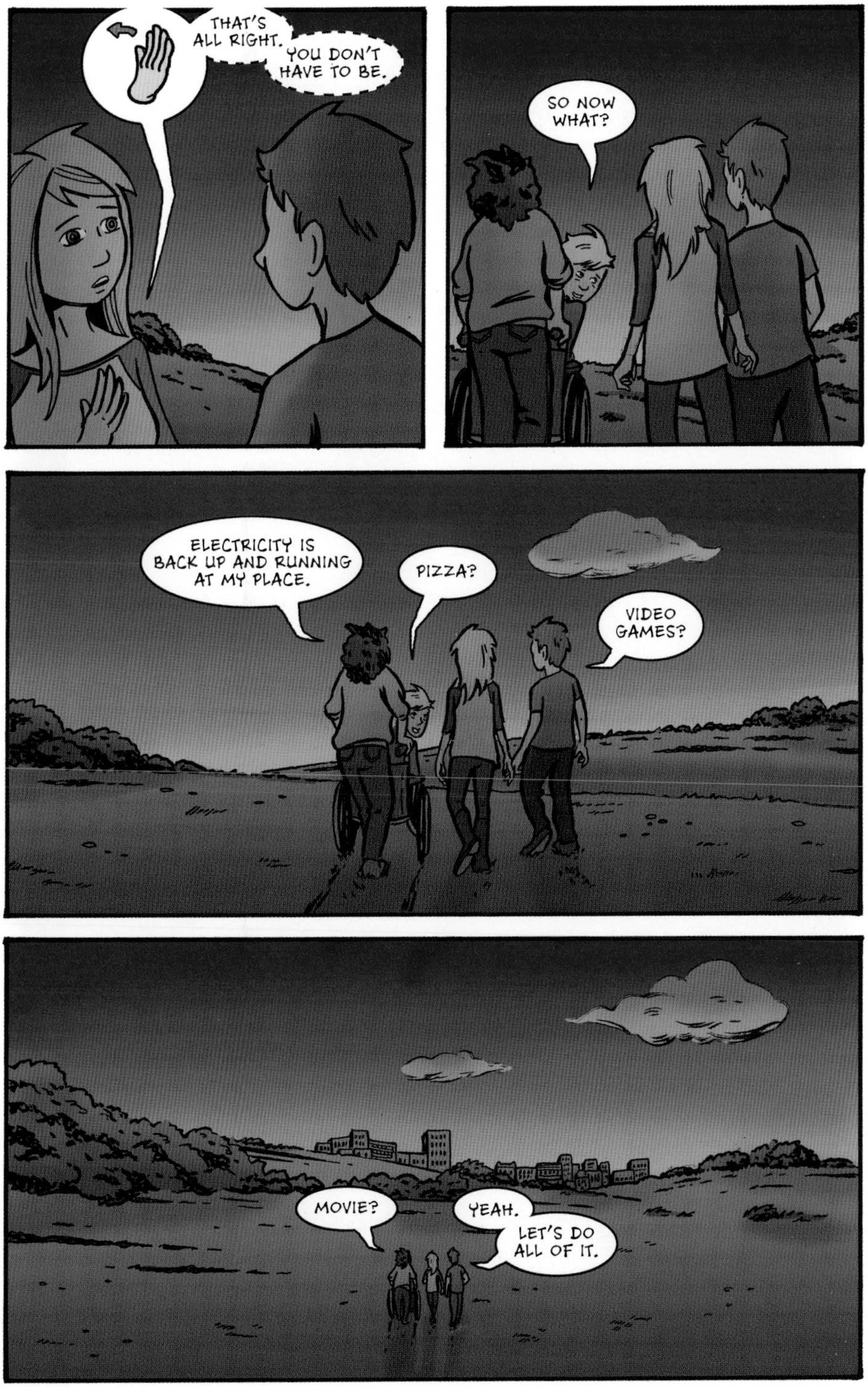
THAT'S ALL RIGHT.
YOU DON'T HAVE TO BE.
SO NOW WHAT?
ELECTRICITY IS BACK UP AND RUNNING AT MY PLACE.
PIZZA?
VIDEO GAMES?
MOVIE?
YEAH.
LET'S DO ALL OF IT.

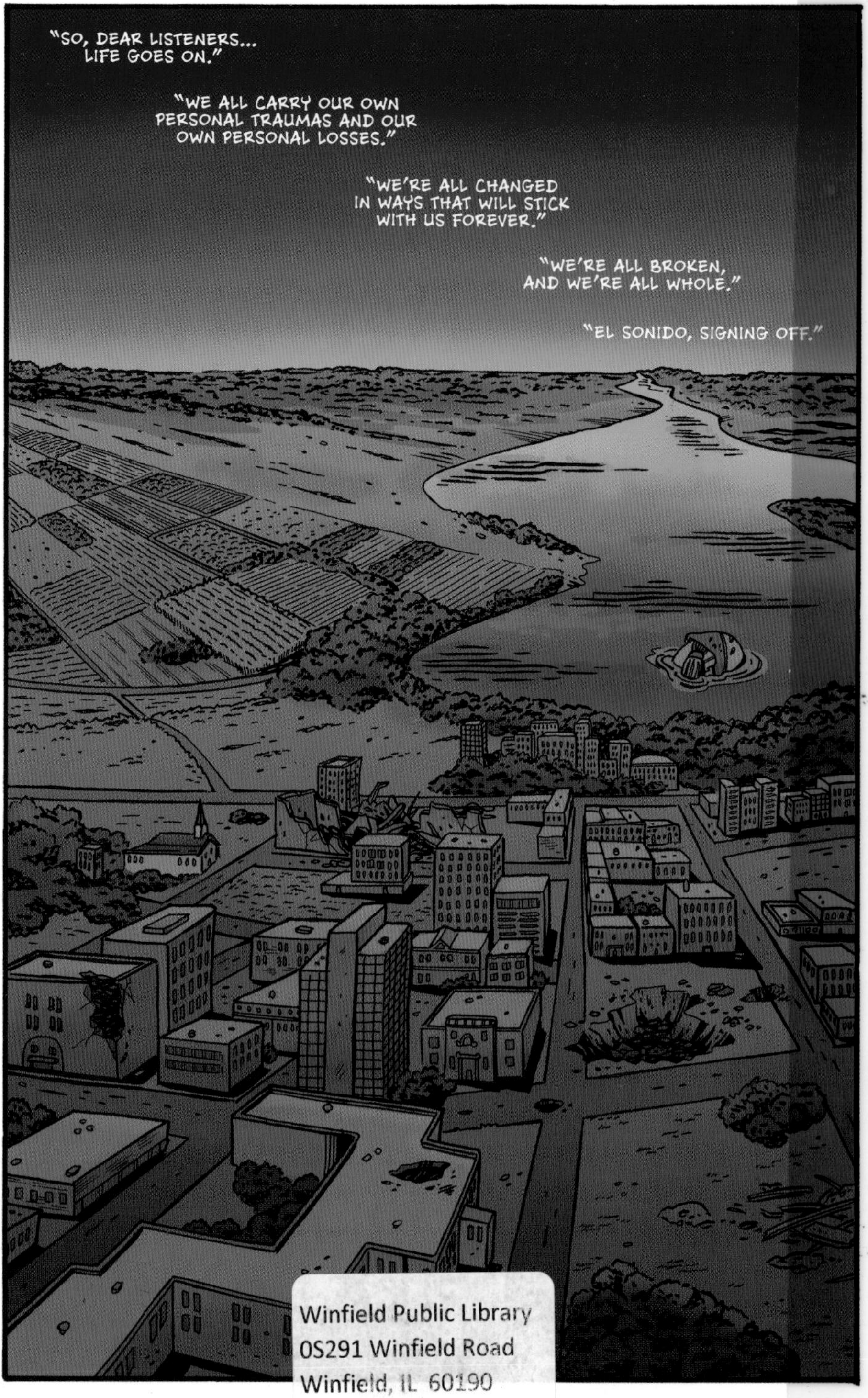
"SO, DEAR LISTENERS... LIFE GOES ON."
"WE ALL CARRY OUR OWN PERSONAL TRAUMAS AND OUR OWN PERSONAL LOSSES."
"WE'RE ALL CHANGED IN WAYS THAT WILL STICK WITH US FOREVER."
"WE'RE ALL BROKEN, AND WE'RE ALL WHOLE."
"EL SONIDO, SIGNING OFF."